GREAT SHORT WORKS

OF

Herman Melville

GREAT SHORT WORKS

OF

Herman Melville

Edited with an Introduction
by Warner Berthoff

PERENNIAL LIBRARY

Harper & Row, Publishers, New York
Grand Rapids, Philadelphia, St. Louis, San Francisco
London, Singapore, Sydney, Tokyo, Toronto

GREAT SHORT WORKS OF HERMAN MELVILLE

CONTENTS

GREAT SHORT WORKS

OF

Herman Melville

INTRODUCTION

BY
WARNER BERTHOFF

BRIMMING over with the creative confidence and ambition he was pouring into the writing of *Moby-Dick*, Herman Melville, in the summer of 1850, published an enthusiastic appreciation of the stories and sketches of his fellow countryman, Nathaniel Hawthorne. This article, the memorable "Hawthorne and His Mosses," is on the whole more revealing of Melville himself at this high point in his hurried public career than of the precise character of Hawthorne's fiction. But it is not superficial; nowhere does it allow us to think that its author has not read deeply into his subject's work, or that the encounter between reader and storyteller has not been extremely direct and full. Melville simply chose to describe his own free part, as well as Hawthorne's, in this literary encounter. He tells about Hawthorne by way of telling about his own participating excitement, and about certain high-flying thoughts—mainly of what it signifies that Hawthorne is an American of the present day and hour—which this response has led him on to. What he has to say, under the licensing disguise of "a Virginian Spending July in Vermont," is not the kind of thing usually met with in critical writing:

> . . . already I feel that this Hawthorne has dropped germinous seeds into my soul. He expands and deepens down, the more I contemplate him; and further and further, shoots his strong New England roots into the hot soil in my Southern soul.

In the era of Romanticism and, in the United States, of New England transcendentalism, it was everybody's custom to appraise works of literature in, broadly speaking, biographical terms. The value of the work was one with the spiritual or existential virtue of the man who had written it, and its function was to give voice to that particular quantum or reserve of virtue, to make it accessible as a source of common good. But Melville as usual overflowed the ideological convention he appropriated. The encounter of reader and author that he describes is not presented as simply a generally edifying or constructive social transaction. It is, in the metaphor used, that one particular transaction whereby life itself is generated and the existence of the race is continued in passion into the future. (Hawthorne, we remember, may have intimated something of the same understanding of the consecrations of the storyteller's calling in a preface written the next year for a new edition of his *Twice-Told Tales* when he described his stories and sketches as "attempts . . . to open an intercourse with the world.") To Melville it was not only the more solemn and profound of Hawthorne's tales or those touched with his peculiar "blackness" that reached out in this way. Pieces like "Buds and Bird Voices" or "The Old Apple Dealer," having their own subtle element of outgoing compassion and melancholy, rose, Melville declared, from "such a depth of tenderness, such a boundless sympathy with all forms of being, such an omnipresent love," that they too had power to open a direct passage from "the intricate, profound heart where they originated."

About storytelling as a social rite, procreative or otherwise, there is more to be said than Melville ventured to say in the Hawthorne article or anywhere else (though a few passing remarks in *The Confidence-Man* on the nature of fiction have gradually been recognized as extraordinarily discerning and comprehensive). What that *more* may be, however, is implicit in his own best practice. His work remains important as much for the ingratiating freedom and inventiveness of its formation, in particular its alertness to the job of beguiling concrete audiences, as for the exemplary humanity of its themes. Indeed the quick responsiveness of compositional arrangement to, at once, the progressive extension of the story and the advance of the reader's expectation is what particularly fixes assent. Quite regularly, these stories shift focus at some key point and momentarily put their emphasis on the storyteller's own resolute efforts to work his way through the narrative occasion and to do it justice, to get it right—or else his willingness to fall silent where the event transcends casual understanding (as in Chapter 22 of *Billy Budd*) rather than falsify its profoundest truth.[1] As much as any ultimate weight-

[1] In those stories with a first-person speaker who is himself a main character—here "Bartleby" is the best example—this effort

iness of theme, with Melville it is this active sense of engagement and risk in the business of getting through his story that gives it plausibility as it goes forward and in the process assists in opening it out until it becomes capable of bearing just that particular weightiness.

A story well told, so that it has the power to enter permanently into the imagination of those who hear it, always tells us two things. It says, "here is what happened"—and it has its say clearly enough in this respect whether or not (as Melville's stories mostly do) it takes on the character of parable or even allegory or, at the least, leads to certain meditative formulations that can stand as autonomous truths. But it will also say something further. It says, "this is what it is like to have knowledge of such happenings, to see in consciousness that they can happen, to undertake the task of opening such knowledge and vision to others." Anyone who passes an ordinary amount of time in the sociable exchange of gossip and anecdote knows how much depends—for interest and for belief, too—on *how* things get said. The more so when the matter is serious: stories that ought to be important and consequential can be so poorly told (or really not "told" at all) that they quite lose currency. The most momentous events reduce to pointless fantasy or rumor in the management of someone who has too little feeling or care for the sequences of reality as they are actually absorbed into consciousness and who merely blurts out their bare substance and result. Melville seems to have understood from the beginning (as well he might, given the strangeness of his first materials) that to tell a tale is to gamble or wager for the reader's, the listener's, continuing acceptance—continuing, that is, beyond the initial "suspension of disbelief" which is the reader's undertaking in the covenant of literature. It is a wager precisely for *confidence;* an offering of testimony that, by forthrightly embracing the pragmatic burden of verification, becomes the better able to persuade others that the game itself is decidedly worth playing, on both sides and for its own sake.

It thus looks, systematically or not, beyond each immediate narrative occasion. Its motives are, in a formal sense, ceremo-

---

merges with the character's dramatic struggle, sometimes comically reluctant, to act out the part that has fallen to him in the story. It may thus issue in a kind of surprising conversion, an unsought-for transformation of consciousness and commitment.

nial and confederating. For the storyteller conspires to draw
his hearer into becoming not simply a believer in the one
particular tale he is telling but a devotee of tales in general,
a true aficionado. In some measure he conceives of transforming his casual reader into a reader-by-vocation, the necessary
partner for his own elected service. ("The demand that I
make of my reader," Joyce remarked, "is that he should
devote his whole life to reading my works.") But in this
task the storyteller serves not only himself but the common
fortune. That is, he engages his readers actively, deliberately,
into that vast unending civil process which men and women
are bound to by their character as, willy-nilly, historical and
imaginative beings: the process of exorcizing the immeasurable entail of past events and making imaginative provision,
so far as can be done, for the uncontrollable onset of present
and future. In a word he fills time, covenanting with his readers to compel time's successions closer to that ideal "fullness"
in which the life we inherit and the life we imagine are not
hopelessly out of joint.[2]

The aim of the storyteller's wager is also, of course, to give
pleasure (and share more or less promptly in the pleasure-
giver's agreeable rewards). As with any art the covenant of
fiction promises enjoyment here and now as well as provision
of the kind described against past and future. (That, after all,
would be the common truth in Melville's sexual metaphor
for his encounter with Hawthorne's tales—and one can find
a further parallel with sexual logistics in the sense communicated in certain of Melville's own narratives that to enter
fully into the engagements of storytelling can be, temporarily
at least, transporting and exhausting.) Except perhaps in a
few special forms—like the *solemn deposition* offered in the
"inside narrative" of *Billy Budd*—the whole vast genre of
prose fiction is primarily intended to entertain. It is hard to
think of a major novelist or storyteller who is not also a first-

---

[2] One may say, risking misunderstanding, that the conspiracy of
fiction is thus, ideally, a religious conspiracy: i.e., a ritual enterprise for the binding together of minds and souls in space (otherwise divided and *un*civil) and in time (otherwise fractured and
*un*historical).

For the reader the case with the best stories corresponds to what
André Gide once remarked of the Christian Gospel: "it is a question not of explaining it but of accepting it."

rate entertainer, in the vulgar sense; a master, according to choice, of high comedy, of one or another robust species of expressive humor, or of some special variety of the preposterous, the grotesque, the absurd. And Melville, certainly, is no exception. A kind of vigorous supervisory humor is his natural idiom as a writer, and one particular attraction of his shorter work is the fresh further display it offers of this prime element in his literary character.

A version of the "contemplative humor" that Melville celebrated in Hawthorne's work is one component in Melville's prose comedy. But its major instrument is something broader and freer, something that on any given page is an end in itself. It is an antic humor, carried by physical gesture as well as meditative fancifulness. What chiefly propels it is, first, a sense of the special interest of those moments in life when, though the self-approving consciousness gives us one set of directions, the creaturely totality of our being mysteriously issues us an altogether different set that abruptly takes command and bends us this way and that, quite against our apparent will; and, second, the corollary sense that these are the moments when our moral history and destiny are really determined. Some of the liveliest sequences in Melville's fiction occur when characters normally at ease with themselves and their attitude to life (like the fine old lawyer of "Bartleby") are overborne by some strange new phenomenon of behavior and carried quite out of themselves by sudden excitement. A passage in *Moby-Dick* nicely summarizes the dialectic of feeling that plays through such sequences:

There are certain queer times and occasions in this strange mixed affair we call life when a man takes this whole universe for a vast practical joke, though the wit thereof he but dimly discerns, and more than suspects that the joke is at nobody's expense but his own. However, nothing dispirits, and nothing seems worth while disputing. He bolts down all events, all creeds, and beliefs, and persuasions, all hard things visible and invisible, never mind how knobby; as an ostrich of potent digestion gobbles down bullets and gun flints. And as for small difficulties and worryings, prospects of sudden disaster, peril of life and limb; all these, and death itself, seem to him only sly, good-natured hits, and jolly punches in the side bestowed by the unseen and unaccountable old joker. That odd sort of wayward mood I am speaking of, comes over a man only in some time of extreme tribulation; it comes in the very midst of his earnestness, so that what just before might have seemed to him a thing most momentous, now seems but a part of the general joke . . . [breeding in him] this free and easy sort of genial, desperado philosophy . . . . (Chapter XLIX, "The Hyena")

The passage gives us in epitome both the character of the fictional world that we can find projected in most of Melville's shorter pieces, and one of the main ways suggested, though not the only one, of looking at this world and surviving what is seen. Also, as a piece of writing it effectively illustrates its own point. The thing to be said is said with a lively humor which convinces by piling up a quick abundance of expressive detail. But it is also said in a manner that presses beyond the conventional limits of comic ingratiation. We feel at once that the "hard things" spoken of are somehow no joke, for all the slapstick of the accompanying image; that *waywardness* and *desperation*, though not necessarily incompatible with a "philosophy" which is genially "free and easy," are more in this case than mere figures of speech. Melville's humor is inseparable from the imaginative intelligence supporting his gravest undertakings in fiction. The impressions of life and destiny it delivers are not materially different from what emerges in those works of his, like "Benito Cereno" and *Billy Budd,* where comic extravagance is subordinated almost completely to wit of another kind, the wit of moral and psychological understanding and of joined narrative sequence which tragic action even more exactingly requires of the writer who attempts it. It is on this ground, among the intense images of spiritual passion and change given to us in Melville's most purely original tales, that we most feel his greatness as a writer, and that his work seems finally to surpass in power and truth even so masterful a humorist as Dickens, from whom in the 1840's and '50's Melville (like Dostoievsky) learned many excellent lessons.

The themes and actions of Melville's shorter tales and the truths they predicate are very likely as profound as interpretive criticism has persistently assumed them to be. He, too, in his broad American way, was a Victorian "sage," who may be read for the wisdom in him. For the most part these themes and actions are clear and explicit in presentation. Melville liked to get things properly explained as well as build up symbolic hints and portents, and when he speaks figuratively, the figures drawn are agreeably circumstantial and definite.

Particularly in the tales of 1853-56 there appears to be, first of all, a fairly constant burden of autobiographical statement. Nearly all remind us somewhere that they are the work of a writer whose literary career seemed by 1853 to have fallen on evil days and who himself, towards the end of his work on *Moby-Dick,* had prophesied that his life had come "to the inmost leaf of the bulb, and that shortly the flower must fall to the mould" (letter to Hawthorne, June, 1851). One after another presents an action of withdrawal, resignation, defeat; of stoic endurance and passive suffering; of isolated and constricted spirits living on, though sometimes with a strange cheerfulness, after wrenching disasters; of measures taken—usually too eccentric to be generally serviceable—against hardly avoidable catastrophe.

The whole frame of action has become less splendid and spacious. Only occasionally are glimpses still given of the kind of "far-off, soft, azure world" ("The Piazza") that figures so largely in the early Polynesian books and *Moby-Dick.* Instead these stories offer, as settings, a series of houses and habitations—the walled law-office and the Tombs in "Bartleby"; the shadowy, decaying slave ship in "Benito Cereno"; the queer misshapen houses of "I and My Chimney" and "Jimmy Rose"; the grimly secluded paper factory which is the "Tartarus of Maids"—that are closed in and oppressive in the extreme. (So the earth itself is presented, in "The Encantadas," as a "great general monastery" and "Potters Field.") The lives of the main characters correspond. Instead of heroic "knights and squires" and figures of "immaculate manliness" of the kind liberally provided in *Moby-Dick,* we find figures of "desperate fortune" ("The Encantadas") who are "afraid of everyone" ("Jimmy Rose"), men who appear "flayed alive," wracked by trouble as if by "the ague" ("Benito Cereno"). Characters may imagine themselves happy and secure, yet be in reality "like the man who, pipe in mouth, was killed one cloudless afternoon long ago in Virginia, by summer lightning; at his own warm open window he was killed, and remained leaning out there upon the dreamy afternoon, till some one touched him, when he fell" ("Bartleby"). "Nature's pride"—the irreducible force of life that is the last inward resort of human dignity—is identified only as a perverse counterforce to "nature's torture" ("The Encantadas: Sketch the Eighth"); it persists as a source of treacherous hope, "a hope which is but mad," depriving its victim even of the consolation of "a sane despair."

As in his earlier books, Melville's statement of these themes is typically reflective as well as figurative and dramatic. In the stories he wrote after 1853 there is still enough of the obstinate seeker after truth and a "definite belief" (as Hawthorne reported of him at their meeting in England in 1856) to supply texts for all manner of philosophical debate. Melville continues to frame his narratives as, among other things, tests of the validity of various great received propositions of religious and moral knowledge. The central New Testament commandment to "charity," for example, is as directly questioned in "Bartleby," the first work published in the 1853-56 period, as it notoriously is in *The Confidence-Man*, the last in this run. But what now becomes equally prominent is the resigned or dryly humorous suggestion that the one sure thing in life is the overturning of received propositions. "Somehow, too," the narrator in "The Apple-Tree Table" remarks, "certain reasonable opinions of mine seemed not so reasonable as before." When the stuff of new awareness materializes, it is not necessarily clarifying. "Truth comes in with darkness," is the concluding strophe (as it may be called) of "The Piazza"; and it comes there with the haunting expression of a particular face, the recollection of one or another puzzling old story. An increasing reserve and restraint are to be felt in these tales with regard to philosophic assessments, and are felt moreover as a positive resource. So, too, certain high dramatic moments are deliberately left undescribed, becoming in fact the more impressive through the narrator's pointed refusal to take them up in his regular fashion. A profounder tact, a more intense respect for persons and what is ultimately required of them, seem responsible for this change of manner, rather than any doctrinaire skepticism or ironic derogation of traditional understanding. "The half shall here remain untold," Melville writes at the darkest point in his narrative of the Chola widow, Hunilla. "Those two unnamed events which befell Hunilla on this isle, let them abide between her and her God. In nature, as in law, it may be libelous to speak some truths." The greatest fiction, perhaps, cannot withdraw into silence in this way. But it is possible to feel a singular humanity, and civility, in writing that chooses to do so out of its own measured strength of intimation.

From 1856 to 1885 Melville gave up prose fiction, as he gave up, in time, the thought of any further public career in literature.[3] But in various renewed experiments during his final years, made possible by his retirement at the end of 1885 from the drudgery of a routine job in the New York Customs House, the tact and forbearance of judgment he had come round to in the middle 1850's are resumed almost as if there had been no interruption. In his last major effort—the long narrative of the handsome sailor, Billy Budd, and what befell him and one or two other "phenomenal men" in the year of the British fleet's Great Mutiny—these qualities become sources of exceptional power. The philosophical restlessness of earlier times seems quite gone, though not the curiosity. Melville's old interest as a storyteller in framing experience into meditative axioms and queries is still a prime motive (so that one way of grasping the general form of *Billy Budd*, the poet Eugenio Montale recognized, is to see that it moves forward not only as, in Montale's terms, a *tale of adventure* crystallizing into a *mystery play* but also as a *critical essay* and *Platonic dialogue*). But the narrative voice is no longer that of a man who can imagine himself either gaining or losing by the outcome of his inquiry. Rather, the various propositions about life which the events of the story yield up are valuable as they help to specify more precisely the quality of manhood celebrated in its main characters: the rare beauty and nobleness of spirit in Billy Budd, the trapped "peacemaker," and the austere personal rectitude of the fatherly Captain who under the rigidities of the martial law must be Billy's executioner.

With these last remarkable figures (and the malignant yet finally pitiful Claggart, for a time their formidable antagonist) the table of personalities and life histories constituted by Melville's later fiction is complete. Ever since *Billy Budd* was first published, readers have felt strongly its unity with

[3] The principal work, however, of this long interval, which was devoted mostly to writing poetry, is a kind of philosophical novel-in-verse, *Clarel* (2v., 1876), offering a remarkable new gallery of fictional characterizations.

Melville's earlier work. In occupying the ground of tragedy it resumes the ambiance approached in "Bartleby," "The Encantadas," "Benito Cereno," and in the dramatic climaxes of *Moby-Dick*. Yet the last word in this moving story is not tragic in accent, though it comes to us as a death-song. It is, instead, Billy's gentle, absolving plea to be allowed as much of beauty and ease in death as he was blessed with in life, and no reader who follows Melville through the full circuit of his life and work can be other than grateful that there could be this music at the close:

I remember Taff the Welshman when he sank,
And his cheek it was like the budding pink.
But me they'll lash me in hammock, drop me deep,
Fathoms down, fathoms down, how I'll dream fast asleep.
I feel it stealing now. Sentry, are you there?
Just ease this darbies at the wrist, and roll me over fair,
I am sleepy and the oozy weeds about me twist.

THE TOWN-HO'S STORY

[As told at the Golden Inn]

NOTE: "The Town-Ho's Story" appeared first in *Harper's New Monthly Magazine* for October, 1851, where it was presented as an excerpt from " 'The Whale' . . . a new work by Mr. Melville, in the press of Harper and Brothers, and now publishing in London by Mr. Bentley." (The same issue coincidentally featured an account of an "Incident During the Mutiny of 1797," that near-revolutionary episode—characteristic of a time, the anonymous author remarks, "more rife with interest and excitement" and "more animated by hope and fear" than the progress-blessed present age—to which Melville himself would return forty years later in *Billy Budd*. The "new work," with its more familiar American title, *Moby-Dick*, went on sale in New York in November, 1851, and was warmly recommended to *Harper's* readers in the December "Literary Notices" column.

As an interpolated chapter "The Town-Ho's Story" serves the purpose of bringing Moby Dick dramatically on stage soon after the revelation of Ahab's scheme of vengeance, and in the appropriate role of superhuman justicer. Otherwise the white whale would not appear, except spectrally, until the end of the book. As a self-contained tale of adventure, and Melville's first published work in this popular mode, the story is proof positive of its author's casual virtuosity in the art of narrative.

THE CAPE of Good Hope, and all the watery region round about there, is much like some noted four corners of a great highway, where you meet more travellers than in any other part.

It was not very long after speaking the Goney that another homeward-bound whaleman, the Town-Ho,* was encountered. She was manned almost wholly by Polynesians. In the short

* The ancient whale-cry upon first sighting a whale from the mast-head, still used by whalemen in hunting the famous Gallipagos terrapin.

Gam that ensued she gave us strong news of Moby Dick. To some the general interest in the White Whale was now wildly heightened by a circumstance of the Town-Ho's story, which seemed obscurely to involve with the whale a certain wondrous, inverted visitation of one of those so-called judgments of God which at times are said to overtake some men. This latter circumstance, with its own particular accompaniments, forming what may be called the secret part of the tragedy about to be narrated, never reached the ears of Captain Ahab or his mates. For that secret part of the story was unknown to the captain of the Town-Ho himself. It was the private property of three confederate white seamen of that ship, one of whom, it seems, communicated it to Tashtego with Romish injunctions of secrecy, but the following night Tashtego rambled in his sleep, and revealed so much of it in that way, that when he was wakened he could not well withhold the rest. Nevertheless, so potent an influence did this thing have on those seamen in the Pequod who came to the full knowledge of it, and by such a strange delicacy, to call it so, were they governed in this matter, that they kept the secret among themselves so that it never transpired abaft the Pequod's main-mast. Interweaving in its proper place this darker thread with the story as publicly narrated on the ship, the whole of this strange affair I now proceed to put on lasting record.

For my humor's sake, I shall preserve the style in which I once narrated it at Lima, to a lounging circle of my Spanish friends, one saint's eve, smoking upon the thick-gilt tiled piazza of the Golden Inn. Of those fine cavaliers, the young Dons, Pedro and Sebastian, were on the closer terms with me; and hence the interluding questions they occasionally put, and which are duly answered at the time.

"Some two years prior to my first learning the events which I am about rehearsing to you, gentlemen, the Town-Ho, Sperm Whaler of Nantucket, was cruising in your Pacific here, not very many days' sail eastward from the eaves of this good Golden Inn. She was somewhere to the northward of the Line. One morning upon handling the pumps, according to daily usage, it was observed that she made more water in her hold than common. They supposed a sword-fish had stabbed her, gentlemen. But the captain, having some unusual reason for believing that rare good luck awaited him in those latitudes; and therefore being very averse to quit them, and the leak not being then considered at all dangerous, though, indeed, they could not find it after searching the hold as low down as was possible in rather heavy weather, the ship still continued her cruisings, the mariners working at the pumps at wide and easy intervals; but no good luck came; more days went by, and not only was the leak yet undiscovered, but it sensibly increased. So much so, that now taking some alarm, the captain, making all sail, stood away for the nearest harbor among the islands, there to have his hull hove out and repaired.

"Though no small passage was before her, yet, if the commonest chance favored, he did not at all fear that his ship would founder by the way, because his pumps were of the best, and being periodically relieved at them, those six-and-thirty men of his could easily keep the ship free; never mind if the leak should double on her. In truth, well nigh the whole of this passage being attended by very prosperous breezes, the Town-Ho had all but certainly arrived in perfect safety at her port without the occurrence of the least fatality, had it not been for the brutal overbearing of Radney, the mate, a Vineyarder, and the bitterly provoked vengeance of Steelkilt, a Lakeman and desperado from Buffalo.

" 'Lakeman!—Buffalo! Pray, what is a Lakeman, and where is Buffalo?' said Don Sebastian, rising in his swinging mat of grass.

"On the eastern shore of our Lake Erie, Don; but—I crave your courtesy—may be, you shall soon hear further of all that. Now, gentlemen, in square-sail brigs and three-masted ships, well nigh as large and stout as any that ever sailed out of your old Callao to far Manilla; this Lakeman, in the landlocked heart of our America, had yet been nurtured by all those agrarian free-booting impressions popularly connected with the open ocean. For in their interflowing aggregate, those grand fresh-water seas of ours—Erie, and Ontario, and Huron, and Superior, and Michigan,—possess an ocean-like expansiveness, with many of the ocean's noblest traits; with many of its rimmed varieties of races and of climes. They contain round archipelagoes of romantic isles, even as the Polynesian waters do; in large part, are shored by two great contrasting nations, as the Atlantic is; they furnish long maritime approaches to our numerous territorial colonies from the East, dotted all round their banks; here and there are frowned upon by batteries, and by the goat-like craggy guns of lofty Mackinaw; they have heard the fleet thunderings of naval

victories; at intervals, they yield their beaches to wild barbarians, whose red painted faces flash from out their peltry
wigwams; for leagues and leagues are flanked by ancient
and unentered forests, where the gaunt pines stand like
serried lines of kings in Gothic genealogies; those same
woods harboring wild Afric beasts of prey, and silken creatures whose exported furs give robes to Tartar Emperors;
they mirror the paved capitals of Buffalo and Cleveland, as
well as Winnebago villages; they float alike the full-rigged merchant ship, the armed cruiser of the State, the steamer, and
the beech canoe; they are swept by Borean and dismasting
blasts as direful as any that lash the salted wave; they know
what shipwrecks are, for out of sight of land, however inland, they have drowned full many a midnight ship with all
its shrieking crew. Thus, gentlemen, though an inlander,
Steelkilt was wild-ocean born, and wild-ocean nurtured; as
much of an audacious mariner as any. And for Radney, though
in his infancy he may have laid him down on the lone Nantucket beach, to nurse at his maternal sea; though in after life
he had long followed our austere Atlantic and your contemplative Pacific; yet was he quite as vengeful and full of social
quarrel as the backwoods seaman, fresh from the latitudes of
buck-horn handled Bowie-knives. Yet was this Nantucketer
a man with some good-hearted traits; and this Lakeman, a
mariner, who though a sort of devil indeed, might yet by
inflexible firmness, only tempered by that common decency
of human recognition which is the meanest slave's right; thus
treated, this Steelkilt had long been retained harmless and
docile. At all events, he had proved so thus far; but Radney
was doomed and made mad, and Steelkilt—but, gentlemen, you shall hear.

"It was not more than a day or two at the furthest after
pointing her prow for her island haven, that the Town-Ho's
leak seemed again increasing, but only so as to require an
hour or more at the pumps every day. You must know that
in a settled and civilized ocean like our Atlantic, for example,
some skippers think little of pumping their whole way across
it; though of a still, sleepy night, should the officer of the
deck happen to forget his duty in that respect, the probability
would be that he and his shipmates would never again remember it, on account of all hands gently subsiding to the bottom.
Nor in the solitary and savage seas far from you to the west-

ward, gentlemen, is it altogether unusual for ships to keep clanging at their pump-handles in full chorus even for a voyage of considerable length; that is, if it lie along a tolerably accessible coast, or if any other reasonable retreat is afforded them. It is only when a leaky vessel is in some very out of the way part of those waters, some really landless latitude, that her captain begins to feel a little anxious.

"Much this way had it been with the Town-Ho; so when her leak was found gaining once more, there was in truth some small concern manifested by several of her company; especially by Radney the mate. He commanded the upper sails to be well hoisted, sheeted home anew, and every way expanded to the breeze. Now this Radney, I suppose, was as little of a coward, and as little inclined to any sort of nervous apprehensiveness touching his own person as any fearless, unthinking creature on land or on sea that you can conveniently imagine, gentlemen. Therefore when he betrayed this solicitude about the safety of the ship, some of the seamen declared that it was only on account of his being a part owner in her. So when they were working that evening at the pumps, there was on this head no small gamesomeness slily going on among them, as they stood with their feet continually overflowed by the rippling clear water; clear as any mountain spring, gentlemen—that bubbling from the pumps ran across the deck, and poured itself out in steady spouts at the lee scupper-holes.

"Now, as you well know, it is not seldom the case in this conventional world of ours—watery or otherwise; that when a person placed in command over his fellow-men finds one of them to be very significantly his superior in general pride of manhood, straightway against that man he conceives an unconquerable dislike and bitterness; and if he have a chance he will pull down and pulverize that subaltern's tower, and make a little heap of dust of it. Be this conceit of mine as it may, gentlemen, at all events Steelkilt was a tall and noble animal with a head like a Roman, and a flowing golden beard like the tasseled housings of your last viceroy's snorting charger; and a brain, and a heart, and a soul in him, gentlemen, which had made Steelkilt Charlemagne, had he been born son to Charlemagne's father. But Radney, the mate, was ugly as a mule; yet as hardy, as stubborn, as malicious. He did not love Steelkilt, and Steelkilt knew it.

"Espying the mate drawing near as he was toiling at the pump with the rest, the Lakeman affected not to notice him, but unawed, went on with his gay banterings.

" 'Aye, aye, my merry lads, it's a lively leak this; hold a cannikin, one of ye, and let's have a taste. By the Lord, it's worth bottling! I tell ye what, men, old Rad's investment must go for it! he had best cut away his part of the hull and tow it home. The fact is, boys, that sword-fish only began the job; he's come back again with a gang of ship-carpenters, saw-fish, and file-fish, and what not; and the whole posse of em are now hard at work cutting and slashing at the bottom; making improvements, I suppose. If old Rad were here now, I'd tell him to jump overboard and scatter 'em. They're playing the devil with his estate, I can tell him. But he's a simple old soul,—Rad, and a beauty too. Boys, they say the rest of his property is invested in looking-glasses. I wonder if he'd give a poor devil like me the model of his nose.'

" 'Damn your eyes! what's that pump stopping for?' roared Radney, pretending not to have heard the sailors' talk. 'Thunder away at it!'

" 'Aye, aye, sir,' said Steelkilt, merry as a cricket. 'Lively, boys, lively, now!' And with that the pump clanged like fifty fire-engines; the men tossed their hats off to it, and ere long that peculiar gasping of the lungs was heard which denotes the fullest tension of life's utmost energies.

"Quitting the pump at last, with the rest of his band, the Lakeman went forward all panting, and sat himself down on the windlass; his face fiery red, his eyes bloodshot, and wiping the profuse sweat from his brow. Now what cozening fiend it was, gentlemen, that possessed Radney to meddle with such a man in that corporeally exasperated state, I know not; but so it happened. Intolerably striding along the deck, the mate commanded him to get a broom and sweep down the planks, and also a shovel, and remove some offensive matters consequent upon allowing a pig to run at large.

"Now, gentlemen, sweeping a ship's deck at sea is a piece of household work which in all times but raging gales is regularly attended to every evening; it has been known to be done in the case of ships actually foundering at the time. Such, gentlemen, is the inflexibility of sea-usages and the instinctive love of neatness in seamen; some of whom would not willingly drown without first washing their faces. But in all vessels this broom business is the prescriptive province of the boys, if boys there be aboard. Besides, it was the stronger men in the Town-Ho that had been divided into gangs, taking turns at the pumps; and being the most athletic seaman of them all, Steelkilt had been regularly assigned captain of one of the gangs; consequently he should have been freed from any trivial business not connected with truly nautical duties, such being the case with his comrades. I mention all these particulars so that you may understand exactly how this affair stood between the two men.

"But there was more than this: the order about the shovel was almost as plainly meant to sting and insult Steelkilt, as though Radney had spat in his face. Any man who has gone sailor in a whale-ship will understand this; and all this and doubtless much more, the Lakeman fully comprehended when the mate uttered his command. But as he sat still for a moment, and as he steadfastly looked into the mate's malignant eye and perceived the stacks of powder-casks heaped up in him and the slow-match silently burning along towards them; as he instinctively saw all this, that strange forbearance and unwillingness to stir up the deeper passionateness in any already ireful being—a repugnance most felt, when felt at all, by really valiant men even when aggrieved—this nameless phantom feeling, gentlemen, stole over Steelkilt.

"Therefore, in his ordinary tone, only a little broken by the bodily exhaustion he was temporarily in, he answered him saying that sweeping the deck was not his business, and he would not do it. And then, without at all alluding to the shovel, he pointed to three lads as the customary sweepers; who, not being billeted at the pumps, had done little or nothing all day. To this, Radney replied with an oath, in a most domineering and outrageous manner unconditionally reiterating his command; meanwhile advancing upon the still seated Lakeman, with an uplifted cooper's club hammer which he had snatched from a cask near by.

"Heated and irritated as he was by his spasmodic toil at the pumps, for all his first nameless feeling of forbearance the sweating Steelkilt could but ill brook this bearing in the mate; but somehow still smothering the conflagration within him, without speaking he remained doggedly rooted to his seat, till at last the incensed Radney shook the hammer within a few inches of his face, furiously commanding him to do his bidding.

"Steelkilt rose, and slowly retreating round the windlass,

steadily followed by the mate with his menacing hammer, deliberately repeated his intention not to obey. Seeing, however, that his forbearance had not the slightest effect, by an awful and unspeakable intimation with his twisted hand he warned off the foolish and infatuated man; but it was to no purpose. And in this way the two went once slowly round the windlass; when, resolved at last no longer to retreat, bethinking him that he had now forborne as much as comported with his humor, the Lakeman paused on the hatches and thus spoke to the officer:

" 'Mr. Radney, I will not obey you. Take that hammer away, or look to yourself.' But the predestinated mate coming still closer to him, where the Lakeman stood fixed, now shook the heavy hammer within an inch of his teeth; meanwhile repeating a string of insufferable maledictions. Retreating not the thousandth part of an inch; stabbing him in the eye with the unflinching poniard of his glance, Steelkilt, clenching his right hand behind him and creepingly drawing it back, told his persecutor that if the hammer but grazed his cheek he (Steelkilt) would murder him. But, gentlemen, the fool had been branded for the slaughter by the gods. Immediately the hammer touched the cheek; the next instant the lower jaw of the mate was stove in his head; he fell on the hatch spouting blood like a whale.

"Ere the cry could go aft Steelkilt was shaking one of the backstays leading far aloft to where two of his comrades were standing their mast-heads. They were both Canallers.

" 'Canallers!' cried Don Pedro. 'We have seen many whaleships in our harbors, but never heard of your Canallers. Pardon: who and what are they?'

" 'Canallers, Don, are the boatmen belonging to our grand Erie Canal. You must have heard of it.'

" 'Nay, Senor; hereabouts in this dull, warm, most lazy, and hereditary land, we know but little of your vigorous North.'

" 'Aye? Well then, Don, refill my cup. Your chicha's very fine; and ere proceeding further I will tell ye what our Canallers are; for such information may throw side-light upon my story.'

"For three hundred and sixty miles, gentlemen, through the entire breadth of the state of New York; through numerous populous cities and most thriving villages; through long, dismal uninhabited swamps, and affluent, cultivated fields, unrivalled for fertility; by billiard-room and bar-room; through the holy-of-holies of great forests; on Roman arches over Indian rivers; through sun and shade; by happy hearts or broken; through all the wide contrasting scenery of those noble Mohawk counties; and especially, by rows of snow-white chapels, whose spires stand almost like milestones, flows one continual stream of Venetianly corrupt and often lawless life. There's your true Ashantee, gentlemen; there howl your pagans; where you ever find them, next door to you; under the long-flung shadow, and the snug patronizing lee of churches. For by some curious fatality, as it is often noted of your metropolitan freebooters that they ever encamp around the halls of justice so sinners, gentlemen, most abound in holiest vicinities.

" 'Is that a friar passing?' said Don Pedro, looking downwards into the crowded plaza, with humorous concern.

" 'Well for our northern friend, Dame Isabella's Inquisition wanes in Lima,' laughed Don Sebastian. 'Proceed, Senor.'

" 'A moment! Pardon!' cried another of the company. 'In the name of all us Limeese, I but desire to express to you, sir sailor, that we have by no means overlooked your delicacy in not substituting present Lima for distant Venice in your corrupt comparison. Oh! do not bow and look surprised; you know the proverb all along this coast—"Corrupt as Lima." It but bears out your saying, too; churches more plentiful than billiard-tables, and for ever open—and "Corrupt as Lima." So, too, Venice; I have been there; the holy city of the blessed evangelist St. Mark!—St. Dominic, purge it! Your cup! Thanks: here I refill; now, you pour out again.'

"Freely depicted in his own vocation, gentlemen, the Canaller would make a fine dramatic hero, so abundantly and picturesquely wicked is he. Like Mark Antony, for days and days along his green-turfed, flowery Nile, he indolently floats, openly toying with his red-cheeked Cleopatra, ripening his apricot thigh upon the sunny deck. But ashore, all this effeminacy is dashed. The brigandish guise which the Canaller so proudly sports; his slouched and gaily-ribboned hat betoken his grand features. A terror to the smiling innocence of the villages through which he floats; his swart visage and bold swagger are not unshunned in cities. Once a vagabond on his own canal, I have received good turns from one of these Canallers; I thank him heartily; would fain be not ungrateful; but it is often one of the prime redeeming qualities of your man of violence, that at times he has as stiff an arm to back a poor stranger in a strait, as to plunder a wealthy one. In sum, gentlemen, what the wildness of this canal life is, is emphatically evinced by this; that our wild whale-fishery contains so many of its most finished graduates, and that scarce any race of mankind, except Sydney men, are so much distrusted by our whaling captains. Nor does it at all diminish the curiousness of this matter, that to many thousands of our rural boys and young men born along its line, the probationary life of the Grand Canal furnishes the sole transition between quietly reaping in a Christian corn-field and recklessly ploughing the waters of the most barbaric seas.

" 'I see! I see!' impetuously exclaimed Don Pedro, spilling his chicha upon his silvery ruffles. 'No need to travel! The world's one Lima. I had thought, now, that at your temperate North the generations were cold and holy as the hills.—But the story.'

"I left off, gentlemen, where the Lakeman shook the backstay. Hardly had he done so, when he was surrounded by the three junior mates and the four harpooneers, who all crowded him to the deck. But sliding down the ropes like baleful comets, the two Canallers rushed into the uproar, and sought to drag their man out of it towards the forecastle. Others of the sailors joined with them in this attempt, and a twisted turmoil ensued; while standing out of harm's way, the valiant captain danced up and down with a whale-pike, calling upon his officers to manhandle that atrocious scoundrel, and smoke him along to the quarter-deck. At intervals, he ran close up to the revolving border of the confusion, and prying into the heart of it with his pike, sought to prick out the object of his resentment. But Steelkilt and his desperadoes were too much for them all; they succeeded in gaining the forecastle deck, where, hastily slewing about three or four large casks in a line with the windlass, these sea-Parisians entrenched themselves behind the barricade.

" 'Come out of that, ye pirates!' roared the captain, now menacing them with a pistol in each hand, just brought to him by the steward. 'Come out of that, ye cut-throats!'

"Steelkilt leaped on the barricade, and striding up and down there, defied the worst the pistols could do; but gave the captain to understand distinctly, that his (Steelkilt's) death would be the signal for a murderous mutiny on the part of all hands. Fearing in his heart lest this might prove but too true, the captain a little desisted, but still commanded the insurgents instantly to return to their duty.

"'Will you promise not to touch us, if we do?' demanded their ringleader.

"'Turn to! turn to!—I make no promise;—to your duty! Do you want to sink the ship, by knocking off at a time like this? Turn to!' and he once more raised a pistol.

"'Sink the ship?' cried Steelkilt. 'Aye, let her sink. Not a man of us turns to, unless you swear not to raise a ropeyarn against us. What say ye, men?' turning to his comrades. A fierce cheer was their response.

"The Lakeman now patrolled the barricade, all the while keeping his eye on the captain, and jerking out such sentences as these:—'It's not our fault; we didn't want it; I told him to take his hammer away; it was boy's business; he might have known me before this; I told him not to prick the buffalo; I believe I have broken a finger here against his cursed jaw; ain't those mincing knives down in the forecastle there, men? look to those handspikes, my hearties. Captain, by God, look to yourself; say the word; don't be a fool; forget it all; we are ready to turn to; treat us decently, and we're your men; but we won't be flogged.'

"'Turn to! I make no promises, turn to, I say!'

"'Look ye, now,' cried the Lakeman, flinging out his arm towards him, 'there are a few of us here (and I am one of them) who have shipped for the cruise, d'ye see; now as you well know, sir, we can claim our discharge as soon as the anchor is down; so we don't want a row; it's not our interest; we want to be peaceable; we are ready to work, but we won't be flogged.'

"'Turn to!' roared the captain.

"Steelkilt glanced round him a moment, and then said:— 'I tell you what it is now, Captain, rather than kill ye, and be hung for such a shabby rascal, we won't lift a hand against ye unless ye attack us; but till you say the word about not flogging us, we don't do a hand's turn.'

"'Down into the forecastle then, down with ye, I'll keep ye there till ye're sick of it. Down ye go.'

"'Shall we?' cried the ringleader to his men. Most of them were against it; but at length, in obedience to Steelkilt, they preceded him down into their dark den, growlingly disappearing, like bears into a cave.

"As the Lakeman's bare head was just level with the planks,

the captain and his posse leaped the barricade, and rapidly drawing over the slide of the scuttle, planted their group of hands upon it, and loudly called for the steward to bring the heavy brass padlock belonging to the companionway. Then opening the slide a little, the captain whispered something down the crack, closed it, and turned the key upon them—ten in number—leaving on deck some twenty or more, who thus far had remained neutral.

"All night a wide-awake watch was kept by all the officers, forward and aft, especially about the forecastle scuttle and fore hatchway; at which last place it was feared the insurgents might emerge, after breaking through the bulkhead below. But the hours of darkness passed in peace; the men who still remained at their duty toiling hard at the pumps, whose clinking and clanking at intervals through the dreary night dismally resounded through the ship.

"At sunrise the captain went forward, and knocking on the deck, summoned the prisoners to work; but with a yell they refused. Water was then lowered down to them, and a couple of handfuls of biscuit were tossed after it; when again turning the key upon them and pocketing it, the captain returned to the quarter-deck. Twice every day for three days this was repeated; but on the fourth morning a confused wrangling, and then a scuffling was heard, as the customary summons was delivered; and suddenly four men burst up from the forecastle, saying they were ready to turn to. The fetid closeness of the air, and a famishing diet, united perhaps to some fears of ultimate retribution, had constrained them to surrender at discretion. Emboldened by this, the captain reiterated his demand to the rest, but Steelkilt shouted up to him a terrific hint to stop his babbling and betake himself where he belonged. On the fifth morning three others of the mutineers bolted up into the air from the desperate arms below that sought to restrain them. Only three were left.

" 'Better turn to, now?' said the captain with a heartless jeer.

" 'Shut us up again, will ye!' cried Steelkilt.

" 'Oh! certainly,' said the captain, and the key clicked.

"It was at this point, gentlemen, that enraged by the defection of seven of his former associates, and stung by the mocking voice that had last hailed him, and maddened by his long entombment in a place as black as the bowels of despair; it was then that Steelkilt proposed to the two Canallers, thus

far apparently of one mind with him, to burst out of their
hole at the next summoning of the garrison; and armed with
their keen mincing knives (long, crescentic, heavy implements
with a handle at each end) run amuck from the bowsprit to
the taffrail; and if by any devilishness of desperation possible,
seize the ship. For himself, he would do this, he said, whether
they joined him or not. That was the last night he should
spend in that den. But the scheme met with no opposition on
the part of the other two; they swore they were ready for that,
or for any other mad thing, for anything in short but a surrender. And what was more, they each insisted upon being
the first man on deck, when the time to make the rush should
come. But to this their leader as fiercely objected, reserving
that priority for himself; particularly as his two comrades
would not yield, the one to the other, in the matter; and both
of them could not be first, for the ladder would but admit one
man at a time. And here, gentlemen, the foul play of these
miscreants must come out.

"Upon hearing the frantic project of their leader, each in
his own separate soul had suddenly lighted, it would seem,
upon the same piece of treachery, namely: to be foremost in
breaking out, in order to be the first of the three, though the
last of the ten, to surrender; and thereby secure whatever small
chance of pardon such conduct might merit. But when Steelkilt made known his determination still to lead them to the
last, they in some way, by some subtle chemistry of villainy,
mixed their before secret treacheries together; and when their
leader fell into a doze, verbally opened their souls to each
other in three sentences; and bound the sleeper with cords,
and gagged him with cords; and shrieked out for the captain
at midnight.

"Thinking murder at hand, and smelling in the dark for
the blood, he and all his armed mates and harpooneers rushed
for the forecastle. In a few minutes the scuttle was opened,
and, bound hand and foot, the still struggling ringleader was
shoved up into the air by his perfidious allies, who at once
claimed the honor of securing a man who had been fully ripe
for murder. But all these were collared, and dragged along
the deck like dead cattle; and, side by side, were seized up into
the mizen rigging, like three quarters of meat, and there they
hung till morning. 'Damn ye,' cried the captain, pacing to and
fro before them, 'the vultures would not touch ye, ye villains!'

"At sunrise he summoned all hands; and separating those

who had rebelled from those who had taken no part in the mutiny, he told the former that he had a good mind to flog them all round—thought, upon the whole, he would do so—he ought to—justice demanded it; but for the present, considering their timely surrender, he would let them go with a reprimand, which he accordingly administered in the vernacular.

" 'But as for you, ye carrion rogues,' turning to the three men in the rigging—'for you, I mean to mince ye up for the try-pots;' and, seizing a rope, he applied it with all his might to the backs of the two traitors, till they yelled no more, but lifelessly hung their heads sideways, as the two crucified thieves are drawn.

" 'My wrist is sprained with ye!' he cried, at last; 'but there is still rope enough left for you, my fine bantam, that wouldn't give up. Take that gag from his mouth, and let us hear what he can say for himself.'

"For a moment the exhausted mutineer made a tremulous motion of his cramped jaws, and then painfully twisting round his head, said in a sort of hiss, 'What I say is this—and mind it well—if you flog me, I murder you!'

" 'Say ye so? then see how ye frighten me'—and the captain drew off with the rope to strike.

" 'Best not,' hissed the Lakeman.

" 'But I must,'—and the rope was once more drawn back for the stroke.

"Steelkilt here hissed out something, inaudible to all but the captain; who, to the amazement of all hands, started back, paced the deck rapidly two or three times, and then suddenly throwing down his rope, said, 'I won't do it—let him go—cut him down: d'ye hear?'

"But as the junior mates were hurrying to execute the order, a pale man, with a bandaged head, arrested them—Radney the chief mate. Ever since the blow, he had lain in his berth; but that morning, hearing the tumult on the deck, he had crept out, and thus far had watched the whole scene. Such was the state of his mouth, that he could hardly speak; but mumbling something about *his* being willing and able to do what the captain dared not attempt, he snatched the rope and advanced to his pinioned foe.

" 'You are a coward!' hissed the Lakeman.

" 'So I am, but take that.' The mate was in the very act of striking, when another hiss stayed his uplifted arm. He paused: and then pausing no more, made good his word, spite of Steelkilt's threat, whatever that might have been. The three men were then cut down, all hands were turned to, and, sullenly worked by the moody seamen, the iron pumps clanged as before.

"Just after dark that day, when one watch had retired below, a clamor was heard in the forecastle; and the two trembling traitors running up, besieged the cabin door, saying they durst not consort with the crew. Entreaties, cuffs, and kicks could not drive them back, so at their own instance they were put down in the ship's run for salvation. Still, no sign of mutiny reappeared among the rest. On the contrary, it seemed, that mainly at Steelkilt's instigation, they had resolved to maintain the strictest peacefulness, obey all orders to the last, and, when the ship reached port, desert her in a body. But in order to insure the speediest end to the voyage, they all agreed to another thing—namely, not to sing out for whales, in case any should be discovered. For, spite of her leak, and spite of all her other perils, the Town-Ho still maintained her mast-heads, and her captain was just as willing to lower for a fish that moment, as on the day his craft first struck the cruising ground; and Radney the mate was quite as ready to change his berth for a boat, and with his bandaged mouth seek to gag in death the vital jaw of the whale.

"But though the Lakeman had induced the seamen to adopt this sort of passiveness in their conduct, he kept his own counsel (at least till all was over) concerning his own proper and private revenge upon the man who had stung him in the ventricles of his heart. He was in Radney the chief mate's watch; and as if the infatuated man sought to run more than half way to meet his doom, after the scene at the rigging, he insisted, against the express counsel of the captain, upon resuming the head of his watch at night. Upon this, and one or two other circumstances, Steelkilt systematically built the plan of his revenge.

"During the night, Radney had an unseamanlike way of sitting on the bulwarks of the quarter-deck, and leaning his arm upon the gunwale of the boat which was hoisted up there, a little above the ship's side. In this attitude, it was well known, he sometimes dozed. There was a considerable vacancy between the boat and the ship, and down between this was the sea. Steelkilt calculated his time, and found that his next trick at the helm would come round at two o'clock, in the morning of the third day from that in which he had been betrayed.

At his leisure, he employed the interval in braiding something very carefully in his watches below.

" 'What are you making there?' said a shipmate.

" 'What do you think? what does it look like?'

" 'Like a lanyard for your bag; but it's an odd one, seems to me.'

" 'Yes, rather oddish,' said the Lakeman, holding it at arm's length before him; 'but I think it will answer. Shipmate, I haven't enough twine,—have you any?'

"But there was none in the forecastle.

" 'Then, I must get some from old Rad;' and he rose to go aft.

" 'You don't mean to go a begging to *him!*' said a sailor.

" 'Why not? Do you think he won't do me a turn, when it's to help himself in the end, shipmate?' and going to the mate, he looked at him quietly, and asked him for some twine to mend his hammock. It was given him—neither twine nor lanyard were seen again; but the next night an iron ball, closely netted, partly rolled from the pocket of the Lakeman's monkey jacket, as he was tucking the coat into his hammock for a pillow. Twenty-four hours after, his trick at the silent helm—nigh to the man who was apt to doze over the grave always ready dug to the seaman's hand—that fatal hour was then to come; and in the fore-ordaining soul of Steelkilt, the mate was already stark and stretched as a corpse, with his forehead crushed in.

"But, gentlemen, a fool saved the would-be murderer from the bloody deed he had planned. Yet complete revenge he had, and without being the avenger. For by a mysterious fatality, Heaven itself seemed to step in to take out of his hands into its own the damning thing he would have done.

"It was just between daybreak and sunrise of the morning of the second day, when they were washing down the decks, that a stupid Teneriffe man, drawing water in the main-chains, all at once shouted out, 'There she rolls! there she rolls!' Jesu, what a whale! It was Moby Dick.

" 'Moby Dick!' cried Don Sebastian; 'St. Dominic! Sir sailor, but do whales have christenings? Whom call you Moby Dick?'

" 'A very white, and famous, and most deadly immortal monster, Don;—but that would be too long a story.'

" 'How? how?' cried all the young Spaniards, crowding.

" 'Nay, Dons, Dons—nay, nay! I cannot rehearse that now. Let me get more into the air, Sirs.'

" 'The chicha! the chicha!' cried Don Pedro; 'our vigorous friend looks faint;—fill up his empty glass!'

"No need, gentlemen; one moment, and I proceed.—Now, gentlemen, so suddenly perceiving the snowy whale within fifty yards of the ship—forgetful of the compact among the crew—in the excitement of the moment, the Teneriffe man had instinctively and involuntarily lifted his voice for the monster, though for some little time past it had been plainly beheld from the three sullen mast-heads. All was now a phrensy. 'The White Whale—the White Whale!' was the cry from captain, mates, and harpooneers, who, undeterred by fearful rumors, were all anxious to capture so famous and precious a fish; while the dogged crew eyed askance, and with curses, the appalling beauty of the vast milky mass, that lit up by a horizontal spangling sun, shifted and glistened like a living opal in the blue morning sea. Gentlemen, a strange fatality pervades the whole career of these events, as if verily mapped out before the world itself was charted. The mutineer was the bowsman of the mate, and when fast to a fish, it was his duty to sit next him, while Radney stood up with his lance in the prow, and haul in or slacken the line, at the word of command. Moreover, when the four boats were lowered, the mate's got the start; and none howled more fiercely with delight than did Steelkilt, as he strained at his oar. After a stiff pull, their harpooneers got fast, and, spear in hand, Radney sprang to the bow. He was always a furious man, it seems, in a boat. And now his bandaged cry was, to beach him on the whale's topmost back. Nothing loath, his bowsman hauled him up and up, through a blinding foam that blent two whitenesses together; till of a sudden the boat struck as against a sunken ledge, and keeling over, spilled out the standing mate. That instant, as he fell on the whale's slippery back, the boat righted, and was dashed aside by the swell, while Radney was tossed over into the sea, on the other flank of the whale. He struck out through the spray, and, for an instant, was dimly seen through that veil, wildly seeking to remove himself from the eye of Moby Dick. But the whale rushed round in a sudden maelstrom; seized the swimmer between his jaws; and rearing high up with him, plunged headlong again, and went down.

"Meantime, at the first tap of the boat's bottom, the Lakeman had slackened the line, so as to drop astern from the whirlpool; calmly looking on, he thought his own thoughts.

But a sudden, terrific, downward jerking of the boat, quickly brought his knife to the line. He cut it; and the whale was free. But, at some distance, Moby Dick rose again, with some tatters of Radney's red woolen shirt, caught in the teeth that had destroyed him. All four boats gave chase again; but the whale eluded them, and finally wholly disappeared.

"In good time, the Town-Ho reached her port—a savage, solitary place—where no civilized creature resided. There, headed by the Lakeman, all but five or six of the foremastmen deliberately deserted among the palms; eventually, as it turned out, seizing a large double war-canoe of the savages, and setting sail for some other harbor.

"The ship's company being reduced to but a handful, the captain called upon the Islanders to assist him in the laborious business of heaving down the ship to stop the leak. But to such unresting vigilance over their dangerous allies was this small band of whites necessitated, both by night and by day, and so extreme was the hard work they underwent, that upon the vessel being ready again for sea, they were in such a weakened condition that the captain durst not put off with them in so heavy a vessel. After taking counsel with his officers, he anchored the ship as far off shore as possible; loaded and ran out his two cannon from the bows; stacked his muskets on the poop; and warning the Islanders not to approach the ship at their peril, took one man with him, and setting the sail of his best whaleboat, steered straight before the wind for Tahiti, five hundred miles distant, to procure a reinforcement to his crew.

"On the fourth day of the sail, a large canoe was descried, which seemed to have touched at a low isle of corals. He steered away from it; but the savage craft bore down on him; and soon the voice of Steelkilt hailed him to heave to, or he would run him under water. The captain presented a pistol. With one foot on each prow of the yoked war-canoes, the Lakeman laughed him to scorn; assuring him that if the pistol so much as clicked in the lock, he would bury him in bubbles and foam.

" 'What do you want of me?' cried the captain.

" 'Where are you bound? and for what are you bound?' demanded Steelkilt; 'no lies.'

" 'I am bound to Tahiti for more men.'

" 'Very good. Let me board you a moment—I come in peace.' With that he leaped from the canoe, swam to the boat; and climbing the gunwale, stood face to face with the captain.

" 'Cross your arms, sir; throw back your head. Now, repeat after me. As soon as Steelkilt leaves me, I swear to beach this boat on yonder island, and remain there six days. If I do not, may lightnings strike me!'

" 'A pretty scholar,' laughed the Lakeman. 'Adios, Senor!' and leaping into the sea, he swam back to his comrades.

"Watching the boat till it was fairly beached, and drawn up to the roots of the cocoa-nut trees, Steelkilt made sail again, and in due time arrived at Tahiti, his own place of destination. There, luck befriended him; two ships were about to sail for France, and were providentially in want of precisely that number of men which the sailor headed. They embarked; and so for ever got the start of their former captain, had he been at all minded to work them legal retribution.

"Some ten days after the French ships sailed, the whale-boat arrived, and the captain was forced to enlist some of the more civilized Tahitians, who had been somewhat used to the sea. Chartering a small native schooner, he returned with them to his vessel; and finding all right there, again resumed his cruisings.

"Where Steelkilt now is, gentlemen, none know; but upon the island of Nantucket, the widow of Radney still turns to the sea which refuses to give up its dead; still in dreams sees the awful White Whale that destroyed him. * * *

" 'Are you through?' said Don Sebastian, quietly.

" 'I am, Don.'

" 'Then I entreat you, tell me if to the best of your own convictions, this your story is in substance really true? It is so passing wonderful! Did you get it from an unquestionable source? Bear with me if I seem to press.'

" 'Also bear with all of us, sir sailor; for we all join in Don Sebastian's suit,' cried the company, with exceeding interest.

" 'Is there a copy of the Holy Evangelists in the Golden Inn, gentlemen?'

" 'Nay,' said Don Sebastian; 'but I know a worthy priest near by, who will quickly procure one for me. I go for it; but are you well advised? this may grow too serious.'

" 'Will you be so good as to bring the priest also,-Don?'

" 'Though there are no Auto-da-Fés in Lima now,' said one of the company to another; 'I fear our sailor friend runs risk of the archiepiscopacy. Let us withdraw more out of the moon-light. I see no need of this.'

" 'Excuse me for running after you, Don Sebastian; but may

I also beg that you will be particular in procuring the largest sized Evangelists you can.'

*   *   *

" 'This is the priest, he brings you the Evangelists,' said Don Sebastian, gravely, returning with a tall and solemn figure.

" 'Let me remove my hat. Now, venerable priest, further into the light, and hold the Holy Book before me that I may touch it.'

" 'So help me, Heaven, and on my honor the story I have told ye, gentlemen, is in substance and its great items, true. I know it to be true; it happened on this ball; I trod the ship; I knew the crew; I have seen and talked with Steelkilt since the death of Radney.' "

BARTLEBY, THE SCRIVENER:
A STORY OF WALL-STREET

NOTE: It is still not possible to reconstruct Melville's literary activity during the sixteen or seventeen months after publication of *Pierre* in the summer of 1852. Documents from this troubled interval refer to works planned or in progress—letters to Hawthorne in the late summer and fall of 1852 outline the pathetic "Agatha" story, and the next April Melville's mother was writing of a "new work, now nearly ready for the press"—but nobody knows what relation, if any, these projects bear to the tales that began appearing in *Harper's* and in *Putnam's Monthly Magazine* late in 1853. The one thing clear is that between *Pierre* and the first installment of "Bartleby, the Scrivener" (*Puntnam's*, November, 1853) Melville altered his character as a producer of fiction, in more ways than one.

What is surely remarkable is that this first independent result of his shift from writing books to writing for magazines should be one of the undisputed masterpieces of nineteenth-century story-telling: Dickensian in its lively vernacular humor, Dostoievskian in its objective pathos and parabolic overtones.

I AM a rather elderly man. The nature of my avocations, for the last thirty years, has brought me into more than ordinary contact with what would seem an interesting and somewhat singular set of men, of whom, as yet, nothing, that I know of, has ever been written—I mean, the law-copyists, or scriveners. I have known very many of them, professionally and privately, and, if I pleased, could relate divers histories, at which good-natured gentlemen might smile, and sentimental souls might weep. But I waive the biographies of all other scriveners, for a few passages in the life of Bartleby, who was a scrivener, the strangest I ever saw, or heard of. While, of other law-copyists, I might write the complete life, of Bartleby nothing of that sort can be done. I believe that no materials exist, for a full and satisfactory biography of this man. It is an irreparable loss to literature. Bartleby was one of those beings of whom nothing is ascertainable, except from the original sources, and, in his case, those are very small. What my own astonished eyes saw of Bartleby, *that* is all I know of him, except, indeed, one vague report, which will appear in the sequel.

Ere introducing the scrivener, as he first appeared to me, it is fit I make some mention of myself, my *employés*, my business, my chambers, and general surroundings; because some such description is indispensable to an adequate understanding of the chief character about to be presented. Imprimis: I am a man who, from his youth upwards, has been filled with a profound conviction that the easiest way of life is the best. Hence, though I belong to a profession proverbially energetic and nervous, even to turbulence, at times, yet nothing of that sort have I ever suffered to invade my peace. I am one of those unambitious lawyers who never address a jury, or in any way draw down public applause; but, in the cool tranquillity of a snug retreat, do a snug business among rich men's bonds, and mortgages, and title-deeds. All who know me, consider me an eminently *safe* man. The late John Jacob Astor, a personage little given to poetic enthusiasm, had no hesitation in pronouncing my first grand point to be prudence; my next, method. I do not speak it in vanity, but simply record the fact, that I was not unemployed in my profession by the late John Jacob Astor; a name which, I admit, I love to repeat; for it hath a rounded and orbicular sound to it, and rings like unto bullion. I will freely add, that I was not insensible to the late John Jacob Astor's good opinion.

Some time prior to the period at which this little history begins, my avocations had been largely increased. The good old office, now extinct in the State of New York, of a Master in Chancery, had been conferred upon me. It was not a very arduous office, but very pleasantly remunerative. I seldom lose my temper; much more seldom indulge in dangerous indignation at wrongs and outrages; but I must be permitted to be rash here and declare, that I consider the sudden and violent abrogation of the office of Master in Chancery, by the new Constitution, as a——premature act; inasmuch as I had counted upon a life-lease of the profits, whereas I only received those of a few short years. But this is by the way.

My chambers were up stairs, at No. — Wall Street. At one end, they looked upon the white wall of the interior of a spacious sky-light shaft, penetrating the building from top to bottom.

This view might have been considered rather tame than otherwise, deficient in what landscape painters call "life." But, if so, the view from the other end of my chambers offered, at least, a contrast, if nothing more. In that direction, my windows commanded an unobstructed view of a lofty brick wall, black by age and everlasting shade; which wall required no spy-glass to bring out its lurking beauties, but, for the benefit of all near-sighted spectators, was pushed up to within ten feet of my window-panes. Owing to the great height of the surrounding buildings, and my chambers being on the second floor, the interval between this wall and mine not a little resembled a huge square cistern.

At the period just preceding the advent of Bartleby, I had two persons as copyists in my employment, and a promising lad as an office-boy. First, Turkey; second, Nippers; third, Ginger Nut. These may seem names, the like of which are not usually found in the Directory. In truth, they were nicknames, mutually conferred upon each other by my three clerks, and were deemed expressive of their respective persons or characters. Turkey was a short, pursy Englishman, of about my own age—that is, somewhere not far from sixty. In the morning, one might say, his face was of a fine florid hue, but after twelve o'clock, meridian—his dinner hour—it blazed like a grate full of Christmas coals; and continued blazing—but, as it were, with a gradual wane—till six o'clock, P. M., or thereabouts; after which, I saw no more of the proprietor of the face, which, gaining its meridian with the sun, seemed to set with it, to rise, culminate, and decline the following day, with the like regularity and undiminished glory. There are many singular coincidences I have known in the course of my life, not the least among which was the fact, that, exactly when Turkey displayed his fullest beams from his red and radiant countenance, just then, too, at that critical moment, began the daily period when I considered his business capacities as seriously disturbed for the remainder of the twenty-four hours. Not that he was absolutely idle, or averse to business then; far from it. The difficulty was, he was apt to be altogether too energetic. There was a strange, inflamed, flurried, flighty recklessness of activity about him. He would be incautious in dipping his pen into his inkstand. All his blots upon my documents were dropped there after twelve 'o'clock, meridian. Indeed, not only would he be reckless, and sadly given to making blots in the afternoon, but, some days, he went further, and was rather noisy. At such times, too, his face flamed with augmented blazonry, as if cannel coal had been heaped on anthracite. He made an unpleasant racket with his chair; spilled his sand-box; in mending his pens, impatiently split them all to pieces, and threw them on the floor in a sudden passion; stood up, and leaned over his table, boxing his papers about in a most indecorous manner, very sad to behold in an elderly man like him. Nevertheless, as he was in many ways a most valuable person to me, and all the time before twelve o'clock, meridian, was the quickest, steadiest creature, too, accomplishing a great deal of work in a style not easily to be matched—for these reasons, I was willing to overlook his eccentricities, though, indeed, occasionally, I remonstrated with him. I did this very gently, however, because, though the civilest, nay, the bland-est and most reverential of men in the morning, yet, in the afternoon, he was disposed, upon provocation, to be slightly rash with his tongue—in fact, insolent. Now, valuing his morn-ing services as I did, and resolved not to lose them—yet, at the same time, made uncomfortable by his inflamed ways after twelve o'clock—and being a man of peace, unwilling by my admonitions to call forth unseemly retorts from him, I took upon me, one Saturday noon (he was always worse on Satur-days) to hint to him, very kindly, that, perhaps, now that he was growing old, it might be well to abridge his labors; in short, he need not come to my chambers after twelve o'clock, but, dinner over, had best go home to his lodgings, and rest himself till tea-time. But no; he insisted upon his afternoon devotions. His countenance became intolerably fervid, as he oratorically assured me—gesticulating with a long ruler at the other end of the room—that if his services in the morning were useful, how indispensable, then, in the afternoon?

"With submission, sir," said Turkey, on this occasion, "I consider myself your right-hand man. In the morning I but marshal and deploy my columns; but in the afternoon I put myself at their head, and gallantly charge the foe, thus"—and he made a violent thrust with the ruler.

"But the blots, Turkey," intimated I.

"True; but, with submission, sir, behold these hairs! I am getting old. Surely, sir, a blot or two of a warm afternoon is not to be severely urged against gray hairs. Old age—even if it blot the page—is honorable. With submission, sir, we *both* are getting old."

This appeal to my fellow-feeling was hardly to be resisted.

At all events, I saw that go he would not. So, I made up my mind to let him stay, resolving, nevertheless, to see to it that, during the afternoon, he had to do with my less important papers.

Nippers, the second on my list, was a whiskered, sallow, and, upon the whole, rather piratical-looking young man, of about five-and-twenty. I always deemed him the victim of two evil powers—ambition and indigestion. The ambition was evinced by a certain impatience of the duties of a mere copyist, an unwarrantable usurpation of strictly professional affairs, such as the original drawing up of legal documents. The indigestion seemed betokened in an occasional nervous testiness and grinning irritability, causing the teeth to audibly grind together over mistakes committed in copying; unnecessary maledictions, hissed, rather than spoken, in the heat of business; and especially by a continual discontent with the height of the table where he worked. Though of a very ingenious mechanical turn, Nippers could never get this table to suit him. He put chips under it, blocks of various sorts, bits of pasteboard, and at last went so far as to attempt an exquisite adjustment, by final pieces of folded blotting-paper. But no invention would answer. If, for the sake of easing his back, he brought the table-lid at a sharp angle well up towards his chin, and wrote there like a man using the steep roof of a Dutch house for his desk, then he declared that it stopped the circulation in his arms. If now he lowered the table to his waistbands, and stooped over it in writing, then there was a sore aching in his back. In short, the truth of the matter was, Nippers knew not what he wanted. Or, if he wanted anything, it was to be rid of a scrivener's table altogether. Among the manifestations of his diseased ambition was a fondness he had for receiving visits from certain ambiguous-looking fellows in seedy coats, whom he called his clients. Indeed, I was aware that not only was he, at times, considerable of a ward-politician, but he occasionally did a little business at the Justices' courts, and was not unknown on the steps of the Tombs. I have good reason to believe, however, that one individual who called upon him at my chambers, and who, with a grand air, he insisted was his client, was no other than a dun, and the alleged title-deed, a bill. But, with all his failings, and the annoyances he caused me, Nippers, like his compatriot Turkey, was a very useful man to me; wrote a neat, swift hand; and, when he chose, was not deficient in a gentlemanly sort

of deportment. Added to this, he always dressed in a gentlemanly sort of way; and so, incidentally, reflected credit upon
my chambers. Whereas, with respect to Turkey, I had much ado
to keep him from being a reproach to me. His clothes were
apt to look oily, and smell of eating-houses. He wore his pantaloons very loose and baggy in summer. His coats were execrable; his hat not to be handled. But while the hat was a
thing of indifference to me, inasmuch as his natural civility
and deference, as a dependent Englishman, always led him to
doff it the moment he entered the room, yet his coat was another matter. Concerning his coats, I reasoned with him; but
with no effect. The truth was, I suppose, that a man with so
small an income could not afford to sport such a lustrous face
and a lustrous coat at one and the same time. As Nippers once
observed, Turkey's money went chiefly for red ink. One winter
day, I presented Turkey with a highly respectable-looking coat
of my own—a padded gray coat, of a most comfortable warmth,
and which buttoned straight up from the knee to the neck. I
thought Turkey would appreciate the favor, and abate his
rashness and obstreperousness of afternoons. But no; I verily
believe that buttoning himself up in so downy and blanket-
like a coat had a pernicious effect upon him—upon the same
principle that too much oats are bad for horses. In fact, precisely as a rash, restive horse is said to feel his oats, so Turkey
felt his coat. It made him insolent. He was a man whom pros-
perity harmed.

Though, concerning the self-indulgent habits of Turkey, I
had my own private surmises, yet, touching Nippers, I was
well persuaded that, whatever might be his faults in other
respects, he was, at least, a temperate young man. But, indeed,
nature herself seemed to have been his vintner, and, at his
birth, charged him so thoroughly with an irritable, brandy-
like disposition, that all subsequent potations were needless.
When I consider how, amid the stillness of my chambers, Nippers would sometimes impatiently rise from his seat, and stooping over his table, spread his arms wide apart, seize the whole
desk, and move it, and jerk it, with a grim, grinding motion
on the floor, as if the table were a perverse voluntary agent,
intent on thwarting and vexing him, I plainly perceive that,
for Nippers, brandy-and-water were altogether superfluous.

It was fortunate for me that, owing to its peculiar cause
—indigestion—the irritability and consequent nervousness of
Nippers were mainly observable in the morning, while in the

afternoon he was comparatively mild. So that, Turkey's paroxysms only coming on about twelve o'clock, I never had to do with their eccentricities at one time. Their fits relieved each other, like guards. When Nippers's was on, Turkey's was off; and *vice versa*. This was a good natural arrangement, under the circumstances.

Ginger Nut, the third on my list, was a lad, some twelve years old. His father was a carman, ambitious of seeing his son on the bench instead of a cart, before he died. So he sent him to my office, as student at law, errand-boy, cleaner and sweeper, at the rate of one dollar a week. He had a little desk to himself, but he did not use it much. Upon inspection, the drawer exhibited a great array of the shells of various sorts of nuts. Indeed, to this quick-witted youth, the whole noble science of the law was contained in a nut-shell. Not the least among the employments of Ginger Nut, as well as one which he discharged with the most alacrity, was his duty as cake and apple purveyor for Turkey and Nippers. Copying law-papers being proverbially a dry, husky sort of business, my two scriveners were fain to moisten their mouths very often with Spitzenbergs, to be had at the numerous stalls nigh the Custom House and Post Office. Also, they sent Ginger Nut very frequently for that peculiar cake—small, flat, round, and very spicy—after which he had been named by them. Of a cold morning, when business was but dull, Turkey would gobble up scores of these cakes, as if they were mere wafers—indeed, they sell them at the rate of six or eight for a penny—the scrape of his pen blending with the crunching of the crisp particles in his mouth. Of all the fiery afternoon blunders and flurried rashnesses of Turkey, was his once moistening a ginger-cake between his lips, and clapping it on to a mortgage, for a seal. I came within an ace of dismissing him then. But he mollified me by making an oriental bow, and saying—

"With submission, sir, it was generous of me to find you in stationery on my own account."

Now my original business—that of a conveyancer and title hunter, and drawer-up of recondite documents of all sorts— was considerably increased by receiving the Master's office. There was now great work for scriveners. Not only must I push the clerks already with me, but I must have additional help.

In answer to my advertisement, a motionless young man one morning stood upon my office threshold, the door being open, for it was summer. I can see that figure now—pallidly neat, pitiably respectable, incurably forlorn! It was Bartleby.

After a few words touching his qualifications, I engaged him, glad to have among my corps of copyists a man of so singularly sedate an aspect, which I thought might operate beneficially upon the flighty temper of Turkey, and the fiery one of Nippers.

I should have stated before that ground-glass folding-doors divided my premises into two parts, one of which was occupied by my scriveners, the other by myself. According to my humor, I threw open these doors, or closed them. I resolved to assign Bartleby a corner by the folding-doors, but on my side of them, so as to have this quiet man within easy call, in case any trifling thing was to be done. I placed his desk close up to a small side-window in that part of the room, a window which originally had afforded a lateral view of certain grimy backyards and bricks, but which, owing to subsequent erections, commanded at present no view at all, though it gave some light. Within three feet of the panes was a wall, and the light came down from far above, between two lofty buildings, as from a very small opening in a dome. Still further to a satisfactory arrangement, I procured a high green folding screen, which might entirely isolate Bartleby from my sight, though not remove him from my voice. And thus, in a manner, privacy and society were conjoined.

At first, Bartleby did an extraordinary quantity of writing. As if long famishing for something to copy, he seemed to gorge himself on my documents. There was no pause for digestion. He ran a day and night line, copying by sunlight and by candle-light. I should have been quite delighted with his application, had he been cheerfully industrious. But he wrote on silently, palely, mechanically.

It is, of course, an indispensable part of a scrivener's business to verify the accuracy of his copy, word by word. Where there are two or more scriveners in an office, they assist each other in this examination, one reading from the copy, the other holding the original. It is a very dull, wearisome, and lethargic affair. I can readily imagine that, to some sanguine temperaments, it would be altogether intolerable. For example, I cannot credit that the mettlesome poet, Byron, would have contentedly sat down with Bartleby to examine a law document of, say five hundred pages, closely written in a crimpy hand.

Now and then, in the haste of business, it had been my habit to assist in comparing some brief document myself, calling Turkey or Nippers for this purpose. One object I had, in placing Bartleby so handy to me behind the screen, was, to avail myself of his services on such trivial occasions. It was on the third day, I think, of his being with me, and before any necessity had arisen for having his own writing examined, that, being much hurried to complete a small affair I had in hand, I abruptly called to Bartleby. In my haste and natural expectancy of instant compliance, I sat with my head bent over the original on my desk, and my right hand extended sideways, and somewhat nervously extended with the copy, so that, immediately upon emerging from his retreat, Bartleby might snatch it and proceed to business without the least delay.

In this very attitude did I sit when I called to him, rapidly stating what it was I wanted him to do—namely, to examine a small paper with me. Imagine my surprise, nay, my consternation, when, without moving from his privacy, Bartleby, in a singularly mild, firm voice, replied, "I would prefer not to."

I sat awhile in perfect silence, rallying my stunned faculties. Immediately it occurred to me that my ears had deceived me, or Bartleby had entirely misunderstood my meaning. I repeated my request in the clearest tone I could assume; but in quite as clear a one came the previous reply, "I would prefer not to."

"Prefer not to," echoed I, rising in high excitement, and crossing the room with a stride. "What do you mean? Are you moon-struck? I want you to help me compare this sheet here—take it," and I thrust it towards him.

"I would prefer not to," said he.

I looked at him steadfastly. His face was leanly composed; his gray eye dimly calm. Not a wrinkle of agitation rippled him. Had there been the least uneasiness, anger, impatience or impertinence in his manner; in other words, had there been anything ordinarily human about him, doubtless I should have violently dismissed him from the premises. But as it was, I should have as soon thought of turning my pale plaster-of-paris bust of Cicero out of doors. I stood gazing at him awhile, as he went on with his own writing, and then reseated myself at my desk. This is very strange, thought I. What had one best do? But my business hurried me. I concluded to forget the matter for the present, reserving it for my future leisure. So, calling Nippers from the other room, the paper was speedily examined.

A few days after this, Bartleby concluded four lengthy documents, being quadruplicates of a week's testimony taken before me in my High Court of Chancery. It became necessary to examine them. It was an important suit, and great accuracy was imperative. Having all things arranged, I called Turkey, Nippers and Ginger Nut, from the next room, meaning to place the four copies in the hands of my four clerks, while I should read from the original. Accordingly, Turkey, Nippers, and Ginger Nut had taken their seats in a row, each with his document in his hand, when I called to Bartleby to join this interesting group.

"Bartleby! quick, I am waiting."

I heard a slow scrape of his chair legs on the uncarpeted floor, and soon he appeared standing at the entrance of his hermitage.

"What is wanted?" said he, mildly.

"The copies, the copies," said I, hurriedly. "We are going to examine them. There"—and I held towards him the fourth quadruplicate.

"I would prefer not to," he said, and gently disappeared behind the screen.

For a few moments I was turned into a pillar of salt, standing at the head of my seated column of clerks. Recovering myself, I advanced towards the screen, and demanded the reason for such extraordinary conduct.

"*Why* do you refuse?"

"I would prefer not to."

With any other man I should have flown outright into a dreadful passion, scorned all further words, and thrust him ignominiously from my presence. But there was something about Bartleby that not only strangely disarmed me, but, in a wonderful manner, touched and disconcerted me. I began to reason with him.

"These are your own copies we are about to examine. It is labor saving to you, because one examination will answer for your four papers. It is common usage. Every copyist is bound to help examine his copy. Is it not so? Will you not speak? Answer!"

"I prefer not to," he replied in a flute-like tone. It seemed to me that, while I had been addressing him, he carefully revolved every statement that I made; fully comprehended the meaning; could not gainsay the irresistible conclusion; but, at the same time, some paramount consideration prevailed with him to reply as he did.

"You are decided, then, not to comply with my request— a request made according to common usage and common sense?"

He briefly gave me to understand, that on that point my judgment was sound. Yes: his decision was irreversible.

It is not seldom the case that, when a man is browbeaten in some unprecedented and violently unreasonable way, he begins to stagger in his own plainest faith. He begins, as it were, vaguely to surmise that, wonderful as it may be, all the justice and all the reason is on the other side. Accordingly, if any disinterested persons are present, he turns to them for some reinforcement for his own faltering mind.

"Turkey," said I, "what do you think of this? Am I not right?"

"With submission, sir," said Turkey, in his blandest tone, "I think that you are."

"Nippers," said I, "what do *you* think of it?"

"I think I should kick him out of the office."

(The reader of nice preceptions will here perceive that, it being morning Turkey's answer is couched in polite and tranquil terms, but Nippers replies in ill-tempered ones. Or, to repeat a previous sentence, Nippers's ugly mood was on duty, and Turkey's off.)

"Ginger Nut," said I, willing to enlist the smallest suffrage in my behalf, "what do *you* think of it?"

"I think, sir, he's a little *luny*," replied Ginger Nut, with a grin.

"You hear what they say," said I, turning towards the screen, "come forth and do your duty."

But he vouchsafed no reply. I pondered a moment in sore perplexity. But once more business hurried me. I determined again to postpone the consideration of this dilemma to my future leisure. With a little trouble we made out to examine the papers without Bartleby, though at every page or two Turkey deferentially dropped his opinion, that this proceeding was quite out of the common; while Nippers, twitching in his chair with a dyspeptic nervousness, ground out, between his set teeth, occasional hissing maledictions against the stubborn oaf behind the screen. And for his (Nippers's) part, this was

the first and the last time he would do another man's business
without pay.

Meanwhile Bartleby sat in his hermitage, oblivious to everything but his own peculiar business there.

Some days passed, the scrivener being employed upon another lengthy work. His late remarkable conduct led me to
regard his ways narrowly. I observed that he never went to
dinner; indeed, that he never went anywhere. As yet I had
never, of my personal knowledge, known him to be outside
of my office. He was a perpetual sentry in the corner. At about
eleven o'clock though, in the morning, I noticed that Ginger
Nut would advance toward the opening in Bartleby's screen,
as if silently beckoned thither by a gesture invisible to me
where I sat. The boy would then leave the office, jingling
a few pence, and reappear with a handful of ginger-nuts,
which he delivered in the hermitage, receiving two of the cakes
for his trouble.

He lives, then, on ginger-nuts, thought I; never eats a dinner,
properly speaking; he must be a vegetarian, then; but no;
he never eats even vegetables, he eats nothing but ginger-nuts.
My mind then ran on in reveries concerning the probable
effects upon the human constitution of living entirely on
ginger-nuts. Ginger-nuts are so called, because they contain
ginger as one of their peculiar constituents and the final flavor-
ing one. Now, what was ginger? A hot, spicy thing. Was Bartleby hot and spicy? Not at all. Ginger, then, had no effect upon
Bartleby. Probably he preferred it should have none.

Nothing so aggravates an earnest person as a passive resistance. If the individual so resisted be of a not inhumane temper,
and the resisting one perfectly harmless in his passivity, then,
in the better moods of the former, he will endeavor charitably
to construe to his imagination what proves impossible to be
solved by his judgment. Even so, for the most part, I regarded
Bartleby and his ways. Poor fellow! thought I, he means no
mischief; it is plain he intends no insolence; his aspect sufficiently evinces that his eccentricities are involuntary. He is useful to me. I can get along with him. If I turn him away, the
chances are he will fall in with some less indulgent employer,
and then he will be rudely treated, and perhaps driven forth
miserably to starve. Yes. Here I can cheaply purchase a delicious self-approval. To befriend Bartleby; to humor him in his
strange wilfulness, will cost me little or nothing, while I lay

up in my soul what will eventually prove a sweet morsel for my conscience. But this mood was not invariable with me. The passiveness of Bartleby sometimes irritated me. I felt strangely goaded on to encounter him in new opposition—to elicit some angry spark from him answerable to my own. But, indeed, I might as well have essayed to strike fire with my knuckles against a bit of Windsor soap. But one afternoon the evil impulse in me mastered me, and the following little scene ensued:

"Bartleby," said I, "when those papers are all copied, I will compare them with you."

"I would prefer not to."

"How? Surely you do not mean to persist in that mulish vagary?"

No answer.

I threw open the folding-doors near by, and, turning upon Turkey and Nippers, exclaimed:

"Bartleby a second time says, he won't examine his papers. What do you think of it, Turkey?"

It was afternoon, be it remembered. Turkey sat glowing like a brass boiler; his bald head steaming; his hands reeling among his blotted papers.

"Think of it?" roared Turkey. "I think I'll just step behind his screen, and black his eyes for him!"

So saying, Turkey rose to his feet and threw his arms into a pugilistic position. He was hurrying away to make good his promise, when I detained him, alarmed at the effect of incautiously rousing Turkey's combativeness after dinner.

"Sit down, Turkey," said I, "and hear what Nippers has to say. What do you think of it, Nippers? Would I not be justified in immediately dismissing Bartleby?"

"Excuse me, that is for you to decide, sir. I think his conduct quite unusual, and, indeed, unjust, as regards Turkey and myself. But it may only be a passing whim."

"Ah," exclaimed I, "you have strangely changed your mind, then—you speak very gently of him now."

"All beer," cried Turkey; "gentleness is effects of beer—Nippers and I dined together to-day. You see how gentle I am, sir. Shall I go and black his eyes?"

"You refer to Bartleby, I suppose. No, not to-day, Turkey," I replied; "pray, put up your fists."

I closed the doors, and again advanced towards Bartleby.

I felt additional incentives tempting me to my fate. I burned to be rebelled against again. I remembered that Bartleby never left the office.

"Bartleby," said I, "Ginger Nut is away; just step around to the Post Office, won't you?" (it was but a three minutes' walk) "and see if there is anything for me."

"I would prefer not to."

"You *will* not?"

"I *prefer* not."

I staggered to my desk, and sat there in a deep study. My blind inveteracy returned. Was there any other thing in which I could procure myself to be ignominiously repulsed by this lean, penniless wight?—my hired clerk? What added thing is there, perfectly reasonable, that he will be sure to refuse to do?

"Bartleby!"

No answer.

"Bartleby," in a louder tone.

No answer.

"Bartleby," I roared.

Like a very ghost, agreeably to the laws of magical invocation, at the third summons, he appeared at the entrance of his hermitage.

"Go to the next room, and tell Nippers to come to me."

"I prefer not to," he respectfully and slowly said, and mildly disappeared.

"Very good, Bartleby," said I, in a quiet sort of serenely-severe self-possessed tone, intimating the unalterable purpose of some terrible retribution very close at hand. At the moment I half intended something of the kind. But upon the whole, as it was drawing towards my dinner-hour, I thought it best to put on my hat and walk home for the day, suffering much from perplexity and distress of mind.

Shall I acknowledge it? The conclusion of this whole business was, that it soon became a fixed fact of my chambers, that a pale young scrivener, by the name of Bartleby, had a desk there; that he copied for me at the usual rate of four cents a folio (one hundred words); but he was permanently exempt from examining the work done by him, that duty being transferred to Turkey and Nippers, out of compliment, doubtless, to their superior acuteness; moreover, said Bartleby was never, on any account, to be dispatched on the most trivial errand of any sort; and that even if entreated to take upon him such a matter, it was generally understood that he would "prefer not to"—in other words, that he would re-fuse point-blank.

As days passed on, I became considerably reconciled to Bartleby. His steadiness, his freedom from all dissipation, his incessant industry (except when he chose to throw himself into a standing revery behind his screen), his great stillness, his unalterableness of demeanor under all circumstances, made him a valuable acquisition. One prime thing was this— *he was always there*—first in the morning, continually through the day, and the last at night. I had a singular confidence in his honesty. I felt my most precious papers perfectly safe in his hands. Sometimes, to be sure, I could not, for the very soul of me, avoid falling into sudden spasmodic passions with him. For it was exceeding difficult to bear in mind all the time those strange peculiarities, privileges, and unheard-of exemp-tions, forming the tacit stipulations on Bartleby's part under which he remained in my office. Now and then, in the eager-ness of dispatching pressing business, I would inadvertently summon Bartleby, in a short, rapid tone, to put his finger, say, on the incipient tie of a bit of red tape with which I was about compressing some papers. Of course, from behind the screen the usual answer, "I prefer not to," was sure to come; and then, how could a human creature, with the common infirmities of our nature, refrain from bitterly exclaiming upon such perverseness—such unreasonableness? However, every added repulse of this sort which I received only tended to lessen the probability of my repeating the inadvertence.

Here it must be said, that, according to the custom of most legal gentlemen occupying chambers in densely-populated law buildings, there were several keys to my door. One was kept by a woman residing in the attic, which person weekly scrubbed and daily swept and dusted my apartments. Another was kept by Turkey for convenience sake. The third I some-times carried in my own pocket. The fourth I knew not who had.

Now, one Sunday morning I happened to go to Trinity Church, to hear a celebrated preacher, and finding myself rather early on the ground I thought I would walk round to my chambers for a while. Luckily I had my key with me; but upon applying it to the lock, I found it resisted by something inserted from the inside. Quite surprised, I called out; when to my consternation a key was turned from within; and thrust-ing his lean visage at me, and holding the door ajar, the apparition of Bartleby appeared, in his shirt-sleeves, and otherwise in a strangely tattered deshabille, saying quietly that he was sorry, but he was deeply engaged just then, and—preferred not admitting me at present. In a brief word or two, he more-over added, that perhaps I had better walk round the block two or three times, and by that time he would probably have concluded his affairs.

Now, the utterly unsurmised appearance of Bartleby, ten-anting my law-chambers of a Sunday morning, with his cadav-erously gentlemanly *nonchalance,* yet withal firm and self-possessed, had such a strange effect upon me, that incontinently I slunk away from my own door, and did as desired. But not without sundry twinges of impotent rebellion against the mild effrontery of this unaccountable scrivener. Indeed, it was his wonderful mildness chiefly, which not only disarmed me, but unmanned me, as it were. For I consider that one, for the time, is a sort of unmanned when he tranquilly permits his hired clerk to dictate to him, and order him away from his own premises. Furthermore, I was full of uneasiness as to what Bartleby could possibly be doing in my office in his shirt-sleeves, and in an otherwise dismantled condition of a Sunday morn-ing. Was anything amiss going on? Nay, that was out of the question. It was not to be thought of for a moment that Bar-tleby was an immoral person. But what could he be doing there —copying? Nay again, whatever might be his eccentricities, Bartleby was an eminently decorous person. He would be the last man to sit down to his desk in any state approaching to nudity. Besides, it was Sunday; and there was something about Bartleby that forbade the supposition that he would by any secular occupation violate the proprieties of the day.

Nevertheless, my mind was not pacified; and full of a restless curiosity, at last I returned to the door. Without hindrance I inserted my key, opened it, and entered. Bartleby was not to be seen. I looked round anxiously, peeped behind his screen; but it was very plain that he was gone. Upon more closely examining the place, I surmised that for an indefinite period Bartleby must have ate, dressed, and slept in my office, and that too without plate, mirror, or bed. The cushioned seat of a rickety old sofa in one corner bore the faint impress of a lean, reclining form. Rolled away under his desk, I found a blanket; under the empty grate, a blacking box and brush; on a chair, a tin basin, with soap and a ragged towel; in a newspaper a few crumbs of ginger-nuts and a morsel of cheese.

Yes, thought I, it is evident enough that Bartleby has been making his home here, keeping bachelor's hall all by himself. Immediately then the thought came sweeping across me, what miserable friendlessness and loneliness are here revealed! His poverty is great; but his solitude, how horrible! Think of it. Of a Sunday, Wall Street is deserted as Petra; and every night of every day it is an emptiness. This building, too, which of weekdays hums with industry and life, at nightfall echoes with sheer vacancy, and all through Sunday is forlorn. And here Bartleby makes his home; sole spectator of a solitude which he has seen all populous—a sort of innocent and transformed Marius brooding among the ruins of Carthage!

For the first time in my life a feeling of overpowering stinging melancholy seized me. Before, I had never experienced aught but a not unpleasing sadness. The bond of a common humanity now drew me irresistibly to gloom. A fraternal melancholy! For both I and Bartleby were sons of Adam. I remembered the bright silks and sparkling faces I had seen that day, in gala trim, swan-like sailing down the Mississippi of Broadway; and I contrasted them with the pallid copyist, and thought to myself, Ah, happiness courts the light, so we deem the world is gay; but misery hides aloof, so we deem that misery there is none. These sad fancyings—chimeras, doubtless, of a sick and silly brain—led on to other and more special thoughts, concerning the eccentricities of Bartleby. Presentiments of strange discoveries hovered round me. The scrivener's pale form appeared to me laid out, among uncaring strangers, in its shivering winding-sheet.

Suddenly I was attracted by Bartleby's closed desk, the key in open sight left in the lock.

I mean no mischief, seek the gratification of no heartless curiosity, thought I; besides, the desk is mine, and its contents, too, so I will make bold to look within. Everything was methodically arranged, the papers smoothly placed. The pigeonholes were deep, and removing the files of documents, I groped into their recesses. Presently I felt something there, and dragged it out. It was an old bandanna handkerchief, heavy and knotted. I opened it, and saw it was a saving's bank.

I now recalled all the quiet mysteries which I had noted in the man. I remembered that he never spoke but to answer; that, though at intervals he had considerable time to himself, yet I had never seen him reading—no, not even a newspaper; that for long periods he would stand looking out, at his pale window behind the screen, upon the dead brick wall; I was quite sure he never visited any refectory or eating-house; while his pale face clearly indicated that he never drank beer like Turkey, or tea and coffee even, like other men; that he never went anywhere in particular that I could learn; never went out for a walk, unless, indeed, that was the case at present; that he had declined telling who he was, or whence he came, or whether he had any relatives in the world; that though so thin and pale, he never complained of ill-health. And more than all, I remembered a certain unconscious air of pallid—how shall I call it?—of pallid haughtiness, say, or rather an austere reserve about him, which had positively awed me into my tame compliance with his eccentricities, when I had feared to ask him to do the slightest incidental thing for me, even though I might know, from his long-continued motionlessness, that behind his screen he must be standing in one of those dead-wall reveries of his.

Revolving all these things, and coupling them with the recently discovered fact, that he made my office his constant abiding place and home, and not forgetful of his morbid moodiness; revolving all these things, a prudential feeling began to steal over me. My first emotions had been those of pure melancholy and sincerest pity; but just in proportion as the forlornness of Bartleby grew and grew to my imagination, did that same melancholy merge into fear, that pity into repulsion. So true it is, and so terrible, too, that up to a certain point the thought or sight of misery enlists our best affections; but, in certain special cases, beyond that point it does not. They err who would assert that invariably this is owing to the inherent selfishness of the human heart. It rather proceeds from a certain hopelessness of remedying excessive and organic ill. To a sensitive being, pity is not seldom pain. And when at last it is perceived that such pity cannot lead to effectual succor, common sense bids the soul be rid of it. What I saw that morning persuaded me that the scrivener was the victim of innate and incurable disorder. I might give alms to his body; but his body did not pain him; it was his soul that suffered, and his soul I could not reach.

I did not accomplish the purpose of going to Trinity Church that morning. Somehow, the things I had seen disqualified me for the time from church-going. I walked homeward, thinking what I would do with Bartleby. Finally, I resolved upon this— I would put certain calm questions to him the next morning, touching his history, etc., and if he declined to answer them openly and unreservedly (and I supposed he would prefer not), then to give him a twenty dollar bill over and above whatever I might owe him, and tell him his services were no longer required; but that if in any other way I could assist him, I would be happy to do so, especially if he desired to return to his native place, whereever that might be, I would willingly help to defray the expenses. Moreover, if, after reaching home, he found himself at any time in want of aid, a letter from him would be sure of a reply.

The next morning came.

"Bartleby," said I, gently calling to him behind his screen.

No reply.

"Bartleby," said I, in a still gentler tone, "come here; I am not going to ask you to do anything you would prefer not to do—I simply wish to speak to you."

Upon this he noiselessly slid into view.

"Will you tell me, Bartleby, where you were born?"

"I would prefer not to."

"Will you tell me *anything* about yourself?"

"I would prefer not to."

"But what reasonable objection can you have to speak to me? I feel friendly towards you."

He did not look at me while I spoke, but kept his glance fixed upon my bust of Cicero, which, as I then sat, was directly behind me, some six inches above my head.

"What is your answer, Bartleby?" said I, after waiting a considerable time for a reply, during which his countenance remained immovable, only there was the faintest conceivable tremor of the white attenuated mouth.

"At present I prefer to give no answer," he said, and retired into his hermitage.

It was rather weak in me I confess, but his manner, on this occasion, nettled me. Not only did there seem to lurk in it a certain calm disdain, but his perverseness seemed ungrateful, considering the undeniable good usage and indulgence he had received from me.

Again I sat ruminating what I should do. Mortified as I was at his behavior, and resolved as I had been to dismiss him when I entered my office, nevertheless I strangely felt something superstitious knocking at my heart, and forbidding me to carry out my purpose, and denouncing me for a villain if I dared to breathe one bitter word against this forlornest of mankind. At last, familiarly drawing my chair behind his screen, I sat down and said: "Bartleby, never mind, then, about revealing your history; but let me entreat you, as a friend, to comply as far as may be with the usages of this office. Say now, you will help to examine papers to-morrow or next day: in short, say now, that in a day or two you will begin to be a little reasonable:—say so, Bartleby."

"At present I would prefer not to be a little reasonable," was his mildly cadaverous reply.

Just then the folding-doors opened, and Nippers approached. He seemed suffering from an unusually bad night's rest, induced by severer indigestion than common. He overheard those final words of Bartleby.

"*Prefer not*, eh?" gritted Nippers—"I'd *prefer* him, if I were you, sir," addressing me—"I'd *prefer* him; I'd give him preferences, the stubborn mule! What is it, sir, pray, that he *prefers* not to do now?"

Bartleby moved not a limb.

"Mr. Nippers," said I, "I'd prefer that you would withdraw for the present."

Somehow, of late, I had got into the way of involuntarily using this word "prefer" upon all sorts of not exactly suitable occasions. And I trembled to think that my contact with the scrivener had already and seriously affected me in a mental way. And what further and deeper aberration might it not yet produce? This apprehension had not been without efficacy in determining me to summary measures.

As Nippers, looking very sour and sulky, was departing, Turkey blandly and deferentially approached.

"With submission, sir," said he, "yesterday I was thinking about Bartleby here, and I think that if he would but prefer to take a quart of good ale every day it would do much towards mending him, and enabling him to assist in examining his papers."

"So you have got the word, too," said I, slightly excited.

"With submission, what word, sir?" asked Turkey, respectfully crowding himself into the contracted space behind the screen, and by so doing, making me jostle the scrivener. "What word, sir?"

"I would prefer to be left alone here," said Bartleby, as if offended at being mobbed in his privacy.

"*That's* the word, Turkey," said I—"*that's* it."

"Oh, *prefer?* oh yes—queer word. I never use it myself. But, sir, as I was saying, if he would but prefer—"

"Turkey," interrupted I, "you will please withdraw."

"Oh certainly, sir, if you prefer that I should."

As he opened the folding-door to retire, Nippers at his desk caught a glimpse of me, and asked whether I would prefer to have a certain paper copied on blue paper or white. He did not in the least roguishly accent the word "prefer." It was plain that it involuntarily rolled from his tongue. I thought to myself, surely I must get rid of a demented man, who already has in some degree turned the tongues, if not the heads of myself and clerks. But I thought it prudent not to break the dismission at once.

The next day I noticed that Bartleby did nothing but stand at his window in his dead-wall revery. Upon asking him why he did not write, he said that he had decided upon doing no more writing.

"Why, how now? what next?" exclaimed I, "do no more writing?"

"No more."

"And what is the reason?"

"Do you not see the reason for yourself?" he indifferently replied.

I looked steadfastly at him, and perceived that his eyes looked dull and glazed. Instantly it occurred to me, that his unexampled diligence in copying by his dim window for the first few weeks of his stay with me might have temporarily impaired his vision.

I was touched. I said something in condolence with him. I hinted that of course he did wisely in abstaining from writing for a while; and urged him to embrace that opportunity of taking wholesome exercise in the open air. This, however, he did not do. A few days after this, my other clerks being absent, and being in a great hurry to dispatch certain letters by the mail, I thought that, having nothing else earthly to do, Bartleby would surely be less inflexible than usual, and carry these letters to the post-office. But he blankly declined. So, much to my inconvenience, I went myself.

Still added days went by. Whether Bartleby's eyes improved or not, I could not say. To all appearance, I thought they did. But when I asked him if they did, he vouchsafed no answer. At all events, he would do no copying. At last, in reply to my urgings, he informed me that he had permanently given up copying.

"What!" exclaimed I; "suppose your eyes should get entirely well—better than ever before—would you not copy then?"

"I have given up copying," he answered, and slid aside.

He remained as ever, a fixture in my chamber. Nay—if that were possible—he became still more of a fixture than before. What was to be done? He would do nothing in the office; why should he stay there? In plain fact, he had now become a mill-stone to me, not only useless as a necklace, but afflictive to bear. Yet I was sorry for him. I speak less than truth when I say that, on his own account, he occasioned me uneasiness. If he would but have named a single relative or friend, I would instantly have written, and urged their taking the poor fellow away to some convenient retreat. But he seemed alone, absolutely alone in the universe. A bit of wreck in the mid-Atlantic. At length, necessities connected with my business tyrannized over all other considerations. Decently as I could, I told Bartleby that in six days' time he must unconditionally leave the office. I warned him to take measures, in the interval, for procuring some other abode. I offered to assist him in this endeavor, if he himself would but take the first step towards a removal. "And when you finally quit me, Bartleby," added I, "I shall see that you go not away entirely unprovided. Six days from this hour, remember."

At the expiration of that period, I peeped behind the screen, and lo! Bartleby was there.

I buttoned up my coat, balanced myself; advanced slowly towards him, touched his shoulder, and said, "The time has come; you must quit this place; I am sorry for you; here is money; but you must go."

"I would prefer not," he replied, with his back still towards me.

"You *must*."

He remained silent.

Now I had an unbounded confidence in this man's common honesty. He had frequently restored to me sixpences and shillings carelessly dropped upon the floor, for I am apt to be very reckless in such shirt-button affairs. The proceeding, then, which followed will not be deemed extraordinary.

"Bartleby," said I, "I owe you twelve dollars on account; here are thirty-two; the odd twenty are yours— Will you take it?" and I handed the bills towards him.

But he made no motion.

"I will leave them here, then," putting them under a weight on the table. Then taking my hat and cane and going to the door, I tranquilly turned and added—"After you have removed your things from these offices, Bartleby, you will of course lock the door—since every one is now gone for the day but you—and if you please, slip your key underneath the mat, so that I may have it in the morning. I shall not see you again; so good-bye to you. If, hereafter, in your new place of abode, I can be of any service to you, do not fail to advise me by letter. Good-bye, Bartleby, and fare you well."

But he answered not a word; like the last column of some ruined temple, he remained standing mute and solitary in the middle of the otherwise deserted room.

As I walked home in a pensive mood, my vanity got the better of my pity. I could not but highly plume myself on my masterly management in getting rid of Bartleby. Masterly I call it, and such it must appear to any dispassionate thinker. The beauty of my procedure seemed to consist in its perfect quietness. There was no vulgar bullying, no bravado of any sort, no choleric hectoring, and striding to and fro across the apartment, jerking out vehement commands for Bartleby to bundle himself off with his beggarly traps. Nothing of the kind. Without loudly bidding Bartleby depart—as an inferior genius might have done—I *assumed* the ground that depart he must; and upon that assumption built all I had to say. The more I thought over my procedure, the more I was charmed with it. Nevertheless, next morning, upon awakening, I had my doubts—I had somehow slept off the fumes of vanity. One of the coolest and wisest hours a man has, is just after he awakes in the morning. My procedure seemed as sagacious as ever—but only in theory. How it would prove in practice—there was the rub. It was truly a beautiful thought to have assumed Bartleby's departure; but, after all, that assumption was simply my own, and none of Bartleby's. The great point was, not whether I had assumed that he would quit me, but whether he would prefer so to do. He was more a man of preferences than assumptions.

After breakfast, I walked down town, arguing the probabilities *pro* and *con*. One moment I thought it would prove a miserable failure, and Bartleby would be found all alive at my office as usual; the next moment it seemed certain that I should find his chair empty. And so I kept veering about.

At the corner of Broadway and Canal Street, I saw quite an excited group of people standing in earnest conversation.

"I'll take odds he doesn't," said a voice as I passed.

"Doesn't go?—done!" said I, "put up your money."

I was instinctively putting my hand in my pocket to produce my own, when I remembered that this was an election day. The words I had overheard bore no reference to Bartleby, but to the success or non-success of some candidate for the mayoralty. In my intent frame of mind, I had, as it were, imagined that all Broadway shared in my excitement, and were debating the same question with me. I passed on, very thankful that the uproar of the street screened my momentary absent-mindedness.

As I had intended, I was earlier than usual at my office door. I stood listening for a moment. All was still. He must be gone. I tried the knob. The door was locked. Yes, my procedure had worked to a charm; he indeed must be vanished. Yet a certain melancholy mixed with this: I was almost sorry for my brilliant success. I was fumbling under the door mat for the key, which Bartleby was to have left there for me, when accidentally my knee knocked against a panel, producing a summoning sound, and in response a voice came to me from within—"Not yet; I am occupied."

It was Bartleby.

I was thunderstruck. For an instant I stood like the man who, pipe in mouth, was killed one cloudless afternoon long ago in Virginia, by summer lightning; at his own warm open window he was killed, and remained leaning out there upon the dreamy afternoon, till some one touched him, when he fell.

"Not gone!" I murmured at last. But again obeying that wondrous ascendancy which the inscrutable scrivener had over me, and from which ascendancy, for all my chafing, I could not completely escape, I slowly went down stairs and out into the street, and while walking round the block, considered what I should next do in this unheard-of perplexity. Turn the man out by an actual thrusting I could not; to drive him away by calling him hard names would not do; calling in the police was an unpleasant idea; and yet, permit him to enjoy his cadaverous triumph over me—this, too, I could not think of. What was to be done? or, if nothing could be done, was there anything further that I could *assume* in the matter? Yes, as before I had prospectively assumed that Bartleby would depart, so now I might retrospectively assume that departed he was. In the legitimate carrying out of this assumption, I might enter my office in a great hurry, and pretending not to see Bartleby at all, walk straight against him as if he were air. Such a proceeding would in a singular degree have the appearance of a home-thrust. It was hardly possible that Bartleby could withstand such an application of the doctrine of assumptions. But upon second thoughts the success of the plan seemed rather dubious. I resolved to argue the matter over with him again.

"Bartleby," said I, entering the office, with a quietly severe expression, "I am seriously displeased. I am pained, Bartleby. I had thought better of you. I had imagined you of such a gentlemanly organization, that in any delicate dilemma a slight hint would suffice—in short, an assumption. But it appears I am deceived. Why," I added, unaffectedly starting, "you have not even touched that money yet," pointing to it, just where I had left it the evening previous.

He answered nothing.

"Will you, or will you not, quit me?" I now demanded in a sudden passion, advancing close to him.

"I would prefer *not* to quit you," he replied, gently emphasizing the *not*.

"What earthly right have you to stay here? Do you pay any rent? Do you pay my taxes? Or is this property yours?"

He answered nothing.

"Are you ready to go on and write now? Are your eyes recovered? Could you copy a small paper for me this morning? or help examine a few lines? or step round to the post-office? In a word, will you do anything at all, to give a coloring to your refusal to depart the premises?"

He silently retired into his hermitage.

I was now in such a state of nervous resentment that I thought it but prudent to check myself at present from further demonstrations. Bartleby and I were alone. I remembered the tragedy of the unfortunate Adams and the still more unfortunate Colt in the solitary office of the latter; and how poor Colt, being dreadfully incensed by Adams, and imprudently permitting himself to get wildly excited, was at unawares hurried into his fatal act—an act which certainly no man could possibly deplore more than the actor himself. Often it had occurred to me in my ponderings upon the subject that had that altercation taken place in the public street, or at a private residence, it would not have terminated as it did. It was the circumstance of being alone in a solitary office, up stairs, of a building entirely unhallowed by humanizing domestic associations—an uncarpeted office, doubtless, of a dusty, haggard sort of appearance—this it must have been, which greatly helped to enhance the irritable desperation of the hapless Colt.

But when this old Adam of resentment rose in me and tempted me concerning Bartleby, I grappled him and threw him. How? Why, simply by recalling the divine injunction: "A new commandment give I unto you, that ye love one another." Yes, this it was that saved me. Aside from higher considerations, charity often operates as a vastly wise and prudent principle—a great safeguard to its possessor. Men have committed murder for jealousy's sake, and anger's sake, and hatred's sake, and selfishness' sake, and spiritual pride's sake; but no man, that ever I heard of, ever committed a diabolical murder for sweet charity's sake. Mere self-interest, then, if no better motive can be enlisted, should, especially with high-tempered men, prompt all beings to charity and philanthropy. At any rate, upon the occasion in question, I strove to drown my exasperated feelings towards the scrivener by benevolently construing his conduct. Poor fellow, poor fellow! thought I, he don't mean anything; and besides, he has seen hard times, and ought to be indulged.

I endeavored, also, immediately to occupy myself, and at the same time to comfort my despondency. I tried to fancy, that in the course of the morning, at such time as might prove agreeable to him, Bartleby, of his own free accord, would emerge from his hermitage and take up some decided line of march in the direction of the door. But no. Half-past twelve o'clock came; Turkey began to glow in the face, overturn his inkstand, and become generally obstreperous; Nippers abated down into quietude and courtesy; Ginger Nut munched his noon apple; and Bartleby remained standing at his window in one of his profoundest dead-wall reveries. Will it be credited? Ought I to acknowledge it? That afternoon I left the office without saying one further word to him.

Some days now passed, during which, at leisure intervals I looked a little into "Edwards on the Will," and "Priestley on Necessity." Under the circumstances, those books induced a salutary feeling. Gradually I slid into the persuasion that these troubles of mine, touching the scrivener, had been all predestinated from eternity, and Bartleby was billeted upon me for some mysterious purpose of an all-wise Providence, which it was not for a mere mortal like me to fathom. Yes, Bartleby, stay there behind your screen, thought I; I shall persecute you no more; you are harmless and noiseless as any of these old chairs; in short, I never feel so private as when I know you are here. At last I see it, I feel it; I penetrate to the predestinated purpose of my life. I am content. Others may have loftier parts to enact; but my mission in this world, Bartleby, is to furnish you with office-room for such period as you may see fit to remain.

I believe that this wise and blessed frame of mind would have continued with me, had it not been for the unsolicited and uncharitable remarks obtruded upon me by my professional friends who visited the rooms. But thus it often is, that the constant friction of illiberal minds wears out at last the best resolves of the more generous. Though to be sure, when I reflected upon it, it was not strange that people entering my office should be struck by the peculiar aspect of the unaccountable Bartleby, and so be tempted to throw out some sinister observations concerning him. Sometimes an attorney, having business with me, and calling at my office, and finding no one but the scrivener there, would undertake to obtain some sort of precise information from him touching my whereabouts; but without heeding his idle talk, Bartleby would remain standing immovable in the middle of the room. So after contemplating him in that position for a time, the attorney would depart, no wiser than he came.

Also, when a reference was going on, and the room full of lawyers and witnesses, and business driving fast, some deeply-occupied legal gentleman present, seeing Bartleby wholly unemployed, would request him to run round to his (the legal gentleman's) office and fetch some papers for him. Thereupon, Bartleby would tranquilly decline, and yet remain idle as before. Then the lawyer would give a great stare, and turn to me. And what could I say? At last I was made aware that all through the circle of my professional acquaintance, a whisper of wonder was running round, having reference to the strange creature I kept at my office. This worried me very much. And as the idea came upon me of his possibly turning out a long-lived man, and keep occupying my chambers, and denying my authority; and perplexing my visitors; and scandalizing my professional reputation; and casting a general gloom over the premises; keeping soul and body together to the last upon his savings (for doubtless he spent but half a dime a day), and in the end perhaps outlive me, and claim possession of my office by right of his perpetual occupancy: as all these dark anticipations crowded upon me more and more, and my friends continually intruded their relentless remarks upon the apparition in my room; a great change was wrought in me. I resolved to gather all my faculties together, and forever rid me of this intolerable incubus.

Ere revolving any complicated project, however, adapted to this end, I first simply suggested to Bartleby the propriety of his permanent departure. In a calm and serious tone, I commended the idea to his careful and mature consideration. But, having taken three days to meditate upon it, he apprised me, that his original determination remained the same; in short, that he still preferred to abide with me.

What shall I do? I now said to myself, buttoning up my coat to the last button. What shall I do? what ought I to do? what does conscience say I *should* do with this man, or, rather, ghost. Rid myself of him, I must; go, he shall. But how? You will not thrust him, the poor, pale, passive mortal—you will not thrust such a helpless creature out of your door? you will not dishonor yourself by such cruelty? No, I will not, I cannot do that. Rather would I let him live and die here, and then mason up his remains in the wall. What, then, will you do? For all your coaxing, he will not budge. Bribes he leaves under your own paper-weight on your table; in short, it is quite plain that he prefers to cling to you.

Then something severe, something unusual must be done. What! surely you will not have him collared by a constable, and commit his innocent pallor to the common jail? And upon what ground could you procure such a thing to be done? —a vagrant, is he? What! he a vagrant, a wanderer, who refuses to budge? It is because he will *not* be a vagrant, then, that you seek to count him *as* a vagrant. That is too absurd. No visible means of support: there I have him. Wrong again: for indubitably he *does* support himself, and that is the only unanswerable proof that any man can show of his possessing the means so to do. No more, then. Since he will not quit me, I must quit him. I will change my offices; I will move elsewhere, and give him fair notice, that if I find him on my new premises I will then proceed against him as a common trespasser.

Acting accordingly, next day I thus addressed him: "I find these chambers too far from the City Hall; the air is unwholesome. In a word, I propose to remove my offices next week, and shall no longer require your services. I tell you this now, in order that you may seek another place."

He made no reply, and nothing more was said.

On the appointed day I engaged carts and men, proceeded to my chambers, and, having but little furniture, everything was removed in a few hours. Throughout, the scrivener remained standing behind the screen, which I directed to be removed the last thing. It was withdrawn; and, being folded up like a huge folio, left him the motionless occupant of a naked room. I stood in the entry watching him a moment, while something from within me upbraided me.

I re-entered, with my hand in my pocket—and—and my heart in my mouth.

"Good-bye, Bartleby; I am going—good-bye, and God some way bless you; and take that," slipping something in his hand. But it dropped upon the floor, and then—strange to say—I tore myself from him whom I had so longed to be rid of.

Established in my new quarters, for a day or two I kept the door locked, and started at every footfall in the passages. When I returned to my rooms, after any little absence, I would pause at the threshold for an instant, and attentively listen, ere applying my key. But these fears were needless. Bartleby never came nigh me.

I thought all was going well, when a perturbed-looking stranger visited me, inquiring whether I was the person who had recently occupied rooms at No. — Wall Street.

Full of forebodings, I replied that I was.

"Then, sir," said the stranger, who proved a lawyer, "you are responsible for the man you left there. He refuses to do any copying; he refuses to do anything; he says he prefers not to; and he refuses to quit the premises."

"I am very sorry, sir," said I, with assumed tranquillity, but an inward tremor, "but, really, the man you allude to is nothing to me—he is no relation or apprentice of mine, that you should hold me responsible for him."

"In mercy's name, who is he?"

"I certainly cannot inform you. I know nothing about him. Formerly I employed him as a copyist; but he has done nothing for me now for some time past."

"I shall settle him, then—good morning, sir."

Several days passed, and I heard nothing more; and, though I often felt a charitable prompting to call at the place and see poor Bartleby, yet a certain squeamishness, of I know not what, withheld me.

All is over with him, by this time, thought I, at last, when, through another week, no further intelligence reached me. But, coming to my room the day after, I found several persons waiting at my door in a high state of nervous excitement.

"That's the man—here he comes," cried the foremost one, whom I recognized as the lawyer who had previously called upon me alone.

"You must take him away, sir, at once," cried a portly person among them, advancing upon me, and whom I knew to be the landlord of No. — Wall Street. "These gentlemen, my tenants, cannot stand it any longer; Mr. B——," pointing to the lawyer, "has turned him out of his room, and he now persists in haunting the building generally, sitting upon the banisters of the stairs by day, and sleeping in the entry by night. Everybody is concerned; clients are leaving the offices; some fears are entertained of a mob; something you must do, and that without delay."

Aghast at this torrent, I fell back before it, and would fain have locked myself in my new quarters. In vain I persisted that Bartleby was nothing to me—no more than to any one else. In vain—I was the last person known to have anything to do with him, and they held me to the terrible account. Fearful, then, of being exposed in the papers (as one person present obscurely threatened), I considered the matter, and, at length, said, that if the lawyer would give me a confidential interview with the scrivener, in his (the lawyer's) own room, I would, that afternoon, strive my best to rid them of the nuisance they complained of.

Going up stairs to my old haunt, there was Bartleby silently sitting upon the banister at the landing.

"What are you doing here, Bartleby?" said I.

"Sitting upon the banister," he mildly replied.

I motioned him into the lawyer's room, who then left us.

"Bartleby," said I, "are you aware that you are the cause of great tribulation to me, by persisting in occupying the entry after being dismissed from the office?"

No answer.

"Now one of two things must take place. Either you must do something, or something must be done to you. Now what

sort of business would you like to engage in? Would you like
to re-engage in copying for some one?"

"No; I would prefer not to make any change."

"Would you like a clerkship in a dry-goods store?"

"There is too much confinement about that. No, I would
not like a clerkship; but I am not particular."

"Too much confinement," I cried, "why, you keep yourself
confined all the time!"

"I would prefer not to take a clerkship," he rejoined, as
if to settle that little item at once.

"How would a bar-tender's business suit you? There is no
trying of the eye-sight in that."

"I would not like it at all; though, as I said before, I am
not particular."

His unwonted wordiness inspirited me. I returned to the
charge.

"Well, then, would you like to travel through the country
collecting bills for the merchants? That would improve your
health."

"No, I would prefer to be doing something else."

"How, then, would going as a companion to Europe, to
entertain some young gentleman with your conversation—
how would that suit you?"

"Not at all. It does not strike me that there is anything
definite about that. I like to be stationary. But I am not particular."

"Stationary you shall be, then," I cried, now losing all patience, and, for the first time in all my exasperating connec-
tion· with him, fairly flying into a passion. "If you do not go
away from these premises before night, I shall feel bound—
indeed, I *am* bound—to—to—to quit the premises myself!"
I rather absurdly concluded, knowing not with what possible
threat to try to frighten his immobility into compliance. Despairing of all further efforts, I was precipitately leaving him,
when a final thought occurred to me—one which had not been
wholly unindulged before.

"Bartleby," said I, in the kindest tone I could assume under
such exciting circumstances, "will you go home with me
now—not to my office, but my dwelling—and remain there
till we can conclude upon some convenient arrangement for
you at our leisure? Come, let us start now, right away."

"No: at present I would prefer not to make any change
at all."

I answered nothing; but, effectually dodging every one
by the suddenness and rapidity of my flight, rushed from the
building, ran up Wall Street towards Broadway, and, jumping into the first omnibus, was soon removed from pursuit.
As soon as tranquillity returned, I distinctly perceived that I
had now done all that I possibly could, both in respect to the
demands of the landlord and his tenants, and with regard
to my own desire and sense of duty, to benefit Bartleby, and
shield him from rude persecution. I now strove to be entirely care-free and quiescent; and my conscience justified
me in the attempt; though, indeed, it was not so successful as
I could have wished. So fearful was I of being again hunted out
by the incensed landlord and his exasperated tenants, that,
surrendering my business to Nippers, for a few days, I drove
about the upper part of the town and through the suburbs,
in my rockaway; crossed over to Jersey City and Hoboken,
and paid fugitive visits to Manhattanville and Astoria. In fact,
I almost lived in my rockaway for the time.

When again I entered my office, lo, a note from the landlord
lay upon the desk. I opened it with trembling hands. It informed me that the writer had sent to the police, and had
Bartleby removed to the Tombs as a vagrant. Moreover, since
I knew more about him than any one else, he wished me to
appear at that place, and make a suitable statement of the
facts. These tidings had a conflicting effect upon me. At first
I was indignant; but, at last, almost approved. The landlord's
energetic, summary disposition, had led him to adopt a procedure which I do not think I would have decided upon myself; and yet, as a last resort, under such peculiar circumstances, it seemed the only plan.

As I afterwards learned, the poor scrivener, when told that
he must be conducted to the Tombs, offered not the slightest
obstacle, but, in his pale, unmoving way, silently acquiesced.

Some of the compassionate and curious by-standers joined
the party; and headed by one of the constables arm-in-arm
with Bartleby, the silent procession filed its way through all
the noise, and heat, and joy of the roaring thoroughfares at
noon.

The same day I received the note, I went to the Tombs, or,
to speak more properly, the Halls of Justice. Seeking the right
officer, I stated the purpose of my call, and was informed that
the individual I described was, indeed, within. I then assured
the functionary that Bartleby was a perfectly honest man, and

greatly to be compassionated, however unaccountably eccentric. I narrated all I knew, and closed by suggesting the idea of letting him remain in as indulgent confinement as possible, till something less harsh might be done—though, indeed, I hardly knew what. At all events, if nothing else could be decided upon, the alms-house must receive him. I then begged to have an interview.

Being under no disgraceful charge, and quite serene and harmless in all his ways, they had permitted him freely to wander about the prison, and, especially, in the inclosed grass-platted yards thereof. And so I found him there, standing all alone in the quietest of the yards, his face towards a high wall, while all around, from the narrow slits of the jail windows, I thought I saw peering out upon him the eyes of murderers and thieves.

"Bartleby!"

"I know you," he said, without looking round—"and I want nothing to say to you."

"It was not I that brought you here, Bartleby," said I, keenly pained at his implied suspicion. "And to you, this should not be so vile a place. Nothing reproachful attaches to you by being here. And see, it is not so sad a place as one might think. Look, there is the sky, and here is the grass."

"I know where I am," he replied, but would say nothing more, and so I left him.

As I entered the corridor again, a broad meat-like man, in an apron, accosted me, and, jerking his thumb over his shoulder, said—"Is that your friend?"

"Yes."

"Does he want to starve? If he does, let him live on the prison fare, that's all."

"Who are you?" asked I, not knowing what to make of such an unofficially speaking person in such a place.

"I am the grub-man. Such gentlemen as have friends here, hire me to provide them with something good to eat."

"Is this so?" said I, turning to the turnkey.

He said it was.

"Well, then," said I, slipping some silver into the grub-man's hands (for so they called him), "I want you to give particular attention to my friend there; let him have the best dinner you can get. And you must be as polite to him as possible."

"Introduce me, will you?" said the grub-man, looking at me

with an expression which seemed to say he was all impatience for an opportunity to give a specimen of his breeding.

Thinking it would prove of benefit to the scrivener, I acquiesced; and, asking the grub-man his name, went up with him to Bartleby.

"Bartleby, this is a friend; you will find him very useful to you."

"Your sarvant, sir, your sarvant," said the grub-man, making a low salutation behind his apron. "Hope you find it pleasant here, sir; nice grounds—cool apartments—hope you'll stay with us some time—try to make it agreeable. What will you have for dinner to-day?"

"I prefer not to dine to-day," said Bartleby, turning away. "It would disagree with me; I am unused to dinners." So saying, he slowly moved to the other side of the inclosure, and took up a position fronting the dead-wall.

"How's this?" said the grub-man, addressing me with a stare of astonishment. "He's odd, ain't he?"

"I think he is a little deranged," said I, sadly.

"Deranged? deranged is it? Well, now, upon my word, I thought that friend of yourn was a gentleman forger; they are always pale and genteel-like, them forgers. I can't help pity 'em—can't help it, sir. Did you know Monroe Edwards?" he added, touchingly, and paused. Then, laying his hand piteously on my shoulder, sighed, "He died of consumption at Sing-Sing. So you weren't acquainted with Monroe?"

"No, I was never socially acquainted with any forgers. But I cannot stop longer. Look to my friend yonder. You will not lose by it. I will see you again."

Some few days after this, I again obtained admission to the Tombs, and went through the corridors in quest of Bartleby; but without finding him.

"I saw him coming from his cell not long ago," said a turnkey, "maybe he's gone to loiter in the yards."

So I went in that direction.

"Are you looking for the silent man?" said another turnkey, passing me. "Yonder he lies—sleeping in the yard there. 'Tis not twenty minutes since I saw him lie down."

The yard was entirely quiet. It was not accessible to the common prisoners. The surrounding walls, of amazing thickness, kept off all sounds behind them. The Egyptian character of the masonry weighed upon me with its gloom. But a soft imprisoned turf grew under foot. The heart of the eternal pyramids, it seemed, wherein, by some strange magic, through the clefts, grass-seed, dropped by birds, had sprung.

Strangely huddled at the base of the wall, his knees drawn up, and lying on his side, his head touching the cold stones, I saw the wasted Bartleby. But nothing stirred. I paused; then went close up to him; stooped over, and saw that his dim eyes were open; otherwise he seemed profoundly sleeping. Something prompted me to touch him. I felt his hand, when a tingling shiver ran up my arm and down my spine to my feet.

The round face of the grub-man peered upon me now. "His dinner is ready. Won't he dine to-day, either? Or does he live without dining?"

"Lives without dining," said I, and closed the eyes.

"Eh!—He's asleep, ain't he?"

"With kings and counselors," murmured I.

* * *

There would seem little need for proceeding further in this history. Imagination will readily supply the meagre recital of poor Bartleby's interment. But, ere parting with the reader, let me say, that if this little narrative has sufficiently interested him, to awaken curiosity as to who Bartleby was, and what manner of life he led prior to the present narrator's making his acquaintance, I can only reply, that in such curiosity I fully share, but am wholly unable to gratify it. Yet here I hardly know whether I should divulge one little item of rumor, which came to my ear a few months after the scrivener's decease. Upon what basis it rested, I could never ascertain; and hence, how true it is I cannot now tell. But, inasmuch as this vague report has not been without a certain suggestive interest to me, however sad, it may prove the same with some others, and so I will briefly mention it. The report was this: that Bartleby had been a subordinate clerk in the Dead Letter Office at Washington, from which he had been suddenly removed by a change in the administration. When I think over this rumor, hardly can I express the emotions which seize me. Dead letters! does it not sound like dead men? Conceive a man by nature and misfortune prone to a pallid hopelessness, can any business seem more fitted to heighten it than that of continually handling these dead letters, and assorting them for the flames? For by the cart-load they are annually burned. Sometimes from out the folded paper the pale clerk takes a ring—the finger it was meant for, perhaps, moulders in the grave; a bank-note sent in swiftest charity—he whom it would relieve, nor eats nor hungers any more; pardon for those who died despairing; hope for those who died unhoping; good tidings for those who died stifled by unrelieved calamities. On errands of life, these letters speed to death.

Ah, Bartleby! Ah, humanity!

COCK-A-DOODLE-DOO! OR
THE CROWING OF THE
NOBLE COCK BENEVENTANO

NOTE: As with "Bartleby," a classically efficient contrast between the narrator's lively tone and the grim substance of his story gives "Cock-A-Doodle-Doo!" an ironic force and suggestiveness that license considerable freedom of interpretation. The alarming parody-reference to Wordsworth's "Resolution and Independence" points to a parable of the true artist's or man-of-imagination's probable career in a "miserable world" full of "horrid accidents"; the title and much of the language of the narration ("oh, noble cock! oh, noble man!") fairly flaunt a bitter sub-theme of men's enslavement to the force of sex; and with the spare, stoical Merrymusk we have yet another Melvillean figure of "dateless endurance," strong of soul against impossible odds and able at last to "die unappalled"—for Melville the ultimate accolade.

"Cock-A-Doodle-Doo!" was published in *Harper's* in December, 1853, the month in which the second half of "Bartleby" appeared in *Putnam's*.

IN ALL parts of the world many high-spirited revolts from rascally despotisms had of late been knocked on the head; many dreadful casualties, by locomotive and steamer, had likewise knocked hundreds of high-spirited travelers on the head (I lost a dear friend in one of them); my own private affairs were also full of despotisms, casualties, and knockings on the head when early one morning in Spring, being too full of hypos to sleep, I sallied out to walk on my hillside pasture.

It was a cool and misty, damp, disagreeable air. The country looked underdone, its raw juices squirting out all round. I buttoned out this squitchy air as well as I could with my lean, double-breasted dress-coat—my overcoat being so long-skirted I only used it in my wagon—and spitefully thrusting my crabstick into the oozy sod, bent my blue form to the steep ascent of the hill. This toiling posture brought my head pretty well earthward, as if I were in the act of butting it against the world. I marked the fact, but only grinned at it with a ghastly grin.

All round me were tokens of a divided empire. The old grass and the new grass were striving together. In the low wet swales the verdure peeped out in vivid green; beyond, on the mountains, lay light patches of snow, strangely relieved against their russet sides; all the humped hills looked like brindled kine in the shivers. The woods were strewn with dry dead boughs, snapped off by the riotous winds of March, while the young trees skirting the woods were just beginning to show the first yellowish tinge of the nascent spray.

I sat down for a moment on a great rotting log nigh the top of the hill, my back to a heavy grove, my face presented toward a wide sweeping circuit of mountains enclosing a rolling, diversified country. Along the base of one long range of heights ran a lagging, fever-and-agueish river, over which was a duplicate stream of dripping mist, exactly corresponding in every meander with its parent water below. Low down, here and there, shreds of vapor listlessly wandered in the air, like abandoned or helmless nations of ships—or very soaky towels hung on criss-cross clothes-lines to dry. Afar, over a distant village lying in a bay of the plain formed by the mountain, there rested a great flat canopy of haze, like a pall. It was the condensed smoke of the chimneys, with the condensed, exhaled breath of the villagers, prevented from dispersion by the imprisoning hills. It was too heavy and lifeless to mount of itself; so there it lay, between the village and the sky, doubtless hiding many a man with the mumps, and many a queasy child.

My eye ranged over the capacious rolling country, and over the mountains, and over the village, and over a farmhouse here and there, and over woods, groves, streams, rocks, fells—and I thought to myself, what a slight mark, after all, does man make on this huge great earth. Yet the earth makes a mark on him. What a horrid accident was that on the Ohio, where my good friend and thirty other good fellows were sloped into eternity at the bidding of a thick-headed engineer, who knew not a valve from a flue. And that crash on the railroad just over yon mountains there, where two infatuate trains ran pell-mell into each other, and climbed and clawed each other's backs; and one locomotive was found fairly shelled, like a chick, inside of a passenger car in the antagonist train; and near a score of noble hearts, a bride and her groom, and an innocent little infant, were all disembarked into the grim hulk of Charon, who ferried them over, all baggageless, to some clinkered iron-foundry or other. Yet what's the use of complaining? What justice of the peace will right this matter? Yea, what's the use of bothering the very heavens about it? Don't the heavens themselves ordain these things—else they could not happen?

A miserable world! Who would take the trouble to make a fortune in it, when he knows not how long he can keep it, for the thousand villains and asses who have the management of railroads and steamboats, and innumerable other vital things in the world. If they would make me Dictator in North America a while, I'd string them up! and hang, draw, and quarter; fry, roast, and boil; stew, grill and devil them, like so many turkey-legs—the rascally numskulls of stokers; I'd set them to stokering in Tartarus—I would.

Great improvements of the age! What! to call the facilitation of death and murder an improvement! Who wants to travel so fast? My grandfather did not, and he was no fool. Hark! here comes that old dragon again—that gigantic gadfly of a Moloch—snort! puff! scream!—here he comes straightbent throught these vernal woods, like the Asiatic cholera cantering on a camel. Stand aside! here he comes, the chartered murderer! the death monopolizer! judge, jury, and hangman all together, whose victims die always without benefit of clergy. For two hundred and fifty miles that iron fiend goes yelling through the land, crying "More! more! more!" Would that fifty conspiring mountains would fall atop of him! And, while they were about it, would they would also fall atop of that smaller dunning fiend, my creditor, who frightens the life out of me more than any locomotive—a lantern-jawed rascal, who seems to run on a railroad track, too, and duns me even on Sunday, all the way to church and back, and comes and sits in the same pew with me, and pretending to be polite and hand me the prayer-book opened at the proper place, pokes his pesky bill under my nose in the very midst of my devotions, and so shoves himself between me and salvation; for how can one keep his temper on such occasions?

I can't pay this horrid man; and yet they say money was never so plentiful—a drug in the market; but blame me if I can get any of the drug, though there never was a sick man more in need of that particular sort of medicine. It's a lie; money ain't plentiful—feel of my pocket. Ha! here's a powder I was going to send to the sick baby in yonder hovel, where the Irish ditcher lives. That baby has the scarlet fever. They say the measles are rife in the country, too, and the varioloid, and the chicken-pox, and it's bad for teething children. And after all, I suppose many of the poor little ones, after going through all this trouble, snap off short; and so they had the measles, mumps, croup, scarlet fever, chicken-pox, cholera morbus, summer-complaint, and all else, in vain! Ah! there's that twinge of the rheumatics in my right shoulder. I got it one night on the North River, when, in a crowded boat, I gave up my berth to a sick lady, and stayed on deck till morning in drizzling weather. There's the thanks one gets for charity! Twinge! Shoot away, ye rheumatics! Ye couldn't lay on worse if I were some villain who had murdered the lady instead of befriending her. Dyspepsia, too—I am troubled with that.

"Hallo! here come the calves, the two-year-olds, just turned out of the barn into the pasture, after six months of cold victuals. What a miserable-looking set, to be sure! A breaking up of a hard winter, that's certain: sharp bones sticking out like elbows; all quilted with a strange stuff dried on their flanks like layers of pancakes. Hair worn quite off too, here and there; and where it ain't pancaked, or worn off, looks like the rubbed sides of mangy old hair-trunks. In fact, they are not six two-years-olds, but six abominable old hair-trunks wandering about here in this pasture.

"Hark! By Jove, what's that? See! the very hair-trunks prick their ears at it, and stand and gaze away down into the rolling country yonder. Hark again! How clear! how musical! how prolonged! What a triumphant thanksgiving of a cock-crow! *"Glory be to God in the highest!"* It says those very words as plain as ever cock did in this world. Why, why, I begin to feel a little in sorts again. It ain't so very misty, after all. The sun yonder is beginning to show himself: I feel warmer.

Hark! There again! Did ever such a blessed cock-crow so ring out over the earth before! Clear, shrill, full of pluck, full of fire, full of fun, full of glee. It plainly says—*"Never say die!"* My friends, it is extraordinary, is it not?

Unwittingly, I found that I had been addressing the two-year-olds—the calves—in my enthusiasm; which shows how one's true nature will betray itself at times in the most unconscious way. For what a very two-year-old, and calf, I had been to fall into the sulks, on a hill-top too, when a cock down in the lowlands there, without discourse of reason, and quite penniless in the world, and with death hanging over him at any moment from his hungry master, sends up a cry like a very laureate celebrating the glorious victory of New Orleans.

Hark! there it goes again! My friends, that must be a Shanghai; no domestic-born cock could crow in such prodigious exulting strains. Plainly, my friends, a Shanghai of the Emperor of China's breed.

But my friends the hair-trunks, fairly alarmed at last by such clamorously-victorious tones, were now scampering off, with their tails flirting in the air, and capering with their legs in clumsy enough sort of style, sufficiently evincing that they had not freely flourished them for the six months last past.

Hark! there again! Whose cock is that? Who in this region can afford to buy such an extraordinary Shanghai? Bless me— it makes my blood bound—I feel wild. What? jumping on this rotten old log here, to flap my elbows and crow too? And just now in the doleful dumps. And all this from the simple crow of a cock. Marvelous cock! But soft—this fellow now crows most lustily; but it's only morning; let's see how he'll crow about noon, and toward nightfall. Come to think of it, cocks crow mostly in the beginning of the day. Their pluck ain't lasting, after all. Yes, yes; even cocks have to succumb to the universal spell of tribulation: jubilant in the beginning, but down in the mouth at the end.

> "*. . . Of fine mornings,*
> *We fine lusty cocks begin our crows in gladness;*
> *But when eve does come we don't crow*
>   *quite so much,*
> *For then cometh despondency and madness.*"

The poet had this very Shanghai in his mind when he wrote that. But stop. There he rings out again, ten times richer, fuller, longer, more obstreperously exulting than before! Why, this is equal to hearing the great bell on St. Paul's rung at a coronation! In fact, that bell ought to be taken down, and this Shanghai put in its place. Such a crow would jollify all London, from Mile End (which is no end) to Primrose Hill (where there ain't any primroses), and scatter the fog.

Well, I have an appetite for my breakfast this morning, if I have not had it for a week before. I meant to have only tea and toast; but I'll have coffee and eggs—no, brown-stout and a beef-steak. I want something hearty. Ah, here comes the down-train: white cars, flashing through the trees like a vein of silver. How cheerfully the steam-pipe chirps! Gay are the passengers. There waves a handkerchief—going down to the city to eat oysters, and see their friends, and drop in at the circus. Look at the mist yonder; what soft curls and undulations round the hills, and the sun weaving his rays among them. See the azure smoke of the village, like the azure tester over a bridal-bed. How bright the country looks there where the river overflowed the meadows. The old grass has to knock under to the new. Well, I feel the better for this walk. Home now, and walk into that steak and crack that bottle of brown-stout; and by the time that's drank—a quart of stout—by that time, I shall feel about as stout as Samson. Come to think of it, that dun may call, though. I'll just visit the woods and cut a club. I'll club him, by jove, if he duns me this day.

Hark! there goes Shanghai again. Shanghai says, "Bravo!" Shanghai says, "Club him!"

Oh, brave cock!

I felt in rare spirits the whole morning. The dun called about eleven. I had the boy Jake send the dun up. I was reading *Tristram Shandy,* and could not go down under the circumstances. The lean rascal (a lean farmer, too—think of that!) entered, and found me seated in an armchair, with my feet on the table, and the second bottle of brown-stout handy, and the book under eye.

"Sit down," said I; "I'll finish this chapter, and then attend to you. Fine morning. Ha! ha!—this a fine joke about my Uncle Toby and the Widow Wadman! Ha! ha! ha! let me read this to you."

"I have no time; I've got my noon *chores* to do."

"To the deuce with your *chores!*" said I. "Don't drop your old tobacco about here, or I'll turn you out."

"Sir!"

"Let me read you this about the Widow Wadman. Said the Widow Wadman—"

"There's my bill, sir."

"Very good. Just twist it up, will you;—it's about my smoking time; and hand a coal, will you, from the hearth yonder!"

"My bill, sir!" said the rascal, turning pale with rage and amazement at my unwonted air (formerly I had always dodged him with a pale face), but too prudent as yet to betray the extremity of his astonishment. "My bill, sir!"—and he stiffly poked it at me.

"My friend," said I, "what a charming morning! How sweet the country looks! Pray, did you hear that extraordinary cock-crow this morning? Take a glass of my stout!"

"*Yours?* First pay your debts before you offer folks *your* stout!"

"You think, then, that, properly speaking, I have no *stout,*" said I, deliberately rising. "I'll undeceive you. I'll show you stout of a superior brand to Barclay and Perkins."

Without more ado, I seized that insolent dun by the slack of his coat— (and being a lean shad-bellied wretch, there was plenty of slack to it)—I seized him that way, tied him with a sailor-knot, and, thrusting his bill between his teeth, introduced him to the open country lying round about my place of abode.

"Jake," said I, "you'll find a sack of blue-nosed potatoes lying under the shed. Drag it here, and pelt this pauper away: he's been begging pence of me, and I know he can work, but he's lazy. Pelt him away, Jake!"

Bless my stars, what a crow! Shanghai sent up such a perfect pæan and *laudamus*—such a trumpet-blast of triumph that my soul fairly snorted in me. Duns!—I could have fought an army of them! Plainly, Shanghai was of the opinion that duns only came into the world to be kicked, banged, bruised, battered, choked, walloped, hammered, drowned, clubbed!

Returning in-doors, when the exultation of my victory over the dun had a little subsided, I fell to musing over the mysterious Shanghai. I had no idea I would hear him so nigh my house. I wondered from what rich gentleman's yard he crowed. Nor had he cut short his crows so easily as I had supposed he would. This Shanghai crowed till midday, at least. Would he keep a-crowing all day? I resolved to learn. Again I ascended the hill. The whole country was now bathed in a rejoicing sun-light. The warm verdure was bursting all round me. Teams were a-field. Birds, newly arrived from the South, were blithely singing in the air. Even the crows cawed with a certain unction, and seemed a shade or two less black than usual.

Hark! there goes the cock! How shall I describe the crow of the Shanghai at noon-tide? His sunrise crow was a whisper to it. It was the loudest, longest, and most strangely musical crow that ever amazed mortal man. I had heard plenty of cock-

crows before, and many fine ones;—but this one! so smooth
and flute-like, in its very clamor—so self-possessed in its very
rapture of exultation—so vast, mounting, swelling, soaring, as
if spurted out from a golden throat, thrown far back. Nor did
it sound like the foolish, vain-glorious crow of some young
sophomorean cock, who knew not the world, and was beginning
life in audacious gay spirits, because in wretched ignorance of
what might be to come. It was the crow of a cock who crowed
not without advice; the crow of a cock who knew a thing or
two; the crow of a cock who had fought the world and got
the better of it, and was now resolved to crow, though the
earth should heave and the heavens should fall. It was a wise
crow; an invincible crow; a philosophic crow; a crow of all
crows.

I returned home once more full of reinvigorated spirits,
with a dauntless sort of feeling. I thought over my debts and
other troubles, and over the unlucky risings of the poor oppressed *peoples* abroad, and over the railroad and steamboat
accidents, and over even the loss of my dear friend, with a
calm, good-natured rapture of defiance, which astounded myself. I felt as though I could meet Death, and invite him to
dinner, and toast the Catacombs with him, in pure overflow
of self-reliance and a sense of universal security.

Toward evening I went up to the hill once more to find
whether, indeed, the glorious cock would prove game even
from the rising of the sun unto the going down thereof. Talk
of Vespers or Curfew!—the evening crow of the cock went
out of his mighty throat all over the land and inhabited it,
like Xerxes from the East with his double-winged host. It was
miraculous. Bless me, what a crow! The cock went game to
roost that night, depend upon it, victorious over the entire
day, and bequeathing the echoes of his thousand crows to
night.

After an unwontedly sound, refreshing sleep I rose early,
feeling like a carriage-spring—light—elliptical—airy—buoy-
ant as sturgeon-nose—and, like a football, bounded up the
hill. Hark! Shanghai was up before me. The early bird that
caught the worm—crowing like a bugle worked by an engine
—lusty, loud, all jubilation. From the scattered farmhouses a
multitude of other cocks were crowing, and replying to each
other's crows. But they were as flageolets to a trombone. Shanghai would suddenly break in, and overwhelm all their crows
with his one domineering blast. He seemed to have nothing

to do with any other concern. He replied to no other crow, but crowed solely by himself, on his own account, in solitary scorn and independence.

Oh, brave cock!—oh, noble Shanghai!—oh, bird rightly offered up by the invincible Socrates, in testimony of his final victory over life.

As I live, thought I, this blessed day will I go and seek out the Shanghai, and buy him, if I have to clap another mortgage on my land.

I listened attentively now, striving to mark from what direction the crow came. But it so charged and replenished, and made bountiful and overflowing all the air, that it was impossible to say from what precise point the exultation came. All that I could decide upon was this: the crow came from out of the East, and not from out of the West. I then considered with myself how far a cock-crow might be heard. In this still country, shut in, too, by mountains, sounds were audible at great distances. Besides, the undulations of the land, the abuttings of the mountains into the rolling hill and valley below, produced strange echoes, and reverberations, and multiplications, and accumulations of resonance, very remarkable to hear, and very puzzling to think of. Where lurked this valiant Shanghai—this bird of cheerful Socrates—the game-fowl Greek who died unappalled? Where lurked he? Oh, noble cock, where are you? Crow once more, my Bantam! my princely, my imperial Shanghai! my bird of the Emperor of China! Brother of the Sun! Cousin of great Jove! where are you?— one crow more, and tell me your number!

Hark! like a full orchestra of the cocks of all nations, forth burst the crow. But where from? There it is; but where? There was no telling, further than it came from out the East.

After breakfast I took my stick and sallied down the road. There were many gentlemen's seats dotting the neighboring country, and I made no doubt that some of these opulent gentlemen had invested a hundred dollar bill in some royal Shanghai recently imported in the ship *Trade Wind,* or the ship *White Squall,* or the ship *Sovereign of the Seas;* for it must needs have been a brave ship with a brave name which bore the fortunes of so brave a cock. I resolved to walk the entire country, and find this noble foreigner out; but thought it would not be amiss to inquire on the way at the humblest homesteads, whether, peradventure, they had heard of a lately-imported Shanghai belonging to any of the gentlemen settlers from the city; for it was plain that no poor farmer, no poor man of any sort, could own such an Oriental trophy—such a Great Bell of St. Paul's swung in a cock's throat.

I met an old man, plowing, in a field nigh the road-side fence.

"My friend, have you heard an extraordinary cock-crow of late?"

"Well, well," he drawled, "I don't know—the Widow Crowfoot has a cock—and Squire Squaretoes has a cock—and I have a cock, and they all crow. But I don't know of any on 'em with 'strordinary crows."

"Good morning to you," said I, shortly; "it's plain that you have not heard the crow of the Emperor of China's chanticleer."

Presently I met another old man mending a tumble-down old rail-fence. The rails were rotten, and at every move of the old man's hand they crumbled into yellow ochre. He had much better let the fence alone, or else get him new rails. And here I must say, that one cause of the sad fact why idiocy more prevails among farmers than any other class of people, is owing to their undertaking the mending of rotten rail-fences in warm, relaxing spring weather. The enterprise is a hopeless one. It is a laborious one; it is a bootless one. It is an enterprise to make the heart break. Vast pains squandered upon a vanity. For how can one make rotten rail-fences stand up on their rotten pins? By what magic put pith into sticks which have lain freezing and baking through sixty consecutive winters and summers? This it is, this wretched endeavor to mend rotten rail-fences with their own rotten rails, which drives many farmers into the asylum.

On the face of the old man in question incipient idiocy was plainly marked. For about sixty rods before him extended one of the most unhappy and desponding broken-hearted Virginia rail-fences I ever saw in my life. While in a field behind, were a set of young steers, possessed as by devils, continually butting at this forlorn old fence, and breaking through it here and there, causing the old man to drop his work and chase them back within bounds. He would chase them with a piece of rail huge as Goliath's beam, but as light as cork. At the first flourish, it crumbled into powder.

"My friend," said I, addressing this woeful mortal, "have you heard an extraordinary cock-crow of late?"

I might as well have asked him if he had heard the death-tick. He stared at me with a long, bewildered, doleful, and unutterable stare, and without reply resumed his unhappy labors.

What a fool, thought I, to have asked such an uncheerful and uncheerable creature about a cheerful cock!

I walked on. I had now descended the high land where my house stood, and being in a low tract could not hear the crow of the Shanghai, which, doubtless, overshot me there. Besides, the Shanghai might be at lunch of corn and oats, or taking a nap, and so interrupted his jubilations for a while.

At length, I encountered, riding along the road, a portly gentleman—nay, a *pursy* one—of great wealth, who had recently purchased him some noble acres, and built him a noble mansion, with a goodly fowl-house attached, the fame whereof spread through all that country. Thought I, Here now is the owner of the Shanghai.

"Sir," said I, "excuse me, but I am a countryman of yours, and would ask, if so be you own any Shanghais?"

"Oh, yes; I have ten Shanghais."

"Ten!" exclaimed I, in wonder, "and do they all crow?"

"Most lustily; every soul of them; I wouldn't own a cock that wouldn't crow."

"Will you turn back, and show me those Shanghais?"

"With pleasure: I am proud of them. They cost me, in the lump, six hundred dollars."

As I walked by the side of his horse, I was thinking to myself whether possibly I had not mistaken the harmoniously combined crowings of ten Shanghais in a squad, for the supernatural crow of a single Shanghai by himself.

"Sir," said I, "is there one of your Shanghais which far exceeds all the others in the lustiness, musicalness, and inspiring effects of his crow?"

"They crow pretty much alike, I believe," he courteously replied. "I really don't know that I could tell their crows apart."

I began to think that, after all, my noble chanticleer might not be in the possession of this wealthy gentleman. However, we went into his fowl-yard, and I saw his Shanghais. Let me say that hitherto I had never clapped eye on this species of imported fowl. I had heard what enormous prices were paid for them, and also that they were of an enormous size, and had somehow fancied they must be of a beauty and brilliancy proportioned both to size and price. What was my surprise, then, to see ten carrot-colored monsters, without the smallest pretension to effulgence of plumage. Immediately, I determined that my royal cock was neither among these, nor could possibly be a Shanghai at all; if these gigantic gallows-bird fowl were fair specimens of the true Shanghai.

I walked all day, dining and resting at a farm-house, inspecting various fowl-yards, interrogating various owners of fowls, hearkening to various crows, but discovered not the mysterious chanticleer. Indeed, I had wandered so far and deviously, that I could not hear his crow. I began to suspect that this cock was a mere visitor in the country, who had taken his departure by the eleven o'clock train for the South, and was now crowing and jubilating somewhere on the verdant banks of Long Island Sound.

But next morning, again I heard the inspiring blast, again felt my blood bound in me, again felt superior to all the ills of life, again felt like turning my dun out of doors. But displeased with the reception given him at his last visit, the dun stayed away. Doubtless being in a huff; silly fellow that he was to take a harmless joke in earnest.

Several days passed, during which I made sundry excursions in the regions roundabout, but in vain sought the cock. Still, I heard him from the hill, and sometimes from the house, and sometimes in the stillness of the night. If at times I would relapse into my doleful dumps, straightway at the sound of the exultant and defiant crow, my soul, too, would turn chanticleer, and clap her wings, and throw back her throat, and breathe forth a cheerful challenge to all the world of woes.

At last, after some weeks I was necessitated to clap another mortgage on my estate, in order to pay certain debts, and among others the one I owed the dun, who of late had commenced a civil-process against me. The way the process was served was a most insulting one. In the private room I had been enjoying myself in the village tavern over a bottle of Philadelphia porter, and some Herkimer cheese, and a roll, and having apprised the landlord, who was a friend of mine, that I would settle with him when I received my next remittances, stepped to the peg where I had hung my hat in the bar-room, to get a choice cigar I had left in the hall, when lo! I found the civil-process enveloping the cigar. When I unrolled the cigar, I unrolled the civil-process, and the constable standing by rolled out, with a thick tongue, "Take notice!" and added, in a whisper, "Put that in your pipe and smoke it!"

I turned short round upon the gentlemen then and there present in that bar-room. Said I, "Gentlemen, is this an honorable—nay, is this a lawful way of serving a civil-process? Behold!"

One and all they were of opinion, that it was a highly inelegant act in the constable to take advantage of a gentleman's lunching on cheese and porter, to be so uncivil as to slip a civil-process into his hat. It was ungenerous; it was cruel; for the sudden shock of the thing coming instanter upon the lunch, would impair the proper digestion of the cheese, which is proverbially not so easy of digestion as blancmange.

Arrived home, I read the process, and felt a twinge of melancholy. Hard world! hard world! Here I am, as good a fellow as ever lived—hospitable—open-hearted—generous to a fault: and the Fates forbid that I should possess the fortune to bless the country with my bounteousness. Nay, while many a stingy curmudgeon rolls in idle gold, I, heart of nobleness as I am, I have civil-processes served on me! I bowed my head, and felt forlorn—unjustly used—abused—unappreciated—in short, miserable.

Hark! like a clarion! yea, like a jolly bolt of thunder with bells to it—came the all-glorious and defiant crow! Ye gods, how it set me up again! Right on my pins! Yea, verily on stilts!

Oh, noble cock!

Plain as cock could speak, it said, "Let the world and all aboard of it go to pot. Do you be jolly, and never say die. What's the world compared to you? What is it, anyhow, but a lump of loam? Do you be jolly!"

Oh, noble cock!

"But, my dear and glorious cock," mused I, upon second thought, "one can't so easily send this world to pot; one can't so easily be jolly with civil-processes in his hat or hand."

Hark! the crow again. Plain as cock could speak, it said, "Hang the process, and hang the fellow that sent it! If you have not land or cash, go and thrash the fellow, and tell him you never mean to pay him. Be jolly!"

Now this was the way—through the imperative intimations of the cock—that I came to clap the added mortgage on my estate; paid all my debts by fusing them into this one added bond and mortgage. Thus made at ease again, I renewed my search for the noble cock. But in vain, though I heard him every day. I began to think there was some sort of deception in this mysterious thing: some wonderful ventriloquist prowled around my barns, or in my cellar, or on my roof, and was minded to be gaily mischievous. But no—what ventriloquist could so crow with such an heroic and celestial crow?

At last, one morning there came to me a certain singular man, who had sawed and split my wood in March—some five-and-thirty cords of it—and now he came for his pay. He was a singular man, I say. He was tall and spare, with a long saddish face, yet somehow a latently joyous eye, which offered the strangest contrast. His air seemed staid, but undepressed. He wore a long, gray, shabby coat, and a big battered hat. This man had sawed my wood at so much a cord. He would stand and saw all day long in a driving snow-storm, and never wink at it. He never spoke unless spoken to. He only sawed. Saw, saw, saw—snow, snow, snow. The saw and the snow went together like two natural things. The first day this man came, he brought his dinner with him, and volunteered to eat it sitting on his buck in the snow-storm. From my window, where I was read-ing Burton's *Anatomy of Melancholy,* I saw him in the act. I burst out of-doors bare-headed. "Good heavens!" cried I, "what are you doing? Come in. *This* your dinner!"

He had a hunk of stale bread and another hunk of salt beef, wrapped in a wet newspaper, and washed his morsels down by melting a handful of fresh snow in his mouth. I took this rash man in-doors, planted him by the fire, gave him a dish of hot pork and beans, and a mug of cider.

"Now," said I, "don't you bring any of your damp dinners here. You work by the job, to be sure; but I'll dine you for all that."

He expressed his acknowledgments in a calm, proud, but not ungrateful way, and dispatched his meal with satisfaction to himself, and me also. It afforded me pleasure to perceive that he quaffed down his mug of cider like a man. I honored him. When I addressed him in the way of business at his buck, I did so in a guardedly respectful and deferential manner. Interested in his singular aspect, struck by his wondrous in-tensity of application at his saw—a most wearisome and dis-gustful occupation to most people—I often sought to gather from him who he was, what sort of a life he led, where he was born, and so on. But he was mum. He came to saw my wood, and eat my dinners—if I chose to offer them—but not to gabble. At first, I somewhat resented his sullen silence under the circumstances. But better considering it, I honored him the more. I increased the respectfulness and deferentialness of my address toward him. I concluded within myself that this man had experienced hard times; that he had had many sore rubs in the world; that he was of a solemn disposition; that he was of the mind of Solomon; that he lived calmly, decorously, temperately; and though a very poor man, was, nevertheless, a highly respectable one. At times I imagined that he might even be an elder or deacon of some small country church. I thought it would not be a bad plan to run this excellent man for President of the United States. He would prove a great reformer of abuses.

His name was Merrymusk. I had often thought how jolly a name for so unjolly a wight. I inquired of people whether they knew Merrymusk. But it was some time before I learned much about him. He was by birth a Marylander, it appeared, who had long lived in the country round about; a wandering man; until within some ten years ago, a thriftless man, though perfectly innocent of crime; a man who would work hard a month with surprising soberness, and then spend all his wages in one riotous night. In youth he had been a sailor, and run away from his ship at Batavia, where he caught the fever, and came nigh dying. But he rallied, reshipped, landed home, found all his friends dead and struck for the Northern interior, where he had since tarried. Nine years back he had married a wife, and now had four children. His wife was become a perfect invalid; one child had the white-swelling, and the rest were rickety. He and his family lived in a shanty on a lonely barren patch nigh the railroad track, where it passed close to the base of a mountain. He had bought a fine cow to have plenty of wholesome milk for his children; but the cow died during an accouchement, and he could not afford to buy another. Still, his family never suffered for lack of food. He worked hard and brought it to them.

Now, as I said before, having long previously sawed my wood, this Merrymusk came for his pay.

"My friend," said I, "do you know of any gentleman hereabouts who owns an extraordinary cock?"

The twinkle glittered quite plain in the wood-sawyer's eye.

"I know of no *gentleman*," he replied, "who has what might well be called an extraordinary cock."

Oh, thought I, this Merrymusk is not the man to enlighten

me. I am afraid I shall never discover this extraordinary cock.

Not having the full change to pay Merrymusk, I gave him his due, as nigh as I could make it, and told him that in a day or two I would take a walk and visit his place, and hand him the remainder. Accordingly one fine morning I sallied forth upon the errand. I had much ado finding the best road to the shanty. No one seemed to know where it was exactly. It lay in a very lonely part of the country, a densely wooded mountain on one side (which I call October Mountain, on account of its bannered aspect in that month), and a thicketed swamp on the other, the railroad cutting the swamp. Straight as a die the railroad cut it; many times a day tantalizing the wretched shanty with the sight of all the beauty, rank, fashion, health, trunks, silver and gold, drygoods and groceries, brides and grooms, happy wives and husbands, flying by the lonely door—no time to stop—flash! here they are—and there they go!—out of sight at both ends—as if that part of the world were only made to fly over, and not to settle upon. And this was about all the shanty saw of what people call "life."

Though puzzled somewhat, yet I knew the general direction where the shanty lay, and on I trudged. As I advanced, I was surprised to hear the mysterious cock crow with more and more distinctness. Is it possible, thought I, that any gentleman owning a Shanghai can dwell in such a lonesome, dreary region? Louder and louder, nigher and nigher, sounded the glorious and defiant clarion. Though somehow I may be out of the track to my wood-sawyer's, I said to myself, yet, thank heaven, I seem to be on the way toward that extraordinary cock. I was delighted with this auspicious accident. On I journeyed; while at intervals the crow sounded most invitingly, and jocundly, and superbly; and the last crow was ever nigher than the former one. At last, emerging from a thicket of elders, straight before me I saw the most resplendent creature that ever blessed the sight of man.

A cock, more like a golden eagle than a cock. A cock, more like a Field-Marshal than a cock. A cock, more like Lord Nelson with all his glittering arms on, standing on the _Vanguard_'s quarter-deck going into battle, than a cock. A cock, more like the Emperor Charlemagne in his robes at Aix-la-Chapelle, than a cock.

Such a cock!

He was of a haughty size, stood haughtily on his haughty legs. His colors were red, gold, and white. The red was on his crest alone, which was a mighty and symmetric crest, like unto Hector's helmet, as delineated on antique shields. His plumage was snowy, traced with gold. He walked in front of the shanty, like a peer of the realm, his crest lifted, his chest heaved out, his embroidered trappings flashing in the light. His pace was wonderful. He looked like some noble foreigner. He looked like some Oriental king in some magnificent Italian opera.

Merrymusk advanced from the door.

"Pray, is not that the Signor Beneventano?"

"Sir?"

"That's the cock," said I, a little embarrassed. The truth was, my enthusiasm had betrayed me into a rather silly inadvertence. I had made a somewhat learned sort of allusion in the presence of an unlearned man. Consequently, upon discovering it by his honest stare, I felt foolish; but carried if off by declaring that *this was the cock.*

Now, during the preceding autumn I had been to the city, and had chanced to be present at a performance of the Italian Opera. In that opera figured in some royal character a certain Signor Beneventano—a man of a tall, imposing person, clad in rich raiment, like to plumage, and with a most remarkable, majestic, scornful stride. The Signor Beneventano seemed on the point of tumbling over backward with exceeding haughtiness. And, for all the world, the proud pace of the cock seemed the very stage-pace of the Signor Beneventano.

Hark! Suddenly the cock paused, lifted his head still higher, ruffled his plumes, seemed inspired, and sent forth a lusty crow. October Mountain echoed it; other mountains sent it back; still others rebounded it; it overran the country round. Now I plainly perceived how it was I had chanced to hear the gladdening sound on my distant hill.

"Good Heavens! do you own the cock? Is that cock yours?"

"Is it my cock!" said Merrymusk, looking slyly gleeful out of the corner of his long, solemn face.

"Where did you get it?"

"It chipped the shell here. I raised it."

"You?"

Hark! Another crow. It might have raised the ghosts of all the pines and hemlocks ever cut down in that country. Marvelous cock! Having crowed, he strode on again, surrounded by a bevy of admiring hens.

"What will you take for Signor Beneventano?"

"Sir?"

"That magic cock!—what will you take for him?"

"I won't sell him."

"I will give you fifty dollars."

"Pooh!"

"One hundred!"

"Pish!"

"Five hundred!"

"Bah!"

"And you a poor man?"

"No: don't I own that cock, and haven't I refused five hundred dollars for him?"

"True," said I, in profound thought, "that's a fact. You won't sell him, then?"

"No."

"Will you give him?"

"No."

"Will you *keep* him, then!" I shouted, in a rage.

"Yes."

I stood awhile admiring the cock, and wondering at the man. At last I felt a redoubled admiration of the one, and a redoubled deference for the other.

"Won't you step in?" said Merrymusk.

"But won't the cock be prevailed upon to join us?" said I.

"Yes. Trumpet! hither, boy! hither!"

The cock turned round, and strode up to Merrymusk.

"Come!"

The cock followed us into the shanty.

"Crow!"

The roof jarred.

Oh, noble cock!

I turned in silence upon my entertainer. There he sat on an old battered chest, in his old battered gray coat, with patches at his knees and elbows, and a deplorably bunged hat. I glanced round the room. Bare rafters overhead, but solid junks of jerked beef hanging from them. Earth floor, but a heap of potatoes in one corner, and a sack of Indian meal in another. A blanket was strung across the apartment at the further end, from which came a woman's ailing voice and the voices of ailing children. But somehow in the ailing of these voices there seemed no complaint.

"Mrs. Merrymusk and children?"

"Yes."

I looked at the cock. There he stood majestically in the middle of the room. He looked like a Spanish grandee caught in a shower, and standing under some peasant's shed. There was a strange supernatural look of contrast about him. He irradiated the shanty; he glorified its meanness. He glorified the battered chest, and tattered gray coat, and the bunged hat. He glorified the very voices which came in ailing tones from behind the screen.

"Oh, father," cried a little sickly voice, "let Trumpet sound again."

"Crow," cried Merrymusk.

The cock threw himself into a posture.

The roof jarred.

"Does not this disturb Mrs. Merrymusk and the sick children?"

"Crow again, Trumpet."

The roof jarred.

"It does not disturb them, then?"

"Didn't you hear 'em *ask* for it?"

"How is it, that your sick family like this crowing?" said I. "The cock is a glorious cock, with a glorious voicĕ, but not exactly the sort of thing for a sick chamber, one would suppose. Do they really like it?"

"Don't *you* like it? Don't it do *you* good? Ain't it inspiring? don't it impart pluck? give stuff against despair?"

"All true," said I, removing my hat with profound humility before the brave spirit disguised in the base coat.

"But then," said I, still with some misgivings, "so loud, so wonderfully clamorous a crow, methinks might be amiss to invalids, and retard their convalescence."

"Crow your best now, Trumpet!"

I leaped from my chair. The cock frightened me, like some overpowering angel in the Apocalypse. He seemed crowing over the fall of wicked Babylon, or crowing over the triumph of righteous Joshua in the vale of Ashkelon. When I regained my composure somewhat, an inquisitive thought occurred to me. I resolved to gratify it.

"Merrymusk, will you present me to your wife and children?"

"Yes. Wife, the gentleman wants to step in."

"He is very welcome," replied a weak voice.

Going behind the curtain, there lay a wasted, but strangely cheerful human face; and that was pretty much all; the body, hid by the counterpane and an old coat, seemed too shrunken to reveal itself through such impediments. At the bedside sat a pale girl, ministering. In another bed lay three children, side by side: three more pale faces.

"Oh, father, we don't mislike the gentleman, but let us see Trumpet, too."

At a word, the cock strode behind the screen, and perched himself on the children's bed. All their wasted eyes gazed at him with a wild and spiritual delight. They seemed to sun themselves in the radiant plumage of the cock.

"Better than a 'pothecary, eh?" said Merrymusk. "This is Dr. Cock himself."

We retired from the sick ones, and I reseated myself again, lost in thought, over this strange household.

"You seem a glorious independent fellow!" said I.

"And I don't think you a fool, and never did. Sir, you are a trump."

"Is there any hope of your wife's recovery?" said I, modestly seeking to turn the conversation.

"Not the least."

"The children?"

"Very little."

"It must be a doleful life, then, for all concerned. This lonely solitude—this shanty—hard work—hard times."

"Haven't I Trumpet? He's the cheerer. He crows through all; crows at the darkest; Glory to God in the highest! continually he crows it."

"Just the import I first ascribed to his crow, Merrymusk, when first I heard it from my hill. I thought some rich nabob owned some costly Shanghai; little weening any such poor man as you owned this lusty cock of a domestic breed."

"*Poor* man like *me?* Why call *me* poor? Don't the cock *I* own glorify this otherwise inglorious, lean, lantern-jawed land? Didn't *my* cock encourage *you?* And *I* give you all this glorification away gratis. I am a great philanthropist. I am a rich man—a very rich man, and a very happy one. Crow, Trumpet."

The roof jarred.

I returned home in a deep mood. I was not wholly at rest concerning the soundness of Merrymusk's views of things, though full of admiration for him. I was thinking on the matter before my door, when I heard the cock crow again. Enough. Merrymusk is right.

Oh, noble cock! oh, noble man!

I did not see Merrymusk for some weeks after this; but hearing the glorious and rejoicing crow, I supposed that all went as usual with him. My own frame of mind remained a rejoicing one. The cock still inspired me. I saw another mortgage piled on my plantation; but only bought another dozen of stout, and a dozen dozen of Philadelphia porter. Some of my relatives died; I wore no mourning, but for three days drank stout in preference to porter, stout being of the darker color. I heard the cock the instant I received the unwelcome tidings.

"Your health in this stout, oh noble cock!"

I thought I would call on Merrymusk again, not having seen or heard of him for some time now. Approaching the place, there were no signs of motion about the shanty. I felt a strange misgiving. But the cock crew from within doors, and the boding vanished. I knocked at the door. A feeble voice bade me enter. The curtain was no longer drawn; the whole house was a hospital now. Merrymusk lay on a heap of old clothes; wife and children were all in their beds. The cock was perched on an old hogshead hoop, swung from the ridge-pole in the middle of the shanty.

"You are sick, Merrymusk," said I, mournfully.

"No, I am well," he feebly answered. "Crow, Trumpet."

I shrunk. The strong soul in the feeble body appalled me. But the cock crew.

The roof jarred.

"How is Mrs. Merrymusk?"

"Well."

"And the children?"

"Well. All well."

The last two words he shouted forth in a kind of wild ecstasy of triumph over ill. It was too much. His head fell back. A white napkin seemed dropped upon his face. Merrymusk was dead.

An awful fear seized me.

But the cock crew.

The cock shook his plumage as if each feather were a banner. The cock hung from the shanty roof as erewhile the trophied flags from the dome of St. Paul's. The cock terrified me with exceeding wonder.

I drew nigh the bedsides of the woman and children. They marked my look of strange affright; they knew what had happened.

"My good man is just dead," breathed the woman lowly. "Tell me true?"

"Dead," said I.

The cock crew.

She fell back, without a sigh and, through long-loving sympathy, was dead.

The cock crew.

The cock shook his plumage over them. The cock crew. The cock seemed in a rapture of benevolent delight. Leaping from the hoop, he strode up majestically to the pile of old clothes, where the wood-sawyer lay, and planted himself, like an armorial supporter, at his side. Then raised one long, musical, triumphant, and final sort of crow, with throat heaved far back, as if he meant the blast to waft the wood-sawyer's soul sheer up to the seventh heavens. Then he strode, king-like, to the woman's bed. Another upturned and exultant crow, mated to the former.

The pallor of the children was changed to radiance. Their faces shone celestially through grime and dirt. They seemed children of emperors and kings, disguised. The cock sprang upon their bed, shook himself, and crowed, and crowed again, and still and still again. He seemed bent upon crowing the souls of the children out of their wasted bodies. He seemed bent upon rejoining instanter this whole family in the upper air. The children seemed to second his endeavors. Far, deep, intense longings for release transfigured them into spirits before my eyes. I saw angels where they lay.

They were dead.

The cock shook his plumage over them. The cock crew. It was now like a Bravo! like a Hurrah! like a Three-times-three! hip! hip! He strode out of the shanty. I followed. He flew upon the apex of the dwelling, spread wide his wings, sounded one supernatural note, and dropped at my feet.

The cock was dead.

If now you visit that hilly region, you will see, nigh the railroad track, just beneath October Mountain, on the other side of the swamp—there you will see a grave-stone, not with skull and cross-bones, but with a lusty cock in act of crowing, chiseled on it, with the words beneath:

> *O death, where is thy sting?*
> *O grave, where is thy victory?*

The wood-sawyer and his family, with the Signor Beneventano, lie in that spot; and I buried them, and planted the stone, which was a stone made to order; and never since then have I felt the doleful dumps, but under all circumstances crow late and early with a continual crow.

COCK-A-DOODLE-DOO!—oo!—oo!—oo!—oo!

THE ENCANTADAS OR
ENCHANTED ISLES

NOTE: Melville's "Encantadas" are the Galapagos Islands, which he had seen at first hand during his South Sea years and which the young Darwin had recently described in his *Diary of the Voyage of H.M.S. Beagle* (1839). When these ten sketches appeared in *Putnam's* (March, April, May, 1854) they bore the pseudonym, "Salvator R. Tarnmoor." But the epigraphs, taken mostly from *The Faerie Queene*, and the thrust of the apocalyptic opening paragraphs, indicate that something other than the fashion for the romantically strange or picturesque governs Melville's presentation, and in fact the pseudonym was dropped when these sketches were reprinted as a unit in *The Piazza Tales* (1856). Of all Melville's work after *Pierre*, "The Encantadas" is perhaps the nearest in vision and address to the descriptive mass of *Moby-Dick*.

Sketch First

THE ISLES AT LARGE

That may not be, said then the Ferryman,
Least we unweeting hap to be fordonne:
For those same Islands, seeming now and than,
Are not firme land, nor any certein wonne,
But stragling plots, which to and fro do ronne
In the wide waters; therefore are they hight
The Wandring Islands: Therefore doe them shonne;
For they have oft drawne many a wan'dring wight
Into most deadly daunger and distressed plight;
For whosoever once hath fastened
His foot thereon, may never it recure,
But wandreth evermore uncertain and unsure.

Darke, dolefull, dreary, like a greedy grave,
That still for carrion carcases doth crave:

On top whereof ay dwelt the ghastly owle,
Shrieking his balefull note, which ever drave
Far from that haunt all other chearefull fowle;
And all about it wandring ghostes did wayle and howle.

TAKE five-and-twenty heaps of cinders dumped here and there
in an outside city lot; imagine some of them magnified into
mountains, and the vacant lot the sea; and you will have a fit
idea of the general aspect of the Encantadas, or Enchanted
Isles. A group rather of extinct volcanoes than of isles; looking
much as the world at large might, after a penal conflagration.

It is to be doubted whether any spot of earth can, in deso-
lateness, furnish a parallel to this group. Abandoned cemeter-
ies of long ago, old cities by piecemeal tumbling to their ruin,
these are melancholy enough; but, like all else which has but
once been associated with humanity, they still awaken in us
some thoughts of sympathy, however sad. Hence, even the Dead
Sea, along with whatever other emotions it may at times in-
spire, does not fail to touch in the pilgrim some of his less un-
pleasurable feelings.

And as for solitariness; the great forests of the north, the
expanses of unnavigated waters, the Greenland ice-fields, are
the profoundest of solitudes to a human observer; still the
magic of their changeable tides and seasons mitigates their
terror; because, though unvisited by men, those forests are
visited by the May; the remotest seas reflect familiar stars even
as Lake Erie does; and in the clear air of a fine Polar day, the
irradiated, azure ice shows beautifully as malachite.

But the special curse, as one may call it, of the Encantadas,
that which exalts them in desolation above Idumea and the
Pole, is, that to them change never comes; neither the change
of seasons nor of sorrows. Cut by the Equator, they know not
autumn, and they know not spring; while already reduced to
the lees of fire, ruin itself can work little more upon them.
The showers refresh the deserts; but in these isles, rain never
falls. Like split Syrian gourds left withering in the sun, they are
cracked by an everlasting drought beneath a torrid sky. "Have
mercy on me," the wailing spirit of the Encantadas seems to
cry, "and send Lazarus that he may dip the tip of his finger in
water and cool my tongue, for I am tormented in this flame."

Another feature in these isles is their emphatic uninhabit-
ableness. It is deemed a fit type of all-forsaken overthrow, that
the jackal should den in the wastes of weedy Babylon; but

the Encantadas refuse to harbor even the outcasts of the beasts. Man and wolf alike disown them. Little but reptile life is here found: tortoises, lizards, immense spiders, snakes and that strangest anomaly of outlandish nature, the *iguana*. No voice, no low, no howl is heard; the chief sound of life here is a hiss.

On most of the isles where vegetation is found at all, it is more ungrateful than the blankness of Atacama. Tangled thickets of wiry bushes, without fruit and without a name, springing up among deep fissures of calcined rock, and treacherously masking them; or a parched growth of distorted cactus trees.

In many places the coast is rock-bound, or, more properly, clinker-bound; tumbled masses of blackish or greenish stuff like the dross of an iron-furnace, forming dark clefts and caves here and there, into which a ceaseless sea pours a fury of foam; overhanging them with a swirl of gray, haggard mist, amidst which sail screaming flights of unearthly birds heightening the dismal din. However calm the sea without, there is no rest for these swells and those rocks; they lash and are lashed, even when the outer ocean is most at peace with itself. On the oppressive, clouded days, such as are peculiar to this part of the watery Equator, the dark, vitrified masses, many of which raise themselves among white whirlpools and breakers in detached and perilous places off the shore, present a most Plutonian sight. In no world but a fallen one could such lands exist.

Those parts of the strand free from the marks of fire, stretch away in wide level beaches of multitudinous dead shells, with here and there decayed bits of sugar-cane, bamboos, and cocoanuts, washed upon this other and darker world from the charming palm isles to the westward and southward; all the way from Paradise to Tartarus; while mixed with the relics of distant beauty you will sometimes see fragments of charred wood and mouldering ribs of wrecks. Neither will any one be surprised at meeting these last, after observing the conflicting currents which eddy throughout nearly all the wide channels of the entire group. The capriciousness of the tides of air sympathizes with those of the sea. Nowhere is the wind so light, baffling, and every way unreliable, and so given to perplexing calms, as at the Encantadas. Nigh a month has been spent by a ship going from one isle to another, though but ninety miles between; for owing to the force of the current, the boats employed to tow barely suffice to keep the craft from sweeping upon the cliffs, but do nothing towards accelerating her voyage. Sometimes it is impossible for a vessel from afar to fetch up with the group itself, unless large allowances for prospective lee-way have been made ere its coming in sight. And yet, at other times, there is a mysterious indraft, which irresistibly draws a passing vessel among the isles, though not bound to them.

True, at one period, as to some extent at the present day, large fleets of whalemen cruised for spermaceti upon what some seamen call the Enchanted Ground. But this, as in due place will be described, was off the great outer isle of Albemarle, away from the intricacies of the smaller isles, where there is plenty of sea-room; and hence, to that vicinity, the above remarks do not altogether apply; though even there the current runs at times with singular force, shifting, too, with as singular a caprice.

Indeed, there are seasons when currents quite unaccountable prevail for a great distance round about the total group, and are so strong and irregular as to change a vessel's course against the helm, though sailing at the rate of four or five miles the hour. The difference in the reckonings of navigators, produced by these causes, along with the light and variable winds, long nourished a persuasion, that there existed two distinct clusters of isles in the parallel of the Encantadas, about a hundred leagues apart. Such was the idea of their earlier visitors, the Buccaneers; and as late as 1750, the charts of that part of the Pacific accorded with the strange delusion. And this apparent fleetingness and unreality of the locality of the isles was most probably one reason for the Spaniards calling them the Encantada, or Enchanted Group.

But not uninfluenced by their character, as they now confessedly exist, the modern voyager will be inclined to fancy that the bestowal of this name might have in part originated in that air of spell-bound desertness which so significantly invests the isles. Nothing can better suggest the aspect of once living things malignly crumbled from ruddiness into ashes. Apples of Sodom, after touching, seem these isles.

However wavering their place may seem by reason of the currents, they themselves, at least to one upon the shore, appear invariably the same: fixed, cast, glued into the very body of cadaverous death.

Nor would the appellation, enchanted, seem misapplied in still another sense. For concerning the peculiar reptile inhabitant of these wilds—whose presence gives the group its second Spanish name, Galapagos—concerning the tortoises found here, most mariners have long cherished a superstition, not more frightful than grotesque. They earnestly believe that all wicked sea-officers, more especially commodores and captains, are at death (and, in some cases, before death) transfromed into tortoises; thenceforth dwelling upon these hot aridities, sole solitary lords of Asphaltum.

Doubtless, so quaintly dolorous a thought was originally inspired by the woe-begone landscape itself; but more particularly, perhaps, by the tortoises. For, apart from their strictly physical features, there is something strangely self-condemned in the appearance of these creatures. Lasting sorrow and penal hopelessness are in no animal form so suppliantly expressed as in theirs; while the thought of their wonderful longevity does not fail to enhance the impression.

Nor even at the risk of meriting the charge of absurdly believing in enchantments, can I restrain the admission that sometimes, even now, when leaving the crowded city to wander out July and August among the Adirondack Mountains, far from the influences of towns and proportionally nigh to the mysterious ones of nature; when at such times I sit me down in the mossy head of some deep-wooded gorge, surrounded by prostrate trunks of blasted pines, and recall, as in a dream, my other and far-distant rovings in the baked heart of the charmed isles; and remember the sudden glimpses of dusky shells, and long languid necks protruded from the leafless thickets; and again have beheld the vitreous inland rocks worn down and grooved into deep ruts by ages and ages of the slow draggings of tortoises in quest of pools of scanty water; I can hardly resist the feeling that in my time I have indeed slept upon evilly enchanted ground.

Nay, such is the vividness of my memory, or the magic of my fancy, that I know not whether I am not the occasional victim of optical delusion concerning the Galapagos. For, often in scenes of social merriment, and especially at revels held by candle-light in old-fashioned mansions, so that shadows are thrown into the further recesses of an angular and spacious room, making them put on a look of haunted undergrowth of lonely woods, I have drawn the attention of my comrades by my fixed gaze and sudden change of air, as I have seemed to see, slowly emerging from those imagined solitudes,

and heavily crawling along the floor, the ghost of a gigantic
tortoise, with "Memento * * * * *" burning in live letters
upon his back.

Sketch Second

TWO SIDES TO A TORTOISE

Most ugly shapes and horrible aspects,
Such as Dame Nature selfe mote feare to see,
Or shame, that ever should so fowle defects
From her most cunning hand escaped bee;
All dreadful pourtraicts of deformitee:
Ne wonder, if these do a man appall;
For all that here at home we dreadfull hold,
Be but as bugs to fearen babes withall,
Compared to the creatures in these isles' entrall.

"Feare nought," then saide the Palmer well aviz'd,
"For these same monsters are not these in deed,
But are into these fearfull shapes disguiz'd."
And lifting up his vertuous staffe on hye,
Then all that dreadfull armie fast can flye
Into great Tethys bosome, where they hidden lye.

IN VIEW of the description given, may one be gay upon the Encantadas? Yes: that is, find one the gaiety, and he will be gay.
And, indeed, sackcloth and ashes as they are, the isles are not
perhaps unmitigated gloom. For while no spectator can deny
their claims to a most solemn and superstitious consideration,
no more than my firmest resolutions can decline to behold
the spectre-tortoise when emerging from its shadowy recess;
yet even the tortoise, dark and melancholy as it is upon the
back, still possesses a bright side; its calipee or breast-plate
being sometimes of a faint yellowish or golden tinge. Moreover, every one knows that tortoises as well as turtles are of such
a make, that if you but put them on their backs you thereby

expose their bright sides without the possibility of their re-covering themselves, and turning into view the other. But after you have done this, and because you have done this, you should not swear that the tortoise has no dark side. Enjoy the bright, keep it turned up perpetually if you can, but be honest, and don't deny the black. Neither should he, who cannot turn the tortoise from its natural position so as to hide the darker and expose his livelier aspect, like a great October pumpkin in the sun, for that cause declare the creature to be one total inky blot. The tortoise is both black and bright. But let us to particulars.

Some months before my first stepping ashore upon the group, my ship was cruising in its close vicinity. One noon we found ourselves off the South Head of Albemarle, and not very far from the land. Partly by way of freak, and partly by way of spying out so strange a country, a boat's crew was sent ashore, with orders to see all they could, and besides, bring back what-ever tortoises they could conveniently transport.

It was after sunset, when the adventurers returned. I looked down over the ship's high side as if looking down over the curb of a well, and dimly saw the damp boat deep in the sea with some unwonted weight. Ropes were dropt over, and presently three huge antediluvian-looking tortoises, after much straining, were landed on deck. They seemed hardly of the seed of earth. We had been abroad upon the waters for five long months, a period amply sufficient to make all things of the land wear a fabulous hue to the dreamy mind. Had three Spanish custom-house officers boarded us then, it is not unlikely that I should have curiously stared at them, felt of them, and stroked them much as savages serve civilized guests. But instead of three custom-house officers, behold these really wondrous tortoises—none of your schoolboy mud-turtles—but black as widower's weeds, heavy as chests of plate, with vast shells medallioned and orbed like shields, and dented and blistered like shields that have breasted a battle, shaggy, too, here and there, with dark green moss, and slimy with the spray of the sea. These mystic creatures, suddenly translated by night from unutterable solitudes to our peopled deck, affected me in a manner not easy to unfold. They seemed newly crawled forth from beneath the foundations of the world. Yea, they seemed the identical tortoises whereon the Hindoo plants this total sphere. With a lantern I inspected them more closely. Such worshipful venerableness of aspect! Such furry greenness mantling the rude peelings and healing the fissures of their shattered shells. I no more saw three tortoises. They expanded—became transfigured. I seemed to see three Roman Coliseums in magnificent decay.

Ye oldest inhabitants of this, or any other isle, said I, pray, give me the freedom of your three walled towns.

The great feeling inspired by these creatures was that of age:—dateless, indefinite endurance. And, in fact, that any other creature can live and breathe as long as the tortoise of the Encantadas, I will not readily believe. Not to hint of their known capacity of sustaining life, while going without food for an entire year, consider that impregnable armor of their living mail. What other bodily being possesses such a citadel wherein to resist the assaults of Time?

As, lantern in hand, I scraped among the moss and beheld the ancient scars of bruises received in many a sullen fall among the marly mountains of the isle—scars strangely widened, swollen, half obliterate, and yet distorted like those sometimes found in the bark of very hoary trees, I seemed an antiquary of a geologist, studying the bird-tracks and ciphers upon the exhumed slates trod by incredible creatures whose very ghosts are now defunct.

As I lay in my hammock that night, overhead I heard the slow weary draggings of the three ponderous strangers along the encumbered deck. Their stupidity or their resolution was so great, that they never went aside for any impediment. One ceased his movements altogether just before the midwatch. At sunrise I found him butted like a battering-ram against the immovable foot of the foremast, and still striving, tooth and nail, to force the impossible passage. That these tortoises are the victims of a penal, or malignant, or perhaps a downright diabolical enchanter, seems in nothing more likely than in that strange infatuation of hopeless toil which so often possesses them. I have known them in their journeyings ram themselves heroically against rocks, and long abide there, nudging, wriggling, wedging, in order to displace them, and so hold on their inflexible path. Their crowning curse is their drudging impulse to straightforwardness in a belittered world.

Meeting with no such hinderance as their companion did, the other tortoises merely fell foul of small stumbling-blocks—buckets, blocks, and coils of rigging—and at times in the act of crawling over them would slip with an astounding rattle to the deck. Listening to these draggings and concussions, I thought me of the haunt from which they came; an isle full of metallic ravines and gulches, sunk bottomlessly into the hearts of splintered mountains, and covered for many miles with inextricable thickets. I then pictured these three straight-forward monsters, century after century, writhing through the shades, grim as blacksmiths; crawling so slowly and ponderously, that not only did toadstools and all fungous things grow beneath their feet, but a sooty moss sprouted upon their backs. With them I lost myself in volcanic mazes; brushed away endless boughs of rotting thickets; till finally in a dream I found myself sitting cross-legged upon the foremost, a Brahmin similarly mounted upon either side, forming a tripod of fore-heads which upheld the universal cope.

Such was the wild nightmare begot by my first impression of the Encantadas tortoise. But next evening, strange to say, I sat down with my shipmates, and made a merry repast from tortoise steaks and tortoise stews; and supper over, out knife, and helped convert the three mighty concave shells into three fanciful soup-tureens, and polished the three flat yellowish calipees into three gorgeous salvers.

Sketch Third

ROCK RODONDO

For they this hight the Rock of vile Reproch,
A daungerous and dreadful place,
To which nor fish nor fowle did once approch,
But yelling meawes, with seagulles hoars and bace,
And cormoyrants, with birds of ravenous race,
Which still sit waiting on that dreadfull clift.

With that the rolling sea resounding soft,
In his big base them fitly answered;
And on the Rock the waves breaking aloft
A solemne meane unto them measured;
Then he the Boteman bad row easily,
And let him heare some part of that rare melody.

Suddeinly an innumerable flight
Of harmefull fowles about them fluttering cride,
And with their wicked wings them oft did smight,
And sore annoyed, groping in that griesly night.
Even all the nation of unfortunate
And fatall birds about them flocked were.

To go up into a high stone tower is not only a very fine thing in itself, but the very best mode of gaining a comprehensive view of the region round about. It is all the better if this tower stand solitary and alone, like that mysterious Newport one, or else be sole survivor of some perished castle.

Now, with reference to the Enchanted Isles, we are fortunately supplied with just such a noble point of observation in a remarkable rock, from its peculiar figure called of old by the Spaniards, Rock Rodondo, or Round Rock. Some two hundred and fifty feet high, rising straight from the sea ten miles from land, with the whole mountainous group to the south and east, Rock Rodondo occupies, on a large scale, very much the position which the famous Campanile or detached Bell-Tower of St. Mark does with respect to the tangled group of hoary edifices around it.

Ere ascending, however, to gaze abroad upon the Encantadas, this sea-tower itself claims attention. It is visible at the distance of thirty miles; and, fully participating in that enchantment which pervades the group, when first seen afar invariably is mistaken for a sail. Four leagues away, of a golden, hazy noon, it seems some Spanish Admiral's ship, stacked up with glittering canvas. *Sail ho! Sail ho! Sail ho!* from all there masts. But coming nigh, the enchanted frigate is transformed apace into a craggy keep.

My first visit to the spot was made in the gray of the morning. With a view of fishing, we had lowered three boats, and pulling some two miles from our vessel, found ourselves just before dawn of day close under the moon-shadow of Rodondo. Its aspect was heightened, and yet softened, by the strange double twilight of the hour. The great full moon burnt in the low west like a half-spent beacon, casting a soft mellow tinge upon the sea like that cast by a waning fire of embers upon a midnight hearth; while along the entire east the invisible sun sent pallid intimations of his coming. The wind was light; the waves languid; the stars twinkled with a faint effulgence; all nature seemed supine with the long night watch, and half-suspended in jaded expectation of the sun. This was the critical hour to catch Rodondo in his perfect mood. The twilight was just enough to reveal every striking point, without tearing away the dim investiture of wonder.

From a broken stair-like base, washed, as the steps of a water-palace, by the waves, the tower rose in entablatures of strata to a shaven summit. These uniform layers, which compose the mass, form its most peculiar feature. For at their lines of junction they project flatly into encircling shelves, from top to bottom, rising one above another in graduated series. And so the eaves of any old barn or abbey are alive with swallows, so were all these rocky ledges with unnumbered sea-fowl. Eaves upon eaves, and nests upon nests. Here and there were long birdlime streaks of a ghostly white staining the tower from sea to air, readily accounting for its sail-like look afar. All would have been bewitchingly quiescent, were it not for the demoniac din created by the birds. Not only were the eaves rustling with them, but they flew densely overhead, spreading themselves into a winged and continually shifting canopy. The tower is the resort of aquatic birds for hundreds of leagues around. To the north, to the east, to the west, stretches nothing but eternal ocean; so that the man-of-war hawk coming from the coasts of North America, Polynesia, or Peru, makes his first land at Rodondo. And yet though Rodondo be terra firma, no land-bird ever lighted on it. Fancy a red-robin or a canary there! What a falling into the hands of the Philistines, when the poor warbler should be surrounded by such locust-flights of strong bandit birds, with long bills cruel as daggers.

I know not where one can better study the Natural History of strange sea-fowl than at Rodondo. It is the aviary of Ocean. Birds light here which never touched mast or tree; hermit-birds, which ever fly alone; cloud-birds, familiar with un-pierced zones of air.

Let us first glance low down to the lowermost shelf of all, which is the widest, too, and but a little space from high-water mark. What outlandish beings are these? Erect as men, but hardly as symmetrical, they stand all round the rock like sculptured caryatides, supporting the next range of eaves above. Their bodies are grotesquely misshapen; their bills short; their feet seemingly legless; while the members at their sides are neither fin, wing, nor arm. And truly neither fish, flesh, nor fowl is the penguin; as an edible, pertaining neither to Carnival nor Lent; without exception the most ambiguous and least lovely creature yet discovered by man. Though dabbling in all three elements, and indeed possessing some rudimental claims to all, the penguin is at home in none. On land it stumps; afloat it sculls; in the air it flops. As if ashamed of her failure, Nature keeps this ungainly child hidden away at the ends of the earth, in the Straits of Magellan, and on the abased sea-story of Rodondo.

But look, what are yon woe-begone regiments drawn up on the next shelf above? what rank and file of large strange fowl? what sea Friars of Orders Gray? Pelicans. Their elongated bills, and heavy leathern pouches suspended thereto, give them the most lugubrious expression. A pensive race, they stand for hours together without motion. Their dull, ashy plumage imparts an aspect as if they had been powdered over with cinders. A penitential bird, indeed, fitly haunting the shores of the clinkered Encantadas, whereon tormented Job himself might have well sat down and scraped himself with potsherds.

Higher up now we mark the gony, or gray albatross, anomaously so called, an unsightly, unpoetic bird, unlike its storied kinsman, which is the snow-white ghost of the haunted Capes of Hope and Horn.

As we still ascend from shelf to shelf, we find the tenants of the tower serially disposed in order of their magnitude:— gannets, black and speckled haglets, jays, sea-hens, sperm-whale-birds, gulls of all varieties:—thrones, princedoms, powers, dominating one above another in senatorial array; while, sprinkled over all, like an ever-repeated fly in a great piece of broidery, the stormy petrel or Mother Cary's chicken sounds his continual challenge and alarm. That this mysterious humming-bird of ocean—which, had it but brilliancy of hue, might, from its evanescent liveliness, be almost called its butterfly, yet whose chirrup under the stern is ominous to mariners as to the peasant the death-tick sounding from behind the chimney jamb—should have its special haunt at the Encantadas, contributes, in the seaman's mind, not a little to their dreary spell.

As day advances the dissonant din augments. With ear-splitting cries the wild birds celebrate their matins. Each moment, flights push from the tower, and join the aerial choir hovering overhead, while their places below are supplied by darting myriads. But down through all this discord of commotion, I hear clear, silver, bugle-like notes unbrokenly falling, like oblique lines of swift-slanting rain in a cascading shower. I gaze far up, and behold a snow-white angelic thing, with one long, lance-like feather thrust out behind. It is the bright, inspiriting chanticleer of ocean, the beauteous bird, from its bestirring whistle of musical invocation, fitly styled the "Boatswain's Mate."

The winged life clouding Rodondo had its full counterpart in the finny hosts which peopled the waters at its base. Below the waterline, the rock seemed one honey-comb of grottoes, affording labyrinthine lurking-places for swarms of fairy fish. All were strange; many exceedingly beautiful; and would have well graced the costliest glass globes in which goldfish are kept for a show. Nothing was more striking than the complete novelty of many individuals of this multitude. Here hues were seen as yet unpainted, and figures which are unengraved.

To show the multitude, avidity, and nameless fearlessness and tameness of these fish, let me say, that often, marking through clear spaces of water—temporarily made so by the concentric dartings of the fish above the surface—certain larger and less unwary wights,. which swam slow and deep, our anglers would cautiously essay to drop their lines down to these last. But in vain; there was no passing the uppermost zone. No sooner did the hook touch the sea, than a hundred infatuates contended for the honor of capture. Poor fish of Rodondo! in your victimized confidence, you are of the number of those who inconsiderately trust, while they do not understand, human nature.

But the dawn is now fairly day. Band after band, the sea-fowl sail away to forage the deep for their food. The tower is left solitary, save the fish-caves at its base. Its birdlime gleams in the golden rays like the whitewash of a tall lighthouse, or the lofty sails of a cruiser. This moment, doubtless, while we know it to be a dead desert rock, other voyagers are taking oaths it is a glad populous ship.

But ropes now, and let us ascend. Yet soft, this is not so easy.

Sketch Fourth

A PISGAH VIEW FROM THE ROCK

That done, he leads him to the highest Mount,
From whence, far off he unto him did shew . . .

IF YOU seek to ascend Rock Rodondo, take the following pre-
scription. Go three voyages round the world as a main-royal-
man of the tallest frigate that floats; then serve a year or two
apprenticeship to the guides who conduct strangers up the Peak
of Teneriffe; and as many more respectively to a rope-dancer,
an Indian juggler, and a chamois. This done, come and be
rewarded by the view from our tower. How we get there, we
alone know. If we sought to tell others, what the wiser were
they? Suffice it, that here at the summit you and I stand. Does
any balloonist, does the outlooking man in the moon, take a
broader view of space? Much thus, one fancies, looks the universe from Milton's celestial battlements. A boundless watery
Kentucky. Here Daniel Boone would have dwelt content.

Never heed for the present yonder Burnt District of the
Enchanted Isles. Look edgeways, as it were, past them, to the
south. You see nothing; but permit me to point out the direction, if not the place, of certain interesting objects in the vast
sea, which, kissing this tower's base, we behold unscrolling itself towards the Antarctic Pole.

We stand now ten miles from the Equator. Yonder, to the
east, some six hundred miles, lies the continent, this Rock
being just about on the parallel of Quito.

Observe another thing here. We are at one of three uninhabited clusters, which, at pretty nearly uniform distances from
the main, sentinel, at long intervals from each other, the entire
coast of South America. In a peculiar manner, also, they terminate the South American character of country. Of the unnumbered Polynesian chains to the westward, not one partakes
of the qualities of the Encantadas or Galapagos, the isles of

San Felix and San Ambrosio, the isles Juan Fernandez and Mas-a-Fuera. Of the first, it needs not here to speak. The second lie a little above the Southern Tropic; lofty, inhospitable, and uninhabitable rocks, one of which, presenting two round hummocks connected by a low reef, exactly resembles a huge double-headed shot. The last lie in the latitude of 33°; high, wild and cloven. Juan Fernandez is sufficiently famous without further description. Mas-a-Fuera is a Spanish name, expressive of the fact, that the isle so called lies *more without,* that is, further off the main than its neighbor Juan. This isle Mas-a-Fuera has a very imposing aspect at a distance of eight or ten miles. Approached in one direction, in cloudy weather, its great overhanging height and rugged contour, and more especially a peculiar slope of its broad summits, give it much the air of a vast iceberg drifting in tremendous poise. Its sides are split with dark cavernous recesses, as an old cathedral with its gloomy lateral chapels. Drawing nigh one of these gorges from sea, after a long voyage, and beholding some tatterdemalion outlaw, staff in hand, descending its steep rocks toward you, conveys a very queer emotion to a lover of the picturesque.

On fishing parties from ships, at various times, I have chanced to visit each of these groups. The impression they give to the stranger pulling close up in his boat under their grim cliffs is, that surely he must be their first discoverer, such, for the most part, is the unimpaired . . . . . silence and solitude. And here, by the way, the mode in which these isles were really first lighted upon by Europeans is not unworthy of mention, especially as what is about to be said, likewise applies to the original discovery of our Encantadas.

Prior to the year 1563, the voyages made by Spanish ships from Peru to Chile, were full of difficulty. Along this coast, the winds from the South most generally prevail; and it had been an invariable custom to keep close in with the land, from a superstitious conceit on the part of the Spaniards, that were they to lose sight of it, the eternal trade-wind would waft them into unending waters, from whence would be no return. Here, involved among tortuous capes and headlands, shoals and reefs, beating, too, against a continual head wind, often light, and sometimes for days and weeks sunk into utter calm, the provincial vessels, in many cases, suffered the extremest hardships, in passages, which at the present day seem to have been incredibly protracted. There is on record in some collections of nautical disasters, an account of one of these ships, which, starting on a voyage whose duration was estimated at ten days, spent four months at sea, and indeed never again entered harbor, for in the end she was cast away. Singular to tell, this craft never encountered a gale, but was the vexed sport of malicious calms and currents. Thrice, out of provisions, she put back to an intermediate port, and started afresh, but only yet again to return. Frequent fogs enveloped her; so that no observation could be had of her place, and once, when all hands were joyously anticipating sight of their destination, lo! the vapors lifted and disclosed the mountains from which they had taken their first departure. In the like deceptive vapors she at last struck upon a reef, whence ensued a long series of calamities too sad to detail.

It was the famous pilot, Juan Fernandez, immortalized by the island named after him, who put an end to these coasting tribulations, by boldly venturing the experiment—as De Gama did before him with respect to Europe—of standing broad out from land. Here he found the winds favorable for getting to the South, and by running westward till beyond the influences of the trades, he regained the coast without difficulty; making the passage which, though in a high degree circuitous, proved far more expeditious than the nominally direct one. Now it was upon these new tracks, and about the year 1670, or thereabouts, that the Enchanted Isles, and the rest of the sentinel groups, as they may be called, were discovered. Though I know of no account as to whether any of them were found inhabited or no, it may be reasonably concluded that they have been immemorial solitudes. But let us return to Rodondo.

Southwest from our tower lies all Polynesia, hundreds of leagues away; but straight west, on the precise line of his parallel, no land rises till your keel is beached upon the Kingsmills, a nice little sail of, say 5000 miles.

Having thus by such distant references—with Rodondo the only possible ones—settled our relative place on the sea, let us consider objects not quite so remote. Behold the grim and charred Enchanted Isles. This nearest crater-shaped headland is part of Albemarle, the largest of the group, being some sixty miles or more long, and fifteen broad. Did you ever lay eye on the real genuine Equator? Have you ever, in the largest sense, toed the Line? Well, that identical crater-shaped headland there, all yellow lava, is cut by the Equator exactly as a knife cuts straight through the centre of a pumpkin pie.

If you could only see so far, just to one side of that same headland, across yon low dikey ground, you would catch sight of the isle of Narborough, the loftiest land of the cluster; no soil whatever; one seamed clinker from top to bottom; abounding in black caves like smithies; its metallic shore ringing under foot like plates of iron; its central volcanoes standing grouped like a gigantic chimney-stack.

Narborough and Albemarle are neighbors after a quite curious fashion. A familiar diagram will illustrate this strange neighborhood:

Cut a channel at the above letter joint, and the middle transverse limb is Narborough, and all the rest is Albemarle. Volcanic Narborough lies in the black jaws of Albemarle like a wolf's red tongue in his open mouth.

If now you desire the population of Albemarle, I will give you, in round numbers, the statistics, according to the most reliable estimates made upon the spot:

Men,	none
Ant-eaters,	unknown
Man-haters,	unknown
Lizards,	500,000
Snakes,	500,000
Spiders,	10,000,000
Salamanders,	unknown
Devils,	do.
Making a clean total of,	11,000,000

exclusive of an incomputable host of fiends, ant-eaters, man-haters and salamanders.

Albemarle opens his mouth towards the setting sun. His distended jaws form a great bay, which Narborough, his tongue, divides into halves, one whereof is called Weather Bay, the other Lee Bay, while the volcanic promontories, terminating his coasts, are styled South Head and North Head. I note this, because these bays are famous in the annals of the Sperm Whale Fishery. The whales come here at certain seasons to calve. When ships first cruised hereabouts, I am told, they used to blockade the entrance of Lee Bay, when their boats going round by Weather Bay, passed through Narborough channel, and so had the Leviathans very neatly in a pen.

The day after we took fish at the base of this Round Tower, we had a fine wind, and shooting round the north headland, suddenly descried a fleet of full thirty sail, all beating to windward like a squadron in line. A brave sight as ever man saw. A most harmonious concord of rushing keels. Their thirty kelsons hummed like thirty harp-strings, and looked as straight whilst they left their parallel traces on the sea. But there proved too many hunters for the game. The fleet broke up, and went their separate ways out of sight, leaving my own ship and two trim gentlemen of London. These last, finding no luck either, likewise vanished· and Lee Bay, with all its appurtenances, and without a rival, devolved to us.

The way of cruising here is this. You keep hovering about the entrance of the· bay, in one beat and out the next. But at times—not always, as in other parts of the group—a race-horse of a current sweeps right across its mouth. So, with all sails set, you carefully ply your tacks. How often, standing at the foremast head at sunrise, with our patient prow pointed in between these isles, did I gaze upon that land, not of cakes, but of clinkers, not of streams of sparkling water, but arrested torrents of tormented lava.

As the ship runs in from the open sea, Narborough presents its side in one dark craggy mass, soaring up some five or six thousand feet, at which point it hoods itself in heavy clouds, whose lowest level fold is as clearly defined against the rocks as the snow-line against the Andes. There is dire mischief going on in that upper dark. There toil the demons of fire, who, at intervals, irradiate the· nights with a strange spectral illumination for miles and miles around,· but unaccompanied by any further demonstration; or else, suddenly announce themselves by terrific concussions, and the full drama of a volcanic erup-tion. The blacker that cloud by day, the more may you look for light by night. Often whalemen have found themselves cruising nigh that burning mountain when all aglow with a ball-room blaze. Or, rather, glass-works, you may call this same vitreous isle of Narborough, with its tall chimney-stacks.

Where we still stand, here on Rodondo, we cannot see all the other isles, but it is a good place from which to point out where they lie. Yonder, though, to the E.N.E., I mark a distant dusky ridge. It is Abington Isle, one of the most northerly of the group; so solitary, remote, and blank, it looks like No-Man's Land seen off our northern shore. I doubt whether two human beings ever touched upon that spot. So far as yon Abington Isle is concerned, Adam and his billions of posterity remain uncreated.

Ranging south of Abington, and quite out of sight behind the long spine of Albemarle, lies James's Isle, so called by the early Buccaneers after the luckless Stuart, Duke of York. Observe here, by the way, that, excepting the isles particularized in comparatively recent times, and which mostly received the names of famous Admirals, the Encantadas were first christened by the Spaniards; but these Spanish names were generally effaced on English charts by the subsequent christenings of the Buccaneers, who, in the middle of the seventeenth century, called them after English noblemen and kings. Of these loyal freebooters and the things which associate their name with the Encantadas, we shall hear anon. Nay, for one little item, immediately; for between James's Isle and Albemarle, lies a fantastic islet, strangely known as "Cowley's Enchanted Isle." But, as all the group is deemed enchanted, the reason must be given for the spell within a spell involved by this particular designation. The name was bestowed by that excellent Buccaneer himself, on his first visit here. Speaking in his published voyages of this spot, he says— "My fancy led me to call it Cowley's Enchanted Isle, for, we having had a Sight of it upon several Points of the Compass, it appear'd always in as many different Forms; sometimes like a ruined Fortification, upon another Point, like a great City, &c." No wonder though, that among the Encantadas all sorts of ocular deceptions and mirages should be met.

That Cowley linked his name with this self-transforming and bemocking isle, suggests the possibility that it conveyed to him some meditative image of himself. At least, as is not impossible, if he were any relative of the mildly-thoughtful and self-upbraiding poet Cowley, who lived about his time, the conceit might seem not unwarranted; for that sort of thing evinced in the naming of this isle runs in the blood, and may be seen in pirates as in poets.

Still south of Jame's Isle lie Jervis Isle, Duncan Isle, Crossman's Isle, Brattle Isle, Wood's Isle, Chatham Isle, and various lesser isles, for the most part an archipelago of aridities, without inhabitant, history, or hope of either in all time to come.

But not far from these are rather notable isles—Barrington, Charles's, Norfolk, and Hood's. Succeeding chapters will reveal some ground for their notability.

Sketch Fifth

THE FRIGATE, AND SHIP FLYAWAY

Looking far foorth into the ocean wide,
A goodly ship with banners bravely dight,
And flag in her top-gallant I espide
Through the maine sea making her merry flight.

ERE quitting Rodondo, it must not be omitted that here, in 1813, the U. S. Frigate *Essex*, Captain David Porter, came near leaving her bones. Lying becalmed one morning with a strong current setting her rapidly towards the rock, a strange sail was descried, which—not out of keeping with alleged enchantments of the neighborhood—seemed to be staggering under a violent wind, while the frigate lay lifeless as if spellbound. But a light air springing up, all sail was made by the frigate in chase of the enemy, as supposed—he being deemed an English whale-ship—but the rapidity of the current was so great, that soon all sight was lost of him; and at meridian, the *Essex*, spite of her drags, was driven so close under the foamlashed cliffs of Rodondo that, for a time, all hands gave her up. A smart breeze, however, at last helped her off, though the escape was so critical as to seem almost miraculous.

Thus saved from destruction herself, she now made use of that salvation to destroy the other vessel, if possible. Renewing the chase in the direction in which the stranger had disappeared, sight was caught of him the following morning. Upon being descried he hoisted American colors and stood away from the *Essex*. A calm ensued; when, still confident that the stranger was an Englishman, Porter dispatched a cutter, not to board the enemy, but to drive back his boats engaged in towing him. The cutter succeeded. Cutters were subsequently sent to capture him; the stranger now showing English colors in place of American. But, when the frigate's boats were within a short distance of their hoped-for prize, another sudden breeze sprang up; the stranger, under all sail, bore off to the westward, and, ere night, was hull down ahead of the *Essex,* which, all this time, lay perfectly becalmed.

This enigmatic craft—American in the morning, and English in the evening—her sails full of wind in a calm—was never again beheld. An enchanted ship no doubt. So, at least, the sailors swore.

This cruise of the *Essex* in the Pacific during the war of 1812, is, perhaps, the strangest and most stirring to be found in the history of the American navy. She captured the furthest wandering vessels; visited the remotest seas and isles; long hovered in the charmed vicinity of the enchanted group; and, finally, valiantly gave up the ghost fighting two English frigates in the harbor of Valparaiso. Mention is made of her here for the same reason that the Buccaneers will likewise receive record; because, like them, by long cruising among the isles, tortoise-hunting upon their shores, and generally exploring them; for these and other reasons, the *Essex* is peculiarly associated with the Encantadas.

Here be it said that you have but three eye-witness authorities worth mentioning touching the Enchanted Isles:—Cowley, the Buccaneer (1684); Colnett, the whaling-ground explorer (1793); Porter, the post captain (1813). Other than these you have but barren, bootless allusions from some few passing voyagers or compilers.

Sketch Sixth

BARRINGTON ISLE AND THE BUCCANEERS

Let us all servile base subjection scorne;
And, as we bee sonnes of the earth so wide,
Let us our fathers heritage divide,
And chalenge to our selves our portions dew

Of all the patrimonie, which a few
Now hold in hugger-mugger in their hand . . .
Lords of the world, and so will wander free,
Where so us listeth, uncontrol'd of anie.

How bravely now we live, how jocund, how
near the first inheritance, without fear, how
free from little troubles!

NEAR two centuries ago Barrington Isle was the resort of that famous wing of the West Indian Buccaneers, which, upon their repulse from the Cuban waters, crossing the Isthmus of Darien, ravaged the Pacific side of the Spanish colonies, and, with the regularity and timing of a modern mail, waylaid the royal treasure-ships plying between Manila and Acapulco. After the toils of piratic war, here they came to say their prayers, enjoy their free-and-easies, count their crackers from the cask, their doubloons from the keg, and measure their silks of Asia with long Toledos for their yard-sticks

As a secure retreat, an undiscoverable hiding-place, no spot in those days could have been better fitted. In the centre of a vast and silent sea, but very little traversed—surrounded by islands, whose inhospitable aspect might well drive away the chance navigator—and yet within a few days' sail of the opulent countries which they made their prey—the unmolested Buccaneers found here that tranquillity which they fiercely denied to every civilized harbor in that part of the world. Here, after stress of weather, or a temporary drubbing at the hands of their vindictive foes, or in swift flight with golden booty, those old marauders came, and lay snugly out of all harm's reach. But not only was the place a harbor of safety, and a bower of ease, but for utility in other things it was most admirable.

Barrington Isle is, in many respects, singularly adapted to careening, refitting, refreshing, and other seamen's purposes. Not only has it good water, and good anchorage, well sheltered from all winds by the high land of Albemarle, but it is the least unproductive isle of the group. Tortoises good for food, trees good for fuel, and long grass good for bedding, abound here, and there are petty natural walks, and several landscapes to be seen. Indeed, though in its locality belonging to the Enchanted group, Barrington Isle is so unlike most of its neighbors, that it would hardly seem of kin to them.

"I once landed on its western side," says a sentimental voyager long ago, "where it faces the black buttress of Albemarle. I walked beneath groves of trees—not very lofty, and not palm trees, or orange trees, or peach trees, to be sure—but, for all that, after a long sea-faring, very beautiful to walk under, even though they supplied no fruit. And here, in calm spaces at the heads of glades, and on the shaded tops of slopes commanding the most quiet scenery—what do you think I saw? Seats which might have served Brahmins and presidents of peace societies. Fine old ruins of what had once been symmetric lounges of stone and turf, they bore every mark both of artificialness and age, and were, undoubtedly, made by the Buccaneers. One had been a long sofa, with back and arms, jus such a sofa as the poet Gray might have loved to throw himself upon, his Crébillon in hand.

"Though they sometimes tarried here for months at a time, and used the spot for a storing-place for spare spars, sails, and casks; yet it is highly improbable that the Buccaneers ever erected dwelling-houses upon the isle. They never were here except their ships remained, and they would most likely have slept on board. I mention this, because I cannot avoid the thought, that it is hard to impute the construction of these romantic seats to any other motive than one of pure peacefulness and kindly fellowship with nature. That the Buccaneers perpetrated the greatest outrages is very true—that some of them were mere cut-throats is not to be denied; but we know that here and there among their host was a Dampier, a Wafer, and a Cowley, and likewise other men, whose worst reproach was their desperate fortunes—whom persecution, or adversity, or secret and unavengeable wrongs, had driven from Christian society to seek the melancholy solitude or the guilty adventures of the sea. At any rate, long as those ruins of seats on Barrington remain, the most singular monuments are furnished to the fact, that all of the Buccaneers were not unmitigated monsters.

"But during my ramble on the isle I was not long in discovering other tokens, of things quite in accordance with those wild traits, popularly, and no doubt truly enough, imputed to the freebooters at large. Had I picked up old sails and rusty hoops I would only have thought of the ship's carpenter and cooper. But I found old cutlasses and daggers reduced to mere threads of rust, which, doubtless, had stuck between Spanish ribs ere now. These were signs of the murderer and robber; the reveler likewise had left his trace. Mixed with shells, fragments of broken jars were lying here and there, high up upon the beach. They were precisely like the jars now used upon the Spanish coast for the wine and Pisco spirits of that country.

"With a rusty dagger-fragment in one hand, and a bit of a wine-jar in another, I sat me down on the ruinous green sofa I have spoken of, and bethought me long and deeply of these same Buccaneers. Could it be possible, that they robbed and murdered one day, reveled the next, and rested themselves by turning meditative philosophers, rural poets, and seat-builders on the third? Not very improbable, after all. For consider the vacillations of a man. Still, strange as it may seem, I must also abide by the more charitable thought; namely, that among these adventurers were some gentlemanly, companionable souls, capable of genuine tranquillity and virtue."

Sketch Seventh

CHARLES'S ISLE AND THE DOG-KING

> *Loe with outragious cry*
> *A thousand villeins round about him swarmd*
> *Out of the rockes and caves adjoyning nye;*
> *Vile caitive wretches, ragged, rude, deformd,*
> *All threatning death, all in straunge manner armd;*
> *Some with unweldy clubs, some with long speares,*
> *Some rusty knives, some staves in fier warmd.*
>
> *We will not be of anie occupation,*
> *Let such vile vassalls borne to base vocation*
> *Drudge in the world, and for their living droyle,*
> *Which have no wit to live withouten toyle.*

SOUTHWEST of Barrington lies Charles's Isle. And hereby hangs a history which I gathered long ago from a shipmate learned in all the lore of outlandish life.

During the successful revolt of the Spanish provinces from

Old Spain, there fought on behalf of Peru a certain Creole adventurer from Cuba, who, by his bravery and good fortune, at length advanced himself to high rank in the patriot army. The war being ended, Peru found itself like many valorous gentlemen, free and independent enough, but with few shot in the locker. In other words, Peru had not wherewithal to pay off its troops. But the Creole—I forget his name—volunteered to take his pay in lands. So they told him he might have his pick of the Enchanted Isles, which were then, as they still remain, the nominal appanage of Peru. The soldier straightway embarks thither, explores the group, returns to Callao, and says he will take a deed of Charles's Isle. Moreover, this deed must stipulate that thenceforth Charles's Isle is not only the sole property of the Creole, but is forever free of Peru, even as Peru of Spain. To be short, this adventurer procures himself to be made in effect Supreme Lord of the Island, one of the princes of the powers of the earth.*

He now sends forth a proclamation inviting subjects to his as yet unpopulated kingdom. Some eighty souls, men and women, respond; and being provided by their leader with necessaries, and tools of various sorts, together with a few cattle and goats, take ship for the promised land; the last arrival on board, prior to sailing, being the Creole himself, accompanied, strange to say, by a disciplined cavalry company of large grim dogs. These, it was observed on the passage, refusing to consort with the emigrants, remained aristocratically grouped around their master on the elevated quarter-deck, casting disdainful glances forward upon the inferior rabble there; much as, from the ramparts, the soldiers of a garrison, thrown into a conquered town, eye the inglorious citizen-mob over which they are set to watch.

Now Charles's Isle not only resembles Barrington Isle in being much more inhabitable than other parts of the group, but it is double the size of Barrington, say forty or fifty miles in circuit.

Safely debarked at last, the company, under direction of their

---

*The American Spaniards have long been in the habit of making presents of islands to deserving individuals. The pilot Juan Fernandez procured a deed of the isle named after him, and for some years resided there before Selkirk came. It is supposed, however, that he eventually contracted the blues upon his princely property, for after a time he returned to the main, and as report goes, became a very garrulous barber in the city of Lima.

lord and patron, forthwith proceeded to build their capital city. They make considerable advance in the way of walls of clinkers, and lava floors, nicely sanded with cinders. On the least barren hills they pasture their cattle, while the goats, adventurers by nature, explore the far inland solitudes for a scanty livelihood of lofty herbage. Meantime, abundance of fish and tortoises supply their other wants.

The disorders incident to settling all primitive regions, in the present case were heightened by the peculiarly untoward character of many of the pilgrims. His Majesty was forced at last to proclaim martial law, and actually hunted and shot with his own hand several of his rebellious subjects, who, with most questionable intentions, had clandestinely encamped in the interior, whence they stole by night, to prowl barefooted on tiptoe round the precincts of the lava-palace. It is to be remarked, however, that prior to such stern proceedings, the more reliable men had been judiciously picked out for an infantry body-guard, subordinate to the cavalry body-guard of dogs. But the state of politics in this unhappy nation may be somewhat imagined, from the circumstance that all who were not of the body-guard were downright plotters and malignant traitors. At length the death penalty was tacitly abolished, owing to the timely thought, that were strict sportsman's justice to be dispensed among such subjects, ere long the Nimrod King would have little or no remaining game to shoot. The human part of the life-guard was now disbanded, and set to work cultivating the soil, and raising potatoes; the regular army now solely consisting of the dog-regiment. These, as I have heard, were of a singularly ferocious character, though by severe training rendered docile to their master. Armed to the teeth, the Creole now goes in state, surrounded by his canine janizaries, whose terrific bayings prove quite as serviceable as bayonets in keeping down the surgings of revolt.

But the census of the isle, sadly lessened by the dispensation of justice, and not materially recruited by matrimony, began to fill his mind with sad mistrust. Some way the population must be increased. Now, from its possessing a little water, and its comparative pleasantness of aspect, Charles's Isle at this period was occasionally visited by foreign whalers. These His Majesty had always levied upon for port charges, thereby contributing to his revenue. But now he had additional designs. By insidious arts he, from time to time, cajoles certain sailors to desert their ships, and enlist beneath his banner.

Soon as missed, their captains crave permission to go and hunt them up. Whereupon His Majesty first hides them very carefully away, and then freely permits the search. In consequence, the delinquents are never found, and the ships retire without them.

Thus, by a two-edged policy of this crafty monarch, foreign nations were crippled in the number of their subjects, and his own were greatly multiplied. He particularly petted these renegado strangers. But alas for the deep-laid schemes of ambitious princes, and alas for the vanity of glory. As the foreign-born Prætorians, unwisely introduced into the Roman state, and still more unwisely made favorites of the Emperors, at last insulted and overturned the throne, even so these lawless mariners, with all the rest of the body-guard and all the populace, broke out into a terrible mutiny, and defied their master. He marched against them with all his dogs. A deadly battle ensued upon the beach. It raged for three hours, the dogs fighting with determined valor, and the sailors reckless of everything but victory. Three men and thirteen dogs were left dead upon the field, many on both sides were wounded, and the king was forced to fly with the remainder of his canine regiment. The enemy pursued, stoning the dogs with their master into the wilderness of the interior. Discontinuing the pursuit, the victors returned to the village on the shore, stove the spirit casks, and proclaimed a Republic. The dead men were interred with the honors of war, and the dead dogs ignominiously thrown into the sea. At last, forced by stress of suffering, the fugitive Creole came down from the hills and offered to treat for peace. But the rebels refused it on any other terms than his unconditional banishment. Accordingly, the next ship that arrived carried away the ex-king to Peru.

The history of the king of Charles's Island furnishes another illustration of the difficulty of colonizing barren islands with unprincipled pilgrims.

Doubtless for a long time the exiled monarch, pensively ruralizing in Peru, which afforded him a safe asylum in his calamity, watched every arrival from the Encantadas, to hear news of the failure of the Republic, the consequent penitence of the rebels, and his own recall to royalty. Doubtless he deemed the Republic but a miserable experiment which would soon explode. But no, the insurgents had confederated themselves into a democracy neither Grecian, Roman, nor American. Nay, it was no democracy at all, but a permanent *Riotocracy*, which gloried in having no law but lawlessness. Great inducements being offered to deserters, their ranks were swelled by accessions of scamps from every ship which touched their shores. Charles's Island was proclaimed the asylum of the oppressed of all navies. Each runaway tar was hailed as a martyr in the cause of freedom, and became immediately installed a ragged citizen of this universal nation. In vain the captains of absconding seamen strove to regain them. Their new compatriots were ready to give any number of ornamental eyes in their behalf. They had few cannon, but their fists were not to be trifled with. So at last it came to pass that no vessels acquainted with the character of that country durst touch there, however sorely in want of refreshment. It became Anathema—a sea Alsatia—the unassailed lurking-place of all sorts of desperadoes, who in the name of liberty did just what they pleased. They continually fluctuated in their numbers. Sailors, deserting ships at other islands, or in boats at sea anywhere in that vicinity, steered for Charles's Isle, as to their sure home of refuge; while, sated with the life of the isle, numbers from time to time crossed the water to the neighboring ones, and there presenting themselves to strange captains as shipwrecked seamen, often succeeded in getting on board vessels bound to the Spanish coast, and having a compassionate purse made up for them on landing there.

One warm night during my first visit to the group, our ship was floating along in languid stillness, when some one on the forecastle shouted "Light ho!" We looked and saw a beacon burning on some obscure land off the beam. Our third mate was not intimate with this part of the world. Going to the captain he said, "Sir, shall I put off in a boat? These must be shipwrecked men."

The captain laughed rather grimly, as, shaking his fist towards the beacon, he rapped out an oath, and said—"No, no, you precious rascals, you don't juggle one of my boats ashore this blessed night. You do well, you thieves—you do benevolently to hoist a light yonder as on a dangerous shoal. It tempts no wise man to pull off and see what's the matter, but bids him steer small and keep off shore—that is Charles's Island; brace up, Mr. Mate, and keep the light astern."

Sketch Eighth

NORFOLK ISLE AND THE CHOLA WIDOW

At last they in an Island did espy
A seemely woman, sitting by the shore,
That with great sorrow and sad agony
Seemed some great misfortune to deplore,
And lowd to them for succour called evermore.

   Blacke hys eye as the midnyghte sky,
   Whyte hys neck as the driven snowe,
   Redde hys cheek as the mornynge lyghte,
   Cold he lys ynne the ground belowe;
     Mie love ys dedde,
     Gon to hys deathe-bedde,
     All under the cactus tree.

   Each lonely scene shall thee restore,
     For thee the tear be duly shed;
   Belov'd till life can charm no more,
     And mourn'd till Pity's self be dead.

FAR to the northeast of Charles's Isle, sequestered from the rest, lies Norfolk Isle; and, however insignificant to most voyagers, to me, through sympathy, that lone island has become a spot made sacred by the strangest trials of humanity.

It was my first visit to the Encantadas. Two days had been spent ashore in hunting tortoises. There was not time to capture many; so on the third afternoon we loosed our sails. We were just in the act of getting under way, the uprooted anchor yet suspended and invisibly swaying beneath the wave, as the good ship gradually turned her heel to leave the isle behind, when the seaman who heaved with me at the windlass paused suddenly, and directed my attention to something moving on the land, not along the beach, but somewhat back, fluttering from a height.

In view of the sequel of this little story, be it here narrated how it came to pass, that an object which partly from its being so small was quite lost to every other man on board, still caught the eye of my handspike companion. The rest of the crew, myself included, merely stood up to our spikes in heaving, whereas, unwontedly exhilarated, at every turn of the ponderous windlass, my belted comrade leaped atop of it, with might and main giving a downward, thewy, perpendicular heave, his raised eye bent in cheery animation upon the slowly receding shore. Being high lifted above all others was the reason he perceived the object, otherwise unperceivable; and this elevation of his eye was owing to the elevation of his spirits; and this again—for truth must out—to a dram of Peruvian pisco, in guerdon for some kindness done, secretly administered to him that morning by our mulatto steward. Now, certainly, pisco does a deal of mischief in the world; yet seeing that, in the present case, it was the means, though indirect, of rescuing a human being from the most dreadful fate, must we not also needs admit that sometimes pisco does a deal of good?

Glancing across the water in the direction pointed out, I saw some white thing hanging from an inland rock, perhaps half a mile from the sea.

"It is a bird; a white-winged bird; perhaps a——no; it is—— it is a handkerchief!"

"Aye, a handkerchief!" echoed my comrade, and with a louder shout apprised the captain.

Quickly now—like the running out and training of a great gun—the long cabin spy-glass was thrust through the mizzen-rigging from the high platform of the poop; whereupon a human figure was plainly seen upon the inland rock, eagerly waving towards us what seemed to be the handkerchief.

Our captain was a prompt, good fellow. Dropping the glass, he lustily ran forward, ordering the anchor to be dropped again; hands to stand by a boat, and lower away.

In a half-hour's time the swift boat returned. It went with six and came with seven; and the seventh was a woman.

It is not artistic heartlessness, but I wish I could but draw in crayons; for this woman was a most touching sight; and crayons, tracing softly melancholy lines, would best depict the mournful image of the dark-damasked Chola widow.

Her story was soon told, and though given in her own strange language was as quickly understood; for our captain, from long trading on the Chilean coast, was well versed in the Span-

ish. A Cholo, or half-breed Indian woman of Payta in Peru,
three years gone by, with her young new-wedded husband
Felip, of pure Castilian blood, and her one only Indian
brother, Truxill, Hunilla had taken passage on the main in a
French whaler, commanded by a joyous man; which vessel,
bound to the cruising grounds beyond the Enchanted Isles,
proposed passing close by their vicinity. The object of the little party was to procure tortoise oil, a fluid which for its great
purity and delicacy is held in high estimation wherever known;
and it is well known all along this part of the Pacific coast.
With a chest of clothes, tools, cooking utensils, a rude apparatus for trying out the oil, some casks of biscuit, and other things,
not omitting two favorite dogs, of which faithful animal all
the Cholos are very fond, Hunilla and her companions were
safely landed at their chosen place; the Frenchman, according to the contract made ere sailing, engaged to take them
off upon returning from a four months' cruise in the westward seas; which interval the three adventurers deemed quite
sufficient for their purposes.

On the isle's lone beach they paid him in silver for their
passage out, the stranger having declined to carry them at
all except upon that condition; though willing to take every
means to insure the due fulfillment of his promise. Felipe had
striven hard to have this payment put off to the period of
the ship's return. But in vain. Still they thought they had, in
another way, ample pledge of the good faith of the Frenchman.
It was arranged that the expenses of the passage home should
not be payable in silver, but in tortoises; one hundred tortoises
ready captured to the returning captain's hand. These the
Cholos meant to secure after their own work was done, against
the probable time of the Frenchman's coming back; and no
doubt in prospect already felt, that in those hundred tortoises
—now somewhere ranging the isle's interior—they possessed
one hundred hostages. Enough: the vessel sailed; the gazing
three on shore answered the loud glee of the singing crew;
and ere evening, the French craft was hull down in the distant
sea, its masts three faintest lines which quickly faded from
Hunilla's eye.

The stranger had given a blithesome promise, and anchored
it with oaths; but oaths and anchors equally will drag; naught
else abides on fickle earth but unkept promises of joy. Contrary winds from out unstable skies, or contrary moods of his
more varying mind, or shipwreck and sudden death in solitary

waves; whatever was the cause, the blithe stranger never was seen again.

Yet, however dire a calamity was here in store, misgivings of it ere due time never disturbed the Cholos' busy minds, now all intent upon the toilsome matter which had brought them hither. Nay, by swift doom coming like the thief at night, ere seven weeks went by, two of the little party were removed from all anxieties of land or sea. No more they sought to gaze with feverish fear, or still more feverish hope, beyond the present's horizon line; but into the furthest future their own silent spirits sailed. By persevering labor beneath that burning sun, Felipe and Truxill had brought down to their hut many scores of tortoises, and tried out the oil, when, elated with their good success, and to reward themselves for such hard work, they, too hastily, made a catamaran, or Indian raft, much used on the Spanish main, and merrily started on a fishing trip, just without a long reef with many jagged gaps, running parallel with the shore, about half a mile from it. By some bad tide or hap, or natural negligence of joyfulness (for though they could not be heard, yet by their gestures they seemed singing at the time), forced in deep water against that iron bar, the ill-made catamaran was overset, and came all to pieces; when dashed by broad-chested swells between their broken logs and the sharp teeth of the reef, both adventurers perished before Hunilla's eyes.

Before Hunilla's eyes they sank. The real woe of this event passed before her sight as some sham tragedy on the stage. She was seated in a rude bower among the withered thickets, crowning a lofty cliff, a little back from the beach. The thickets were so disposed, that in looking upon the sea at large she peered out from among the branches as from the lattice of a high balcony. But upon the day we speak of here, the better to watch the adventure of those two hearts she loved, Hunilla had withdrawn the branches to one side, and held them so. They formed an oval frame, through which the bluely boundless sea rolled like a painted one. And there, the invisible painter painted to her view the wave-tossed and disjointed raft, its once level logs slantingly upheaved, as raking masts, and the four struggling arms undistinguishable among them; and then all subsided into smooth-flowing creamy waters, slowly drifting the splintered wreck; while first and last, no sound of any sort was heard. Death in a silent picture; a dream of the eye; such vanishing shapes as the mirage shows.

So instant was the scene, so trance-like its mild pictorial effect, so distant from her blasted bower and her common sense of things, that Hunilla gazed and gazed, nor raised a finger or a wail. But as good to sit thus dumb, in stupor staring on that dumb show, for all that otherwise might be done. With half a mile of sea between, how could her two enchanted arms aid those four fated ones? The distance long, the time one sand. After the lightning is beheld, what fool shall stay the thunder-bolt? Felipe's body was washed ashore, but Truxill's never came; only his gay, braided hat of golden straw—that same sunflower thing he waved to her, pushing from the strand—and now, to the last gallant, it still saluted her. But Felipe's body floated to the marge, with one arm encirclingly outstretched. Lock-jawed in grim death, the lover-husband softly clasped his bride, true to her even in death's dream. Ah, Heaven, when man thus keeps his faith, wilt Thou be faithless who created the faithful one? But they cannot break faith who never plighted it.

It needs not to be said what nameless misery now wrapped the lonely widow. In telling her own story she passed this almost entirely over, simply recounting the event. Construe the comment of her features as you might, from her mere words little would you have weened that Hunilla was herself the heroine of her tale. But not thus did she defraud us of our tears. All hearts bled that grief could be so brave.

She but showed us her soul's lid, and the strange ciphers thereon engraved; all within, with pride's timidity, was withheld. Yet was there one exception. Holding out her small olive hand before her captain, she said in mild and slowest Spanish, "Señor, I buried him," then paused, struggled as against the writhed coilings of a snake, and cringing suddenly, leaped up, repeating in impassioned pain, "I buried him, my life, my soul!"

Doubtless, it was by half-unconscious, automatic motions of her hands, that this heavy-hearted one performed the final office for Felipe, and planted a rude cross of withered sticks —no green ones might be had—at the head of that lonely grave, where rested now in lasting uncomplaint and quiet haven he whom untranquil seas had overthrown.

But some dull sense of another body that should be interred, of another cross that should hallow another grave—unmade as yet—some dull anxiety and pain touching her undiscovered brother, now haunted the oppressed Hunilla. Her hands fresh from the burial earth, she slowly went back to the beach, with unshaped purposes wandering there, her spell-bound eye bent upon the incessant waves. But they bore nothing to her but a dirge, which maddened her to think that murderers should mourn. As time went by, and these things came less dreamingly to her mind, the strong persuasions of her Romish faith, which sets peculiar store by consecrated urns, prompted her to resume in waking earnest that pious search which had but been begun as in somnambulism. Day after day, week after week, she trod the cindery beach, till at length a double motive edged every eager glance. With equal longing she now looked for the living and the dead; the brother and the captain; alike vanished, never to return. Little accurate note of time had Hunilla taken under such emotions as were hers, and little, outside herself, served for calendar or dial. As to poor Crusoe in the self-same sea, no saint's bell pealed forth the lapse of week or month; each day went by unchallenged; no chanticleer announced those sultry dawns, no lowing herds those poisonous nights. All wonted and steadily recurring sounds, human or humanized by sweet fellowship with man, but one stirred that torrid trance—the cry of dogs; save which naught but the rolling sea invaded it, an all-pervading monotone; and to the widow that was the least loved voice she could have heard.

No wonder, that as her thoughts now wandered to the unreturning ship, and were beaten back again, the hope against hope so struggled in her soul, that at length she desperately said, "Not yet, not yet; my foolish heart runs on too fast." So she forced patience for some further weeks. But to those whom earth's sure indraft draws, patience or impatience is still the same.

Hunilla now sought to settle precisely in her mind, to an hour, how long it was since the ship had sailed; and then, with the same precision, how long a space remained to pass. But this proved impossible. What present day or month it was she could not say. Time was her labyrinth, in which Hunilla was entirely lost.

And now follows——

Against my own purposes a pause descends upon me here. One knows not whether nature doth not impose some secrecy upon him who has been privy to certain things. At least, it is to be doubted whether it be good to blazon such. If some books are deemed most baneful and their sale forbid, how, then, with deadlier facts, not dreams of doting men? Those whom books will hurt will not be proof against events. Events, not books, should be forbid. But in all things man sows upon the wind, which bloweth just there whither it listeth; for ill or good, man cannot know. Often ill comes from the good, as good from ill.

When Hunilla——

Dire sight it is to see some silken beast long dally with a golden lizard ere she devour. More terrible, to see how feline Fate will sometimes dally with a human soul, and by a nameless magic make it repulse a sane despair with a hope which is but mad. Unwittingly I imp this cat-like thing, sporting with the heart of him who reads; for if he feel not he reads in vain.

——"The ship sails this day, to-day," at last said Hunilla to herself; "this gives me certain time to stand on; without certainty I go mad. In loose ignorance I have hoped and hoped; now in firm knowledge I will but wait. Now I live and no longer perish in bewilderings. Holy Virgin, aid me! Thou wilt waft back the ship. Oh, past length of weary weeks—all to be dragged over—to buy the certainty of to-day, I freely give ye, though I tear ye from me!"

As mariners, tost in tempest on some desolate ledge, patch them a boat out of the remnants of their vessel's wreck, and launch it in the self-same waves, see here Hunilla, this lone shipwrecked soul, out of treachery invoking trust. Humanity, thou strong thing, I worship thee, not in the laureled victor, but in this vanquished one.

Truly Hunilla leaned upon a reed, a real one; no metaphor: a real Eastern reed. A piece of hollow cane, drifted from unknown isles, and found upon the beach, its once jagged ends rubbed smoothly even as by sand-paper; its golden glazing gone. Long ground between the sea and land, upper and nether stone, the unvarnished substance was filed bare, and wore another polish now, one with itself, the polish of its agony. Circular lines at intervals cut all round this surface, divided it into six panels of unequal length. In the first were scored the days, each tenth one marked by a longer and deeper notch; the second was scored for the number of sea-fowl eggs for sustenance, picked out from the rocky nests; the third, how many fish had been caught from the shore; the fourth, how many small tortoises found inland; the fifth, how many days of sun; the sixth, of clouds; which last, of the two, was the greater one. Long night of busy numbering, misery's mathematics, to weary her too-wakeful soul to sleep; yet sleep for that was none.

The panel of the days was deeply worn—the long tenth notches half effaced, as alphabets of the blind. Ten thousand times the longing widow had traced her finger over the bamboo—dull flute, which played on, gave no sound—as if counting birds flown by in air would hasten tortoises creeping through the woods.

After the one hundred and eightieth day no further mark was seen; that last one was the faintest, as the first the deepest.

"There were more days," said our Captain; "many, many more; why did you not go on and notch them, too, Hunilla?"

"Señor, ask me not."

"And meantime, did no other vessel pass the isle?"

"Nay, Señor;—but——"

"You do not speak; but *what*, Hunilla?"

"Ask me not, Señor."

"You saw ships pass, far away; you waved to them; they passed on;—was that it, Hunilla?"

"Señor, be it as you say."

Braced against her woe, Hunilla would not, durst not trust the weakness of her tongue. Then when our Captain asked whether any whale-boats had——

But no, I will not file this thing complete for scoffing souls to quote, and call it firm proof upon their side. The half shall here remain untold. Those two unnamed events which befell Hunilla on this isle, let them abide between her and her God. In nature, as in law, it may be libelous to speak some truths.

Still, how it was that, although our vessel had lain three days anchored nigh the isle, its one human tenant should not have discovered us till just upon the point of sailing, never to revisit so lone and far a spot, this needs explaining ere the sequel come.

The place where the French captain had landed the little party was on the further and opposite end of the isle. There, too, it was that they had afterwards built their hut. Nor did the widow in her solitude desert the spot where her loved ones had dwelt with her, and where the dearest of the twain now slept his last long sleep, and all her plaints awaked him not, and he of husbands the most faithful during life.

Now, high broken land rises between the opposite extremities of the isle. A ship anchored at one side is invisible from the other. Neither is the isle so small, but a considerable company might wander for days through the wilderness of one side, and never be seen, or their halloos heard, by any stranger holding aloof on the other. Hence Hunilla, who naturally associated the possible coming of ships with her own part of the isle, might to the end have remained quite ignorant of the presence of our vessel, were it not for a mysterious presentiment borne to her, so our mariners averred, by this isle's enchanted air. Nor did the widow's answer undo the thought.

"How did you come to cross the isle this morning, then, Hunilla?" said our Captain.

"Señor, something came flitting by me. It touched my cheek, my heart, Señor."

"What do you say, Hunilla?"

"I have said, Señor, something came through the air."

It was a narrow chance. For when in crossing the isle Hunilla gained the high land in the centre, she must then for the first have perceived our masts, and also marked that their sails were being loosed, perhaps even heard the echoing chorus of the windlass song. The strange ship was about to sail, and she behind. With all haste she now descends the height on the hither side, but soon loses sight of the ship among the sunken jungles at the mountain's base. She struggles on through the withered branches, which seek at every step to bar her path, till she comes to the isolated rock, still some way from the water. This she climbs, to reassure herself. The ship is still in plainest sight. But now, worn out with over-tension, Hunilla all but faints; she fears to step down from her giddy perch; she is fain to pause, there where she is, and as a last resort catches the turban from her head, unfurls and waves it over the jungles towards us.

During the telling of her story the mariners formed a voiceless circle round Hunilla and the Captain; and when at length the word was given to man the fastest boat, and pull round to the isle's thither side, to bring away Hunilla's chest and the tortoise oil, such alacrity of both cheery and sad obedience seldom before was seen. Little ado was made. Already the anchor had been recommitted to the bottom, and the ship swung calmly to it.

But Hunilla insisted upon accompanying the boat as indispensable pilot to her hidden hut. So being refreshed with the best the steward could supply, she started with us. Nor did ever any wife of the most famous admiral, in her husband's barge, receive more silent reverence of respect than poor Hunilla from this boat's crew.

Rounding many a vitreous cape and bluff, in two hours' time we shot inside the fatal reef; wound into a secret cove, looked up along a green many-gabled lava wall, and saw the island's solitary dwelling.

It hung upon an impending cliff, sheltered on two sides by tangled thickets, and half-screened from view in front by juttings of the rude stairway, which climbed the precipice from the sea. Built of canes, it was thatched with long, mildewed grass. It seemed an abandoned hay-rick, whose haymakers were now no more. The roof inclined but one way; the eaves coming to within two feet of the ground. And here was a simple apparatus to collect the dews, or rather doubly-distilled and finest winnowed rains, which, in mercy or in mockery, the night-skies sometimes drop upon these blighted Encantadas. All along beneath the eaves, a spotted sheet, quite weather-stained, was spread, pinned to short, upright stakes, set in the shallow sand. A small clinker, thrown into the cloth, weighed its middle down, thereby straining all moisture into a calabash placed below. This vessel supplied each drop of water ever drunk upon the isle by the Cholos. Hunilla told us the calabash would sometimes, but not often, be half filled overnight. It held six quarts, perhaps. "But," said she, "we were used to thirst. At sandy Payta, where I live, no shower from heaven ever fell; all the water there is brought on mules from the inland vales."

Tied among the thickets were some twenty moaning tortoises, supplying Hunilla's lonely larder; while hundreds of vast tableted black bucklers, like displaced, shattered tomb-stones of dark slate, were also scattered round. These were the skeleton backs of those great tortoises from which Felipe and Truxill had made their precious oil. Several large calabashes and two goodly kegs we filled with it. In a pot near by were the caked crusts of a quantity which had been permitted to evaporate. "They meant to have strained it off next day," said Hunilla, as she turned aside.

I forgot to mention the most singular sight of all, though the first that greeted us after landing.

Some ten small, soft-haired, ringleted dogs, of a beautiful breed, peculiar to Peru, set up a concert of glad welcomings when we gained the beach, which was responded to by Hun-

ila. Some of these dogs had, since her widowhood, been
born upon the isle, the progeny of the two brought from Payta.
Owing to the jagged steeps and pitfalls, tortuous thickets,
sunken cleft sand perilous intricacies of all sorts in the interior,
Hunilla, admonished by the loss of one favorite among them,
never allowed these delicate creatures to follow her in her occasional birds'-nests climbs and other wanderings; so that,
through long habituation, they offered not to follow, when that
morning she crossed the land, and her own soul was then too
full of other things to heed their lingering behind. Yet, all
along she had so clung to them, that, besides what moisture
they lapped up at early daybreak from the small scoop-holes
among the adjacent rocks, she had shared the dew of her calabash among them; never laying by any considerable store
against those prolonged and utter droughts which, in some
disastrous seasons, warp these isles.

Having pointed out, at our desire, what few things she would
like transported to the ship—her chest, the oil, not omitting
the live tortoises which she intended for a grateful present
to our Captain—we immediately set to work, carrying them to
the boat down the long, sloping stair of deeply-shadowed rock.
While my comrades were thus employed, I looked and Hunilla
had disappeared.

It was not curiosity alone, but, it seems to me, something
different mingled with it, which prompted me to drop my
tortoise, and once more gaze slowly around. I remembered
the husband buried by Hunilla's hands. A narrow pathway led
into a dense part of the thickets. Following it through many
mazes, I came out upon a small, round, open space, deeply
chambered there.

The mound rose in the middle; a bare heap of finest sand,
like that unverdured heap found at the bottom of an hour-
glass run out. At its head stood the cross of withered sticks;
the dry, peeled bark still fraying from it; its transverse limb
tied up with rope, and forlornly adroop in the silent air.

Hunilla was partly prostrate upon the grave; her dark head
bowed, and lost in her long, loosened Indian hair; her hands
extended to the cross-foot, with a little brass crucifix clasped
between; a crucifix worn featureless, like an ancient graven
knocker long plied in vain. She did not see me, and I made
no noise, but slid aside, and left the spot.

A few moments ere all was ready for our going, she reappeared among us. I looked into her eyes, but saw no tear.

There was something which seemed strangely haughty in her air, and yet it was the air of woe. A Spanish and an Indian grief, which would not visibly lament. Pride's height in vain abased to proneness on the rack; nature's pride subduing nature's torture.

Like pages the small and silken dogs surrounded her, as she slowly descended towards the beach. She caught the two most eager creatures in her arms—"*Tita mia! Tomotita mia!*"—and fondling them, inquired how many could we take on board.

The mate commanded the boat's crew; not a hard-hearted man, but his way of life had been such that in most things, even in the smallest, simple utility was his leading motive.

"We cannot take them all, Hunilla; our supplies are short; the winds are unreliable; we may be a good many days going to Tumbez. So take those you have, Hunilla; but no more."

She was in the boat; the oarsmen, too, were seated, all save one, who stood ready to push off and then spring himself. With the sagacity of their race, the dogs now seemed aware that they were in the very instant of being deserted upon a barren strand. The gunwales of the boat were high; its prow—presented inland—was lifted; so owing to the water, which they seemed instinctively to shun, the dogs could not well leap into the little craft. But their busy paws hard scraped the prow, as it had been some farmer's door shutting them out from shelter in a winter storm. A clamorous agony of alarm. They did not howl, or whine; they all but spoke.

"Push off! Give way!" cried the mate. The boat gave one heavy drag and lurch, and next moment shot swiftly from the beach, turned on her heel, and sped. The dogs ran howling along the water's marge; now pausing to gaze at the flying boat, then motioning as if to leap in chase, but mysteriously withheld themselves; and again ran howling along the beach. Had they been human beings, hardly would they have more vividly inspired the sense of desolation. The oars were plied as confederate feathers of two wings. No one spoke. I looked back upon the beach, and then upon Hunilla, but her face was set in a stern dusky calm. The dogs crouching in her lap vainly licked her rigid hands. She never looked behind her, but sat motionless, till we turned a promontory of the coast and lost all sights and sounds astern. She seemed as one who, having experienced the sharpest of mortal pangs, was henceforth content to have all lesser heart-strings riven, one by one. To Hunilla, pain seemed so necessary, that pain in other

beings, though by love and sympathy made her own, was un-
repiningly to be borne. A heart of yearning in a frame of steel.
A heart of earthly yearning, frozen by the frost which falleth
from the sky.

The sequel is soon told. After a long passage, vexed by calms
and baffling winds, we made the little port of Tumbez in
Peru, there to recruit the ship. Payta was not very distant.
Our captain sold the tortoise oil to a Tumbez merchant; and
adding to the silver a contribution from all hands, gave it to
our silent passenger, who knew not what the mariners had
done.

The last seen of lone Hunilla she was passing into Payta
town, riding upon a small gray ass; and before her on the
ass's shoulders, she eyed the jointed workings of the beast's
armorial cross.

Sketch Ninth

HOOD'S ISLE AND THE HERMIT OBERLUS

*That darkesome glen they enter, where they find
That cursed man, low sitting on the ground,
Musing full sadly in his sullein mind;
His griesie lockes, long growen and unbound,
Disordred hong about his shoulders round,
And hid his face; through which his hollow eyne
Lookt deadly dull, and stared as astound;
His raw-bone cheekes, through penurie and pine,
Were shronke into his jawes, as he did never dine.
His garment nought but many ragged clouts,
With thornes together pind and patched was,
The which his naked sides he wrapt abouts.*

SOUTHEAST of Crossman's Isle lies Hood's Isle, or McCain's Be-
clouded Isle; and upon its south side is a vitreous cove with a
wide strand of dark pounded black lava, called Black Beach,
or Oberlus's Landing. It might fitly have been styled Charon's.

It received its name from a wild white creature who spent many years here; in the person of a European bringing into this savage region qualities more diabolical than are to be found among any of the surrounding cannibals.

About half a century ago, Oberlus deserted at the above-named island, then, as now, a solitude. He built himself a den of lava and clinkers, about a mile from the Landing, subsequently called after him, in a vale, or expanded gulch, containing here and there among the rocks about two acres of soil capable of rude cultivation; the only place on the isle not too blasted for that purpose. Here he succeeded in raising a sort of degenerate potatoes and pumpkins, which from time to time he exchanged with needy whalemen passing, for spirits or dollars.

His appearance, from all accounts, was that of the victim of some malignant sorceress; he seemed to have drunk of Circe's cup; beast-like; rags insufficient to hide his nakedness; his be-freckled skin blistered by continual exposure to the sun; nose flat; countenance contorted, heavy, earthy; hair and beard unshorn, profuse, and of fiery red. He struck strangers much as if he were a volcanic creature thrown up by the same convulsion which exploded into sight the .isle. All bepatched and coiled asleep in his lonely lava den among the mountains, he looked, they say, as a heaped drift of withered leaves, torn from autumn trees, and so left in some hidden nook by the whirling halt for an instant of a fierce night-wind, which then ruthlessly sweeps on, somewhere else to repeat the capricious act. It is also reported to have been the strangest sight, this same Oberlus, of a sultry, cloudy morning, hidden under his shocking old black tarpaulin hat, hoeing potatoes among the lava. So warped and crooked was his strange nature, that the very handle of his hoe seemed gradually to have shrunk and twisted in his grasp, being a wretched bent stick, elbowed more like a savage's war-sickle than a civilized hoe-handle. It was his mysterious custom upon a first encounter with a stranger ever to present his back; possibly, because that was his better side, since it revealed the least. If the encounter chanced in his garden, as it sometimes did—the new-landed strangers going from the sea-side straight through the gorge, to hunt up the queer green-grocer reported doing business here—Oberlus for a time hoed on, unmindful of all greeting, jovial or bland; as the curious stranger would turn to face him, the recluse, hoe in hand, as diligently would avert himself; bowed over, and sullenly revolving round his murphy hill. Thus far for hoeing. When planting, his whole aspect and all his gestures were so malevolently and uselessly sinister and secret, that he seemed rather in act of dropping poison into wells than potatoes into soil. But among his lesser and more harmless marvels was an idea he ever had, that his visitors came equally as well led by longings to behold the mighty hermit Oberlus in his royal state of solitude, as simply to obtain potatoes, or find whatever company might be upon a barren isle. It seems incredible that such a being should possess such vanity; a misanthrope be conceited; but he really had his notion; and upon the strength of it, often gave himself amusing airs to captains. But after all, this is somewhat of a piece with the well-known eccentricity of some convicts, proud of that very hatefulness which makes them notorious. At other times, another unaccountable whim would seize him, and he would long dodge advancing strangers round the clinkered corners of his hut; sometimes like a stealthy bear, he would slink through the withered thickets up the mountains, and refuse to see the human face.

Except his occasional visitors from the sea, for a long period, the only companions of Oberlus were the crawling tortoises; and he seemed more than degraded to their level, having no desires for a time beyond theirs, unless it were for the stupor brought on by drunkenness. But sufficiently debased as he appeared, there yet lurked in him, only awaiting occasion for discovery, a still further proneness. Indeed, the sole superiority of Oberlus over the tortoises was his possession of a larger capacity of degradation; and along with that, something like an intelligent will to it. Moreover, what is about to be revealed, perhaps will show, that selfish ambition, or the love of rule for its own sake, far from being the peculiar infirmity of noble minds, is shared by beings which have no mind at all. No creatures are so selfishly tyrannical as some brutes; as any one who has observed the tenants of the pasture must occasionally have observed.

"This island's mine by Sycorax my mother," said Oberlus to himself, glaring round upon his haggard solitude. By some means, barter or theft—for in those days ships at intervals still kept touching at his Landing—he obtained an old musket, with a few charges of powder and ball. Possessed of arms, he was stimulated to enterprise, as a tiger that first feels the coming of its claws. The long habit of sole dominion over every object round him, his almost unbroken solitude, his never encountering humanity except on terms of misanthropic independence, or mercantile craftiness, and even such encounters being comparatively but rare; all this must have gradually nourished in him a vast idea of his own importance, together with a pure animal sort of scorn for all the rest of the universe.

The unfortunate Creole, who enjoyed his brief term of royalty at Charles's Isle was perhaps in some degree influenced by not unworthy motives; such as prompt other adventurous spirits to lead colonists into distant regions and assume political pre-eminence over them. His summary execution of many of his Peruvians is quite pardonable, considering the desperate characters he had to deal with; while his offering canine battle to the banded rebels seems under the circumstances altogether just. But for this King Oberlus and what shortly follows, no shade of palliation can be given. He acted out of mere delight in tyranny and cruelty, by virtue of a quality in him inherited from Sycorax his mother. Armed now with that shocking blunderbuss, strong in the thought of being master of that horrid isle, he panted for a chance to prove his potency upon the first specimen of humanity which should fall unbefriended into his hands.

Nor was he long without it. One day he spied a boat upon the beach, with one man, a negro, standing by it. Some distance off was a ship, and Oberlus immediately knew how matters stood. The vessel had put in for wood, and the boat's crew had gone into the thickets for it. From a convenient spot he kept watch of the boat, till presently a straggling company appeared loaded with billets. Throwing these on the beach, they again went into the thickets, while the negro proceeded to load the boat.

Oberlus now makes all haste and accosts the negro, who, aghast at seeing any living being inhabiting such a solitude, and especially so horrific a one, immediately falls into a panic, not at all lessened by the ursine suavity of Oberlus, who begs the favor of assisting him in his labors. The negro stands with several billets on his shoulder, in act of shouldering others; and Oberlus, with a short cord concealed in his bosom, kindly proceeds to lift those other billets to their place. In so doing, he persists in keeping behind the negro, who, rightly suspicious of this, in vain dodges about to gain the front of Oberlus but Oberlus dodges also; till at last, weary of this boot-

less attempt at treachery, or fearful of being surprised by
the remainder of the party, Oberlus runs off a little space to
a bush, and fetching his blunderbuss, savagely commands the
negro to desist work and follow him. He refuses. Whereupon,
presenting his piece, Oberlus snaps at him. Luckily the blunderbuss misses fire; but by this time, frightened out of his wits,
the negro, upon a second intrepid summons, drops his billets,
surrenders at discretion, and follows on. By a narrow defile
familiar to him, Oberlus speedily removes out of sight of the
water.

On their way up the mountains he exultingly informs the
negro that henceforth he is to work for him, and be his slave,
and that his treatment would entirely depend on his future
conduct. But Oberlus, deceived by the first impulsive cowardice
of the black, in an evil moment slackens his vigilance. Passing
through a narrow way, and perceiving his leader quite off
his guard, the negro, a powerful fellow, suddenly grasps him
in his arms, throws him down, wrests his musketoon from him,
ties his hands with the monster's own cord, shoulders him,
and returns with him down to the boat. When the rest of the
party arrive, Oberlus is carried on board the ship. This proved
an Englishman, and a smuggler; a sort of craft not apt to be
over-charitable. Oberlus is severely whipped, then handcuffed,
taken ashore, and compelled to make known his habitation
and produce his property. His potatoes, pumpkins, and tortoises, with a pile of dollars he had hoarded from his mercantile operations were secured on the spot. But while the too vindictive smugglers were busy destroying his hut and garden,
Oberlus makes his escape into the mountains, and conceals
himself there in impenetrable recesses, only known to himself,
till the ship sails, when he ventures back, and by means of an
old file which he sticks into a tree, contrives to free himself from
his handcuffs.

Brooding among the ruins of his hut, and the desolate clinkers and extinct volcanoes of this outcast isle, the insulted misanthrope now meditates a signal revenge upon humanity,
but conceals his purposes. Vessels still touch the Landing at
times; and by and by Oberlus is enabled to supply them with
some vegetables.

Warned by his former failure in kidnapping strangers, he
now pursues a quite different plan. When seamen come ashore,
he makes up to them like a free-and-easy comrade, invites
them to his hut, and with whatever affability his red-haired

grimness may assume, entreats them to drink his liquor and be merry. But his guests need little pressing; and so, soon as rendered insensible, are tied hand and foot, and pitched among the clinkers, are there concealed till the ship departs, when, finding themselves entirely dependent upon Oberlus, alarmed at his changed demeanor, his savage threats, and above all, that shocking blunderbuss, they willingly enlist under him, becoming his humble slaves, and Oberlus the most incredible of tyrants. So much so, that two or three perish beneath his initiating process. He sets the remainder—four of them—to breaking the caked soil; transporting upon their backs loads of loamy earth, scooped up in moist clefts among the mountains; keeps them on the roughest fare; presents his piece at the slightest hint of insurrection; and in all respects converts them into reptiles at his feet—plebeian garter-snakes to this Lord Anaconda.

At last, Oberlus contrives to stock his arsenal with four rusty cutlasses, and an added supply of powder and ball intended for his blunderbuss. Remitting in good part the labor of his slaves, he now approves himself a man, or rather devil, of great abilities in the way of cajoling or coercing others into acquiescence with his own ulterior designs, however at first abhorrent to them. But indeed, prepared for almost any eventual evil by their previous lawless life, as a sort of ranging Cow-Boys of the sea, which had dissolved within them the whole moral man, so that they were ready to concrete in the first offered mold of baseness now; rotted down from manhood by their hopeless misery on the isle; wonted to cringe in all things to their lord, himself the worst of slaves; these wretches were now become wholly corrupted to his hands. He used them as creatures of an inferior race; in short, he gaffles his four animals, and makes murderers of them; out of cowards fitly manufacturing bravoes.

Now, sword or dagger, human arms are but artificial claws and fangs, tied on like false spurs to the fighting cock. So, we repeat, Oberlus, czar of the isle, gaffles his four subjects; that is, with intent of glory, puts four rusty cutlasses into their hands. Like any other autocrat, he had a noble army now.

It might be thought a servile war would hereupon ensue. Arms in the hands of trodden slaves? how indiscreet of Emperor Oberlus! Nay, they had but cutlasses—sad old scythes enough— he a blunderbuss, which by its blind scatterings of all sorts of boulders, clinkers, and other scoria would annihilate all four

mutineers, like four pigeons at one shot. Besides, at first he
did not sleep in his accustomed hut; every lurid sunset, for a
time, he might have been seen wending his way among the
riven mountains, there to secrete himself till dawn in some sulphurous pitfall, undiscoverable to his gang; but finding this
at last too troublesome, he now each evening tied his slaves
hand and foot, hid the cutlasses, and thrusting them into his
barracks, shut to the door, and lying down before it, beneath
a rude shed lately added, slept out the night, blunderbuss in
hand.

It is supposed that not content with daily parading over a
cindery solitude at the head of his fine army, Oberlus now meditated the most active mischief; his probable object being to
surprise some passing ship touching at his dominions, massacre
the crew, and run away with her to parts unknown. While
these plans were simmering in his head, two ships touch in
company at the isle, on the opposite side to his; when his designs undergo a sudden change.

The ships are in want of vegetables, which Oberlus promises
in great abundance, provided they send their boats round to
his Landing, so that the crews may bring the vegetables from
his garden; informing the two captains, at the same time, that
his rascals—slaves and soldiers—had become so abominably
lazy and good-for-nothing of late, that he could not make them
work by ordinary inducements, and did not have the heart to
be severe with them.

The arrangement was agreed to, and the boats were sent
and hauled upon the beach. The crews went to the lava hut;
but to their surprise nobody was there. After waiting till their
patience was exhausted, they returned to the shore, when lo,
some stranger—not the Good Samaritan either—seems to have
very recently passed that way. Three of the boats were broken
in a thousand pieces, and the fourth was missing. By hard toil
over the mountains and through the clinkers, some of the strangers succeeded in returning to that side of the isle where the
ships lay, when fresh boats are sent to the relief of the rest of
the hapless party.

However amazed at the treachery of Oberlus, the two captains, afraid of new and still more mysterious atrocities—and
indeed, half imputing such strange events to the enchantments
associated with these isles—perceive no security but in instant
flight; leaving Oberlus and his army in quiet possession of the
stolen boat.

On the eve of sailing they put a letter in a keg, giving the Pacific Ocean intelligence of the affair, and moored the keg in the bay. Some time subsequent, the keg was opened by another captain chancing to anchor there, but not until after he had dispatched a boat round to Oberlus's Landing. As may be readily surmised, he felt no little inquietude till the boat's return; when another letter was handed him, giving Oberlus's version of the affair. This precious document had been found pinned half-mildewed to the clinker wall of the sulphurous and deserted hut. It ran as follows: showing that Oberlus was at least an accomplished writer, and no mere boor; and what is more, was capable of the most tristful eloquence.

"Sir: I am the most unfortunate ill-treated gentleman that lives. I am a patriot, exiled from my country by the cruel hand of tyranny.

"Banished to these Enchanted Isles, I have again and again besought captains of ships to sell me a boat, but always have been refused, though I offered the handsomest prices in Mexican dollars. At length an opportunity presented of possessing myself of one and I did not let it slip.

"I have been long endeavoring, by hard labor and much solitary suffering, to accumulate something to make myself comfortable in a virtuous though unhappy old age; but at various times have been robbed and beaten by men professing to be Christians.

"To-day I sail from the Enchanted group in the good boat Charity bound to the Feejee Isles.

FATHERLESS OBERLUS

"P.S.—Behind the clinkers, nigh the oven, you will find the old fowl. Do not kill it; be patient; I leave it setting; if it shall have any chicks, I hereby bequeath them to you, whoever you may be. But don't count your chicks before they are hatched."

The fowl proved a starveling rooster, reduced to a sitting posture by sheer debility.

Oberlus declares that he was bound to the Feejee Isles; but this was only to throw pursuers on a false scent. For, after a long time, he arrived, alone in his open boat, at Guayaquil. As his miscreants were never again beheld on Hood's Isle, it is supposed, either that they perished for want of water on the passage to Guayaquil, or, what is quite as probable, were thrown overboard by Oberlus, when he found the water growing scarce.

From Guayaquil Oberlus proceeded to Payta; and there, with that nameless witchery peculiar to some of the ugliest animals, wound himself into the affections of a tawny damsel; prevailing upon her to accompany him back to his Enchanted Isle; which doubtless he painted as a Paradise of flowers, not a Tartarus of clinkers.

But unfortunately for the colonization of Hood's Isle with a choice variety of animated nature, the extraordinary and devilish aspect of Oberlus made him to be regarded in Payta as a highly suspicious character. So that being found concealed one night, with matches in his pocket, under the hull of a small vessel just ready to be launched, he was seized and thrown into jail.

The jails in most South American towns are generally of the least wholesome sort. Built of huge cakes of sunburnt brick, and containing but one room, without windows or yard, and but one door heavily grated with wooden bars, they present both within and without the grimmest aspect. As public edifices they conspicuously stand upon the hot and dusty Plaza, offering to view, through the gratings, their villainous and hopeless inmates, burrowing in all sorts of tragic squalor. And here, for a long time, Oberlus was seen; the central figure of a mongrel and assassin band; a creature whom it is religion to detest, since it is philanthropy to hate a misanthrope.

Note.—They who may be disposed to question the possibility of the character above depicted, are referred to the 2d vol. of Porter's *Voyage into the Pacific*, where they will recognize many sentences, for expedition's sake derived verbatim from thence, and incorporated here; the main difference—save a few passing reflections—between the two accounts being, that the present writer has added to Porter's facts accessory ones picked up in the Pacific from reliable sources; and where facts conflict, has naturally preferred his own authorities to Porter's. As, for instance, *his* authorities place Oberlus on Hood's Isle: Porters', on Charles's Isle. The letter found in the hut is also somewhat different; for while at the Encantadas he was informed that, not only did it evince a certain clerkliness, but was full of the strangest satiric effrontery which does not adequately appear in Porter's version. I accordingly altered it to suit the general character of its author.

Sketch Tenth

RUNAWAYS, CASTAWAYS, SOLITARIES, GRAVE-STONES, ETC.

And all about old stockes and stubs of trees,
Whereon nor fruit nor leafe was ever seen,
Did hang upon the ragged rocky knees;
On which had many wretches hanged beene.

SOME relics of the hut of Oberlus partially remain to this day at the head of the clinkered valley. Nor does the stranger, wandering among other of the Enchanted Isles, fail to stumble upon still other solitary abodes, long abandoned to the tortoise and the lizard. Probably few parts of earth have, in modern times, sheltered so many solitaries. The reason is, that these isles are situated in a distant sea, and the vessels which occasionally visit them are mostly all whalers, or ships bound on dreary and protracted voyages, exempting them in a good degree from both the oversight and the memory of human law. Such is the character of some commanders and some seamen, that under these untoward circumstances, it is quite impossible but that scenes of unpleasantness and discord should occur between them. A sullen hatred of the tyrannic ship will seize the sailor, and he gladly exchanges it for isles, which, though blighted as by a continual sirocco and burning breeze, still offer him, in their labyrinthine interior, a retreat beyond the possibility of capture. To flee the ship in any Peruvian or Chilean port, even the smallest and most rustical, is not unattended with great risk of apprehension, not to speak of jaguars. A reward of five pesos sends fifty dastardly Spaniards into the wood, who, with long knives, scour them day and night in eager hopes of securing their prey. Neither is it, in general, much easier to escape pursuit at the isles of Polynesia. Those of them which have felt a civilizing influence present the same difficulty to the runaway with the Peruvian ports, the advanced natives being quite as mercenary and keen of knife and scent as the retrograde Spaniards; while, owing to the bad odor in which all Europeans lie, in the minds of aboriginal savages who have chanced to hear aught of them, to desert the ship among primitive Polynesians, is, in most cases, a hope not unforlorn. Hence the Enchanted Isles become the voluntary tarrying place of all sorts of refugees; some of whom too sadly experience the fact, that flight from tyranny does not of itself insure a safe asylum, far less a happy home.

Moreover, it has not seldom happened that hermits have been made upon the isles by the accidents incident to tortoise-hunting. The interior of most of them is tangled and difficult of passage beyond description; the air is sultry and stifling; an intolerable thirst is provoked, for which no running stream offers its kind relief. In a few hours, under an equatorial sun, reduced by these causes to entire exhaustion, woe betide the straggler at the Enchanted Isles! Their extent is such as to forbid an adequate search, unless weeks are devoted to it. The impatient ship waits a day or two; when, the missing man remaining undiscovered, up goes a stake on the beach, with a letter of regret, and a keg of crackers and another of water tied to it, and away sails the craft.

Nor have there been wanting instances where the inhumanity of some captains has led them to wreak a secure revenge upon seamen who have given their caprice or pride some singular offense. Thrust ashore upon the scorching marl, such mariners are abandoned to perish outright, unless by solitary labors they succeed in discovering some precious driblets of moisture oozing from a rock or stagnant in a mountain pool.

I was well acquainted with a man, who, lost upon the Isle of Narborough, was brought to such extremes by thirst, that at last he only saved his life by taking that of another being. A large hair-seal came upon the beach. He rushed upon it, stabbed it in the neck, and then throwing himself upon the panting body quaffed at the living wound; the palpitations of the creature's dying heart injected life into the drinker.

Another seaman, thrust ashore in a boat upon an isle at which no ship ever touched, owing to its peculiar sterility and the shoals about it, and from which all other parts of the group were hidden—this man, feeling that it was sure death to remain there, and that nothing worse than death menaced him in quitting it, killed two seals, and inflating their skins, made a float, upon which he transported himself to Charles's Island, and joined the republic there.

But men, not endowed with courage equal to such desperate attempts, find their only resource in forthwith seeking some watering-place, however precarious or scanty; building a hut; catching tortoises and birds; and in all respects preparing for a hermit life, till tide or time, or a passing ship arrives to float them off.

At the foot of precipices on many of the isles, small rude basins in the rocks are found, partly filled with rotted rubbish or vegetable decay, or overgrown with thickets, and sometimes a little moist; which, upon examination, reveal plain tokens of artificial instruments employed in hollowing them out, by some poor castaway or still more miserable runaway. These basins are made in places where it was supposed some scanty drops of dew might exude into them from the upper crevices.

The relics of hermitages and stone basins are not the only signs of vanishing humanity to be found upon the isles. And, curious to say, that spot which of all others in settled communities is most animated, at the Enchanted Isles presents the most dreary of aspects. And though it may seem very strange to talk of post-offices in this barren region, yet post-offices are occasionally to be found there. They consist of a stake and a bottle. The letters being not only sealed, but corked. They are geneially deposited by captains of Nantucketers for the benefit of passing fishermen, and contain statements as to what luck they had in whaling or tortoise-hunting. Frequently, however, long months and months, whole years glide by and no applicant appears. The stake rots and falls, presenting no very exhilarating object.

If now it be added that grave-stones, or rather grave-boards, are also discovered upon some of the isles, the picture will be complete.

Upon the beach of James's Isle, for many years, was to be seen a rude finger-post, pointing inland. And, perhaps, taking it for some signal of possible hospitality in this otherwise desolate spot—some good hermit living there with his maple dish —the stranger would follow on in the path thus indicated, till at last he would come out in a noiseless nook, and find his only welcome, a dead man—his sole greeting the inscription over a grave. Here, in 1813, fell in a daybreak duel, a lieutenant of the U.S. frigate *Essex*, aged twenty-one: attaining his majority in death.

It is but fit that, like those old monastic institutions of Europe, whose inmates go not out of their own walls to be inurned, but are entombed there where they die, the Encantadas, too, should bury their own dead, even as the great general monastery of earth does hers.

It is known that burial in the ocean is a pure necessity of sea-faring life, and that it is only done when land is far astern, and not clearly visible from the bow. Hence, to vessels cruising in the vicinity of the Enchanted Isles, they afford a convenient Potters Field. The interment over, some good-natured forecastle poet and artist seizes his paint-brush, and inscribes a doggerel epitaph. When, after a long lapse of time, other good-natured seamen chance to come upon the spot, they usually make a table of the mound, and quaff a friendly can to the poor soul's repose.

As a specimen of these epitaphs, take the following found in a bleak gorge of Chatham Isle:

> *Oh, Brother Jack, as you pass by,*
> *As you are now, so once was I.*
> *Just so game, and just so gay,*
> *But now, alack, they've stopped my pay.*
> *No more I peep out of my blinkers,*
> *Here I be—tucked in with clinkers!*

THE TWO TEMPLES

dedicated to Sheridan Knowles

NOTE: So far as we know, this pair of sketches was the only one of Melville's magazine contributions between 1853 and 1856 to be rejected. *Putnam's* editor, the capable Charles Briggs, explained that though the description was "exquisite" and the satire "pungent," "the religious sensibilities of the public" had to be considered (letter to Melville, May 12, 1854). If, however, "Temple First"—"marble-buttressed, stained-glassed, spic-and-span new"—and the "fat-paunched, beadle-faced man" guarding its doors had not been immediately identifiable as New York's fashionable Grace Church and its warden, "The Two Temples" probably would have been accepted. The remarkable thing about Melville's three-year career as a writer for the magazines is how free from censorship and the squeamishness of editors he appears to have been. By the 1870's and '80's story-writers like Cable, Howells, Mark Twain and Henry James or, in England, Thomas Hardy seem a good deal more constrained in this respect.

"Temple Second" derives from Melville's trip to Europe in 1849. Its description of "Babylonian" London on Saturday night may be compared with Poe's in "The Man of the Crowd" (1840) or Dostoievsky's in *Winter Notes on Summer Impressions* (1863)—or with innumerable London scenes in Dickens, whose *Bleak House* had been serialized by *Harper's* during 1852 and 1853. The treatment here of the theme of "charity" may or may not shed light on *The Confidence-Man* (1857), Melville's last and longest work of this period.

TEMPLE FIRST

"THIS is too bad," said I, "here have I tramped this blessed Sunday morning, all the way from the Battery, three long miles, for this express purpose, prayerbook under arm; here I am, I say, and, after all, I can't get in.

"Too bad. And how disdainful the great, fat-paunched, beadle-faced man looked, when, in answer to my humble petition, he said they had no galleries. Just the same as if he'd said, they didn't entertain poor folks. But I'll wager something that had my new coat been done last night, as the false tailor- promised, and had I, arrayed therein this bright morning, tickled the fat-paunched, beadle-faced man's palm with a bank-note, then, gallery or no gallery, I would have had a fine seat in this marble-buttressed, stained-glassed, spic-and-span new temple.

"Well, here I am in the porch, very politely bowed out of the nave. I suppose I'm excommunicated; excluded, anyway. —That's a noble string of flashing carriages drawn up along the curb; those champing horses too have a haughty curve to their foam-flecked necks. Property of those 'miserable sinners' inside, I presume. I don't a bit wonder they unreservedly confess to such misery as *that*.—See the gold hat-bands, too, and other gorgeous trimmings, on those glossy groups of low-voiced gossipers near by. If I were in England now, I should think those chaps a company of royal dukes, right honorable barons, etc. As it is, though, I guess they are only lackeys.—By the way, here I dodge about, as if I wanted to get into their aristocratic circle. In fact, it looks a sort of lackeyish to be idly standing outside a fine temple, cooling your heels, during service.—I had best move back to the Battery again, peeping into my prayerbook as I go.—But hold, don't I see a small door? Just in there, to one side, if I don't mistake, is a very low and very narrow vaulted door. No one seems to go that way. Ten to one, that identical door leads up into the tower. And now that I think of it, there is usually in these splendid, new-fashioned Gothic Temples, a curious little window high over the orchestra and everything else, away up among the gilded clouds of the ceiling's frescoes; and that little window, seems to me, if one could, but get there, ought to command a glorious bird's-eye view of the entire field of operations below.—I guess I'll try it. No one in the porch now. The beadle-faced man is smoothing down some ladies' cushions, far up the broad aisle, I dare say. Softly now. If the small door ain't locked, I shall have stolen a march upon the beadle-faced man, and secured a humble seat in the sanctuary, in spite of him.—Good! Thanks for this! The door is not locked. Bell-ringer forgot to lock it, no doubt. Now, like any felt-footed grimalkin, up I steal among the leads."

Ascending some fifty stone steps along a very narrow curving stair-way, I found myself on a blank platform forming the second story of the huge square tower.

I seemed inside some magic-lantern. On three sides, three gigantic Gothic windows of richly dyed glass, filled the otherwise meagre place with all sorts of sunrises and sunsets, lunar and solar rainbows, falling stars, and other flaming fire-works and pyrotechnics. But after all, it was but a gorgeous dungeon; for I couldn't look out, any more than if I had been the occupant of a basement cell in "the Tombs." With some pains, and care not to do any serious harm, I contrived to scratch a minute opening in a great purple star forming the centre of the chief compartment of the middle window; when peeping through, as through goggles, I ducked my head in dismay. The beadle-faced man, with no hat on his head, was just in the act of driving three ragged little boys into the middle of the street; and how could I help trembling at the apprehension of his discovering a rebellious caitiff like me peering down on him from the tower? For, in stealing up here, I had set at naught his high authority. He whom he thought effectually ejected had burglariously returned. For a moment I was almost ready to bide my chance and get to the sidewalk again with all dispatch. But another Jacob's ladder of lofty steps,—wooden ones, this time—allured me to another and still higher flight, —in sole hopes of gaining the one secret window where I might, at distance, take part in the proceedings.

Presently I noticed something which, owing to the first marvellous effulgence of the place, had remained unseen till now. Two strong ropes, dropping through holes in the rude ceiling high overhead, fell a sheer length of sixty feet, right through the center of the space, and dropped in coils upon the floor of the huge magic-lantern. Bell-ropes these, thought I, and quaked. For if the beadle-faced man should learn that a grimalkin was somewhere prowling about the edifice, how easy for him to ring the alarm. Hark!—ah, that's only the organ—yes—it's the *"Venite, exultemus Domine."* Though an insider in one respect, yet am I but an outsider in another. But for all that, I will not be defrauded of my natural rights. Uncovering my head, and taking out my book, I stood erect, midway up the tall Jacob's ladder, as if standing among the congregation; and in spirit, if not in place, participated in those devout exultings. That over, I continued my upward path; and after crossing sundry minor platforms and irregular landings all the while on a general ascent, at last I was delighted by catching sight of a small round window in the otherwise dead-wall side of the tower, where the tower attached

itself to the main building. In front of the window was a rude
narrow gallery, used as a bridge to cross from the lower stairs
on one side to the upper stairs on the opposite.

As I drew nigh the spot, I well knew from the added clearness with which the sound of worship came to me, that the
window did indeed look down upon the entire interior. But
I was hardly prepared to find that no pane of glass, stained
or unstained, was to stand between me and the far-under aisles
and altar. For the purpose of ventilation, doubtless, the opening had been left unsupplied with sash of any sort. But a sheet
of fine-woven, gauzy wire-work was in place of that. When,
all eagerness, and open book in hand, I first advanced to stand
before the window, I involuntarily shrank, as from before the
mouth of a furnace, upon suddenly feeling a forceful puff of
strange, heated air, blown, as by a blacksmith's bellows, full
into my face and lungs. Yes, thought I, this window is doubtless for ventilation. Nor is it quite so comfortable as I fancied
it might be. But beggars must not be choosers. The furnace
which makes the people below there feel so snug and cosy in
their padded pews, is to me, who stand here upon the naked
gallery, cause of grievous trouble. Besides, though my face is
scorched, my back is frozen. But I won't complain. Thanks for
this much, anyway,—that by hollowing one hand to my ear,
and standing a little sideways out of the more violent rush of
the torrid current, I can at least hear the priest sufficiently to
make my responses in the proper place. Little dream the good
congregation away down there, that they have a faithful clerk
away up here. Here, too, is a fitter place for sincere devotions,
where, though I see, I remain unseen. Depend upon it, no
Pharisee would have my pew. I like it, and admire it, too, because it is so very high. Height, somehow, hath devotion in
it. The archangelic anthems are raised in a lofty place. All
the good shall go to such an one. Yes, Heaven is high.

As thus I mused, the glorious organ burst, like an earthquake,
almost beneath my feet; and I heard the invoking cry— "Gov-
ern them and *lift* them up forever!" Then down I gazed upon
the standing human mass, far, far below, whose heads, gleaming in the many-colored window-stains, showed like beds of
spangled pebbles, flashing in a Cuban sun. So, at least, I knew
they needs would look, if but the wire-woven screen were
drawn aside. That wire-woven screen had the effect of casting
crape upon all I saw. Only by making allowances for the crape,
could I gain a right idea of the scene disclosed.

Surprising, most surprising, too, it was. As said before, the window was a circular one; the part of the tower where I stood was dusky-dark; its height above the congregation-floor could not have been less than ninety or a hundred feet; the whole interior temple was lit by naught but glass dimmed, yet glorified with all imaginable rich and russet hues; the approach to my strange look-out, through perfect solitude, and along rude and dusty ways, enhanced the theatric wonder of the populous spectacle of this sumptuous sanctuary. Book in hand, responses on my tongue, standing in the very posture of devotion, I could not rid my soul of the intrusive thought, that, through some necromancer's glass, I looked down upon some sly enchanter's show.

At length the lessons being read, the chants chanted, the white-robed priest, a noble-looking man, with a form like the incomparable Talma's, gave out from the reading-desk the hymn before the sermon, and then through a side door vanished from the scene. In good time I saw the same Talma-like and noble-looking man reappear through the same side door, his white apparel wholly changed for black.

By the melodious tone and persuasive gesture of the speaker, and the all-approving attention of the throng, I knew the sermon must be eloquent, and well adapted to an opulent auditory; but owing to the priest's changed position from the reading-desk, to the pulpit, I could not so distinctly hear him now as in the previous rites. The text, however,—repeated at the outset, and often after quoted,—I could not but plainly catch:—"Ye are the salt of the earth."

At length the benediction was pronounced over the mass of low-inclining foreheads; hushed silence, intense motionlessness followed for a moment, as if the congregation were one of buried, not of living men; when, suddenly, miraculously, like the general rising at the Resurrection, the whole host came to their feet, amid a simultaneous roll, like a great drumbeat, from the enrapturing, overpowering organ. Then, in three freshets—all gay sprightly nods and becks—the gilded brooks poured down the gilded aisles.

Time for me, too, to go, thought I, as snatching one last look upon the imposing scene, I clasped my book and put it in my pocket. The best thing I can do just now, is to slide out unperceived amid the general crowd. Hurrying down the great length of ladder, I soon found myself at the base of the last stone step of the final flight; but started aghast—the door was locked! The bell-ringer, or more probably that forever-prying suspicious-looking beadle-faced man has done this. He would not let me in at all at first, and now, with the greatest inconsistency, he will not let me out. But what is to be done? Shall I knock on the door? That will never do. It will only frighten the crowd streaming by, and no one can adequately respond to my summons, except the beadle-faced man; and if he sees me, he will recognize me, and perhaps roundly rate me—poor, humble worshipper—before the entire public. No, I won't knock. But what then?

Long time I thought, and thought, till at last all was hushed again. Presently a clicking sound admonished me that the church was being closed. In sudden desperation, I gave a rap on the door. But too late. It was not heard. I was left alone and solitary in a temple which but a moment before was more populous than many villages.

A strange trepidation of gloom and loneliness gradually stole over me. Hardly conscious of what I did, I reascended the stone steps: higher and higher still, and only paused, when once more I felt the hot-air blast from the wire-woven screen. Snatching another peep down into the vast arena, I started at its hushed desertness. The long ranges of grouped columns down the nave, and clusterings of them into copses about the corners of the transept; together with the subdued, dim-streaming light from the autumnal glasses; all assumed a secluded and deep-wooded air. I seemed gazing from Pisgah into the forests of old Canaan. A Puseyitish painting of a Madonna and Child, adorning a lower window, seemed showing to me the sole tenants of this painted wilderness—the true Hagar and her Ishmael.—

With added trepidation I stole softly back to the magic-lantern platform; and revived myself a little by peeping through the scratch, upon the unstained light of open day.—But what is to be done, thought I, again.

I descended to the door; listened there; heard nothing. A third time climbing the stone steps, once more I stood in the magic-lantern, while the full nature of the more than awkwardness of my position came over me.

The first persons who will re-enter the temple, mused I, will doubtless be the beadle-faced man, and the bell-ringer. And the first man to come up here, where I am, will be the latter. Now what will be his natural impressions upon first descrying an unknown prowler here? Rather disadvantageous to said prowler's moral character. Explanations will be vain. Circumstances are against me. True, I may hide, till he retires again. But how do I know, that he will then leave the door unlocked? Besides, in a position of affairs like this, it is generally best, I think, to anticipate discovery, and by magnanimously announcing yourself, forestall an inglorious detection. But how announce myself? Already have I knocked, and no response. That moment, my eye, impatiently ranging roundabout, fell upon the bell-ropes. They suggested the usual signal made at dwelling-houses to convey tidings of a stranger's presence. But I was not an outside caller; alas, I was an inside prowler.—But one little touch of that bell-rope would be sure to bring relief. I have an appointment at three o'clock. The beadle-faced man must naturally reside very close by the church. He well knows the peculiar ring of his own bell. The slightest possible hum would bring him flying to the rescue. Shall I, or shall I not?—But I may alarm the neighborhood. Oh no; the merest tinkle, not by any means a loud vociferous peal. Shall I? Better voluntarily bring the beadle-faced man to me, than be involuntarily dragged out from this most suspicious hiding-place. I have to face him, first or last. Better now than later.—Shall I?—

No more. Creeping to the rope, I gave it a cautious twitch. No sound. A little less warily. All was dumb. Still more strongly. Horrors! my hands, instinctively clapped to my ears, only served to condense the appalling din. Some undreamed-of mechanism seemed to have been touched. The bell must have thrice revolved on its thunderous axis, multiplying the astounding reverberation.

My business is effectually done, this time, thought I, all in a tremble. Nothing will serve me now but the reckless confidence of innocence reduced to desperation.

In less than five minutes, I heard a running noise beneath me; the lock of the door clicked, and up rushed the beadle-faced man, the perspiration starting from his cheeks.

"You! Is it *you*? The man I turned away this very morning, skulking here? *You* dare to touch that bell? Scoundrel!"

And ere I could defend myself, seizing me irresistibly in his powerful grasp, he tore me along by the collar, and dragging me down the stairs, thrust me into the arms of three policemen, who, attracted by the sudden toll of the bell, had gathered curiously about the porch.

All remonstrances were vain. The beadle-faced man was

bigoted against me. Represented as a lawless violator, and a remorseless disturber of the Sunday peace, I was conducted to the Halls of Justice. Next morning, my rather gentlemanly appearance procured me a private hearing from the judge. But the beadle-faced man must have made a Sunday night call on him. Spite of my coolest explanations, the circumstances of the case were deemed so exceedingly suspicious, that only after paying a round fine, and receiving a stinging reprimand, was I permitted to go at large, and pardoned for having humbly indulged myself in the luxury of public worship.

TEMPLE SECOND

A STRANGER in London on Saturday night, and without a copper! What hospitalities may such an one expect? What shall I do with myself this weary night? My landlady won't receive me in her parlor. I owe her money. She looks like flint on me. So in this monstrous rabblement must I crawl about till, say ten o'clock, and then slink home to my unlighted bed.

The case was this: the week following my inglorious expulsion from the transatlantic temple, I had packed up my trunks and damaged character, and repaired to the paternal, loving town of Philadelphia. There chance threw into my way an interesting young orphan lady and her aunt-duenna; the lady rich as Cleopatra, but not as beautiful; the duenna lovely as Charmian, but not so young. For the lady's health, prolonged travel had been prescribed. Maternally connected in old England, the lady chose London for her primal port. But ere securing their passage, the two were looking round for some young physician, whose disengagement from pressing business might induce him to accept, on a moderate salary, the post of private Æsculapius and knightly companion to the otherwise unprotected pair. The most necessary was this, as not only the voyage to England was intended, but an extensive European tour, to follow.

Enough. I came; I saw; I was made the happy man. We sailed. We landed on the other side; when, after two weeks of agonized attendance on the vacillations of the lady, I was very cavalierly dismissed, on the score, that the lady's maternal relations had persuaded her to try, through the winter, the salubrious climate of the foggy Isle of Wight, in preference to the fabulous blue atmosphere of the Ionian Isles. So much for national prejudice. (Nota Bene: The lady was in a sad decline.)

Having, ere sailing, been obliged to anticipate nearly a quarter's pay to foot my outfit bills, I was dismally cut adrift in Fleet Street without a solitary shilling. By disposing, at certain pawnbrokers, of some of my less indispensable apparel, I had managed to stave off the more slaughterous onsets of my landlady, while diligently looking about for any business that might providentially appear.

So on I drifted amid those indescribable crowds which every seventh night pour and roar through each main artery and block the by-veins of great London, the Leviathan. Saturday Night it was; and the markets and the shops, and every stall and counter were crushed with the one unceasing tide. A whole Sunday's victualling for three millions of human bodies, was going on. Few of them equally hungry with my own, as through my spent lassitude, the unscrupulous human whirlpools eddied me aside at corners, as any straw is eddied in the Norway Maelstrom. What dire suckings into oblivion must such swirling billows know. Better perish mid myriad sharks in mid-Atlantic, than die a penniless stranger in Babylonian London. Forlorn, outcast, without a friend, I staggered on through three millions of my own human kind. The fiendish gaslights, shooting their Tartarean rays across the muddy, sticky streets, lit up the pitiless and pitiable scene.

Well, well, if this were but Sunday now, I might conciliate some kind female pew-opener, and rest me in some inn-like chapel, upon some stranger's outside bench. But it is Saturday night. The end of the weary week, and all but the end of weary me.

Disentangling myself at last from those skeins of Pande-monian lanes which snarl one part of the metropolis between Fleet Street and Holborn, I found myself at last in a wide and far less noisy street, a short and shopless one, leading up from the Strand, and terminating at its junction with a crosswise avenue. The comparative quietude of the place was inex-pressively soothing. It was like emerging upon the green en-closure surrounding some Cathedral church, where sanctity makes all things still. Two lofty brilliant lights attracted me in this tranquil street. Thinking it might prove some moral or religious meeting, I hurried towards the spot; but was sur-prised to see two tall placards announcing the appearance that night of the stately Macready in the part of Cardinal Richelieu. Very few loiterers hung about the place, the hour being rather late, and the play-bill hawkers mostly departed, or keeping entirely quiet. This theatre, indeed, as I afterwards discovered, was not only one of the best in point of acting, but likewise one of the most decorous in its general management, inside and out. In truth, the whole neighborhood, as it seemed to me—issuing from the jam and uproar of those turbulent tides against which, or borne on irresistibly by which, I had so long been swimming—the whole neighborhood, I say, of this pleasing street seemed in good keeping with the character imputed to its theatre.

Glad to find one blessèd oasis of tranquillity, I stood leaning against a column of the porch, and striving to lose my sadness in running over one of the huge placards. No one molested me. A tattered little girl, to be sure, approached, with a hand-bill extended, but marking me fore narrowly, retreated; her strange skill in physiognomy at once enabling her to determine that I was penniless. As I read, and read— for the placard, of enormous dimensions, contained minute particulars of each successive scene in the enacted play —gradually a strong desire to witness this celebrated Macready in this his celebrated part stole over me. By one act, I might rest my jaded limbs, and more than jaded spirits. Where else could I go for rest, unless I crawled into my cold and lonely bed far up in an attic of Craven Street, looking down upon the muddy Phlegethon of the Thames. Besides, what I wanted was not merely rest, but cheer; the making one of many pleased and pleasing human faces; the getting into a genial humane assembly of my kind; such as, at its best and highest, is to be found in the unified multitude of a devout congregation. But no such assemblies were accessible that night, even if my unbefriended and rather shabby air would overcome the scruples of those fastidious gentry with red gowns and long gilded staves, who guard the portals of the first-class London tabernacles from all profanation of a poor forlorn and fainting wanderer like me. Not inns, but ecclesiastical hotels, where the pews are the rented chambers.

No use to ponder, thought I, at last; it is Saturday night, not Sunday; and so, a theatre only can receive me. So powerfully in the end did the longing to get into the edifice come over me, that I almost began to think of pawning my overcoat for admittance. But from this last infatuation I was providentially withheld by a sudden cheery summons, in a voice unmistakably benevolent. I turned, and saw a man who seemed to be some sort of a working-man.

"Take it," said he, holding a plain red ticket towards me, full in the gas-light. "You want to go in; I know you do. Take it. I am suddenly called home. There—hope you'll enjoy yourself. Good-bye."

Blankly and mechanically, I had suffered the ticket to be thrust into my hand, and now stood quite astonished, bewildered, and for the time, ashamed. The plain fact was, I had received charity; and for the first time in my life. Often in the course of my strange wanderings I had needed charity, but never had asked it, and certainly never, ere this blessed night, had been offered it. And a stranger, and in the very maw of the roaring London, too! Next moment my sense of foolish shame departed, and I felt a queer feeling in my left eye, which, as sometimes is the case with people, was the weaker one; probably from being on the same side with the heart.

I glanced round eagerly. But the kind giver was no longer in sight. I looked upon the ticket. I understood. It was one of those checks given to persons inside a theatre when for any cause they desire to step out a moment. Its presentation ensures unquestioned readmittance.

"Shall I use it?" mused I.—What? It's charity.—But if it be gloriously right to do a charitable deed, can it be ingloriously wrong to receive its benefit?—No one knows you; go boldly in.—Charity.—Why these unvanquishable scruples? All your life, naught but charity sustains you, and all others in the world. Maternal charity nursed you as a babe; paternal charity fed you as a child; friendly charity got you your profession; and to the charity of every man you meet this night in London, are you indebted for your unattempted life. Any knife, any hand of all the millions of knives and hands in London, has you this night at its mercy. You, and all mortals, live but by sufferance of your charitable kind; charitable by omission, not performance.—Stush for your self-upbraidings, and pitiful, poor, shabby pride, you friendless man without a purse. —Go in.

Debate was over. Marking the direction from which the stranger had accosted me, I stepped that way; and soon saw a low-vaulted, inferior-looking door on one side of the edifice. Entering, I wandered on and up, and up and on again, through various doubling stairs and wedge-like, ill-lit passages, whose bare boards much reminded me of my ascent of the Gothic tower on the ocean's far-other side. At last I gained a lofty platform, and saw a fixed human countenance facing me from a mysterious window of a sort of sentry-box or closet. Like some saint in a shrine, the countenance was illuminated by two smoky candles. I divined the man. I exhibited my diploma, and he nodded me to a little door beyond; while a sudden burst of orchestral music admonished me I was now very near my destination, and also revived the memory of the organ-anthems I had heard while on the ladder of the tower at home.

Next moment, the wire-woven gauzy screen of the ventilating window in that same tower seemed enchantedly reproduced before me. The same hot blast of stifling air once more rushed into my lungs. From the same dizzy altitude, through the same fine-spun, vapory crapey air; far, far down upon just such a packed mass of silent human beings; listening to just such grand harmonies; I stood within the topmost gallery of the temple. But hardly alone and silently as before. This time I had company. Not of the first circles, and certainly not of the dress-circle; but most acceptable, right welcome, cheery company, to otherwise uncompanioned me. Quiet, well-pleased working-men, and their glad wives and sisters, with here and there an aproned urchin, with all-absorbed, bright face, vermilioned by the excitement and the heated air, hovering like a painted cherub over the vast human firmament below. The height of the gallery was in truth appalling. The rail was low. I thought of deep-sea-leads, and the mariner in the vessel's chains, drawing up the line, with his long-drawn musical accompaniment. And, like beds of glittering coral, through the deep sea of azure smoke, there, far down, I saw the jewelled necks and white sparkling arms of crowds of ladies in the semi-cirque. But, in the interval of two acts, again the orchestra was heard; some inspiring national anthem now was played. As the volumed sound came undulating up, and broke in showery spray and foam of melody against our gallery rail, my head involuntarily was bowed, my hand instinctively sought my pocket. Only by a second thought did I check my momentary lunacy and remind myself that this time I had no small morocco book with me, and that this was not the house of prayer.

Quickly was my wandering mind—preternaturally affected by the sudden translation from the desolate street to this bewildering and blazing spectacle—arrested in its wanderings, by feeling at my elbow a meaning nudge; when turning suddenly, I saw a sort of coffee-pot, and pewter mug hospitably presented to me by a ragged, but good-natured looking boy.

"Thank you," said I, "I won't take any coffee, I guess."

"Coffee?—I guess?—ain't you a Yankee?"

"Aye, boy; true blue."

"Well, dad's gone to Yankee-land, a-seekin' of his fortin; so take a penny mug of ale, do, Yankee, for poor dad's sake."

Out from the tilted coffee-pot-looking can, came a coffee-colored stream, and a small mug of humming ale was in my hand.

"I don't want it, boy. The fact is, my boy, I have no penny by me. I happened to leave my purse at my lodgings."

"Never do you mind, Yankee; drink to honest dad."

"With all my heart, you generous boy; here's immortal life to him!"

He stared at my strange burst, smiled merrily, and left me, offering his coffee-pot in all directions, and not in vain.

'Tis not always poverty to be poor, mused I; one may fare well without a penny. A ragged boy may be a prince-like benefactor.

Because that unpurchased penny-worth of ale revived my drooping spirits strangely. Stuff was in that barley malt; a most sweet bitterness in those blessed hops. God bless the glorious boy!

The more I looked about me in this lofty gallery, the more was I delighted with its occupants. It was not spacious. It was, if anything, rather contracted, being the very cheapest portion of the house, where very limited attendance was expected; embracing merely the very crown of the top-most semicircle; and so commanding, with a sovereign outlook, and imperial downlook, the whole theatre, with the expanded stage directly opposite, though some hundred feet below. As at the tower, peeping into the transatlantic temple, so stood I here, at the very main-mast-head of all the interior edifice.

Such was the decorum of this special theatre, that nothing objectionable was admitted within its walls. With an unhurt eye of perfect love, I sat serenely in the gallery, gazing upon the pleasing scene, around me and below. Neither did it abate from my satisfaction, to remember, that Mr. Macready, the chief actor of the night, was an amiable gentleman, combining the finest qualities of social and Christian respectability, with the highest excellence in his particular profession; for which last he had conscientiously done much, in many ways, to refine, elevate, and chasten.

But now the curtain rises, and the robed cardinal advances. How marvellous this personal resemblance! He looks every inch to be the self-same, stately priest I saw irradiated by the glow-worm dyes of the pictured windows from my high tower-pew. And shining as he does, in the rosy reflexes of these stained walls and gorgeous galleries, the mimic priest down there; he too seems lit by Gothic blazonings.—Hark! The same measured, courtly, noble tone. See! the same imposing attitude. Excellent actor is this Richelieu!

He disappears behind the scenes. He slips, no doubt, into the Green Room. He reappears somewhat changed in his habiliments. Do I dream, or is it genuine memory that recalls some similar thing seen through the woven wires?

The curtain falls. Starting to their feet, the enraptured thousands sound their responses, deafeningly; unmistakably sincere. Right from the undoubted heart. I have no duplicate in my memory of this. In earnestness of response, this second temple stands unmatched. And hath mere mimicry done this? What is it then to act a part?

But now the music surges up again, and borne by that rolling billow, I, and all the gladdened crowd, are harmoniously attended to the street.

I went home to my lonely lodging, and slept not much that night, for thinking of the First Temple and the Second Temple; and how that, a stranger in a strange land, I found sterling charity in the one; and at home, in my own land, was thrust out from the other.

POOR MAN'S PUDDING AND
RICH MAN'S CRUMBS

NOTE: Like Dickens, Melville had a rich sense of how
confrontations with poverty and suffering exposed the hollowness of conventional moral attitudes. As an American democrat he felt with special force "the practical misery and
infamy of poverty" in a new world which habitually pronounced itself blessed by a special providence. It may have
been a Dickensian sense of the uses of indirection that led
Melville to set these two raspingly satirical sketches (*Harper's*,
June, 1854) forty years in the past.

Picture First

POOR MAN'S PUDDING

"YOU SEE," said Poet Blandmour, enthusiastically—as some
forty years ago we walked along the road in a soft, moist
snow-fall, toward the end of March—"you see, my friend, that
the blessed almoner, Nature, is in all things beneficent; and
not only so, but considerate in her charities, as any discreet
human philanthropist might be. This snow, now, which seems
so unseasonable, is in fact just what a poor husbandman needs.
Rightly is this soft March snow, falling just before seed-time,
rightly is it called 'Poor Man's Manure.' Distilling from kind
heaven upon the soil, by a gentle penetration it nourishes every
clod, ridge, and furrow. To the poor farmer it is as good as
the rich farmer's farm-yard enrichments. And the poor man
has no trouble to spread it, while the rich man has to spread
his."

"Perhaps so," said I, without equal enthusiasm, brushing
some of the damp flakes from my chest. "It may be as you
say, dear Blandmour. But tell me, how is it that the wind
drives yonder drifts of 'Poor Man's Manure' off poor Coulter's

two-acre patch here, and piles it up yonder on rich Squire
Teamster's twenty-acre field?"

"Ah! to be sure—yes—well; Coulter's field, I suppose, is
sufficiently moist without further moistenings. Enough is as
good as a feast, you know."

"Yes," replied I, "of this sort of damp fare," shaking another shower of the damp flakes from my person. "But tell
me, this warm spring-snow may answer very well, as you say;
but how is it with the cold snows of the long, long winters
here?"

"Why, do you not remember the words of the Psalmist?
—'The Lord giveth snow like wool;' meaning not only that
snow is white as wool, but warm, too, as wool. For the only
reason, as I take it, that wool is comfortable, is because air
is entangled, and therefore warmed among its fibres. Just so,
then, take the temperature of a December field when covered
with this snow-fleece, and you will no doubt find it several
degrees above that of the air. So, you see, the winter's snow
itself is beneficent; under the pretense of frost—a sort of gruff
philanthropist—actually warming the earth, which afterward
is to be fertilizingly moistened by these gentle flakes of March."

"I like to hear you talk, dear Blandmour; and, guided by
your benevolent heart, can only wish to poor Coulter plenty
of this 'Poor man's Manure.' "

"But that is not all," said Blandmour, eagerly. "Did you
never hear of the 'Poor Man's Eye-water?' "

"Never."

"Take this soft March snow, melt it, and bottle it. It keeps
pure as alcohol. The very best thing in the world for weak
eyes. I have a whole demijohn of it myself. But the poorest
man, afflicted in his eyes, can freely help himself to this
same all-bountiful remedy. Now, what a kind provision is
that!"

"Then 'Poor Man's Manure' is 'Poor Man's Eye-water' too?"

"Exactly. And what could be more economically contrived?
One thing answering two ends—ends so very distinct."

"Very distinct, indeed."

"Ah! that is your way. Making sport of earnest. But never
mind. We have been talking of snow; but common rain-water
—such as falls all the year round—is still more kindly. Not
to speak of its known fertilizing quality as to fields, consider
it in one of its minor lights. Pray, did you ever hear of a 'Poor
Man's Egg?' "

"Never. What is that, now?"

"Why, in making some culinary preparations of meal and flour, where eggs are recommended in the receipt-book, a substitute for the eggs may be had in a cup of cold rain-water, which acts as leaven. And so a cup of cold rain-water thus used is called by housewives a 'Poor Man's Egg.' And many rich men's housekeepers sometimes use it."

"But only when they are out of hen's eggs, I presume, dear Blandmour. But your talk is—I sincerely say it—most agreeable to me. Talk on."

"Then there's 'Poor Man's Plaster' for wounds and other bodily harms; an alleviative and curative, compounded of simple, natural things; and so, being very cheap, is accessible to the poorest of sufferers. Rich men often use 'Poor Man's Plaster.' "

"But not without the judicious advice of a fee'd physician, dear Blandmour."

"Doubtless, they first consult the physician; but that may be an unnecessary precaution."

"Perhaps so. I do not gainsay it. Go on."

"Well, then, did you ever eat of a 'Poor Man's Pudding'?"

"I never so much as heard of it before."

"Indeed! Well, now you shall eat of one; and you shall eat it, too, as made, unprompted, by a poor man's wife, and you shall eat it at a poor man's table, and in a poor man's house. Come now, and if after this eating, you do not say that a 'Poor Man's Pudding' is as relishable as a rich man's, I will give up the point altogether; which briefly is: that, through kind Nature, the poor, out of their very poverty, extract comfort."

Not to narrate any more of our conversations upon this subject (for we had several—I being at that time the guest of Blandmour in the country, for the benefit of my health, suffice it that, acting upon Blandmour's hint, I introduced myself into Coulter's house on a wet Monday noon (for the snow had thawed), under the innocent pretense of craving a pedestrian's rest and refreshment for an hour or two.

I was greeted, not without much embarrassment—owing, I suppose, to my dress—but still with unaffected and honest kindness. Dame Coulter was just leaving the wash-tub to get ready her one o'clock meal against her good man's return from a deep wood about a mile distant among the hills, where he was chopping by day's-work—seventy-five cents per day —and found himself. The washing being done outside the

main building, under an infirm-looking old shed, the dame
stood upon a half-rotten, soaked board to protect her feet, as
well as might be, from the penetrating damp of the bare
ground; hence she looked pale and chill. But her paleness
had still another and more secret cause—the paleness of a
mother to be. A quiet, fathomless heart-trouble, too, couched
beneath the mild, resigned blue of her soft and wife-like eye.
But she smiled upon me, as apologizing for the unavoidable
disorder of a Monday and a washing-day, and, conducting
me into the kitchen, set me down in the best seat it had—an
old-fashioned chair of an enfeebled constitution.

I thanked her; and sat rubbing my hands before the ineffectual low fire, and—unobservantly as I could—glancing
now and then about the room, while the good woman, throwing on more sticks, said she was sorry the room was no warmer.
Something more she said, too—not repiningly, however—of
the fuel, as old and damp; picked-up sticks in Squire Teamster's forest, where her husband was chopping the sappy logs
of the living tree for the Squire's fires. It needed not her remark, whatever it was, to convince me of the inferior quality
of the sticks; some being quite mossy and toad-stooled with
long lying bedded among the accumulated dead leaves of
many autumns. They made a sad hissing, and vain spluttering enough.

"You must rest yourself here till dinner-time, at least," said
the dame; "what I have you are heartily welcome to."

I thanked her again, and begged her not to heed my presence in the least, but go on with her usual affairs.

I was struck by the aspect of the room. The house was old,
and constitutionally damp. The window-sills had beads of
exuded dampness upon them. The shriveled sashes shook
in their frames, and the green panes of glass were clouded
with the long thaw. On some little errand the dame passed
into an adjoining chamber, leaving the door partly open. The
floor of that room was carpetless, as the kitchen's was. Nothing but bare necessaries were about me; and those not of the
best sort. Not a print on the wall; but an old volume of Doddridge lay on the smoked chimney-shelf.

"You must have walked a long way, sir; you sigh so with
weariness."

"No, I am not nigh so weary as yourself, I dare say."

"Oh, but I am accustomed to that; *you* are not, I should
think," and her soft, sad blue eye ran over my dress. "But I

must sweep these shavings away; husband made him a new axe-helve this morning before sunrise, and I have been so busy washing, that I have had no time to clear up. But now they are just the thing I want for the fire. They'd be much better though, were they not so green."

Now if Blandmour were here, thought I to myself, he would call those green shavings "Poor Man's Matches," or "Poor Man's Tinder," or some pleasant name of that sort.

"I do not know," said the good woman, turning round to me again—as she stirred among her pots on the smoky fire—"I do not know how you will like our pudding. It is only rice, milk, and salt boiled together."

"Ah, what they call 'Poor Man's Pudding,' I suppose you mean."

A quick flush, half resentful, passed over her face.

"*We* do not call it so, sir," she said, and was silent.

Upbraiding myself for my inadvertence, I could not but again think to myself what Blandmour would have said, had he heard those words and seen that flush.

At last a slow, heavy footfall was heard; then a scraping at the door, and another voice said, "Come, wife; come, come —I must be back again in a jiff—if you say I *must* take all my meals at home, you must be speedy; because the Squire— Good day, sir," he exclaimed, now first catching sight of me as he entered the room. He turned toward his wife, inquiringly, and stood stock-still, while the moisture oozed from his patched boots to the floor.

"This gentleman stops here awhile to rest and refresh: he will take dinner with us, too. All will be ready now in a trice; so sit down on the bench, husband, and be patient, I pray. You see, sir," she continued, turning to me, "Willian there wants, of mornings, to carry a cold meal into the woods with him, to save the long one o'clock walk across the fields to and fro. But I won't let him. A warm dinner is more than pay for the long walk."

"I don't know about that," said William, shaking his head. "I have often debated in my mind whether it really paid. There's not much odds, either way, between a wet walk after hard work, and a wet dinner before it. But I like to oblige a good wife like Martha. And you know, sir, that women will have their whimsies."

"I wish they all had as kind whimsies as your wife has," said I.

"Well, I've heard that some women ain't all maple-sugar; but, content with dear Martha, I don't know much about others."

"You find rare wisdom in the woods," mused I.

"Now, husband, if you ain't too tired, just lend a hand to draw the table out."

"Nay," said I, "let him rest, and let me help."

"No," said William, rising.

"Sit still," said his wife to me.

The table set, in due time we all found ourselves with plates before us.

"You see what we have," said Coulter—"salt pork, rye-bread, and pudding. Let me help you. I got this pork of the Squire; some of his last year's pork, which he let me have on account. It isn't quite so sweet as this year's would be; but I find it hearty enough to work on, and that's all I eat for. Only let the rheumatiz and other sicknesses keep clear of me, and I ask no flavors or favors from any. But you don't eat of the pork!"

"I see," said the wife, gently and gravely, "that the gentleman knows the difference between this year's and last year's pork. But perhaps he will like the pudding."

I summoned up all my self-control, and smilingly assented to the proposition of the pudding, without by my looks casting any reflections upon the pork. But, to tell the truth, it was quite impossible for me (not being ravenous, but only a little hungry at the time) to eat of the latter. It had a yellowish crust all round it, and was rather rankish, I thought, to the taste. I observed, too, that the dame did not eat of it, though she suffered some to be put on her plate and pretended to be busy with it when Coulter looked that way. But she ate of the rye-bread, and so did I.

"Now, then, for the pudding," said Coulter. "Quick, wife; the Squire sits in his sitting-room window, looking far out across the fields. His time-piece is true."

"He don't play the spy on you, does he?" said I.

"Oh, no!—I don't say that. He's a good enough man. He gives me work. But he's particular. Wife, help the gentleman. You see, sir, if I lose the Squire's work, what will become of—" and, with a look for which I honored humanity, with sly significance he glanced toward his wife; then, a little changing his voice, instantly continued—"that fine horse I am going to buy."

"I guess," said the dame, with a strange, subdued sort of inefficient pleasantry—"I guess that fine horse you sometimes so merrily dream of will long stay in the Squire's stall. But sometimes his man gives me a Sunday ride."

"A Sunday ride!" said I.

"You see," resumed Coulter, "wife loves to go to church; but the nighest is four miles off, over yon snowy hills. So she can't walk it; and I can't carry her in my arms, though I have carried her up-stairs before now. But, as she says, the Squire's man sometimes gives her a lift on the road; and for this cause it is that I speak of a horse I am going to have one of these fine sunny days. And already, before having it, I have christened it 'Martha.' But what am I about? Come, come, wife! the pudding! Help the gentleman, do! The Squire! the Squire! —think of the Squire! and help round the pudding. There, one—two—three mouthfuls must do me. Good-bye, wife. Goodbye, sir. I'm off."

And, snatching his soaked hat, the noble Poor Man hurriedly went out into the soak and the mire.

I suppose now, thinks I to myself, that Blandmour would poetically say, He goes to take a Poor Man's Saunter.

"You have a fine husband," said I to the woman, as we were now left together.

"William loves me this day as on the wedding-day, sir. Some hasty words, but never a harsh one. I wish I were better and stronger for his sake, And, oh! sir, both for his sake and mine," (and the soft, blue, beautiful eyes turned into two well-springs) "how I wish little William and Martha lived—it is so lonely-like now. William named after him, and Martha for me."

When a companion's heart of itself overflows, the best one can do is to do nothing. I sat looking down on my as yet untasted pudding.

"You should have seen little William, sir. Such a bright, manly boy, only six years old—cold, cold now!"

Plunging my spoon into the pudding, I forced some into my mouth to stop it.

"And little Martha— Oh! sir, she was the beauty! Bitter, bitter! but needs must be borne."

The mouthful of pudding now touched my palate, and touched it with a mouldy, briny taste. The rice, I knew, was of that damaged sort sold cheap; and the salt from the last year's pork barrel.

"Ah, sir, if those little ones yet to enter the world were the same little ones which so sadly have left it; returning friends, not strangers, strangers, always strangers! Yet does a mother soon learn to love them; for certain, sir, they come from where the others have gone. Don't you believe that, sir? Yes, I know all good people must. But, still, still—and I fear it is wicked, and very black-hearted, too—still, strive how I may to cheer me with thinking of little William and Martha in heaven, and with reading Dr. Doddridge there—still, still does dark grief leak in, just like the rain through our roof. I am left so lonesome now; day after day, all the day long, dear William is gone; and all the damp day long grief drizzles and drizzles down on my soul. But I pray to God to forgive me for this; and for the rest, manage it as well as I may."

Bitter and mouldy is the "Poor Man's Pudding," groaned I to myself, half choked with but one little mouthful of it, which would hardly go down.

I could stay no longer to hear of sorrows for which the sincerest sympathies could give no adequate relief; of a fond persuasion, to which there could be furnished no further proof than already was had—a persuasion, too, of that sort which much speaking is sure more or less to mar; of causeless self-upbraidings, which no expostulations could have dispelled. I offered no pay for hospitalities gratuitous and honorable as those of a prince. I knew that such offerings would have been more than declined; charity resented.

The native American poor never lose their delicacy or pride; hence, though unreduced to the physical degradation of the European pauper, they yet suffer more in mind than the poor of any other people in the world. Those peculiar social sensibilities nourished by our own peculiar political principles, while they enhance the true dignity of a prosperous American, do but minister to the added wretchedness of the unfortunate, first, by prohibiting their acceptance of what little random relief charity may offer; and, second, by furnishing them with the keenest appreciation of the smarting distinction between their ideal of universal equality and their grindstone experience of the practical misery and infamy of poverty—a misery and infamy which is, ever has been, and ever will be, precisely the same in India, England, and America.

Under pretense that my journey called me forthwith, I bade the dame good-bye; shook her cold hand; looked my last into her blue, resigned eye, and went out into the wet. But cheerless as it was, the damp, damp, damp—the heavy atmosphere charged with all sorts of incipiencies—I yet became conscious, by the suddenness of the contrast, that the house air I had quitted was laden down with that peculiar deleterious quality, the height of which—insufferable to some visitants—will be found in a poor-house ward.

This ill-ventilation in winter of the rooms of the poor—a thing, too, so stubbornly persisted in—is usually charged upon them as their disgraceful neglect of the most simple means to health. But the instinct of the poor is wiser than we think. The air which ventilates, likewise *cools*. And to any shiverer, ill-ventilated warmth is better than well-ventilated cold. Of all the preposterous assumptions of humanity over humanity, nothing exceeds most of the criticisms made on the habits of the poor by the well-housed, well-warmed, and well-fed.

*   *   *

"Blandmour," said I that evening, as after tea I sat on his comfortable sofa, before a blazing fire, with one of his two ruddy little children on my knee, "you are not what may rightly be called a rich man; you have a fair competence; no more. Is it not so? Well, then, I do not include *you*, when I say, that if ever a Rich Man speaks prosperously to me of a Poor Man, I shall set it down as—I won't mention the word."

Picture Second

RICH MAN'S CRUMBS

IN THE year 1814, during the summer following my first taste of the "Poor Man's Pudding," a sea-voyage was recommended to me by my physician. The Battle of Waterloo having closed the long drama of Napoleon's wars, many strangers were visiting Europe. I arrived in London at the time the victorious princes were there assembled enjoying the Arabian Nights' hospitalities of a grateful and gorgeous aristocracy, and the courtliest of gentlemen and kings—George the Prince Regent.

I had declined all letters but one to my banker. I wandered about for the best reception an adventurous traveler can have —the reception, I mean, which unsolicited chance and accident throw in his venturous way.

But I omit all else to recount one hour's hap under the lead of a very friendly man, whose acquaintance I made in the open street of Cheapside. He wore a uniform, and was some sort of a civic subordinate; I forget exactly what. He was off duty that day. His discourse was chiefly of the noble charities of London. He took me to two or three, and made admiring mention of many more.

"But," said he, as we turned into Cheapside again, "if you are at all curious about such things, let me take you—if it be not too late—to one of the most interesting of all—our Lord Mayor's Charities, sir; nay, the charities not only of a Lord Mayor, but I may truly say, in this one instance, of emperors, regents, and kings. You remember the event of yesterday?"

"That sad fire on the river-side, you mean, unhousing so many of the poor?"

"No. The grand Guildhall Banquet to the princes. Who can forget it? Sir, the dinner was served on nothing but solid silver and gold plate, worth at the least £200,000—that is, 1,000,000 of your dollars; while the mere expenditure of meats, wines, attendance and upholstery, etc., cannot be footed under £25,000—125,000 dollars of your hard cash."

"But, surely, my friend, you do not call that charity—feeding kings at that rate?"

"No. The feast came first—yesterday; and the charity after —to-day. How else would you have it, where princes are concerned? But I think we shall be quite in time—come; here we are at King Street, and down there is Guildhall. Will you go?"

"Gladly, my good friend. Take me where you will. I came but to roam and see."

Avoiding the main entrance of the hall, which was barred, he took me through some private way, and we found ourselves in a rear blind-walled place in the open air. I looked round amazed. The spot was grimy as a back-yard in the Five Points. It was packed with a mass of lean, famished, ferocious creatures, struggling and fighting for some mysterious precedency, and all holding soiled blue tickets in their hands.

"There is no other way," said my guide; "we can only get in with the crowd. Will you try it? I hope you have not on your drawing-room suit? What do you say? It will be well worth your sight. So noble a charity does not often offer. The one following the annual banquet of Lord Mayor's day—fine a charity as that certainly is—is not to be mentioned with what will be seen to-day. Is it, aye?"

As he spoke, a basement door in the distance was thrown open, and the squalid mass made a rush for the dark vault beyond.

I nodded to my guide, and sideways we joined in with the rest. Ere long we found our retreat cut off by the yelping crowd behind, and I could not but congratulate myself on having a civic, as well as civil guide; one, too, whose uniform made evident his authority.

It was just the same as if I were pressed by a mob of cannibals on some pagan beach. The beings round me roared with famine. For in this mighty London misery but maddens. In the country it softens. As I gazed on the meagre, murderous pack, I thought of the blue eye of the gentle wife of poor Coulter. Some sort of curved, glittering steel thing (not a sword; I know not what it was), before worn in his belt, was now flourished overhead by my guide, menacing the creatures to forebear offering the stranger violence.

As we drove, slow and wedge-like, into the gloomy vault, the howls of the mass reverberated. I seemed seething in the Pit with the Lost. On and on, through the dark and the damp, and then up a stone stairway to a wide portal; when, diffusing, the pestiferous mob poured in bright day between painted walls and beneath a painted dome. I thought of the anarchic sack of Versailles.

A few moments more and I stood bewildered among the beggars in the famous Guildhall.

Where I stood—where the thronged rabble stood, less than twelve hours before sat His Imperial Majesty, Alexander of Russia; His Royal Majesty, Frederic William, King of Prussia; His Royal Highness, George, Prince Regent of England; His world-renowned Grace, the Duke of Wellington; with a mob of magnificoes, made up of conquering field-marshals, earls, counts, and innumerable other nobles of mark.

The walls swept to and fro, like the foliage of a forest, with blazonings of conquerors' flags. Naught outside the hall was visible. No windows were within four-and-twenty feet of the floor. Cut off from all other sights, I was hemmed in by one splendid spectacle—splendid, I mean, everywhere but as the eye fell toward the floor. *That* was foul as a hovel's—as a kennel's; the naked boards being strewed with the smaller and more wasteful fragments of the feast, while the two long parallel lines, up and down the hall, of now unrobed, shabby, dirty pine-tables were piled with less trampled wrecks. The

dyed banners were in keeping with the last night's kings; the
floor suited the beggars of to-day. The banners looked down
upon the floor as from his balcony Dives upon Lazarus. A line
of liveried men kept back with their staves the impatient jam
of the mob, who, otherwise, might have instantaneously converted the Charity into a Pillage. Another body of gowned
and gilded officials distributed the broken meats—the cold
victuals and crumbs of kings. One after another the beggars
held up their dirty blue tickets, and were served with the
plundered wreck of a pheasant, or the rim of a pasty—like
the detached crown of an old hat—the solids and meats stolen
out.

"What a noble charity!" whispered my guide. "See that
pasty now, snatched by that pale girl; I dare say the Emperor
of Russia ate of that last night."

"Very probably," murmured I; "it looks as though some
omnivorous Emperor or other had had a finger in that pie."

"And see yon pheasant, too—there—*that* one—the boy in
the torn shirt has it now—look! The Prince Regent might
have dined off that."

The two breasts were gouged ruthlessly out, exposing the
bare bones, embellished with the untouched pinions and
legs.

"Yes, who knows!" said my guide, "his Royal Highness the
Prince Regent might have eaten of that identical pheasant."

"I don't doubt it," murmured I, "he is said to be uncommonly fond of the breast. But where is Napoleon's head in a
charger? I should fancy *that* ought to have been the principal
dish."

"You are merry. Sir, even Cossacks are charitable here in
Guildhall. Look! the famous Platoff, the Hetman himself— (he
was here last night with the rest)—no doubt he thrust a lance
into yon fat pork-pie there. Look! the old shirtless man has it
now. How he licks his chops over it, little thinking of or
thanking the good, kind Cossack that left it him! Ah! another—
a stouter—has grabbed it. It falls; bless my soul!—the dish is
quite empty—only a bit of the hacked crust."

"The Cossacks, my friend, are said to be immoderately fond
of fat," observed I. "The Hetman was hardly so charitable as
you thought."

"A noble charity, upon the whole, for all that. See, even
Gog and Magog yonder, at the other end of the hall, fairly
laugh out their delight at the scene."

"But don't you think, though," hinted I, "that the sculptor, whoever he was, carved the laugh too much into a grin—a sort of sardonical grin?"

"Well, that's as you take it, sir. But see—now I'd wager a guinea the Lord Mayor's lady dipped her golden spoon into yonder golden-hued jelly. See, the jelly-eyed old body has slipped it, in one broad gulp, down his throat!"

"Peace to that jelly!" breathed I.

"What a generous, noble, magnanimous charity this is! Unheard of in any country but England, which feeds her very beggars with golden-hued jellies."

"But not three times every day, my friend. And do you really think that jellies are the best sort of relief you can furnish to beggars? Would not plain beef and bread, with something to do, and be paid for, be better?"

"But plain beef and bread were not eaten here. Emperors, and prince-regents, and kings, and field-marshals don't often dine on plain beef and bread. So the leavings are according. Tell me, can you expect that the crumbs of kings can be like the crumbs of squirrels?"

"*You!* I mean *you!* stand aside, or else be served and away! Here, take this pasty, and be thankful that you taste of the same dish with Her Grace the Duchess of Devonshire. Graceless ragamuffin, do you hear?"

These words were bellowed at me through the din by a red-gowned official nigh the board.

"Surely he does not mean *me*," said I to my guide; "he has not confounded *me* with the rest."

"One is known by the company he keeps," smiled my guide. "See! not only stands your hat awry and bunged on your head, but your coat is fouled and torn. Nay," he cried to the red-gown, "this is an unfortunate friend; a simple spectator, I assure you."

"Ah! is that you, old lad?" responded the red-gown, in familiar recognition of my guide—a personal friend, as it seemed. "Well, convey your friend out forthwith. Mind the grand crash; it will soon be coming; hark! now! away with him!"

Too late. The last dish had been seized. The yet unglutted mob raised a fierce yell, which wafted the banners like a strong gust, and filled the air with a reek as from sewers. They surged against the tables, broke through all barriers, and billowed over the hall—their bare tossed arms like the dashed ribs of a wreck. It seemed to me as if a sudden impotent fury of fell envy possessed them. That one half-hour's peep at the mere remnants of the glories of the Banquets of Kings, the unsatisfying mouthfuls of disembowelled pasties, plundered pheasants, and half-sacked jellies, served to remind them of the intrinsic contempt of the alms. In this sudden mood, or whatever mysterious thing it was that now seized them, these Lazaruses seemed ready to spew up in repentant scorn the contumelious crumbs of Dives.

"This way, this way! stick like a bee to my back," intensely whispered my guide. "My friend there has answered my beck, and thrown open yon private door for us two. Wedge—wedge in—quick—there goes your bunged hat—never stop for your coat-tail—hit that man—strike him down! hold! jam! now! now! wrench along for your life! ha! here we breathe freely; thank God! You faint. Ho!"

"Never mind. This fresh air revives me."

I inhaled a few more breaths of it, and felt ready to proceed.

"And now conduct me, my good friend, by some front passage into Cheapside, forthwith. I must home."

"Not by the sidewalk though. Look at your dress. I must get a hack for you."

"Yes, I suppose so," said I, ruefully eying my tatters, and then glancing in envy at the close-bodied coat and flat cap of my guide, which defied all tumblings and tearings.

"There, now, sir," said the honest fellow, as he put me into the hack, and tucked in me and my rags, "when you get back to your own country, you can say you have witnessed the greatest of all England's noble charities. Of course, you will make reasonable allowances for the unavoidable jam. Good-bye. Mind, Jehu"—addressing the driver on the box—"this is a *gentleman* you carry. He is just from the Guildhall Charity, which accounts for his appearance. Go on now. London Tavern, Fleet Street, remember, is the place."

*   *   *

"Now, Heaven in its kind mercy save me from the noble charities of London," sighed I, as that night I lay bruised and battered on my bed; "and Heaven save me equally from the 'Poor Man's Pudding' and the 'Rich Man's Crumbs.' "

THE HAPPY FAILURE:
A STORY OF THE RIVER HUDSON

NOTE: In outline this short tale (*Harper's*, July, 1854) seems a straightforward skit on standard American characteristics in the extravagant era of internal improvements and Jacksonian venture-capitalism, when the construction of Great Hydraulic-Hydrostatic Apparatuses for draining swamps and the collapse of dreams of quick and everlasting fortune through some ingenious secret invention were everyday occurrences. But as soon as Melville puts words in the mouth of his narrator's raptly earnest uncle—a character halfway over from Hawthorne's obsessed scientist-inventors to Mark Twain's fantastic Colonel Sellers—deeper and stranger notes are sounded (though not much developed or sustained). A story written by Herman Melville in 1854 dealing with ten years of dedicated invention sunk in sudden failure, after which the inventor appears relieved of a tormenting burden and is described as being himself again, must be assumed open to autobiographical reading.

THE appointment was that I should meet my elderly uncle at the river-side, precisely at nine in the morning. The skiff was to be ready, and the apparatus to be brought down by his grizzled old black man. As yet, the nature of the wonderful experiment remained a mystery to all but the projector.

I was first on the spot. The village was high up the river, and the inland summer sun was already oppressively warm. Presently I saw my uncle advancing beneath the trees, hat off, and wiping his brow; while far behind staggered poor old Yorpy, with what seemed one of the gates of Gaza on his back.

"Come, hurrah, stump along, Yorpy!" cried my uncle, impatiently turning round every now and then.

Upon the black's staggering up to the skiff, I perceived that the great gate of Gaza was transformed into a huge, shabby, oblong box, hermetically sealed. The sphinx-like blankness of the box quadrupled the mystery in my mind.

"Is *this* the wonderful apparatus?" said I, in amazement.

"Why, it's nothing but a battered old dry-goods box, nailed up. And is *this* the thing, uncle, that is to make you a million of dollars ere the year be out? What a forlorn-looking, lack-lustre, old ash-box it is."

"Put it into the skiff!" roared my uncle to Yorpy, without heeding my boyish disdain. "Put it in, you grizzle-headed cherub—put it in carefully, carefully! If the box bursts, my everlasting fortune collapses."

"Bursts?—collapses?" cried I, in alarm. "It ain't full of combustibles? Quick! let me go to the further end of the boat!"

"Sit still, you simpleton!" cried my uncle again. "Jump in, Yorpy, and hold on to the box like grim death while I shove off. Carefully! carefully! you dunderheaded black! Mind t'other side of the box, I say! Do you mean to destroy the box?"

"Duyvel take de pox!" muttered old Yorpy, who was a sort of Dutch African. "De pox has been my cuss for de ten long 'ear."

"Now, then, we're off—take an oar, youngster; you, Yorpy, clinch the box fast. Here we go now. Carefully! carefully! You, Yorpy, stop shaking the box! Easy! easy! there's a big snag. Pull now. Hurrah! deep water at last! Now give way, youngster, and away to the island."

"The island!" said I. "There's no island hereabouts."

"There is ten miles above the bridge, though," said my uncle, determinately.

"Ten miles off! Pull that old dry-goods box ten miles up the river in this blazing sun!"

"All that I have to say," said my uncle, firmly, "is that we are bound to Quash Island."

"Mercy, uncle! If I had known of this great long pull of ten mortal miles in this fiery sun, you wouldn't have juggled *me* into the skiff so easy. What's *in* that box?—paving-stones? See how the skiff settles down under it. I won't help pull a box of paving-stones ten miles. What's the use of pulling 'em?"

"Look you, simpleton," quoth my uncle, pausing upon his suspended oar. "Stop rowing, will ye! Now then, if you don't want to share in the glory of my experiment; if you are wholly indifferent to halving its immortal renown; I say, sir, if you care not to be present at the first trial of my Great Hydraulic-Hydrostatic Apparatus for draining swamps and marshes, and converting them, at the rate of one acre the hour, into fields more fertile than those of the Genessee; if you care not, I repeat, to have this proud thing to tell—in far future days, when poor old I shall have been long dead and gone, boy—to your children, and your children's children; in that case, sir, you are free to land forthwith."

"Oh, uncle! I did not mean—"

"No words, sir! Yorpy, take his oar, and help pull him ashore."

"But, my dear uncle; I declare to you that—"

"Not a syllable, sir; you have cast open scorn upon the Great Hydraulic-Hydrostatic Apparatus. Yorpy, put him ashore, Yorpy. It's shallow here again. Jump out, Yorpy, and wade with him ashore."

"Now, my dear, good, kind uncle, do but pardon me this one time, and I will say just nothing about the apparatus."

"Say nothing about it! When it is my express end and aim it shall be famous! Put him ashore, Yorpy."

"Nay, uncle, I *will* not give up my oar. I have an oar in this matter, and I mean to keep it. You shall not cheat me out of my share of your glory."

"Ah, now there—that's sensible. You may stay, youngster. Pull again now."

We were all silent for a time, steadily plying our way. At last I ventured to break water once more.

"I am glad, dear uncle, you have revealed to me at last the nature and end of your great experiment. It is the effectual draining of swamps; an attempt, dear uncle, in which, if you do but succeed (as I know you will), you will earn the glory denied to a Roman emperor. He tried to drain the Pontine marsh, but failed."

"The world has shot ahead the length of its own diameter since then," quoth my uncle, proudly. "If that Roman emperor were here, I'd show him what can be done in the present enlightened age."

Seeing my good uncle so far mollified now as to be quite self-complacent, I ventured another remark.

"This is a rather severe, hot pull, dear uncle."

"Glory is not to be gained, youngster, without pulling hard for it—against the stream, too, as we do now. The natural tendency of man, in the mass, is to go down with the universal current into oblivion."

"But why pull so far, dear uncle, upon the present occasion? Why pull ten miles for it? You do but propose, as I understand it, to put to the actual test this admirable invention of yours. And could it not be tested almost anywhere?"

"Simple boy," quoth my uncle, "would you have some malignant spy steal from me the fruits of ten long years of high-hearted, persevering endeavor? Solitary in my scheme, I go to a solitary place to test it. If I fail—for all things are possible—no one out of the family will know it. If I succeed, secure in the secrecy of my invention, I can boldly demand any price for its publication."

"Pardon me, dear uncle; you are wiser than I."

"One would think years and gray hairs should bring wisdom, boy."

"Yorpy there, dear uncle; think you his grizzled locks thatch a brain improved by long life?"

"Am I Yorpy, boy? Keep to your oar!"

Thus padlocked again, I said no further word till the skiff grounded on the shallows, some twenty yards from the deep-wooded isle.

"Hush!" whispered my uncle, intensely; "not a word now!" and he sat perfectly still, slowly sweeping with his glance the whole country around, even to both banks of the here wide-expanded stream.

"Wait till that horseman, yonder, passes!" he whispered again, pointing to a speck moving along a lofty river-side road, which perilously wound on midway up a long line of broken bluffs and cliffs. "There—he's out of sight now, behind the copse. Quick! Yorpy! Carefully, though! Jump overboard, and shoulder the box, and—Hold!"

We were all mute and motionless again.

"Ain't that a boy, sitting like Zacchæus in yonder tree of the orchard on the other bank? Look, youngster—young eyes are better than old—don't you see him?"

"Dear uncle, I see the orchard, but I can't see any boy."

"He's a spy—I know he is," suddenly said my uncle, disregardful of my answer, and intently gazing, shading his eyes with his flattened hand. "Don't touch the box, Yorpy. Crouch! crouch down, all of ye!"

"Why, uncle—there—see—the boy is only a withered white bough. I see it very plainly now."

"You don't see the tree I mean," quoth my uncle, with a decided air of relief, "but never mind; I defy the boy. Yorpy, jump out, and shoulder the box. And now then, youngster, off with your shoes and stockings, roll up your trowsers legs, and follow me. Carefully, Yorpy, carefully. That's more precious than a box of gold, mind."

"Heavy as de gelt, anyhow," growled Yorpy, staggering and splashing in the shallows beneath it.

"There, stop under the bushes there—in among the flags —so—gently, gently—there, put it down just there. Now, youngster, are you ready? Follow—tiptoes, tiptoes!"

"I can't wade in this mud and water on my tiptoes, uncle; and I don't see the need of it either."

"Go ashore, sir—instantly!"

"Why, uncle, I *am* ashore."

"Peace! follow me, and no more."

Crouching in the water in complete secrecy, beneath the bushes and among the tall flags, my uncle now stealthily produced a hammer and wrench from one of his enormous pockets, and presently tapped the box. But the sound alarmed him.

"Yorpy," he whispered, "go you off to the right, behind the bushes, and keep watch. If you see anyone coming, whistle softly. Youngster, you do the same to the left."

We obeyed; and presently, after considerable hammering and supplemental tinkering, my uncle's voice was heard in the utter solitude, loudly commanding our return.

Again we obeyed, and now found the cover of the box removed. All eagerness, I peeped in, and saw a surprising multiplicity of convoluted metal pipes and syringes of all sorts and varieties, all sizes and calibres, inextricably inter-wreathed together in one gigantic coil. It looked like a huge nest of anacondas and adders.

"Now then, Yorpy," said my uncle, all animation, and flushed with the foretaste of glory, "do you stand this side, and be ready to tip when I give the word. And do you, youngster, stand ready to do as much for the other side. Mind, don't budge it the fraction of a barley-corn till I say the word. All depends on a proper adjustment."

"No fear, uncle. I will be careful as a lady's tweezers."

"I s'ant lift de heavy pox," growled old Yorpy, "till de wort pe given; no fear o' dat."

"Oh boy," said my uncle now, upturning his face devotionally, while a really noble gleam irradiated his gray eyes, locks, and wrinkles; "oh boy! this, *this* is the hour which for ten long years has, in the prospect, sustained me through all my painstaking obscurity. Fame will be the sweeter because it comes at the last; the truer, because it comes to an old man like me, not to a boy like you. Sustainer! I glorify Thee."

He bowed over his venerable head, and—as I live—something like a shower-drop somehow fell from my face into the shallows.

"Tip!"

We tipped.

"A little more!"

We tipped a little more.

"A *leetle* more!"

We tipped a *leetle* more.

"Just a *leetle*, very *leetle* bit more."

With great difficulty we tipped just a *leetle*, very *leetle* more.

All this time my uncle was diligently stooping over, and striving to peep in, up, and under the box where the coiled anacondas and adders lay; but the machine being now fairly immersed, the attempt was wholly vain.

He rose erect, and waded slowly all round the box; his countenance firm and reliant, but not a little troubled and vexed.

It was plain something or other was going wrong. But as I was left in utter ignorance as to the mystery of the contrivance, I could not tell where the difficulty lay, or what was the proper remedy.

Once more, still more slowly, still more vexedly, my uncle waded round the box, the dissatisfaction gradually deepening, but still controlled, and still with hope at the bottom of it.

Nothing could be more sure than that some anticipated effect had, as yet, failed to develop itself. Certain I was, too, that the waterline did not lower about my legs.

"Tip it a *leetle* bit—very *leetle* now."

"Dear uncle, it is tipped already as far as it can be. Don't you see it rests now square on its bottom?"

"You, Yorpy, take your black hoof from under the box!"

This gust of passion on the part of my uncle made the matter seem still more dubious and dark. It was a bad symptom, I thought.

"Surely you *can* tip it just a *leetle* more!"

"Not a hair, uncle."

"Blast and blister the cursed box, then!" roared my uncle, in a terrific voice, sudden as a squall. Running at the box, he dashed his bare foot into it, and with astonishing power all but crushed in the side. Then, seizing the whole box, he disemboweled it of all its anacondas and adders, and, tearing and wrenching them, flung them right and left over the water.

"Hold, hold, my dear, dear uncle!—do, for Heaven's sake, desist. Don't destroy so, in one frantic moment, all your long calm years of devotion to one darling scheme. Hold, I conjure!"

Moved by my vehement voice and uncontrollable tears, he paused in his work of destruction, and stood steadfastly eying me, or rather blankly staring at me, like one demented.

"It is not yet wholly ruined, dear uncle; come put it together now. You have hammer and wrench; put it together again, and try it once more. While there is life there is hope."

"While there is life hereafter there is *despair*," he howled.

"Do, do now, dear uncle—here, here, put these pieces together; or, if that can't be done without more tools, try a *section* of it—that will do just as well. Try it once; try, uncle."

My persistent persuasiveness told upon him. The stubborn stump of hope, plowed at and uprooted in vain, put forth one last miraculous green sprout.

Steadily and carefully culling out of the wreck some of the more curious-looking fragments, he mysteriously involved them together, and then, clearing out the box, slowly inserted them there, and ranging Yorpy and me as before, bade us tip the box once again.

We did so; and as no perceptible effect yet followed, I was each moment looking for the previous command to tip the box over yet more, when, glancing into my uncle's face, I started aghast. It seemed pinched, shriveled into mouldy whiteness, like a mildewed grape. I dropped the box, and sprang toward him just in time to prevent his fall.

Leaving the woeful box where we had dropped it, Yorpy and I helped the old man into the skiff, and silently pulled from Quash Isle.

How swiftly the current now swept us down! How hardly before had we striven to stem it! I thought of my poor uncle's saying, not an hour gone by, about the universal drift of the mass of humanity toward utter oblivion.

"Boy!" said my uncle at last, lifting his head.

I looked at him earnestly, and was gladdened to see that the terrible blight of his face had almost departed.

"Boy, there's not much left in an old world for an old man to invent."

I said nothing.

"Boy, take my advice, and never try to invent anything but —happiness."

I said nothing.

"Boy, about ship, and pull back for the box."

"Dear uncle!"

"It will make a good wood-box, boy. And faithful old Yorpy can sell the old iron for tobacco-money."

"Dear massa! dear old massa! dat be very fust time in de ten long 'ear yoo hab mention kindly old Yorpy. I tank yoo, dear old massa; I tank yoo so kindly. Yoo is yourself again in de ten long 'ear."

"Aye, long ears enought," sighed my uncle; "Æsopian ears. But it's all over now. Boy, I'm glad I've failed. I say, boy, failure has made a good old man of me. It was horrible at first, but I'm glad I've failed. Praise be to God for the failure!"

His face kindled with a strange, rapt earnestness. I have never forgotten that look. If the event made my uncle a good old man, as he called it, it made me a wise young one. Example did for me the work of experience.

When some years had gone by, and my dear old uncle began to fail, and, after peaceful days of autumnal content, was gathered gently to his fathers—faithful old Yorpy closing his eyes—as I took my last look at his venerable face, the pale resigned lips seemed to move. I seemed to hear again his deep, fervent cry—"Praise be to God for the failure!"

THE LIGHTNING-ROD MAN

NOTE: It has been stated as a matter hardly worth discussion that this story's "whole interest lies below the surface"; and the projection of the narrator as an eccentric semi-hermit trying to live at peace in a naturally unstable world but beleaguered in the sanctuary of his own house by fools and villains is frequent enough in Melville's work of the mid-1850's to justify, again, an autobiographical (or testamentary, or psychoanalytical) interpretation. "The Lightning-Rod Man" (*Putnam's*, August, 1854) is also what a single reading makes transparently clear: a straightforward light satire against the new breed of huckstering salvation-salesmen spawned by the breakup of the old religious consensus, and more generally against all those who would make their living by preying on the natural fears of others.

Like so many of Melville's sympathetic characters the narrator here has the agreeable weakness, under pressure, of getting caught up in sudden "involuntary" responses. Like Dickens, Melville was a master of the comedy of involuntary gesture.

WHAT grand irregular thunder, thought I, standing on my hearth-stone among the Acroceraunian hills, as the scattered bolts boomed overhead, and crashed down among the valleys, every bolt followed by zigzag irradiations, and swift slants of sharp rain, which audibly rang, like a charge of spear-points, on my low shingled roof. I suppose, though, that the mountains hereabouts break and churn up the thunder, so that it is far more glorious here than on the plain. Hark!—some one at the door. Who is this that chooses a time of thunder for making calls? And why don't he, man-fashion, use the knocker, instead of making that doleful undertaker's clatter with his fist against the hollow panel? But let him in. Ah, here he comes. "Good day, sir:" an entire stranger. "Pray be seated." What is that strange-looking walking-stick he carries: "A fine thunderstorm, sir."

"Fine?—Awful!"

"You are wet. Stand here on the hearth before the fire."

"Not for worlds!"

The stranger still stood in the exact middle of the cottage, where he had first planted himself. His singularity impelled a closer scrutiny. A lean, gloomy figure. Hair dark and lank, mattedly streaked over his brow. His sunken pitfalls of eyes were ringed by indigo halos, and played with an innocuous sort of lightning: the gleam without the bolt. The whole man was dripping. He stood in a puddle on the bare oak floor: his strange walking-stick vertically resting at his side.

It was a polished copper rod, four feet long, lengthwise attached to a neat wooden staff, by insertion into two balls of greenish glass, ringed with copper bands. The metal rod terminated at the top tripodwise, in three keen tines, brightly gilt. He held the thing by the wooden part alone.

"Sir," said I, bowing politely, "have I the honor of a visit from that illustrious god, Jupiter Tonans? So stood he in the Greek statue of old, grasping the lightning-bolt. If you be he, or his viceroy, I have to thank you for this noble storm you have brewed among our mountains. Listen: that was a glorious peal. Ah, to a lover of the majestic, it is a good thing to have the Thunderer himself in one's cottage. The thunder grows finer for that. But pray be seated. This old rush-bottomed arm-chair, I grant, is a poor substitute for your evergreen throne on Olympus; but, condescend to be seated."

While I thus pleasantly spoke, the stranger eyed me, half in wonder, and half in a strange sort of horror; but did not move a foot.

"Do, sir, be seated; you need to be dried ere going forth again."

I planted the chair invitingly on the broad hearth, where a little fire had been kindled that afternoon to dissipate the dampness, not the cold; for it was early in the month of September.

But without heeding my solicitation, and still standing in the middle of the floor, the stranger gazed at me portentously and spoke.

"Sir," said he, "excuse me; but instead of my accepting your invitation to be seated on the hearth there, I solemnly warn *you*, that you had best accept *mine*, and stand with me in the middle of the room. Good Heavens!" he cried, starting—"there is another of those awful crashes. I warn you, sir, quit the hearth."

"Mr. Jupiter Tonans," said I, quietly rolling my body on the stone, "I stand very well here."

"Are you so horridly ignorant, then," he cried, "as not to know, that by far the most dangerous part of a house, during such a terrific tempest as this, is the fire-place?"

"Nay, I did not know that," involuntarily stepping upon the first board next to the stone.

The stranger now assumed such an unpleasant air of successful admonition, that—quite involuntarily again—I stepped back upon the hearth, and threw myself into the erectest, proudest posture I could command. But I said nothing.

"For Heaven's sake," he cried, with a strange mixture of alarm and intimidation—"for Heaven's sake, get off the hearth! Know you not, that the heated air and soot are conductors;—to say nothing of those immense iron fire-dogs? Quit the spot—I conjure—I command you."

"Mr. Jupiter Tonans, I am not accustomed to be commanded in my own house."

"Call me not by that pagan name. You are profane in this time of terror."

"Sir, will you be so good as to tell me your business? If you seek shelter from the storm, you are welcome, so long as you be civil; but if you come on business, open it forthwith. Who are you?"

"I am a dealer in lightning-rods," said the stranger, softening his tone; "my special business is—Merciful Heaven! what a crash!—Have you ever been struck—your premises, I mean? No? It's best to be provided,"—significantly rattling his metallic staff on the floor,—"by nature, there are no castles in thunderstorms; yet, say but the word, and of this cottage I can make a Gibraltar by a few waves of this wand. Hark, what Himalayas of concussions!"

"You interrupted yourself; your special business you were about to speak of."

"My special business is to travel the country for orders for lightning-rods. This is my specimen rod;" tapping his staff; "I have the best of references"—fumbling in his pockets. "In Criggan last month, I put up three-and-twenty rods on only five buildings."

"Let me see. Was it not at Criggan last week, about midnight on Saturday, that the steeple, the big elm, and the assembly-room cupola were struck? Any of your rods there?"

"Not on the tree and cupola, but the steeple."

"Of what use is your rod, then?"

"Of life-and-death use. But my workman was heedless. In fitting the rod at top to the steeple, he allowed a part of the metal to graze the tin sheeting. Hence the accident. Not my fault, but his. Hark!"

"Never mind. That clap burst quite loud enough to be heard without finger-pointing. Did you hear of the event at Montreal last year? A servant girl struck at her bed-side with a rosary in her hand; the beads being metal. Does your beat extend into the Canadas?"

"No. And I hear that there, iron rods only are in use. They should have *mine,* which are copper. Iron is easily fused. Then they draw out the rod so slender, that it has not body enough to conduct the full electric current. The metal melts; the building is destroyed. My copper rods never act so. Those Canadians are fools. Some of them knob the rod at the top, which risks a deadly explosion, instead of imperceptibly carrying down the current into the earth, as this sort of rod does. *Mine* is the only true rod. Look at it. Only one dollar a foot."

"This abuse of your own calling in another might make one distrustful with respect to yourself."

"Hark! The thunder becomes less muttering. It is nearing us, and nearing the earth, too. Hark! One crammed crash! All the vibrations made one by nearness. Another flash. Hold."

"What do you?" I said, seeing him now instantaneously relinquishing his staff, lean intently forward towards the window, with his right fore and middle fingers on his left wrist.

But ere the words had well escaped me, another exclamation escaped him.

"Crash! only three pulses—less than a third of a mile off —yonder, somewhere in that wood. I passed three stricken oaks there, ripped out new and glittering. The oak draws lightning more than other timber, having iron in solution in its sap. Your floor here seems oak."

"Heart-of-oak. From the peculiar time of your call upon me, I suppose you purposely select stormy weather for your journeys. When the thunder is roaring, you deem it an hour peculiarly favorable for producing impressions favorable to your trade."

"Hark!—Awful!"

"For one who would arm others with fearlessness, you seem

unbeseemingly timorous yourself. Common men choose fair weather for their travels you choose thunder-storms; and yet———"

"That I travel in thunder-storms, I grant; but not without particular precautions, such as only a lightning-rod man may know. Hark! Quick—look at my specimen rod. Only one dollar a foot."

"A very fine rod, I dare say. But what are these particular precautions of yours? Yet first let me close yonder shutters; the slanting rain is beating through the sash. I will bar up."

"Are you mad? Know you not that yon iron bar is a swift conductor? Desist."

"I will simply close the shutters, then, and call my boy to bring me a wooden bar. Pray, touch the bell-pull there."

"Are you frantic? That bell-wire might blast you. Never touch bell-wire in a thunder-storm, nor ring a bell of any sort."

"Nor those in belfries? Pray, will you tell me where and how one may be safe in a time like this? Is there any part of my house I may touch with hopes of my life?"

"There is; but not where you now stand. Come away from the wall. The current will sometimes run down a wall, and— a man being a better conductor than a wall—it would leave the wall and run into him. Swoop! *That* must have fallen very nigh. That must have been globular lightning."

"Very probably. Tell me at once, which is, in your opinion, the safest part of this house?"

"This room, and this one spot in it where I stand. Come hither."

"The reasons first."

"Hark!—after the flash the gust—the sashes shiver—the house, the house!—Come hither to me!"

"The reasons, if you please."

"Come hither to me!"

"Thank you again, I think I will try my old stand—the hearth. And now, Mr. Lightning-rod man, in the pauses of the thunder, be so good as to tell me your reasons for esteeming this one room of the house the safest, and your own one stand-point there the safest spot in it."

There was now a little cessation of the storm for a while. The Lightning-rod man seemed relieved, and replied:—

"Your house is a one-storied house, with an attic and a cellar; this, room is between. Hence its comparative safety. Because lightning sometimes passes from the clouds to the earth,

and sometimes from the earth to the clouds. Do you comprehend?—and I choose the middle of the room, because, if the
lightning should strike the house at all, it would come down
the chimney or walls; so, obviously, the further you are from
them, the better. Come hither to me, now."

"Presently. Something you just said, instead of alarming
me, has strangely inspired confidence."

"What have I said?"

"You said that sometimes lightning flashes from the earth
to the clouds."

"Aye, the returning-stroke, as it is called; when the earth,
being overcharged with the fluid, flashes its surplus upward."

"The returning-stroke; that is, from earth to sky. Better
and better. But come here on the hearth and dry yourself."

"I am better here, and better wet."

"How?"

"It is the safest thing you can do—Hark, again!—to get
yourself thoroughly drenched in a thunder-storm. Wet clothes
are better conductors than the body; and so, if the lightning
strike, it might pass down the wet clothes without touching
the body. The storm deepens again. Have you a rug in the
house? Rugs are non-conductors. Get one, that I may stand on
it here, and you, too. The skies blacken—it is dusk at noon.
Hark!—the rug, the rug!"

I gave him one; while the hooded mountains seemed closing and tumbling into the cottage.

"And now, since our being dumb will not help us," said I,
resuming my place, "let me hear your precautions in traveling during thunder-storms."

"Wait till this one is passed."

"Nay, proceed with the precautions. You stand in the safest
possible place according to your own account. Go on."

"Briefly, then. I avoid pine-trees, high houses, lonely barns,
upland pastures, running water, flocks of cattle and sheep, a
crowd of men. If I travel on foot—as to-day—I do not walk
fast; if in my buggy, I touch not its back or sides; if on horse-
back, I dismount and lead the horse. But of all things, I avoid
tall men."

"Do I dream? Man avoid man? and in danger-time, too."

"Tall men in a thunder-storm I avoid. Are you so grossly
ignorant as not to know, that the height of a six-footer is
sufficient to discharge an electric cloud upon him? Are not
lonely Kentuckians, ploughing, smit in the unfinished fur-

row? Nay, if the six-footer stand by running water, the cloud will sometimes *select* him as its conductor to that running water. Hark! Sure, yon black pinnacle is split. Yes, a man is a good conductor. The lightning goes through and through a man, but only peels a tree. But sir, you have kept me so long answering your questions, that I have not yet come to business. Will you order one of my rods? Look at this specimen one? See: it is of the best of copper. Copper's the best conductor. Your house is low; but being upon the mountains, that lowness does not one whit depress it. You mountaineers are most exposed. In mountainous countries the lightning-rod man should have most business. Look at the specimen, sir. One rod will answer for a house so small as this. Look over these recommendations. Only one rod, sir; cost, only twenty dollars. Hark! There go all the granite Taconics and Hoosics dashed together like pebbles. By the sound, that must have struck something. An elevation of five feet above the house, will protect twenty feet radius all about the rod. Only twenty dollars, sir—a dollar a foot. Hark!—Dreadful!—Will you order? Will you buy? Shall I put down your name? Think of being a heap of charred offal, like a haltered horse burnt in his stall; and all in one flash!"

"You pretended envoy extraordinary and minister plenipotentiary to and from Jupiter Tonans," laughed I; "you mere man who come here to put you and your pipestem between clay and sky, do you think that because you can strike a bit of green light from the Leyden jar, that you can thoroughly avert the supernal bolt? Your rod rusts, or breaks, and where are you? Who has empowered you, you Tetzel, to peddle round your indulgences from divine ordinations? The hairs of our heads are numbered, and the days of our lives. In thunder as in sunshine, I stand at ease in the hands of my God. False negotiator, away! See, the scroll of the storm is rolled back; the house is unharmed; and in the blue heavens I read in the rainbow, that the Deity will not, of purpose, make war on man's earth."

"Impious wretch!" foamed the stranger, blackening in the face as the rainbow beamed, "I will publish your infidel notions."

"Begone! move quickly! if quickly you can, you that shine forth into sight in moist times like the worm."

The scowl grew blacker on his face; the indigo-circles enlarged round his eyes as the storm-rings round the midnight moon. He sprang upon me, his tri-forked thing at my heart.

I seized it; I snapped it; I dashed it; I trod it; and dragging the dark lightning-king out of my door, flung his elbowed, copper sceptre after him.

But spite of my treatment, and spite of my dissuasive talk of him to my neighbors, the Lightning-rod man still dwells in the land; still travels in storm-time, and drives a brave trade with the fears of man.

THE FIDDLER

NOTE: Autobiographical reference is, once more, unavoidable with this sketch of an artistic prodigy vanished into anonymity after a brilliant short career and enduring his long obscure after-existence in a kind of subdued serenity, acknowledging "facts" however painful or discouraging but reserving judgment as to their ultimate meaning. "The Fiddler" was carried by *Harper's* in September, 1854.

So MY poem is damned, and immortal fame is not for me! I am nobody forever and ever. Intolerable fate!

Snatching my hat, I dashed down the criticism, and rushed out into Broadway, where enthusiastic throngs were crowding to a circus in a side-street near by, very recently started, and famous for a capital clown.

Presently my old friend Standard rather boisterously accosted me.

"Well met, Helmstone, my boy! Ah! what's the matter? Haven't been committing murder? Ain't flying justice? You look wild!"

"You have seen it, then?" said I, of course referring to the criticism.

"Oh yes; I was there at the morning performance. Great clown, I assure you. But here comes Hautboy. Hautboy—Helmstone."

Without having time or inclination to resent so mortifying a mistake, I was instantly soothed as I gazed on the face of the new acquaintance so unceremoniously introduced. His person was short and full, with a juvenile, animated cast to it. His complexion rurally ruddy; his eye sincere, cheery, and gray. His hair alone betrayed that he was not an overgrown boy. From his hair I set him down as forty or more.

"Come, Standard," he gleefully cried to my friend, "are you not going to the circus? The clown is inimitable, they say. Come; Mr. Helmstone, too—come both; and circus over, we'll take a nice stew and punch at Taylor's."

The sterling content, good humor, and extraordinary ruddy, sincere expression of this most singular new acquaintance acted upon me like magic. It seemed mere loyalty to human nature to accept an invitation from so unmistakably kind and honest a heart.

During the circus performance I kept my eye more on Hautboy than on the celebrated clown. Hautboy was the sight for me. Such genuine enjoyment as his struck me to the soul with a sense of the reality of the thing called happiness. The jokes of the clown he seemed to roll under his tongue as ripe magnum bonums. Now the foot, now the hand, was employed to attest his grateful applause. At any hit more than ordinary, he turned upon Standard and me to see if his rare pleasure was shared. In a man of forty I saw a boy of twelve; and this too without the slightest abatement of my respect. Because all was so honest and natural, every expression and attitude so graceful with genuine good-nature, that the marvelous juvenility of Hautboy assumed a sort of divine and immortal air, like that of some forever youthful god of Greece.

But much as I gazed upon Hautboy, and much as I admired his air, yet that desperate mood in which I had first rushed from the house had not so entirely departed as not to molest me with momentary returns. But from these relapses I would rouse myself, and swiftly glance round the broad amphitheatre of eagerly interested and all-applauding human faces. Hark! claps, thumps, deafening huzzas; the vast assembly seemed frantic with acclamation; and what, mused I, has caused all this? Why, the clown only comically grinned with one of his extra grins.

Then I repeated in my mind that sublime passage in my poem, in which Cleothemes the Argive vindicates the justice of the war. Aye, aye, thought I to myself, did I now leap into the ring there, and repeat that identical passage, nay, enact the whole tragic poem before them, would they applaud the poet as they applaud the clown? No! They would hoot me, and call me doting or mad. Then what does this prove? Your infatuation or their insensibility? Perhaps both; but indubitably the first. But why wail? Do you seek admiration from the admirers of a buffoon? Call to mind the saying of the Athenian, who, when the people vociferously applauded in the forum, asked his friend in a whisper, what foolish thing had he said?

Again my eye swept the circus, and fell on the ruddy radiance of the countenance of Hautboy. But its clear honest cheeriness disdained my disdain. My intolerant pride was rebuked. And yet Hautboy dreamed not what magic reproof to a soul like mine sat on his laughing brow. At the very instant I felt the dart of the censure, his eye twinkled, his hand waved, his voice was lifted in jubilant delight at another joke of the inexhaustible clown.

Circus over, we went to Taylor's. Among crowds of others, we sat down to our stews and punches at one of the small marble tables. Hautboy sat opposite to me. Though greatly subdued from its former hilarity, his face still shone with gladness. But added to this was a quality not so prominent before: a certain serene expression of leisurely, deep good sense. Good sense and good humor in him joined hands. As the conversation proceeded between the brisk Standard and him—for I said little or nothing—I was more and more struck with the excellent judgment he evinced. In most of his remarks upon a variety of topics Hautboy seemed intuitively to hit the exact line between enthusiasm and apathy. It was plain that while Hautboy saw the world pretty much as it was, yet he did not theoretically espouse its bright side nor its dark side. Rejecting all solutions, he but acknowledged facts. What was sad in the world he did not superficially gainsay; what was glad in it he did not cynically slur; and all which was to him personally enjoyable, he gratefully took to his heart. It was plain, then—so it seemed at that moment, at least—that his extraordinary cheerfulness did not arise either from deficiency of feeling or thought.

Suddenly remembering an engagement, he took up his hat, bowed pleasantly, and left us.

"Well, Helmstone," said Standard, inaudibly drumming on the slab, "what do you think of your new acquaintance?"

The two last words tingled with a peculiar and novel significance.

"New acquaintance indeed," echoed I. "Standard, I owe you a thousand thanks for introducing me to one of the most singular men I have ever seen. It needed the optical sight of such a man to believe in the possibility of his existence."

"You rather like him, then," said Standard, with ironical dryness.

"I hugely love and admire him, Standard. I wish I were Hautboy."

"Ah? That's a pity, now. There's only one Hautboy in the world."

This last remark set me to pondering again, and somehow it revived my dark mood.

"His wonderful cheerfulness, I suppose," said I, sneering with spleen, "originates not less in a felicitous fortune than in a felicitous temper. His great good sense is apparent; but great good sense may exist without sublime endowments. Nay, I take it, in certain cases, that good sense is simply owing to the absence of those. Much more, cheerfulness. Unpossessed of genius, Hautboy is eternally blessed."

"Ah? You would not think him an extraordinary genuis, then?"

"Genius? What! such a short, fat fellow a genius! Genius, like Cassius, is lank."

"Ah? But could you not fancy that Hautboy might formerly have had genius, but luckily getting rid of it, at last fatted up?"

"For a genius to get rid of his genius is as impossible as for a man in the galloping consumption to get rid of that."

"Ah? You speak very decidedly."

"Yes, Standard," cried I, increasing in spleen, "your cheery Hautboy, after all, is no pattern, no lesson for you and me. With average abilities; opinions clear, because circumscribed; passions docile, because they are feeble; a temper hilarious, because he was born to it—how can your Hautboy be made a reasonable example to a handy fellow like you, or an ambitious dreamer like me? Nothing tempts him beyond common limit; in himself he has nothing to restrain. By constitution he is exempted from all moral harm. Could ambition but prick him; had he but once heard applause, or endured contempt, a very different man would your Hautboy be. Acquiescent and calm from the cradle to the grave, he obviously slides through the crowd."

"Ah?"

"Why do you say Ah to me so strangely whenever I speak?"

"Did you ever hear of Master Betty?"

"The great English prodigy, who long ago ousted the Siddons and the Kembles from Drury Lane, and made the whole town run mad with acclamation?"

"The same," said Standard, once more inaudibly drumming on the slab.

I looked at him perplexed. He seemed to be holding the master-key of our theme in mysterious reserve; seemed to be throwing out his Master Betty, too, to puzzle me only the more.

"What under heaven can Master Betty, the great genius and prodigy, an English boy twelve years old, have to do with the poor commonplace plodder, Hautboy, an American of forty?"

"Oh, nothing in the least. I don't imagine that they ever saw each other. Besides, Master Betty must be dead and buried long ere this."

"Then why cross the ocean, and rifle the grave to drag his remains into this living discussion?"

"Absent-mindedness, I suppose. I humbly beg pardon. Proceed with your observations on Hautboy. You think he never had genius, quite too contented, and happy and fat for that —ah? You think him no pattern for men in general? affording no lesson of value to neglected merit, genius ignored, or impotent presumption rebuked?—all of which three amount to much the same thing. You admire his cheerfulness, while scorning his commonplace soul. Poor Hautboy, how sad that your very cheerfulness should, by a by-blow, bring you despite!"

"I don't say I scorn him; you are unjust. I simply declare that he is no pattern for me."

A sudden noise at my side attracted my ear. Turning, I saw Hautboy again, who very blithely reseated himself on the chair he had left.

"I was behind time with my engagement," said Hautboy, "so thought I would run back and rejoin you. But come, you have sat long enough here. Let us go to my rooms. It is only a five minutes' walk."

"If you will promise to fiddle for us, we will," said Standard.

Fiddle! thought I—he's a jiggumbob *fiddler*, then? No wonder genius declines to measure its pace to a fiddler's bow. My spleen was very strong on me now.

"I will gladly fiddle you your fill," replied Hautboy to Standard. "Come on."

In a few minutes we found ourselves in the fifth story of a sort of storehouse, in a lateral street to Broadway. It was curiously furnished with all sorts of odd furniture which seemed to have been obtained, piece by piece, at auctions of old-fashioned household stuff. But all was charmingly clean and cozy.

Pressed by Standard, Hautboy forthwith got out his dented old fiddle and, sitting down on a tall rickety stool, played away right merrily at "Yankee Doodle" and other off-handed, dashing, and disdainfully care-free airs. But common as were the tunes, I was transfixed by something miraculously superior in the style. Sitting there on the old stool, his rusty hat sideways cocked on his head, one foot dangling adrift, he plied the bow of an enchanter. All my moody discontent, every vestige of peevishness, fled. My whole splenetic soul capitulated to the magical fiddle.

"Something of an Orpheus, ah?" said Standard, archly nudging me beneath the left rib.

"And I, the charmed Bruin," murmured I.

The fiddle ceased. Once more, with redoubled curiosity, I gazed upon the easy, indifferent Hautboy. But he entirely baffled inquisition.

When, leaving him, Standard and I were in the street once more, I earnestly conjured him to tell me who, in sober truth, this marvelous Hautboy was.

"Why, haven't you seen him? And didn't you yourself lay his whole anatomy open on the marble slab at Taylor's? What more can you possibly learn? Doubtless, your own masterly insight has already put you in possession of all."

"You mock me, Standard. There is some mystery here. Tell me, I entreat you, who is Hautboy?"

"An extraordinary genius, Helmstone," said Standard, with sudden ardor, "who in boyhood drained the whole flagon of glory; whose going from city to city was a going from triumph to triumph. One who has been an object of wonder to the wisest, been caressed by the loveliest, received the open homage of thousands on thousands of the rabble. But to-day he walks Broadway and no man knows him. With you and me, the elbow of the hurrying clerk, and the pole of the remorseless omnibus, shove him. He who has a hundred times been crowned with laurels, now wears, as you see, a bunged beaver. Once fortune poured showers of gold into his lap, as showers of laurel leaves upon his brow. To-day, from house to house he hies, teaching fiddling for a living. Crammed once with fame, he is now hilarious without it. *With* genius and *without* fame, he is happier than a king. More a prodigy now than ever."

"His true name?"

"Let me whisper it in your ear."

"What! Oh, Standard, myself, as a child, have shouted myself hoarse applauding that very name in the theatre."

"I have heard your poem was not very handsomely received," said Standard, now suddenly shifting the subject.

"Not a word of that, for Heaven's sake!" cried I. "If Cicero, traveling in the East, found sympathetic solace for his grief in beholding the arid overthrow of a once gorgeous city, shall not my petty affair be as nothing, when I behold in Hautboy the vine and the rose climbing the shattered shafts of his tumbled temple of Fame?"

Next day I tore all my manuscripts, bought me a fiddle, and went to take regular lessons of Hautboy.

THE PARADISE OF BACHELORS
AND THE TARTARUS OF MAIDS

NOTE: The first half of this double sketch (*Harper's*, April, 1855) is another by-product of Melville's London visit in 1849, and one of many stories (and poems, and narrative episodes) offering the bachelor's free and easy life as an image of earthly happiness. Paired with the more openly allegorical fantasia of the second part, in which the operations of a Berkshire Hills paper factory appear to represent the tyrannical machinery of sex and masculine domination, it seems something less—and more—than a piece of social commentary. The whole work, though casually organized, vibrates with imaginative obsession.

I

THE PARADISE OF BACHELORS

IT LIES not far from Temple Bar.

Going to it, by the usual way, is like stealing from a heated plain into some cool, deep glen, shady among harboring hills.

Sick with the din and soiled with the mud of Fleet Street —where the Benedick tradesmen are hurrying by, with ledger-lines ruled along their brows, thinking upon rise of bread and fall of babies—you adroitly turn a mystic corner—not a street—glide down a dim, monastic way, flanked by dark, sedate, and solemn piles, and still wending on, give the whole care-worn world the slip, and, disentangled, stand beneath the quiet cloisters of the Paradise of Bachelors.

Sweet are the oases in Sahara: charming the isle-groves of August prairies; delectable pure faith amidst a thousand perfidies; but sweeter, still more charming, most delectable, the dreamy Paradise of Bachelors, found in the stony heart of stunning London.

In mild meditation pace the cloisters; take your pleasure,

sip your leisure, in the garden waterward; go linger in the ancient library; go worship in the sculptured chapel; but little have you seen, just nothing do you know, not the sweet kernel have you tasted, till you dine among the banded Bachelors, and see their convivial eyes and glasses sparkle. Not dine in bustling commons, during term-time, in the hall; but tranquilly, by private hint, at a private table; some fine Templar's hospitably invited guest.

Templar? That's a romantic name. Let me see. Brian de Bois-Guilbert was a Templar, I believe. Do we understand you to insinuate that those famous Templars still survive in modern London? May the ring of their armed heels be heard, and the rattle of their shields, as in mailed prayer the monk-knights kneel before the consecrated Host? Surely a monk-knight were a curious sight picking his way along the Strand, his gleaming corselet and snowy surcoat spattered by an omnibus. Long-bearded, too, according to his order's rule; his face fuzzy as a pard's; how would the grim ghost look among the crop-haired, close-shaven citizens? We know indeed—sad history recounts it—that a moral blight tainted at last this sacred Brotherhood. Though no sworded foe might outskill them in the fence, yet the worm of luxury crawled beneath their guard, gnawing the core of knightly troth, nibbling the monastic vow, till at last the monk's austerity relaxed to wassailing, and the sworn knights-bachelors grew to be but hypocrites and rakes.

But for all this, quite unprepared were we to learn that Knights-Templars (if at all in being) were so entirely secularized as to be reduced from carving out immortal fame in glorious battling for the Holy Land, to the carving of roast-mutton at a dinner-board. Like Anacreon, do these degenerate Templars now think it sweeter far to fall in banquet than in war? Or, indeed, how can there be any survival of that famous order? Templars in modern London! Templars in their red-cross mantles smoking cigars at the Divan! Templars crowded in a railway train, till, stacked with steel helmet, spear, and shield, the whole train looks like one elongated locomotive!

No. The genuine Templar is long since departed. Go view the wondrous tombs in the Temple Church; see there the rigidly-haughty forms stretched out, with crossed arms upon their stilly hearts, in everlasting and undreaming rest. Like the years before the flood, the bold Knights-Templars are no more.

Nevertheless, the name remains, and the nominal society, and the ancient grounds, and some of the ancient edifices. But the iron heel is changed to a boot of patent-leather; the long two-handed sword to a one-handed quill; the monk-giver of gratuitous ghostly counsel now counsels for a fee; the defender of the sarcophagus (if in good practice with his weapon) now has more than one case to defend; the vowed opener and clearer of all highways leading to the Holy Sepulchre, now has it in particular charge to check, to clog, to hinder, and embarrass all the courts and avenues of Law; the knight-combatant of the Saracen, breasting spear-points at Acre, now fights law-points in Westminster Hall. The helmet is a wig. Struck by Time's enchanter's wand, the Templar is to-day a Lawyer.

But, like many others tumbled from proud glory's height —like the apple, hard on the bough but mellow on the ground —the Templar's fall has but made him all the finer fellow.

I dare say those old warrior-priests were but gruff and grouty at the best; cased in Birmingham hardware, how could their crimped arms give yours or mine a hearty shake? Their proud, ambitious, monkish souls clasped shut, like horn-book missals; their very faces clapped in bomb-shells; what sort of genial men were these? But best of comrades, most affable of hosts, capital diner is the modern Templar. His wit and wine are both of sparkling brands.

The church and cloisters, courts and vaults, lanes and passages, banquet-halls, refectories, libraries, terraces, gardens, broad walks, domiciles, and dessert-rooms, covering a very large space of ground, and all grouped in central neighborhood, and quite sequestered from the old city's surrounding din; and everything about the place being kept in most bachelor-like particularity, no part of London offers to a quiet wight so agreeable a refuge.

The Temple is, indeed, a city by itself. A city with all the best appurtenances, as the above enumeration shows. A city with a park to it, and flower-beds, and a riverside—the Thames flowing by as openly, in one part, as by Eden's primal garden flowed the mild Euphrates. In what is now the Temple Garden the old Crusaders used to exercise their steeds and lances; the modern Templars now lounge on the benches beneath the trees, and, switching their patent-leather boots, in gay discourse exercise at repartee.

Long lines of stately portraits in the banquet-halls, show what great men of mark—famous nobles, judges, and Lord

Chancellors—have in their time been Templars. But all Templars are not known to universal fame; though, if the having warm hearts and warmer welcomes, full minds and fuller cellars, and giving good advice and glorious dinners, spiced with rare divertisements of fun and fancy, merit immortal mention, set down, ye muses, the names of R. F. C. and his imperial brother.

Though to be a Templar, in the one true sense, you must needs be a lawyer, or a student at the law, and be ceremoniously enrolled as member of the order, yet as many such, though Templars, do not reside within the Temple's precincts, though they may have their offices there, just so, on the other hand, there are many residents of the hoary old domiciles who are not admitted Templars. If being, say, a lounging gentleman and bachelor, or a quiet, unmarried, literary man, charmed with the soft seclusion of the spot, you much desire to pitch your shady tent among the rest in this serene encampment, then you must make some special friend among the order, and procure him to rent, in his name but at your charge, whatever vacant chamber you may find to suit.

Thus, I suppose, did Dr. Johnson, that nominal Benedick and widower but virtual bachelor, when for a space he resided here. So, too, did that undoubted bachelor and rare good soul, Charles Lamb. And hundreds more, of sterling spirits, Brethren of the Order of Celibacy, from time to time have dined, and slept, and tabernacled here. Indeed, the place is all a honey-comb of offices and domiciles. Like any cheese, it is quite perforated through and through in all directions with the snug cells of bachelors. Dear, delightful spot! Ah! when I bethink me of the sweet hours there passed, enjoying such genial hospitalities beneath those time-honored roofs, my heart only finds due utterance through poetry; and, with a sigh, I softly sing, "Carry me back to old Virginny!"

Such then, at large, is the Paradise of Bachelors. And such I found it one pleasant afternoon in the smiling month of May, when, sallying from my hotel in Trafalgar Square, I went to keep my dinner-appointment with that fine Barrister, Bachelor, and Bencher, R. F. C. (he *is* the first and second, and *should be* the third; I hereby nominate him), whose card I kept fast pinched between my gloved forefinger and thumb, and every now and then snatched still another look at the pleasant address inscribed beneath the name, "No. ——, Elm Court, Temple."

At the core he was a right bluff, care-free, right comfortable, and most companionable Englishman. If on a first acquaintance he seemed reserved, quite icy in his air—patience; this Champagne will thaw. And if it never do, better frozen Champagne than liquid vinegar.

There were nine gentlemen, all bachelors, at the dinner. One was from "No. —, King's Beach Walk, Temple"; a second, third, and fourth, and fifth, from various courts or passages christened with some similarly rich resounding syllables. It was, indeed, a sort of Senate of the Bachelors, sent to this dinner from widely scattered districts, to represent the general celibacy of the Temple. Nay, it was, by representation, a Grand Parliament of the best Bachelors in universal London; several of those present being from distant quarters of the town, noted immemorial seats of lawyers and unmarried men—Lincoln's Inn, Furnival's Inn; and one gentleman, upon whom I looked with a sort of collateral awe, hailed from the spot where Lord Verulam once abode a bachelor—Gray's Inn.

The apartment was well up toward heaven. I know not how many strange old stairs I climbed to get to it. But a good dinner, with famous company, should be well earned. No doubt our host had his dining-room so high with a view to secure the prior exercise necessary to the due relishing and digesting of it.

The furniture was wonderfully unpretending, old, and snug. No new shining mahogany, sticky with undried varnish; no uncomfortably luxurious ottomans, and sofas too fine to use, vexed you in this sedate apartment. It is a thing which every sensible American should learn from every sensible Englishman, that glare and glitter, gim-cracks and gewgaws, are not indispensable to domestic solacement. The American Benedick snatches, down-town, a tough chop in a gilded show-box; the English bachelor leisurely dines at home on that incomparable South Down of his, off a plain deal board.

The ceiling of the room was low. Who wants to dine under the dome of St. Peter's? High ceilings! If that is your demand, and the higher the better, and you be so very tall, then go dine out with the topping giraffe in the open air.

In good time the nine gentlemen sat down to nine covers, and soon were fairly under way.

If I remember right, ox-tail soup inaugurated the affair. Of a rich russet hue, its agreeable flavor dissipated my first confounding of its main ingredient with teamsters' gads and the raw-hides of ushers. (By way of interlude, we here drank a little claret.) Neptune's was the next tribute rendered—turbot coming second; snow-white, flaky, and just gelatinous enough, not too turtleish in its unctuousness.

(At this point we refreshed ourselves with a glass of sherry.) After these light skirmishers had vanished, the heavy artillery of the feast marched in, led by that well-known English generalissimo, roast beef. For aides-de-camp we had a saddle of mutton, a fat turkey, a chicken-pie, and endless other savory things; while for avant-couriers came nine silver flagons of humming ale.. This heavy ordnance having departed on the track of the light skirmishers, a picked brigade of game-fowl encamped upon the board, their camp-fires lit by the ruddiest of decanters.

Tarts and puddings followed, with innumerable niceties; then cheese and crackers. (By way of ceremony, simply, only to keep up good old fashions, we here each drank a glass of good old port.)

The cloth was now removed; and, like Blucher's army coming in at the death on the field of Waterloo, in marched a fresh detachment of bottles, dusty with their hurried march.

All these manœuvrings of the forces were superintended by a surprising old field-marshal (I can not school myself to call him by the inglorious name of waiter), with snowy hair and napkin, and a head like Socrates. Amidst all the hilarity of the feast, intent on important business, he disdained to smile. Venerable man!

I have above endeavored to give some slight schedule of the general plan of operations. But any one knows that a good, genial dinner is a sort of pell-mell, indiscriminate affair, quite baffling to detail in all particulars. Thus, I spoke of taking a glass of claret, and a glass of sherry, and a glass of port, and a mug of ale—all at certain specific periods and times. But those were merely the state bumpers, so to speak. Innumerable impromptu glasses were drained between the periods of those grand imposing ones.

The nine bachelors seemed to have the most tender concern for each other's health. All the time, in flowing wine, they most earnestly expressed their sincerest wishes for the entire well-being and lasting hygiene of the gentleman on the right and on the left. I noticed that when one of these kind bachelors desired a little more wine (just for his stomach's sake, like Timothy), he would not help himself to it unless some other bachelor would join him. It seemed held something indelicate, selfish, and unfraternal, to be seen taking a lonely, unparticipated glass. Meantime, as the wine ran apace, the spirits of the company grew more and more to perfect genialness and unconstraint. They related all sorts of pleasant stories. Choice experiences in their private lives were now brought out, like choice brands of Moselle or Rhenish, only kept for particular company. One told us how mellowly he lived when a student at Oxford; with various spicy anecdotes of most frank-hearted noble lords, his liberal companions. Another bachelor, a gray-headed man, with a sunny face, who, by his own account, embraced every opportunity of leisure to cross over into the Low Countries, on sudden tours of inspection of the fine old Flemish architecture there—this learned, white-haired, sunny-faced old bachelor excelled in his descriptions of the elaborate splendors of those old guild-halls, town-halls, and stadthold-houses, to be seen in the land of the ancient Flemings. A third was a great frequenter of the British Museum, and knew all about scores of wonderful antiquities, of Oriental manuscripts, and costly books without a duplicate. A fourth had lately returned from a trip to Old Granada, and, of course, was full of Saracenic scenery. A fifth had a funny case in law to tell. A sixth was erudite in wines. A seventh had a strange characteristic anecdote of the private life of the Iron Duke, never printed, and never before announced in any public or private company. An eighth had lately been amusing his evenings, now and then, with translating a comic poem of Pulci's. He quoted for us the more amusing passages.

And so the evening slipped along, the hours told, not by a water-clock, like King Alfred's, but a wine-chronometer. Meantime the table seemed a sort of Epsom Heath; a regular ring, where the decanters galloped round. For fear one decanter should not with sufficient speed reach his destination, another was sent express after him to hurry him; and then a third to hurry the second; and so on with a fourth and fifth. And throughout all this nothing loud, nothing unmannerly, nothing turbulent. I am quite sure, from the scrupulous gravity and austerity of his air, that had Socrates, the field-marshal, perceived aught of indecorum in the company he served, he would have forthwith departed without giving warning. I afterward learned that, during the repast, an invalid bachelor in an adjoining chamber enjoyed his first sound refreshing slumber in three long, weary weeks.

It was the very perfection of quiet absorption of good living, good drinking, good feeling, and good talk. We were a band of brothers. Comfort—fraternal, household comfort, was the grand trait of the affair. Also, you could plainly see that these easy-hearted men had no wives or children to give an anxious thought. Almost all of them were travelers, too; for bachelors alone can travel freely, and without any twinges of their consciences touching desertion of the fireside.

The thing called pain, the bugbear styled trouble—those two legends seemed preposterous to their bachelor imaginations. How could men of liberal sense, ripe scholarship in the world, and capacious philosophical and convivial understandings—how could they suffer themselves to be imposed upon by such monkish fables? Pain! Trouble! As well talk of Catholic miracles. No such thing.—Pass the sherry, sir.—Pooh, pooh! Can't be!—The port, sir, if you please. Nonsense; don't tell me so.—The decanter stops with you, sir, I believe.

And so it went.

Not long after the cloth was drawn our host glanced significantly upon Socrates, who, solemnly stepping to a stand, returned with an immense convolved horn, a regular Jericho horn, mounted with polished silver, and otherwise chased and curiously enriched; not omitting two life-like goats' heads, with four more horns of solid silver, projecting from opposite sides of the mouth of the noble main horn.

Not having heard that our host was a performer on the bugle, I was surprised to see him lift this horn from the table, as if he were about to blow an inspiring blast. But I was relieved from this, and set quite right as touching the purposes of the horn, by his now inserting his thumb and forefinger into its mouth; whereupon a slight aroma was stirred up, and my nostrils were greeted with the smell of some choice Rappee. It was a mull of snuff. It went the rounds. Capital idea this, thought I, of taking snuff about this juncture. This goodly fashion must be introduced among my countrymen at home, further ruminated I.

The remarkable decorum of the nine bachelors—a decorum not to be affected by any quantity of wine—a decorum unassailable by any degree of mirthfulness—this was again set in a forcible light to me, by now observing that, though they took snuff very freely, yet not a man so far violated the proprieties, or so far molested the invalid bachelor in the adjoining room as to indulge himself in a sneeze. The snuff was snuffed silently, as if it had been some fine innoxious powder brushed off the wings of butterflies.

But fine though they be, bachelors' dinners, like bachelors' lives, can not endure forever. The time came for breaking up. One by one the bachelors took their hats, and two by two, and arm-in-arm they descended, still conversing, to the flagging of the court; some going to their neighboring chambers to turn over the *Decameron* ere retiring for the night; some to smoke a cigar, promenading in the garden on the cool river-side; some to make for the street, call a hack, and be driven snugly to their distant lodgings.

I was the last lingerer.

"Well," said my smiling host, "what do you think of the Temple here, and the sort of life we bachelors make out to live in it?"

"Sir," said I, with a burst of admiring candor—"Sir, this is the very Paradise of Bachelors!"

II

THE TARTARUS OF MAIDS

It LIES not far from Woedolor Mountain in New England. Turning to the East, right out from among bright farms and sunny meadows, nodding in early June with odorous grasses, you enter ascendingly among bleak hills. These gradually close in upon a dusky pass, which, from the violent Gulf Stream of air unceasingly driving between its cloven walls of haggard rock, as well as from the tradition of a crazy spinster's hut having long ago stood somewhere hereabouts, is called the Mad Maid's Bellows-pipe.

Winding along at the bottom of the gorge is a dangerously narrow wheel-road, occupying the bed of a former torrent.

Following this road to its highest point, you stand as within a Dantean gateway. From the steepness of the walls here, their strangely ebon hue, and the sudden contraction of the gorge, this particular point is called the Black Notch. The ravine now expandingly descends into a great, purple, hopper-shaped hollow, far sunk among many Plutonian, shaggy-wooded mountains. By the country people this hollow is called the Devil's Dungeon. Sounds of torrents fall on all sides upon the ear. These rapid waters unite at last in one turbid brick-colored stream, boiling through a flume among enormous boulders. They call this strange-colored torrent Blood River. Gaining a dark precipice it wheels suddenly to the West, and makes one maniac spring of sixty feet into the arms of a stunted wood of gray-haired pines, between which it thence eddies on its further way down to the invisible low-lands.

Conspicuously crowning a rocky bluff high to one side, at the cataract's verge, is the ruin of an old saw-mill, built in those primitive times when vast pines and hemlocks superabounded throughout the neighboring region. The black-mossed bulk of those immense, rough-hewn, and spike-knotted logs, here and there tumbled all together, in long abandonment and decay, or left in solitary, perilous projection over the cataract's gloomy brink, impart to this rude wooden ruin not only much of the aspect of one of rough-quarried stone, but also a sort of feudal, Rhineland, and Thurmberg look, derived from the pinnacled wildness of the neighboring scenery.

Not far from the bottom of the Dungeon stands a large whitewashed building, relieved, like some great whited sepulchre, against the sullen background of mountain-side firs, and other hardy evergreens, inaccessibly rising in grim terraces for some two thousand feet.

The building is a paper-mill.

Having embarked on a large scale in the seedsman's business (so extensively and broadcast, indeed, that at length my seeds were distributed through all the Eastern and Northern States, and even fell into the far soil of Missouri and the Carolinas), the demand for paper at my place became so great, that the expenditure soon amounted to a most important item in the general account. It need hardly be hinted how paper comes into use with seedsmen, as envelopes. These are mostly made of yellowish paper, folded square; and when filled, are all but flat, and being stamped, and superscribed with the nature of the seeds contained, assume not a little the appearance of business-letters ready for the mail. Of these small envelopes I used an incredible quantity—several hundreds of thousands in a year. For a time I had purchased my paper from the wholesale dealers in a neighboring town. For economy's sake, and partly for the adventure of the trip, I now resolved to cross the mountains, some sixty miles, and order my future paper at the Devil's Dungeon paper-mill.

The sleighing being uncommonly fine toward the end of January, and promising to hold so for no small period, in spite of the bitter cold I started one gray Friday noon in my pung, well fitted with buffalo and wolf robes; and, spending one night on the road, next noon came in sight of Woedolor Mountain.

The far summit fairly smoked with frost; white vapors curled up from its white-wooded top, as from a chimney. The intense congelation made the whole country look like one petrifaction. The steel shoes of my pung craunched and gritted over the vitreous, chippy snow, as if it had been broken glass. The forests here and there skirting the route, feeling the same all-stiffening influence, their inmost fibres penetrated with the cold, strangely groaned—not in the swaying branches merely, but likewise in the vertical trunk—as the fitful gusts remorselessly swept through them. Brittle with excessive frost, many colossal tough-grained maples, snapped in twain like pipe-stems, cumbered the unfeeling earth.

Flaked all over with frozen sweat, white as a milky ram, his nostrils at each breath sending forth two horn-shaped shoots of heated respiration, Black, my good horse, but six years old, started at a sudden turn, where, right across the track—not ten minutes fallen—an old distorted hemlock lay, darkly undulatory as an anaconda.

Gaining the Bellows-pipe, the violent blast, dead from behind, all but shoved my high-backed pung up-hill. The gust shrieked through the shivered pass, as if laden with lost spirits bound to the unhappy world. Ere gaining the summit, Black, my horse, as if exasperated by the cutting wind, slung out with his strong hind legs, tore the light pung straight up-hill, and sweeping grazingly through the narrow notch, sped downward madly past the ruined saw-mill. Into the Devil's Dungeon horse and cataract rushed together.

With might and main, quitting my seat and robes, and standing backward, with one foot braced against the dashboard, I rasped and churned the bit, and stopped him just in time to avoid collision, at a turn, with the bleak nozzle of a rock, couchant like a lion in the way—a roadside rock.

At first I could not discover the paper-mill.

The whole hollow gleamed with the white, except, here and there, where a pinnacle of granite showed one wind-swept angle bare. The mountains stood pinned in shrouds—a pass of Alpine corpses. Where stands the mill? Suddenly a whirring, humming sound broke upon my ear. I looked, and there, like an arrested avalanche, lay the large whitewashed factory. It was subordinately surrounded by a cluster of other and smaller buildings, some of which, from their cheap, blank air, great length, gregarious windows, and comfortless expression, no doubt were boarding-houses of the operatives. A snow-white hamlet amidst the snows. Various rude, irregular squares and courts resulted from the somewhat picturesque clusterings of these buildings, owing to the broken, rocky nature of the ground, which forbade all method in their relative arrangement. Several narrow lanes and alleys, too, partly blocked with snow fallen from the roof, cut up the hamlet in all directions.

When, turning from the traveled highway, jingling with bells of numerous farmers—who, availing themselves of the fine sleighing, were dragging their wood to market—and frequently diversified with swift cutters dashing from inn to inn of the scattered villages—when, I say, turning from that bustling main-road, I by degrees wound into the Mad-Maid's Bellows-pipe, and saw the grim Black Notch beyond, then something latent, as well as something obvious in the time and scene, strangely brought back to my mind my first sight of dark and grimy Temple Bar. And when Black, my horse, went darting through the Notch, perilously grazing its rocky wall, I remembered being in a runaway London omnibus, which in much the same sort of style, though by no means at an equal rate, dashed through the ancient arch of Wren. Though the two objects did by no means completely correspond, yet this partial inadequacy but served to tinge the similitude not less with the vividness than the disorder of a dream. So that, when upon reining up at the protruding rock I at last caught sight of the quaint groupings of the factory-buildings, and with the traveled highway and the Notch behind, found myself all alone, silently and privily stealing through deep-cloven passages into this sequestered spot, and saw the long, high-gabled main factory edifice, with a rude tower—for hoisting heavy boxes—at one end, standing among its crowded outbuildings and boarding-houses, as the Temple Church amidst the surrounding offices and dormitories, and when the marvelous retirement of this mysterious mountain nook fastened its whole spell upon me, then, what memory lacked, all tributary imagination furnished, and I said to myself, "This is the very counterpart of the Paradise of Bachelors, but snowed upon, and frost-painted to a sepulchre."

Dismounting and warily picking my way down the dangerous declivity—horse and man both sliding now and then upon the icy ledges—at length I drove, or the blast drove me, into the largest square, before one side of the main edifice. Piercingly and shrilly the shotted blast blew by the corner; and redly and demoniacally boiled Blood River at one side. A long wood-pile, of many scores of cords, all glittering in mail of crusted ice, stood crosswise in the square. A row of horse-posts, their north sides plastered with adhesive snow, flanked the factory wall. The bleak frost packed and paved the square as with some ringing metal.

The inverted similitude recurred—"The sweet, tranquil Temple garden, with the Thames bordering its green beds," strangely meditated I.

But where are the gay bachelors?

Then, as I and my horse stood shivering in the wind-spray, a girl ran from a neighboring dormitory door, and throwing her thin apron over her bare head, made for the opposite building.

"One moment, my girl; is there no shed hereabouts which I may drive into?"

Pausing, she turned upon me a face pale with work, and blue with cold; an eye supernatural with unrelated misery. "Nay," faltered I, "I mistook you. Go on; I want nothing."

Leading my horse close to the door from which she had come, I knocked. Another pale, blue girl appeared, shivering in the doorway as, to prevent the blast, she jealously held the door ajar.

"Nay, I mistake again. In God's name shut the door. But hold, is there no man about?"

That moment a dark-complexioned, well-wrapped personage passed, making for the factory door, and spying him coming, the girl rapidly closed the other one.

"Is there no horse-shed here, sir?"

"Yonder, to the wood-shed," he replied, and disappeared inside the factory.

With much ado I managed to wedge in horse and pung between the scattered piles of wood all sawn and split. Then, blanketing my horse, and piling my buffalo on the blanket's top, and tucking in its edges well around the breast-band and breeching, so that the wind might not strip him bare, I tied him fast, and ran lamely for the factory door, stiff with frost, and cumbered with my driver's dread-naught.

Immediately I found myself standing in a spacious place, intolerably lighted by long rows of windows, focusing inward the snowy scene without.

At rows of blank-looking counters sat rows of blank-looking girls, with blank, white folders in their blank hands, all blankly folding blank paper.

In one corner stood some huge frame of ponderous iron, with a vertical thing like a piston periodically rising and falling upon a heavy wooden block. Before it—its tame minister —stood a tall girl, feeding the iron animal with half-quires of rose-hued note-paper which, at every downward dab of the piston-like machine, received in the corner the impress of a wreath of roses. I looked from the rosy paper to the pallid cheek, but said nothing.

Seated before a long apparatus, strung with long, slender strings like any harp, another girl was feeding it with foolscap sheets which, so soon as they curiously traveled from her on the cords, were withdrawn at the opposite end of the machine by a second girl. They came to the first girl·blank; they went to the second girl ruled.

I looked upon the first girl's brow, and saw it was young and fair; I looked upon the second girl's brow, and saw it was ruled and wrinkled. Then, as I still looked, the two—for some small variety to the monotony—changed places; and where had stood the young, fair brow, now stood the ruled and wrinkled one.

Perched high upon a narrow platform, and still higher upon a high stool crowning it, sat another figure serving some other iron animal; while below the platform sat her mate in some sort of reciprocal attendance.

Not a syllable was breathed. Nothing was heard but the low, steady overruling hum of the iron animals. The human voice was banished from the spot. Machinery—that vaunted slave of humanity—here stood menially served by human beings, who served mutely and cringingly as the slave serves the Sultan. The girls did not so much seem accessory wheels to the general machinery as mere cogs to the wheels.

All this scene around me was instantaneously taken in at one sweeping glance—even before I had proceeded to unwind the heavy fur tippet from around my neck. But as soon as this fell from me, the dark-complexioned man, standing close by, raised a sudden cry, and seizing my arm, dragged me out into the open air, and without pausing for a word instantly caught up some congealed snow and began rubbing both my cheeks.

"Two white spots like the whites of your eyes," he said; "man, your cheeks are frozen."

"That may well be," muttered I; " 'tis some wonder the frost of the Devil's Dungeon strikes in no deeper. Rub away."

Soon a horrible, tearing pain caught at my reviving cheeks. Two gaunt blood-hounds, one on each side, seemed mumbling them. I seemed Actæon.

Presently, when all was over, I re-entered the factory, made known my business, concluded it satisfactorily, and then begged to be conducted throughout the place to view it.

"Cupid is the boy for that," said the dark-complexioned man. "Cupid!" and by this odd fancy-name calling a dimpled, red-cheeked, spirited-looking, forward little fellow, who was rather impudently, I thought, gliding about among the passive-looking girls—like a gold-fish through hueless waves—yet doing nothing in particular that I could see, the man bade him lead the stranger through the edifice.

"Come first and see the water-wheel," said this lively lad, with the air of boyishly-brisk importance.

Quitting the folding-room, we crossed some damp, cold boards, and stood beneath a great wet shed, incessantly showering with foam, like the green barnacled bow of some East Indiaman in a gale. Round and round here went the enormous revolutions of the dark colossal water-wheel, grim with its one immutable purpose.

"This sets our whole machinery a-going, sir; in every part of all these buildings; where the girls work and all."

I looked, and saw that the turbid waters of Blood River had not changed their hue by coming under the use of man.

"You make only blank paper; no printing of any sort, I suppose? All blank paper, don't you?"

"Certainly; what else should a paper-factory make?"

The lad here looked at me as if suspicious of my common-sense.

"Oh, to be sure!" said I, confused and stammering; "it only struck me as so strange that red waters should turn out pale chee—paper, I mean."

He took me up a wet and rickety stair to a great light room, furnished with no visible thing but rude, manger-like receptacles running all round its sides: and up to these mangers, like so many mares haltered to the rack, stood rows of girls. Before each was vertically thrust up a long, glittering scythe, immovably fixed at bottom to the manger-edge. The curve of the scythe, and its having no snath to it, made it look exactly like a sword. To and fro, across the sharp edge, the girls forever dragged long strips of rags, washed white, picked from baskets at one side; thus ripping asunder every seam, and converting the tatters almost into lint. The air swam with the fine, poisonous particles, which from all sides darted, subtilely, as motes in sunbeams, into the lungs.

"This is the rag-room," coughed the boy.

"You find it rather stifling here," coughed I, in answer; "but the girls don't cough."

"Oh, they are used to it."

"Where do you get such hosts of rags?" picking up a handful from a basket.

"Some from the country round about; some from far over sea—Leghorn and London."

"'Tis not unlikely, then," murmured I, "that among these heaps of rags there may be some old shirts, gathered from the dormitories of the Paradise of Bachelors. But the buttons are all dropped off. Pray, my lad, do you ever find any bachelors' buttons hereabouts?"

"None grow in this part of the country. The Devil's Dungeon is no place for flowers."

"Oh! you mean the *flowers* so called—the Bachelor's Buttons?"

"And was not that what you asked about? Or did you mean the gold bosom-buttons of our boss, Old Bach, as our whispering girls all call him?"

"The man, then, I saw below is a bachelor, is he?"

"Oh, yes, he's a Bach."

"The edges of those swords, they are turned outward from the girls, if I see right; but their rags and fingers fly so, I can not distinctly see."

"Turned outward."

Yes, murmured I to myself; I see it now; turned outward; and each erected sword is so borne, edge-outward before each girl. If my reading fails me not, just so, of old, condemned state-prisoners went from the hall of judgment to their doom: an officer before, bearing a sword, its edge turned outward, in significance of their fatal sentence. So, through consumptive pallors of this blank, raggy life, go these white girls to death.

"Those scythes look very sharp," again turning toward the boy.

"Yes; they have to keep them so. Look!"

That moment two of the girls, dropping their rags, plied each a whet-stone up and down the sword-blade. My unaccustomed blood curdled at the sharp shriek of the tormented steel.

Their own executioners; themselves whetting the very swords that slay them; meditated I.

"What makes those girls so sheet-white, my lad?"

"Why"—with a roguish twinkle, pure ignorant drollery, not knowing heartlessness—"I suppose the handling of such white bits of sheets all the time makes them so sheety."

"Let us leave the rag-room now, my lad."

More tragical and more inscrutably mysterious than any mystic sight, human or machine, throughout the factory, was the strange innocence of cruel-heartedness in this usage-hardened boy.

"And now," said he, cheerily, "I suppose you want to see our great machine, which cost us twelve thousand dollars only last autumn. That's the machine that makes the paper, too. This way, sir."

Following him, I crossed a large, bespattered place, with two great round vats in it, full of a white, wet, woolly-looking stuff, not unlike the albuminous part of an egg, soft-boiled.

"There," said Cupid, tapping the vats carelessly, "these are the first beginnings of the paper, this white pulp you see. Look how it swims bubbling round and round, moved by the paddle here. From hence it pours from both vats into that one common channel yonder, and so goes, mixed up and leisurely, to the great machine. And now for that."

He led me into a room, stifling with a strange, blood-like, abdominal heat, as if here, true enough, were being finally developed the germinous particles lately seen.

Before me, rolled out like some long Eastern manuscript, lay stretched one continuous length of iron frame-work—multitudinous and mystical, with all sorts of rollers, wheels, and cylinders, in slowly-measured and unceasing motion.

"Here first comes the pulp now," said Cupid, pointing to the highest end of the machine. "See; first it pours out and spreads itself upon this wide, sloping board; and then—look—slides, thin and quivering, beneath the first roller there. Follow on now, and see it as it slides from under that to the next cylinder. There; see how it has become just a very little less pulpy now. One step more, and it grows still more to some slight consistence. Still another cylinder, and it is so knitted—though as yet mere dragon-fly wing—that it forms an air-bridge here, like a suspended cobweb, between two more separated rollers; and flowing over the last one, and under again, and doubling about there out of sight for a minute among all those mixed cylinders you indistinctly see, it reappears here, looking now at last a little less like pulp and more like paper, but still quite delicate and defective yet awhile. But —a little further onward, sir, if you please—here now, at this further point, it puts on something of a real look, as if it might turn out to be something you might possibly handle in the end. But it's not yet done, sir. Good way to travel yet, and plenty more of cylinders must roll it."

"Bless my soul!" said I, amazed at the elongation, interminable convolutions, and deliberate slowness of the machine; "it must take a long time for the pulp to pass from end to end, and come out paper."

"Oh! not so long," smiled the precocious lad, with a superior and patronizing air; "only nine minutes. But look; you may try it for yourself. Have you a bit of paper? Ah! here's a bit on the floor. Now mark that with any word you please, and let me dab it on here, and we'll see how long before it comes out at the other end."

"Well, let me see," said I, taking out my pencil; "come, I'll mark it with your name."

Bidding me take out my watch, Cupid adroitly dropped the inscribed slip on an exposed part of the incipient mass.

Instantly my eye marked the second-hand on my dial-plate.

Slowly I followed the slip, inch by inch; sometimes pausing for full half a minute as it disappeared beneath inscrutable groups of the lower cylinders, but only gradually to emerge again; and so, on, and on, and on—inch by inch; now in open sight, sliding along like a freckle on the quivering sheet; and then again wholly vanished; and so, on, and on, and on —inch by inch; all the time the main sheet growing more and more to final firmness—when, suddenly, I saw a sort of paper-fall, not wholly unlike a water-fall; a scissory sound smote my ear, as of some cord being snapped; and down dropped an unfolded sheet of perfect foolscap, with my "Cupid" half faded out of it, and still moist and warm.

My travels were at an end, for here was the end of the machine.

"Well, how long was it?" said Cupid.

"Nine minutes to a second," replied I, watch in hand.

"I told you so."

For a moment a curious emotion filled me, not wholly unlike that which one might experience at the fulfillment of some mysterious prophecy. But how absurd, thought I again; the thing is a mere machine, the essence of which is unvarying punctuality and precision.

Previously absorbed by the wheels and cylinders, my attention was now directed to a sad-looking woman standing by.

"That is rather an elderly person so silently tending the machine-end here. She would not seem wholly used to it either."

"Oh," knowingly whispered Cupid, through the din, "she only came last week. She was a nurse formerly. But the business is poor in these parts, and she's left it. But look at the paper she is piling there."

"Aye, foolscap," handling the piles of moist, warm sheets, which continually were being delivered into the woman's waiting hands. "Don't you turn out anything but foolscap at this machine?"

"Oh, sometimes, but not often, we turn out finer work—cream-laid and royal sheets, we call them. But foolscap being in chief demand, we turn out foolscap most."

It was very curious. Looking at that blank paper continually dropping, dropping, dropping, my mind ran on in wonderings of those strange uses to which those thousand sheets eventually would be put. All sorts of writings would be writ on those now vacant things—sermons, lawyers' briefs, physicians' prescriptions, love-letters, marriage certificates, bills of divorce, registers of births, death-warrants, and so on, without end. Then, recurring back to them as they here lay all blank, I could not but bethink me of that celebrated comparison of John Locke, who, in demonstration of his theory that man had no innate ideas, compared the human mind at birth to a sheet of blank paper; something destined to be scribbled on, but what sort of characters no soul might tell.

Pacing slowly to and fro along the involved machine, still humming with its play, I was struck as well by the inevitability as the evolvement-power in all its motions.

"Does that thin cobweb there," said I, pointing to the sheet in its more imperfect stage, "does that never tear or break? It is marvelous fragile, and yet this machine it passes through is so mighty."

"It never is known to tear a hair's point."

"Does it never stop—get clogged?"

"No. It *must* go. The machinery makes it go just *so;* just that very way, and at that very pace you there plainly *see* it go. The pulp can't help going."

Something of awe now stole over me, as I gazed upon this inflexible iron animal. Always, more or less, machinery of this ponderous, elaborate sort strikes, in some moods, strange dread into the human heart, as some living, panting Behemoth might. But what made the thing I saw so specially terrible to me was the metallic necessity, the unbudging fatality which governed it. Though, here and there, I could not follow the thin, gauzy vail of pulp in the course of its more mysterious or entirely invisible advance, yet it was indubitable that, at those points where it eluded me, it still marched on in unvarying docility to the autocratic cunning of the machine. A fascination fastened on me. I stood spell-bound and wandering in my soul. Before my eyes—there, passing in slow procession along the wheeling cylinders, I seemed to see, glued to the pallid incipience of the pulp, the yet more pallid faces of all the pallid girls I had eyed that heavy day. Slowly, mournfully, beseechingly, yet unresistingly, they gleamed along, their agony dimly outlined on the imperfect paper, like the print of the tormented face on the handkerchief of Saint Veronica.

"Halloa! the heat of the room is too much for you," cried Cupid, staring at me.

"No—I am rather chill, if anything."

"Come out, sir—out—out," and, with the protecting air of a careful father, the precocious lad hurried me outside.

In a few moments, feeling revived a little, I went into the folding-room—the first room I had entered, and where the desk for transacting business stood, surrounded by the blank counters and blank girls engaged at them.

"Cupid here has led me a strange tour," said I to the dark-complexioned man before mentioned, whom I had ere this discovered not only to be an old bachelor, but also the principal proprietor. "Yours is a most wonderful factory. Your great machine is a miracle of inscrutable intricacy."

"Yes, all our visitors think it so. But we don't have many. We are in a very out-of-the-way corner here. Few inhabitants, too. Most of our girls come from far-off villages."

"The girls," echoed I, glancing round at their silent forms. "Why is it, sir, that in most factories, female operatives, of whatever age, are indiscriminately called girls, never women?"

"Oh! as to that—why, I suppose, the fact of their being generally unmarried—that's the reason, I should think. But it never struck me before. For our factory here, we will not have married women; they are apt to be off-and-on too much. We want none but steady workers: twelve hours to the day, day after day, through the three hundred and sixty-five days, excepting Sundays, Thanksgiving, and Fast-days. That's our rule. And so, having no married women, what females we have are rightly enough called girls."

"Then these are all maids," said I, while some pained homage to their pale virginity made me involuntarily bow.

"All maids."

Again the strange emotion filled me.

"Your cheeks look whitish yet, sir," said the man, gazing at me narrowly. "You must be careful going home. Do they pain you at all now? It's a bad sign, if they do."

"No doubt, sir," answered I, "when once I have got out of the Devil's Dungeon, I shall feel them mending."

"Ah, yes; the winter air in valleys, or gorges, or any sunken place, is far colder and more bitter than elsewhere. You would hardly believe it now, but it is colder here than at the top of Woedolor Mountain."

"I dare say it is, sir. But time presses me; I must depart."

With that, remuffling myself in dread-naught and tippet, thrusting my hands into my huge seal-skin mittens, I sallied out into the nipping air, and found poor Black, my horse, all cringing and doubled up with the cold.

Soon, wrapped in furs and meditations, I ascended from the Devil's Dungeon.

At the Black Notch I paused, and once more bethought me of Temple Bar. Then, shooting through the pass, all alone with inscrutable nature, I exclaimed—Oh! Paradise of Bachelors! and oh! Tartarus of Maids!

THE BELL-TOWER

NOTE: "The Bell-Tower" (*Putnam's*, August, 1855) is in conception the most Hawthornesque of Melville's stories and in performance the most inept. The writing is arthritically clumsy; the Faustian (or Frankensteinian) parable is both labored and erratic in its progression; and the moralizing last paragraph makes you wish it might be proved that somebody else was the real author. Melville, however, thought well enough of the piece to include it in *The Piazza Tales* along with his other *Putnam's* work, and it was anthologized in later nineteenth-century collections like the Stedman-Hutchinson *Library of American Literature* (1889).

> *Like negroes, these powers own man sullenly;*
> *mindful of their higher master; while serving,*
> *plot revenge.*
>
> *The world is apoplectic with high-living of*
> *ambition; and apoplexy has its fall.*
>
> *Seeking to conquer a larger liberty, man but*
> *extends the empire of necessity.*
>
> *from a private MS.*

IN THE south of Europe, nigh a once frescoed capital, now with dank mould cankering its bloom, central in a plain, stands what, at distance, seems the black mossed stump of some immeasurable pine, fallen, in forgotten days, with Anak and the Titan.

As all along where the pine tree falls, its dissolution leaves a mossy mound—last-flung shadow of the perished trunk; never lengthening, never lessening; unsubject to the fleet falsities of the sun; shade immutable, and true gauge which cometh by prostration—so westward from what seems the stump, one steadfast spear of lichened ruin veins the plain.

From that tree-top, what birded chimes of silver throats had rung. A stone pine; a metallic aviary in its crown: the Bell-Tower, built by the great mechanician, the unblest foundling, Bannadonna.

Like Babel's, its base was laid in a high hour of renovated earth, following the second deluge, when the waters of the Dark Ages had dried up, and once more the green appeared. No wonder that, after so long and deep submersion, the jubilant expectation of the race should, as with Noah's sons, soar into Shinar aspiration.

In firm resolve, no man in Europe at that period went beyond Bannadonna. Enriched through commerce with the Levant, the state in which he lived voted to have the noblest Bell-Tower in Italy. His repute assigned him to be architect.

Stone by stone, month by month, the tower rose. Higher, higher; snail-like in pace, but torch or rocket in its pride.

After the masons would depart, the builder, standing alone upon its ever-ascending summit, at close of every day, saw that he overtopped still higher walls and trees. He would tarry till a late hour there, wrapped in schemes of other and still loftier piles. Those who of saints' days thronged the spot—hanging to the rude poles of scaffolding, like sailors on yards, or bees on boughs, unmindful of lime and dust, and falling chips of stone—their homage not the less inspirited him to self-esteem.

At length the holiday of the Tower came. To the sound of viols, the climax-stone slowly rose in air, and, amid the firing of ordnance, was laid by Bannadonna's hands upon the final course. Then mounting it, he stood erect, alone, with folded arms, gazing upon the white summits of blue inland Alps, and whiter crests of bluer Alps off-shore—sights invisible from the plain. Invisible, too, from thence was that eye he turned below, when, like the cannon booms, came up to him the people's combustions of applause.

That which stirred them so was, seeing with what serenity the builder stood three hundred feet in the air, upon an un-railed perch. This none but he durst do. But his periodic standing upon the pile, in each stage of its growth—such discipline had its last result.

Little remained now but the bells. These, in all respects, must correspond with their receptacle.

The minor ones were prosperously cast. A highly enriched one followed, of a singular make, intended for suspension in a manner before unknown. The purpose of this bell, its rotary motion, and connection with the clock-work, also executed at the time, will, in the sequel, receive mention.

In the one erection, bell-tower and clock-tower were united, though, before that period, such structures had commonly been built distinct; as the Campanile and Torre dell' Orologio of St. Mark to this day attest.

But it was upon the great state-bell that the founder lavished his more daring skill. In vain did some of the less elated magistrates here caution him; saying that though truly the tower was Titanic, yet limit should be set to the dependent weight of its swaying masses. But undeterred, he prepared his mammoth mold, dented with mythological devices; kindled his fires of balsamic firs; melted his tin and copper, and, throwing in much plate, contributed by the public spirit of the nobles, let loose the tide.

The unleashed metals bayed like hounds. The workmen shrunk. Through their fright, fatal harm to the bell was dreaded. Fearless as Shadrach, Bannadonna, rushing through the glow, smote the chief culprit with his ponderous ladle. From the smitten part, a splinter was dashed into the seething mass, and at once was melted in.

Next day a portion of the work was heedfully uncovered. All seemed right. Upon the third morning, with equal satisfaction, it was bared still lower. At length, like some old Theban king, the whole cooled casting was disinterred. All was fair except in one strange spot. But as he suffered no one to attend him in these inspections, he concealed the blemish by some preparation which none knew better to devise.

The casting of such a mass was deemed no small triumph for the caster; one, too, in which the state might not scorn to share. The homicide was overlooked. By the charitable that deed was but imputed to sudden transports of esthetic passion, not to any flagitious quality. A kick from an Arabian charger; not sign of vice, but blood.

His felony remitted by the judge, absolution given him by the priest, what more could even a sickly conscience have desired!

Honoring the tower and its builder with another holiday, the republic witnessed the hoisting of the bells and clock-work amid shows and pomps superior to the former.

Some months of more than usual solitude on Bannadonna's part ensued. It was not unknown that he was engaged upon something for the belfry, intended to complete it, and surpass all that had gone before. Most people imagined that the design would involve a casting like the bells. But those who thought they had some further insight, would shake their heads, with hints, that not for nothing did the mechanician keep so secret. Meantime, his seclusion failed not to invest his work with more or less of that sort of mystery pertaining to the forbidden.

Ere long he had a heavy object hoisted to the belfry, wrapped in a dark sack or cloak—a procedure sometimes had in the case of an elaborate piece of sculpture, or statue, which, being intended to grace the front of a new edifice, the architect does not desire exposed to critical eyes, till set up, finished, in its appointed place. Such was the impression now. But, as the object rose, a statuary present observed, or thought he did, that it was not entirely rigid, but was, in a manner, pliant. At last, when the hidden thing had attained its final height, and, obscurely seen from below, seemed almost of itself to step into the belfry, as if with little assistance from the crane, a shrewd old blacksmith present ventured the suspicion that it was but a living man. This surmise was thought a foolish one, while the general interest failed not to augment.

Not without demur from Bannadonna, the chief-magistrate of the town, with an associate—both elderly men—followed what seemed the image up the tower. But, arrived at the belfry, they had little recompense. Plausibly entrenching himself behind the conceded mysteries of his art, the mechanician withheld present explanation. The magistrates glanced toward the cloaked object, which, to their surprise, seemed now to have changed its attitude, or else had before been more perplexingly concealed by the violent muffling action of the wind without. It seemed now seated upon some sort of frame, or chair, contained within the domino. They observed that nigh the top, in a sort of square, the web of the cloth, either from accident or design, had its warp partly withdrawn, and the cross threads plucked out here and there, so as to form a sort of woven grating. Whether it were the low wind or no, stealing through the stone lattice-work, or only their own perturbed imaginations, is uncertain, but they thought they discerned a slight sort of fitful, spring-like motion, in the domino. Nothing, however incidental or insignificant, escaped their uneasy eyes. Among other things, they pried out, in a corner, an earthen cup, partly corroded and partly encrusted, and one whispered to the other, that this cup was just such a one as might, in mockery, be offered to the lips of some brazen statue, or, perhaps, still worse.

But, being questioned, the mechanician said, that the cup was simply used in his founder's business, and described the purpose; in short, a cup to test the condition of metals in fusion. He added, that it had got into the belfry by the merest chance.

Again, and again, they gazed at the domino, as at some suspicious incognito at a Venetian masque. All sorts of vague apprehensions stirred them. They even dreaded lest, when they should descend, the mechanician, though without a flesh and blood companion, for all that, would not be left alone.

Affecting some merriment at their disquietude, he begged to relieve them, by extending a coarse sheet of workman's canvas between them and the object.

Meantime he sought to interest them in his other work; nor, now that the domino was out of sight, did they long remain insensible to the artistic wonders lying round them; wonders hitherto beheld but in their unfinished state; because, since hoisting the bells, none but the caster had entered within the belfry. It was one trait of his, that, even in details, he would not let another do what he could, without too great loss of time, accomplish for himself. So, for several preceding weeks, whatever hours were unemployed in his secret design, had been devoted to elaborating the figures on the bells.

The clock-bell, in particular, now drew attention. Under a patient chisel, the latent beauty of its enrichments, before obscured by the cloudings incident to casting, that beauty in its shyest grace, was now revealed. Round and round the bell, twelve figures of gay girls, garlanded, hand-in-hand, danced in a choral ring—the embodied hours.

"Bannadonna," said the chief, "this bell excels all else. No added touch could here improve. Hark!" hearing a sound, "was that the wind?"

"The wind, Excellenza," was the light response. "But the figures, they are not yet without their faults. They need some touches yet. When those are given, and the——block yonder," pointing towards the canvas screen, "when Haman there, as I merrily call him,—him? *it*, I mean——when Haman is fixed on this, his lofty tree, then, gentlemen, will I be most happy to receive you here again."

The equivocal reference to the object caused some return of restlessness. However, on their part, the visitors forbore further allusion to it, unwilling, perhaps, to let the foundling see how easily it lay within his plebeian art to stir the placid dignity of nobles.

"Well, Bannadonna," said the chief, "how long ere you are

ready to set the clock going, so that the hour shall be sounded?
Our interest in you, not less than in the work itself, makes us
anxious to be assured of your success. The people, too,—why,
they are shouting now. Say the exact hour when you will be
ready."

"To-morrow, Excellenza, if you listen for it,—or should you
not, all the same—strange music will be heard. The stroke of
one shall be the first from yonder bell," pointing to the bell,
adorned with girls and garlands, "that stroke shall fall there,
where the hand of Una clasps Dua's. The stroke of one shall
sever that loved clasp. To-morrow, then, at one o'clock, as
struck here, precisely here," advancing and placing his finger
upon the clasp, "the poor mechanic will be most happy once
more to give you liege audience, in this his littered shop. Farewell till then, illustrious magnificoes, and hark ye for your
vassal's stroke."

His still, Vulcanic face hiding its burning brightness like a
forge, he moved with ostentatious deference towards the scuttle,
as if so far to escort their exit. But the junior magistrate, a
kind-hearted man, troubled at what seemed to him a certain
sardonical disdain, lurking beneath the foundling's humble
mien, and in Christian sympathy more distressed at it on his
account than on his own, dimly surmising what might be the
final fate of such a cynic solitaire, nor perhaps uninfluenced
by the general strangeness of surrounding things, this good
magistrate had glanced sadly, sideways from the speaker, and
thereupon his foreboding eye had started at the expression
of the unchanging face of the Hour Una.

"How is this, Bannadonna?" he lowly asked, "Una looks
unlike her sisters."

"In Christ's name, Bannadonna," impulsively broke in the
chief, his attention, for the first attracted to the figure, by his
associate's remark, "Una's face looks just like that of Deborah, the prophetess, as painted by the Florentine, Del Fonca."

"Surely, Bannadonna," lowly resumed the milder magistrate,
"you meant the twelve should wear the same jocundly abandoned air. But see, the smile of Una seems but a fatal one.
'Tis different."

While his mild associate was speaking, the chief glanced,
inquiringly, from him to the caster, as if anxious to mark how
the discrepancy would be accounted for. As the chief stood,
his advanced foot was on the scuttle's curb.

Bannadonna spoke:

"Excellenza, now that, following your keener eye, I glance upon the face of Una, I do, indeed perceive some little variance. But look all round the bell, and you will find no two faces entirely correspond. Because there is a law in art—— but the cold wind is rising more; these lattices are but a poor defense. Suffer me, magnificoes, to conduct you, at least, partly on your way. Those in whose well-being there is a public stake, should be heedfully attended."

"Touching the look of Una you were saying, Bannadonna, that there was a certain law in art," observed the chief, as the three now descended the stone shaft, "pray, tell me, then——."

"Pardon; another time, Excellenza;—the tower is damp."

"Nay, I must rest, and hear it now. Here,—here is a wide landing, and through this leeward slit, no wind, but ample light. Tell us of your law; and at large."

"Since, Excellenza, you insist, know that there is a law in art, which bars the possibility of duplicates. Some years ago, you may remember, I graved a small seal for your republic, bearing, for its chief device, the head of your own ancestor, its illustrious founder. It becoming necessary, for the customs' use, to have innumerable impressions for bales and boxes, I graved an entire plate, containing one hundred of the seals. Now, though, indeed, my object was to have those hundred heads identical, and though, I dare say, people think them so, yet, upon closely scanning an uncut impression from the plate, no two of those five-score faces, side by side, will be found alike. Gravity is the air of all; but, diversified in all. In some, benevolent; in some, ambiguous; in two or three, to a close scrutiny, all but incipiently malign, the variation of less than a hair's breadth in the linear shadings round the mouth sufficing to all this. Now, Excellenza, transmute that general gravity into joyousness, and subject it to twelve of those variations I have described, and tell me, will you not have my hours here, and Una one of them? But I like——."

"Hark! is that—a football above?"

"Mortar, Excellenza; sometimes it drops to the belfry-floor from the arch where the stonework was left undressed. I must have it seen to. As I was about to say: for one, I like this law forbidding duplicates. It evokes fine personalities. Yes, Excellenza, that strange, and—to you—uncertain smile, and those fore-looking eyes of Una, suit Bannadonna very well."

"Hark!—sure we left no soul above?"

"No soul, Excellenza; rest assured, no *soul*.—Again the mortar."

"It fell not while we were there."

"Ah, in your presence, it better knew its place, Excellenza," blandly bowed Bannadonna.

"But, Una," said the milder magistrate, "she seemed intently gazing on you; one would have almost sworn that she picked you out from among us three."

"If she did, possibly, it might have been her finer apprehension, Excellenza."

"How, Bannadonna? I do not understand you."

"No consequence, no consequence, Excellenza—but the shifted wind is blowing through the slit. Suffer me to escort you on; and then, pardon, but the toiler must to his tools."

"It may be foolish, Signor," said the milder magistrate, as, from the third landing, the two now went down unescorted, "but, somehow, our great mechanician moves me strangely. Why, just now, when he so superciliously replied, his walk seemed Sisera's, God's vain foe, in Del Fonca's painting. And that young, sculptured Deborah, too. Aye, and that——."

"Tush, tush, Signor!" returned the chief. "A passing whim. Deborah?—Where's Jael, pray?"

"Ah," said the other, as they now stepped upon the sod, "ah, Signor, I see you leave your fears behind you with the chill and gloom; but mine, even in this sunny air, remain. Hark!"

It was a sound from just within the tower door, whence they had emerged. Turning, they saw it closed.

"He has slipped down and barred us out," smiled the chief; "but it is his custom."

Proclamation was now made, that the next day, at one hour after meridian, the clock would strike, and—thanks to the mechanician's powerful art—with unusual accompaniments. But what those should be, none as yet could say. The announcement was received with cheers.

By the looser sort, who encamped about the tower all night, lights were seen gleaming through the topmost blind-work, only disappearing with the morning sun. Strange sounds, too, were heard, or were thought to be, by those whom anxious watching might not have left mentally undisturbed— sounds, not only of some ringing implement, but also—so they said—half-suppressed screams and plainings, such as might have issued from some ghostly engine, overplied.

Slowly the day drew on; part of the concourse chasing the weary time with songs and games, till, at last, the great blurred sun rolled, like a football, against the plain.

At noon, the nobility and principal citizens came from the town in cavalcade; a guard of soldiers, also, with music, the more to honor the occasion.

Only one hour more. Impatience grew. Watches were held in hands of feverish-men, who stood, now scrutinizing their small dial-plates, and then, with neck thrown back, gazing toward the belfry, as if the eye might foretell that which could only be made sensible to the ear; for, as yet, there was no dial to the tower-clock.

The hour-hands of a thousand watches now verged within a hair's breadth of the figure I. A silence, as of the expectation of some Shiloh, pervaded the swarming plain. Suddenly a dull, mangled sound—naught ringing in it; scarcely audible, indeed, to the outer circles of the people—that dull sound dropped heavily from the belfry. At the same moment, each man stared at his neighbor blankly. All watches were upheld. All hour-hands were at—had passed—the figure I. No bell-stroke from the tower. The multitude became tumultuous.

Waiting a few moments, the chief magistrate, commanding silence, hailed the belfry, to know what thing unforeseen had happened there.

No response.

He hailed again and yet again.

All continued hushed.

By his order, the soldiers burst in the tower-door; when, stationing guards to defend it from the now surging mob, the chief, accompanied by his former associate, climbed the winding stairs. Half-way up, they stopped to listen. No sound. Mounting faster, they reached the belfry; but, at the threshold, started at the spectacle disclosed. A spaniel, which, unbeknown to them, had followed them thus far, stood shivering as before some unknown monster in a brake: or, rather, as if it snuffed footsteps leading to some other world.

Bannadonna lay, prostrate and bleeding, at the base of the bell which was adorned with girls and garlands. He lay at the feet of the hour Una; his head coinciding, in a vertical line, with her left hand, clasped by the hour Dua. With downcast face impending over him, like Jael over nailed Sisera in the tent, was the domino; now no more becloaked.

It had limbs, and seemed clad in a scaly mail, lustrous as a dragon-beetle's. It was manacled, and its clubbed arms were uplifted, as if, with its manacles, once more to smite its already smitten victim. One advanced foot of it was inserted beneath the dead body, as if in the act of spurning it.

Uncertainty falls on what now followed.

It were but natural to suppose that the magistrates would, at first, shrink from immediate personal contact with what they saw. At the least, for a time, they would stand in involuntary doubt; it may be, in more or less of horrified alarm. Certain it is, that an arquebuss was called for from below. And some add, that its report, followed by a fierce whiz, as of the sudden snapping of a main-spring, with a steely din, as if a stack of sword-blades should be dashed upon a pavement, these blended sounds came ringing to the plain, attracting every eye far upward to the belfry, whence, through the lattice-work, thin wreaths of smoke were curling.

Some averred that it was the spaniel, gone mad by fear, which was shot. This, others denied. True it was, the spaniel never more was seen; and, probably, for some unknown reason, it shared the burial now to be related of the domino. For, whatever the preceding circumstances may have been, the first instinctive panic over, or else all ground of reasonable fear removed, the two magistrates, by themselves, quickly rehooded the figure in the dropped cloak wherein it had been hoisted. The same night, it was secretly lowered to the ground, smuggled to the beach, pulled far out to sea, and sunk. Nor to any after urgency, even in free convivial hours, would the twain ever disclose the full secrets of the belfry.

From the mystery unavoidably investing it, the popular solution of the foundling's fate involved more or less of supernatural agency. But some few less unscientific minds pretended to find little difficulty in otherwise accounting for it. In the chain of circumstantial inferences drawn, there may, or may not, have been some absent or defective links. But, as the explanation in question is the only one which tradition has explicitly preserved, in dearth of better, it will here be given. But, in the first place, it is requisite to present the supposition entertained as to the entire motive and mode, with their origin, of the secret design of Bannadonna; the minds above-mentioned assuming to penetrate as well into his soul as into the event. The disclosure will indirectly involve reference to peculiar matters, none of the clearest, beyond the immediate subject.

At that period, no large bell was made to sound otherwise than as at present, by agitation of a tongue within, by means of ropes, or percussion from without, either from cumbrous machinery, or stalwart watchmen, armed with heavy hammers, stationed in the belfry, or in sentry-boxes on the open roof, according as the bell was sheltered or exposed.

It was from observing these exposed bells, with their watchmen, that the foundling, as was opined, derived the first suggestion of his scheme. Perched on a great mast or spire, the human figure, viewed from below, undergoes such a reduction in its apparent size, as to obliterate its intelligent features. It evinces no personality. Instead of bespeaking volition, its gestures rather resemble the automatic ones of the arms of a telegraph.

Musing, therefore, upon the purely Punchinello aspect of the human figure thus beheld, it had indirectly occurred to Bannadonna to devise some metallic agent, which should strike the hour with its mechanic hand, with even greater precision than the vital one. And, moreover, as the vital watchman on the roof, sallying from his retreat at the given periods, walked to the bell with uplifted mace, to smite it, Bannadonna had resolved that his invention should likewise possess the power of locomotion, and, along with that, the appearance, at least, of intelligence and will.

If the conjectures of those who claimed acquaintance with the intent of Bannadonna be thus far correct, no unenterprising spirit could have been his. But they stopped not here; intimating that though, indeed, his design had, in the first place, been prompted by the sight of the watchman, and confined to the devising of a subtle substitute for him: yet, as is not seldom the case with projectors, by insensible gradations, proceeding from comparatively pigmy aims to Titanic ones, the original scheme had, in its anticipated eventualities, at last, attained to an unheard-of degree of daring. He still bent his efforts upon the locomotive figure for the belfry, but only as a partial type of an ulterior creature, a sort of elephantine Helot, adapted to further, in a degree scarcely to be imagined, the universal conveniences and glories of humanity; supplying nothing less than a supplement to the Six Days' Work; stocking the earth with a new serf, more useful than the ox, swifter then the dolphin, stronger than the lion, more cunning than the ape, for industry an ant, more fiery than serpents, and yet, in patience, another ass. All excellences of all

God-made creatures, which served man, were here to receive advancement, and then to be combined in one. Talus was to have been the all-accomplished Helot's name. Talus, iron slave to Bannadonna, and, through him, to man.

Here, it might well be thought that, were these last conjectures as to the foundling's secrets not erroneous, then must he have been hopelessly infected with the craziest chimeras of his age; far outgoing Albert Magus and Cornelius Agrippa. But the contrary was averred. However marvelous his design, however apparently transcending not alone the bounds of human invention, but those of divine creation, yet the proposed means to be employed were alleged to have been confined within the sober forms of sober reason. It was affirmed that, to a degree of more than skeptic scorn, Bannadonna had been without sympathy for any of the vain-glorious irrationalities of his time. For example, he had not concluded, with the visionaries among the metaphysicians, that between the finer mechanic forces and the ruder animal vitality some germ of correspondence might prove discoverable. As little did his scheme partake of the enthusiasm of some natural philosophers, who hoped, by physiological and chemical inductions, to arrive at a knowledge of the source of life, and so qualify themselves to manufacture and improve upon it. Much less had he aught in common with the tribe of alchemists, who sought, by a species of incantations to evoke same surprising vitality from the laboratory. Neither had he imagined, with certain sanguine theosophists, that, by faithful adoration of the Highest, unheard of powers would be vouchsafed to man. A practical materialist, what Bannadonna had aimed at was to have been reached, not by logic, not by crucible, not by conjuration, not by altars; but by plain vice-bench and hammer. In short, to solve nature, to steal into her, to intrigue beyond her, to procure some one else to bind her to his hand; —these, one and all, had not been his objects; but, asking no favors from any element or any being, of himself, to rival her, outstrip her, and rule her. He stooped to conquer. With him, common sense was theurgy; machinery, miracle; Prometheus, the heroic name for machinist; man, the true God.

Nevertheless, in his initial step, so far as the experimental automaton for the belfry was concerned, he allowed fancy some little play; or, perhaps, what seemed his fancifulness was but his utilitarian ambition collaterally extended. In figure, the creature for the belfry should not be likened after the human pattern, nor any animal one, nor after the ideals, however wild, of ancient fable, but equally in aspect as in organism be an original production; the more terrible to behold, the better.

Such, then, were the suppositions as to the present scheme, and the reserved intent. How, at the very threshold, so un-looked-for a catastrophe overturned all, or rather, what was the conjecture here, is now to be set forth.

It was thought that on the day preceding the fatality, his visitors having left him, Bannadonna had unpacked the bel-fry image, adjusted it, and placed it in the retreat provided— a sort of sentry-box in one corner of the belfry; in short, through-out the night, and for some part of the ensuing morn-ing, he had been engaged in arranging everything connected with the domino; the issuing from the sentry-box each sixty minutes; sliding along a grooved way, like a railway; advanc-ing to the clock-bell, with uplifted manacles; striking it at one of the twelve junctions of the four-and-twenty hands; then wheeling, circling the bell and retiring to its post, there to bide for another sixty minutes, when the same process was to be repeated; the bell, by a cunning mechanism, meantime turn-ing on its vertical axis, so as to present, to the descending mace, the clasped hands of the next two figures, when it would strike two, three, and so on, to the end. The musical metal in this time-bell being so managed in the fusion, by some art, perishing with its originator, that each of the clasps of the four-and-twenty hands should give forth its own peculiar re-sonance when parted.

But on the magic metal, the magic and metallic stranger never struck but that one stroke, drove but that one nail, sev-ered but that one clasp, by which Bannadonna clung to his ambitious life. For, after winding up the creature in the sentry-box, so that, for the present, skipping the intervening hours, it should not emerge till the hour of one, but should then infallibly emerge, and, after deftly oiling the grooves whereon it was to slide, it was surmised that the mechanician must then have hurried to the bell, to give his final touches to its sculpture. True artist, he here became absorbed; and absorption still further intensified, it may be, by his striving to abate that strange look of Una; which, though, before others, he had treated with such unconcern, might not, in secret, have been without its thorn.

And so, for the interval, he was oblivious of his creature;

which, not oblivious of him, and true to its creation, and true to its heedful winding up, left its post precisely at the given moment; along its well-oiled route, slid noiselessly toward its mark; and, aiming at the hand of Una, to ring one clangorous note, dully smote the intervening brain of Bannadonna, turned backwards to it; the manacled arms then instantly up-springing to their hovering poise. The falling body clogged the thing's return; so, there it stood, still impending over Bannadonna, as if whispering some postmortem terror. The chisel lay dropped from the hand, but beside the hand; the oil-flask spilled across the iron track.

In his unhappy end, not unmindful of the rare genius of the mechanician, the republic decreed him a stately funeral. It was resolved that the great bell—the one whose casting had been jeopardized through the timidity of the ill-starred workmen—should be rung upon the entrance of the bier into the cathedral. The most robust man of the country round was assigned the office of bell-ringer.

But as the pall-bearers entered the cathedral porch, naught but a broken and disastrous sound, like that of some lone Alpine land-slide, fell from the tower upon their ears. And then, all was hushed.

Glancing backwards, they saw the groined belfry crashed sideways in. It afterwards appeared that the powerful peasant, who had the bell-rope in charge, wishing to test at once the full glory of the bell, had swayed down upon the rope with one concentrate jerk. The mass of quaking metal, too ponderous for its frame, and strangely feeble somewhere at its top, loosed from its fastening, tore sideways down, and tumbling in one sheer fall, three hundred feet to the soft sward below, buried itself inverted and half out of sight.

Upon its disinterment, the main fracture was found to have started from a small spot in the ear; which, being scraped, revealed a defect, deceptively minute, in the casting; which defect must subsequently have been pasted over with some unknown compound.

The remolten metal soon reassumed its place in the tower's repaired superstructure. For one year the metallic choir of birds sang musically in its belfry-bough-work of sculptured blinds and traceries. But on the first anniversary of the tower's completion—at early dawn, before the concourse had surrounded it—an earthquake came; one loud crash was heard.

The stone-pine, with its bower of songsters, lay overthrown upon the plain.

So the blind slave obeyed its blinder lord; but, in obedience, slew him. So the creator was killed by the creature. So the bell was too heavy for the tower. So the bell's main weakness was where man's blood had flawed it. And so pride went before the fall.

BENITO CERENO

NOTE: There have been extreme differences of opinion about the artistic merits of this long story, as well as about its philosophical meaning, its bearing—as a work of the 1850's—on the slavery crisis, and even so basic a matter as the author's attitude (forgiving? patronizing? contemptuous or worse?) toward the right-thinking American captain through whose eyes and shifting impressions the circumstances of the action are given to us. A critical "casebook" has been published. I have set down some of my own views on these issues in another place (*The Example of Melville*, 150–158) and offer only the barest summary of them here: that the form of the story is an odd one for a work of this length, being essentially a *riddle* and therefore requiring to be twice told, once for trial and once for confirmation; that the matching of form and substance is extraordinarily tactful (and free-handed, original); and that the story is, in brief, a work of the first rank by one of the great creative masters of narrated—as opposed to dramatized —fiction.

Robert Lowell's brilliant stage version of "Benito Cereno," and yet his failure, for all his play's solid theatrical virtue, not to vulgarize the strong but quite unparaphrasable burden of Melville's development of the story, have doubly re-emphasized the singular authority of the original work.

"Benito Cereno" was published in *Putnam's*, October, November, December, 1855. The present text is that of the slightly revised version printed in *The Piazza Tales*. Melville based the story on an episode he had found in an 1817 *Narrative of Voyages and Travels in the Northern and Southern Hemispheres* written by an actual Amasa Delano of Duxbury, Massachusetts, and containing the court documents from which he adapted the depositions that follow the main narrative and unravel its riddling mysteries. "Benito Cereno" was the second work he had built up on the basis of an existing document; the novel *Israel Potter*, which ran serially in *Putnam's* from July, 1854, through March, 1855, derives from an old life-history Melville found in a London bookstall in 1849.

IN THE year 1799, Captain Amasa Delano, of Duxbury, in Massachusetts, commanding a large sealer and general trader, lay at anchor with a valuable cargo, in the harbor of Santa Maria—a small, desert, uninhabited island toward the southern extremity of the long coast of Chile. There he had touched for water.

On the second day, not long after dawn, while lying in his berth, his mate came below, informing him that a strange sail was coming into the bay. Ships were then not so plenty in those waters as now. He rose, dressed, and went on deck.

The morning was one peculiar to that coast. Everything was mute and calm; everything gray. The sea, though undulated into long roods of swells, seemed fixed, and was sleeked at the surface like waved lead that has cooled and set in the smelter's mold. The sky seemed a gray surtout. Flights of troubled gray fowl, kith and kin with flights of troubled gray vapors among which they were mixed, skimmed low and fitfully over the waters, as swallows over meadows before storms. Shadows present, foreshadowing deeper shadows to come.

To Captain Delano's surprise, the stranger, viewed through the glass, showed no colors; though to do so upon entering a haven, however uninhabited in its shores, where but a single other ship might be lying, was the custom among peaceful seamen of all nations. Considering the lawlessness and loneliness of the spot, and the sort of stories, at that day, associated with those seas, Captain Delano's surprise might have deepened into some uneasiness had he not been a person of a singularly undistrustful good-nature, not liable, except on extraordinary and repeated incentives, and hardly then, to indulge in personal alarms, any way involving the imputation of malign evil in man. Whether, in view of what humanity is capable, such a trait implies, along with a benevolent heart, more than ordinary quickness and accuracy of intellectual perception, may be left to the wise to determine.

But whatever misgivings might have obtruded on first seeing the stranger, would almost, in any seaman's mind, have been dissipated by observing that, the ship, in navigating into the harbor, was drawing too near the land; a sunken reef making out off her bow. This seemed to prove her a stranger, indeed, not only to the sealer, but the island; consequently, she could be no wonted freebooter on that ocean. With no small interest, Captain Delano continued to watch her—a proceeding not much facilitated by the vapors partly mantling the hull, through which the far matin light from her cabin streamed equivocally enough; much like the sun—by this time hemisphered on the rim of the horizon, and, apparently, in company with the strange ship entering the harbor—which, wimpled by the same low, creeping clouds, showed not unlike a Lima intriguante's one sinister eye peering across the Plaza from the Indian loop-hole of her dusk *saya-y-manto*.

It might have been but a deception of the vapors, but, the longer the stranger was watched the more singular appeared her manœuvres. Ere long it seemed hard to decide whether she meant to come in or no—what she wanted, or what she was about. The wind, which had breezed up a little during the night, was now extremely light and baffling, which the more increased the apparent uncertainty of her movements.

Surmising, at last, that it might be a ship in distress, Captain Delano ordered his whale-boat to be dropped, and, much to the wary opposition of his mate, prepared to board her, and, at the least, pilot her in. On the night previous, a fishing party of the seamen had gone a long distance to some detached rocks out of sight from the sealer, and, an hour or two before daybreak, had returned, having met with no small success. Presuming that the stranger might have been long off soundings, the good captain put several baskets of the fish, for presents, into his boat, and so pulled away. From her continuing too near the sunken reef, deeming her in danger, calling to his men, he made all haste to apprise those on board of their situation. But, some time ere the boat came up, the wind, light though it was, having shifted, had headed the vessel off, as well as partly broken the vapors from about her.

Upon gaining a less remote view, the ship, when made signally visible on the verge of the leaden-hued swells, with the shreds of fog here and there raggedly furring her, appeared like a whitewashed monastery after a thunder-storm, seen perched upon some dun cliff among the Pyrenees. But it was no purely fanciful resemblance which now, for a moment, almost led Captain Delano to think that nothing less than a ship-load of monks was before him. Peering over the bulwarks were what really seemed, in the hazy distance, throngs of dark cowls; while, fitfully, revealed through the open port-holes, other dark moving figures were dimly descried, as of Black Friars pacing the cloisters.

Upon a still nigher approach, this appearance was modified, and the true character of the vessel was plain—a Spanish merchantman of the first class, carrying negro slaves, amongst other valuable freight, from one colonial port to another. A very large, and, in its time, a very fine vessel, such as in those days were at intervals encountered along that main;

sometimes superseded Acapulco treasure-ships, or retired frigates of the Spanish king's navy, which, like superannuated Italian palaces, still, under a decline of masters, preserved signs of former state.

As the whale-boat drew more and more nigh, the cause of the peculiar pipe-clayed aspect of the stranger was seen in the slovenly neglect pervading her. The spars, ropes, and great part of the bulwarks, looked woolly, from long unacquaintance with the scraper, tar, and the brush. Her keel seemed laid, her ribs put together, and she launched, from Ezekiel's Valley of Dry Bones.

In the present business in which she was engaged, the ship's general model and rig appeared to have undergone no material change from their original warlike and Froissart pattern. However, no guns were seen.

The tops were large and were railed about with what had once been octagonal net-work, all now in sad disrepair. These tops hung overhead like three ruinous aviaries, in one of which was seen perched, on a ratlin, a white noddy, a strange fowl, so called from its lethargic, somnambulistic character, being frequently caught by hand at sea. Battered and mouldy, the castellated forecastle seemed some ancient turret, long ago taken by assault, and then left to decay. Toward the stern, two high-raised quarter galleries—the balustrades here and there covered with dry, tindery sea-moss—opening out from the unoccupied state-cabin, whose dead-lights, for all the mild weather, were hermetically closed and calked—these tenantless balconies hung over the sea as if it were the grand Venetian canal. But the principal relic of faded grandeur was the ample oval of the shield-like stern-piece, intricately carved with the arms of Castile and Leon, medallioned about by groups of mythological or symbolical devices; uppermost and central of which was a dark satyr in a mask, holding his foot on the prostrate neck of a writhing figure, likewise masked.

Whether the ship had a figure-head, or only a plain beak, was not quite certain, owing to canvas wrapped about that part, either to protect it while undergoing a refurbishing, or else decently to hide its decay. Rudely painted or chalked, as in a sailor freak, along the forward side of a sort of pedestal below the canvas, was the sentence, *"Seguid vuestro jefe,"* (follow your leader); while upon the tarnished head-boards, near by, appeared, in stately capitals, once gilt, the ship's name, "SAN DOMINICK," each letter streakingly corroded with tricklings of copper-spike rust; while, like mourning weeds, dark festoons of sea-grass slimily swept to and fro over the name, with every hearse-like roll of the hull.

As, at last, the boat was hooked from the bow along toward the gangway amidship, its keel, while yet some inches separated from the hull, harshly grated as on a sunken coral reef. It proved a huge bunch of conglobated barnacles adhering below the water to the side like a wen—a token of baffling airs and long calms passed somewhere in those seas.

Climbing the side, the visitor was at once surrounded by a clamorous throng of whites and blacks, but the latter outnumbering the former more than could have been expected, negro transportation-ship as the stranger in port was. But, in one language, and as with one voice, all poured out a common tale of suffering; in which the negresses, of whom there were not a few, exceeded the others in their dolorous vehemence. The scurvy, together with the fever, had swept off a great part of their number, more especially the Spaniards. Off Cape Horn they had narrowly escaped shipwreck; then, for days together, they had lain tranced without wind; their provisions were low; their water next to none; their lips that moment were baked.

While Captain Delano was thus made the mark of all eager tongues; his one eager glance took in all faces, with every other object about him.

Always upon first boarding a large and populous ship at sea, especially a foreign one, with a nondescript crew such as Lascars or Manila men, the impression varies in a peculiar way from that produced by first entering a strange house with strange inmates in a strange land. Both house and ship—the one by its walls and blinds, the other by its high bulwarks like ramparts—hoard from view their interiors till the last moment; but in the case of the ship there is this addition: that the living spectacle it contains, upon its sudden and complete disclosure, has, in contrast with the blank ocean which zones it, something of the effect of enchantment. The ship seems unreal; these strange costumes, gestures, and faces, but a shadowy tableau just emerged from the deep, which directly must receive back what it gave.

Perhaps it was some such influence, as above is attempted to be described, which, in Captain Delano's mind, heightened whatever, upon a staid scrutiny, might have seemed unusual;

especially the conspicuous figures of four elderly grizzled negroes, their heads like black, doddered willow tops, who, in
venerable contrast to the tumult below them, were couched,
sphynx-like, one on the starboard cat-head, another on the lar-
board, and the remaining pair face to face on the opposite
bulwarks above the main-chains. They each had bits of unstranded old junk in their hands, and, with a sort of stoical
self-content, were picking the junk into oakum, a small heap
of which lay by their sides. They accompanied the task with a
continuous, low, monotonous chant; droning and drooling
away like so many gray-headed bag-pipers playing a funeral
march.

The quarter-deck rose into an ample elevated poop, upon
the forward verge of which, lifted, like the oakum-pickers,
some eight feet above the general throng, sat along in a row,
separated by regular spaces, the cross-legged figures of six
other blacks; each with a rusty hatchet in his hand, which,
with a bit of brick and a rag, he was engaged like a scullion
in scouring; while between each two was a small stack of hatchets, their rusted edges turned forward awaiting a like operation. Though occasionally the four oakum-pickers would
briefly address some person or persons in the crowd below, yet
the six hatchet-polishers neither spoke to others, nor breathed
a whisper among themselves, but sat intent upon their task,
except at intervals, when, with the peculiar love in negroes
of uniting industry with pastime, two and two they sideways
clashed their hatchets together, like cymbals, with a barbarous
din. All six, unlike the generality, had the raw aspect of unsophisticated Africans.

But that first comprehensive glance which took in those ten
figures, with scores less conspicuous, rested but an instant upon
them, as, impatient of the hubbub of voices, the visitor turned
in quest of whomsoever it might be that commanded the ship.

But as if not unwilling to let nature make known her own
case among his suffering charge, or else in despair of restrain-
ing it for the time, the Spanish captain, a gentlemanly, re-
served-looking, and rather young man to a stranger's eye,
dressed with singular richness, but bearing plain traces of recent sleepless cares and disquietudes, stood passively by, leaning against the main-mast, at one moment casting a dreary,
spiritless look upon his excited people, at the next an unhappy
glance toward his visitor. By his side stood a black of small

stature, in whose rude face, as occasionally, like a shepherd's dog, he mutely turned it up into the Spaniard's, sorrow and affection were equally blended.

Struggling through the throng, the American advanced to the Spaniard, assuring him of his sympathies, and offering to render whatever assistance might be in his power. To which the Spaniard returned for the present but grave and ceremonious acknowledgments, his national formality dusked by the saturnine mood of ill-health.

But losing no time in mere compliments, Captain Delano, returning to the gangway, had his baskets of fish brought up; and as the wind still continued light, so that some hours at least must elapse ere the ship could be brought to the anchorage, he bade his men return to the sealer, and fetch back as much water as the whale-boat could carry, with whatever soft bread the steward might have, all the remaining .pumpkins on board, with a box of sugar, and a dozen of his private bottles of cider.

Not many minutes after the boat's pushing off, to the vexation of all, the wind entirely died away, and the tide turning, began drifting back the ship helplessly seaward. But trusting this would not long last, Captain Delano sought, with good hopes, to cheer up the strangers, feeling no small satisfaction that, with persons in their condition, he could—thanks to his frequent voyages along the Spanish main—converse with some freedom in their native tongue.

While left alone with them, he was not long in observing some things tending to heighten his first impressions; but surprise was lost in pity, both for the Spaniards and blacks, alike evidently reduced from scarcity of water and provisions; while long-continued suffering seemed to have brought out the less good-natured qualities of the negroes, besides, at the same time, impairing the Spaniard's authority over them. But, under the circumstances, precisely this condition of things was to have been anticipated. In armies, navies, cities, or families, in nature herself, nothing more relaxes good order than misery. Still, Captain Delano was not without the idea, that had Benito Cereno been a man of greater energy, misrule would hardly have come to the present pass. But the debility, constitutional or induced by hardships, bodily and mental, of the Spanish captain,· was too obvious to be overlooked. A prey to settled dejection, as if long mocked with hope he would not now indulge it, even when it had ceased to be a mock, the prospect of that day, or evening at furthest, lying at anchor, with plenty of water for his people, and a brother captain to counsel and befriend, seemed in no perceptible degree to encourage him. His mind appeared unstrung, if not still more seriously affected. Shut up in these oaken walls, chained to one dull round of command, whose unconditionality cloyed him, like some hypochondriac abbot he moved slowly about, at times suddenly pausing, starting, or staring, biting his lip, biting his finger-nail, flushing, paling, twitching his beard, with other symptoms of an absent or moody mind. This distempered spirit was lodged, as before hinted, in as distempered a frame. He was rather tall, but seemed never to have been robust, and now with nervous suffering was almost worn to a skeleton. A tendency to some pulmonary complaint appeared to have been lately confirmed. His voice was like that of one with lungs half gone—hoarsely suppressed, a husky whisper. No wonder that, as in this state he tottered about, his private servant apprehensively followed him. Sometimes the negro gave his master his arm, or took his handkerchief out of his pocket for him; performing these and similar offices with that affectionate zeal which transmutes into something filial or fraternal acts in themselves but menial; and which has gained for the negro the repute of making the most pleasing body-servant in the world; one, too, whom a master need be on no stiffly superior terms with, but may treat with familiar trust; less a servant than a devoted companion.

Marking the noisy indocility of the blacks in general, as well as what seemed the sullen inefficiency of the whites, it was not without humane satisfaction that Captain Delano witnessed the steady good conduct of Babo.

But the good conduct of Babo, hardly more than the ill-behavior of others, seemed to withdraw the half-lunatic Don Benito from his cloudy languor. Not that such precisely was the impression made by the Spaniard on the mind of his visitor. The Spaniard's individual unrest was, for the present, but noted as a conspicuous feature in the ship's general affliction. Still, Captain Delano was not a little concerned at what he could not help taking for the time to be Don Benito's unfriendly indifference towards himself. The Spaniard's manner, too, conveyed a sort of sour and gloomy disdain, which he seemed at no pains to disguise. But this the American in charity ascribed to the harassing effects of sickness, since, in former instances, he had noted that there are peculiar natures on whom prolonged physical suffering seems to cancel every social instinct of kindness; as if, forced to black bread themselves, they deemed it but equity that each person coming nigh them should, indirectly, by some slight or affront, be made to partake of their fare.

But ere long Captain Delano bethought him that, indulgent as he was at the first, in judging the Spaniard, he might not, after all, have exercised charity enough. At bottom it was Don Benito's reserve which displeased him; but the same reserve was shown towards all but his faithful personal attendant. Even the formal reports which, according to sea-usage, were, at stated times, made to him by some petty underling, either a white, mulatto or black, he hardly had patience enough to listen to, without betraying contemptuous aversion. His manner upon such occasions was, in its degree, not unlike that which might be supposed to have been his imperial countryman's, Charles V, just previous to the anchoritish retirement of that monarch from the throne.

This splenetic disrelish of his place was evinced in almost every function pertaining to it. Proud as he was moody, he condescended to no personal mandate. Whatever special orders were necessary, their delivery was delegated to his body-servant, who in turn transferred them to their ultimate destination, through runners, alert Spanish boys or slave boys, like pages or pilot-fish within easy call continually hovering round Don Benito. So that to have beheld this undemonstrative invalid gliding about, apathetic and mute, no landsman could have dreamed that in him was lodged a dictatorship beyond which, while at sea, there was no earthly appeal.

Thus, the Spaniard, regarded in his reserve, seemed the involuntary victim of mental disorder. But, in fact, his reserve might, in some degree, have proceeded from design. If so, then here was evinced the unhealthy climax of that icy though conscientious policy, more or less adopted by all commanders of large ships, which, except in signal emergencies, obliterates alike the manifestation of sway with every trace of sociality; transforming the man into a block, or rather into a loaded cannon, which, until there is call for thunder, has nothing to say.

Viewing him in this light, it seemed but a natural token of the perverse habit induced by a long course of such hard self-restraint, that, notwithstanding the present condition of his ship, the Spaniard should still persist in a demeanor, which, however harmless, or, it may be, appropriate, in a well-ap-

pointed vessel, such as the *San Dominick* might have been at
the outset of the voyage, was anything but judicious now. But
the Spaniard, perhaps, thought that it was with captains as
with gods: reserve, under all events, must still be their cue.
But probably this appearance of slumbering dominion might
have been but an attempted disguise to conscious imbecility—
not deep policy, but shallow device. But be all this as it might,
whether Don Benito's manner was designed or not, the more
Captain Delano noted its pervading reserve, the less he felt
uneasiness at any particular manifestation of that reserve towards himself.

Neither were his thoughts taken up by the captain alone.
Wonted to the quiet orderliness of the sealer's comfortable
family of a crew, the noisy confusion of the *San Dominick's*
suffering host repeatedly challenged his eye. Some prominent
breaches, not only of discipline but of decency, were observed.
These Captain Delano could not but ascribe, in the main, to
the absence of those subordinate deck-officers to whom, along
with higher duties, is intrusted what may be styled the police
department of a populous ship. True, the old oakum-pickers
appeared at times to act the part of monitorial constables to
their countrymen, the blacks; but though occasionally succeeding in allaying trifling outbreaks now and then between
man and man, they could do little or nothing toward estab-
lishing general quiet. The *San Dominick* was in the condition
of a transatlantic emigrant ship, among whose multitude of
living freight are some individuals, doubtless, as little troublesome as crates and bales; but the friendly remonstrances of
such with their ruder companions are of not so much avail as
the unfriendly arm of the mate. What the *San Dominick*
wanted was, what the emigrant ship has, stern superior officers. But on these decks not so much as a fourth-mate was to
be seen.

The visitor's curiosity was roused to learn the particulars
of those mishaps which had brought about such absenteeism,
with its consequences; because, though deriving some inkling
of the voyage from the wails which at the first moment had
greeted him, yet of the details no clear understanding had
been had. The best account would, doubtless, be given by the
captain. Yet at first the visitor was loth to ask it, unwilling to
provoke some distant rebuff. But plucking up courage, he at
last accosted Don Benito, renewing the expression of his benevolent interest, adding, that did he (Captain Delano) but

know the particulars of the ship's misfortunes, he would, perhaps, be better able in the end to relieve them. Would Don Benito favor him with the whole story?

Don Benito faltered; then, like some somnambulist suddenly interfered with, vacantly stared at his visitor, and ended by looking down on the deck. He maintained this posture so long, that Captain Delano, almost equally disconcerted, and involuntarily almost as rude, turned suddenly from him, walking forward to accost one of the Spanish seamen for the desired information. But he had hardly gone five paces, when, with a sort of eagerness, Don Benito invited him back, regretting his momentary absence of mind, and professing readiness to gratify him.

While most part of the story was being given, the two captains stood on the after part of the main-deck, a privileged spot, no one being near but the servant.

"It is now a hundred and ninety days," began the Spaniard, in his husky whisper, "that this ship, well officered and well manned, with several cabin passengers—some fifty Spaniards in all—sailed from Buenos Ayres bound to Lima, with a general cargo, hardware, Paraguay tea and the like—and," pointing forward, "that parcel of negroes, now not more than a hundred and fifty, as you see, but then numbering over three hundred souls. Off Cape Horn we had heavy gales. In one moment, by night, three of my best officers, with fifteen sailors, were lost, with the main-yard; the spar snapping under them in the slings, as they sought, with heavers, to beat down the icy sail. To lighten the hull, the heavier sacks of maté were thrown into the sea, with most of the water-pipes lashed on deck at the time. And this last necessity it was, combined with the prolonged detentions afterwards experienced, which eventually brought about our chief causes of suffering. When——"

Here there was a sudden fainting attack of his cough, brought on, no doubt, by his mental distress. His servant sustained him, and drawing a cordial from his pocket placed it to his lips. He a little revived. But unwilling to leave him unsupported while yet imperfectly restored, the black with one arm still encircled his master, at the same time keeping his eye fixed on his face, as if to watch for the first sign of complete restoration, or relapse, as the event might prove.

The Spaniard proceeded, but brokenly and obscurely, as one in a dream.

—"Oh, my God! rather than pass through what I have, with joy I would have hailed the most terrible gales; but——"

His cough returned and with increased violence; this subsiding, with reddened lips and closed eyes he fell heavily against his supporter.

"His mind wanders. He was thinking of the plague that followed the gales," plaintively sighed the servant; "my poor, poor master!" wringing one hand, and with the other wiping the mouth. "But be patient, Señor," again turning to Captain Delano, "these fits do not last long; master will soon be himself."

Don Benito reviving, went on; but as this portion of the story was very brokenly delivered, the substance only will here be set down.

It appeared that after the ship had been many days tossed in storms off the Cape, the scurvy broke out, carrying off numbers of the whites and blacks. When at last they had worked round into the Pacific, their spars and sails were so damaged, and so inadequately handled by the surviving mariners, most of whom were become invalids, that, unable to lay her northerly course by the wind, which was powerful, the unmanageable ship, for successive days and nights, was blown northwestward, where the breeze suddenly deserted her, in unknown waters, to sultry calms. The absence of the water-pipes now proved as fatal to life as before their presence had menaced it. Induced, or at least aggravated, by the more than scanty allowance of water, a malignant fever followed the scurvy; with the excessive heat of the lengthened calm, making such short work of it as to sweep away, as by billows, whole families of the Africans, and a yet larger number, proportionably, of the Spaniards, including, by a luckless fatality, every remaining officer on board Consequently, in the smart west winds eventually following the calm, the already rent sails, having to be simply dropped, not furled, at need, had been gradually reduced to the beggars' rags they were now. To procure substitutes for his lost sailors, as well as supplies of water and sails, the captain, at the earliest opportunity, had made for Valdivia, the southernmost civilized port of Chile and South America; but upon nearing the coast the thick weather had prevented him from so much as sighting that harbor. Since which period, almost without a crew, and almost without canvas and almost without water, and, at intervals, giving its added dead to the sea, the *San Dominick* had been battledored about by contrary winds, inveigled by currents, or grown weedy in calms. Like a man lost in woods, more than once she had doubled upon her own track.

"But throughout these calamities," huskily continued Don Benito, painfully turning in the half embrace of his servant, "I have to thank those negroes you see, who, though to your inexperienced eyes appearing unruly, have, indeed, conducted themselves with less of restlessness than even their owner could have thought possible under such circumstances."

Here he again fell faintly back. Again his mind wandered; but he rallied, and less obscurely proceeded.

"Yes, their owner was quite right in assuring me that no fetters would be needed with his blacks; so that while, as is wont in this transportation, those negroes have always remained upon deck—not thrust below, as in the Guineamen—they have, also, from the beginning, been freely permitted to range within given bounds at their pleasure."

Once more the faintness returned—his mind roved—but, recovering, he resumed:

"But it is Babo here to whom, under God, I owe not only my own preservation, but likewise to him, chiefly, the merit is due, of pacifying his more ignorant brethren, when at intervals tempted to murmurings."

"Ah, master," sighed the black, bowing his face, "don't speak of me; Babo is nothing; what Babo has done was but duty."

"Faithful fellow!" cried Captain Delano. "Don Benito, I envy you such a friend; slave I cannot call him."

As master and man stood before him, the black upholding the white, Captain Delano could not but bethink him of the beauty of that relationship which could present such a spectacle of fidelity on the one hand and confidence on the other. The scene was heightened by the contrast in dress, denoting their relative positions. The Spaniard wore a loose Chile jacket of dark velvet; white small-clothes and stockings, with silver buckles at the knee and instep; a high-crowned sombrero, of fine grass; a slender sword, silver mounted, hung from a knot in his sash—the last being an almost invariable adjunct, more for utility than ornament, of a South American gentleman's dress to this hour. Excepting when his occasional nervous contortions brought about disarray, there was a certain precision in his attire curiously at variance with the unsightly disorder around; especially in the belittered Ghetto, forward of the mainmast, wholly occupied by the blacks.

The servant wore nothing but wide trowsers, apparently, from their coarseness and patches, made out of some old topsail; they were clean, and confined at the waist by a bit of unstranded rope, which, with his composed, deprecatory air at times, made him look something like a begging friar of St. Francis.

However unsuitable for the time and place, at least in the blunt-thinking American's eyes, and however strangely surviving in the midst of all his afflictions, the toilette of Don Benito might not, in fashion at least, have gone beyond the style of the day among South Americans of his class. Though on the present voyage sailing from Buenos Ayres, he had avowed himself a native and resident of Chile, whose inhabitants had not so generally adopted the plain coat and once plebeian pantaloons; but, with a becoming modification, adhered to their provincial costume, picturesque as any in the world. Still, relatively to the pale history of the voyage, and his own pale face, there seemed something so incongruous in the Spaniard's apparel, as almost to suggest the image of an invalid courtier tottering about London streets in the time of the plague.

The portion of the narrative which, perhaps, most excited interest, as well as some surprise, considering the latitudes in question, was the long calms spoken of, and more particularly the ship's so long drifting about: Without communicating the opinion, of course, the American could not but impute at least part of the detentions both to clumsy seamanship and faulty navigation. Eying Don Benito's small, yellow hands, he easily inferred that the young captain had not got into command at the hawse-hole, but the cabin-window; and if so, why wonder at incompetence, in youth, sickness, and gentility united?

But drowning criticism in compassion, after a fresh repetition of his sympathies, Captain Delano, having heard out his story, not only engaged, as in the first place, to see Don Benito and his people supplied in their immediate bodily needs, but, also, now further promised to assist him in procuring a large permanent supply of water, as well as some sails and rigging; and, though it would involve no small embarrassment to himself, yet he would spare three of his best seamen for temporary deck-officers; so that without delay the ship might proceed to Concepcion, there fully to refit for Lima, her destined port.

Such generosity was not without its effect, even upon the invalid. His face lighted up; eager and hectic, he met the honest glance of his visitor. With gratitude he seemed overcome.

"This excitement is bad for master," whispered the servant, taking his arm, and with soothing words gently drawing him aside.

When Don Benito returned, the American was pained to observe that his hopefulness, like the sudden kindling in his cheek, was but febrile and transient.

Ere long, with a joyless mien, looking up towards the poop, the host invited his guest to accompany him there, for the benefit of what little breath of wind might be stirring.

As during the telling of the story, Captain Delano had once or twice started at the occasional cymballing of the hatchet-polishers, wondering why such an interruption should be allowed, especially in that part of the ship, and in the ears of an invalid; and moreover, as the hatchets had anything but an attractive look, and the handlers of them still less so, it was, therefore, to tell the truth, not without some lurking reluctance, or even shrinking, it may be, that Captain Delano, with apparent complaisance, acquiesced in his host's invitation. The more so, since, with an untimely caprice of punctilio, rendered distressing by his cadaverous aspect, Don Benito, with Castilian bows, solemnly insisted upon his guest's preceding him up the ladder leading to the elevation; where, one on each side of the last step, sat for armorial supporters and sentries two of the ominous file. Gingerly enough stepped good Captain Delano between them, and in the instant of leaving them behind, like one running the gauntlet, he felt an apprehensive twitch in the calves of his legs.

But when, facing about, he saw the whole file, like so many organ-grinders, still stupidly intent on their work, unmindful of everything beside, he could not but smile at his late fidgety panic.

Presently, while standing with his host, looking forward upon the decks below, he was struck by one of those instances of insubordination previously alluded to. Three black boys, with two Spanish boys, were sitting together on the hatches, scraping a rude wooden platter, in which some scanty mess had recently been cooked. Suddenly, one of the black boys, enraged at a word dropped by one of his white companions, seized a knife, and, though called to forbear by one of the oakum-pickers, struck the lad over the head, inflicting a gash from which blood flowed.

In amazement, Captain Delano inquired what this meant. To which the pale Don Benito dully muttered, that it was merely the sport of the lad.

"Pretty serious sport, truly," rejoined Captain Delano. "Had such a thing happened on board the *Bachelor's Delight*, instant punishment would have followed."

At these words the Spaniard turned upon the American one of his sudden, staring, half-lunatic looks; then, relapsing into his torpor, answered, "Doubtless, doubtless, Señor."

Is it, thought Captain Delano, that this hapless man is one of those paper captains I've known, who by policy wink at what by power they cannot put down? I know no sadder sight than a commander who has little of command but the name.

"I should think, Don Benito," he now said, glancing towards the oakum-picker who had sought to interfere with the boys, "that you would find it advantageous to keep all your blacks employed, especially the younger ones, no matter at what useless task, and no matter what happens to the ship. Why, even with my little band, I find such a course indispensable. I once kept a crew on my quarter-deck thrumming mats for my cabin, when, for three days, I had given up my ship—mats, men, and all—for a speedy loss, owing to the violence of a gale, in which we could do nothing but helplessly drive before it."

"Doubtless, doubtless," muttered Don Benito.

"But," continued Captain Delano, again glancing upon the oakum-pickers and then at the hatchet-polishers, near by, "I see you keep some, at least, of your host employed."

"Yes," was again the vacant response.

"Those old men there, shaking their pows from their pulpits," continued Captain Delano, pointing to the oakum-pickers, "seem to act the part of old dominies to the rest, little heeded as their admonitions are at times. Is this voluntary on their part, Don Benito, or have you appointed them shepherds to your flock of black sheep?"

"What posts they fill, I appointed them," rejoined the Spaniard, in an acrid tone, as if resenting some supposed satiric reflection.

"And these others, these Ashantee conjurors here," continued Captain Delano, rather uneasily eying the brandished steel of the hatchet-polishers, where, in spots, it had been brought to a shine, "this seems a curious business they are at, Don Benito?"

"In the gales we met," answered the Spaniard, "what of our general cargo was not thrown overboard was much damaged by the brine. Since coming into calm weather, I have had several cases of knives and hatchets daily brought up for overhauling and cleaning."

"A prudent idea, Don Benito. You are part owner of ship and cargo, I presume; but none of the slaves, perhaps?"

"I am owner of all you see," impatiently returned Don Benito, "except the main company of blacks, who belonged to my late friend, Alexandro Aranda."

As he mentioned this name, his air was heart-broken; his knees shook; his servant supported him.

Thinking he divined the cause of such unusual emotion, to confirm his surmise, Captain Delano, after a pause, said: "And may I ask, Don Benito, whether—since a while ago you spoke of some cabin passengers—the friend, whose loss so afflicts you, at the outset of the voyage accompanied his blacks?"

"Yes."

"But died of the fever?"

"Died of the fever. Oh, could I but——" Again quivering, the Spaniard paused.

"Pardon me," said Captain Delano, lowly, "but I think that, by a sympathetic experience, I conjecture, Don Benito, what it is that gives the keener edge to your grief. It was once my hard fortune to lose, at sea, a dear friend, my own brother, then supercargo. Assured of the welfare of his spirit, its departure I could have borne like a man: but that honest eye, that honest hand—both of which had so often met mine—and that warm heart; all, all—like scraps to the dogs—to throw all to the sharks! It was then I vowed never to have for fellow-voyager a man I loved, unless, unbeknown to him, I had provided every requisite, in case of a fatality, for embalming his mortal part for interment on shore. Were your friend's remains now on board this ship, Don Benito, not thus strangely would the mention of his name affect you."

"On board this ship?" echoed the Spaniard. Then, with horrified gestures, as directed against some spectre, he unconsciously fell into the ready arms of his attendant, who, with a silent appeal toward Captain Delano, seemed beseeching him not again to broach a theme so unspeakably distressing to his master.

This poor fellow now, thought the pained American, is the victim of that sad superstition which associates goblins with the deserted body of man, as ghosts with an abandoned house. How unlike are we made! What to me, in like case, would have been a solemn satisfaction, the bare suggestion, even, terrifies the Spaniard into this trance. Poor Alexandro Aranda! what would you say could you here see your friend—who, on former voyages, when you, for months, were left behind, has, I dare say, often longed, and longed, for one peep at you—now transported with terror at the least thought of having you anyway nigh him.

At this moment, with a dreary grave-yard toll, betokening a flaw, the ship's forecastle bell, smote by one of the grizzled oakum-pickers, proclaimed ten o'clock, through the leaden calm; when Captain Delano's attention was caught by the moving figure of a gigantic black, emerging from the general crowd below, and slowly advancing towards the elevated poop. An iron collar was about his neck, from which depended a chain, thrice wound round his body; the terminating links padlocked together at a broad band of iron, his girdle.

"How like a mute Atufal moves," murmured the servant.

The black mounted the steps of the poop, and, like a brave prisoner, brought up to receive sentence, stood in unquailing muteness before Don Benito, now recovered from his attack.

At the first glimpse of his approach, Don Benito had started, a resentful shadow swept over his face; and, as with the sudden memory of bootless rage, his white lips glued together.

This is some mulish mutineer, thought Captain Delano, surveying, not without a mixture of admiration, the colossal form of the negro.

"See, he waits your question, master," said the servant.

Thus reminded, Don Benito, nervously averting his glance, as if shunning, by anticipation, some rebellious response, in a disconcerted voice, thus spoke:—

"Atufal, will you ask my pardon, now?"

The black was silent.

"Again, master," murmured the servant, with bitter upbraiding eying his countryman, "Again, master; he will bend to master yet."

"Answer," said Don Benito, still averting his glance, "say but the one word, *pardon,* and your chains shall be off."

Upon this, the black, slowly raising both arms, let them lifelessly fall, his links clanking, his head bowed; as much as to say, "No, I am content."

"Go," said Don Benito, with inkept and unknown emotion. Deliberately as he had come, the black obeyed.

"Excuse me, Don Benito," said Captain Delano, "but this scene surprises me; what means it, pray?"

"It means that that negro alone, of all the band, has given me peculiar cause of offense. I have put him in chains; I——"

Here he paused; his hand to his head, as if there were a swimming there, or a sudden bewilderment of memory had come over him; but meeting his servant's kindly glance seemed reassured, and proceeded:—

"I could not scourge such a form. But I told him he must ask my pardon. As yet he has not. At my command, every two hours he stands before me."

"And how long has this been?"

"Some sixty days."

"And obedient in all else? And respectful?"

"Yes."

"Upon my conscience, then," exclaimed Captain Delano, impulsively, "he has a royal spirit in him, this fellow."

"He may have some right to it," bitterly returned Don Benito, "he says he was king in his own land."

"Yes," said the servant, entering a word, "those slits in Atufal's ears once held wedges of gold; but poor Babo here, in his own land, was only a poor slave; a black man's slave was Babo, who now is the white's."

Somewhat annoyed by these conversational familiarities, Captain Delano turned curiously upon the attendant, then glanced inquiringly at his master; but, as if long wonted to these little informalities, neither master nor man seemed to understand him.

"What, pray, was Atufal's offense, Don Benito?" asked Captain Delano; "if it was not something very serious, take a fool's advice, and, in view of his general docility, as well as in some natural respect for his spirit, remit him his penalty."

"No, no, master never will do that," here murmured the servant to himself, "proud Atufal must first ask master's pardon. The slave there carries the padlock, but master here carries the key."

His attention thus directed, Captain Delano now noticed for the first, that, suspended by a slender silken cord, from Don

Benito's neck, hung a key. At once, from the servant's muttered syllables, divining the key's purpose, he smiled and said: —"So, Don Benito—padlock and key—significant symbols, truly."

Biting his lip, Don Benito faltered.

Though the remark of Captain Delano, a man of such native simplicity as to be incapable of satire or irony, had been dropped in playful allusion to the Spaniard's singularly evidenced lordship over the black; yet the hypochondriac seemed some way to have taken it as a malicious reflection upon his confessed inability thus far to break down, at least, on a verbal summons, the entrenched will of the slave. Deploring this supposed misconception, yet despairing of correcting it, Captain Delano shifted the subject; but finding his companion more than ever withdrawn, as if still sourly digesting the lees of the presumed affront above-mentioned, by and by Captain Delano likewise became less talkative, oppressed, against his own will, by what seemed the secret vindictiveness of the morbidly sensitive Spaniard. But the good sailor, himself of a quite contrary disposition, refrained, on his part, alike from the appearance as from the feeling of resentment, and if silent, was only so from contagion.

Presently the Spaniard, assisted by his servant, somewhat discourteously crossed over from his guest; a procedure which, sensibly enough, might have been allowed to pass for idle caprice of ill-humor, had not master and man, lingering round the corner of the elevated skylight, begun whispering together in low voices. This was unpleasing. And more: the moody air of the Spaniard, which at times had not been without a sort of valetudinarian stateliness, now seemed anything but dignified; while the menial familiarity of the servant lost its original charm of simple-hearted attachment.

In his embarrassment, the visitor turned his face to the other side of the ship. By so doing, his glance accidentally fell on a young Spanish sailor, a coil of rope in his hand, just stepped from the deck to the first round of the mizzen-rigging. Perhaps the man would not have been particularly noticed, were it not that, during his ascent to one of the yards, he, with a sort of covert intentness, kept his eye fixed on Captain Delano, from whom, presently, it passed, as if by a natural sequence, to the two whisperers.

His own attention thus redirected to that quarter, Captain Delano gave a slight start. From something in Don Benito's manner just then, it seemed as if the visitor had, at least partly, been the subject of the withdrawn consultation going on—a conjecture as little agreeable to the guest as it was little flattering to the host.

The singular alternations of courtesy and ill-breeding in the Spanish captain were unaccountable, except on one of two suppositions—innocent lunacy, or wicked imposture.

But the first idea, though it might naturally have occurred to an indifferent observer, and, in some respect, had not hitherto been wholly a stranger to Captain Delano's mind, yet, now that, in an incipient way, he began to regard the stranger's conduct something in the light of an intentional affront, of course the idea of lunacy was virtually vacated. But if not a lunatic, what then? Under the circumstances, would a gentleman, nay, any honest boor, act the part now acted by his host? The man was an imposter. Some low-born adventurer, masquerading as an oceanic grandee; yet so ignorant of the first requisites of mere gentlemanhood as to be betrayed into the present remarkable indecorum. That strange ceremoniousness, too, at other times evinced, seemed not uncharacteristic of one playing a part above his real level. Benito Cereno—Don Benito Cereno—a sounding name. One, too, at that period, not unknown, in the surname, to supercargoes and sea captains trading along the Spanish Main, as belonging to one of the most enterprising and extensive mercantile families in all those provinces; several members of it having titles; a sort of Castilian Rothschild, with a noble brother, or cousin, in every great trading town of South America. The alleged Don Benito was in early manhood, about twenty-nine or thirty. To assume a sort of roving cadetship in the maritime affairs of such a house, what more likely scheme for a young knave of talent and spirit? But the Spaniard was a pale invalid. Never mind. For even to the degree of simulating mortal disease, the craft of some tricksters had been known to attain. To think that, under the aspect of infantile weakness, the most savage energies might be couched—those velvets of the Spaniard but the silky paw to his fangs.

From no train of thought did these fancies come; not from within, but from without; suddenly, too, and in one throng, like hoar frost; yet as soon to vanish as the mild sun of Captain Delano's good-nature regained its meridian.

Glancing over once more towards his host—whose side-face, revealed above the skylight, was now turned towards him—

he was struck by the profile, whose clearness of cut was re-
fined by the thinness, incident to ill-health, as well as ennobled
about the chin by the beard. Away with suspicion. He was a
true off-shoot of a true hidalgo Cereno.

Relieved by these and other better thoughts, the visitor,
lightly humming a tune, now began indifferently pacing the
poop, so as not to betray to Don Benito that he had at all mis-
trusted incivility, much less duplicity; for such mistrust would
yet be proved illusory, and by the event; though, for the present, the circumstance which had provoked that distrust remained unexplained. But when that little mystery should
have been cleared up, Captain Delano thought he might extremely regret it, did he allow Don Benito to become aware
that he had indulged in ungenerous surmises. In short, to the
Spaniard's black-letter text, it was best, for a while, to leave
open margin.

Presently, his pale face twitching and overcast, the Spaniard,
still supported by his attendant, moved over towards his guest,
when, with even more than his usual embarrassment, and a
strange sort of intriguing intonation in his husky whisper, the
following conversation began:—

"Señor, may I ask how long you have lain at this isle?"

"Oh, but a day or two, Don Benito."

"And from what port are you last?"

"Canton."

"And there, Señor, you exchanged your sealskins for teas
and silks, I think you said?"

"Yes. Silks, mostly."

"And the balance you took in specie, perhaps?"

Captain Delano, fidgeting a little, answered—

"Yes; some silver, not a very great deal though."

"Ah—well. May I ask how many men have you, Señor?"

Captain Delano slightly started, but answered—

"About five-and-twenty, all told."

"And at present, Señor, all on board, I suppose?"

"All on board, Don Benito," replied the Captain, now with
satisfaction.

"And will be to-night, Señor?"

At this last question, following so many pertinacious ones,
for the soul of him Captain Delano could not but look very
earnestly at the questioner, who, instead of meeting the glance,
with every token of craven discomposure dropped his eyes to
the deck; presenting an unworthy contrast to his servant, who,

just then, was kneeling at his feet, adjusting a loose shoe-buckle; his disengaged face meantime, with humble curiosity, turned openly up into his master's downcast one.

The Spaniard, still with a guilty shuffle, repeated his question:

"And—and will be to-night, Señor?"

"Yes, for aught I know," returned Captain Delano—"but nay," rallying himself into fearless truth, "some of them talked of going off on another fishing party about midnight."

"Your ships generally go—go more or less armed, I believe, Señor?"

"Oh, a six-pounder or two, in case of emergency," was the intrepidly indifferent reply, "with a small stock of muskets, sealing-spears, and cutlasses, you know."

As he thus responded, Captain Delano again glanced at Don Benito, but the latter's eyes were averted; while abruptly and awkwardly shifting the subject, he made some peevish allusion to the calm, and then, without apology, once more, with his attendant, withdrew to the opposite bulwarks, where the whispering was resumed.

At this moment, and ere Captain Delano could cast a cool thought upon what had just passed, the young Spanish sailor, before mentioned, was seen descending from the rigging. In act of stooping over to spring inboard to the deck, his voluminous, unconfined frock, or shirt, of coarse woolen, much spotted with tar, opened out far down the chest, revealing a soiled under-garment of what seemed the finest linen, edged, about the neck, with a narrow blue ribbon, sadly faded and worn. At this moment the young sailor's eye was again fixed on the whisperers, and Captain Delano thought he observed a lurking significance in it, as if silent signs, of some Freemason sort, had that instant been interchanged.

This once more impelled his own glance in the direction of Don Benito, and, as before, he could not but infer that himself formed the subject of the conference. He paused. The sound of the hatchet-polishing fell on his ears. He cast another swift side-look at the two. They had the air of conspirators. In connection with the late questionings, and the incident of the young sailor, these things now begat such return of involuntary suspicion, that the singular guilelessness of the American could not endure it. Plucking up a gay and humorous expression, he crossed over to the two rapidly, saying:—"Ha, Don

Benito, your black here seems high in your trust; a sort of privy-counselor, in fact."

Upon this, the servant looked up with a good-natured grin, but the master started as from a venomous bite. It was a moment or two before the Spaniard sufficiently recovered himself to reply; which he did, at last, with cold constraint:—"Yes, Señor, I have trust in Babo."

Here Babo, changing his previous grin of mere animal humor into an intelligent smile, not ungratefully eyed his master.

Finding that the Spaniard now stood silent and reserved, as if involuntarily, or purposely giving hint that his guest's proximity was inconvenient just then, Captain Delano, unwilling to appear uncivil even to incivility itself, made some trivial remark and moved off; again and again turning over in his mind the mysterious demeanor of Don Benito Cereno.

He had descended from the poop, and, wrapped in thought, was passing near a dark hatchway, leading down into the steerage, when, perceiving motion there, he looked to see what moved. The same instant there was a sparkle in the shadowy hatchway, and he saw one of the Spanish sailors, prowling there, hurriedly placing his hand in the bosom of his frock, as if hiding something. Before the man could have been certain who it was that was passing, he slunk below out of sight. But enough was seen of him to make it sure that he was the same young sailor before noticed in the rigging.

What was that which so sparkled? thought Captain Delano. It was no lamp—no match—no live coal. Could it have been a jewel? But how come sailors with jewels?—or with silk-trimmed under-shirts either? Has he been robbing the trunks of the dead cabin-passengers? But if so, he would hardly wear one of the stolen articles on board ship here. Ah, ah—if, now, that was, indeed, a secret sign I saw passing between this suspicious fellow and his captain awhile since; if I could only be certain that, in my uneasiness, my senses did not deceive me, then——

Here, passing from one suspicious thing to another, his mind revolved the strange questions put to him concerning his ship.

By a curious coincidence, as each point was recalled, the black wizards of Ashantee would strike up with their hatchets, as in ominous comment on the white stranger's thoughts. Pressed by such enigmas and portents, it would have been almost against nature, had not, even into the least distrustful heart, some ugly misgiving obtruded.

Observing the ship, now helplessly fallen into a current, with enchanted sails, drifting with increased rapidity seaward; and noting that, from a lately intercepted projection of the land, the sealer was hidden, the stout mariner began to quake at thoughts which he barely durst confess to himself. Above all, he began to feel a ghostly dread of Don Benito. And yet, when he roused himself, dilated his chest, felt himself strong on his legs, and coolly considered it—what did all these phantoms amount to?

Had the Spaniard any sinister scheme, it must have reference not so much to him (Captain Delano) as to his ship (the *Bachelor's Delight*). Hence the present drifting away of the one ship from the other, instead of favoring any such possible scheme, was, for the time, at least, opposed to it. Clearly any suspicion, combining such contradictions, must need be delusive. Besides, was it not absurd to think of a vessel in distress —a vessel by sickness almost dismanned of her crew—a vessel whose inmates were parched for water—was it not a thousand times absurd that such a craft should, at present, be of a piratical character; or her commander, either for himself or those under him, cherish any desire but for speedy relief and refreshment? But then, might not general distress, and thirst in particular, be affected? And might not that same undiminished Spanish crew, alleged to have perished off to a remnant, be at that very moment lurking in the hold? On heart-broken pretense of entreating a cup of cold water, fiends in human form had got into lonely dwellings, nor retired until a dark deed had been done. And among the Malay pirates, it was no unusual thing to lure ships after them into their treacherous harbors, or entice boarders from a declared enemy at sea, by the spectacle of thinly manned or vacant decks, beneath which prowled a hundred spears with yellow arms ready to upthrust them through the mats. Not that Captain Delano had entirely credited such things. He had heard of them—and now, as stories, they recurred. The present destination of the ship was the anchorage. There she would be near his own vessel. Upon gaining that vicinity, might not the *San Dominick*, like a slumbering volcano, suddenly let loose energies now hid?

He recalled the Spaniard's manner while telling his story. There was a gloomy hesitancy and subterfuge about it. It was just the manner of one making up his tale for evil purposes, as he goes. But if that story was not true, what was the truth? That the ship had unlawfully come into the Spaniard's possession? But in many of its details, especially in reference to the more calamitous parts, such as the fatalities among the seamen, the consequent prolonged beating about, the past sufferings from obstinate calms, and still continued suffering from thirst; in all these points, as well as others, Don Benito's story had corroborated not only the wailing ejaculations of the indiscriminate multitude, white and black, but likewise—what seemed impossible to be counterfeit—by the very expression and play of every human feature, which Captain Delano saw. If Don Benito's story was, throughout, an invention, then every soul on board, down to the youngest negress, was his carefully drilled recruit in the plot: an incredible inference. And yet, if there was ground for mistrusting his veracity, that inference was a legitimate one.

But those questions of the Spaniard. There, indeed, one might pause. Did they not seem put with much the same object with which the burglar or assassin, by day-time, reconnoitres the walls of a house? But, with ill purposes, to solicit such information openly of the chief person endangered, and so, in effect, setting him on his guard; how unlikely a procedure was that? Absurd, then, to suppose that those questions had been prompted by evil designs. Thus, the same conduct, which, in this instance, had raised the alarm, served to dispel it. In short, scarce any suspicion or uneasiness, however apparently reasonable at the time, which was not now, with equally apparent reason, dismissed.

At last he began to laugh at his former forebodings; and laugh at the strange ship for, in its aspect, someway siding with them, as it were; and laugh, too, at the odd-looking blacks, particularly those old scissors-grinders, the Ashantees; and those bed-ridden old knitting women, the oakum-pickers; and almost at the dark Spaniard himself, the central hobgoblin of all.

For the rest, whatever in a serious way seemed enigmatical, was now good-naturedly explained away by the thought that, for the most part, the poor invalid scarcely knew what he was about; either sulking in black vapors, or putting idle questions without sense or object. Evidently, for the present, the man was not fit to be intrusted with the ship. On some benevolent plea withdrawing the command from him, Captain Delano would yet have to send her to Concepcion, in charge of his second mate, a worthy person and good navigator—a plan not

more convenient for the *San Dominick* than for Don Benito;
for, relieved from all anxiety, keeping wholly to his cabin, the
sick man, under the good nursing of his servant, would, probably, by the end of the passage, be in a measure restored to
health, and with that he should also be restored to authority.

Such were the American's thoughts. They were tranquilliz-
ing. There was a difference between the idea of Don Benito's
darkly pre-ordaining Captain Delano's fate, and Captain
Delano's lightly arranging Don Benito's. Nevertheless, it was
not without something of relief that the good seaman presently perceived his whale-boat in the distance. Its absence had
been prolonged by unexpected detention at the sealer's side,
as well as its returning trip lengthened by the continual reces-
sion of the goal.

The advancing speck was observed by the blacks. Their
shouts attracted the attention of Don Benito, who, with a return of courtesy, approaching Captain Delano, expressed satisfaction at the coming of some supplies, slight and temporary
as they must necessarily prove.

Captain Delano responded; but while doing so, his attention was drawn to something passing on the deck below:
among the crowd climbing the landward bulwarks, anxiously
watching the coming boat, two blacks, to all appearances accidentally incommoded by one of the sailors, violently pushed
him aside, which the sailor someway resenting, they dashed
him to the deck, despite the earnest cries of the oakum-pickers.

"Don Benito," said Captain Delano quickly, "do you see
what is going on there? Look!"

But, seized by his cough, the Spaniard staggered, with both
hands to his face, on the point of falling. Captain Delano
would have supported him, but the servant was more alert,
who, with one hand sustaining his master, with the other applied the cordial. Don Benito restored, the black withdrew his
support, slipping aside a little, but dutifully remaining within
call of a whisper. Such discretion was here evinced as quite
wiped away, in the visitor's eyes, any blemish of impropriety
which might have attached to the attendant, from the indecorous conferences before mentioned; showing, too, that if the
servant were to blame, it might be more the master's fault than
his own, since, when left to himself, he could conduct thus well.

His glance called away from the spectacle of disorder to
the more pleasing one before him, Captain Delano could not
avoid again congratulating his host upon possessing such a

servant, who, though perhaps a little too forward now and then, must upon the whole be invaluable to one in the invalid's situation.

"Tell me, Don Benito," he added, with a smile—"I should like to have your man here, myself—what will you take for him? Would fifty doubloons be any object?"

"Master wouldn't part with Babo for a thousand doubloons," murmured the black, overhearing the offer, and taking it in earnest, and, with the strange vanity of a faithful slave, appreciated by his master, scorning to hear so paltry a valuation put upon him by a stranger. But Don Benito, apparently hardly yet completely restored, and again interrupted by his cough, made but some broken reply.

Soon his physical distress became so great, affecting his mind, too, apparently, that, as if to screen the sad spectacle, the servant gently conducted his master below.

Left to himself, the American, to while away the time till his boat should arrive, would have pleasantly accosted some one of the few Spanish seamen he saw; but recalling something that Don Benito had said touching their ill conduct, he refrained; as a shipmaster indisposed to countenance cowardice or unfaithfulness in seamen.

While, with these thoughts, standing with eye directed forward towards that handful of sailors, suddenly he thought that one or two of them returned the glance and with a sort of meaning. He rubbed his eyes, and looked again; but again seemed to see the same thing. Under a new form, but more obscure than any previous one, the old suspicions recurred, but, in the absence of Don Benito, with less of panic than before. Despite the bad account given of the sailors, Captain Delano resolved forthwith to accost one of them. Descending the poop, he made his way through the blacks, his movement drawing a queer cry from the oakum-pickers, prompted by whom, the negroes, twitching each other aside, divided before him; but, as if curious to see what was the object of this deliberate visit to their Ghetto, closing in behind, in tolerable order, followed the white stranger up. His progress thus proclaimed as by mounted kings-at-arms, and escorted as by a Kaffir guard of honor, Captain Delano, assuming a good-humored, off-handed air, continued to advance; now and then saying a blithe word to the negroes, and his eye curiously surveying the white faces, here and there sparsely mixed in with the blacks, like stray white pawns venturously involved in the ranks of the chess-men opposed.

While thinking which of them to select for this purpose, he chanced to observe a sailor seated on the deck engaged in tar-ring the strap of a large clock, a circle of blacks squatted round him inquisitively eying the process.

The mean employment of the man was in contrast with something superior in his figure. His hand, black with con-tinually thrusting it into the tar-pot held for him by a negro, seemed not naturally allied to his face, a face which would have been a very fine one but for its haggardness. Whether this haggardness had aught to do with criminality, could not be determined; since, as intense heat and cold, though unlike, produce like sensations, so innocence and guilt, when, through casual association with mental pain, stamping any visible im-press, use one seal—a hacked one.

Not again that this reflection occurred to Captain Delano at the time, charitable man as he was. Rather another idea. Because observing so singular a haggardness combined with a dark eye, averted as in trouble and shame, and then again re-calling Don Benito's confessed ill opinion of his crew, insensi-bly he was operated upon by certain general notions which, while disconnecting pain and abashment from virtue, invaria-bly link them with vice.

If, indeed, there be any wickedness on board this ship, thought Captain Delano, be sure that man there has fouled his hand in it, even as now he fouls it in the pitch. I don't like to accost him. I will speak to this other, this old Jack here on the windlass.

He advanced to an old Barcelona tar, in ragged red breeches and dirty night-cap, cheeks trenched and bronzed, whiskers dense as thorn hedges. Seated between two sleepy-looking Africans, this mariner, like his younger shipmate, was employed upon some rigging—splicing a cable—the sleepy-looking blacks performing the inferior function of holding the outer parts of the ropes for him.

Upon Captain Delano's approach, the man at once hung his head below its previous level; the one necessary for busi-ness. It appeared as if he desired to be thought absorbed, with more than common fidelity, in his task. Being addressed, he glanced up, but with what seemed a furtive, diffident air, which sat strangely enough on his weather-beaten visage, much as if a grizzly bear, instead of growling and biting, should simper and cast sheep's eyes. He was asked several questions concerning the voyage—questions purposely referring to several particulars in Don Benito's narrative, not previously corroborated by those impulsive cries greeting the visitor on first coming on board. The questions were briefly answered, confirming all that remained to be confirmed of the story. The negroes about the windlass joined in with the old sailor; but, as they became talkative, he by degrees became mute, and at length quite glum, seemed morosely unwilling to answer more questions, and yet, all the while, this ursine air was somehow mixed with his sheepish one.

Despairing of getting into unembarrassed talk with such a centaur, Captain Delano, after glancing round for a more promising countenance, but seeing none, spoke pleasantly to the blacks to make way for him; and so, amid various grins and grimaces, returned to the poop, feeling a little strange at first, he could hardly tell why, but upon the whole with regained confidence in Benito Cereno.

How plainly, thought he, did that old whiskerando yonder betray a consciousness of ill desert. No doubt, when he saw me coming, he dreaded lest I, apprised by his captain of the crew's general misbehavior, came with sharp words for him, and so down with his head. And yet—and yet, now that I think of it, that very old fellow, if I err not, was one of those who seemed so earnestly eying me here awhile since. Ah, these currents spin one's head round almost as much as they do the ship. Ha, there now's a pleasant sort of sunny sight; quite sociable, too.

His attention had been drawn to a slumbering negress, partly disclosed through the lacework of some rigging, lying, with youthful limbs carelessly disposed, under the lee of the bulwarks, like a doe in the shade of a woodland rock. Sprawling at her lapped breasts, was her wide-awake fawn, stark naked, its black little body half lifted from the deck, crosswise with its dam's; its hands, like two paws, clambering upon her; its mouth and nose ineffectually rooting to get at the mark; and meantime giving a vexatious half-grunt, blending with the composed snore of the negress.

The uncommon vigor of the child at length roused the mother. She started up, at a distance facing Captain Delano. But as if not at all concerned at the attitude in which she had been caught, delightedly she caught the child up, with maternal transports, covering it with kisses.

There's naked nature, now; pure tenderness and love, thought Captain Delano, well pleased.

This incident prompted him to remark the other negresses more particularly than before. He was gratified with their manners: like most uncivilized women, they seemed at once tender of heart and tough of constitution; equally ready to die for their infants or fight for them. Unsophisticated as leopardesses; loving as doves. Ah! thought Captain Delano, these, perhaps, are some of the very women whom Ledyard saw in Africa, and gave such a noble account of.

These natural sights somehow insensibly deepened his confidence and ease. At last he looked to see how his boat was getting on; but it was still pretty remote. He turned to see if Don Benito had returned; but he had not.

To change the scene, as well as to please himself with a leisurely observation of the coming boat, stepping over into the mizzen-chains, he clambered his way into the starboard quarter-gallery—one of those abandoned Venetian-looking water-balconies previously mentioned—retreats cut off from the deck. As his foot pressed the half-damp, half-dry sea-mosses matting the place, and a chance phantom cats-paw—an islet of breeze, unheralded, unfollowed—as this ghostly cats-paw came fanning his cheek; as his glance fell upon the row of small, round dead-lights—all closed like coppered eyes of the coffined—and the state-cabin door, once connecting with the gallery, even as the dead-lights had once looked out upon it, but now calked fast like a sarcophagus lid; and to a purple-black, tarred-over panel, threshold, and post; and he bethought him of the time, when that state-cabin and this state-balcony had heard the voices of the Spanish king's officers, and the forms of the Lima viceroy's daughters had perhaps leaned where he stood —as these and other images flitted through his mind, as the cats-paw through the calm, gradually he felt rising a dreamy inquietude, like that of one who alone on the prairie feels unrest from the repose of the noon.

He leaned against the carved balustrade, again looking off toward his boat; but found his eye falling upon the ribbon grass, trailing along the ship's water-line, straight as a border of green box; and parterres of sea-weed, broad ovals and crescents, floating nigh and far, with what seemed long formal alleys between, crossing the terraces of swells, and sweeping round as if leading to the grottoes below. And overhanging all was the balustrade by his arm, which, partly stained with pitch and partly embossed with moss, seemed the charred ruin of some summer-house in a grand garden long running to waste.

Trying to break one charm, he was but becharmed anew. Though upon the wide sea, he seemed in some far inland country; prisoner in some deserted chateau, left to stare at empty grounds, and peer out at vague roads, where never wagon or wayfarer passed.

But these enchantments were a little disenchanted as his eye fell on the corroded main-chains. Of an ancient style, massy and rusty in link, shackle and bolt, they seemed even more fit for the ship's present business than the one for which she had been built.

Presently he thought something moved nigh the chains. He rubbed his eyes, and looked hard. Groves of rigging were about the chains; and there, peering from behind a great stay, like an Indian from behind a hemlock, a Spanish sailor, a marling-spike in his hand, was seen, who made what seemed an imperfect gesture towards the balcony, but immediately, as if alarmed by some advancing step along the deck within, vanished into the recesses of the hempen forest, like a poacher.

What meant this? Something the man had sought to communicate, unbeknown to any one, even to his captain. Did the secret involve aught unfavorable to his captain? Were those previous misgivings of Captain Delano's about to be verified? Or, in his haunted mood at the moment, had some random, unintentional motion of the man, while busy with the stay, as if repairing it, been mistaken for a significant beckoning?

Not unbewildered, again he gazed off for his boat. But it was temporarily hidden by a rocky spur of the isle. As with some eagerness he bent forward, watching for the first shooting view of its beak, the balustrade gave way before him like charcoal. Had he not clutched an outreaching rope he would have fallen into the sea. The crash, though feeble, and the fall, though hollow, of the rotten fragments, must have been overheard. He glanced up. With sober curiosity peering down upon him was one of the old oakum-pickers, slipped from his perch to an outside boom; while below the old negro, and, invisible to him, reconnoitering from a port-hole like a fox from the mouth of its den, crouched the Spanish sailor again. From something suddenly suggested by the man's air, the mad idea now darted into Captain Delano's mind, that Don Benito's plea of indisposition, in withdrawing below, was but a pretense: that he was engaged there maturing his plot, of which the sailor, by some means gaining an inkling, had a mind to warn the stranger against; incited, it may be, by gratitude for a kind word on first boarding the ship. Was it from foreseeing some possible interference like this, that Don Benito had, beforehand, given such a bad character of his sailors, while praising the negroes; though, indeed, the former seemed as docile as the latter the contrary? The whites, too, by nature, were the shrewder race. A man with some evil design, would he not be likely to speak well of that stupidity which was blind to his depravity, and malign that intelligence from which it might not be hidden? Not unlikely, perhaps. But if the whites had dark secrets concerning Don Benito, could then Don Benito be any way in complicity with the blacks? But they were too stupid. Besides, who ever heard of a white so far a renegade as to apostatize from his very species almost, by leaguing in against it with negroes? These difficulties recalled former ones. Lost in their mazes, Captain Delano, who had now regained the deck, was uneasily advancing along it, when he observed a new face; an aged sailor seated cross-legged near the main hatchway. His skin was shrunk up with wrinkles like a pelican's empty pouch; his hair frosted; his countenance grave and composed. His hands were full of ropes, which he was working into a large knot. Some blacks were about him obligingly dipping the strands for him, here and there, as the exigencies of the operation demanded.

Captain Delano crossed over to him, and stood in silence surveying the knot; his mind, by a not uncongenial transition, passing from its own entanglements to those of the hemp. For intricacy, such a knot he had never seen in an American ship, nor indeed any other. The old man looked like an Egyptian priest, making Gordian knots for the temple of Ammon. The knot seemed a combination of double-bowline-knot, treble-crown-knot, back-handed-well-knot, knot-in-and-out-knot, and jamming-knot.

At last, puzzled to comprehend the meaning of such a knot, Captain Delano addressed the knotter:—

"What are you knotting there, my man?"

"The knot," was the brief reply, without looking up.

"So it seems; but what is it for?"

"For some one else to undo," muttered back the old man,

plying his fingers harder than ever, the knot being now nearly completed.

While Captain Delano stood watching him, suddenly the old man threw the knot towards him, saying in broken English —the first heard in the ship—something to this effect: "Undo it, cut it, quick." It was said lowly, but with such condensation of rapidity, that the long, slow words in Spanish, which had preceded and followed, almost operated as covers to the brief English between.

For a moment, knot in hand, and knot in head, Captain Delano stood mute; while, without further heeding him, the old man was now intent upon other ropes. Presently there was a slight stir behind Captain Delano. Turning, he saw the chained negro, Atufal, standing quietly there. The next moment the old sailor rose, muttering, and, followed by his subordinate negroes, removed to the forward part of the ship, where in the crowd he disappeared.

An elderly negro, in a clout like an infant's, and with a pepper and salt head, and a kind of attorney air, now approached Captain Delano. In tolerable Spanish, and with a good-natured, knowing wink, he informed him that the old knotter was simple-witted, but harmless; often playing his odd tricks. The negro concluded by begging the knot, for of course the stranger would not care to be troubled with it. Unconsciously, it was handed to him. With a sort of congé, the negro received it, and, turning his back, ferreted into it like a detective custom-house officer after smuggled laces. Soon, with some African word, equivalent to pshaw, he tossed the knot overboard.

All this is very queer now, thought Captain Delano, with a qualmish sort of emotion; but, as one feeling incipient seasickness, he strove, by ignoring the symptoms, to get rid of the malady. Once more he looked off for his boat. To his delight, it was now again in view, leaving the rocky spur astern.

The sensation here experienced, after at first relieving his uneasiness, with unforeseen efficacy soon began to remove it. The less distant sight of that well-known boat—showing it, not as before, half blended with the haze, but with outline defined, so that its individuality, like a man's, was manifest; that boat, *Rover* by name, which, though now in strange seas, had often pressed the beach of Captain Delano's home, and, brought to its threshold for repairs, had familiarly lain there, as a Newfoundland dog; the sight of that household boat evoked a thousand trustful associations, which, contrasted with previous suspicions, filled him not only with lightsome confidence, but somehow with half humorous self-reproaches at his former lack of it.

"What, I, Amasa Delano—Jack of the Beach, as they called me when a lad—I, Amasa; the same that, duck-satchel in hand, used to paddle along the water-side to the school-house made from the old hulk—I, little Jack of the Beach, that used to go berrying with cousin Nat and the rest; I to be murdered here at the ends of the earth, on board a haunted pirate-ship by a horrible Spaniard? Too nonsensical to think of! Who would murder Amasa Delano? His conscience is clean. There is some one above. Fie, fie, Jack of the Beach! you are a child indeed; a child of the second childhood, old boy; you are beginning to dote and drool, I'm afraid."

Light of heart and foot, he stepped aft, and there was met by Don Benito's servant, who, with a pleasing expression, responsive to his own present feelings, informed him that his master had recovered from the effects of his coughing fit, and had just ordered him to go present his compliments to his good guest, Don Amasa, and say that he (Don Benito) would soon have the happiness to rejoin him.

There now, do you mark that? again thought Captain Delano, walking the poop. What a donkey I was. This kind gentleman who here sends me his kind compliments, he, but ten minutes ago, dark-lantern in hand, was dodging round some old grindstone in the hold, sharpening a hatchet for me, I thought. Well, well; these long calms have a morbid effect on the mind, I've often heard, though I never believed it before. Ha! glancing towards the boat; there's *Rover;* good dog; a white bone in her mouth. A pretty big bone though, seems to me.—What? Yes, she has fallen afoul of the bubbling tide-rip there. It sets her the other way, too, for the time. Patience.

It was now about noon, though, from the grayness of everything, it seemed to be getting towards dusk.

The calm was confirmed. In the far distance, away from the influence of land, the leaden ocean seemed laid out and leaded up, its course finished, soul gone, defunct. But the current from landward, where the ship was, increased; silently sweeping her further and further towards the tranced waters beyond.

Still, from his knowledge of those latitudes, cherishing hopes of a breeze, and a fair and fresh one, at any moment, Captain Delano, despite present prospects, buoyantly counted upon bringing the *San Dominick* safely to anchor ere night. The distance swept over was nothing; since, with a good wind, ten minutes' sailing would retrace more than sixty minutes' drifting. Meantime, one moment turning to mark *Rover* fighting the tide-rip, and the next to see Don Benito approaching, he continued walking the poop.

Gradually he felt a vexation arising from the delay of his boat; this soon merged into uneasiness; and at last—his eye falling continually, as from a stage-box into the pit, upon the strange crowd before and below him, and, by and by, recognizing there the face—now composed to indifference—of the Spanish sailor who had seemed to beckon from the main-chains—something of his old trepidations returned.

Ah, thought he—gravely enough—this is like the ague: because it went off, it follows not that it won't come back.

Though ashamed of the relapse, he could not altogether subdue it; and so, exerting his good-nature to the utmost insensibly he came to a compromise.

Yes, this is a strange craft; a strange history, too, and strange folks on board. But—nothing more.

By way of keeping his mind out of mischief till the boat should arrive, he tried to occupy it with turning over and over, in a purely speculative sort of way, some lesser peculiarities of the captain and crew. Among others, four curious points recurred:

First, the affair of the Spanish lad assailed with a knife by the slave boy; an act winked at by Don Benito. Second, the tyranny in Don Benito's treatment of Atufal, the black; as if a child should lead a bull of the Nile by the ring in his nose. Third, the trampling of the sailor by the two negroes; a piece of insolence passed over without so much as a reprimand. Fourth, the cringing submission to their master, of all the ship's underlings, mostly blacks; as if by the least inadvertence they feared to draw down his despotic displeasure.

Coupling these points, they seemed somewhat contradictory. But what then, thought Captain Delano, glancing towards his now nearing boat—what then? Why, Don Benito is a very capricious commander. But he is not the first of the sort I have seen; though it's true he rather exceeds any other. But as a nation—continued he in his reveries—these Spaniards are all an odd set; the very word Spaniard has a curious, conspirator, Guy-Fawkish twang to it. And yet, I dare say, Spaniards in the main are as good folks as any in Duxbury, Massachusetts. Ah good! At last *Rover* has come.

As, with its welcome freight, the boat touched the side, the oakum-pickers, with venerable gestures, sought to restrain the blacks, who, at the sight of three gurried water-casks in its bottom, and a pile of wilted pumpkins in its bow, hung over the bulwarks in disorderly raptures.

Don Benito, with his servant, now appeared; his coming, perhaps, hastened by hearing the noise. Of him Captain Delano sought permission to serve out the water, so that all might share alike, and none injure themselves by unfair excess. But sensible, and, on Don Benito's account, kind as this offer was, it was received with what seemed impatience; as if aware that he lacked energy as a commander, Don Benito, with the true jealousy of weakness, resented as an affront any interference. So, at least, Captain Delano inferred.

In another moment the casks were being hoisted in, when some of the eager negroes accidentally jostled Captain Delano, where he stood by the gangway; so that, unmindful of Don Benito, yielding to the impulse of the moment, with good-natured authority he bade the blacks stand back; to enforce his words making use of a half-mirthful, half-menacing gesture. Instantly the blacks paused, just where they were, each negro and negress suspended in his or her posture, exactly as the word had found them—for a few seconds continuing so— while, as between the responsive posts of a telegraph, an unknown syllable ran from man to man among the perched oakum-pickers. While the visitor's attention was fixed by this scene, suddenly the hatchet-polishers half rose, and a rapid cry came from Don Benito.

Thinking that at the signal of the Spaniard he was about to be massacred, Captain Delano would have sprung for his boat, but paused, as the oakum-pickers, dropping down into the crowd with earnest exclamations, forced every white and every negro back, at the same moment, with gestures friendly and familiar, almost jocose, bidding him, in substance, not be a fool. Simultaneously the hatchet-polishers resumed their seats, quietly as so many tailors, and at once, as if nothing had happened, the work of hoisting in the casks was resumed, whites and blacks singing at the tackle.

Captain Delano glanced towards Don Benito. As he saw his meagre form in the act of recovering itself from reclining in the servant's arms, into which the agitated invalid had fallen, he could not but marvel at the panic by which himself had been surprised, on the darting supposition that such a commander, who, upon a legitimate occasion, so trivial, too, as it now appeared, could lose all self-command, was, with energetic iniquity, going to bring about his murder.

The casks being on deck, Captain Delano was handed a number of jars and cups by one of the steward's aids, who, in the name of his captain, entreated him to do as he had proposed—dole out the water. He complied, with republican impartiality as to this republican element, which always seeks one level, serving the oldest white no better than the youngest black; excepting, indeed, poor Don Benito, whose condition, if not rank, demanded an extra allowance. To him, in the first place, Captain Delano presented a fair pitcher of the fluid; but, thirsting as he was for it, the Spaniard quaffed not a drop until after several grave bows and salutes. A reciprocation of courtesies which the sight-loving Africans hailed with clapping of hands.

Two of the less wilted pumpkins being reserved for the cabin table, the residue were minced up on the spot for the general regalement. But the soft bread, sugar, and bottled cider, Captain Delano would have given the whites alone, and in chief Don Benito; but the latter objected; which disinterestedness not a little pleased the American; and so mouthfuls all around were given alike to whites and blacks; excepting one bottle of cider, which Babo insisted upon setting aside for his master.

Here it may be observed that as, on the first visit of the boat, the American had not permitted his men to board the ship, neither did he now; being unwilling to add to the confusion of the decks.

Not uninfluenced by the peculiar good-humor at present prevailing, and for the time oblivious of any but benevolent thoughts, Captain Delano, who, from recent indications, counted upon a breeze within an hour or two at furthest, dispatched the boat back to the sealer, with orders for all the hands that could be spared immediately to set about rafting casks to the watering-place and filling them. Likewise he bade word be carried to his chief officer, that if, against present expectation, the ship was not brought to anchor by sunset, he need be under no concern; for as there was to be a full moon that night, he (Captain Delano) would remain on board ready to play the pilot, come the wind soon or late.

As the two Captains stood together, observing the departing boat—the servant, as it happened, having just spied a spot
on his master's velvet sleeve, and silently engaged rubbing it
out—the American expressed his regrets that the *San Dominick* had no boats; none, at least, but the unseaworthy old
hulk of the long-boat, which, warped as a camel's skeleton in
the desert, and almost as bleached, lay pot-wise inverted amidships, one side a little tipped, furnishing a subterranean sort
of den for family groups of the blacks, mostly women and
small children; who, squatting on old mats below, or perched
above in the dark dome, on the elevated seats, were descried,
some distance within, like a social circle of bats, sheltering in
some friendly cave; at intervals, ebon flights of naked boys
and girls, three or four years old, darting in and out of the
den's mouth.

"Had you three or four boats now, Don Benito," said Captain Delano, "I think that, by tugging at the oars, your negroes
here might help along matters some. Did you sail from port
without boats, Don Benito?"

"They were stove in the gales, Señor."

"That was bad. Many men, too, you lost then. Boats and
men. Those must have been hard gales, Don Benito."

"Past all speech," cringed the Spaniard.

"Tell me, Don Benito," continued his companion with increased interest, "tell me, were these gales immediately off the
pitch of Cape Horn?"

"Cape Horn?—who spoke of Cape Horn?"

"Yourself did, when giving me an account of your voyage,"
answered Captain Delano, with almost equal astonishment at
this eating of his own words, even as he ever seemed eating his
own heart, on the part of the Spaniard. "You yourself, Don
Benito, spoke of Cape Horn," he emphatically repeated.

The Spaniard turned, in a sort of stopping posture, pausing an instant, as one about to make a plunging exchange of
elements, as from air to water.

At this moment a messenger-boy, a white, hurried by, in the
regular performance of his function carrying the last expired
half-hour forward to the forecastle, from the cabin time-piece,
to have it struck at the ship's large bell.

"Master," said the servant, discontinuing his work on the
coat sleeve, and addressing the rapt Spaniard with a sort of
timid apprehensiveness, as one charged with a duty, the discharge of which, it was foreseen, would prove irksome to the

very person who had imposed it, and for whose benefit it was intended, "master told me never mind where he was, or how engaged, always to remind him, to a minute, when shaving-time comes. Miguel has gone to strike the half-hour afternoon. It is *now*, master. Will master go into the cuddy?"

"Ah—yes," answered the Spaniard, starting, as from dreams into realities; then turning upon Captain Delano, he said that ere long he could resume the conversation.

"Then if master means to talk more to Don Amasa," said the servant, "why not let Don Amasa sit by master in the cuddy, and master can talk, and Don Amasa can listen, while Babo here lathers and strops."

"Yes," said Captain Delano, not unpleased with this sociable plan, "yes, Don Benito, unless you had rather not, I will go with you."

"Be it so, Señor."

As the three passed aft, the American could not but think it another strange instance of his host's capriciousness, this being shaved with such uncommon punctuality in the middle of the day. But he deemed it more than likely that the servant's anxious fidelity had something to do with the matter; inasmuch as the timely interruption served to rally his master from the mood which had evidently been coming upon him.

The place called the cuddy was a light deck-cabin formed by the poop, a sort of attic to the large cabin below. Part of it had formerly been the quarters of the officers; but since their death all the partitionings had been thrown down, and the whole interior converted into one spacious and airy marine hall; for absence of fine furniture and picturesque disarray of odd appurtenances, somewhat answering to the wide, cluttered hall of some eccentric bachelor-squire in the country, who hangs his shooting-jacket and tobacco-pouch on deer antlers, and keeps his fishing-rod, tongs, and walking-stick in the same corner.

The similitude was heightened, if not originally suggested, by glimpses of the surrounding sea; since, in one aspect, the country and the ocean seem cousins-german.

The floor of the cuddy was matted. Overhead, four or five old muskets were stuck into horizontal holes along the beams. On one side was a claw-footed old table lashed to the deck; a thumbed missal on it, and over it a small, meagre crucifix attached to the bulk-head. Under the table lay a dented cutlass or two, with a hacked harpoon, among some melancholy old rigging, like a heap of poor friars' girdles. There were also two long, sharp-ribbed settees of Malacca cane, black with age, and uncomfortable to look at as inquisitors' racks, with a large, misshapen arm-chair, which, furnished with a rude barber's crotch at the back, working with a screw, seemed some grotesque engine of torment. A flag-locker was in one corner, open, exposing various colored bunting, some rolled up, others half unrolled, still others tumbled. Opposite was a cumbrous washstand, of black mahogany, all of one block, with a pedestal, like a font, and over it a railed shelf, containing combs, brushes, and other implements of the toilet. A torn hammock of stained grass swung near; the sheets tossed, and the pillow wrinkled up like a brow, as if whoever slept here slept but illy, with alternate visitations of sad thoughts and bad dreams.

The further extremity of the cuddy, overhanging the ship's stern, was pierced with three openings, windows or port-holes, according as men or cannon might peer, socially or unsocially, out of them. At present neither men nor cannon were seen, though huge ring-bolts and other rusty iron fixtures of the wood-work hinted of twenty-four-pounders.

Glancing towards the hammock as he entered, Captain Delano said, "You sleep here, Don Benito?"

"Yes, Señor, since we got into mild weather."

"This seems a sort of dormitory, sitting-room, sail-loft, chapel, armory, and private closet all together, Don Benito," added Captain Delano, looking round.

"Yes, Señor; events have not been favorable to much order in my arrangements."

Here the servant, napkin on arm, made a motion as if waiting his master's good pleasure. Don Benito signified his readiness, when, seating him in the Malacca arm-chair, and for the guest's convenience drawing opposite one of the settees, the servant commenced operations by throwing back his master's collar and loosening his cravat.

There is something in the negro which, in a peculiar way, fits him for avocations about one's person. Most negroes are natural valets and hair-dressers; taking to the comb and brush congenially as to the castanets, and flourishing them apparently with almost equal satisfaction. There is, too, a smooth tact about them in this employment, with a marvelous, noiseless, gliding briskness, not ungraceful in its way, singularly pleasing to behold, and still more so to be the manipulated subject of. And above all is the great gift of good-humor. Not the mere grin or laugh is here meant. Those were unsuitable. But a certain easy cheerfulness, harmonious in every glance and gesture; as though God had set the whole negro to some pleasant tune.

When to this is added the docility arising from the unaspiring contentment of a limited mind, and that susceptibility of blind attachment sometimes inhering in indisputable inferiors, one readily perceives why those hypochondriacs, Johnson and Byron—it may be, something like the hypochondriac Benito Cereno—took to their hearts, almost to the exclusion of the entire white race, their serving men, the negroes, Barber and Fletcher. But if there be that in the negro which exempts him from the inflicted sourness of the morbid or cynical mind, how, in his most prepossessing aspects, must he appear to a benevolent one? When at ease with respect to exterior things, Captain Delano's nature was not only benign, but familiarly and humorously so. At home, he had often taken rare satisfaction in sitting in his door, watching some free man of color at his work or play. If on a voyage he chanced to have a black sailor, invariably he was on chatty and half-gamesome terms with him. In fact, like most men of a good, blithe heart, Captain Delano took to negroes, not philanthropically, but genially, just as other men to Newfoundland dogs.

Hitherto, the circumstances in which he found the *San Dominick* had repressed the tendency. But in the cuddy, relieved from his former uneasiness, and, for various reasons, more sociably inclined than at any previous period of the day, and seeing the colored servant, napkin on arm, so debonair about his master, in a business so familiar as that of shaving, too, all his old weakness for negroes returned.

Among other things, he was amused with an odd instance of the African love of bright colors and fine shows, in the black's informally taking from the flag-locker a great piece of bunting of all hues, and lavishly tucking it under his master's chin for an apron.

The mode of shaving among the Spaniards is a little different from what it is with other nations. They have a basin, specifically called a barber's basin, which on one side is scooped out, so as accurately to receive the chin, against which it is closely held in lathering; which is done, not with a brush, but with soap dipped in the water of the basin and rubbed on the face.

In the present instance salt-water was used for lack of better; and the parts lathered were only the upper lip, and low down under the throat, all the rest being cultivated beard.

The preliminaries being somewhat novel to Captain Delano, he sat curiously eying them, so that no conversation took place, nor, for the present, did Don Benito appear disposed to renew any.

Setting down his basin, the negro searched among the razors, as for the sharpest, and having found it, gave it an additional edge by expertly stropping it on the firm, smooth, oily skin of his open palm; he then made a gesture as if to begin, but midway stood suspended for an instant, one hand elevating the razor, the other professionally dabbling among the bubbling suds on the Spaniard's lank neck. Not unaffected by the close sight of the gleaming steel, Don Benito nervously shuddered; his usual ghastliness was heightened by the lather, which lather, again, was intensified in its hue by the contrasting sootiness of the negro's body. Altogether the scene was somewhat peculiar, at least to Captain Delano, nor, as he saw the two thus postured, could he resist the vagary, that in the black he saw a headsman, and in the white a man at the block. But this was one of those antic conceits, appearing and vanishing in a breath, from which, perhaps, the best regulated mind is not always free.

Meantime the agitation of the Spaniard had a little loosened the bunting from around him, so that one broad fold swept curtain-like over the chair-arm to the floor, revealing, amid a profusion of armorial bars and ground-colors—black, blue, and yellow—a closed castle in a blood-red field diagonal with a lion rampant in a white.

"The castle and the lion," exclaimed Captain Delano— "why, Don Benito, this is the flag of Spain you use here. It's well it's only I, and not the King, that sees this," he added, with a smile, "but"—turning towards the black—"it's all one, I suppose, so the colors be gay," which playful remark did not fail somewhat to tickle the negro.

"Now, master," he said, readjusting the flag, and pressing the head gently further back into the crotch of the chair; "now, master," and the steel glanced nigh the throat.

Again Don Benito faintly shuddered.

"You must not shake so, master. See, Don Amasa, master always shakes when I shave him. And yet master knows I never yet have drawn blood, though it's true, if master will shake so,

I may some of these times. Now, master," he continued. "And now, Don Amasa, please go on with your talk about the gale, and all that; master can hear, and, between times, master can answer."

"Ah yes, these gales," said Captain Delano; "but the more I think of your voyage, Don Benito, the more I wonder, not at the gales, terrible as they must have been, but at the disastrous interval following them. For here, by your account, have you been these two months and more getting from Cape Horn to Santa Maria, a distance which I myself, with a good wind, have sailed in a few days. True, you had calms, and long ones, but to be becalmed for two months, that is, at least, unusual. Why, Don Benito, had almost any other gentleman told me such a story, I should have been half disposed to a little incredulity."

Here an involuntary expression came over the Spaniard, similar to that just before on the deck, and whether it was the start he gave, or a sudden gawky roll of the hull in the calm, or a momentary unsteadiness of the servant's hand, however it was, just then the razor drew blood, spots of which stained the creamy lather under the throat: immediately the black barber drew back his steel, and, remaining in his professional attitude, back to Captain Delano, and face to Don Benito, held up the trickling razor, saying, with a sort of half humorous sorrow, "See, master—you shook so—here's Babo's first blood."

No sword drawn before James the First of England, no assassination in that timid King's presence, could have produced a more terrified aspect than was now presented by Don Benito.

Poor fellow, thought Captain Delano, so nervous he can't even bear the sight of barber's blood; and this unstrung, sick man, is it credible that I should have imagined he meant to spill all my blood, who can't endure the sight of one little drop of his own? Surely, Amasa Delano, you have been beside yourself this day. Tell it not when you get home, sappy Amasa. Well, well, he looks like a murderer, doesn't he? More like as if himself were to be done for. Well, well, this day's experience shall be a good lesson.

Meantime, while these things were running through the honest seaman's mind, the servant had taken the napkin from his arm, and to Don Benito had said—"But answer Don

Amasa, please, master, while I wipe this ugly stuff off the razor, and strop it again."

As he said the words, his face was turned half round, so as to be alike visible to the Spaniard and the American, and seemed, by its expression, to hint, that he was desirous, by getting his master to go on with the conversation, considerately to withdraw his attention from the recent annoying accident. As if glad to snatch the offered relief, Don Benito resumed, rehearsing to Captain Delano, that not only were the calms of unusual duration, but the ship had fallen in with obstinate currents; and other things he added, some of which were but repetitions of former statements, to explain how it came to pass that the passage from Cape Horn to Santa Maria had been so exceedingly long; now and then mingling with his words, incidental praises, less qualified than before, to the blacks, for their general good conduct. These particulars were not given consecutively, the servant, at convenient times, using his razor, and so, between the intervals of shaving, the story and panegyric went on with more than usual huskiness.

To Captain Delano's imagination, now again not wholly at rest, there was something so hollow in the Spaniard's manner, with apparently some reciprocal hollowness in the servant's dusky comment of silence, that the idea flashed across him, that possibly master and man, for some unknown purpose, were acting out, both in word and deed, nay, to the very tremor of Don Benito's limbs, some juggling play before him. Neither did the suspicion of collusion lack apparent support, from the fact of those whispered conferences before mentioned. But then, what could be the object of enacting this play of the barber before him? At last, regarding the notion as a whimsy, insensibly suggested, perhaps, by the theatrical aspect of Don Benito in his harlequin ensign, Captain Delano speedily banished it.

The shaving over, the servant bestirred himself with a small bottle of scented waters, pouring a few drops on the head, and then diligently rubbing; the vehemence of the exercise causing the muscles of his face to twitch rather strangely.

His next operation was with comb, scissors, and brush; going round and round, smoothing a curl here, clipping an unruly-whisker-hair there, giving a graceful sweep to the temple-lock, with other impromptu touches evincing the hand of a master; while, like any resigned gentleman in barber's hands, Don Benito bore all, much less uneasily, at least, than he had

done the razoring; indeed, he sat so pale and rigid now, that
the negro seemed a Nubian sculptor finishing off a white
statue-head.

All being over at last, the standard of Spain removed, tumbled up, and tossed back into the flag-locker, the negro's warm
breath blowing away any stray hair which might have lodged
down his master's neck; collar and cravat readjusted; a speck
of lint whisked off the velvet lapel; all this being done, backing off a little space, and pausing with an expression of subdued self-complacency, the servant for a moment surveyed his
master, as, in toilet at least, the creature of his own tasteful
hands.

Captain Delano playfully complimented him upon his
achievement; at the same time congratulating Don Benito.

But neither sweet waters, nor shampooing, nor fidelity, nor
sociality, delighted the Spaniard. Seeing him relapsing into
forbidding gloom, and still remaining seated, Captain Delano,
thinking that his presence was undesired just then, withdrew,
on pretense of seeing whether, as he had prophesied, any signs
of a breeze were visible.

Walking forward to the main-mast, he stood awhile thinking over the scene, and not without some undefined misgivings, when he heard a noise near the cuddy, and turning, saw
the negro, his hand to his cheek. Advancing, Captain Delano
perceived that the cheek was bleeding. He was about to ask
the cause, when the negro's wailing soliloquy enlightened
him.

"Ah, when will master get better from his sickness; only the
sour heart that sour sickness breeds made him serve Babo so;
cutting Babo with the razor, because, only by accident, Babo
had given master one little scratch; and for the first time in
so many a day, too. Ah, ah, ah," holding his hand to his face.

Is it possible, thought Captain Delano; was it to wreak in
private his Spanish spite against this poor friend of his, that
Don Benito, by his sullen manner, impelled me to withdraw?
Ah, this slavery breeds ugly passions in man.—Poor fellow!

He was about to speak in sympathy to the negro, but with
a timid reluctance he now re-entered the cuddy.

Presently master and man came forth; Don Benito leaning
on his servant as if nothing had happened.

But a sort of love-quarrel, after all, thought Captain Delano.

He accosted Don Benito, and they slowly walked together.

They had gone but a few paces, when the steward—a tall, rajah-looking mulatto, orientally set off with a pagoda turban formed by three or four Madras handkerchiefs wound about his head, tier on tier—approaching with a salaam, announced lunch in the cabin.

On their way thither, the two captains were preceded by the mulatto, who, turning round as he advanced, with continual smiles and bows, ushered them on, a display of elegance which quite completed the insignificance of the small bare-headed Babo, who, as if not unconscious of inferiority, eyed askance the graceful steward. But in part, Captain Delano imputed his jealous watchfulness to that peculiar feeling which the full-blooded African entertains for the adulterated one. As for the steward, his manner, if not bespeaking much dignity of self-respect, yet evidenced his extreme desire to please; which is doubly meritorious, as at once Christian and Chesterfieldian.

Captain Delano observed with interest that while the complexion of the mulatto was hybrid, his physiognomy was European—classically so.

"Don Benito," whispered he, "I am glad to see this usher-of-the-golden-rod of yours; the sight refutes an ugly remark once made to me by a Barbados planter; that when a mulatto has a regular European face, look out for him; he is a devil. But see, your steward here has features more regular than King George's of England; and yet there he nods, and bows, and smiles; a king, indeed—the king of kind hearts and polite fellows. What a pleasant voice he has, too."

"He has, Señor."

"But tell me, has he not, so far as you have known him, always proved a good, worthy fellow?" said Captain Delano, pausing, while with a final genuflexion the steward disappeared into the cabin; "come, for the reason just mentioned, I am curious to know."

"Francesco is a good man," somewhat sluggishly responded Don Benito, like a phlegmatic appreciator, who would neither find fault nor flatter.

"Ah, I thought so. For it were strange, indeed, and not very creditable to us white-skins, if a little of our blood mixed with the African's, should, far from improving the latter's quality, have the sad effect of pouring vitriolic acid into black broth; improving the hue, perhaps, but not the wholesomeness."

"Doubtless, doubtless, Señor, but"—glancing at Babo—"not

to speak of negroes, your planter's remark I have heard applied to the Spanish and Indian intermixtures in our provinces. But I know nothing about the matter," he listlessly added.

And here they entered the cabin.

The lunch was a frugal one. Some of Captain Delano's fresh fish and pumpkins, biscuit and salt beef, the reserved bottle of cider, and the *San Dominick*'s last bottle of Canary.

As they entered, Francesco, with two or three colored aids, was hovering over the table giving the last adjustments. Upon perceiving their master they withdrew, Francesco making a smiling congé, and the Spaniard, without condescending to notice it, fastidiously remarking to his companion that he relished not superfluous attendance.

Without companions, host and guest sat down, like a childless married couple, at opposite ends of the table, Don Benito waving Captain Delano to his place, and, weak as he was, insisting upon that gentleman being seated before himself.

The negro placed a rug under Don Benito's feet, and a cushion behind his back, and then stood behind, not his master's chair, but Captain Delano's. At first, this a little surprised the latter. But it was soon evident that, in taking his position, the black was still true to his master; since by facing him he could the more readily anticipate his slightest want.

"This is an uncommonly intelligent fellow of yours, Don Benito," whispered Captain Delano across the table.

"You say true, Señor."

During the repast, the guest again reverted to parts of Don Benito's story, begging further particulars here and there. He inquired how it was that the scurvy and fever should have committed such wholesale havoc upon the whites, while destroying less than half of the blacks. As if this question reproduced the whole scene of plague before the Spaniard's eyes, miserably reminding him of his solitude in a cabin where before he had had so many friends and officers round him, his hand shook, his face became hueless, broken words escaped; but directly the sane memory of the past seemed replaced by insane terrors of the present. With starting eyes he stared before him at vacancy. For nothing was to be seen but the hand of his servant pushing the Canary over towards him. At length a few sips served partially to restore him. He made random reference to the different constitution of races,

enabling one to offer more resistance to certain maladies than
another. The thought was new to his companion.

Presently Captain Delano, intending to say something to
his host concerning the pecuniary part of the business he had
undertaken for him, especially—since he was strictly account-
able to his owners—with reference to the new suit of sails, and
other things of that sort; and naturally preferring to conduct
such affairs in private, was desirous that the servant should
withdraw; imagining that Don Benito for a few minutes could
dispense with his attendance. He, however, waited awhile;
thinking that, as the conversation proceeded, Don Benito,
without being prompted, would perceive the propriety of the
step.

But it was otherwise. At last catching his host's eye, Captain Delano, with a slight backward gesture of his thumb,
whispered, "Don Benito, pardon me, but there is an interference with the full expression of what I have to say to you."

Upon this the Spaniard changed countenance; which was
imputed to his resenting the hint, as in some way a reflection
upon his servant. After a moment's pause, he assured his guest
that the black's remaining with them could be of no disserv-
ice; because since losing his officers he had made Babo (whose
original office, it now appeared, had been captain of the
slaves) not only his constant attendant and companion, but in
all things his confidant.

After this, nothing more could be said; though, indeed,
Captain Delano could hardly avoid some little tinge of irrita-
tion upon being left ungratified in so inconsiderable a wish,
by one, too, for whom he intended such solid services. But it
is only his querulousness, thought he; and so filling his glass
he proceeded to business.

The price of the sails and other matter was fixed upon. But
while this was being done, the American observed that, though
his original offer of assistance had been hailed with hectic animation, yet now, when it was reduced to a business transaction, indifference and apathy were betrayed. Don Benito, in
fact, appeared to submit to hearing the details more out of
regard to common propriety, than from any impression that
weighty benefit to himself and his voyage was involved.

Soon, his manner became still more reserved. The effort
was vain to seek to draw him into social talk. Gnawed by his
splenetic mood, he sat twitching his beard, while to little pur-

pose the hand of his servant, mute as that on the wall, slowly pushed over the Canary.

Lunch being over, they sat down on the cushioned transom; the servant placing a pillow behind his master. The long continuance of the calm had now affected the atmosphere. Don Benito sighed heavily, as if for breath.

"Why not adjourn to the cuddy?" said Captain Delano. "There is more air there." But the host sat silent and motionless.

Meantime his servant knelt before him, with a large fan of feathers. And Francesco coming in on tiptoes, handed the negro a little cup of aromatic waters, with which at intervals he chafed his master's brow; smoothing the hair along the temples as a nurse does a child's. He spoke no word. He only rested his eye on his master's, as if, amid all Don Benito's distress, a little to refresh his spirit by the silent sight of fidelity.

Presently the ship's bell sounded two o'clock; and through the cabin windows a slight rippling of the sea was discerned; and from the desired direction.

"There," exclaimed Captain Delano, "I told you so, Don Benito, look!"

He had risen to his feet, speaking in a very animated tone, with a view the more to rouse his companion. But though the crimson curtain of the stern-window near him that moment fluttered against his pale cheek, Don Benito seemed to have even less welcome for the breeze than the calm.

Poor fellow, thought Captain Delano, bitter experience has taught him that one ripple does not make a wind, any more than one swallow a summer. But he is mistaken for once. I will get his ship in for him, and prove it.

Briefly alluding to his weak condition, he urged his host to remain quietly where he was, since he (Captain Delano) would with pleasure take upon himself the responsibility of making the best use of the wind.

Upon gaining the deck, Captain Delano started at the unexpected figure of Atufal, monumentally fixed at the threshold, like one of those sculptured porters of black marble guarding the porches of Egyptian tombs.

But this time the start was, perhaps, purely physical. Atufal's presence, singularly attesting docility even in sullenness, was contrasted with that of the hatchet-polishers, who in patience evinced their industry; while both spectacles showed, that lax as Don Benito's general authority might be, still, whenever he chose to exert it, no man so savage or colossal but must, more or less, bow.

Snatching a trumpet which hung from the bulwarks, with a free step Captain Delano advanced to the forward edge of the poop, issuing his orders in his best Spanish. The few sailors and many negroes, all equally pleased, obediently set about heading the ship towards the harbor.

While giving some directions about setting a lower stu'n-sail, suddenly Captain Delano heard a voice faithfully repeating his orders. Turning, he saw Babo, now for the time acting, under the pilot, his original part of captain of the slaves. This assistance proved valuable. Tattered sails and warped yards were soon brought into some trim. And no brace or halyard was pulled but to the blithe songs of the inspirited negroes.

Good fellows, thought Captain Delano, a little training would make fine sailors of them. Why see, the very women pull and sing too. These must be some of those Ashantee negresses that make such capital soldiers, I've heard. But who's at the helm? I must have a good hand there.

He went to see.

The *San Dominick* steered with a cumbrous tiller, with large horizontal pulleys attached. At each pulley-end stood a subordinate black, and between them, at the tiller-head, the responsible post, a Spanish seaman, whose countenance evinced his due share in the general hopefulness and confidence at the coming of the breeze.

He proved the same man who had behaved with so shame-faced an air on the windlass.

"Ah,—it is you, my man," exclaimed Captain Delano— "well, no more sheep's eyes now;—look straight forward and keep the ship so. Good hand, I trust? And want to get into the harbor, don't you?"

The man assented with an inward chuckle, grasping the tiller-head firmly. Upon this, unperceived by the American, the two blacks eyed the sailor intently.

Finding all right at the helm, the pilot went forward to the forecastle, to see how matters stood there.

The ship now had way enough to breast the current. With the approach of evening, the breeze would be sure to freshen.

Having done all that was needed for the present, Captain Delano, giving his last orders to the sailors, turned aft to report affairs to Don Benito in the cabin; perhaps additionally incited to rejoin him by the hope of snatching a moment's private chat while the servant was engaged upon deck.

From opposite sides, there were, beneath the poop, two approaches to the cabin; one further forward than the other, and consequently communicating with a longer passage. Marking the servant still above, Captain Delano, taking the nighest entrance—the one last named, and at whose porch Atufal still stood—hurried on his way, till, arrived at the cabin threshold, he paused an instant, a little to recover from his eagerness. Then, with the words of his intended business upon his lips, he entered. As he advanced toward the seated Spaniard, he heard another footstep, keeping time with his. From the opposite door, a salver in hand, the servant was likewise advancing.

"Confound the faithful fellow," thought Captain Delano; "what a vexatious coincidence."

Possibly, the vexation might have been something different, were it not for the brisk confidence inspired by the breeze. But even as it was, he felt a slight twinge, from a sudden indefinite association in his mind of Babo with Atufal.

"Don Benito," said he, "I give you joy; the breeze will hold, and will increase. By the way, your tall man and time-piece, Atufal, stands without. By your order, of course?"

Don Benito recoiled, as if at some bland satirical touch, delivered with such adroit garnish of apparent good breeding as to present no handle for retort.

He is like one flayed alive, thought Captain Delano; where may one touch him without causing a shrink?

The servant moved before his master, adjusting a cushion; recalled to civility, the Spaniard stiffly replied: "You are right. The slave appears where you saw him, according to my command; which is, that if at the given hour I am below, he must take his stand and abide my coming."

"Ah now, pardon me, but that is treating the poor fellow like an ex-king indeed. Ah, Don Benito," smiling, "for all the license you permit in some things, I fear lest, at bottom, you are a bitter hard master."

Again Don Benito shrank; and this time, as the good sailor thought, from a genuine twinge of his conscience.

Again conversation became constrained. In vain Captain Delano called attention to the now perceptible motion of the keel gently cleaving the sea; with lack-lustre eye, Don Benito returned words few and reserved.

By and by, the wind having steadily risen, and still blowing right into the harbor, bore the *San Dominick* swiftly on. Rounding a point of land, the sealer at distance came into open view.

Meantime Captain Delano had again repaired to the deck, remaining there some time. Having at last altered the ship's course, so as to give the reef a wide berth, he returned for a few moments below.

I will cheer up my poor friend, this time, thought he.

"Better and better, Don Benito," he cried as he blithely re-entered: "there will soon be an end to your cares, at least for a while. For when, after a long, sad voyage, you know, the anchor drops into the haven, all its vast weight seems lifted from the captain's heart. We are getting on famously, Don Benito. My ship is in sight. Look through this side-light here; there she is; all a-taunt-o! The *Bachelor's Delight*, my good friend. Ah, how this wind braces one up. Come, you must take a cup of coffee with me this evening. My old steward will give you as fine a cup as ever any sultan tasted. What say you, Don Benito, will you?"

At first, the Spaniard glanced feverishly up, casting a longing look towards the sealer, while with mute concern his servant gazed into his face. Suddenly the old ague of coldness returned, and droppong back to his cushions he was silent.

"You do not answer. Come, all day you have been my host; would you have hospitality all on one side?"

"I cannot go," was the response.

"What? It will not fatigue you. The ships will lie together as near as they can, without swinging foul. It will be little more than stepping from deck to deck; which is but as from room to room. Come, come, you must not refuse me."

"I cannot go," decisively and repulsively repeated Don Benito.

Renouncing all but the last appearance of courtesy, with a sort of cadaverous sullenness, and biting his thin nails to the quick, he glanced, almost glared, at his guest, as if impatient that a stranger's presence should interfere with the full indulgence of his morbid hour. Meantime the sound of the parted waters came more and more gurglingly and merrily in at the windows; as reproaching him for his dark spleen; as telling him that, sulk as he might, and go mad with it, nature cared not a jot; since, whose fault was it, pray?

But the foul mood was now at its depth, as the fair wind at its height.

There was something in the man so far beyond any mere unsociality or sourness previously evinced, that even the forbearing good-nature of his guest could no longer endure it. Wholly at a loss to account for such demeanor, and deeming sickness with eccentricity, however extreme, no adequate excuse, well satisfied, too, that nothing in his own conduct could justify it, Captain Delano's pride began to be roused. Himself became reserved. But all seemed one to the Spaniard. Quitting him, therefore, Captain Delano once more went to the deck.

The ship was now within less than two miles of the sealer. The whale-boat was seen darting over the interval.

To be brief, the two vessels, thanks to the pilot's skill, ere long in neighborly style lay anchored together.

Before returning to his own vessel, Captain Delano had intended communicating to Don Benito the smaller details of the proposed services to be rendered. But, as it was, unwilling anew to subject himself to rebuffs, he resolved, now that he had seen the *San Dominick* safely moored, immediately to quit her, without further allusion to hospitality or business. Indefinitely postponing his ulterior plans, he would regulate his future actions according to future circumstances. His boat was ready to receive him; but his host still tarried below. Well, thought Captain Delano, if he has little breeding, the more need to show mine. He descended to the cabin to bid a ceremonious, and, it may be, tacitly rebukeful adieu. But to his great satisfaction, Don Benito, as if he began to feel the weight of that treatment with which his slighted guest had, not indecorously, retaliated upon him, now supported by his servant, rose to his feet, and grasping Captain Delano's hand, stood tremulous; too much agitated to speak. But the good augury hence drawn was suddenly dashed, by his resuming all his previous reserve, with augmented gloom, as, with half-averted eyes, he silently reseated himself on his cushions. With a corresponding return of his own chilled feelings, Captain Delano bowed and withdrew.

He was hardly midway in the narrow corridor, dim as a tunnel, leading from the cabin to the stairs, when a sound, as of the tolling for execution in some jail-yard, fell on his ears. It was the echo of the ship's flawed bell, striking the hour, drearily reverberated in this subterranean vault. Instantly, by a fatality not to be withstood, his mind, responsive to the portent, swarmed with superstitious suspicions. He paused. In images far swifter than these sentences, the minutest details of all his former distrusts swept through him.

Hitherto, credulous good-nature had been too ready to furnish excuses for reasonable fears. Why was the Spaniard, so superfluously punctilious at times, now heedless of common propriety in not accompanying to the side his departing guest? Did indisposition forbid? Indisposition had not forbidden more irksome exertion that day. His last equivocal demeanor recurred. He had risen to his feet, grasped his guest's hand, motioned toward his hat; then, in an instant, all was eclipsed in sinister muteness and gloom. Did this imply one brief, repentant relenting at the final moment, from some iniquitous plot, followed by remorseless return to it? His last glance seemed to express a calamitous, yet acquiescent farewell to Captain Delano forever. Why decline the invitation to visit the sealer that evening? Or was the Spaniard less hardened than the Jew, who refrained not from supping at the board of him whom the same night he meant to betray? What imported all those day-long enigmas and contradictions, except they were intended to mystify, preliminary to some stealthy blow? Atufal, the pretended rebel, but punctual shadow, that moment lurked by the threshold without. He seemed a sentry, and more. Who, by his own confession, had stationed him there? Was the negro now lying in wait?

The Spaniard behind—his creature before: to rush from darkness to light was the involuntary choice.

The next moment, with clenched jaw and hand, he passed Atufal, and stood unharmed in the light. As he saw his trim ship lying peacefully at anchor, and almost within ordinary call; as he saw his household boat, with familiar faces in it, patiently rising and falling on the short waves by the *San Dominick*'s side; and then, glancing about the decks where he stood, saw the oakum-pickers still gravely plying their fingers; and heard the low, buzzing whistle and industrious hum of the hatchet-polishers, still bestirring themselves over their endless occupation; and more than all, as he saw the benign aspect of nature, taking her innocent repose in the evening; the screened sun in the quiet camp of the west shining out like the mild light from Abraham's tent; as charmed eye and ear took in all these, with the chained figure of the black, clenched jaw and hand relaxed. Once again he smiled at the phantoms which had mocked him, and felt something like a tinge of re-morse, that, by harboring them even for a moment, he should, by implication, have betrayed an atheist doubt of the ever-watchful Providence above.

There was a few minutes' delay, while, in obedience to his orders, the boat was being hooked along to the gangway. Dur-ing this interval, a sort of saddened satisfaction stole over Cap-tain Delano, at thinking of the kindly offices he had that day discharged for a stranger. Ah, thought he, after good actions one's conscience is never ungrateful, however much so the benefited party may be.

Presently, his foot, in the first act of descent into the boat, pressed the first round of the side-ladder, his face presented in-ward upon the deck. In the same moment, he heard his name courteously sounded; and, to his pleased surprise, saw Don Benito advancing—an unwonted energy in his air, as if, at the last moment, intent upon making amends for his recent dis-courtesy. With instinctive good feeling, Captain Delano, with-drawing his foot, turned and reciprocally advanced. As he did so, the Spaniard's nervous eagerness increased, but his vital energy failed; so that, the better to support him, the serv-ant, placing his master's hand on his naked shoulder, and gen-tly holding it there, formed himself into a sort of crutch.

When the two captains met, the Spaniard again fervently took the hand of the American, at the same time casting an earnest glance into his eyes, but, as before, too much over-come to speak.

I have done him wrong, self-reproachfully thought Captain Delano; his apparent coldness has deceived me; in no instance has he meant to offend.

Meantime, as if fearful that the continuance of the scene might too much unstring his master, the servant seemed anx-ious to terminate it. And so still presenting himself as a crutch, and walking between the two captains, he advanced with them towards the gangway; while still, as if full of kindly contrition, Don Benito would not let go the hand of Captain Delano, but retained it in his, across the black's body.

Soon they were standing by the side, looking over into the boat, whose crew turned up their curious eyes. Waiting a mo-ment for the Spaniard to relinquish his hold, the now em-barrassed Captain Delano lifted his foot, to overstep the threshold of the open gangway; but still Don Benito would not let go his hand. And yet, with an agitated tone, he said,

"I can go no further; here I must bid you adieu. Adieu, my dear, dear Don Amasa. Go—go!" suddenly tearing his hand loose, "go, and God guard you better than me, my best friend."

Not unaffected, Captain Delano would now have lingered; but catching the meekly admonitory eye of the servant, with a hasty farewell he descended into his boat, followed by the continual adieus of Don Benito, standing rooted in the gangway.

Seating himself in the stern, Captain Delano, making a last salute, ordered the boat shoved off. The crew had their oars on end. The bowsmen pushed the boat a sufficient distance for the oars to be lengthwise dropped. The instant that was done, Don Benito sprang over the bulwarks, falling at the feet of Captain Delano; at the same time calling towards his ship, but in tones so frenzied, that none in the boat could understand him. But, as if not equally obtuse, three sailors, from three different and distant parts of the ship, splashed into the sea, swimming after their captain, as if intent upon his rescue.

The dismayed officer of the boat eagerly asked what this meant. To which, Captain Delano, turning a disdainful smile upon the unaccountable Spaniard, answered that, for his part, he neither knew nor cared; but it seemed as if Don Benito had taken it into his head to produce the impression among his people that the boat wanted to kidnap him. "Or else—give way for your lives," he wildly added, starting at a clattering hubbub in the ship, above which rang the tocsin of the hatchet-polishers; and seizing Don Benito by the throat he added, "this plotting pirate means murder!" Here, in apparent verification of the words, the servant, a dagger in his hand, was seen on the rail overhead, poised, in the act of leaping, as if with desperate fidelity to befriend his master to the last; while, seemingly to aid the black, the three white sailors were trying to clamber into the hampered bow. Meantime, the whole host of negroes, as if inflamed at the sight of their jeopardized captain, impended in one sooty avalanche over the bulwarks.

All this, with what preceded, and what followed, occurred with such involutions of rapidity, that past, present, and future seemed one.

Seeing the negro coming, Captain Delano had flung the Spaniard aside, almost in the very act of clutching him, and, by the unconscious recoil, shifting his place, with arms thrown

up, so promptly grappled the servant in his descent, that with
dagger presented at Captain Delano's heart, the black seemed
of purpose to have leaped there as to his mark. But the
weapon was wrenched away, and the assailant dashed down
into the bottom of the boat, which now with disentangled oars,
began to speed through the sea.

At this juncture, the left hand of Captain Delano, on one
side, again clutched the half-reclining Don Benito, heedless
that he was in a speechless faint, while his right foot, on the
other side, ground the prostrate negro; and his right arm
pressed for added speed on the after oar, his eye bent forward,
encouraging his men to their utmost.

But here, the officer of the boat, who had at last succeeded
in beating off the towing sailors, and was now, with face
turned aft, assisting the bowsman at his oar, suddenly called
to Captain Delano, to see what the black was about; while a
Portuguese oarsman shouted to him to give heed to what the
Spaniard was saying.

Glancing down at his feet, Captain Delano saw the freed
hand of the servant aiming with a second dagger—a small one,
before concealed in his wool—with this he was snakishly writhing up from the boat's bottom, at the heart of his master, his
countenance lividly vindictive, expressing the centred purpose
of his soul; while the Spaniard, half-choked, was vainly shrinking away, with husky words, incoherent to all but the Portuguese.

That moment, across the long-benighted mind of Captain
Delano, a flash of revelation swept, illuminating, in unanticipated clearness, his host's whole mysterious demeanor, with
every enigmatic event of the day, as well as the entire past voyage of the *San Dominick*. He smote Babo's hand down, but
his own heart smote him harder. With infinite pity he withdrew his hold from Don Benito. Not Captain Delano, but Don
Benito, the black, in leaping into the boat, had intended to
stab.

Both the black's hands were held, as, glancing up towards
the *San Dominick*, Captain Delano, now with scales dropped
from his eyes, saw the negroes, not in misrule, not in tumult,
not as if frantically concerned for Don Benito, but with mask
torn away, flourishing hatchets, and knives, in ferocious piratical revolt. Like delirious black dervishes, the six Ashantees
danced on the poop. Prevented by their foes from springing
into the water, the Spanish boys were hurrying up to the top-

most spars, while such of the few Spanish sailors, not already in the sea, less alert, were descried, helplessly mixed in, on deck, with the blacks.

Meantime Captain Delano hailed his own vessel, ordering the ports up, and the guns run out. But by this time the cable of the *San Dominick* had been cut; and the fag-end, in lashing out, whipped away the canvas shroud about the beak, suddenly revealing, as the bleached hull swung round towards the open ocean, death for the figure-head, in a human skeleton; chalky comment on the chalked words below, *"Follow your leader."*

At the sight, Don Benito, covering his face, wailed out: " 'Tis he, Aranda! my murdered, unburied friend!"

Upon reaching the sealer, calling for ropes, Captain Delano bound the negro, who made no resistance, and had him hoisted to the deck. He would then have assisted the now almost helpless Don Benito up the side; but Don Benito, wan as he was, refused to move, or be moved, until the negro should have been first put below out of view. When, presently assured that it was done, he no more shrank from the ascent.

The boat was immediately dispatched back to pick up the three swimming sailors. Meantime, the guns were in readiness, though, owing to the *San Dominick* having glided somewhat astern of the sealer, only the aftermost one could be brought to bear. With this, they fired six times; thinking to cripple the fugitive ship by bringing down her spars. But only a few inconsiderable ropes were shot away. Soon the ship was beyond the gun's range, steering broad out of the bay; the blacks thickly clustering round the bowsprit, one moment with taunting cries towards the whites, the next with upthrown gestures hailing the now dusky moors of ocean—cawing crows escaped from the hand of the fowler.

The first impulse was to slip the cables and give chase. But, upon second thoughts, to pursue with whale-boat and yawl seemed more promising.

Upon inquiring of Don Benito what fire-arms they had on board the *San Dominick,* Captain Delano was answered that they had none that could be used; because, in the earlier stages of the mutiny, a cabin-passenger, since dead, had secretly put out of order the locks of what few muskets there were. But with all his remaining strength, Don Benito entreated the American not to give chase, either with ship or boat; for the negroes had already proved themselves such desperadoes, that, in case of a present assault, nothing but a total massacre of the whites could be looked for. But, regarding this warning as coming from one whose spirit had been crushed by misery, the American did not give up his design.

The boats were got ready and armed. Captain Delano ordered his men into them. He was going himself when Don Benito grasped his arm.

"What! have you saved my life, Señor, and are you now going to throw away your own?"

The officers also, for reasons connected with their interests and those of the voyage, and a duty owing to the owners, strongly objected against their commander's going. Weighing their remonstrances a moment, Captain Delano felt bound to remain; appointing his chief mate—an athletic and resolute man, who had been a privateer's-man—to head the party. The more to encourage the sailors, they were told, that the Spanish captain considered his ship good as lost; that she and her cargo, including some gold and silver, were worth more than a thousand doubloons. Take her, and no small part should be theirs. The sailors replied with a shout.

The fugitives had now almost gained an offing. It was nearly night; but the moon was rising. After hard, prolonged pulling, the boats came up on the ship's quarters, at a suitable distance laying upon their oars to discharge their muskets. Having no bullets to return, the negroes sent their yells. But, upon the second volley, Indian-like, they hurled their hatchets. One took off a sailor's fingers. Another struck the whale-boat's bow, cutting off the rope there, and remaining stuck in the gunwale like a woodman's axe. Snatching it, quivering from its lodgment, the mate hurled it back. The returned gauntlet now stuck in the ship's broken quarter-gallery, and so remained.

The negroes giving too hot a reception, the whites kept a more respectful distance. Hovering now just out of reach of the hurtling hatchets, they, with a view to the close encounter which must soon come, sought to decoy the blacks into entirely disarming themselves of their most murderous weapons in a hand-to-hand fight, by foolishly flinging them, as missiles, short of the mark, into the sea. But, ere long, perceiving the stratagem, the negroes desisted, though not before many of them had to replace their lost hatchets with hand-spikes; an exchange which, as counted upon, proved, in the end, favorable to the assailants.

Meantime, with a strong wind, the ship still clove the water; the boats alternately falling behind, and pulling up, to discharge fresh volleys.

The fire was mostly directed towards the stern, since there, chiefly, the negroes, at present, were clustering. But to kill or maim the negroes was not the object. To take them, with the ship, was the object. To do it, the ship must be boarded; which could not be done by boats while she was sailing so fast.

A thought now struck the mate. Observing the Spanish boys still aloft, high as they could get, he called to them to descend to the yards, and cut adrift the sails. It was done. About this time, owing to causes hereafter to be shown, two Spaniards, in the dress of sailors, and conspicuously showing themselves, were killed; not by volleys, but by deliberate marksman's shots; while, as it afterwards appeared, by one of the general discharges, Atufal, the black, and the Spaniard at the helm likewise were killed. What now, with the loss of the sails, and loss of leaders, the ship became unmanageable to the negroes.

With creaking masts, she came heavily round to the wind; the prow slowly swinging into view of the boats, its skeleton gleaming in the horizontal moonlight, and casting a gigantic ribbed shadow upon the water. One extended arm of the ghost seemed beckoning the whites to avenge it.

"Follow your leader!" cried the mate; and, one on each bow, the boats boarded. Sealing-spears and cutlasses crossed hatchets and hand-spikes. Huddled upon the long-boat amidships, the negresses raised a wailing chant, whose chorus was the clash of the steel.

For a time, the attack wavered; the negroes wedging themselves to beat it back; the half-repelled sailors, as yet unable to gain a footing, fighting as troopers in the saddle, one leg sideways flung over the bulwarks, and one without, plying their cutlasses like carters' whips. But in vain. They were almost overborne, when, rallying themselves into a squad as one man, with a huzza, they sprang inboard, where, entangled, they involuntarily separated again. For a few breaths' space, there was a vague, muffled, inner sound, as of submerged sword-fish rushing hither and thither through shoals of black-fish. Soon, in a reunited band, and joined by the Spanish seamen, the whites came to the surface, irresistibly driving the negroes toward the stern. But a barricade of casks and sacks, from side to side, had been thrown up by the main-mast. Here the negroes faced about, and though scorning peace or truce, yet fain would have had respite. But, without pause, overleaping the barrier, the unflagging sailors again closed. Exhausted, the blacks now fought in despair. Their red tongues lolled, wolf-like, from their black mouths. But the pale sailors' teeth were set; not a word was spoken; and in five minutes more, the ship was won.

Nearly a score of the negroes were killed. Exclusive of those by the balls, many were mangled; their wounds—mostly inflicted by the long-edged sealing-spears, resembling those shaven ones of the English at Preston Pans, made by the poled scythes of the Highlanders. On the other side, none were killed, though several were wounded; some severely, including the mate. The surviving negroes were temporarily secured, and the ship, towed back into the harbor at midnight, once more lay anchored.

Omitting the incidents and arrangements ensuing, suffice it that, after two days spent in refitting, the ships sailed in company for Concepcion, in Chile, and thence for Lima, in Peru; where, before the vice-regal courts, the whole affair, from the beginning, underwent investigation.

Though, midway on the passage, the ill-fated Spaniard, relaxed from constraint, showed some signs of regaining health with free-will; yet, agreeably to his own foreboding, shortly before arriving at Lima, he relapsed, finally becoming so reduced as to be carried ashore in arms. Hearing of his story and plight, one of the many religious institutions of the City of Kings opened an hospitable refuge to him, where both physician and priest were his nurses, and a member of the order volunteered to be his one special guardian and consoler, by night and by day.

The following extracts, translated from one of the official Spanish documents, will, it is hoped, shed light on the preceding narrative, as well as, in the first place, reveal the true port of departure and true history of the *San Dominick's* voyage, down to the time of her touching at the island of Santa Maria.

But, ere the extracts come, it may be well to preface them with a remark.

The document selected, from among many others, for partial translation, contains the deposition of Benito Cereno; the first taken in the case. Some disclosures therein were, at the time, held dubious for both learned and natural reasons. The tribunal inclined to the opinion that the deponent, not undisturbed in his mind by recent events, raved of some things

which could never have happened. But subsequent depositions of the surviving sailors, bearing out the revelations of
their captain in several of the strangest particulars, gave credence to the rest. So that the tribunal, in its final decision,
rested its capital sentences upon statements which, had they
lacked confirmation, it would have deemed it but duty to re-
ject.

I, DON JOSÉ DE ABOS AND PADILLA, *His Majesty's Notary
for the Royal Revenue, and Register of this Province, and
Notary Public of the Holy Crusade of this Bishoprick, &c.*

*Do certify and declare, as much as is requisite in law, that,
in the criminal cause commenced the twenty-fourth of the
month of September, in the year seventeen hundred and
ninety-nine, against the negroes of the ship* San Dominick,
the following declaration before me was made:

Declaration of the first Witness, DON BENITO CERENO.

*The same day and month and year, His Honor, Doctor
Juan Martinez de Rozas, Councilor of the Royal Audience
of this Kingdom, and learned in the law of this Intendency,
ordered the captain of the ship* San Dominick, *Don Benito
Cereno, to appear; which he did in his litter, attended by
the monk Infelez; of whom he received the oath, which he
took by God, our Lord, and a Sign of the Cross; under which
he promised to tell the truth of whatever he should know
and should be asked;—and being interrogated agreeably to
the tenor of the act, commencing the process, he said, that
on the twentieth of May last, he set sail with his ship from
the port of Valparaiso, bound to that of Callao; loaded with
the produce of the country beside thirty cases of hardware
and one hundred and sixty blacks, of both sexes, mostly belonging to Don Alexandro Aranda, gentleman, of the City of
Mendoza; that the crew of the ship consisted of thirty-six
men, beside the persons who went as passengers; that the
negroes were in part as follows:*

[Here, in the original, follows a list of some fifty names,
descriptions, and ages, compiled from certain recovered documents of Aranda's and also from recollections of the deponent,
from which portions only are extracted.]

—One, from about eighteen to nineteen years, named José, and this was the man that waited upon his master, Don Alexandro, and who speaks well the Spanish, having served him four or five years; * * * a mulatto, named Francesco, the cabin steward, of a good person and voice, having sung in the Valparaiso churches, native of the province of Buenos Ayres, aged about thirty-five years. * * * A smart negro, named Dago, who had been for many years a grave-digger among the Spaniards, aged forty-six years. * * * Four old negroes, born in Africa, from sixty to seventy, but sound, calkers by trade, whose names are as follows:—the first was named Mure, and he was killed (as was also his son named Diamelo); the second, Nacta; the third, Yola, likewise killed; the fourth, Ghofan; and six full-grown negroes, aged from thirty to forty-five, all raw, and born among the Ashantees— Matinqui, Yau, Lecbe, Mapenda, Yambaio, Akim; four of whom were killed; * * * a powerful negro named Atufal, who being supposed to have been a chief in Africa, his owner set great store by him. *_ * * And a small negro of Senegal, but some years among the Spaniards, aged about thirty, which negro's name was Babo; * * * that he does not remember the names of the others, but that still expecting the residue of Don Alexandro's papers will be found, will then take due account of them all, and remit to the court; * * * and thirty-nine women and children of all ages.

[The catalogue over, the deposition goes on:]

* * * That all the negroes slept upon deck, as is customary in this navigation, and none wore fetters, because the owner, his friend Aranda, told him that they were all tractable; * * * that on the seventh day after leaving port, at three o'clock in the morning, all the Spaniards being asleep except the two officers on the watch, who were the boatswain, Juan Robels, and the carpenter, Juan Bautista Gayete, and the helmsman and his boy, the negroes revolted suddenly, wounded dangerously the boatswain and the carpenter, and successively killed eighteen men of those who were sleeping upon deck, some with hand-spikes and hatchets, and others by throwing them alive overboard, after tying them; that of the Spaniards upon deck, they left about seven, as he thinks, alive and tied, to manœuvre the ship, and three or four

more, who hid themselves, remained also alive. Although in
the act of revolt the negroes made themselves masters of the
hatchway, six or seven wounded went through it to the cockpit, without any hindrance on their part; that during the act
of revolt, the mate and another person, whose name he does
not recollect, attempted to come up through the hatchway,
but being quickly wounded, were obliged to return to the
cabin; that the deponent resolved at break of day to come
up the companion-way, where the negro Babo was, being the
ringleader, and Atufal, who assisted him, and having spoken
to them, exhorted them to cease committing such atrocities,
asking them, at the same time, what they wanted and intended
to do, offering, himself, to obey their commands; that notwithstanding this, they threw, in his presence, three men,
alive and tied, overboard; that they told the deponent to
come up, and that they would not kill him; which having
done, the negro Babo asked him whether there were in those
seas any negro countries where they might be carried, and he
answered them, No; that the negro Babo afterwards told him
to carry them to Senegal, or to the neighboring islands of St.
Nicholas; and he answered, that this was impossible, on account of the great distance, the necessity involved of rounding Cape Horn, the bad condition of the vessel, the want of
provisions, sails, and water; but that the negro Babo replied
to him he must carry them in any way; that they would do
and conform themselves to everything the deponent should
require as to eating and drinking; that after a long conference, being absolutely compelled to please them, for they
threatened to kill all the whites if they were not, at all
events, carried to Senegal, he told them that what was most
wanting for the voyage was water; that they would go near
the coast to take it, and thence they would proceed on their
course; that the negro Babo agreed to it; and the deponent
steered towards the intermediate ports, hoping to meet some
Spanish or foreign vessel that would save them; that within
ten or eleven days they saw the land, and continued their
course by it in the vicinity of Nasca; that the deponent observed that the negroes were now restless and mutinous, because he did not effect the taking in of water, the negro Babo
having required, with threats, that it should be done, without
fail, the following day; he told him he saw plainly that the
coast was steep, and the rivers designated in the maps were
not to be found, with other reasons suitable to the circum-

*stances; that the best way would be to go to the island of Santa
Maria, where they might water easily, it being a solitary island,
as the foreigners did; that the deponent did not go to Pisco,
that was near, nor make any other port of the coast, because
the negro Babo had intimated to him several times, that he
would kill all the whites the very moment he should perceive
any city, town, or settlement of any kind on the shores to
which they should be carried: that having determined to go to
the island of Santa Maria, as the deponent had planned, for
the purpose of trying whether, on the passage or near the island itself, they could find any vessel that should favor them,
or whether he could escape from it in a boat to the neighboring coast of Arauco, to adopt the necessary means he immediately changed his course, steering for the island; that the negroes Babo and Atufal held daily conferences, in which they
discussed what was necessary for their design of returning to
Senegal, whether they were to kill all the Spaniards, and particularly the deponent; that eight days after parting from the
coast of Nasca, the deponent being on the watch a little after
day-break, and soon after the negroes had their meeting, the
negro Babo came to the place where the deponent was, and
told him that he had determined to kill his master, Don Alexandro Aranda, both because he and his companions could not
otherwise be sure of their liberty, and that to keep the seamen
in subjection, he wanted to prepare a warning of what road
they should be made to take did they or any of them oppose
him; and that, by means of the death of Don Alexandro, that
warning would best be given; but, that what this last meant,
the deponent did not at the time comprehend, nor could not,
further than that the death of Don Alexandro was intended;
and moreover the negro Babo proposed to the deponent to
call the mate Raneds, who was sleeping in the cabin, before
the thing was done, for fear, as the deponent understood it,
that the mate, who was a good navigator, should not be killed
with Don Alexandro and the rest; that the deponent, who was
the friend, from youth, of Don Alexandro, prayed and conjured, but all was useless; for the negro Babo answered him
that the thing could not be prevented, and that all the Spaniards risked their death if they should attempt to frustrate his
will in this matter, or any other; that, in this conflict, the deponent called the mate, Raneds, who was forced to go apart,
and immediately the negro Babo commanded the Ashantee
Matinqui and the Ashantee Lecbe to go and commit the mur-*

der; that those two went down with hatchets to the berth of
Don Alexandro; that, yet half alive and mangled, they dragged
him on deck; that they were going to throw him overboard in
that state, but the negro Babo stopped them, bidding the murder be completed on the deck before him, which was done,
when, by his orders, the body was carried below, forward; that
nothing more was seen of it by the deponent for three days;
* * * that Don Alonzo Sidonia, an old man, long resident at
Valparaiso, and lately appointed to a civil office in Peru,
whither he had taken passage, was at the time sleeping in the
berth opposite Don Alexandro's; that awakening at his cries,
surprised by them, and at the sight of the negroes with their
bloody hatchets in their hands, he threw himself into the sea
through a window which was near him, and was drowned,
without it being in the power of the deponent to assist or take
him up; * * * that a short time after killing Aranda, they
brought upon deck his cousin-german, of middle-age, Don
Francisco Masa, of Mendoza, and the young Don Joaquin,
Marques de Aramboalaza, then lately from Spain, with his
Spanish servant Ponce, and the three young clerks of Aranda,
José Morairi, Lorenzo Bargas, and Hermenegildo Gandix, all
of Cadiz; that Don Joaquin and Hermenegildo Gandix, the
negro Babo, for purposes hereafter to appear, preserved alive;
but Don Francisco Masa, José Morairi, and Lorenzo Bargas,
with Ponce the servant, beside the boatswain, Juan Robles, the
boatswain's mates, Manuel Viscaya and Roderigo Hurta, and
four of the sailors, the negro Babo ordered to be thrown alive
into the sea, although they made no resistance, nor begged for
anything else but mercy; that the boatswain, Juan Robles,
who knew how to swim, kept the longest above water, making
acts of contrition, and, in the last words he uttered, charged
this deponent to cause mass to be said for his soul to our
Lady of Succor; * * * that, during the three days which followed, the deponent, uncertain what fate had befallen the
remains of Don Alexandro, frequently asked the negro Babo
where they were, and, if still on board, whether they were to
be preserved for interment ashore, entreating him so to order
it; that the negro Babo answered nothing till the fourth day,
when at sunrise, the deponent coming on deck, the negro
Babo showed him a skeleton, which had been substituted for
the ship's proper figure-head—the image of Cristobal Colon,
the discoverer of the New World; that the negro Babo asked
him whose skeleton that was, and whether, from its whiteness,

*he should not think it a white's; that, upon discovering his
face, the negro Babo, coming close, said words to this effect:
"Keep faith with the blacks from here to Senegal, or you shall
in spirit, as now in body, follow your leader," pointing to the
prow; * * * that the same morning the negro Babo took by
succession each Spaniard forward, and asked him whose
skeleton that was, and whether, from its whiteness, he should
not think it a white's; that each Spaniard covered his face;
that then to each the negro Babo repeated the words in the
first place said to the deponent; * * * that they (the Spaniards), being then assembled aft, the negro Babo harangued
them, saying that he had now done all; that the deponent (as
navigator for the negroes) might pursue his course, warning
him and all of them that they should, soul and body, go the
way of Don Alexandro, if he saw them (the Spaniards) speak
or plot anything against them (the negroes)—a threat which
was repeated every day; that, before the events last mentioned, they had tied the cook to throw him overboard, for it
is not known what thing they heard him speak, but finally the
negro Babo spared his life, at the request of the deponent;
that a few days after, the deponent, endeavoring not to omit
any means to preserve the lives of the remaining whites, spoke
to the negroes peace and tranquillity, and agreed to draw up
a paper, signed by the deponent and the sailors who could
write, as also by the negro Babo, for himself and all the
blacks, in which the deponent obliged himself to carry them
to Senegal, and they not to kill any more, and he formally to
make over to them the ship, with the cargo, with which they
were for that time satisfied and quieted. * * * But the next
day, the more surely to guard against the sailors' escape, the
negro Babo commanded all the boats to be destroyed but the
long-boat, which was unseaworthy, and another, a cutter in
good condition, which knowing it would yet be wanted for
towing the water casks, he had it lowered down into the
hold. * * **

[Various particulars of the prolonged and perplexed navigation ensuing here follow, with incidents of a calamitous calm,
from which portion one passage is extracted, to wit:]

*—That on the fifth day of the calm, all on board suffering
much from the heat, and want of water, and five having died
in fits, and mad, the negroes became irritable, and for a*

*chance gesture, which they deemed suspicious—though it was
harmless—made by the mate, Raneds, to the deponent in the
act of handing a quadrant, they killed him; but that for this
they afterwards were sorry, the mate being the only remaining navigator on board, except the deponent.*

*   *   *

*—That omitting other events, which daily happened, and
which can only serve uselessly to recall past misfortunes and
conflicts, after seventy-three days' navigation, reckoned from
the time they sailed from Nasca, during which they navigated
under a scanty allowance of water, and were afflicted with the
calms before mentioned, they at last arrived at the island of
Santa Maria, on the seventeenth of the month of August, at
about six o'clock in the afternoon, at which hour they cast
anchor very near the American ship,* Bachelor's Delight, *which
lay in the same bay, commanded by the generous Captain
Amasa Delano; but at six o'clock in the morning, they had
already descried the port, and the negroes became uneasy, as
soon as at distance they saw the ship, not having expected to
see one there; that the negro Babo pacified them, assuring
them that no fear need be had; that straightway he ordered the
figure on the bow to be covered with canvas, as for repairs,
and had the decks a little set in order; that for a time the
negro Babo and the negro Atufal conferred; that the negro
Atufal was for sailing away, but the negro Babo would not,
and, by himself, cast about what to do; that at last he came
to the deponent, proposing to him to say and do all that the
deponent declares to have said and done to the American
captain;* *   *   * *that the negro Babo warned him that if he
varied in the least, or uttered any word, or gave any look that
should give the least intimation of the past events or present
state, he would instantly kill him, with all his companions,
showing a dagger, which he carried hid, saying something
which, as he understood it, meant that that dagger would be
alert as his eye; that the negro Babo then announced the plan
to all his companions, which pleased them; that he then, the
better to disguise the truth, devised many expedients, in
some of them uniting deceit and defense; that of this sort
was the device of the six Ashantees before named, who were
his bravoes; that them he stationed on the break of the poop,
as if to clean certain hatchets (in cases, which were part of*

*the cargo), but in reality to use them, and distribute them at
need, and at a given word he told them; that, among other
devices, was the device of presenting Atufal, his right hand
man, as chained, though in a moment the chains could be
dropped; that in every particular he informed the deponent
what part he was expected to enact in every device, and what
story he was to tell on every occasion, always threatening him
with instant death if he varied in the least: that, conscious
that many of the negroes would be turbulent, the negro Babo
appointed the four aged negroes, who were calkers, to keep
what domestic order they could on the decks; that again and
again he harangued the Spaniards and his companions, informing them of his intent, and of his devices, and of the invented
story that this deponent was to tell; charging them lest any of
them varied from that story; that these arrangements were
made and matured during the interval of two or three hours,
between their first sighting the ship and the arrival on board
of Captain Amasa Delano; that this happened about half-past
seven o'clock in the morning, Captain Amasa Delano coming
in his boat, and all gladly receiving him; that the deponent,
as well as he could force himself, acting then the part of
principal owner, and a free captain of the ship, told Captain
Amasa Delano, when called upon, that he came from Buenos
Ayres, bound to Lima, with three hundred negroes; that off
Cape Horn, and in a subsequent fever, many negroes had
died; that also, by similar casualties, all the sea-officers and the
greatest part of the crew had died.*

*   *   *

[And so the deposition goes on, circumstantially recounting
the fictitious story dictated to the deponent by Babo, and
through the deponent imposed upon Captain Delano; and
also recounting the friendly offers of Captain Delano, with
other things, but all of which is here omitted. After the
fictitious story, etc., the deposition proceeds:]

—*That the generous Captain Amasa Delano remained on board
all the day, till he left the ship anchored at six o'clock in the
evening, deponent speaking to him always of his pretended
misfortunes, under the fore-mentioned principles, without having had it in his power to tell a single word, or give him the
least hint, that he might know the truth and state of things;*

*because the negro Babo, performing the office of an officious
servant with all the appearance of submission of the humble
slave, did not leave the deponent one moment; that this was
in order to observe the deponent's actions and words, for the
negro Babo understands well the Spanish; and besides, there
were thereabout some others who were constantly on the
watch, and likewise understood the Spanish;* * * * *that upon
one occasion, while deponent was standing on the deck conversing with Amasa Delano, by a secret sign the negro Babo
drew him (the deponent) aside, the act appearing as if
originating with the deponent; that then, he being drawn
aside, the negro Babo proposed to him to gain from Amasa
Delano full particulars about his ship, and crew, and arms;
that the deponent asked "For what?" that the negro Babo
answered he might conceive; that, grieved at the prospect of
what might overtake the generous Captain Amasa Delano, the
deponent at first refused to ask the desired questions, and used
every argument to induce the negro Babo to give up this new
design; that the negro Babo showed the point of his dagger;
that, after the information had been obtained, the negro Babo
again drew him aside, telling him that that very night he
(the deponent) would be captain of two ships, instead of one,
for that, great part of the American's ship's crew being to be
absent fishing, the six Ashantees, without any one else, would
easily take it; that at this time he said other things to the same
purpose; that no entreaties availed; that, before Amasa
Delano's coming on board, no hint had been given touching
the capture of the American ship; that to prevent this project
the deponent was powerless;* * * * *—that in some things his
memory is confused, he cannot distinctly recall every event;
* * * * *—that as soon as they had cast anchor at six o'clock
in the evening, as has before been stated, the American
Captain took leave, to return to his vessel; that upon a sudden
impulse, which the deponent believes to have come from
God and his angels, he, after the farewell had been said, followed the generous Captain Amasa Delano as far as the
gunwale, where he stayed, under pretense of taking leave,
until Amasa Delano should have been seated in his boat; that
on shoving off, the deponent sprang from the gunwale into
the boat, and fell into it, he knows not how, God guarding
him; that—*

[Here, in the original, follows the account of what further

happened at the escape, and how the *San Dominick* was retaken, and of the passage to the coast; including in the recital many expressions of "eternal gratitude" to the "generous Captain Amasa Delano." The deposition then proceeds with recapitulatory remarks, and a partial renumeration of the negroes, making record of their individual part in the past events, with a view to furnishing, according to command of the court, the data whereon to found the criminal sentences to be pronounced. From this portion is the following:]

—*That he believes that all the negroes, though not in the first place knowing to the design of revolt, when it was accomplished, approved it.* * * * *That the negro, José, eighteen years old, and in the personal service of Don Alexandro, was the one who communicated the information to the negro Babo about the state of things in the cabin, before the revolt; that this is known, because, in the preceding nights, he used to come from his berth, which was under his master's, in the cabin, to the deck where the ringleader and his associates were, and had secret conversations with the negro Babo, in which he was several times seen by the mate; that, one night, the mate drove him away twice;* * * * *that this same negro José was the one who, without being commanded to do so by the negro Babo, as Lecbe and Matinqui were, stabbed his master, Don Alexandro, after he had been dragged half-lifeless to the deck;* * * * *that the mulatto steward, Francesco, was of the first band of revolters, that he was, in all things, the creature and tool of the negro Babo; that, to make his court, he, just before a repast in the cabin, proposed, to the negro Babo, poisoning a dish for the generous Captain Amasa Delano; this is known and believed, because the negroes have said it; but that the negro Babo, having another design, forbade Francesco;* * * * *that the Ashantee Lecbe was one of the worst of them; for that, on the day the ship was retaken, he assisted in the defense of her, with a hatchet in each hand, with one of which he wounded, in the breast, the chief mate of Amasa Delano, in the first act of boarding; this all knew; that, in sight of the deponent, Lecbe struck with a hatchet, Don Francisco Masa, when, by the negro Babo's orders, he was carrying him to throw him overboard alive, beside participating in the murder, before mentioned, of Don Alexandro Aranda, and others of the cabin-passengers; that, owing to the fury with which the Ashantees fought in the engagement with* *the boats, but this Lecbe and Yau survived; that Yau was bad as Lecbe; that Yau was the man who, by Babo's command, willingly prepared the skeleton of Don Alexandro, in a way the negroes afterwards told the deponent, but which he, so long as reason is left him, can never divulge; that Yau and Lecbe were the two who, in a calm by night, riveted the skeleton to the bow; this also the negroes told him; that the negro Babo was he who traced the inscription below it; that the negro Babo was the plotter from first to last; he ordered every murder, and was the helm and keel of the revolt; that Atufal was his lieutenant in all; but Atufal, with his own hand, committed no murder; nor did the negro Babo; * * * that Atufal was shot, being killed in the fight with the boats, ere boarding; * * * that the negresses of age, were knowing to the revolt, and testified themselves satisfied at the death of their master, Don Alexandro; that, had the negroes not re-strained them, they would have tortured to death, instead of simply killing, the Spaniards slain by command of the negro Babo; that the negresses used their utmost influence to have the deponent made away with; that in the various acts of murder, they sang songs and danced—not gaily, but solemnly; and before the engagement with the boats, as well as during the action, they sang melancholy songs to the negroes, and that this melancholy tone was more inflaming than a different one would have been, and was so intended; that all this is believed, because the negroes have said it;—that of the thirty-six men of the crew, exclusive of the passengers (all of whom are now dead), which the deponent had knowledge of, six only remained alive, with four cabin-boys and ship-boys, not included with the crew; * * * —that the negroes broke an arm of one of the cabin-boys and gave him strokes with hatchets.*

[Then follow various random disclosures referring to various periods of time. The following are extracted:]

—That during the presence of Captain Amasa Delano on board, some attempts were made by the sailors, and one by Hermenegildo Gandix, to convey hints to him of the true state of affairs; but that these attempts were ineffectual, owing to fear of incurring death, and, furthermore, owing to the devices which offered contradictions to the true state of affairs, as well as owing to the generosity and piety of Amasa Delano

*incapable of sounding such wickedness; * * * that Luys Galgo, a sailor about sixty years of age, and formerly of the King's navy, was one of those who sought to convey tokens to Captain Amasa Delano; but his intent, though undiscovered, being suspected, he was, on a pretense, made to retire out of sight, and at last into the hold, and there was made away with. This the negroes have since said; * * * that one of the ship-boys feeling, from Captain Amasa Delano's presence, some hopes of release, and not having enough prudence, dropped some chance word respecting his expectations, which being overheard and understood by a slave-boy with whom he was eating at the time, the latter struck him on the head with a knife, inflicting a bad wound, but of which the boy is now healing; that likewise, not long before the ship was brought to anchor, one of the seamen, steering at the time, endangered himself by letting the blacks remark some expression in his countenance, arising from a cause similar to the above; but this sailor, by his heedful after conduct, escaped; * * * that these statements are made to show the court that from the beginning to the end of the revolt, it was impossible for the deponent and his men to act otherwise than they did; * * * —that the third clerk, Hermenegildo Gandix, who before had been forced to live among the seamen, wearing a seaman's habit, and in all respects appearing to be one for the time, he, Gandix, was killed by a musket ball fired through mistake from the boats before boarding; having in his fright run up the mizzen-rigging, calling to the boats—"don't board," lest upon their boarding the negroes should kill him; that this inducing the Americans to believe he some way favored the cause of the negroes, they fired two balls at him, so that he fell wounded from the rigging, and was drowned in the sea; * * * —that the young Don Joaquin, Marques de Aramboalaza, like Hermenegildo Gandix, the third clerk, was degraded to the office and appearance of a common seaman; that upon one occasion when Don Joaquin shrank, the negro Babo commanded the Ashantee Lecbe to take tar and heat it, and pour it upon Don Joaquin's hands; * * * —that Don Joaquin was killed owing to another mistake of the Americans, but one impossible to be avoided, as upon the approach of the boats, Don Joaquin, with a hatchet tied edge out and upright to his hand, was made by the negroes to appear on the bulwarks; whereupon, seen with arms in his hands and in a questionable attitude, he was shot for a renegade seaman;*

* * * —that on the person of Don Joaquin was found secreted a jewel, which, by papers that were discovered, proved to have been meant for the shrine of our Lady of Mercy in Lima; a votive offering, beforehand prepared and guarded, to attest his gratitude, when he should have landed in Peru, his last destination, for the safe conclusion of his entire voyage from Spain; * * * —that the jewel, with the other effects of the late Don Joaquin, is in the custody of the brethren of the Hospital de Sacerdotes, awaiting the disposition of the honorable court; * * * —that, owing to the condition of the deponent, as well as the haste in which the boats departed for the attack, the Americans were not forewarned that there were, among the apparent crew, a passenger and one of the clerks disguised by the negro Babo; * * *. —that, beside the negroes killed in the action, some were killed after the capture and re-anchoring at night, when shackled to the ring-bolts on deck; that these deaths were committed by the sailors, ere they could be prevented. That so soon as informed of it, Captain Amasa Delano used all his authority, and, in particular with his own hand, struck down Martinez Gola, who, having found a razor in the pocket of an old jacket of his, which one of the shackled negroes had on, was aiming it at the negro's throat; that the noble Captain Amasa Delano also wrenched from the hand of Bartholomew Barlo a dagger, secreted at the time of the massacre of the whites, with which he was in the act of stabbing a shackled negro, who, the same day, with another negro, had thrown him down and jumped upon him; * * * —that, for all the events, befalling through so long a time, during which the ship was in the hands of the negro Babo, he cannot here give account; but that, what he has said is the most substantial of what occurs to him at present, and is the truth under the oath which he has taken; which declaration he affirmed and ratified, after hearing it read to him.

He said that he is twenty-nine years of age, and broken in body and mind; that when finally dismissed by the court, he shall not return home to Chile, but betake himself to the monastery on Mount Agonia without; and signed with his honor, and crossed himself, and, for the time, departed as he came, in his litter, with the monk Infelez, to the Hospital de Sacerdotes.   BENITO CERENO.

DOCTOR ROZAS

If the Deposition have served as the key to fit into the lock of the complications which precede it, then, as a vault whose door has been flung back, the *San Dominick*'s hull lies open to-day.

Hitherto the nature of this narrative, besides rendering the intricacies in the beginning unavoidable, has more or less required that many things, instead of being set down in the order of occurrence, should be retrospectively, or irregularly given; this last is the case with the following passages, which will conclude the account:

During the long, mild voyage to Lima, there was, as before hinted, a period during which the sufferer a little recovered his health, or, at least in some degree, his tranquility. Ere the decided relapse which came, the two captains had many cordial conversations—their fraternal unreserve in singular contrast with former withdrawments.

Again and again it was repeated, how hard it had been to enact the part forced on the Spaniard by Babo.

"Ah, my dear friend," Don Benito once said, "at those very times when you thought me so morose and ungrateful, nay, when, as you now admit, you have thought me plotting your murder, at those very times my heart was frozen; I could not look at you, thinking of what, both on board this ship and your own, hung, from other hands, over my kind benefactor. And as God lives, Don Amasa, I know not whether desire for my own safety alone could have nerved me to that leap into your boat, had it not been for the thought that, did you, unenlightened, return to your ship, you, my best friend, with all who might be with you, stolen upon, that night, in your hammocks, would never in this world have wakened again. Do but think how you walked this deck, how you sat in this cabin, every inch of ground mined into honey-combs under you. Had I dropped the least hint, made the least advance towards an understanding between us, death, explosive death—yours as mine—would have ended the scene."

"True, true," cried Captain Delano, starting, "you have saved my life, Don Benito, more than I yours; saved it, too, against my knowledge and will."

"Nay, my friend," rejoined the Spaniard, courteous even to the point of religion, "God charmed your life, but you saved mine. To think of some things you did—those smilings and chattings, rash pointings and gesturings. For less than these, they slew my mate, Raneds; but you had the Prince of Heaven's safe-conduct through all ambuscades."

"Yes, all is owing to Providence, I know: but the temper of my mind that morning was more than commonly pleasant, while the sight of so much suffering, more apparent than real, added to my good-nature, compassion, and charity, happily interweaving the three. Had it been otherwise, doubtless, as you hint, some of my interferences might have ended unhappily enough. Besides, those feelings I spoke of enabled me to get the better of momentary distrust, at times when acuteness might have cost me my life, without saving another's. Only at the end did my suspicions get the better of me, and you know how wide of the mark they then proved."

"Wide, indeed," said Don Benito, sadly; "you were with me all day; stood with me, sat with me, talked with me, looked at me, ate with me, drank with me; and yet, your last act was to clutch for a monster, not only an innocent man, but the most pitiable of all men. To such degree may malign machinations and deceptions impose. So far may even the best man err, in judging the conduct of one with the recesses of whose condition he is not acquainted. But you were forced to it; and you were in time undeceived. Would that, in both respects, it was so ever, and with all men."

"You generalize, Don Benito; and mournfully enough. But the past is passed; why moralize upon it? Forget it. See, yon bright sun has forgotten it all, and the blue sea, and the blue sky; these have turned over new leaves."

"Because they have no memory," he dejectedly replied; "because they are not human."

"But these mild trades that now fan your cheek, do they not come with a human-like healing to you? Warm friends, steadfast friends are the trades."

"With their steadfastness they but waft me to my tomb, Señor," was the foreboding response.

"You are saved," cried Captain Delano, more and more astonished and pained; "you are saved: what has cast such a shadow upon you?"

"The negro."

There was silence, while the moody man sat, slowly and unconsciously gathering his mantle about him, as if it were a pall.

There was no more conversation that day.

But if the Spaniard's melancholy sometimes ended in muteness upon topics like the above, there were others upon which he never spoke at all; on which, indeed, all his old reserves were piled. Pass over the worst, and, only to elucidate, let an item or two of these be cited. The dress, so precise and costly, worn by him on the day whose events have been narrated, had not willingly been put on. And that silver-mounted sword, apparent symbol of despotic command, was not, indeed, a sword, but the ghost of one. The scabbard, artificially stiffened, was empty.

As for the black—whose brain, not body, had schemed and led the revolt, with the plot—his slight frame, inadequate to that which it held, had at once yielded to the superior muscular strength of his captor, in the boat. Seeing all was over, he uttered no sound, and could not be forced to. His aspect seemed to say, since I cannot do deeds, I will not speak words. Put in irons in the hold, with the rest, he was carried to Lima. During the passage, Don Benito did not visit him. Nor then, nor at any time after, would he look at him. Before the tribunal he refused. When pressed by the judges he fainted. On the testimony of the sailors alone rested the legal identity of Babo.

Some months after, dragged to the gibbet at the tail of a mule, the black met his voiceless end. The body was burned to ashes; but for many days, the head, that hive of subtlety, fixed on a pole in the Plaza, met, unabashed, the gaze of the whites; and across the Plaza looked towards St. Bartholomew's church, in whose vaults slept then, as now, the recovered bones of Aranda: and across the Rimac bridge looked towards the monastery, on Mount Agonia without; where, three months after being dismissed by the court, Benito Cereno, borne on the bier, did, indeed, follow his leader.

JIMMY ROSE

NOTE: This New York tale (*Harper's*, November, 1855) turns on one more of those "sudden and terrible reverses," plunging its victim into poverty and estrangement in some queer out-of-the-way relic of a house, that came to haunt Melville's imagination. It is not necessary to identify the wreck of the two vessels from China which completes Jimmy's ruin with the market failure of the exotically freighted *Moby-Dick* and *Pierre,* or with the loss of the printed stock of all his books in the Harper's fire of 1853, in order to feel an element of personal absorption in the telling. The familiar relationship between observing narrator and the story's chief actor is particularly close in "Jimmy Rose"—they are old friends, the narrator winds up living in Jimmy's queer retreat, and so on —to the point of raising at least the possibility that "Jimmy" is to be taken as an *alter ego*, a possibility rather insisted on by the refrain, "poor Jimmy—God guard us all—poor Jimmy Rose!"

A TIME ago, no matter how long precisely, I, an old man, removed from the country to the city, having become unexpected heir to a great old house in a narrow street of one of the lower wards, once the haunt of style and fashion, full of gay parlors and bridal chambers; but now, for the most part, transformed into counting-rooms and warehouses. There bales and boxes usurp the place of sofas; day-books and ledgers are spread where once the delicious breakfast toast was buttered. In those old wards the glorious old soft-waffle days are over.

Nevertheless, in this old house of mine, so strangely spared, some monument of departed days survived. Nor was this the only one. Amidst the warehouse ranges some few other dwellings likewise stood. The street's transmutation was not yet complete. Like those old English friars and nuns, long haunting the ruins of their retreats after they had been despoiled, so some few strange old gentlemen and ladies still lingered in the neighborhood and would not, could not, might not quit it. And I thought that when, one spring, emerging from my white-blossoming orchard, my own white hairs and white ivory-headed cane were added to their loitering census, that those poor old souls insanely fancied the ward was looking up—the tide of fashion setting back again.

For many years the old house had been unoccupied by an owner; those into whose hands it from time to time had passed having let it out to various shifting tenants; decayed old townspeople, mysterious recluses, or transient, ambiguous-looking foreigners.

While from certain cheap furbishings to which the exterior had been subjected, such as removing a fine old pulpit-like porch crowning the summit of six lofty steps, and set off with a broad-brimmed sounding-board overshadowing the whole, as well as replacing the original heavy window-shutters (each pierced with a crescent in the upper panel to admit an Oriental and moony light into the otherwise shut-up rooms of a sultry morning in July) with frippery Venetian blinds; while, I repeat, the front of the house hereby presented an incongruous aspect, as if the graft of modernness had not taken in its ancient stock; still, however it might fare without, within little or nothing had been altered. The cellars were full of great grim, arched bins of blackened brick, looking like the ancient tombs of Templars, while overhead were shown the first-floor timbers, huge, square, and massive, all red oak, and through long eld, of a rich and Indian color. So large were those timbers, and so thickly ranked, that to walk in those capacious cellars was much like walking along a line-of-battle ship's gun-deck.

All the rooms in each story remained just as they stood ninety years ago, with all their heavy-molded, wooden cornices, paneled wainscots, and carved and inaccessible mantels of queer horticultural and zoological devices. Dim with longevity, the very covering of the walls still preserved the patterns of the times of Louis XVI. In the largest parlor (the drawing-room, my daughters called it, in distinction from two smaller parlors, though I did not think the distinction indispensable) the paper hangings were in the most gaudy style. Instantly we knew such paper could only have come from Paris—genuine Versailles paper—the sort of paper that might have hung in Marie Antoinette's boudoir. It was of great diamond lozenges, divided by massive festoons of roses (onions, ·Biddy the girl said they were, but my wife soon changed Biddy's mind on that head); and in those lozenges, one and all, as in an over-arbored garden-cage, sat a grand series of gorgeous illustrations of the natural history of the most imposing Parisian-looking birds:

parrots, macaws, and peacocks, but mostly peacocks. Real
Prince Esterhazys of birds: all rubies, diamonds, and Orders
of the Golden Fleece. But, alas! the north side of this old apartment presented a strange look: half mossy and half mildew,
something as ancient forest trees on their north sides, to which
particular side the moss most clings, and where, they say, internal decay first strikes. In short, the original resplendence of
the peacocks had been sadly dimmed on that north side of the
room, owing to a small leak in the eaves, from which the rain
had slowly trickled its way down the wall, clean down to the
first floor. This leak the irreverent tenants, at that period occupying the premises, did not see fit to stop, or rather, did not
think it worth their while, seeing that they only kept their fuel
and dried their clothes in the parlor of the peacocks. Hence
many of the once glowing birds seemed as if they had their
princely plumage bedraggled in a dusty shower. Most mournfully their starry trains were blurred. Yet so patiently and so
pleasantly, nay, here and there so ruddily did they seem to bide
their bitter doom, so much of real elegance still lingered in
their shapes, and so full, too, seemed they of a sweet engaging
pensiveness, meditating all day long, for years and years, among
their faded bowers, that though my family repeatedly adjured
me (especially my wife, who, I fear, was too young for me) to
destroy the whole hen-roost, as Biddy called it, and cover the
walls with a beautiful, nice, genteel, cream-colored paper, despite all entreaties, I could not be prevailed upon, however
submissive in other things.

But chiefly would I permit no violation of the old parlor of
the peacocks or room of roses (I call it by both names), on account of its long association in my mind with one of the original proprietors of the mansion—the gentle Jimmy Rose.

Poor Jimmy Rose!

He was among my earliest acquaintances. It is not many
years since he died; and I and two other tottering old fellows
took hack, and in sole procession followed him to his grave.

Jimmy was born a man of moderate fortune. In his prime
he had an uncommonly handsome person: large and manly,
with bright eyes of blue, brown curling hair, and cheeks that
seemed painted with carmine, but it was health's genuine
bloom, deepened by the joy of life. He was by nature a great
ladies' man, and like most deep adorers of the sex, never tied
up his freedom of general worship by making one willful sacrifice of himself at the altar.

now that I bethink me, I recall how I had more than once observed this same middle-aged gentleman, and how that toward the close of one of Jimmy's dinners he would sit at the table pretending to be earnestly talking with beaming Jimmy, but all the while, with a half-furtive sort of tremulous eagerness and hastiness, pour down glass after glass of noble wine, as if now, while Jimmy's bounteous sun was at meridian, was the time to make his selfish hay.

At last I met a person famed for his peculiar knowledge of whatever was secret or withdrawn in the histories and habits of noted people. When I inquired of this person where Jimmy could possibly be, he took me close to Trinity Church rail, out of the jostling of the crowd, and whispered me, that Jimmy had the evening before entered an old house of his (Jimmy's), in C— Street, which old house had been for a time untenanted. The inference seemed to be that perhaps Jimmy might be lurking there now. So getting the precise locality, I bent my steps in that direction, and at last halted before the house containing the room of roses. The shutters were closed, and cobwebs were spun in their crescents. The whole place had a dreary, deserted air. The snow lay unswept, drifted in one billowy heap against the porch, no footprint tracking it. Whoever was within, surely that lonely man was an abandoned one. Few or no people were in the street; for even at that period the fashion of the street had departed from it, while trade had not as yet occupied what its rival had renounced.

Looking up and down the sidewalk a moment, I softly knocked at the door. No response. I knocked again, and louder. No one came. I knocked and rung both; still without effect. In despair I was going to quit the spot, when, as a last resource, I gave a prolonged summons, with my utmost strength, upon the heavy knocker, and then again stood still; while from various strange old windows up and down the street, various strange old heads were thrust out in wonder at so clamorous a stranger. As if now frightened from its silence, a hollow, husky voice addressed me through the keyhole.

"Who are you?" it said.

"A friend."

"Then shall you not come in," replied the voice, more hollowly than before.

"Great Heaven! this is not Jimmy Rose," thought I, starting. This is the wrong house. I have been misdirected. But still, to make all sure, I spoke again.

"Is James Rose within there?"

No reply.

Once more I spoke:

"I am William Ford; let me in."

"Oh, I can not, I can not! I am afraid of everyone."

It *was* Jimmy Rose!

"Let me in, Rose; let me in, man. I am your friend."

"I will not. I can trust no man now."

"Let me in, Rose; trust at least one, in me."

"Quit the spot, or—"

With that I heard a rattling against the huge lock, not made by any key, as if some small tube were being thrust into the keyhole. Horrified, I fled fast as feet could carry me.

I was a young man then, and Jimmy was not more than forty. It was five-and-twenty years ere I saw him again. And what a change. He whom I expected to behold—if behold at all—dry, shrunken, meagre, cadaverously fierce with misery and misanthropy—amazement! the old Persian roses bloomed in his cheeks. And yet poor as any rat; poor in the last dregs of poverty; a pauper beyond alms-house pauperism; a promenading pauper in a thin, thread-bare, careful coat; a pauper with wealth of polished words; a courteous, smiling, shivering gentleman.

Ah, poor, poor Jimmy—God guard us all—poor Jimmy Rose!

Though at the first onset of his calamity, when creditors, once fast friends, pursued him as carrion for jails; though then, to avoid their hunt, as well as the human eye, he had gone and denned in the old abandoned house; and there, in his loneliness, had been driven half mad, yet time and tide had soothed him down to sanity. Perhaps at bottom Jimmy was too thoroughly good and kind to be made from any cause a man-hater. And doubtless it at last seemed irreligious to Jimmy even to shun mankind.

Sometimes sweet sense of duty will entice one to bitter doom. For what could be more bitter than now, in abject need, to be seen of those—nay, crawl and visit them in an humble sort, and be tolerated as an old eccentric, wandering in their parlors—who once had known him richest of the rich, and gayest of the gay? Yet this Jimmy did. Without rudely breaking him right down to it, fate slowly bent him more and more to the lowest deep. From an unknown quarter he received an income of some seventy dollars, more or less. The principal he would never touch, but, by various models of eking it out, managed to live on the interest. He lived in an attic, where he supplied himself with food. He took but one regular repast a day—meal and milk—and nothing more, unless procured at others' tables. Often, about the tea-hour, he would drop in upon some old acquaintance, clad in his neat, forlorn frock coat, with worn velvet sewed upon the edges of the cuffs, and a similar device upon the hems of his pantaloons, to hide that dire look of having been grated off by rats. On Sunday he made a point of always dining at some fine house or other.

It is evident that no man could with impunity be allowed to lead this life unless regarded as one who, free from vice, was by fortune brought so low that the plummet of pity alone could reach him. Not much merit redounded to his entertainers because they did not thrust the starving gentleman forth when he came for his poor alms of tea and toast. Some merit had been theirs had they clubbed together and provided him, at small cost enough, with a sufficient income to make him, in point of necessaries, independent of the daily dole of charity; charity not sent to him, either, but charity for which he had to trudge round to their doors.

But the most touching thing of all were those roses in his cheeks; those ruddy roses in his nipping winter. How they bloomed; whether meal and milk, and tea and toast could keep them flourishing; whether now he painted them; by what strange magic they were made to blossom so; no son of man might tell. But there they bloomed. And besides the roses, Jimmy was rich in smiles. He smiled ever. The lordly door which received him to his eleemosynary teas, knew no such smiling guest as Jimmy. In his prosperous days the smile of Jimmy was famous far and wide. It should have been trebly famous now.

Wherever he went to tea, he had all of the news of the town to tell. By frequenting the reading-rooms, as one privileged through harmlessness, he kept himself informed of European affairs and the last literature, foreign and domestic. And of this, when encouragement was given, he would largely talk. But encouragement was not always given. At certain houses, and not a few, Jimmy would drop in about ten minutes before the tea-hour, and drop out again about ten minutes after it; well knowing that his further presence was not indispensable to the contentment or felicity of his host.

How forlorn it was to see him so heartily drinking the generous tea, cup after cup, and eating the flavorous bread and

butter, piece after piece, when, owing to the lateness of the dinner hour with the rest, and the abundance of that one grand
meal with them, no one besides Jimmy touched the bread and
butter, or exceeded a single cup of Souchong. And knowing
all this very well, poor Jimmy would try to hide his hunger,
and yet gratify it, too, by striving hard to carry on a sprightly
conversation with his hostess, and throwing in the eagerest
mouthfuls with a sort of absent-minded air, as if he ate merely
for custom's sake, and not starvation's.

Poor, poor Jimmy—God guard us all—poor Jimmy Rose!

Neither did Jimmy give up his courtly ways. Whenever
there were ladies at the table, sure were they of some fine
word; though, indeed, toward the close of Jimmy's life, the
young ladies rather thought his compliments somewhat musty,
smacking of cocked hats and small-clothes—nay, of old pawnbrokers' shoulder-lace and sword belts. For there still lingered
in Jimmy's address a subdued sort of martial air; he having in
his palmy days been, among other things, a general of the State
militia. There seems a fatality in these militia generalships.
Alas! I can recall more than two or three gentlemen who from
militia generals became paupers. I am afraid to think why
this is so. Is it that this military leaning in a man of an un-
military heart—that is, a gentle, peaceable heart—is an indication of some weak love of vain display? But ten to one it is not
so. At any rate, it is unhandsome, if not unchristian, in the
happy, too much to moralize on those who are not so.

So numerous were the houses that Jimmy visited, or so cautious was he in timing his less welcome calls, that at certain
mansions he only dropped in about once a year or so. And
annually, upon seeing at that house the blooming Miss Frances
or Miss Arabella, he would profoundly bow in his forlorn
old coat, and with his soft, white hand take hers in gallant
wise, saying, "Ah, Miss Arabella, these jewels here are bright
upon these fingers; but brighter would they look were it not
for those still brighter diamonds of your eyes!"

Though in thy own need thou hadst no pence to give the
poor, thou, Jimmy, still hadst alms to give the rich. For not
the beggar chattering at the corner pines more after bread
than the vain heart after compliment. The rich in their craving glut, as the poor in their craving want, we have with us always. So, I suppose, thought Jimmy Rose.

But all women are not vain, or if a little grain that way in-

clined, more than redeem it all with goodness. Such was the
sweet girl that closed poor Jimmy's eyes. The only daughter of
an opulent alderman, she knew Jimmy well, and saw to him
in his declining days. During his last sickness, with her own
hands she carried him jellies and blancmange; made tea for
him in his attic, and turned the poor old gentleman in his bed.
And well hadst thou deserved it, Jimmy, at that fair creature's
hands; well merited to have thy old eyes closed by woman's
fairy fingers, who through life, in riches and in poverty, was
still woman's sworn champion and devotee.

I hardly know that I should mention here one little incident
connected with this young lady's ministrations, and poor Jimmy's reception of them. But it is harm to neither; I will tell it.

Chancing to be in town, and hearing of Jimmy's illness, I
went to see him. And there in his lone attic I found the lovely
ministrant. Withdrawing upon seeing another visitor, she left
me alone with him. She had brought some little delicacies,
and also several books, of such a sort as are sent by serious-
minded well-wishers to invalids in a serious crisis. Now whether
it was repugnance at being considered next door to death, or
whether it was but the natural peevishness brought on by the
general misery of his state; however it was, as the gentle girl
withdrew, Jimmy, with what small remains of strength were
his, pitched the books into the furthest corner, murmuring,
"Why will she bring me this sad old stuff? Does she take me
for a pauper? Thinks she to salve a gentleman's heart with
Poor Man's Plaster?"

Poor, poor Jimmy—God guard us all—poor Jimmy Rose!

Well, well, I am an old man, and I suppose these tears I
drop are driblets from my dotage. But Heaven be praised,
Jimmy needs no man's pity now.

Jimmy Rose is dead!

Meantime, as I sit within the parlor of the peacocks—that
chamber from which his husky voice had come ere threatening
me with the pistol—I still must meditate upon his strange example, whereof the marvel is, how after that gay, dashing,
nobleman's career, he could be content to crawl through life,
and peep about among the marbles and mahoganies for contumelious tea and toast, where once like a very Warwick he
had feasted the huzzaing world with Burgundy and venison.

And every time I look at the wilted resplendence of those
proud peacocks on the wall, I bethink me of the withering

change in Jimmy's once resplendent pride of state. But still again, every time I gaze upon those festoons of perpetual roses, mid which the faded peacocks hang, I bethink me of those undying roses which bloomed in ruined Jimmy's cheek.

Transplanted to another soil, all the unkind past .forgot, God grant that Jimmy's roses may immortally survive!

I AND MY CHIMNEY

NOTE: The speaker in this extended monologue is of the same moral type as those in "Jimmy Rose" and "The Lightning-Rod Man": genial and essentially forbearing despite a rather melancholy old man's understanding of the world's incorrigible heartlessness in its dealings with men (and of humankind's corresponsive folly), but increasingly inclined to keep at a safe distance from it and stick fast to certain inoffensive private comforts. But what is he really saying? Is the vast overbuilt chimney—dominating the cramped house it all too abundantly warms, full of mysterious and perhaps treasure-filled recesses, yet razeed across the top like a beheaded king—a personal symbol? Is the story as a whole an allegory of the tragicomedy of its author's imaginative life and failing career? The ease and charm of its workmanship create a narrative surface that echoes back almost any interpretation one urges upon it. At the least there is no denying that in "I and My Chimney" (*Putnam's*, March, 1856) Melville appears on the happiest of compositional terms with the outlook he is projecting.

I AND my chimney, two gray-headed old smokers, reside in the country. We are, I may say, old settlers here; particularly my old chimney, which settles more and more every day.

Though I always say, *I and my chimney,* as Cardinal Wolsey used to say, *I and my King,* yet this egotistic way of speaking, wherein I take precedence of my chimney, is hardly borne out by the facts; in everything, except the above phrase, my chimney taking precedence of me.

Within thirty feet of the turf-sided road, my chimney—a huge, corpulent old Harry VIII of a chimney—rises full in front of me and all my possessions. Standing well up a hillside, my chimney, like Lord Rosse's monster telescope, swung vertical to hit the meridian moon, is the first object to greet the approaching traveler's eye, nor is it the last which the sun salutes. My chimney, too, is before me in receiving the first-fruits of the seasons. The snow is on its head ere on my hat; and every spring, as in a hollow beech tree, the first swallows build their nests in it.

But it is within doors that the pre-eminence of my chimney is most manifest. When in the rear room, set apart for that object, I stand to receive my guests (who, by the way, call more, I suspect, to see my chimney than me), I then stand, not so much before, as, strictly speaking, behind my chimney, which is, indeed, the true host. Not that I demur. In the presence of my betters, I hope I know my place.

From this habitual precedence of my chimney over me, some even think that I have got into a sad rearward way altogether; in short, from standing behind my old-fashioned chimney so much, I have got to be quite behind the age, too, as well as running behind-hand in everything else. But to tell the truth, I never was a very forward old fellow, nor what my farming neighbors call a forehanded one. Indeed, those rumors about my behindhandedness are so far correct, that I have an odd sauntering way with me sometimes of going about with my hands behind my back. As for my belonging to the rear-guard in general, certain it is, I bring up the rear of my chimney—which, by the way, is this moment before me—and that, too, both in fancy and fact. In brief, my chimney is my superior; my superior by I know not how many heads and shoulders; my superior, too, in that humbly bowing over with shovel and tongs, I much minister to it; yet never does it minister, or incline over to me; but, if anything, in its settlings, rather leans the other way.

My chimney is grand seignior here—the one great domineering object, not more of the landscape, than of the house; all the rest of which house, in each architectural arrangement, as may shortly appear, is, in the most marked manner, accommodated, not to my wants, but to my chimney's, which, among other things, has the centre of the house to himself, leaving but the odd holes and corners to me.

But I and my chimney must explain; and, as we are both rather obese, we may have to expatiate.

In those houses which are strictly double houses—that is, where the hall is in the middle—the fire-places usually are on opposite sides; so that while one member of the household is warming himself at a fire built into a recess of the north wall, say another member, the former's own brother, perhaps, may be holding his feet to the blaze before a hearth in the south wall—the two thus fairly sitting back to back. Is this well? Be it put to any man who has a proper fraternal feeling. Has it not a sort of sulky appearance? But very probably this style of chimney building originated with some architect afflicted with a quarrelsome family.

Then again, almost every modern fire-place has its separate flue—separate throughout, from hearth to chimney-top. At least such an arrangement is deemed desirable. Does not this look egotistical, selfish? But still more, all these separate flues, instead of having independent masonry establishments of their own, or instead of being grouped together in one federal stock in the middle of the house—instead of this, I say, each flue is surreptitiously honeycombed into the walls; so that these last are here and there, or indeed almost anywhere, treacherously hollow, and, in consequence, more or less weak. Of course, the main reason of this style of chimney building is to economize room. In cities, where lots are sold by the inch, small space is to spare for a chimney constructed on magnanimous principles; and, as with most thin men, who are generally tall, so with such houses, what is lacking in breadth must be made up in height. This remark holds true even with regard to many very stylish abodes, built by the most stylish of gentlemen. And yet, when that stylish gentleman, Louis le Grand of France, would build a palace for his lady friend, Madame de Maintenon, he built it but one story high—in fact, in the cottage style. But then, how uncommonly quadrangular, spacious, and broad—horizontal acres, not vertical ones. Such is the palace which, in all its one-storied magnificence of Languedoc marble, in the garden of Versailles, still remains to this day. Any man can buy a square foot of land and plant a liberty-pole on it; but it takes a king to set apart whole acres for a grand Trianon.

But nowadays it is different; and furthermore, what originated in a necessity has been mounted into a vaunt. In towns there is large rivalry in building tall houses. If one gentleman builds his house four stories high, and another gentleman comes next door and builds five stories high, then the former, not to be looked down upon that way, immediately sends for his architect and claps a fifth and a sixth story on top of his previous four. And, not till the gentleman has achieved his aspiration, not till he has stolen over the way by twilight and observed how his sixth story soars beyond his neighbor's fifth—not till then does he retire to his rest with satisfaction.

Such folks, it seems to me, need mountains for neighbors, to take this emulous conceit of soaring out of them.

If, considering that mine is a very wide house, and by no

means lofty, aught in the above may appear like interested pleading, as if I did but fold myself about in the cloak of a general proposition, cunningly to tickle my individual vanity beneath it, such misconception must vanish upon my frankly conceding that land adjoining my alder swamp was sold last month for ten dollars an acre, and thought a rash purchase at that; so that for wide houses hereabouts there is plenty of room, and cheap. Indeed, so cheap—dirt cheap—is the soil, that our elms thrust out their roots in it, and hang their great boughs over it, in the most lavish and reckless way. Almost all our crops, too, are sown broadcast, even peas and turnips. A farmer among us, who should go about his twenty-acre field, poking his finger into it here and there, and dropping down a mustard seed, would be thought a penurious, narrow-minded husbandman. The dandelions in the river-meadows, and the forget-me-nots along the mountain roads, you see at once they are put to no economy in space. Some seasons, too, our rye comes up, here and there a spear, sole and single like a church-spire. It doesn't care to crowd itself where it knows there is such a deal of room. The world is wide, the world is all before us, says the rye. Weeds, too, it is amazing how they spread. No such thing as arresting them—some of our pastures being a sort of Alsatia for the weeds. As for the grass, every spring it is like Kossuth's rising of what he calls the peoples. Mountains, too, a regular camp-meeting of them. For the same reason, the same all-sufficiency of room, our shadows march and countermarch, going through their various drills and masterly evolutions, like the old imperial guard on the Champs de Mars. As for the hills, especially where the roads cross them, the supervisors of our various towns have given notice to all concerned, that they can come and dig them down and cart them off, and never a cent to pay, no more than for the privilege of picking blackberries. The stranger who is buried here, what liberal-hearted landed proprietor among us grudges him his six feet of rocky pasture?

Nevertheless, cheap, after all, as our land is, and much as it is trodden under foot, I, for one, am proud of it for what it bears; and chiefly for its three great lions—the Great Oak, Ogg Mountain, and my chimney.

Most houses here, are but one and a half stories high; few exceed two. That in which I and my chimney dwell, is in width nearly twice its height, from sill to eaves—which accounts for the magnitude of its main content—besides, showing that in this house, as in this country at large, there is abundance of space, and to spare, for both of us.

The frame of the old house is of wood—which but the more sets forth the solidity of the chimney, which is of brick. And as the great wrought nails, binding the clapboards, are unknown in these degenerate days, so are the huge bricks in the chimney walls. The architect of the chimney must have had the pyramid of Cheops before him; for, after that famous structure, it seems modeled, only its rate of decrease towards the summit is considerably less, and it is truncated. From the exact middle of the mansion it soars from the cellar, right up through each successive floor, till, four feet square, it breaks water from the ridgepole of the roof, like an anvil-headed whale, through the crest of a billow. Most people, though, liken it, in that part, to a razeed observatory, masoned up.

The reason for its peculiar appearance above the roof touches upon rather delicate ground. How shall I reveal that, forasmuch as many years ago the original gable roof of the old house had become very leaky, a temporary proprietor hired a band of woodmen, with their huge, crosscut saws, and went to sawing the old gable roof clean off. Off it went, with all its birds' nests, and dormer windows. It was replaced with a modern roof, more fit for a railway wood-house than an old country gentleman's abode. This operation—razeeing the structure some fifteen feet—was, in effect upon the chimney, something like the falling of the great spring tides. It left uncommon low water all about the chimney—to abate which appearance, the same person now proceeds to slice fifteen feet off the chimney itself, actually beheading my royal old chimney—a regicidal act which, were it not for the palliating fact that he was a poulterer by trade, and, therefore, hardened to such neck-wringings, should send that former proprietor down to posterity in the same cart with Cromwell.

Owing to its pyramidal shape, the reduction of the chimney inordinately widened its razeed summit. Inordinately, I say, but only in the estimation of such as have no eye to the picturesque. What care I, if, unaware that my chimney, as a free citizen of this free land, stands upon an independent basis of its own, people passing it wonder how such a brick-kiln, as they call it, is supported upon mere joists and rafters? What care I? I will give a traveler a cup of switchel, if he want it;

but am I bound to supply him with a sweet taste? Men of cultivated minds see, in my old house and chimney, a goodly old
elephant-and-castle.

All feeling hearts will sympathize with me in what I am
now about to add. The surgical operation, above referred to,
necessarily brought into the open air a part of the chimney
previously under cover, and intended to remain so and, therefore, not built of what are called weather-bricks. In consequence, the chimney, though of a vigorous constitution, suffered not a little from so naked an exposure; and, unable to
acclimate itself, ere long began to fail—showing blotchy symptoms akin to those in measles. Whereupon travelers, passing my
way, would wag their heads, laughing: "See that wax nose—
how it melts off!" But what cared I? The same travelers would
travel across the sea to view Kenilworth peeling away, and for
a very good reason: that of all artists of the picturesque, decay
wears the palm—I would say, the ivy. In fact, I've often thought
that the proper place for my old chimney is ivied old England.

In vain my wife—with what probably ulterior intent will,
ere long, appear—solemnly warned me, that unless something
were done, and speedily, we should be burnt to the ground,
owing to the holes crumbling through the aforesaid blotchy
parts, where the chimney joined the roof. "Wife," said I, "far
better that my house should burn down, than that my chimney
should be pulled down, though but a few feet. They call it a
wax nose; very good; not for me to tweak the nose of my superior." But at last the man who has a mortgage on the house
dropped me a note, reminding me that, if my chimney was allowed to stand in that invalid condition, my policy of insurance would be void. This was a sort of hint not to be neglected. All the world over, the picturesque yields to the pock-
etesque. The mortgagor cared not, but the mortgagee did.

So another operation was performed. The wax nose was
taken off, and a new one fitted on. Unfortunately for the expression—being put up by a squint-eyed mason who, at the
time, had a bad stitch in the same side—the new nose stands a
little awry, in the same direction.

Of one thing, however, I am proud. The horizontal dimensions of the new part are unreduced.

Large as the chimney appears upon the roof, that is nothing to its spaciousness below. At its base in the cellar, it is precisely twelve feet square; and hence covers precisely one hundred and forty-four superficial feet. What an appropriation of

terra firma for a chimney, and what a huge load for this earth! In fact, it was only because I and my chimney formed no part of his ancient burden, that that stout peddler, Atlas of old, was enabled to stand up so bravely under his pack. The dimensions given may, perhaps, seem fabulous. But, like those stones at Gilgal, which Joshua set up for a memorial of having passed over Jordan, does not my chimney remain, even unto this day?

Very often I go down into my cellar, and attentively survey that vast square of masonry. I stand long, and ponder over, and wonder at it. It has a druidical look, away down in the umbrageous cellar there, whose numerous vaulted passages, and far glens of gloom, resemble the dark, damp depths of primeval woods. So strongly did this conceit steal over me, so deeply was I penetrated with wonder at the chimney, that one day—when I was a little out of my mind, I now think—getting a spade from the garden, I set to work, digging round the foundation, especially at the corners thereof, obscurely prompted by dreams of striking upon some old, earthen-worn memorial of that by-gone day when, into all this gloom, the light of heaven entered, as the masons laid the foundation-stones, peradventure sweltering under an August sun, or pelted by a March storm. Plying my blunted spade, how vexed was I by that ungracious interruption of a neighbor who, calling to see me upon some business, and being informed that I was below, said I need not be troubled to come up, but he would go down to me; and so, without ceremony, and without my having been forewarned, suddenly discovered me, digging in my cellar.

"Gold digging, sir?"

"Nay, sir," answered I, starting, "I was merely—ahem!—merely—I say I was merely digging—round my chimney."

"Ah, loosening the soil, to make it grow. Your chimney, sir, you regard as too small, I suppose; needing further development, especially at the top?"

"Sir!" said I, throwing down the spade, "do not be personal. I and my chimney—"

"Personal?"

"Sir, I look upon this chimney less as a pile of masonry than as a personage. It is the king of the house. I am but a suffered and inferior subject."

In fact, I would permit no gibes to be cast at either myself or my chimney; and never again did my visitor refer to it in my hearing, without coupling some compliment with the mention. It well deserves a respectful consideration. There it stands, solitary and alone—not a council-of-ten flues, but, like his sacred majesty of Russia, a unit of an autocrat.

Even to me, its dimensions, at times, seem incredible. It does not look so big—no, not even in the cellar. By the mere eye, its magnitude can be but imperfectly comprehended, because only one side can be received at one time; and said side can only present twelve feet, linear measure. But then, each other side also is twelve feet long; and the whole obviously forms a square; and twelve times twelve is one hundred and forty-four. And so, an adequate conception of the magnitude of this chimney is only to be got at by a sort of process in the higher mathematics, by a method somewhat akin to those whereby the surprising distances of fixed stars are computed.

It need hardly be said, that the walls of my house are entirely free from fire-places. These all congregate in the middle —in the one grand central chimney, upon all four sides of which are hearths—two tiers of hearths—so that when, in the various chambers, my family and guests are warming themselves of a cold winter's night, just before retiring, then, though at the time they may not be thinking so, all their faces mutually look towards each other, yea, all their feet point to one centre; and, when they go to sleep in their beds, they all sleep round one warm chimney, like so many Iroquois Indians, in the woods, round their one heap of embers. And just as the Indian's fire serves, not only to keep them comfortable, but also to keep off wolves, and other savage monsters, so my chimney, by its obvious smoke at top, keeps off prowling burglars from the towns—for what burglar or murderer would dare break into an abode from whose chimney issues such a continual smoke—betokening that if the inmates are not stirring, at least fires are, and in case òf an alarm, candles may readily be lighted, to say nothing of muskets.

But stately as is the chimney—yea, grand high altar as it is, right worthy for the celebration of high mass before the Pope of Rome, and all his cardinals—yet what is there perfect in this world? Caius Julius Caesar, had he not been so inordinately great, they say that Brutus, Cassius, Antony, and the rest, had been greater. My chimney, were it not so mighty in its magnitude, my chambers had been larger. How often has my wife ruefully told me, that my chimney, like the English aristocracy, casts a contracting shade all round it. She avers that endless domestic inconveniences arise—more particularly from the chimney's stubborn central locality. The grand objection with her is, that it stands midway in the place where a fine entrance-hall ought to be. In truth, there is no hall whatever to the house—nothing but a sort of square landing-place, as you enter from the wide front door. A roomy enough landing-place, I admit, but not attaining to the dignity of a hall. Now, as the front door is precisely in the middle of the front of the house, inwards it faces the chimney. In fact, the opposite wall of the landing-place is formed solely by the chimney; and hence—owing to the gradual tapering of the chimney—is a little less than twelve feet in width. Climbing the chimney in this part, is the principal stair-case—which, by three abrupt turns, and three minor landing-places, mounts to the second floor, where, over the front door, runs a sort of narrow gallery, something less than twelve feet long, leading to chambers on either hand. This gallery, of course, is railed; and so on, looking down upon the stairs, and all those landing-places together, with the main one at bottom, resembles not a little a balcony for musicians, in some jolly old abode, in times Elizabethan. Shall I tell a weakness? I cherish the cobwebs there, and many a time arrest Biddy in the act of brushing them with her broom, and have many a quarrel with my wife and daughters about it.

Now the ceiling, so to speak, of the place where you enter the house, that ceiling is, in fact, the ceiling of the second floor, not the first. The two floors are made one here; so that ascending this turning stairs, you seem going up into a kind of soaring tower, or light-house. At the second landing, midway up the chimney, is a mysterious door, entering to a mysterious closet; and here I keep mysterious cordials, of a choice, mysterious flavor, made so by the constant nurturing and subtle ripening of the chimney's gentle heat, distilled through that warm mass of masonry. Better for wines is it than voyages to the Indias; my chimney itself a tropic. A chair by my chimney in a November day is as good for an invalid as a long season spent in Cuba. Often I think how grapes might ripen against my chimney. How my wife's geraniums bud there! Bud in December. Her eggs, too—can't keep them near the chimney, on account of hatching. Ah, a warm heart has my chimney.

How often my wife was at me about that projected grand entrance-hall of hers, which was to be knocked clean through the chimney, from one end of the house to the other, and astonish all guests by its generous amplitude. "But, wife," said I, "the chimney—consider the chimney: if you demolish the foundation, what is to support the superstructure?" "Oh, that will rest on the second floor." The truth is, women know next to nothing about the realities of architecture. However, my wife still talked of running her entries and partitions. She spent many long nights elaborating her plans; in imagination building her boasted hall through the chimney, as though its high mightiness were a mere spear of sorrel-top. At last, I gently reminded her that, little as she might fancy it, the chimney was a fact—a sober, substantial fact, which, in all her plannings, it would be well to take into full consideration. But this was not of much avail.

And here, respectfully craving her permission, I must say a few words about this enterprising wife of mine. Though in years nearly old as myself, in spirit she is young as my little sorrel mare, Trigger, that threw me last fall. What is extraordinary, though she comes of a rheumatic family, she is straight as a pine, never has any aches; while for me with the sciatica, I am sometimes as crippled up as any old apple tree. But she has not so much as a toothache. As for her hearing—let me enter the house in my dusty boots, and she away up in the attic. And for her sight—Biddy, the housemaid, tells other people's housemaids, that her mistress will spy a spot on the dresser straight through the pewter platter, put up on purpose to hide it. Her faculties are alert as her limbs and her senses. No danger of my spouse dying of torpor. The longest night in the year I've known her lie awake, planning her campaign for the morrow. She is a natural projector. The maxim, "Whatever is, is right," is not hers. Her maxim is, Whatever is, is wrong; and what is more, must be altered; and what is still more, must be altered right away. Dreadful maxim for the wife of a dozy old dreamer like me, who dote on seventh days as days of rest, and, out of a sabbatical horror of industry, will, on a week-day, go out of my road a quarter of a mile, to avoid the sight of a man at work.

That matches are made in heaven, may be, but my wife would have been just the wife for Peter the Great, or Peter the Piper. How she would have set in order that huge littered empire of the one, and with indefatigable painstaking picked the peck of pickled peppers for the other.

But the most wonderful thing is, my wife never thinks of her end. Her youthful incredulity, as to the plain theory, and still plainer fact of death, hardly seems Christian. Advanced in years, as she knows she must be, my wife seems to think that she is to' teem on, and be inexhaustible forever. She doesn't believe in old age. At that strange promise in the plain of Mamre, my old wife, unlike old Abraham's, would not have jeeringly laughed within herself.

Judge how to me, who, sitting in the comfortable shadow of my chimney, smoking my comfortable pipe, with ashes not unwelcome at my feet, and ashes not unwelcome all but in my mouth; and who am thus in a comfortable sort of not unwelcome, though, indeed, ashy enough way, reminded of the ultimate exhaustion even of the most fiery life; judge how to me this unwarrantable vitality in my wife must come, sometimes, it is true, with a moral and a calm, but oftener with a breeze and a ruffle.

If the doctrine be true, that in wedlock contraries attract, by how cogent a fatality must I have been drawn to my wife! While spicily impatient of present and past, like a glass of ginger-beer she overflows with her schemes; and, with like energy as she puts down her foot, puts down her preserves and her pickles, and lives with them in a continual future; or ever full of expectations both from time and space, is ever restless for newspapers, and ravenous for letters. Content with the years that are gone, taking no thought for the morrow, and looking for no new thing from any person or quarter whatever, I have not a single scheme or expectation on earth, save in unequal resistance of the undue encroachment of hers.

Old myself, I take to oldness in things; for that cause mainly loving old Montaigne, and old cheese, and old wine; and eschewing young people, hot rolls, new books, and early potatoes, and very fond of my old claw-footed chair, and old club-footed Deacon White, my neighbor, and that still nigher old neighbor, my betwisted old grape-vine, that of a summer evening leans in his elbow for cosy company at my window-sill, while I, within doors, lean over mine to meet his; and above all, high above all, am fond of my high-manteled old chimney. But she, out of that infatuate juvenility of hers, takes to nothing but newness; for that cause mainly, loving new cider in autumn, and in spring, as if she were own daughter of Nebuchadnezzar, fairly raving after all sorts of salads and spinaches, and more particularly green cucumbers (though all the time nature rebukes such unsuitable young hankerings in so elderly a person, by never permitting such things to agree with her), and has an itch after recently-discovered fine prospects (so no grave-yard be in the background), and also after Sweden-borgianism, and the Spirit Rapping philosophy, with other new views, alike in things natural and unnatural; and immortally hopeful, is forever making new flower-beds even on the north side of the house, where the bleak mountain wind would scarce allow the wiry weed called hard-hack to gain a thorough footing; and on the road-side sets out mere pipe-stems of young elms; though there is no hope of any shade from them, except over the ruins of her great granddaughters' grave-stones; and won't wear caps, but plaits her gray hair; and takes the Ladies' Magazine for the fashions, and always buys her new almanac a month before the new year; and rises at dawn; and to the warmest sunset turns a cold shoulder; and still goes on at odd hours with her new course of history, and her French, and her music; and likes young company; and offers to ride young colts; and sets out young suckers in the orchard; and has a spite against my elbowed old grape-vine, and my club-footed old neighbor, and my claw-footed old chair, and above all, high above all, would fain persecute, unto death, my high-manteled old chimney. By what perverse magic, I a thousand times think, does such a very autumnal old lady have such a very vernal young soul? When I would remonstrate at times, she spins round on me with, "Oh, don't you grumble, old man (she always calls me old man), it's I, young I, that keep you from stagnating." Well, I suppose it is so. Yea, after all, these things are well ordered. My wife, as one of her poor relations, good soul, intimates, is the salt of the earth, and none the less the salt of my sea, which otherwise were unwholesome. She is its monsoon, too, blowing a brisk gale over it, in the one steady direction of my chimney.

Not insensible of her superior energies, my wife has frequently made me propositions to take upon herself all the responsibilities of my affairs. She is desirous that, domestically, I should abdicate; that, renouncing further rule, like the venerable Charles V, I should retire into some sort of monastery. But indeed, the chimney excepted, I have little authority to lay down. By my wife's ingenious application of the principle that certain things belong of right to female jurisdiction, I find myself, through my easy compliances, insensibly stripped by degrees of one masculine prerogative after another. In a dream I go about my fields, a sort of lazy, happy-go-lucky, good-for-nothing, loafing, old Lear. Only by some sudden revelation am I reminded who is over me; as year before last, one day seeing in one corner of the premises fresh deposits of mysterious boards and timbers, the oddity of the incident at length begat serious meditation. "Wife," said I, "whose boards and timbers are those I see near the orchard there? Do you know anything about them, wife? Who put them there? You know I do not like the neighbors to use my land that way; they should ask permission first."

She regarded me with a pitying smile.

"Why, old man, don't you know I am building a new barn? Didn't you know that, old man?"

This is the poor old lady that was accusing me of tyrannizing over her.

To return now to the chimney. Upon being assured of the futility of her proposed hall, so long as the obstacle remained, for a time my wife was for a modified project. But I could never exactly comprehend it. As far as I could see through it, it seemed to involve the general idea of a sort of irregular archway, or elbowed tunnel, which was to penetrate the chimney at some convenient point under the stair-case, and carefully avoiding dangerous contact with the fire-places, and particularly steering clear of the great interior flue, was to conduct the enterprising traveler from the front door all the way into the dining-room in the remote rear of the mansion. Doubtless it was a bold stroke of genius, that plan of hers, and so was Nero's when he schemed his grand canal through the Isthmus of Corinth. Nor will I take oath, that, had her project been accomplished, then, by help of lights hung at judicious intervals through the tunnel, some Belzoni or other might have succeeded in future ages in penetrating through the masonry, and actually emerging into the dining-room, and once there, it would have been inhospitable treatment of such a traveler to have denied him a recruiting meal.

But my bustling wife did not restrict her objections, nor in the end confine her proposed alterations to the first floor. Her ambition was of the mounting order. She ascended with her schemes to the second floor, and so to the attic. Perhaps there was some small ground for her discontent with things as they were. The truth is, there was no regular passage-way up stairs or down, unless we again except that little orchestra-gallery before mentioned. And all this was owing to the chimney, which my gamesome spouse seemed despitefully to regard as the bully of the house. On all its four sides, nearly all the chambers sidled up to the chimney for the benefit of a fire-place. The chimney would not go to them; they must needs go to it. The consequence was, almost every room, like a philosophical system, was in itself an entry, or passage-way to other rooms, and systems of rooms—a whole suite of entries, in fact. Going through the house, you seem to be forever going somewhere, and getting nowhere. It is like losing one's self in the woods; round and round the chimney you go, and if you arrive at all, it is just where you started, and so you begin again, and again get nowhere. Indeed—though I say it not in the way of fault-finding at all—never was there so labyrinthine an abode. Guests will tarry with me several weeks and every now and then, be anew astonished at some unforeseen apartment.

The puzzling nature of the mansion, resulting from the chimney, is peculiarly noticeable in the dining-room, which has no less than nine doors, opening in all directions, and into all sorts of paces. A stranger, for the first time entering this dining-room, and naturally taking no special heed at what door he entered, will, upon rising to depart, commit the strangest blunders. Such, for instance, as opening the first door that comes handy, and finding himself stealing up stairs by the back passage. Shutting that door, he will proceed to another, and be aghast at the cellar yawning at his feet. Trying a third, he surprises the housemaid at her work. In the end, no more relying on his own unaided efforts, he procures a trusty guide in some passing person, and in good time successfully emerges. Perhaps as curious a blunder as any, was that of a certain stylish young gentleman, a great exquisite, in whose judicious eyes my daughter Anna had found especial favor. He called upon the young lady one evening, and found her alone in the dining-room at her needle-work. He stayed rather late; and after abundance of superfine discourse, all the while retaining his hat and cane, made his profuse adieus, and with repeated graceful bows proceeded to depart, after the fashion of courtiers from the Queen, and by so doing, opening a door at random, with one hand placed behind, very effectually succeeded in backing himself into a dark pantry, where he carefully shut himself up, wondering there was no light in the entry. After several strange noises as of a cat among the crockery, he reappeared through the same door, looking uncommonly crest-fallen, and, with a deeply embarrassed air, requested my daughter to designate at which of the nine he should find exit. When the mischievous Anna told me the story, she said it was surprising how unaffected and matter-of-fact the young gentle-

man's manner was after his reappearance. He was more candid than ever, to be sure; having inadvertently thrust his white
kids into an open drawer of Havana sugar, under the impression, probably, that being what they call "a sweet fellow," his
route might possibly lie in that direction.

Another inconvenience resulting from the chimney is the
bewilderment of a guest in gaining his chamber, many strange
doors lying between him and it. To direct him by finger-
posts would look rather queer; and just as queer in him to be
knocking at every door on his route, like London's city guest,
the king, at Temple Bar.

Now, of all these things and many, many more, my family
continually complained. At last my wife came out with her
sweeping proposition—in toto to abolish the chimney.

"What!" said I, "abolish the chimney? To take out the back-
bone of anything, wife, is a hazardous affair. Spines out of
backs, and chimneys out of houses, are not to be taken like
frosted lead-pipes from the ground. Besides," added I, "the
chimney is the one grand permanence of this abode. If undisturbed by innovators, then in future ages, when all the house
shall have crumbled from it, this chimney will still survive—a
Bunker Hill monument. No, no, wife, I can't abolish my back-
bone."

So said I then. But who is sure of himself, especially an old
man, with both wife and daughters ever at his elbow and
ear? In time, I was persuaded to think a little better of it; in
short, to take the matter into preliminary consideration. At
length it came to pass that a master-mason—a rough sort of
architect—one Mr. Scribe, was summoned to a conference. I
formally introduced him to my chimney. A previous introduction from my wife had introduced him to myself. He had been
not a little employed by that lady, in preparing plans and
estimates for some of her extensive operations in drainage.
Having, with much ado, extorted from my spouse the promise
that she would leave us to an unmolested survey, I began by
leading Mr. Scribe down to the root of the matter, in the cellar.
Lamp in hand, I descended; for though up stairs it was noon,
below it was night.

We seemed in the pyramids; and I, with one hand holding
my lamp overhead, and with the other pointing out, in the obscurity, the hoar mass of the chimney, seemed some Arab
guide, showing the cob-webbed mausoleum of the great god
Apis.

"This is a most remarkable structure, sir," said the master-mason, after long contemplating it in silence, "a most remarkable structure, sir."

"Yes," said I, complacently, "every one says so."

"But large as it appears above the roof, I would not have inferred the magnitude of this foundation, sir," eying it critically.

Then taking out his rule, he measured it.

"Twelve feet square; one hundred and forty-four square feet! Sir, this house would appear to have been built simply for the accommodation of your chimney."

"Yes, my chimney and me. Tell me candidly, now," I added, "would you have such a famous chimney abolished?"

"I wouldn't have it in a house of mine, sir, for a gift," was the reply. "It's a losing affair altogether, sir. Do you know, sir, that in retaining this chimney, you are losing, not only one hundred and forty-four square feet of good ground, but likewise a considerable interest upon a considerable principal?"

"How?"

"Look, sir," said he, taking a bit of red chalk from his pocket, and figuring against a whitewashed wall, "twenty times eight is so and so; then forty-two times thirty-nine is so and so—ain't it, sir? Well, add those together, and subtract this here, then that makes so and so," still chalking away.

To be brief, after no small ciphering, Mr. Scribe informed me that my chimney contained, I am ashamed to say how many thousand and odd valuable bricks.

"No more," said I fidgeting. "Pray now, let us have a look above."

In that upper zone we made two more circumnavigations for the first and second floors. That done, we stood together at the foot of the stairway by the front door; my hand upon the knob, and Mr. Scribe hat in hand.

"Well, sir," said he, a sort of feeling his way, and, to help himself, fumbling with his hat, "well, sir, I think it can be done."

"What, pray, Mr. Scribe; *what* can be done?"

"Your chimney, sir; it can without rashness be removed, I think."

"*I* will think of it, too, Mr. Scribe," said I, turning the knob, and bowing him towards the open space without, "I will *think* of it, sir; it demands consideration; much obliged to ye; good morning, Mr. Scribe."

"It is all arranged, then," cried my wife with great glee, bursting from the nighest room.

"When will they begin?" demanded my daughter Julia.

"To-morrow?" asked Anna.

"Patience, patience, my dears," said I, "such a big chimney is not to be abolished in a minute."

Next morning it began again.

"You remember the chimney," said my wife.

"Wife," said I, "it is never out of my house, and never out of my mind."

"But when is Mr. Scribe to begin to pull it down?" asked Anna.

"Not to-day, Anna," said I.

"*When*, then?" demanded Julia, in alarm.

Now, if this chimney of mine was, for size, a sort of belfry, for ding-donging at me about it, my wife and daughters were a sort of bells, always chiming together, or taking up each other's melodies at every pause, my wife the key-clapper of all. A very sweet ringing, and pealing, and chiming, I confess; but then, the most silvery of bells may, sometimes, dismally toll, as well as merrily play. And as touching the subject in question, it became so now. Perceiving a strange relapse of opposition in me, wife and daughters began a soft and dirge-like, melancholy tolling over it.

At length my wife, getting much excited, declared to me, with pointed finger, that so long as that chimney stood, she should regard it as the monument of what she called my broken pledge. But finding this did not answer, the next day she gave me to understand that either she or the chimney must quit the house.

Finding matters coming to such a pass, I and my pipe philosophized over them awhile, and finally concluded between us, that little as our hearts went with the plan, yet for peace's sake, I might write out the chimney's death-warrant and, while my hand was in, scratch a note to Mr. Scribe.

Considering that I, and my chimney, and my pipe, from having been so much together, were three great cronies, the facility with which my pipe consented to a project so fatal to the goodliest of our trio; or rather, the way in which I and my pipe, in secret, conspired together, as it were, against our unsuspicious old comrade—this may seem rather strange, if not suggestive of sad reflections upon us two. But, indeed, we sons of clay, that is my pipe and I, are no whit better than the rest. Far from us, indeed, to have volunteered the betrayal of our crony. We are of a peaceable nature, too. But that love of peace it was which made us false to a mutual friend, as soon as his cause demanded a vigorous vindication. But I rejoice to add, that better and braver thoughts soon returned, as will now briefly be set forth.

To my note, Mr. Scribe replied in person.

Once more we made a survey, mainly now with a view to a pecuniary estimate.

"I will do it for five hundred dollars," said Mr. Scribe at last, again hat in hand.

"Very well, Mr. Scribe, I will think of it," replied I, again bowing him to the door.

Not unvexed by this, for the second time, unexpected response, again he withdrew, and from my wife and daughters again burst the old exclamations.

The truth is, resolve how I would, at the last pinch I and my chimney could not be parted.

"So Holofernes will have his way, never mind whose heart breaks for it," said my wife next morning, at breakfast, in that half-didactic, half-reproachful way of hers, which is harder to bear than her most energetic assault. Holofernes, too, is with her a pet name for any fell domestic despot. So, whenever, against her most ambitious innovations, those which saw me quite across the grain, I, as in the present instance, stand with however little steadfastness on the defence, she is sure to call me Holofernes, and ten to one takes the first opportunity to read aloud, with a suppressed emphasis, of an evening, the first newspaper paragraph about some tyrannic day-laborer who, after being for many years the Caligula of his family, ends by beating his long-suffering spouse to death, with a garret door wrenched off its hinges, and then, pitching his little innocents out of the window, suicidally turns inward towards the broken wall scored with the butcher's and baker's bills, and so rushes headlong to his dreadful account.

Nevertheless, for a few days, not a little to my surprise, I heard no further reproaches. An intense calm pervaded my wife, but beneath which, as in the sea, there was no knowing what portentous movements might be going on. She frequently went abroad, and in a direction which I thought not unsuspicious; namely, in the direction of New Petra, a griffin-like house of wood and stucco, in the highest style of ornamental art, graced with four chimneys in the form of erect dragons spouting smoke from their nostrils; the elegant modern residence of Mr. Scribe, which he had built for the purpose of a standing advertisement, not more of his taste as an architect, than his solidity as a master-mason.

At last, smoking my pipe one morning, I heard a rap at the door, and my wife, with an air unusually quiet for her, brought me a note. As I have no correspondents except Solomon, with who, in his sentiments, at least, I entirely correspond, the note occasioned me some little surprise, which was not diminished upon reading the following:

New Petra, April 1st.

Sir:—During my last examination of your chimney, possibly you may have noted that I frequently applied my rule to it in a manner apparently unnecessary. Possibly also, at the same time, you might have observed in me more or less of perplexity, to which, however, I refrained from giving any verbal expression.

I now feel it obligatory upon me to inform you of what was then but a dim suspicion, and as such would have been unwise to give utterance to, but which now, from various subsequent calculations assuming no little probability, it may be important that you should not remain in further ignorance of.

It is my solemn duty to warn you, sir, that there is architectural cause to conjecture that somewhere concealed in your chimney is a reserved space, hermetically closed, in short, a secret chamber, or rather closet. How long it has been there, it is for me impossible to say. What it contains is hid, with itself, in darkness. But probably a secret closet would not have been contrived except for some extraordinary object, whether for the concealment of treasure, or what other purpose, may be left to those better acquainted with the history of the house to guess.

But enough: in making this disclosure, sir, my conscience is eased. Whatever step you choose to take upon it is, of course, a matter of indifference to me; though, I confess, as respects the character of the closet, I cannot but share in a natural curiosity.

Trusting that you may be guided aright, in determining whether it is Christian-like knowingly to reside in a house, hidden in which is a secret closet,

I remain,

With much respect,

yours very humbly,

HIRAM SCRIBE

My first thought upon reading this note was, not of the alleged mystery of manner to which, at the outset, it alluded —for none such had I at all observed in the master-mason during his surveys—but of my late kinsman, Captain Julian Dacres, long a ship-master and merchant in the Indian trade, who, about thirty years ago, and at the ripe age of ninety, died a bachelor, and in this very house, which he had built. He was supposed to have retired into this country with a large fortune. But to the general surprise, after being at great cost in building himself this mansion, he settled down into a sedate, reserved, and inexpensive old age, which by the neighbors was thought all the better for his heirs; but lo! upon opening the will, his property was found to consist but of the house and grounds, and some ten thousand dollars in stocks; but the place, being found heavily mortgaged, was in consequence sold. Gossip had its day, and left the grass quietly to creep over the captain's grave, where he still slumbers in a privacy as unmolested as if the billows of the Indian Ocean, instead of the billows of inland verdure, rolled over him. Still, I remembered, long ago, hearing strange solutions whispered by the country people for the mystery involving his will, and, by reflex, himself; and that, too, as well in conscience as purse. But people who could circulate the report (which they did), that Captain Julian Dacres had, in his day, been a Borneo pirate, surely were not worthy of credence in their collateral notions. It is queer what wild whimsies of rumors will, like toadstools, spring up about any eccentric stranger who, settling down among a rustic population, keeps quietly to himself. With some, inoffensiveness would seem a prime cause of offense. But what chiefly had led me to scout at these rumors, particuarly as referring to concealed treasure, was the circumstance, that the stranger (the same who razeed the roof and the chimney) into whose hands the estate had passed on my kinsman's death, was of that sort of character, that had there been the least ground for those reports, he would speedily have tested them, by tearing down and rummaging the walls.

Nevertheless, the note of Mr. Scribe, so strangely recalling the memory of my kinsman, very naturally chimed in with what had been mysterious, or at least unexplained, about him; vague flashings of ingots united in my mind with vague gleamings of skulls. But the first cool thought soon dismissed such chimeras; and, with a calm smile, I turned towards my wife, who, meantime, had been sitting near by, impatient enough, I dare say, to know who could have taken it into his head to write me a letter.

"Well, old man," said she, "who is it from, and what is it about?"

"Read it, wife," said I, handing it.

Read it she did, and then—such an explosion! I will not pretend to describe her emotions, or repeat her expressions. Enough that my daughters were quickly called in to share the excitement. Although they had never before dreamed of such a revelation as Mr. Scribe's, yet upon the first suggestion they instinctively saw the extreme likelihood of it. In corroboration, they cited first my kinsman, and second, my chimney; alleging that the profound mystery involving the former, and the equally profound masonry involving the latter, though both acknowledged facts, were alike preposterous on any other supposition than the secret closet.

But all this time I was quietly thinking to myself: Could it be hidden from me that my credulity in this instance would operate very favorably to a certain plan of theirs? How to get to the secret closet, or how to have any certainty about it at all, without making such fell work with the chimney as to render its set destruction superfluous? That my wife wished to get rid of the chimney, it needed no reflection to show; and that Mr. Scribe, for all his pretended disinterestedness, was not opposed to pocketing five hundred dollars by the operation, seemed equally evident. That my wife had, in secret, laid heads together with Mr. Scribe, I at present refrain from affirming. But when I consider her enmity against my chimney, and the steadiness with which at the last she is wont to carry out her schemes, if by hook or by crook she can, especially after having been once baffled, why, I scarcely knew at what step of hers to be surprised.

Of one thing only was I resolved, that I and my chimney should not budge.

In vain all protests. Next morning I went out into the road, where I had noticed a diabolical-looking old gander that, for its doughty exploits in the way of scratching into forbidden inclosures, had been rewarded by its master with a portentous, four-pronged, wooden decoration, in the shape of a collar of the Order of the Garotte. This gander I cornered, and rummaging out its stiffest quill, plucked it, took it home, and making a stiff pen, inscribed the following stiff note:

Chimney Side, April 2.

Mr. Scribe.

Sir:—For your conjecture, we return you our joint thanks and compliments, and beg leave to assure you, that

We shall remain,

Very faithfully,

The same,

I AND MY CHIMNEY.

Of course, for this epistle we had to endure some pretty sharp raps. But having at last explicitly understood from me that Mr. Scribe's note had not altered my mind one jot, my wife, to move me, among other things said, that if she remembered aright, there was a statute placing the keeping in private houses of secret closets on the same unlawful footing with the keeping of gunpowder. But it had no effect.

A few days after, my spouse changed her key.

It was nearly midnight, and all were in bed but ourselves, who sat up, one in each chimney-corner; she, needles in hand, indefatigably knitting a sock; I, pipe in mouth, indolently weaving my vapors.

It was one of the first of the chill nights in autumn. There was a fire on the hearth, burning low. The air without was torpid and heavy; the wood, by an oversight, of the sort called soggy.

"Do look at the chimney," she began; "can't you see that something must be in it?"

"Yes, wife. Truly there is smoke in the chimney, as in Mr. Scribe's note."

"Smoke? Yes, indeed, and in my eyes, too. How you two wicked old sinners do smoke!—this wicked old chimney and you."

"Wife," said I, "I and my chimney like to have a quiet smoke together, it is true, but we don't like to be called names."

"Now, dear old man," said she, softening down, and a little shifting the subject, "when you think of that old kinsman of yours, you *know* there must be a secret closet in this chimney."

"Secret ash-hole, wife, why don't you have it? Yes, I dare say there is a secret ash-hole in the chimney; for where do all the ashes go to that we drop down the queer hole yonder?"

"I know where they go to; I've been there almost as many times as the cat."

"What devil, wife, prompted you to crawl into the ash-hole! Don't you know that St. Dunstan's devil emerged from the ash-hole? You will get your death one of these days, exploring all about as you do. But supposing there be a secret closet, what then?"

"What, then? why what should be in a secret closet but—"

"Dry bones, wife," broke in I with a puff, while the sociable old chimney broke in with another.

"There again! Oh, how this wretched old chimney smokes," wiping her eyes with her handkerchief. "I've no doubt the reason it smokes so is, because that secret closet interferes with the flue. Do see, too, how the jambs here keep settling; and it's down hill all the way from the door to this hearth. This horrid old chimney will fall on our heads yet; depend upon it, old man."

"Yes, wife, I do depend on it; yes, indeed, I place every dependence on my chimney. As for its settling, I like it. I, too, am settling, you know, in my gait. I and my chimney are settling together, and shall keep settling, too, till as in a great feather-bed, we shall both have settled away clean out of sight. But this secret oven; I mean, secret closet of yours, wife; where exactly do you suppose that secret closet is?"

"That is for Mr. Scribe to say."

"But suppose he cannot say exactly; what, then?"

"Why, then he can prove, I am sure, that it must be somewhere or other in this horrid old chimney."

"And if he can't prove that; what, then?"

"Why, then, old man," with a stately air, "I shall say little more about it."

"Agreed, wife," returned I, knocking my pipe-bowl against the jamb, "and now, to-morrow, I will a third time send for Mr. Scribe. Wife, the sciatica takes me; be so good as to put this pipe on the mantel."

"If you get the step-ladder for me, I will. This shocking old chimney, this abominable old-fashioned old chimney's mantels are so high, I can't reach them."

No opportunity, however trivial, was overlooked for a subordinate fling at the pile.

Here, by way of introduction, it should be mentioned, that besides the fire-places all round it, the chimney was, in the most haphazard way, excavated on each floor for certain curious out-of-the-way cupboards and closets, of all sorts and sizes, clinging here and there, like nests in the crotches of some old oak. On the second floor these closets were by far the most irregular and numerous. And yet this should hardly have been so, since the theory of the chimney was, that it pyramidically diminished as it ascended. The abridgment of its square on the roof was obvious enough; and it was supposed that the reduction must be methodically graduated from bottom to top.

"Mr. Scribe," said I when, the next day, with an eager aspect, that individual again came, "my object in sending for you this morning is, not to arrange for the demolition of my chimney, nor to have any particular conversation about it, but simply to allow you every reasonable facility for verifying, if you can, the conjecture communicated in your note."

Though in secret not a little crestfallen, it may be, by my phlegmatic reception, so different from what he had looked for; with much apparent alacrity he commenced the survey; throwing open the cupboards on the first floor, and peering into the closets on the second; measuring one within, and then comparing that measurement with the measurement without. Removing the fire-boards, he would gaze up the flues. But no sign of the hidden work yet.

Now, on the second floor the rooms were the most rambling conceivable. They, as it were, dovetailed into each other. They were of all shapes; not one mathematically square room among them all—a peculiarity which by the master-mason had not been unobserved. With a significant, not to say portentous expression, he took a circuit of the chimney, measuring the area of each room around it; then going down stairs, and out of doors, he measured the entire ground area; then compared the sum total of all the areas of all the rooms on the second floor with the ground area; then, returning to me in no small excitement, announced that there was a difference of no less than two hundred and odd square feet—room enough, in all conscience, for a secret closet.

"But, Mr. Scribe," said I, stroking my chin, "have you allowed for the walls, both main and sectional? They take up some space, you know."

"Ah, I had forgotten that," tapping his forehead; "but," still ciphering on his paper, "that will not make up the deficiency."

"But, Mr. Scribe, have you allowed for the recesses of so many fire-places on a floor, and for the fire-walls, and the flues; in short, Mr. Scribe, have you allowed for the legitimate chimney itself—some one hundred and forty-four square feet or thereabouts, Mr. Scribe?"

"How unaccountable. That slipped my mind, too."

"Did it, indeed, Mr. Scribe?"

He faltered a little, and burst forth with, "But we must not allow one hundred and forty-four square feet for the legitimate chimney. My position is, that within those undue limits the secret closet is contained."

I eyed him in silence a moment; then spoke:

"Your survey is concluded, Mr. Scribe; be so good now as to lay your finger upon the exact part of the chimney wall where you believe this secret closet to be; or would a witch-hazel wand assist you, Mr. Scribe?"

"No, sir, but a crow-bar would," he, with temper, rejoined.

Here, now, thought I to myself, the cat leaps out of the bag. I looked at him with a calm glance, under which he seemed somewhat uneasy. More than ever now I suspected a plot. I remembered what my wife had said about abiding by the decision of Mr. Scribe. In a bland way, I resolved to buy up the decision of Mr. Scribe.

"Sir," said I, "really I am much obliged to you for this survey. It has quite set my mind at rest. And no doubt you, too, Mr. Scribe, must feel much relieved. Sir," I added, "you have made three visits to the chimney. With a business man, time is money. Here are fifty dollars, Mr. Scribe. Nay, take it. You have earned it. Your opinion is worth it. And by the way," as he modestly received the money—"have you any objections to give me a—a—little certificate—something, say, like a steamboat certificate, certifying that you, a competent surveyor, have surveyed my chimney, and found no reason to believe any unsoundness; in short, any—any secret closet in it. Would you be so kind, Mr. Scribe?"

"But, but, sir," stammered he with honest hesitation.

"Here, here are pen and paper," said I, with entire assurance.

Enough.

That evening I had the certificate framed and hung over the dining-room fire-place, trusting that the continual sight of it would forever put at rest at once the dreams and stratagems of my household.

But, no. Inveterately bent upon the extirpation of that noble old chimney, still to this day my wife goes about it, with my daughter Anna's geological hammer, tapping the wall all over, and then holding her ear against it, as I have seen the physicians of life insurance companies tap a man's chest, and then incline over for the echo. Sometimes of nights she almost frightens one, going about on this phantom errand, and still following the sepulchral response of the chimney, round and round, as if it were leading her to the threshold of the secret closet.

"How hollow it sounds," she will hollowly cry. "Yes, I declare," with an emphatic tap, "there is a secret closet here. Here, in this very spot. Hark! How hollow!"

"Pshaw! wife, of course it is hollow. Who ever heard of a solid chimney?"

But nothing avails. And my daughters take after, not me, but their mother.

Sometimes all three abandon the theory of the secret closet, and return to the genuine ground of attack—the unsightliness of so cumbrous a pile, with comments upon the great addition of room to be gained by its demolition, and the fine effect of the projected grand hall, and the convenience resulting from the collateral running in one direction and another of their various partitions. Not more ruthlessly did the Three Powers partition away poor Poland, than my wife and daughters would fain partition away my chimney.

But seeing that, despite all, I and my chimney still smoke our pipes, my wife reoccupies the ground of the secret closet, enlarging upon what wonders are there, and what a shame it is, not to seek it out and explore it.

"Wife," said I, upon one of these occasions, "why speak more of that secret closet, when there before you hangs contrary testimony of a master-mason, elected by yourself to decide. Besides, even if there were a secret closet, secret it should remain, and secret it shall. Yes, wife, here for once I must say my say. Infinite sad mischief has resulted from the profane

bursting open of secret recesses. Though standing in the heart of this house, though hitherto we have all nestled about it, unsuspicious of aught hidden within, this chimney may or may not have a secret closet. But if it have, it is my kinsman's. To break into that wall would be to break into his breast. And that wall-breaking wish of Momus I account the wish of a church-robbing gossip and knave. Yes, wife, a vile eaves-dropping varlet was Momus."

"Moses?—Mumps? Stuff with your mumps and your Moses!"

The truth is, my wife, like all the rest of the world, cares not a fig for my philosophical jabber. In dearth of other philosophical companionship, I and my chimney have to smoke and philosophize together. And sitting up so late as we do at it, a mighty smoke it is that we two smoky old philosophers make.

But my spouse, who likes the smoke of my tobacco as little as she does that of the soot, carries on her war against both. I live in continual dread lest, like the golden bowl, the pipes of me and my chimney shall yet be broken. To stay that mad project of my wife's, naught answers. Or, rather, she herself is incessantly answering, incessantly besetting me with her terrible alacrity for improvement, which is a softer name for destruction. Scarce a day I do not find her with her tape-measure, measuring for her grand hall, while Anna holds a yard-stick on one side, and Julia looks approvingly on from the other. Mysterious intimations appear in the nearest village paper, signed "Claude," to the effect that a certain structure, standing on a certain hill, is a sad blemish to an otherwise lovely landscape. Anonymous letters arrive, threatening me with I know not what, unless I remove my chimney. Is it my wife, too, or who, that sets up the neighbors to badgering me on the same subject, and hinting to me that my chimney, like a huge elm, absorbs all moisture from my garden? At night, also, my wife will start as from sleep, professing to hear ghostly noises from the secret closet. Assailed on all sides, and in all ways, small peace have I and my chimney.

Were it not for the baggage, we would together pack up, and remove from the country.

What narrow escapes have been ours! Once I found in a drawer a whole portfolio of plans and estimates. Another time, upon returning after a day's absence, I discovered my wife standing before the chimney in earnest conversation with a person whom I at once recognized as a meddlesome architectural reformer, who, because he had no gift for putting up anything, was ever intent upon pulling down; in various parts of the country having prevailed upon half-witted old folks to destroy their old-fashioned houses, particularly the chimneys.

But worst of all was, that time I unexpectedly returned at early morning from a visit to the city, and upon approaching the house, narrowly escaped three brickbats which fell, from high aloft, at my feet. Glancing up, what was my horror to see three savages, in blue jean overalls, in the very act of commencing the long-threatened attack. Aye, indeed, thinking of those three brickbats, I and my chimney have had narrow escapes.

It is now some seven years since I have stirred from home. My city friends all wonder why I don't come to see them, as in former times. They think I am getting sour and unsocial. Some say that I have become a sort of mossy old misanthrope, while all the time the fact is, I am simply standing guard over my mossy old chimney; for it is resolved between me and my chimney, that I and my chimney will never surrender.

THE 'GEES

NOTE: Very little that Melville wrote fails to generate some sort of satirical or symbolic resonance. The "'Gees" of this little sketch (*Harper's*, March, 1856) are a version of an actual race of crossbred Portuguese sailors familiar in the North Atlantic fisheries and ports. But the ironic stress on this race's aboriginal "incivility" and on its submissiveness when "green" and subtle recalcitrance when "ripe" and "knowing" may carry an allusion to the character of the working classes in general within the exploitative order of modern economic life—if not indeed, in a work of the 1850's, to slavery itself and its human consequences.

IN RELATING TO my friends various passages of my sea-goings, I have at times had occasion to allude to that singular people the 'Gees, sometimes as casual acquaintances, sometimes as shipmates. Such allusions have been quite natural and easy. For instance, I have said *The two 'Gees,* just as another would say *The two Dutchmen,* or *The two Indians.* In fact, being myself so familiar with 'Gees, it seemed as if all the rest of the world must be. But not so. My auditors have opened their eyes as much as to say, "What under the sun is a 'Gee?" To enlighten them I have repeatedly had to interrupt myself, and not without detriment to my stories. To remedy which inconvenience, a friend hinted the advisability of writing out some account of the 'Gees, and having it published. Such as they are, the following memoranda spring from that happy suggestion:

The word *'Gee* (g hard) is an abbreviation, by seamen, of *Portuguee,* the corrupt form of *Portuguese.* As the name is a curtailment, so the race is a residuum. Some three centuries ago certain Portuguese convicts were sent as a colony to Fogo, one of the Cape de Verds, off the northwest coast of Africa, an island previously stocked with an aboriginal race of negroes, ranking pretty high in incivility, but rather low in stature and morals. In course of time, from the amalgamated generation all the likelier sort were drafted off as food for powder, and the ancestors of the since called 'Gees were left as the *caput mortuum*, or melancholy remainder.

Of all men seamen have strong prejudices, particularly in the matter of race. They are bigots here. But when a creature of inferior race lives among them, an inferior tar, there seems no bound to their disdain. Now, as ere long will be hinted, the 'Gee, though of an aquatic nature, does not, as regards higher qualifications, make the best of sailors. In short, by seamen the abbreviation 'Gee was hit upon in pure contumely; the degree of which may be partially inferred from this, that with them the primitive word Portuguee itself is a reproach; so that 'Gee, being a subtle distillation from that word, stands, in point of relative intensity to it, as attar of roses does to rose-water. At times, when some crusty old sea-dog has his spleen more than usually excited against some luckless blunderer of Fogo his shipmate, it is marvelous the prolongation of taunt into which he will spin out the one little exclamatory monosyllable Ge-e-e-e-e!

The Isle of Fogo, that is, "Fire Isle," was so called from its volcano, which, after throwing up an infinite deal of stones and ashes, finally threw up business altogether, from its broadcast bounteousness having become bankrupt. But thanks to the volcano's prodigality in its time, the soil of Fogo is such as may be found of a dusty day on a road newly Macadamized. Cut off from farms and gardens, the staple food of the inhabitants is fish, at catching which they are expert. But none the less do they relish ship-biscuit, which, indeed, by most islanders, barbarous or semi-barbarous, is held a sort of lozenge.

In his best estate the 'Gee is rather small (he admits it), but, with some exceptions, hardy; capable of enduring extreme hard work, hard fare, or hard usage, as the case may be. In fact, upon a scientific view, there would seem a natural adaptability in the 'Gee to hard times generally. A theory not uncorroborated by his experiences; and furthermore, that kindly care of Nature in fitting him for them, something as for his hard rubs with a hardened world Fox the Quaker fitted himself, namely, in a tough leather suit from top to toe. In other words, the 'Gee is by no means of that exquisitely delicate sensibility expressed by the figurative adjective thin-skinned. His physicals and spirituals are in singular contrast. The 'Gee has a great appetite, but little imagination; a large eyeball, but small insight. Biscuit he crunches, but sentiment he eschews.

His complexion is hybrid; his hair ditto; his mouth disproportionally large, as compared with his stomach; his neck short; but his head round, compact, and betokening a solid understanding.

Like the negro, the 'Gee has a peculiar savor, but a different one—a sort of wild, marine, gamy savor, as in the sea-bird called haglet. Like venison, his flesh is firm but lean.

His teeth are what are called butter-teeth, strong, durable, square, and yellow. Among captains at a loss for better discourse during dull, rainy weather in the horse-latitudes, much debate has been had whether his teeth are intended for carnivorous or herbivorous purposes, or both conjoined. But as on his isle the 'Gee eats neither flesh nor grass, this inquiry would seem superfluous.

The native dress of the 'Gee is, like his name, compendious. His head being by nature well thatched, he wears no hat. Wont to wade much in the surf, he wears no shoes. He has a serviceably hard heel, a kick from which is by the judicious held almost as dangerous as one from a wild zebra.

Though for a long time back no stranger to the seafaring people of Portugal, the 'Gee, until a comparatively recent period, remained almost undreamed of by seafaring Americans. It is now some forty years since he first became known to certain masters of our Nantucket ships, who commenced the practice of touching at Fogo, on the outward passage, there to fill up vacancies among their crews arising from the short supply of men at home. By degrees the custom became pretty general, till now the 'Gee is found aboard of almost one whaler out of three. One reason why they are in request is this: An unsophisticated 'Gee coming on board a foreign ship never asks for wages. He comes for biscuit. He does not know what other wages mean, unless cuffs and buffets be wages, of which sort he receives a liberal allowance, paid with great punctuality, besides perquisites of punches thrown in now and then. But for all this, some persons there are, and not unduly biassed by partiality to him either, who still insist that the 'Gee never gets his due.

His docile services being thus cheaply to be had, some captains will go the length of maintaining that 'Gee sailors are preferable, indeed every way, physically and intellectually, superior to American sailors—such captains complaining, and justly, that American sailors, if not decently treated, are apt to give serious trouble.

But even by their most ardent admirers it is not deemed prudent to sail a ship with none but 'Gees, at least if they chance to be all green hands, a green 'Gee being of all green things the greenest. Besides, owing to the clumsiness of their feet ere improved by practice in the rigging, green 'Gees are wont, in no inconsiderable numbers, to fall overboard the first dark, squally night; insomuch that when unreasonable owners insist with a captain against his will upon a green 'Gee crew fore and aft, he will ship twice as many 'Gees as he would have shipped of Americans, so as to provide for all contingencies.

The 'Gees are always ready to be shipped. Any day one may go to their isle, and on the showing of a coin of biscuit over the rail, may load down to the water's edge with them.

But though any number of 'Gees are ever ready to be shipped, still it is by no means well to take them as they come. There is a choice even in 'Gees.

Of course the 'Gee has his private nature as well as his public coat. To know 'Gees—to be a sound judge of 'Gees—one must study them, just as to know and be a judge of horses one must study horses. Simple as for the most part are both horse and 'Gee, in neither case can knowledge of the creature come by intuition. How unwise, then, in those ignorant young captains who, on their first voyage, will go and ship their 'Gees at Fogo without any preparatory information, or even so much as taking convenient advice from a 'Gee jockey. By a 'Gee jockey is meant a man well versed in 'Gees. Many a young captain has been thrown and badly hurt by a 'Gee of his own choosing. For notwithstanding the general docility of the 'Gee when green, it may be otherwise with him when ripe. Discreet captains won't have such a 'Gee. "Away with that ripe 'Gee!" they cry; "that smart 'Gee; that knowing 'Gee! Green 'Gees for me!"

For the benefit of inexperienced captains about to visit Fogo, the following may be given as the best way to test a 'Gee: Get square before him, at, say three paces, so that the eye, like a shot, may rake the 'Gee fore and aft, at one glance taking in his whole make and build—how he looks about the head, whether he carry it well; his ears, are they over-lengthy? How fares it in the withers? His legs, does the 'Gee stand strongly on them? His knees, any Belshazzar symptoms there? How stands it in the region of the brisket? etc., etc.

Thus far for bone and bottom. For the rest, draw close to,

and put the centre of the pupil of your eye—put it, as it were, right into the 'Gee's eye; even as an eye-stone, gently, but firmly slip it in there, and then note what speck or beam of viciousness, if any, will be floated out.

All this and much more must be done; and yet after all, the best judge may be deceived. But on no account should the shipper negotiate for his 'Gee with any middle-man, himself a 'Gee. Because such an one must be a knowing 'Gee, who will be sure to advise the green 'Gee what things to hide and what to display, to hit the skipper's fancy; which, of course, the knowing 'Gee supposes to lean toward as much physical and moral excellence as possible. The rashness of trusting to one of these middle-men was forcibly shown in the case of the 'Gee who by his countrymen was recommended to a New Bedford captain as one of the most agile 'Gees in Fogo. There he stood straight and stout, in a flowing pair of man-of-war's-man's trowsers, uncommonly well filled out. True, he did not step around much at the time. But that was diffidence. Good. They shipped him. But at the first taking in of sail the 'Gee hung fire. Come to look, both trowser-legs were full of elephantiasis. It was a long sperm-whaling voyage. Useless as so much lumber, at every port prohibited from being dumped ashore, that elephantine 'Gee, ever crunching biscuit, for three weary years was trundled round the globe.

Grown wise by several similar experiences, old Captain Hosea Kean, of Nantucket, in shipping a 'Gee, at present manages matters thus: He lands at Fogo in the night; by secret means gains information where the likeliest 'Gee wanting to ship lodges; whereupon with a strong party he surprises all the friends and acquaintances of that 'Gee; putting them under guard with pistols at their heads; then creeps cautiously toward the 'Gee, now lying wholly at unawares in his hut, quite relaxed from all possibility of displaying aught deceptive in his appearance. Thus silently, thus suddenly, thus unannounced, Captain Kean bursts upon his 'Gee, so to speak, in the very bosom of his family. By this means, more than once, unexpected revelations have been made. A 'Gee, noised abroad for a Hercules in strength and an Apollo Belvidere for beauty, of a sudden is discovered all in a wretched heap; forlornly adroop as upon crutches, his legs looking as if broken at the cart-wheel. Solitude is the house of candor, according to Captain Kean. In the stall, not the street, he says, resides the real nag.

The innate disdain of regularly bred seamen toward 'Gees receives an added edge from this. The 'Gees undersell them, working for biscuit where the sailors demand dollars. Hence, any thing said by sailors to the prejudice of 'Gees should be received with caution. Especially that jeer of theirs, that monkey-jacket was originally so called from the circumstance that that rude sort of shaggy garment was first known in Fogo. They often call a monkey-jacket a 'Gee-jacket. However this may be, there is no call to which the 'Gee will with more alacrity respond than the word "Man!"

Is there any hard work to be done, and the 'Gees stand round in sulks? "Here, my men!" cries the mate. How they jump. But ten to one when the work is done, it is plain 'Gee again. "Here, 'Gee! you 'Ge-e-e-e!" In fact, it is not unsurmised, that only when extraordinary stimulus is needed, only when an extra strain is to be got out of them, are these hapless 'Gees ennobled with the human name.

As yet, the intellect of the 'Gee has been little cultivated. No well-attested educational experiment has been tried upon him. It is said, however, that in the last century a young 'Gee was by a visionary Portuguese naval officer sent to Salamanca University. Also, among the Quakers of Nantucket, there has been talk of sending five comely 'Gees, aged sixteen, to Dartmouth College; that venerable institution, as is well known, having been originally founded partly with the object of finishing off wild Indians in the classics and higher mathematics. Two qualities of the 'Gee which, with his docility, may be justly regarded as furnishing a hopeful basis for his intellectual training, are his excellent memory, and still more excellent credulity.

The above account may, perhaps, among the ethnologists, raise some curiosity to see a 'Gee. But to see a 'Gee there is no need to go all the way to Fogo, no more than to see a Chinaman to go all the way to China. 'Gees are occasionally to be encountered in our sea-ports, but more particularly in Nantucket and New Bedford. But these 'Gees are not the 'Gees of Fogo. That is, they are no longer green 'Gees. They are sophisticated 'Gees, and hence liable to be taken for naturalized citizens badly sunburnt. Many a Chinaman, in new coat and pantaloons, his long queue coiled out of sight in one of Genin's hats, has promenaded Broadway, and been taken merely for an eccentric Georgia planter. The same with 'Gees; a stranger need have a sharp eye to know a 'Gee, even if he see him.

Thus much for a general sketchy view of the 'Gee. For further and fuller information apply to any sharp-witted American whaling captain, but more especially to the before-mentioned old Captain Hosea Kean, of Nantucket, whose address at present is "Pacific Ocean."

THE APPLE-TREE TABLE OR
ORIGINAL SPIRITUAL
MANIFESTATIONS

NOTE: For several pages this last of Melville's mid-1850's magazine pieces (*Harper's*, May, 1856) promises as much entertainment as "I and My Chimney" and in much the same serio-comic vein. But despite palpable efforts to keep the thing going, the narration quite noticeably runs out of steam and drags to a flat, anti-climactic ending. The case seems symptomatic of the radical faltering of Melville's creative *élan* by 1856 and of the state of exhaustion and discouragement he had fallen into.

WHEN I first saw the table, dingy and dusty, in the furthest corner of the old hopper-shaped garret, and set out with broken, be-crusted, old purple vials and flasks, and a ghostly, dismantled old quarto, it seemed just such a necromantic little old table as might have belonged to Friar Bacon. Two plain features it had, significant of conjurations and charms —the circle and tripod; the slab being round, supported by a twisted little pillar, which, about a foot from the bottom, sprawled out into three crooked legs, terminating in three cloven feet. A very satanic-looking little old table, indeed.

In order to convey a better idea of it, some account may as well be given of the place it came from. A very old garret of a very old house in an old-fashioned quarter of one of the oldest towns in America. This garret had been closed for years. It was thought to be haunted; a rumor, I confess, which, however absurd (in my opinion), I did not, at the time of purchasing, very vehemently contradict; since, not improbably, it tended to place the property the more conveniently within my means.

It was, therefore, from no dread of the reputed goblins aloft, that, for five years after first taking up my residence in the house, I never entered the garret. There was no special inducement. The roof was well slated, and thoroughly tight. The company that insured the house waived all visitation of the garret; why, then, should the owner be over-anxious about it?—particularly as he had no use for it, the house having ample room below. Then the key of the stair-door leading to it was lost. The lock was a huge, old-fashioned one. To open it, a smith would have to be called; an unnecessary trouble, I thought. Besides, though I had taken some care to keep my two daughters in ignorance of the rumor above-mentioned, still, they had, by some means, got an inkling of it, and were well enough pleased to see the entrance to the haunted ground closed. It might have remained so for a still longer time, had it not been for my accidentally discovering, in a corner of our glen-like, old, terraced garden, a large and curious key, very old and rusty, which I, at once, concluded must belong to the garret-door—a supposition which, upon trial, proved correct. Now, the possession of a key to anything at once provokes a desire to unlock and explore; and this, too, from a mere instinct of gratification, irrespective of any particular benefit to accrue.

Behold me, then, turning the rusty old key, and going up, alone, into the haunted garret.

It embraced the entire area of the mansion. Its ceiling was formed by the roof, showing the rafters and boards on which the slates were laid. The roof shedding the water four ways from a high point in the centre, the space beneath was much like that of a general's marquee—only midway broken by a labyrinth of timbers, for braces, from which waved innumerable cobwebs that, of a summer's noon, shone like Bagdad tissues and gauzes. On every hand, some strange insect was seen, flying, or running, or creeping, on rafter and floor.

Under the apex of the roof was a rude, narrow, decrepit step-ladder, something like a Gothic pulpit-stairway, leading to a pulpit-like platform, from which a still narrower ladder—a sort of Jacob's ladder—led some ways higher to the lofty scuttle. The slide of this scuttle was about two feet square, all in one piece, furnishing a massive frame for a single small pane of glass, inserted into it like a bull's-eye. The light of the garret came from this sole source, filtrated through a dense curtain of cobwebs. Indeed, the whole stairs, and platform, and ladder, were festooned, and carpeted, and canopied with cobwebs; which, in funereal accumulations, hung, too, from the groined, murky ceiling, like the Carolina moss in the cypress forest. In these cobwebs swung, as in aerial catacombs, myriads of all tribes of mummied insects.

Climbing the stairs to the platform, and pausing there, to recover my breath, a curious scene was presented. The sun was about half-way up. Piercing the little sky-light, it slopingly bored a rainbowed tunnel clear across the darkness of the garret. Here, millions of butterfly moles were swarming. Against the sky-light itself, with a cymbal-like buzzing, thousands of insects clustered in a golden mob.

Wishing to shed a clearer light through the place, I sought to withdraw the scuttle-slide. But no sign of latch or hasp was visible. Only after long peering, did I discover a little padlock, imbedded, like an oyster at the bottom of the sea, amid matted masses of weedy webs, chrysalides, and insectivorous eggs. Brushing these away, I found it locked. With a crooked nail, I tried to pick the lock, when scores of small ants and flies, half-torpid, crawled forth from the key-hole and, feeling the warmth of the sun in the pane, began frisking around me. Others appeared. Presently, I was overrun by them. As if incensed at this invasion of their retreat, countless bands darted up from below, beating about my head like hornets. At last, with a sudden jerk, I burst open the scuttle. And ah! what a change. As from the gloom of the grave and the companionship of worms, man shall at last rapturously rise into the living greenness and glory immortal, so, from my cob-webbed old garret, I thrust forth my head into the balmy air, and found myself hailed by the verdant tops of great trees, growing in the little garden below—trees, whose leaves soared high above my topmost slate.

Refreshed by this outlook, I turned inward to behold the garret, now unwontedly lit up. Such humped masses of obsolete furniture. An old escritoire, from whose pigeonholes sprang mice, and from whose secret drawers came subterranean squeakings, as from chipmunks' holes in the woods; and broken-down old chairs, with strange carvings, which seemed fit to seat a conclave of conjurors. And a rusty, iron-bound chest, lidless, and packed full of mildewed old documents; one of which, with a faded red ink-blot at the end, looked as if it might have been the original bone that Doctor Faust gave to Mephistopheles. And, finally, in the least lighted corner of all, where was a profuse litter of indescribable old rubbish—among which was a broken telescope, and a celestial globe staved in —stood the little old table, one hoofed foot, like that of the Evil One, dimly revealed through the cobwebs. What a thick dust, half paste, had settled upon the old vials and flasks; how their once liquid contents had caked, and how strangely looked the mouldy old book in the middle—Cotton Mather's *Magnalia*.

Table and book I removed below, and had the dislocations of the one and the tatters of the other repaired. I resolved to surround this sad little hermit of a table, so long banished from genial neighborhood, with all the kindly influences of warm urns, warm fires, and warm hearts; little dreaming what all this warm nursing would hatch.

I was pleased by the discovery that the table was not of the ordinary mahogany, but of apple-tree wood, which age had darkened nearly to walnut. It struck me as being quite an appropriate piece of furniture for our cedar-parlor—so called, from its being, after the old fashion, wainscoted with that wood. The table's round slab, or *orb*, was so contrived as to be readily changed from a horizontal to a perpendicular position; so that, when not in use, it could be snugly placed in a corner. For myself, wife, and two daughters, I thought it would make a nice little breakfast and tea-table. It was just the thing for a whist table, too. And I also pleased myself with the idea, that it would make a famous reading-table.

In these fancies, my wife, for one, took little interest. She disrelished the idea of so unfashionable and indigent-looking a stranger as the table intruding into the polished society of more prosperous furniture. But when, after seeking its fortune at the cabinet-maker's, the table came home, varnished over, bright as a guinea, no one exceeded my wife in a gracious reception of it. It was advanced to an honorable position in the cedar-parlor.

But, as for my daughter Julia, she never got over her strange emotions upon first accidentally encountering the table. Unfortunately, it was just as I was in the act of bringing it down from the garret. Holding it by the slab, I was carrying it before me, one cobwebbed hoof thrust out, which weird object, at a turn of the stairs, suddenly touched my girl, as she was ascending; whereupon, turning, and seeing no living creature—for I was quite hidden behind my shield—seeing nothing, indeed, but the apparition of the Evil One's foot, as it seemed, she cried out, and there is no knowing what might have followed, had I not immediately spoken.

From the impression thus produced, my poor girl, of a very nervous temperament, was long recovering. Superstitiously grieved at my violating the forbidden solitude above, she associated in her mind the cloven-footed table with the reputed goblins there. She besought me to give up the idea of domesticating the table. Nor did her sister fail to add her entreaties. Between my girls there was a constitutional sympathy. But my matter-of-fact wife had now declared in the table's favor. She was not wanting in firmness and energy. To her, the prejudices of Julia and Anna were simply ridiculous. It was her maternal duty, she thought, to drive such weakness away. By degrees, the girls, at breakfast and tea, were induced to sit down with us at the table. Continual proximity was not without effect. By and by, they would sit pretty tranquilly, though Julia, as much as possible, avoided glancing at the hoofed feet, and, when at this I smiled, she would look at me seriously—as much as to say, Ah, papa, you, too, may yet do the same. She prophesied that, in connection with the table, something strange would yet happen. But I would only smile the more, while my wife indignantly chided.

Meantime, I took particular satisfaction in my table, as a night reading-table. At a ladies' fair, I bought me a beautifully worked reading-cushion, and, with elbow leaning thereon, and hand shading my eyes from the light, spent many a long hour—nobody by, but the queer old book I had brought down from the garret.

All went well, till the incident now about to be given—an incident, be it remembered, which, like every other in this narration, happened long before the time of the "Fox Girls."

It was late on a Saturday night in December. In the little old cedar-parlor, before the little old apple-tree table, I was sitting up, as usual, alone. I had made more than one effort to get up and go to bed; but I could not. I was, in fact, under a sort of fascination. Somehow, too, certain reasonable opinions of mine seemed not so reasonable as before. I felt nervous. The truth was, that though, in my previous night-readings, Cotton Mather had but amused me, upon this particular night he terrified me. A thousand times I had laughed at such stories. Old wives' fables, I thought, however entertaining. But now, how different. They began to put on the aspect of reality. Now, for the first time it struck me that this was no romantic Mrs. Radcliffe who had written the *Magnalia*, but a practical, hardworking, earnest, upright man, a learned doctor, too, as well as a good Christian and orthodox clergyman. What possible motive could such a man have to deceive? His style had all the plainness and unpoetic boldness of truth. In the most straightforward way, he laid before me detailed accounts of New England witchcraft, each important item corroborated by respectable townsfolk, and, of not a few of the most surprising, he himself had been eye-witness. Cotton Mather testified whereof he had seen. But, is it possible? I asked myself. Then I remembered that Dr. Johnson, the matter-of-fact compiler of a dictionary, had been a believer in ghosts, besides many other sound, worthy men. Yielding to the fascination, I read deeper and deeper into the night. At last, I found myself starting at the least chance sound, and yet wishing that it were not so very still.

A tumbler of warm punch stood by my side, with which beverage, in a moderate way, I was accustomed to treat myself every Saturday night; a habit, however, against which my good wife had long remonstrated; predicting that, unless I gave it up, I would yet die a miserable sot. Indeed, I may here mention that, on the Sunday mornings following my Saturday nights, I had to be exceedingly cautious how I gave way to the slightest impatience at any accidental annoyance; because such impatience was sure to be quoted against me as evidence of the melancholy consequence of over-night indulgence. As for my wife, she, never sipping punch, could yield to any little passing peevishness as much as she pleased.

But, upon the night in question, I found myself wishing that, instead of my usual mild mixture, I had concocted some potent draught. I felt the need of stimulus. I wanted something to hearten me against Cotton Mather—doleful, ghostly, ghastly Cotton Mather. I grew more and more nervous. Nothing but fascination kept me from fleeing the room. The candles burnt low, with long snuffs, and huge winding-sheets. But I durst not raise the snuffers to them. It would make too much noise. And yet, previously, I had been wishing for noise. I read on and on. My hair began to have a sensation. My eyes felt strained; they pained me. I was conscious of it. I knew I was injuring them. I knew I should rue this abuse of them next day; but I read on and on. I could not help it. The skinny hand was on me.

All at once—Hark!

My hair felt like growing grass.

A faint sort of inward rapping or rasping—a strange, inexplicable sound, mixed with a slight kind of woodpecking or ticking.

Tick! Tick!

Yes, it was a faint sort of ticking.

I looked up at my great Strasbourg clock in one corner. It was not that. The clock had stopped.

Tick! Tick!

Was it my watch?

According to her usual practice at night, my wife had, upon retiring, carried my watch off to our chamber to hang it up on its nail.

I listened with all my ears.

Tick! Tick!

Was it a death-tick in the wainscot?

With a tremulous step I went all round the room, holding my ear to the wainscot.

No; it came not from the wainscot.

Tick! Tick!

I shook myself. I was ashamed of my fright.

Tick! Tick!

It grew in precision and audibleness. I retreated from the wainscot. It seemed advancing to meet me.

I looked round and round, but saw nothing, only one cloven foot of the little apple-tree table.

Bless me, said I to myself, with a sudden revulsion, it must be very late; ain't that my wife calling me? Yes, yes; I must to bed. I suppose all is locked up. No need to go the rounds.

The fascination had departed, though the fear had increased. With trembling hands, putting Cotton Mather out of sight, I soon found myself, candle-stick in hand, in my chamber, with a peculiar rearward feeling, such as some truant dog may feel. In my eagerness to get well into the chamber, I stumbled against a chair.

"Do try and make less noise, my dear," said my wife from the bed. "You have been taking too much of that punch, I fear. That sad habit grows on you. Ah, that I should ever see you thus staggering at night into your chamber."

"Wife, wife," hoarsely whispered I, "there is—is something tick—ticking in the cedar-parlor."

"Poor old man—quite out of his mind—I knew it would be so. Come to bed; come and sleep it off."

"Wife, wife!"

"Do, do come to bed. I forgive you. I won't remind you of it to-morrow. But you must give up the punch-drinking, my dear. It quite gets the better of you."

"Don't exasperate me," I cried, now truly beside myself; "I will quit the house!"

"No, no! not in that state. Come to bed, my dear. I won't say another word."

The next morning, upon waking, my wife said nothing about the past night's affair, and, feeling no little embarrassment myself, especially at having been thrown into such a panic, I also was silent. Consequently, my wife must still have ascribed my singular conduct to a mind disordered, not by ghosts, but by punch. For my own part, as I lay in bed watching the sun in the panes, I began to think that much midnight reading of Cotton Mather was not good for man; that it had a morbid influence upon the nerves, and gave rise to hallucinations. I resolved to put Cotton Mather permanently aside. That done, I had no fear of any return of the ticking. Indeed, I began to think that what seemed the ticking in the room, was nothing but a sort of buzzing in my ear.

As is her wont, my wife having preceded me in rising, I made a deliberate and agreeable toilet. Aware that most disorders of the mind have their origin in the state of the body, I made vigorous use of the flesh-brush, and bathed my head with New England rum, a specific once recommended to me as good for buzzing in the ear. Wrapped in my dressing-gown, with cravat nicely adjusted, and finger-nails neatly trimmed, I complacently descended to the little cedar-parlor to breakfast.

What was my amazement to find my wife on her knees, rummaging about the carpet nigh the little apple-tree table, on which the morning meal was laid, while my daughters, Julia and Anna, were running about the apartment distracted.

"Oh, papa, papa!" cried Julia, hurrying up to me, "I knew it would be so. The table, the table!"

"Spirits! spirits!" cried Anna, standing far away from it, with pointed finger.

"Silence!" cried my wife. "How can I hear it, if you make such a noise? Be still. Come here, husband; was this the ticking you spoke of? Why don't you move? Was this it? Here, kneel down and listen to it. Tick, tick, tick!—don't you hear it now?"

"I do, I do," cried I, while my daughters besought us both to come away from the spot.

Tick, tick, tick!

Right from under the snowy cloth, and the cheerful urn,

and the smoking milk-toast, the unaccountable ticking was heard.

"Ain't there a fire in the next room, Julia?" said I. "Let us breakfast there, my dear," turning to my wife—"let us go—leave the table—tell Biddy to remove the things."

And so saying, I was moving towards the door in high self-possession, when my wife interrupted me.

"Before I quit this room, I will see into this ticking," she said with energy. "It is something that can be found out, depend upon it. I don't believe in spirits, especially at breakfast-time. Biddy! Biddy! Here, carry these things back to the kitchen," handing the urn. Then, sweeping off the cloth, the little table lay bare to the eye.

"It's the table, the table!" cried Julia.

"Nonsense," said my wife. "Who ever heard of a ticking table? It's on the floor. Biddy! Julia! Anna! move everything out of the room—table and all. Where are the tack-hammers?"

"Heavens, mamma—you are not going to take up the carpet?" screamed Julia.

"Here's the hammers, marm," said Biddy, advancing tremblingly.

"Hand them to me, then," cried my wife; for poor Biddy was, at long gun-distance, holding them out as if her mistress had the plague.

"Now, husband, do you take up that side of the carpet, and I will this." Down on her knees she then dropped, while I followed suit.

The carpet being removed, and the ear applied to the naked floor, not the slightest ticking could be heard.

"The table—after all, it is the table," cried my wife. "Biddy, bring it back."

"Oh no, marm, not I, please, marm," sobbed Biddy.

"Foolish creature!—Husband, do you bring it."

"My dear," said I, "we have plenty of other tables; why be so particular?"

"Where is that table?" cried my wife, contemptuously, regardless of my gentle remonstrance.

"In the wood-house, marm. I put it away as far as ever I could, marm," sobbed Biddy.

"Shall I go to the wood-house for it, or will you?" said my wife, addressing me in a frightful, business-like manner.

Immediately I darted out of the door, and found the little apple-tree table, upside down, in one of my chipbins. I hurriedly returned with it, and once more my wife examined it attentively. Tick, tick, tick! Yes, it was the table.

"Please, marm," said Biddy, now entering the room, with hat and shawl—"please, marm, will you pay me my wages?"

"Take your hat and shawl off directly," said my wife; "set this table again."

"Set it," roared I, in a passion, "set it, or I'll go for the police."

"Heavens! heavens!" cried my daughters, in one breath. "What will become of us!—Spirits! Spirits!"

"Will you set the table?" cried I, advancing upon Biddy.

"I will, I will—yes, marm—yes, master—I will, I will. Spirits!—Holy Vargin!"

"Now, husband," said my wife, "I am convinced that, whatever it is that causes this ticking, neither the ticking nor the table can hurt us; for we are all good Christians, I hope. I am determined to find out the cause of it, too, which time and patience will bring to light. I shall breakfast on no other table but this, so long as we live in this house. So, sit down, now that all things are ready again, and let us quietly breakfast. My dears," turning to Julia and Anna, "go to your room, and return composed. Let me have no more of this childishness."

Upon occasion my wife was mistress in her house.

During the meal, in vain was conversation started again and again; in vain my wife said something brisk to infuse into others an animation akin to her own. Julia and Anna, with heads bowed over their tea-cups, were still listening for the tick. I confess, too, that their example was catching. But, for the time, nothing was heard. Either the ticking had died quite away, or else, slight as it was, the increasing uproar of the street, with the general hum of day, so contrasted with the repose of night and early morning, smothered the sound. At the lurking inquietude of her companions, my wife was indignant; the more so, as she seemed to glory in her own exemption from panic. When breakfast was cleared away she took my watch and, placing it on the table, addressed the supposed spirits in it, with a jocosely defiant air: "There, tick away, let us see who can tick loudest!"

All that day, while abroad, I thought of the mysterious table. Could Cotton Mather speak true? Were there spirits? And would spirits haunt a tea-table? Would the Evil One dare show his cloven hoof in the bosom of an innocent family? I shuddered when I thought that I myself, against the solemn warnings of my daughters, had willfully introduced the cloven hoof there. Yea, three cloven feet. But, towards noon, this sort of feeling began to wear off. The continual rubbing against so many practical people in the street brushed such chimeras away from me. I remembered that I had not acquitted myself very intrepidly either on the previous night or in the morning. I resolved to regain the good opinion of my wife.

To evince my hardihood the more signally, when tea was dismissed, and the three rubbers of whist had been played, and no ticking had been heard—which the more encouraged me— I took my pipe and, saying that bedtime had arrived for the rest, drew my chair towards the fire, and, removing my slippers, placed my feet on the fender, looking as calm and composed as old Democritus in the tombs of Abdera, when one midnight the mischievous little boys of the town tried to frighten that sturdy philosopher with spurious ghosts.

And I thought to myself, that the worthy old gentleman had set a good example to all times in his conduct on that occasion. For, when at the dead hour, intent on his studies, he heard the strange sounds, he did not so much as move his eyes from his page, only simply said: "Boys, little boys, go home. This is no place for you. You will catch cold here." The philosophy of which words lies here: that they imply the foregone conclusion, that any possible investigation of any possible spiritual phenomena was absurd; that upon the first face of such things, the mind of a sane man instinctively affirmed them a humbug, unworthy the least attention; more especially if such phenomena appear in tombs, since tombs are peculiarly the place of silence, lifelessness, and solitude; for which cause, by the way, the old man, as upon the occasion in question, made the tombs of Abdera his place of study.

Presently I was alone, and all was hushed. I laid down my pipe, not feeling exactly tranquil enough now thoroughly to enjoy it. Taking up one of the newspapers, I began, in a nervous, hurried sort of way, to read by the light of a candle placed on a small stand drawn close to the fire. As for the apple-tree table, having lately concluded that it was rather too low for a reading-table, I thought best not to use it as such that night. But it stood not very distant in the middle of the room.

Try as I would, I could not succeed much at reading. Somehow I seemed all ear and no eye; a condition of intense auricular suspense. But ere long it was broken.

Tick, tick, tick!

Though it was not the first time I had heard that sound; nay, though I had made it my particular business on this occasion to wait for that sound, nevertheless, when it came, it seemed unexpected, as if a cannon had boomed through the window.

Tick! tick! tick!

I sat stock-still for a time, thoroughly to master, if possible, my first discomposure. Then rising, I looked pretty steadily at the table; went up to it pretty steadily; took hold of it pretty steadily; but let it go pretty quickly; then paced up and down, stopping every moment or two, with ear pricked to listen. Meantime, within me, the contest between panic and philosophy remained not wholly decided.

Tick! tick! tick!

With appalling distinctness the ticking now rose on the night.

My pulse fluttered—my heart beat. I hardly know what might not have followed, had not Democritus just then come to the rescue. For shame, said I to myself, what is the use of so fine an example of philosophy, if it cannot be followed? Straightway I resolved to imitate it, even to the old sage's occupation and attitude.

Resuming my chair and paper, with back presented to the table, I remained thus for a time, as if buried in study; when, the ticking still continuing, I drawled out, in as indifferent and dryly jocose a way as I could: "Come, come, Tick, my boy, fun enough for to-night."

Tick! tick! tick!

There seemed a sort of jeering defiance in the ticking now. It seemed to exult over the poor affected part I was playing. But much as the taunt stung me, it only stung me into persistence. I resolved not to abate one whit in my mode of address.

"Come, come, you make more and more noise, Tick, my boy; too much of a joke—time to have done."

No sooner said than the ticking ceased. Never was responsive obedience more exact. For the life of me, I could not help turning round upon the table, as one would upon some reasonable being, when—could I believe my senses? I saw something moving, or wriggling, or squirming upon the slab of the table. It shone like a glow-worm. Unconsciously, I grasped the poker that stood at hand. But bethinking me how absurd to attack a glow-worm with a poker, I put it down. How long I sat spell-bound and staring there, with my body presented one way and my face another, I cannot say; but at length I rose, and, buttoning my coat up and down, made a sudden intrepid forced march full upon the table. And there, near the centre of the slab, as I live, I saw an irregular little hole, or, rather, a short nibbled sort of crack, from which (like a butterfly escaping its chrysalis) the sparkling object, whatever it might be, was struggling. Its motion was the motion of life. I stood becharmed. Are there, indeed, spirits, thought I; and is this one? No; I must be dreaming. I turned my glance off to the red fire on the hearth, then back to the pale lustre on the table. What I saw was no optical illusion, but a real mravel. The tremor was increasing, when, once again, Democritus befriended me. Supernatural coruscation as it appeared, I strove to look at the strange object in a purely scientific way. Thus viewed, it appeared some new sort of small shining beetle or bug, and, I thought, not without something of a hum to it, too.

I still watched it, and with still increasing self-possession. Sparkling and wriggling, it still continued its throes. In another moment it was just on the point of escaping its prison. A thought struck me. Running for a tumbler, I clapped it over the insect just in time to secure it.

After watching it a while longer under the tumbler, I left all as it was, and, tolerably composed, retired.

Now, for the soul of me, I could not, at that time, comprehend the phenomenon. A live bug come out of a dead table? A fire-fly bug come out of a piece of ancient lumber, for one knows not how many years stored away in an old garret? Was ever such a thing heard of, or even dreamed of? How got the bug there? Never mind. I bethought me of Democritus, and resolved to keep cool. At all events, the mystery of the ticking was explained. It was simply the sound of the gnawing and filing, and tapping of the bug, in eating its way out. It was satisfactory to think that there was an end forever to the ticking. I resolved not to let the occasion pass without reaping some credit from it.

"Wife," said I, next morning, "you will not be troubled with any more ticking in our table. I have put a stop to all that."

"Indeed, husband," said she, with some incredulity.

"Yes, wife," returned I, perhaps a little vain-gloriously. "I have put a quietus upon that ticking. Depend upon it. the ticking will trouble you no more."

In vain she besought me to explain myself. I would not gratify her; being willing to balance any previous trepidation I might have betrayed, by leaving room now for the imputation of some heroic feat whereby I had silenced the ticking. It was a sort of innocent deceit by implication, quite harmless, and, I thought, of utility.

But when I went to breakfast, I saw my wife kneeling at the table again, and my girls looking ten times more frightened than ever.

"Why did you tell me that boastful tale?" said my wife indignantly. "You might have known how easily it would be found out. See this crack, too; and here is the ticking again, plainer than ever."

"Impossible," I exclaimed; but upon applying my ear, sure enough, tick! tick! tick! The ticking was there.

Recovering myself the best way I might, I demanded the bug.

"Bug?" screamed Julia. "Good heavens, papa!"

"I hope, sir, you have been bringing no bugs into this house," said my wife, severely.

"The bug, the bug!" I cried; "the bug under the tumbler."

"Bugs in tumblers!" cried the girls; "not *our* tumblers, papa? You have not been putting bugs into our tumblers? Oh, what does—what *does* it all mean?"

"Do you see this hole, this crack here?" said I, putting my finger on the spot.

"That I do," said my wife, with high displeasure. "And how did it come there? What have you been doing to the table?"

"Do you see this crack?" repeated I, intensely.

"Yes, yes," said Julia; "that was what frightened me so; it looks so like witch-work."

"Spirits! spirits!" cried Anna.

"Silence!" said my wife. "Go on, sir, and tell us what you know of the crack."

"Wife and daughters," said I, solemnly, "out of that crack, or hole, while I was sitting all alone here last night, a wonderful—"

Here, involuntarily, I paused, fascinated by the expectant attitudes and bursting eyes of Julia and Anna.

"What, what?" cried Julia.

"A bug, Julia."

"A bug?" cried my wife. "A bug come out of this table? And what did you do with it?"

"Clapped it under a tumbler."

"Biddy! Biddy!" cried my wife, going to the door. "Did you see a tumbler here on this table when you swept the room?"

"Sure I did, marm, and a 'bomnable bug under it."

"And what did you do with it?" demanded I.

"Put the bug in the fire, sir, and rinsed out the tumbler ever so many times, marm."

"Where is that tumbler?" cried Anna. "I hope you scratched it—marked it some way. I'll never drink out of that tumbler; never put it before me, Biddy. A bug—a bug! Oh, Julia! Oh, mamma! I feel it crawling all over me, even now. Haunted table!"

"Spirits! spirits!" cried Julia.

"My daughters," said their mother, with authority in her eyes, "go to your chamber till you can behave more like reasonable creatures. Is it a bug—a bug that can frighten you out of what little wits you ever had? Leave the room. I am astonished. I am pained by such childish conduct."

"Now tell me," said she, addressing me, as soon as they had withdrawn, "now tell me truly, did a bug really come out of this crack in the table?"

"Wife, it is even so."

"Did you see it come out?"

"I did."

She looked earnestly at the crack, leaning over it.

"Are you sure?" said she, looking up, but still bent over.

"Sure, sure."

She was silent. I began to think that the mystery of the thing began to tell even upon her. Yes, thought I, I shall presently see my wife shaking and shuddering, and, who knows, calling in some old dominie to exorcise the table, and drive out the spirits.

"I'll tell you what we'll do," said she suddenly, and not without excitement.

"What, wife?" said I, all eagerness, expecting some mystical proposition; "what, wife?"

"We will rub this table all over with that celebrated roach powder I've heard of."

"Good gracious! Then you don't think it's spirits?"

"Spirits?"

The emphasis of scornful incredulity was worthy of Democritus himself.

"But this ticking—this ticking?" said I.

"I'll whip that out of it."

"Come, come, wife," said I, "you are going too far the other way, now. Neither roach powder nor whipping will cure this table. It's a queer table, wife; there's no blinking it."

"I'll have it rubbed, though," she replied, "well rubbed;" and calling Biddy, she bade her get wax and brush, and give the table a vigorous manipulation. That done, the cloth was again laid, and we sat down to our morning meal; but my daughters did not make their appearance. Julia and Anna took no breakfast that day.

When the cloth was removed, in a business-like way my wife went to work with a dark colored cement, and hermetically closed the little hole in the table.

My daughters looking pale, I insisted upon taking them out for a walk that morning, when the following conversation ensued:

"My worst presentiments about that table are being verified, papa," said Julia; "not for nothing was that intimation of the cloven foot on my shoulder."

"Nonsense," said I. "Let us go into Mrs. Brown's, and have an ice-cream."

The spirit of Democritus was stronger on me now. By a curious coincidence, it strengthened with the strength of the sunlight.

"But is it not miraculous," said Anna, "how a bug should come out of a table?"

"Not at all, my daughter. It is a very common thing for bugs to come out of wood. You yourself must have seen them coming out of the ends of the billets on the hearth."

"Ah, but that wood is almost fresh from the woodland. But the table is at least a hundred years old."

"What of that?" said I, gaily. "Have not live toads been found in the hearts of dead rocks, as old as creation?"

"Say what you will, papa, I feel it is spirits," said Julia. "Do, do now, my dear papa, have that haunted table removed from the house."

"Nonsense," said I.

By another curious coincidence, the more they felt frightened, the more I felt brave.

Evening came.

"This ticking," said my wife; "do you think that another bug will come of this continued ticking?"

Curiously enough, that had not occurred to me before. I

had not thought of there being twins of bugs. But now, who knew—there might be even triplets.

I resolved to take precautions and, if there was to be a second bug, infallibly secure it. During the evening, the ticking was again heard. About ten o'clock I clapped a tumbler over the spot, as near as I could judge of it by my ear. Then we all retired, and locking the door of the cedar-parlor, I put the key in my pocket.

In the morning, nothing was to be seen, but the ticking was heard. The trepidation of my daughters returned. They wanted to call in the neighbors. But to this my wife was vigorously opposed. We should be the laughing-stock of the whole town. So it was agreed that nothing should be disclosed. Biddy received strict charges; and, to make sure, was not allowed that week to go to confession, lest she should tell the priest.

I stayed home all that day, every hour or two bending over the table, both eye and ear. Towards night, I thought the ticking grew more distinct, and seemed divided from my ear by a thinner and thinner partition of the wood. I thought, too, that I perceived a faint heaving up, or bulging of the wood, in the place where I had placed the tumbler. To put an end to the suspense, my wife proposed taking a knife and cutting into the wood there; but I had a less impatient plan; namely, that she and I should sit up with the table that night, as, from present symptoms, the bug would probably make its appearance before morning. For myself, I was curious to see the first advent of the thing—the first dazzle of the chick as it chipped the shell.

The idea struck my wife not unfavorably. She insisted that both Julia and Anna should be of the party, in order that the evidence of their senses should disabuse their minds of all nursery nonsense. For that spirits should tick, and that spirits should take unto themselves the form of bugs, was, to my wife, the most foolish of all foolish imaginations. True, she could not account for the thing; but she had all confidence that it could be, and would yet be, somehow explained, and that to her entire satisfaction. Without knowing it herself, my wife was a female Democritus. For my own part, my present feelings were of a mixed sort. In a strange and not unpleasing way, I gently oscillated between Democritus and Cotton Mather. But to my wife and daughters I assumed to be pure Democritus— a jeerer at all tea-table spirits whatever.

So, laying in a good supply of candles and crackers, all four of us sat up with the table, and at the same time sat round it. For a while my wife and I carried on an animated conversation. But my daughters were silent. Then my wife and I would have had a rubber of whist, but my daughters could not be prevailed upon to join. So we played whist with two dummies, literally; my wife won the rubber, and, fatigued with victory, put away the cards.

Half past eleven o'clock. No sign of the bug. The candles began to burn dim. My wife was just in the act of snuffing them, when a sudden, violent, hollow, resounding, rumbling thumping was heard.

Julia and Anna sprang to their feet.

"All well!" cried a voice from the street. It was the watchman, first ringing down his club on the pavement, and then following it up with this highly satisfactory verbal announcement.

"All well! Do you hear that, my girls?" said I, gaily.

Indeed it was astonishing how brave as Bruce I felt in company with three women, and two of them half frightened out of their wits.

I rose for my pipe, and took a philosophic smoke.

Democritus forever, thought I.

In profound silence, I sat smoking, when lo!—pop! pop! pop!—right under the table, a terrible popping.

This time we all four sprang up, and my pipe was broken.

"Good heavens! what's that?"

"Spirits! spirits!" cried Julia.

"Oh, oh, oh!" cried Anna.

"Shame," said my wife, "it's that new bottled cider, in the cellar, going off. I told Biddy to wire the bottles to-day."

I shall here transcribe from memoranda, kept during part of the night:

One o'clock. No sign of the bug. Ticking continues. Wife getting sleepy.

Two o'clock. No sign of the bug. Ticking intermittent. Wife fast asleep.

Three o'clock. No sign of the bug. Ticking pretty steady. Julia and Anna getting sleepy.

Four o'clock. No sign of the bug. Ticking regular, but not spirited. Wife, Julia, and Anna, all fast asleep in their chairs.

Five o'clock. No sign of the bug. Ticking faint. Myself feeling drowsy. The rest still asleep.

So far the journal.

—Rap! rap! rap!

A terrific, portentous rapping against a door.

Startled from our dreams, we started to our feet.

Rap! rap! rap!

Julia and Anna shrieked.

I cowered in the corner.

"You fools!" cried my wife, "it's the baker with the bread."

Six o'clock.

She went to throw back the shutters, but ere it was done, a cry came from Julia. There, half in and half out its crack, there wriggled the bug, flashing in the room's general dimness like a fiery opal.

Had this bug had a tiny sword by its side—a Damascus sword —and a tiny necklace round its neck—a diamond necklace— and a tiny gun in its claw—a brass gun—and a tiny manuscript in its mouth—a Chaldee manuscript—Julia and Anna could not have stood more charmed.

In truth, it was a beautiful bug—a Jew jeweler's bug—a bug like a sparkle of a glorious sunset.

Julia and Anna had never dreamed of such a bug. To them, bug had been a word synonymous with hideousness. But this was a seraphical bug; or, rather, all it had of the bug was the B, for it was beautiful as a butterfly.

Julia and Anna gazed and gazed. They were no more alarmed. They were delighted.

"But how got this strange, pretty creature into the table?" cried Julia.

"Spirits can get anywhere," replied Anna.

"Pshaw!" said my wife.

"Do you hear any more ticking?" said I.

They all applied their ears, but heard nothing.

"Well, then, wife and daughters, now that it is all over, this very morning I will go and make inquiries about it."

"Oh, do, papa," cried Julia, "do go and consult Madame Pazzi, the conjuress."

"Better go and consult Professor Johnson, the naturalist," said my wife.

"Bravo, Mrs. Democritus!" said I, "Professor Johnson is the man."

By good fortune I found the professor in. Informing him briefly of the incident, he manifested a cool, collected sort of interest, and gravely accompanied me home. The table was produced, the two openings pointed out, the bug displayed, and the details of the affair set forth; my wife and daughters being present.

"And now, Professor," said I, "what do you think of it?"

Putting on his spectacles, the learned professor looked hard at the table, and gently scraped with his pen-knife into the holes, but said nothing.

"Is it not an unusual thing, this?" anxiously asked Anna.

"Very unusual, Miss."

At which Julia and Anna exchanged significant glances.

"But is it not wonderful, very wonderful?" demanded Julia.

"Very wonderful, Miss."

My daughters exchanged still more significant glances, and Julia, emboldened, again spoke.

"And must you not admit, sir, that it is the work of—of—of sp—?"

"Spirits? No," was the crusty rejoinder.

"My daughters," said I, mildly, "you should remember that this is not Madame Pazzi, the conjuress, you put your questions to, but the eminent naturalist, Professor Johnson. And now, Professor," I added, "be pleased to explain. Enlighten our ignorance."

Without repeating all that the learned gentleman said—for, indeed, though lucid, he was a little prosy—let the following summary of his explication suffice.

The incident was not wholly without example. The wood of the table was apple-tree, a sort of tree much fancied by various insects. The bugs had come from eggs laid inside the bark of the living tree in the orchard. By careful examination of the position of the hole from which the last bug had emerged, in relation to the cortical layers of the slab, and then allowing for the inch and a half along the grain, ere the bug had eaten its way entirely out, and then computing the whole number of cortical layers in the slab, with a reasonable conjecture for the number cut off from the outside, it appeared that the egg must have been laid in the tree some ninety years, more or less, before the tree could have been felled. But between the felling of the tree and the present time, how long might that be? It was a very old-fashioned table. Allow eighty years for the age of the table, which would make one hundred and fifty years that the bug had lain in the egg. Such, at least, was Professor Johnson's computation.

"Now, Julia," said I, "after that scientific statement of the case (though, I confess, I don't exactly understand it), where are your spirits? It is very wonderful as it is, but where are your spirits?"

"Where, indeed?" said my wife.

"Why, now, she did not *really* associate this purely natural phenomenon with any crude, spiritual hypothesis, did she?" observed the learned professor, with a slight sneer.

"Say what you will," said Julia, holding up, in the covered tumbler, the glorious, lustrous, flashing live opal, "say what you will, if this beauteous creature be not a spirit, it yet teaches a spiritual lesson. For if, after one hundred and fifty years' entombment, a mere insect comes forth at last into light, itself an effulgence, shall there be no glorified resurrection for the spirit of man? Spirits! spirits!" she exclaimed, with rapture, "I still believe in spirits, only now I believe in them with delight, when before I but thought of them with terror."

The mysterious insect did not long enjoy its radiant life; it expired the next day. But my girls have preserved it. Embalmed in a silver vinaigrette, it lies on the little apple-tree table in the pier of the cedar-parlor.

And whatever lady doubts this story, my daughters will be happy to show her both the bug and the table, and point out to her, in the repaired slab of the latter, the two sealing-wax drops designating the exact place of the two holes made by the two bugs, something in the same way in which are marked the spots where the cannon balls struck Brattle Street Church.

THE PIAZZA

NOTE: This rhapsodizing parable-sketch, which introduces
The Piazza Tales, was written probably in January or February of 1856. Besides resuming familiar themes of all the
work of these years—the illusoriness of visionary hopes; discouragement and stoical endurance ("weariness and wakefulness together"); the torment of thinking—"The Piazza"
contains a very curious exercise in style which anticipates
Melville's long later absorption in writing poetry. This is the
experiment with audibly metrical prose that develops in the
passage (beginning with an allusion to Spenser) describing the
narrator's "inland voyage" to the fairy-land of his vision
(". . . the way now lay where path was none,/ and none
might go but by himself,/ and only go by daring./ Through
blackberry bushes that tried to pluck me back,/ though I but
strained towards fruitless growths/ of mountain-laurel," and
so on).

> *"With fairest flowers,*
> *Whilst summer lasts, and I live here, Fidele—"*

WHEN I removed into the country, it was to occupy an old-fashioned farm-house, which had no piazza—a deficiency the
more regretted, because not only did I like piazzas, as somehow combining the coziness of in-doors with the freedom of
out-doors, and it is so pleasant to inspect your thermometer
there, but the country round about was such a picture, that in
berry time no boy climbs hill or crosses vale without coming
upon easels planted in every nook, and sunburnt painters
painting there. A very paradise of painters. The circle of the
stars cut by the circle of the mountains. At least, so looks it
from the house; though, once upon the mountains, no circle
of them can you see. Had the site been chosen five rods off,
this charmed ring would not have been.

The house is old. Seventy years since, from the heart of the
Hearth Stone Hills, they quarried the Kaaba, or Holy Stone,
to which, each Thanksgiving, the social pilgrims used to come.
So long ago, that, in digging for the foundation, the workmen used both spade and axe, fighting the Troglodytes of

those subterranean parts—sturdy roots of a sturdy wood, encamped upon what is now a long land-slide of sleeping
meadow, sloping away off from my poppy-bed. Of that knit
wood, but one survivor stands—an elm, lonely through steadfastness.

Whoever built the house, he builded better than he knew;
or else Orion in the zenith flashed down his Damocles' sword
to him some starry night, and said, "Build there." For how,
otherwise, could it have entered the builder's mind, that, upon
the clearing being made, such a purple prospect would be his?
—nothing less than Greylock, with all his hills about him, like
Charlemagne among his peers.

Now, for a house, so situated in such a country, to have no
piazza for the convenience of those who might desire to feast
upon the view, and take their time and ease about it, seemed
as much of an omission as if a picture-gallery should have no
bench; for what but picture-galleries are the marble halls of
these same limestone hills?—galleries hung, month after month
anew, with pictures ever fading into pictures ever fresh. And
beauty is like piety—you cannot run and read it; tranquillity
and constancy, with, now-a-days, an easy chair, are needed. For
though, of old, when reverence was in vogue, and indolence
was not, the devotees of Nature, doubtless, used to stand and
adore—just as, in the cathedrals of those ages, the worshipers
of a higher Power did—yet, in these times of failing faith and
feeble knees, we have the piazza and the pew.

During the first year of my residence, the more leisurely to
witness the coronation of Charlemagne (weather permitting,
they crown him every sunrise and sunset), I chose me, on the
hill-side bank near by, a royal lounge of turf—a green velvet
lounge, with long, moss-padded back; while at the head,
strangely enough, there grew (but, I suppose, for heraldry)
three tufts of blue violets in a field-argent of wild strawberries;
and a trellis, with honey-suckle, I set for canopy. Very majesti-
cal lounge, indeed. So much so, that here, as with the reclining
majesty of Denmark in his orchard, a sly ear-ache invaded me.
But, if damps abound at times in Westminster Abbey, because
it is so old, why not within this monastery of mountains,
which is older?

A piazza must be had.

The house was wide—my fortune narrow; so that, to build
a panoramic piazza, one round and round, it could not be—
although, indeed, considering the matter by rule and square,

the carpenters, in the kindest way, were anxious to gratify my furthest wishes, at I've forgotten how much a foot.

Upon but one of the four sides would prudence grant me what I wanted. Now, which side?

To the east, that long camp of the Hearth Stone Hills, fading far away towards Quito; and every fall, a small white flake of something peering suddenly, of a coolish morning, from the topmost cliff—the season's new-dropped lamb, its earliest fleece; and then the Christmas dawn, draping those dun highlands with redbarred plaids and tartans—goodly sight from your piazza, that. Goodly sight; but, to the north is Charlemagne—can't have the Hearth Stone Hills with Charlemagne.

Well, the south side. Apple-trees are there. Pleasant, of a balmy morning, in the month of May, to sit and see that orchard, white-budded, as for a bridal; and, in October, one green arsenal yard; such piles of ruddy shot. Very fine, I grant; but, to the north is Charlemagne.

The west side, look. An upland pasture, alleying away into a maple wood at top. Sweet, in opening spring, to trace upon the hill-side, otherwise gray and bare—to trace, I say, the oldest paths by their streaks of earliest green. Sweet, indeed, I can't deny; but, to the north is Charlemagne.

So Charlemagne, he carried it. It was not long after 1848; and, somehow, about that time, all round the world, these kings, they had the casting vote, and voted for themselves.

No sooner was ground broken, than all the neighborhood, neighbor Dives, in particular, broke, too—into a laugh. Piazza to the north! Winter piazza! Wants, of winter midnights, to watch the Aurora Borealis, I suppose; hope he's laid in good store of Polar muffs and mittens.

That was in the lion month of March. Not forgotten are the blue noses of the carpenters, and how they scouted at the greenness of the cit, who would build his sole piazza to the north. But March don't last forever; patience, and August comes. And then, in the cool elysium of my northern bower, I, Lazarus in Abraham's bosom, cast down the hill a pitying glance on poor old Dives, tormented in the purgatory of his piazza to the south.

But, even in December, this northern piazza does not repel —nipping cold and gusty though it be, and the north wind, like any miller, bolting by the snow, in finest flour—for then, once more, with frosted beard, I pace the sleety deck, weathering Cape Horn.

In summer, too, Canute-like; sitting here, one is often reminded of the sea. For not only do long ground-swells roll the slanting grain, and little wavelets of the grass ripple over upon the low piazza, as their beach, and the blown down of dandelions is wafted like the spray, and the purple of the mountains is just the purple of the billows, and a still August noon broods upon the deep meadows, as a calm upon the Line; but the vastness and the lonesomeness are so oceanic, and the silence and the sameness, too, that the first peep of a strange house, rising beyond the trees, is for all the world like spying, on the Barbary coast, an unknown sail.

And this recalls my inland voyage to fairy-land. A true voyage; but, take it all in all, interesting as if invented.

From the piazza, some uncertain object I had caught, mysteriously snugged away, to all appearance, in a sort of purpled breast-pocket, high up in a hopper-like hollow, or sunken angle, among the northwestern mountains—yet, whether, really, it was on a mountain-side, or a mountain-top, could not be determined; because, though, viewed from favorable points, a blue summit, peering up away behind the rest, will, as it were, talk to you over their heads, and plainly tell you, that, though he (the blue summit) seems among them, he is not of them (God forbid!), and, indeed, would have you know that he considers himself—as, to say truth, he has good right—by several cubits their superior, nevertheless, certain ranges, here and there double-filed, as in platoons, so shoulder and follow up upon one another, with their irregular shapes and heights, that, from the piazza, a nigher and lower mountain will, in most states of the atmosphere, effacingly shade itself away into a higher and further one; that an object, bleak on the former's crest, will, for all that, appear nested in the latter's flank. These mountains, somehow, they play at hide-and-seek, and all before one's eyes.

But, be that as it may, the spot in question was, at all events, so situated as to be only visible, and then but vaguely, under certain witching conditions of light and shadow.

Indeed, for a year or more, I knew not there was such a spot, and might, perhaps, have never known, had it not been for a wizard afternoon in autumn—late in autumn—a mad poet's afternoon; when the turned maple woods in the broad basin below me, having lost their first vermilion tint, dully smoked, like smouldering towns, when flames expire upon their prey; and rumor had it, that this smokiness in the general air was not all Indian summer—which was not used to be so sick a thing, however mild—but, in great part, was blown from far-off forests, for weeks on fire, in Vermont; so that no wonder the sky was ominous as Hecate's cauldron—and two sportsmen, crossing a red stubble buck-wheat field, seemed guilty Macbeth and foreboding Banquo; and the hermit-sun, hutted in an Adullam cave, well towards the south, according to his season, did little else but, by indirect reflection of narrow rays shot down a Simplon pass among the clouds, just steadily paint one small, round, strawberry mole upon the wan cheek of Northwestern hills. Signal as a candle. One spot of radiance, where all else was shade.

Fairies there, thought I; some haunted ring where fairies dance.

Time passed; and the following May, after a gentle shower upon the mountains—a little shower islanded in misty seas of sunshine; such a distant shower—and sometimes two, and three, and four of them, all visible together in different parts —as I love to watch from the piazza, instead of thunderstorms, as I used to, which wrap old Greylock, like a Sinai, till one thinks swart Moses must be climbing among scathed hemlocks there; after, I say, that gentle shower, I saw a rainbow, resting its further end just where, in autumn, I had marked the mole. Fairies there, thought I; remembering that rainbows bring out the blooms, and that, if one can but get to the rainbow's end, his fortune is made in a bag of gold. Yon rainbow's end, would I were there, thought I. And none the less I wished it, for now first noticing what seemed some sort of glen, or grotto, in the mountain side; at least, whatever it was, viewed through the rainbow's medium, it glowed like the Potosi mine. But a work-a-day neighbor said, no doubt it was but some old barn —an abandoned one, its broadside beaten in, the acclivity its background. But I, though I had never been there, I knew better.

A few days after, a cheery sunrise kindled a golden sparkle in the same spot as before. The sparkle was of that vividness, it seemed as if it could only come from glass. The building, then—if building, after all, it was—could, at least, not be a barn, much less an abandoned one; stale hay ten years musting in it. No; if aught built by mortal, it must be a cottage; perhaps long vacant and dismantled, but this very spring magically fitted up and glazed.

Again, one noon, in the same direction, I marked, over

dimmed tops of terraced foliage, a broader gleam, as of a silver buckler, held sunwards over some croucher's head; which gleam, experience in like cases taught, must come from a roof newly shingled. This, to me, made pretty sure the recent occupancy of that far cot in fairy-land.

Day after day, now, full of interest in my discovery, what time I could spare from reading the *Midsummer-Night's Dream*, and all about Titania, wishfully I gazed off towards the hills; but in vain. Either troops of shadows, an imperial guard, with slow pace and solemn, defiled along the steeps; or, routed by pursuing light, fled broadcast from east to west —old wars of Lucifer and Michael; or the mountains, though unvexed by these mirrored sham fights in the sky, had an atmosphere otherwise unfavorable for fairy views. I was sorry; the more so, because I had to keep my chamber for some time after—which chamber did not face those hills.

At length, when pretty well again, and sitting out, in the September morning, upon the piazza, and thinking to myself, when, just after a little flock of sheep, the farmer's banded children passed, a-nutting, and said, "How sweet a day"—it was, after all, but what their fathers call a weather-breeder —and, indeed, was become so sensitive through my illness, as that I could not bear to look upon a Chinese creeper of my adoption, and which, to my delight, climbing a post of the piazza, had burst out in starry bloom, but now, if you removed the leaves a little, showed millions of strange, cankerous worms, which, feeding upon those blossoms, so shared their blessed hue, as to make it unblessed evermore—worms, whose germs had doubtless lurked in the very bulb which, so hopefully, I had planted: in this ingrate peevishness of my weary convalescence, was I sitting there; when, suddenly looking off, I saw the golden mountain-window, dazzling like a deep-sea dolphin. Fairies there, thought I, once more; the queen of fairies at her fairy window; at any rate, some glad mountain-girl; it will do me good, it will cure this weariness, to look on her. No more; I'll launch my yawl—ho, cheerly, heart! and push away for fairy-land—for rainbow's end, in fairy-land.

How to get to fairy-land, by what road, I did not know; nor could any one inform me; not even one Edmund Spenser, who had been there—so he wrote me—further than that to reach fairy-land, it must be voyaged to, and with faith. I took the fairy-mountain's bearings, and the first fine day, when strength permitted, got into my yawl—high-pommeled, leather one—cast off the fast, and away I sailed, free voyager as an autumn leaf. Early dawn; and, sallying westward, I sowed the morning before me.

Some miles brought me nigh the hills; but out of present sight of them. I was not lost; for road-side golden-rods, as guide-posts, pointed, I doubted not, the way to the golden window. Following them, I came to a lone and languid region, where the grass-grown ways were traveled but by drowsy cattle, that, less waked than stirred by day, seemed to walk in sleep. Browse, they did not—the enchanted never eat. At least, so says Don Quixote, that sagest sage that ever lived.

On I went, and gained at last the fairy-mountain's base, but saw yet no fairy ring. A pasture rose before me. Letting down five mouldering bars—so moistly green, they seemed fished up from some sunken wreck—a wigged old Aries, long-visaged, and with crumpled horn, came snuffing up; and then, retreating, decorously led on along a milky-way of white-weed, past dim-clustering Pleiades and Hyades, of small forget-me-nots; and would have led me further still his astral path, but for golden flights of yellow-birds—pilots, surely, to the golden window, to one side flying before me, from bush to bush, towards deep woods—which woods themselves were luring—and, somehow, lured, too, by their fence, banning a dark road, which, however dark, led up. I pushed through; when Aries, renouncing me now for some lost soul, wheeled, and went his wiser way. Forbidding and forbidden ground—to him.

A winter wood road, matted all along with winter-green. By the side of pebbly waters—waters the cheerier for their solitude; beneath swaying fir-boughs, petted by no season, but still green in all, on I journeyed—my horse and I: on, by an old saw-mill, bound down and hushed with vines, that his grating voice no more was heard; on, by a deep flume clove through snowy marble, vernal-tinted, where freshet eddies had, on each side, spun out empty chapels in the living rock; on, where Jacks-in-the-pulpit, like their Baptist namesake, preached but to the wilderness; on, where a huge, cross-grain block, fern-bedded, showed where, in forgotten times, man after man had tried to split it, but lost his wedges for his pains —which wedges yet rusted in their holes; on, where, ages past, in step-like ledges of a cascade, skull-hollow pots had been churned out by ceaseless whirling of a flintstone—ever wearing, but itself unworn; on, by wild rapids pouring into a secret pool, but soothed by circling there awhile, issued forth serenely; on, to less broken ground, and by a little ring, where, truly, fairies must have danced, or else some wheel-tire been heated—for all was bare; still on, and up, and out into a hanging orchard, where maidenly looked down upon me a crescent moon, from morning.

My horse hitched low his head. Red apples rolled before him; Eve's apples; seek-no-furthers. He tasted one, I another; it tasted of the ground. Fairy-land not yet, thought I, flinging my bridle to a humped old tree, that crooked out an arm to catch it. For the way now lay where path was none, and none might go but by himself, and only go by daring. Through blackberry brakes that tried to pluck me back, though I but strained towards fruitless growths of mountain-laurel; up slippery steeps to barren heights, where stood none to welcome. Fairy-land not yet, thought I, though the morning is here before me.

Foot-sore enough and weary, I gained not then my journey's end, but came ere long to a craggy pass, dipping towards growing regions still beyond. A zigzag road, half overgrown with blueberry bushes, here turned among the cliffs. A rent was in their ragged sides; through it a little track branched off, which, upwards threading that short defile, came breezily out above, to where the mountain-top, part sheltered northward, by a taller brother, sloped gently off a space, ere darkly plunging; and here, among fantastic rocks, reposing in a herd, the foot-track wound, half beaten, up to a little, low-storied, grayish cottage, capped, nun-like, with a peaked roof.

On one slope, the roof was deeply weather-stained, and, nigh the turfy eaves-trough, all velvet-napped; no doubt the snail-monks founded mossy priories there. The other slope was newly shingled. On the north side, doorless and windowless, the clapboards, innocent of paint, were yet green as the north side of lichened pines, or copperless hulls of Japanese junks, becalmed. The whole base, like those of the neighboring rocks, was rimmed about with shaded streaks of richest sod; for, with hearth-stones in fairy-land, the natural rock, though housed, preserves to the last, just as in open fields, its fertilizing charm; only, by necessity, working now at a remove, to the sward without. So, at least, says Oberon, grave authority in fairy lore. Though setting Oberon aside, certain it is, that, even in the common world, the soil, close up to farm-houses, as close up to pasture rocks, is, even though untended, ever richer than it is a few rods off—such gentle, nurturing heat is radiated there.

But with this cottage, the shaded streaks were richest in its front and about its entrance, where the ground-sill, and especially the door-sill had, through long eld, quietly settled down.

No fence was seen, no inclosure. Near by—ferns, ferns, ferns; further—woods, woods, woods; beyond—mountains, mountains, mountains; then—sky, sky, sky. Turned out in ærial commons, pasture for the mountain moon. Nature, and but nature, house and all; even a low cross-pile of silver birch, piled openly, to season; up among whose silvery sticks, as through the fencing of some sequestered grave, sprang vagrant raspberry bushes—willful assertors of their right of way.

The foot-track, so dainty narrow, just like a sheep-track, led through long ferns that lodged. Fairy-land at last, thought I; Una and her lamb dwell here. Truly, a small abode—mere palanquin, set down on the summit, in a pass between two worlds, participant of neither.

A sultry hour, and I wore a light hat, of yellow sinnet, with white duck trowsers—both relics of my tropic seagoing. Clogged in the muffling ferns, I softly stumbled, staining the knees a sea-green.

Pausing at the threshold, or rather where threshold once had been, I saw, through the open door-way, a lonely girl, sewing at a lonely window. A pale-cheeked girl, and fly-specked window, with wasps about the mended upper panes. I spoke. She shyly started, like some Tahiti girl, secreted for a sacrifice, first catching sight, through palms, of Captain Cook. Recovering, she bade me enter; with her apron brushed off a stool; then silently resumed her own. With thanks I took the stool; but now, for a space, I, too, was mute. This, then, is the fairy-mountain house, and here, the fairy queen sitting at her fairy window.

I went up to it. Downwards, directed by the tunneled pass, as through a leveled telescope, I caught sight of a far-off, soft, azure world. I hardly knew it, though I came from it.

"You must find this view very pleasant," said I, at last.

"Oh, sir," tears starting in her eyes, "the first time I looked out of this window, I said 'never, never shall I weary of this.'"

"And what wearies you of it now?"

"I don't know," while a tear fell; "but it is not the view, it is Marianna."

Some months back, her brother, only seventeen, had come

hither, a long way from the other side, to cut wood and burn coal, and she, elder sister, had accompanied him. Long had they been orphans, and now, sole inhabitants of the sole house upon the mountain. No guest came, no traveler passed. The zigzag, perilous road was only used at seasons by the coal wagons. The brother was absent the entire day, sometimes the entire night. When at evening, fagged out, he did come home, he soon left his bench, poor fellow, for his bed; just as one, at last, wearily quits that, too, for still deeper rest. The bench, the bed, the grave.

Silent I stood by the fairy window, while these things were being told.

"Do you know," said she at last, as stealing from her story, "do you know who lives yonder?—I have never been down into that country—away off there, I mean; that house, that marble one," pointing far across the lower landscape; "have you not caught it? there, on the long hill-side: the field before, the woods behind; the white shines out against their blue; don't you mark it? the only house in sight."

I looked; and after a time, to my surprise, recognized, more by its position than its aspect, or Marianna's description, my own abode, glimmering much like this mountain one from the piazza. The mirage haze made it appear less a farm-house than King Charming's palace.

"I have often wondered who lives there; but it must be some happy one; again this morning was I thinking so."

"Some happy one," returned I, starting; "and why do you think that? You judge some rich one lives there?"

"Rich or not, I never thought; but it looks so happy, I can't tell how; and it is so far away. Sometimes I think I do but dream it is there. You should see it in a sunset."

"No doubt the sunset gilds it finely; but not more than the sunrise does this house, perhaps."

"This house? The sun is a good sun, but it never gilds this house. Why should it? This old house is rotting. That makes it so mossy. In the morning, the sun comes in at this old window, to be sure—boarded up, when first we came; a window I can't keep clean, do what I may—and half burns, and nearly blinds me at my sewing, besides setting the flies and wasps astir—such flies and wasps as only lone mountain houses know. See, here is the curtain—this apron—I try to shut it out with them. It fades it, you see. Sun gild this house? not that ever Marianna saw."

"Because when this roof is gilded most, then you stay here within."

"The hottest, weariest hour of day, you mean? Sir, the sun gilds not this roof. It leaked so, brother newly shingled all one side. Did you not see it? The north side, where the sun strikes most on what the rain has wetted. The sun is a good sun; but this roof, it first scorches, and then rots. An old house. They went West, and are long dead, they say, who built it. A mountain house. In winter no fox could den in it. That chimney-place has been blocked up with snow, just like a hollow stump."

"Yours are strange fancies, Marianna."

"They but reflect the things."

"Then I shou'd have said, 'These are strange things,' rather than, 'Yours are strange fancies.' "

"As you will;" and took up her sewing.

Something in those quiet words, or in that quiet act, it made me mute again; while, noting, thro gh the fairy window, a broad shadow stealing on, as cast by some gigantic condor, floating at brooding poise on outstretched wings, I marked how, by its deeper and inclusive dusk, it wiped away into itself all lesser shades of rock or fern.

"You watch the cloud," said Marianna.

"No, a shadow; a cloud's, no doubt—though that I cannot see. How did you know it? Your eyes are on your work."

"It dusked my work. There, now the cloud is gone, Tray comes back."

"How?"

"The dog, the shaggy dog. At noon, he steals off, of himself, to change his shape—returns, and lies down awhile, nigh the door. Don't you see him? His head is turned round at you; though, when you came, he looked before him."

"Your eyes rest but on your work; what do you speak of?"

"By the window, crossing."

"You mean this shaggy shadow—the nigh one? And yes, now that I mark it, it is not unlike a large, black Newfoundland dog. The invading shadow gone, the invaded one returns. But I do not see what casts it."

"For that, you must go without."

"One of those grassy rocks, no doubt."

"You see his head, his face?"

"The shadow's? You speak as if *you* saw it, and all the time your eyes are on your work."

"Tray looks at you," still without glancing up; "this is his hour; I see him."

"Have you, then, so long sat at this mountain-window where but clouds and vapors pass, that, to you, shadows are as things, though you speak of them as of phantoms; that by familiar knowledge, working like a second sight, you can, without looking for them, tell just where they are though, as having mice-like feet, they creep about, and come and go; that, to you, these lifeless shadows are as living friends, who, though out of sight, are not out of mind, even in their faces—is it so?"

"That way I never thought of it. But the friendliest one, that used to soothe my weariness so much, coolly quivering on the ferns, it was taken from me, never to return, as Tray did just now. The shadow of a birch. The tree was struck by lightning, and brother cut it up. You saw the cross-pile out-doors—the buried root lies under it; but not the shadow. That is flown, and never will come back, nor ever anywhere stir again."

Another cloud here stole along, once more blotting out the dog, and blackening all the mountain; while the stillness was so still, deafness might have forgot itself, or else believed that noiseless shadow spoke.

"Birds, Marianna, singing-birds, I hear none; I hear nothing. Boys and bob-o-links, do they never come a-berrying up here?"

"Birds, I seldom hear; boys, never. The berries mostly ripe and fall—few, but me, the wiser."

"But yellow-birds showed me the way—part way, at least."

"And then flew back. I guess they play about the mountain-side, but don't make the top their home. And no doubt you think that, living so lonesome here, knowing nothing, hearing nothing—little, at least, but sound of thunder and the fall of trees—never reading, seldom speaking, yet ever wakeful, this is what gives me my strange thoughts—for so you call them—this weariness and wakefulness together. Brother, who stands and works in open air, would I could rest like him; but mine is mostly but dull woman's work—sitting, sitting, restless sitting."

"But, do you not go walk at times? These woods are wide."

"And lonesome; lonesome, because so wide. Sometimes, 'tis true, of afternoons, I go a little way, but soon come back again. Better feel lone by hearth, than rock. The shadows hereabouts I know—those in the woods are strangers."

"But the night?"

"Just like the day. Thinking, thinking—a wheel I cannot stop; pure want of sleep it is that turns it."

"I have heard that, for this wakeful weariness, to say one's prayers, and then lay one's head upon a fresh hop pillow——"

"Look!"

Through the fairy window, she pointed down the steep to a small garden patch near by—mere pot of rifled loam, half round din by shattering rocks—each re, side by side, some feet apart, nipped and puny, two hop-vines climbed two poles, and, gaining their tip ends, would have then joined over in an upward clasp, but the baffled shoots, groping awhile in empty air, trailed back whence they sprung.

"You have tried the pillow, then?"

"Yes."

"And prayer?"

"Prayer and pillow."

"Is there no other cure, or charm?"

"Oh, if I could but once get to yonder house, and but look upon whoever the happy being is that lives there! A foolish thought: why do I think it? Is it that I live so lonesome, and know nothing?"

"I, too, know nothing; and, therefore, cannot answer; but, for your sake, Marianna, well could wish that I were that happy one of the happy house you dream you see; for then you would behold him now, and, as you say, this weariness might leave you."

—Enough. Launching my yawl no more for fairy-land, I stick to the piazza. It is my box-royal; and this amphitheatre, my theatre of San Carlo. Yes, the scenery is magical—the illusion so complete. And Madam Meadow Lark, my prima donna, plays her grand engagement here; and, drinking in her sunrise note, which, Memnon-like, seems struck from the golden window, how far from me the weary face behind it.

But, every night, when the curtain falls, truth comes in with darkness. No light shows from the mountains. To and fro I walk the piazza deck, haunted by Marianna's face, and many as real a story.

THE MARQUIS DE GRANDVIN

NOTE: At his death in 1891 Herman Melville left in manuscript a number of prose tales and sketches that were not published until the Constable edition in the 1920's. Most of these were written to accompany poems, in the manner of the title piece for the volume, *John Marr and Other Sailors*, which Melville did publish privately in 1888. The Marquis de Grandvin and his American "friend and disciple" Jack Gentian are the speakers in a pair of long poems ("At the Hostelry," "An Afternoon in Naples") retrospectively reviewing certain convivial days and nights in the old times before Garibaldi and Cavour.

These poems and, more particularly, the prose sketch here reprinted, develop yet another portrait of that type of genial, humane, frank companionability—most likely to flourish in the bachelor state—which Melville's imagination always treated with special indulgence. He has here no real story to put forward; but in praising the rare virtue of this "Lord Bountiful" of the occasions of good fellowship, he again acts out as narrator that effort of intercession on behalf of his subject, assuming a kind of trusteeship for the man's character and memory, which gives form to more than one of his greater achievements, most notably "Bartleby" and *Moby-Dick*.

A COUNTRYMAN of Lafayette and Bartholdi, this gentleman is not unknown to some Americans, more especially perhaps, to some of us New Yorkers. He is an honorary member of most of the Fifth Avenue clubs, anything but unwelcome at their chance gatherings, while at their premeditated banquets his appearance—and he always happily times it—is commonly hailed by a plausive clapping of hands simultaneous with the vocal salutation. But a person of genial temper is not only very likely to be a popular man's man, but also, and beyond that, a favourite with the ladies. For it is something less venial than mere error in the old philosopher penally branded with a horrible name—misogynist, I think—and a soggy soul he must have been; it was something less venial than error in him to say, as he did, that women, however apt to that grand passion which makes the one divine rapture of life, have nevertheless a constitutional incapacity for good-fellowship, that is, in the masculine acceptation of the term. Assuredly, Hymen knows, too few of them practically demonstrate their capacity for it. Some musky dew-drops from the Garden expelled Eve unwillingly carried away quivering in her hair. More than man, she partakes of the paradisiac spirit. Under favourable conditions evincing a quicker aptitude to pleasure than man. How alert to twine the garland for the holiday! How instinctively prompt for that faint semblance of Eden, the picnic in the greenwood!

Now there is something in the fine, open, cheery aspect of the Marquis de Grandvin that conveys a thrill to those frames so exquisitely strung to happiness. Not invariably running the risk of incurring dark clouds from their lords, the dames and sisters of the Benedicks of the clubs, at their balls and parties, cast upon the Marquis that kindled merry glance which, according to the old French epic whose theme is Roncesvalles, the ladies bestowed upon Roland; not alone smitten by the fame and taken with the person of that noble accredited nephew of Charlemagne, but rightly inferring him to be not more a David against the Saracen than a champion against still more flagitious infidels, impugners of the sex. Yes, it is by instinct that all superior women recognise in this gentleman a cordial friend. Nor do they approve him the less for his friendly alliance with his charming sphere. This is a verity not out of keeping with another, namely, this feminine appreciation of the Marquis, gracious though it be, hardly extends to such of his qualities as partake of the Grand Style, as one may say, the highly elevated style; a style apparently demanding for its due appreciation a robust habit, in short, the masculine habit. For the most part, it is for his less exalted qualities that the ladies approve de Grandvin. They approve him for the way in which he contributes to those amenities and gaieties in which the sexes upon common ground participate, and wherein, thanks to their gallantry of good-nature, the countrymen of the Marquis de Grandvin have always excelled.

The foregoing hints as to what is the standing in America, or at least among some of us Americans, of the genial foreigner here ushered into a regard less exclusive, that, by patriotic intention goes before the recital, show that not alone in his own sweet France are the blended suavity and power of his genius estimated at their just rate, but that in the high circles of every European capital he is received with even more than good-will.

Though the subject of this theme, de Grandvin, be a patrician of hereditary mark, he was not consulted in the matter of his progenitors. At any rate, his cosmopolitan sympathies, transcending his class, go out to mankind. Under auspicious circumstances make his acquaintance, and whatever your degree in the social scale, you will find him friendly company, cordial and frank; without condescension, a solemn popery he was never guilty of.

As to his title, if here he be introduced as the Marquis, it is only because his troops of friends on both sides of the water, not excluding ever. the Levellers among them, insist upon retaining for him an inherited prefix which he himself long ago renounced; and doubtless for the reason that any appellative at all savouring of arbitrary rank is unsuitable to a man of liberal and catholic mind.

In defence of their insistent employment of the title, a caprice hardly compatible with their political principles, the Levellers of his acquaintance, candid in inconsistency, freely admit that somehow there is something in it felicitously befitting the character innately noble of de Grandvin.

But some fuller account of this genial paragon, upon whom are concentred the otherwise diverging suffrages of the divers parties in Church and State—some account less restricted by considerations of space—is in course of preparation, and if clamorously demanded, may hereafter appear. For the present purpose it will be enough, perhaps, if an outlined picture or two serve to suggest the filled portrait.

Though not so plentiful as our peaches in a good year, there are men of such noble quality that being in their company enriches and mellows one. The wisdom they by contact give out is not celibate and sterile like Solomon's, but wedded to enjoyment, and hence productive. They would seem to be a confirmation of the otherwise disputable maxim of Spinoza, that every advance in joy implies an ascent in the scale of intelligence and capability. The influence of such a man insensibly disposes one to gentle charities, brave conceptions, heroic virtues. They have a suggestion of the potentialities in the unvitiated Adam, a creature, according to hallowed authority, originally created but a little lower than the angels. Almost invariably these men have physical beauty; and the moral charm is in keeping with that, apparently a spontaneous emanation from it. It is as golden wine down in a golden chalice, where, seen through the lustre suffusing the shadow, the delicious fluid looks to be the exuded gathered sap of the precious metal.

It was of the Marquis de Grandvin that the landscape painter, B. Hobbema Brown, an inoffensive sort of theoretical misanthrope, with a treacherous flow of loving-kindness in him—to borrow one of his own eccentric phrases; the same B. Hobbema who, were his significant reticence on the point, no unwise thing in him, by the way, conjecturally rendered into words, would seem in his own private judgment to have been treated illiberally enough by the art-dealers, art-critics, and academic hanging-committees, to say nothing of the art public; well, it was of some other than the Marquis that Hobbema B., returning in moonlight from a choice assemblage, where he had been introduced to him, and undergone the inevitable fascination of the contact; it was of him that Brown enthusiastically exclaimed to his companion: 'What a godsend to meet such a man! He is a set-off against the battalions of his contraries. Between you and me, mankind taken in a lump are the gods' job-lot; but, by heaven, the race that can produce a Marquis de Grandvin is not promiscuously to be contemned!'

See there how the talismanic something in the sort of nature here indicated can operate upon another nature though of a temper not favourably disposed to receive its benign influence.

In the casual outcome of such a character, gay fancies and suggestions without stint, sallies of wit and bonhomie, all sharing more or less in a certain lyric glow; herein the spiritual bounty to us would seem to be an unconsciousness in the almoner, involving, too, an indifference or unconcern as to who may appropriate, or as to what purpose the appropriation may be applied. In this particular, what recks the Marquis de Grandvin, for example? He is the ripe peach-tree shedding its abundance, careless of the garner; he is the Prince of Golconda at the ball, some of whose innumerable diamond buttons drop from his raiment unheeded by him in the chance fleeting rubs and collisions of the dance.

But how transitory these prodigal improvident ones can prove!—and once gone, how soon all but good as forgotten! True, were an example here demanded, one adapted for popular illustration, not readily could it be supplied. Literature will not furnish it, since these natures, never directly expressing themselves in literature, have no memorial place in its records. Neither are they Alexanders and Napoleons that the fame which is all but independent of literature should trumpet them. Nevertheless, in local tradition, and comparatively recent, I do find a citable instance which, though below the grade, say, of a de Grandvin, and but in a minor way to the purpose, may perhaps for these reasons serve the better to actualise the general truth, in a measure bring it home.

Rufus Choate, the Boston advocate, when inspired to his best before an audience, how he exhilarated and elevated and transported his hearers. But he is gone; and all those fireworks of elfish passion and wit, where are they? Vainly in the Ceramicus of the libraries will you seek any enduring monument of that oratorical pyrotechnist. As well ransack the museums of Natural History for the bottled-up tail of Encke's comet. What shall we say, then? Are there natures strong to draw and enthrall, yet whose influence is like that of the magnet, only operative as a bodily presence? Yes, withdraw the magnet and all is over. And holds this true as to the Marquis de Grandvin? Yea, and shall he also at last vanish, sailing into the boundless Nil, leaving no phosphorescent wake or magic moon-glade behind? Shall naught remain of his cherub sparkle and spirit? —nothing of all those ineffable qualities that make him what Raphael, Milton's affable archangel, would be seen to be were he commissioned hither to dissuade mankind from ever perpetrating an inhumanity or a pun? And, oh, thou Admirable Crichton, nay, a thousandfold more admirable than he, for art thou not kindly as wise?—of all thy more sustained sallies of bright fantasy and humour, let alone thy erratic coruscations, shall nothing be crystallised into permanence? Nothing at last remain of our Lord Bountiful but the empty larder and void dusty bin? When we laud thee departed, shall the infidel twit us with—What were his assets? If the very plenitude and variety of thy shining gifts, and the preoccupation of thy social charm, if these indispose thee to drudge it as an 'author,' or operate as disqualifications; will no painstaking aspirant for the literary fame essay the task of methodising thee, or some little segment of thee, into the literary form? But even thy foremost disciple, Jack Gentian, though out of humble emulation he strive to follow thy devious footing, yet thy brow is among the stars; he ventures not to lift his head to thy height.

But I—ah, brimmed with thy genial flood—I, here, in the small hour, not long returned from a richer than Plato's

'Banquet,' where thou didst pour from thy cornucopia, with a hand redundant as that of Millet's seed-sower, the profusion of thy good things; I, audacious as I am, resolved upon an emprise.

The Marquis, methought, though glorious, is not of the gods, the more reproach to their synod; but I will make them yield a place for him on their golden benches; I will make him an Immortal! How? Monumentalise him to the remotest posterity in a book fragrant as violets, yet lasting as the Pyramids!

Yes, and as the prophets of old, announcing the mind of their deity, in some instances dramatically put on his personality, even so will I assume that of de Grandvin. How otherwise, indeed? since he it is that kindles me, inspires me, usurps me. I will snatch at those themes—New Italy and the Old Masters—wherein this very night we heard him so sportively romance. I will render the fine festivity of his tone, as well as the loftier touch; catch the rhythm of the waves of his seas of invention; swim out there; in short, I did by implication say to myself an insane thing—I will imitate the inimitable!

The issue of the temerarious resolve, how humiliating! And no wonder. The inordinate aim, and the inadequate achievement! The soaring ambition of the balloon, and its abrupt drop at a fatal puncture!

You who have basked in the vital beams of the Marquis, place not in contrast his own radiant aspect side by side with the dim delineation of him in the preceding sketch. And, for the attempted rendering of his thought and style in the piece to follow, take charitable example from the Persian, who in his comment upon the Icelandic version of the fervid orientalisms of Sadi and Hafiz, made humane allowance for the inherent difficulties and presumably numb fingers of the translator in penning it.

THREE "JACK GENTIAN SKETCHES"

NOTE: These three sketches (published in the Constable edition in 1924, along with other "Gentian" fragments) go somewhat beyond the simple celebration of bachelorhood and wine-bibbing geniality, subjects on which even Melville can become tiresome. Both Major Gentian's Roman pride as a descendant of Revolutionary patriots and as himself a decorated veteran of Grant's Wilderness campaign, and yet his refusal from the first to speak a word against the Southern opponent or—in an era of increasingly gaudy G.A.R. celebrations—to observe any patriotic holiday but the 4th of July, are described with unreserved sympathy. They become the occasion for brief final affirmations of that American-democratic spirit of Christian charity and reconciliation that Melville never lost imaginative faith in; that sense of the unity of mankind in the tragic accumulations of its history which he had once thought American authors especially would be free to express.

1. Portrait of a Gentleman

JOHN GENTIAN, ESQ., or Major Gentian, or the Dean, or the Major or Jack—for all these styles are his according to circumstances and the person mentioning or addressing him—is one of those socially notable characters whose names for all the notability will be found rather in the trustworthy City Directory than in the not-always-reliable Biographical Dictionary. Accordingly in the former "John Gentian" is set down as hailing from the "Burgundy Club," the street and number of the club-house duly and accurately given. In brief, John Gentian is a bachelor having chambers on an upper story of the club-house, a privilege which at his solicitation was cheerfully accorded him, as by seniority of membership, to say nothing of happy qualifications in his character, Dean of the Chapter of *Burgundians*, for so do they denominate themselves, the brethren of that congenial fraternity.

This captain of the good fellows belongs to a transplanted

shoot of Southern stock for two generations taking root and branching out in the North, within the borders of a State which, thanks to its relative geographical position and circumstances originating in that, least partakes of a sectional spirit. For now a fair period, ever since the latter part of 1865, the Dean has gone on in what would seem to be the after-mission of his life, namely, the dispensing of those less abbreviated greetings on the Avenue and considerate old-school hospitalities of the board, hardly practicable for the "business-man" of our day, or, for that matter, the man of leisure either, unless abounding in natural benevolence backed up by its desirable concomitant, a comfortable bank account. Do not infer, however, that there is aught of Count D'Orsay superannuated, or Sir Charles Grandison, become senile, in our Dean of the Burgundians. He is no prodigal in airs and graces, and, on the contrary, sometimes takes singular liberties with etiquette, not out of ignorance, to be sure, or the Leveller's contempt; no, but from a certain impulsive straightforwardness at times, hardly compatible with the abstract theory of a formalised gentlemanhood. Furthermore, he of late has permitted himself an easy latitude in his dress, evincing a lack of proper reverence for mercers and the mode. But yet more astray, he will, upon provocation—say, at some story of perfidy or brutal behavior—incontinently rap out an expletive, startling to the ladies as Brandt's flourished tomahawk at the London masked ball long ago. Then again, as if there were no end to his derelictions, he, when convenient to him, thinks nothing of carrying a brown paper parcel in the street rather than trouble the shopkeeper to send some inexpensive small matter to his rooms. Notwithstanding these deviations from the conventionally correct, there is that in the look of Major Gentian, something in the "cut of his jib," as the sailors say, if not in the end of his coat, that involuntarily inspires respect, yes, even in cabby himself. Cabby, before club-house or theatre, poised on the curb, expectant of the prey, would never dream of hailing him (*the Dean*) with the ambiguous "*Gent.*" Should he do so, whether out of ignorance or sly impudence, the Major would have to hold his temper well in hand to obviate a violent breach of the peace. To *Boss* he objects not, that Dutch monosyllable having an honest bovine sound to it, and being, in fact, a natural localism of a city first settled by the Hollander; and if *master* be not the word's exact equivalent, it would be difficult to find one.

The Major's propensity is to occasional unlicensed emphasis in his talk, a thing assuredly not commendable in anybody, very likely contracted from certain experiences, namely, his adventures in early life among our frontiersmen. Nor could his subsequent campaignings during our Civil War have served to displace the secular expletives by Biblical ejaculations such as those attributed to Cromwell's pious troopers, though, indeed, the historical sceptics of our time have suggested doubts as to whether even these same martial deacons for all their psalmody in the tents did not during active operations against the foe indulge more or less in that "horrible swearing" wherewith "the army in Flanders" stands preeminently charged. To terrorise, if possible, this pertains to the true function of a soldier in the field. The point is energetically put by a Roman consul, one of those schooling his infantry on the eve of an eye-to-eye and hand-to-hand encounter of ancient war. To the same purpose is a well-known passage in Shakespeare. But there are various modes of terrorising as a preliminary to closely engaging. The Chinese Achilles, for example, hurls at the foe missiles of an unmentionable name in English, and which explode an abomination of stench. The sequence is hot air, though disagreeable, and what is "horrible swearing" but the same? It is perhaps equally efficacious, and, in military ethics, why may not either be used as an adjunct to the artillery? But alas for the oathing. It becomes a habit, and so in times of peace is mechanically resorted to by the retired Christian veteran when there is no military call for it. In short, a soldier's or sailor's oath, however shocking to ears polite, is, at least when the man is not actually engaged in tussle with the foe public or private, but an idiocratic form given to whatever meaning may lurk in such phrases as Bless my soul! Thunder! Goodness gracious!

If, however, sin be not of the heart but the tongue, a theological opinion to which some would seem to incline, then woe to no few of our warriors in the late Civil Unhappiness. For, in that case, who but an orthodox Calvinist can with any adequacy appreciate the sublime disinterestedness of their patriotism, since from his point of view, not alone did our heroes jeopardise their lives for us, but mortally endangered their souls. And for what? Oh futility! in the attempts to terrorise enemies who, being our own countrymen, of course, refused to be terrified, though in the end fate, working through force, made them succumb.

Though of all men Jack be the least exclusive as to the company he keeps, and is anything but bumptious in his manner, there have not been wanting detractors who have insinuated a charge against him rather serious in a democratic community, namely, not alone a tendency to the aristocratic in general, but a weakness for certain gewgaws, that savour of the monarchical. True, at certain grand banquets, where as an honorary guest he sits at the high table, banquets more especially of those national societies wherewith our cosmopolitan city abounds—the St. Denis; St. Nicholas, St. Patrick, St. George, St. Andrew; on these occasions the Major a little lays himself open to invidious suspicion by wearing on his left lapel the eagle wings in gold of the Cincinnati, a venerable order whereof he who still reigns "first in the hearts of his countrymen" was the original head. This decoration descended to the Major from his great-grandfather, a South Carolinian, a white-haired captain of infantry at the battle of Saratoga Springs, who therefore, being eligible as a Revolutionary officer, was enrolled in the order upon its formation just after the Peace.

Now, an inherited badge of the Cincinnati, every American however ultra in his democracy, must allow to be something of which no other American need be ashamed. As the Major himself once demanded, and with some animation—"Compared with this bit of old gold," tapping it with his hand, "what is the insignia of the Knights of the Golden Fleece or the Knights of the Spanish Order of the Holy Ghost? Gimcracks, sir! and the last, in fact as in name, but a ghostly sort of vanity."

2. *To Major John Gentian, Dean of the Burgundy Club*

WITH THY rare single-mindedness, so resented by the ambidextrous double-dealers, a virtue putting thee in a worldly sense almost as much at disadvantage with them as thy single arm (the other lost in the Wilderness under Grant) assuredly would in a personal encounter; the genial humour of thy club-chat, garnished, as not unfrequently it is, even like to a holiday barn, with sprigs of classic parsley set about it or inserted cloves of old English proverbs, or yet older Latin ones equally commonplace, yet never losing the verity in them, their preservative spice; thy yellow, wrinkled parchment from Harvard hung up framed in thy bachelor quarters (so convenient to the Club); thy cherished eagle of the Society of the Cincinnati, a golden insignia thou polishest up and sportest on occasion; and—be it never omitted—thy high relish for the qualities of M. de Grandvin, through frequent communion with whom thou hast caught much of his generous spirit enhancing what is naturally thine own, yes, and something of his beaming aspect as well; insomuch that unto thee—after him—belong all the titles of good fellowship. Dean of the Burgundians, but I love thee! Though some of the points just cited might of themselves avail to denote thee, Dean, two other characteristics there are which peradventure may serve to signalise. Though a soldier of the Civil War, and a gazetted one, thou at all times, even upon that legal holiday which has undesignedly become the annual commemoration of that war, refrainest from wearing on thy person any memorial thereof. And, ever since the Peace, even as during the entire military contest, no superfluous syllable ever fell from thy lips touching the Southern half of thy country.

Now, as to the personal memorial, honourably worn by so many, if thou declined to wear it, was this because thou wert in sympathy with the spirit of thy deplored New England friend, Charles Sumner—whom, for what was sterling in him, thou didst so sincerely honour, though far from sharing in all his advocated measures? Years ago Grant and Lee joined hands at Appomattox. Art thou such an old-fashioned Roman in thy patriotism that thou wouldst consign to oblivion the fact that thy countrymen, claiming the van of Adam's alleged advance, were but yesterday plunged in patricidal strife? And, for thy never being a partisan animadverter, is that because for all the free thought that beats in thy brain, at heart thou art the captive of Christ, yea, even something of a Christian, and though but dimly conscious of it, perhaps, art not unmindful of the divine text which implies that if sinners abound they are not in vain demarked from the saints by any parallel of latitude. Or, rather, that there are no saints, but that all mankind, not excluding Americans, are sinners—miserable sinners, as even no few Bostonians themselves nowadays contritely respond in the liturgy.

However this be, both the omission and the abstention referred to are in significant contrast with thy words relative to that elder war wherein thy grandfather was one of the "rebels," a contrast emphasised though involuntarily in thy social utterances upon every recurrence of our one national holiday

On the fourth morning of each July, about the tenth hour by the club clock, spruced up in thy goodly person and decked at lapel with the golden eagle suspended by the white-bordered blue ribbon, an order which Washington and Lafayette and thy grandfather and father wore before thee, thou takest thy customary place at the club's bay-window. There thou comfortably settlest thyself till lunch-time, discoursing at whiles with whomsoever may, fortunately for himself, happen to be at hand.

Now thy Fourth-of-July outgivings, though indeed yearly varying in expression, yet in spirit are much the same. Dost thou remember all that thou saidest on the last Fourth, Major? Hardly. But I do; and will try to refresh thy memory by reproducing it, with some accompanying circumstances, and as if all were of to-day.

After gazing out of the open window for a time, noting the strange Sabbatarian quiet of the Avenue, on other week-days so abounding with diversified life, thou mutterest to thyself a strange litany of lamentations touching the general falling-off in the old-time celebration. "Well, well," thou mutterest, "it is getting along now in its second century, this anniversary, and nearly everything falls off with years. In Victoria's reign is Guy Fawkes' Day what it was in Elizabeth's? I trow not. *Sic transit, Sic transit!*"

Here some swift return of thought to its everyday channel causes thee suddenly to wheel in thy revolving chair and face inward. Thou remarkest the vacant lounges and sofas, thou absorbest the drear silence. Is it the tabernacle on a week-day? Evidently, thou bethinkest thee of the many absentees. Anon, with thy ample white handkerchief mopping the beads from thy brow, thou exclaimest, "Shame upon them! Why, even the thermometer, though a creature metallic, is more sensitive than these renegades to the momentous occasion. Sure, the mercury rises to it! But they—they run from it. Now degenerate, not only from their sires, but their own boyhood. Ah, my good sir," giving another impulsive turn to the revolving chair so as directly to face the one person present, a somewhat reserved gentleman of mature years engaged in methodically refolding a letter just perused, "Ah, my good sir, it is your boy who is your true patriot. *He* made on the *Third* for Long Branch or elsewhere? Nay, sir, on the Third, if not before, he lays in his ammunition, his powder-crackers; at early dawn on the blessed

Fourth he crams his breeches-pockets with them, and though in his heedless enthusiasm, mixing them up there with his matches, they get ignited and suddenly begin going off like minute-guns hurried up, making him a spluttering blunderbuss to himself and the crowd, what recks he if but luckily he come out of it unharmed? Another boy, a yet more devoted young acolyte of the Salii, should repeated discharges at last burst his toy-cannon, and he go to Hades for it, what then? *Ducit amor patriae!* That's the inscription, sir, on General Worth's monument you and I pass every day. Ten to one you never noticed it—the inscription, I mean. Ah, but he was a paladin, a homespun paladin, General Worth. And happy in his sur-name, though indeed his *worth* was of another sort than that of the purse."

"And did you personally know the General, Dean?" inquires the solitary auditor, his curiosity here doing away with a taci-turnity seldom yielding but through the persuasive mediation of wine. "Did you, personally, know the General, sir?" "Ay, in-deed!" And, after losing thee in revery awhile, and reminis-cently ejaculating something to thyself, "The last time I saw Will Worth was on the night-boat coming down from Albany —by Jove, it seems but a week or two ago—he then being bound for Mexico to pay his military respects to General Santa Anna in the field. But he came back horizontal who went forth so erect! Ay, but like the great Gustavus, sir, from Lützen field, if dirged yet laurelled. Pray, sir, can you repeat the battle-names on the monumental shaft? Chermbusco, Buena Vista, Resaca de la Palma, San Antonio, Cerro Gordo. There's a val-ley for you of vowels and victory! Ay, and Monterey, too, that superb dash of arms, one inspiring my chivalric friend, Charlie Fenno Hoffman—remember Charlie, sir? No, no; you don't go back so far—inspired his fine lyric." Now, after a moment's pause, to rally the memory belike, thou didst kindle, and springing from thy seat, leaving it spinning on its pivot, thy adorned chest expanded, thou didst sonorously declaim this stanza:—

> "The foe himself recoiled aghast,
>   When striking where he strongest lay,
> We swoopt his flanking batteries past,
> And braving full their murderous blast
>   Stormed home the towers of Monterey!"

Then reseating thee, a little panting, and pressing one hand to thy side: "Ay, stirring deeds beget stirring rhymes. But stirring rhymes bestir overmuch the cardiac arteries in an old fellow like me. Well, well," in reaction lapsing into a muffled mutter, a sort of audible musing, "Well, well—they are gone, both gone, hero and bard—long ago. *Sic transit.*—They sleep, sleep.—*In pace, in pace—Requiescant!*"

And slowly removing thy gold-rimmed glasses and assiduously rubbing them with thy ample handkerchief, in tone a bit tremulous, thou addressest the mild gentleman thy hearer. "The heat of this unwonted season, sir, would not be so inconvenient but for the confounded humidity dampening one's spectacles so. But where, where now was I? Astraying I've been: Let me see——" shutting thine eyes and clapping a hand to brow, "ah, yes, yes—patriotism of boyhood. Well, such a spluttering blunderbuss as I was speaking of a while ago, or rather such a *feu de joie in persona* our venerable friend, Judge van Groot, inadvertently made himself as a boy, recruiting his fagged patriotism on doughnuts and cider in one of those booths which in *auld lang syne* belted about our City Hall Park every Fourth. I hear the sharp, quick percussion even now—see the lad starting up, clapping his hands to his exploding powder-houses, and yet more rapidly withdrawing them, till the booth-keeper put him out by dashing a handy bucket of cider on his trowsers. That was—bless my soul—nigh threescore years ago!—And now? Yesterday with one foot in prunella, his Honour limped off to Saratoga, and, I dare say, sir, without so much as a single powder-cracker in his vest pocket; nay, and very likely never once recalling the circumstances that Saratoga as a great Revolutionary battlefield, or giving name to one, is signally associated with this blessed day." Then after a few moments of meditative silence, "Myndert van Groot is—let me see—yes, about mine own age. His bay-tree, though planted by the rivers of Burgundy, won't flourish more than a hundred years longer.—Well, well—*tempus* does *fugit—Memento mori!*—die we must—consign to dust—leave all!" Here, settling back in thy chair, thine eyes fixed upon vacancy, thou murmurest from thy Horace in quite other tones than those which late rolled forth the Monterey stanza:—

> "The purple vineyard's luscious stores,
> Secured by trebly bolted doors,

Excite in vain your care;
Soon shall the rich and sparkling hoard
Flow largely o'er the festive board
Of your unsparing heir."

Silence again. Then, suddenly brisking up, "But *à propos,* as
the Marquis says"; and, pulling out thy big watch, "ay, the
lunch hour is at hand. Tobias, hither, thou Rose of Sharon,"
summoning a ruddy-cheeked young servitor, "go, see if the
steward has ordered it as I directed, kept that *Chambertin* three
leagues from his refrigerator and the bottles in readiness to be
gently immersed up to the neck—mind, up to the neck in a
water-cooler, the water of its natural temperature at this season. Go, lad, it is important." Then turning to the quiet listener, "Sir, for myself I am not so particular about these matters, but the two friends I expect to dine with me—Jerry Bland
and Captain Don Tempest of the Navy—well, you know them
—are; and one must humour the peculiar tastes of one's friends,
you know." Here, suddenly reminded that an immediate courtesy was due. "Of course, my good sir, you will join us. Nay, I
insist upon it. Not good for a man to be alone, especially on
the immortal Fourth. Tobias, come back. Tut, he's gone. William! Go, say we will dine at the round table in the south-west
corner, and let there be four covers—four, mind."

Even so, Major, or much so, on the last Fourth, sitting in
the club parlour didst thou by turns ruminate and expatiate,
and humorously rail and feelingly evoke the bygone and glow
as in the poetic fervour of youth, and involuntarily sigh the
sigh of old philosophy, till in the end the home-sense of the
eternal sagacity of all things did but result in awakening in
thee but the more vividly thy relish for life and the *Chambertin.*

But on the forenoon of each thirtieth of May, seated—minus
the aforesaid historic decoration—in thy reserved corner of
the club balcony, in graven sort thou lookest down on the
floral march of the *Grand Army.* Then seemed thou even less
intent on returning the greetings from some hale comrade in
the ranks, or less hearty hero borne along in open barouche;
less dwelling, too, on the processional wains of nodding flowers, followed close by nodding plumes of the escort—to thee
and the other veterans—a new generation of Mars—less absorbed by all this, than musing on the many mounds those
same flowers ere nightfall shall dress. Thy constitutional good

spirits seem strangely overcast that day. Thou forgoest the banquet. Nevertheless, it is observable that in the balcony thy empty sleeve is disposed more picturesquely, nay, somehow more conspicuously on that aforesaid thirtieth of every May, than on any other morning of the year. It more catches the eye. Now and then, during pauses in the procession, the crowd on the sidewalk below glance up at it, and expressively, and thou turnest not aside.

"Ah, Major," I said, "I love thee; yes, and it is as much for thy queer little human foibles as thy not-so-common virtues. Come now, for all thy annual megrims, prouder art thou of that empty sleeve of thine than even of thy grandfather's Revolutionary insignia, for *this* thou didst but inherit, the other, conferred on thee at first hand, and by the God of Battles."

Not often dost thou discuss the tactics of thy Virginia campaigns, but what things hast thou told us of its byplay—the scouting, the foraging, the riding up to lovely mansions garrisoned by a faithful old slave or two, servants to lovely damsels more terrible than Mars in their feminine indignation at the insolent invader; in other instances being coquettishly served at an improvised lunch on some broad old piazza by less implacable beauties reduced by the calamities to dispensing hospitality for the enemy's greenbacks. In such and similar passages of the war thou aboundest, passages luckily not susceptible of being formalised into professed history.

But the better for the felicity of thy friends, thou hast more than one string to thy harp, Major. Did any listener ever tire of thy reminiscences of European travel? What signifies that they date so far back, before some of us were born? Even so do sundry inestimable vintages in the Club's cellar. Pleasant it is when weary of the never-ending daily news, the same sort of thing forever, how pleasant to be spirited back by a tale, by some veteran's living voice and eloquent gestures, to a period that is no news at all, a time prior to those more pronounced changes which have come over so few portions of that ancient and manifold world across the Atlantic, a world to which we are bound by unsunderable ties of genealogy.

Highly, Major, didst thou relish that title whereby, as regards so many of us Americans, a rare son of New England with happiest simplicity designated that Elder England, from which his progenitor came—*Our Old Home*. But if thy filial appreciation of the historic Past has something of Nathaniel

Hawthorne in it, the medium, Dean, through which thou re-
callest it, viewing it as through an irradiated vapour, this is
not without a touch of *our incomparable friend,* the Marquis. He, as well thou knowest, never is so happy, never so
blissfully serene, as when wandering in a haze along that enchanted beach.

Among all thy over-sea reminiscences not the least entertaining to us juniors is thy liberal version of that famous *Afternoon in Naples.* In the wee hours, more especially if inspired
by the beaming presence of M. de Grandvin, how affluent
hast thou been on that theme; how vivid in description; and,
for the rest, how frolic, pathetic, indignant, philosophic; and
throughout how catholic and humane. But shall such a recital
be confined to the small group of the convivially elect, brothers
of the *Burgundy?* Savours that not a little of the exclusive?
Have a care, Dean. With even more than is implied in that
term, one not lightly to be applied in a democracy, thou hast,
unbeknown to thee, perhaps, been reproached.

When General Grant, a bigot for his friends—and thou
wert one of his military family in the field—when he, as President, nominated thee consul at that very Naples thou so en-
tertainest us with, what whisper, doubtless started by some rival applicant, what ridiculous whisper, was it buzzed in the
lobbies, that in spite even of Grant's nomination, stranded
thee unconfirmed by the Senate? But "Pshaw!" thou exclaimest,
amused at the enthusiasm of sophomores, when, ending thy
Neapolitan romance we contendingly fire away with:—

"Bravissimo!"

"Encore!"

"Write it out, Major!"

"Put it in verse!"

"Good, it will immortalise thee!"

"And consider, Dean, the glory redounding to the Club!"

To all which thy expression "Pshaw!" and the politely proffered snuff-box by way of an added parry, and little more do
we get from thee, O Dean of the Burgundians!

Well, Major, what thou in thy impatience of pen-drudgery
and indifference to any reputation except that old-fashioned
one of being a man of honour; what thou, for these reasons,
perchance, never couldst be persuaded to undertake, I, even
I, unsolicited have had the temerity to essay.

And in so doing I have adopted thy earlier rendering of
That Afternoon in Naples ere yet thou begannest to exclaim,

"I don't know what the dogs is the reason, but I can't remember anything", that version seeming to me akin to what engravers call the first-proofs, less free from the blur that ensues after repeated impressions from the plate. Moreover, not unmindful of the enthusiastic injunction, "Put it in verse," I have after a fashion done accordingly. As to the interspersed ballads and ditties—at the which, peradventure, thou mayest stare even as Rip van Winkle, after his resurrection, did at his son—I do assure thee, Dean, they are essentially but thoughts and conceits of thine own, the product of seeds which planted and spontaneously developing in me, eventually effloresced into rhyme.

But to soften the liberty here taken, as well as the licence throughout, yes, and not without hope to propitiate and even please thee, I have so contrived matters that thou personated the part here allotted thee at the special instance of M. de Grandvin; thus in a literary way associating thee with one whose social companionship thou so unaffectedly lovest, and whose magnanimous spirit thou art ever fain to imbibe. Vale!

3. Jack Gentian
(Omitted from the final sketch of him.)

TRUE, hardly to-day art thou what formerly thou wast. Thou thyself sometimes hintest that thy decline has even more than begun. With which confession for warrant some there be—alas for them! who in private are not slow to contribute confirmatory words and enlarge thereon.

"Failing?" says one. "To be sure! And how manifest the signs. In July you see him parrying the sun with his big white umbrella green-line; nevertheless, ere the straw hats yet begin to disappear from the promenade, reassuming his slouched felt sombrero he betakes himself to the street's sunny side." "I have noted that," says another; "but—will you believe it?—late I espied him musing on a shaded bench in Madison Square; in the forenoon it was, too, not far from a seated file of disreputable nondescripts, non-producers in deplorable attire, plunged in lugubrious reveries on their doubtless misspent lives. Yes, and presently he rose, and after looking about him went straight up to a solitary old vagabond, and standing before him seemed making personal inquiries of him, and concluded by putting hand in pocket and bestowing something upon him. Now seems not that an indication of impaired senses?—deliberately to put a premium on improvidence and thriftlessness, or worse?" "You go a little too far there," observes a middle-aged merchant and vestryman, the comfortable president of a charity; "the Major was always benevolent, as officially I have reason to know, always benevolent, but too often, as I hear, unsystematically so; and this unwisdom may very likely increase with years. But I hardly thought that he had any way so far decayed in his sense of what is beseeming in a gentleman whatever his years, as publicly to idle, and in business hours, and in such vicinity as you mention. Besides, those Madison Square benches so frequented by the untidy, how can some of them be otherwise than infected, yes, and with vermin. Dare me," in a tone of real concern, "it were almost enough to banish him from respectable society were it not the esteemed Major and the Dean."

"And with a warm deposit at his bank, too; forget not that, my good sir," gravely observed a waggish young berry-brown cynic in yachtsman's attire, secretly amused at all this. Whereat the respectable vestryman with some severity, "Sir, that has nothing to do with the matter. This is America, Christian America, thank God; where, be it what it may, one's bank account is of no account whatever in an American's estimate of a fellow American." Upon which the elders cast a quiet glance toward the young gentleman, significant of their sense that he had been justly rebuked; and the rebuked wag, as conscious of the fact, assumed a contrite demeanour into which, however, he contrived to infuse a twinkle of irony.

"I was at Mrs. Jones's dinner," volunteered another sexagenarian in an arrested stage of development between the ear and the silk purse; "I was at Mrs. Jones's dinner the other evening—and, by the way, there was twenty-three million represented by the group, twenty-three million dollars, think of that, so I computed it—and between certain parties there was some random talk about Major Gentian, to the effect that he did well in resigning his place as a leading director of the Dime Savings Bank, considering that he had generally outlived his usefulness."

"The Major ought to have an attendant," says a sunken-cheeked, heron-legged bachelor of uncertain years, a sort of man the natural product of the clubs and club-life, so at least the moralising enemies of clubs would doubtless maintain; "he

ought to have an attendant, at any rate it will come to that before long. Tom Dutcher tells me that at Newport last season,
instead of sedately sitting in white waistcoat and armchair on
piazza talking stocks and dividends like most respectable old
worthies of his kind, the Major more than ever before took to
skylarking with those immature little specimens of humanity,
obstreperous enough of themselves, Malthusian superfluities
of the household, the chastisement of intemperate wedlock,
and the bane, as we all have experienced, of many summer resorts. But you know second childhood has a natural affinity for
the first."

"To be sure!" chimes in a young Crœsus of complexion
pink and white, recently returned from a four-in-hand coach-
ing trip in Scotland. "To be sure! And how tediously, too,
does he repeat in the smoking-room of the *Come-and-Goes,*
where he occasionally resorts, his musty old romances of
travel, and every version varies from the other. His memory
is like wares at the auction—*going, going,* and anon it will be
gone."

"Yes," says yet another, "I was talking with him at the
'Windsor yesterday, and his sporadic ideas were like fishing
smacks lost in a Newfoundland fog."

"Very much so," solemnly remarks a clerical-looking citizen,
a politician high in municipal office; "very much so indeed.
But have you observed one little circumstance, gentlemen, and
weighed its significance as a marked symptom—at least some of
it—of that irreparable change that, alas, comes with years? Major Gentian, though a soldier on the right side in the war, besides being of double Revolutionary descent—so I am told—
nevertheless is far from being that sanguine New Yorker he
used to be, and which in true patriotism we are all bound to
be? What is this, I would like to know, but the natural optimist
doting into the deplorable pessimist."

Indeed, Dean, but they do cut and come again at thee, yes,
even say these things of thee and more. But never a Burgun-
dian among them, our Club harbouring none of that kidney.
Outsiders they are, the profane; the seniors, some of them,
confirmed tipplers of tea, a decoction that enlarges the spleen
and warpest the brain, or lightly floating the spirit for a while
at last lands it in a dry place. However, I will not gainsay
these young roosters and old hens, since on some points upon
which they click-clock the basis of their talk is true enough.
But in the crooked mouth of the invidious, imparting its own

twist to all it utters, in effect even veracity lies. Fail thou yet mayest, Major, but never degenerate. Thou mayest *outlive thy usefulness* (execrable phrase!) but never thy loving-kindness. To the last thou wilt be Jack Gentian; not too dignified to be humane; a democrat, though less of the stump than the heart. And should mortal decline come—which Heaven long defer —and the Black Brunswicker lay siege to thee in thy bachelor tower, thy compatriots, those who best know the true temper of thy genial spirit, would still call thee *Jack* as in the days of their youth, and though debility should then tongue-tie thee, thou wouldst still respond to them out of thy waning eyes.

JOHN MARR

NOTE: The special pathos of this sketch, written as prologue to one of several poems commemorating the long-vanished glory days of certain old forecastle sailors, has to do not only with John Marr's longing for a now phantomlike past but also his inability to find anyone who can listen to his reminiscence understandingly. The autobiographical relevance, with an author who once thought to make his living and coincidentally serve his democratic faith as a teller of tales, hardly needs comment.

JOHN MARR, toward the close of the last century born in America of a mother unknown, and from boyhood up to maturity a sailor under divers flags, disabled at last from further maritime life by a crippling wound received at close quarters with pirates of the Keys, eventually betakes himself for a livelihood to less active employment ashore. There, too, he transfers his rambling disposition acquired as a seafarer.

After a variety of removals, at first as a sail-maker from sea-port to sea-port, then adventurously inland as a rough bench-carpenter, he, finally, in the last-named capacity, settles down about the year 1838 upon what was then a frontier-prairie, sparsely sprinkled with small oak-groves and yet fewer log-houses of a little colony but recently from one of our elder inland States. Here, putting a period to his rovings, he marries.

Ere long a fever, the bane of new settlements on teeming loam, and whose sallow livery was certain to show itself, after an interval, in the complexions of too many of these people, carries off his young wife and infant child. In one coffin, put together by his own hands, they are committed with meager rites to the earth—another mound, though a small one, in the wide prairie, not far from where the mound-builders of a race only conjecturable had left their pottery and bones, one common clay, under a strange terrace serpentine in form.

With an honest stillness in his general mien—swarthy and black-browed, with eyes that could soften or flash, but never harden, yet disclosing at times a melancholy depth—this kinless man had affections which, once placed, not readily could be dislodged or resigned to a substituted object. Being now arrived at middle-life, he resolves never to quit the soil that holds the only beings ever connected with him by love in the family tie. His log-house he lets to a new-comer, one glad enough to get it, and dwells with the household.

While the acuter sense of his bereavement becomes mollified by time, the void at heart abides. Fain, if possible, would he fill that void by cultivating social relations yet nearer than before with a people whose lot he purposes sharing to the end —relations superadded to that mere work-a-day bond arising from participation in the same outward hardships, making reciprocal helpfulness a matter of course. But here, and nobody to blame, he is obstructed.

More familiarly to consort, men of a practical turn must sympathetically converse, and upon topics of real life. But, whether as to persons or events, one cannot always be talking about the present, much less speculating about the future; one must needs recur to the past, which, with the mass of men, where the past is in any personal way a common inheritance, supplies to most practical natures the basis of sympathetic communion.

But the past of John Marr was not the past of these pioneers. Their hands had rested on the plow-tail, his upon the ship's helm. They knew but their own kind and their own usages; to him had been revealed something of the checkered globe. So limited unavoidably was the mental reach, and by consequence the range of sympathy, in this particular band of domestic emigrants, hereditary tillers of the soil, that the ocean, but a hearsay to their fathers, had now through yet deeper inland removal become to themselves little more than a rumor traditional and vague.

They were a staid people; staid through habituation to monotonous hardship; ascetics by necessity not less than through moral bias; nearly all of them sincerely, however narrowly, religious. They were kindly at need, after their fashion; but to a man wonted—as John Marr in his previous homeless sojournings could not but have been—to the free-and-easy tavern-clubs affording cheap recreation of an evening in certain old and comfortable sea-port towns of that time, and yet more familiar with the companionship afloat of the sailors of the same period, something was lacking. That something was geniality, the flower of life springing from some sense of joy in it, more or less. This their lot could not give to these hard-working endurers of the dispiriting malaria,—men to whom a holiday never came,—and they had too much of uprightness and no art at all or desire to affect what they did not really feel. At a corn-husking, their least grave of gatherings, did the lonehearted mariner seek to divert his own thoughts from sadness, and in some degree interest theirs, by adverting to aught removed from the crosses and trials of their personal surroundings, naturally enough he would slide into some marine story or picture, but would soon recoil upon himself and be silent, finding no encouragement to proceed. Upon one such occasion an elderly man—a blacksmith, and at Sunday gatherings an earnest exhorter—honestly said to him, "Friend, we know nothing of that here."

Such unresponsiveness in one's fellow-creatures set apart from factitious life, and by their vocation—in those days little helped by machinery—standing, as it were, next of kin to Nature; this, to John Marr, seemed of a piece with the apathy of Nature herself as envisaged to him here on a prairie where none but the perished mound-builders had as yet left a durable mark.

The remnant of Indians thereabout—all but exterminated in their recent and final war with regular white troops, a war waged by the Red Men for their native soil and natural rights—had been coerced into the occupancy of wilds not very far beyond the Mississippi—wilds *then*, but now the seats of municipalities and States. Prior to that, the bisons, once streaming countless in processional herds, or browsing as in an endless battle-line over, these vast aboriginal pastures, had retreated, dwindled in number, before the hunters, in main a race distinct from the agricultural pioneers, though generally their advance-guard. Such a double exodus of man and beast left the plain a desert, green or blossoming indeed, but almost as forsaken as the Siberian Obi. Save the prairie-hen, sometimes startled from its lurking-place in the rank grass; and, in their migratory season, pigeons, high overhead on the wing, in dense multitudes eclipsing the day like a passing storm-cloud; save these—there being no wide woods with their underwood—birds were strangely few.

Blank stillness would for hours reign unbroken on this prairie. "It is the bed of a dried-up sea," said the companionless sailor—no geologist—to himself, musing at twilight upon the fixed undulations of that immense alluvial expanse bounded only by the horizon, and missing there the stir that, to alert eyes and ears, animates at all times the apparent solitudes of the deep.

But a scene quite at variance with one's antecedents may yet prove suggestive of them. Hooped round by a level rim, the prairie was to John Marr a reminder of ocean.

With some of his former shipmates, *chums* on certain cruises, he had contrived, prior to this last and more remote removal, to keep up a little correspondence at odd intervals. But from tidings of anybody or any sort he, in common with the other settlers, was now cut off; quite cut off, except from such news as might be conveyed over the grassy billows by the last-arrived prairie-schooner—the vernacular term, in those parts and times, for the emigrant-wagon arched high over with sail-cloth, and voyaging across the vast champaign. There was no reachable post-office as yet; not even the rude little receptive box with lid and leather hinges, set up at convenient intervals on a stout stake along some solitary green way, affording a perch for birds, and which, later in the unintermitting advance of the frontier, would perhaps decay into a mossy monument, attesting yet another successive overleaped limit of civilized life; a life which in America can to-day hardly be said to have any western bound but the ocean that washes Asia. Throughout these plains, now in places overpopulous with towns over-opulent; sweeping plains, elsewhere fenced off in every direction into flourishing farms—pale townsmen and hale farmers alike, in part, the descendants of the first sallow settlers; a region that half a century ago produced little for the sustenance of man, but to-day launching its superabundant wheat-harvest on the world;—of this prairie, now everywhere intersected with wire and rail, hardly can it be said that at the period here written of there was so much as a traceable road. To the long-distance traveller the oak-groves, wide apart, and varying in compass and form; these, with recent settlements, yet more widely separate, offered some landmarks; but otherwise he steered by the sun. In early midsummer, even going but from one log-encampment to the next, a journey it might be of hours or good part of a day, travel was much like navigation. In some more enriched depressions between the long, green, graduated swells, smooth as those of ocean becalmed receiving and subduing to its own tranquillity the voluminous surge raised by some far-off hurricane of days previous, here

one would catch the first indication of advancing strangers
either in the distance, as a far sail at sea, by the glistening white
canvas of the wagon, the wagon itself wading through the rank
vegetation and hidden by it, or, failing that, when near to, in
the ears of the team, peeking, if not above the tall tiger-lilies,
yet above the yet taller grass.

Luxuriant, this wilderness; but, to its denizen, a friend left
behind anywhere in the world seemed not alone absent to sight,
but an absentee from existence.

Though John Marr's shipmates could not all have departed
life, yet as subjects of meditation they were like phantoms of
the dead. As the growing sense of his environment threw him
more and more upon retrospective musings, these phantoms,
next to those of his wife and child, became spiritual companions, losing something of their first indistinctness and putting
on at last a dim semblance of mute life; and they were lit by
that aureola circling over any object of the affections in the
past for reunion with which an imaginative heart passionately
yearns.

He invokes there visionary ones,—striving, as it were, to get
into verbal communion with them, or, under yet stronger illusion, reproaching them for their silence:—

> Since as in night's deck-watch ye show,
> Why, lads, so silent here to me,
> Your watchmate of times long ago?
> Once, for all the darkling sea,
> You your voices raised how clearly,
> Striking in when tempest sung;
> Hoisting up the storm-sail cheerly,
> *Life is storm—let storm!* you rung.
> Taking things as fated merely,
> Child-like though the world ye spanned;
> Nor holding unto life too dearly,
> Ye who hold your lives in hand—
> Skimmers, who on oceans four
> Petrels were, and larks ashore.
>
> O, not from memory lightly flung,
> Forgot, like strains no more availing,
> The heart to music haughtier strung;

Nay, frequent near me, never staleing,
Whose good feeling kept ye young.
Like tides that enter creek or stream,
Ye come, ye visit me, or seem
Swimming out from seas of faces,
Alien myriads memory traces,
To enfold me in a dream!

I yearn as ye. But rafts that strain,
Parted, shall they lock again?
Twined we were, entwined, then riven,
Ever to new embracements driven,
Shifting gulf-weed of the main!
And how if one here shift no more,
Lodged by the flinging surge ashore?
Nor less, as now, in eve's decline,
Your shadowy fellowship is mine.
Ye float around me, form and feature:—
Tattooings, ear-rings, love-locks curled;
Barbarians of man's simpler nature,
Unworldly servers of the world.
Yea, present all, and dear to me,
Though shades, or scouring China's sea.

Whither, whither, merchant-sailors,
Whitherward now in roaring gales?
Competing still, ye huntsman-whalers,
In leviathan's wake what boat prevails?
And man-of-war's men, whereaway?
If now no dinned drum beat to quarters
On the wilds of midnight waters—
Foemen looming through the spray;
Do yet your gangway lanterns, streaming,
Vainly strive to pierce below,
When, tilted from the slant plank gleaming,
A brother you see to darkness go?

But, gunmates lashed in shotted canvas,
If where long watch-below ye keep,
Never the shrill *"All hands up hammocks!"*
Breaks the spell that charms your sleep,
And summoning trumps might vainly call,

And booming guns implore—
A beat, a heart-beat musters all,
One heart-beat at heart-core.
It musters. But to clasp, retain;
To see you at the halyards main—
To hear your chorus once again!

DANIEL ORME

NOTE: Another brief exercise in the mode of elegiac commemoration, "Daniel Orme" is probably directly contemporary with *Billy Budd*. It, too, may have been meant as prologue to a poem. Manuscript markings indicate that the story proper (such as it is) was to begin with the third paragraph in the text that follows. But the two prefatory paragraphs are retained here because they suggest how stories commonly developed in Melville's mind; how, starting from some memorable impression of a man's appearance or aspect, he would seek out "the career and experience" that produced it; and how the pursuit of this inquiry might lead at last to some insoluble mystery, all ordinary information proving but "unreliable gossip." It is precisely the presentational logic of *Billy Budd*.

A PROFOUND portrait-painter like Titian or our famous countryman Stewart, what such an observer sees in any face he may earnestly study, that essentially is the man. To disentangle his true history from contemporary report is superfluous. Not so with us who are scarce Titians and Stewarts. Occasionally we are struck by some exceptional aspect instantly awakening our interest. But it is an interest that in its ignorance is full of commonplace curiosity. We try to ascertain from somebody the career and experience of the man, or may seek to obtain the information from himself. But what we hear from others may prove but unreliable gossip, and he himself, if approached, prove uncommunicative. In short, in most instances he turns out to be like a meteoric stone in a field. There it lies. The neighbours have their say about it, and an odd enough say it may prove. But what is it? Whence did it come? In what unimaginable sphere did it get that strange, igneous, metallic look, the kine now cropping the dewy grass about it?

Any attempt to depict such a character as is here suggested must be an imperfect one. Nevertheless, it is a man of this description who is the subject of the present essay at a sketch.

A sailor's name as it appears on a crew-list is not always his real name, nor in every instance does it indicate his country. This premised, be it said that by the name at the head of this

424

writing long went an old man-of-war's man of whose earlier history it may verily be said that nobody knew anything but himself; and it was idle to seek it in that quarter. Conscientious, constantly so, in discharging his duties, the respect of his officers naturally followed. And for his fellow-sailors, if none had reason to like one so unlike themselves, none dared to take the slightest liberties with him. Any approach to it, and his eye was a tutoring and deterring one. Getting in years at last, he was retired as captain of a top, and assigned to a lower grade and post, namely, at the foot of the mainmast, his business there being simply to stand by, to let go, and make fast. But even this, with the night-watches, ere long exacted too much from a sailor, a septuagenarian. In brief, he belays his last halyard, and slips into obscure moorings ashore. Whatever his disposition may originally have been, there, in his latter cruise at least, had he been specially noted for his unsociability. Not that he was gruff like some marine veterans with the lumbago, nor stealthily taciturn like an Indian; but moody, frequently muttering to himself. And from such muttered soliloquy he would sometimes start, and with a look or gesture so uncheerfully peculiar that the Calvinistic imagination of a certain frigate's chaplain construed it into remorseful condemnation of some dark deed in the past.

His features were large, strong, cast as in iron; but the effect of a cartridge explosion had peppered all below the eyes with dense dottings of black-blue. When according to custom he as mainmast man used to doff his hat in less laconic speech with the officer-of-the-deck, his tanned brow showed like October's tawny moon revealed in crescent above an ominous cloud. Along with his moody ways, was it this uncanny physical aspect, the result of a mere chance, was it this, and this alone, that had suggested the germ of the rumour among certain afterguardsmen that in earlier life he had been a bucanier of the Keys and the Gulf, one of Lafitte's murderous crew? Certain it is, he had once served on a letter-of-marque.

In stature, though bowed somewhat in the shoulders, akin to the champion of Gath. Hands heavy and hard; short nails like withered horn. A powerful head, and shaggy. An iron-gray beard broad as a commodore's pennant, and about the mouth indelibly streaked with the moodily dribbled tobacco juice of all his cruises. In his day watch-below silently couched by himself on the gun-deck in a bay between black cannon, he might have suggested an image of the Great Grizzly of the California

Sierras, his coat the worse for wear, grim in his last den awaiting the last hour.

In his shore moorings—hard by the waters, not very far from
the docks—what with his all-night-in and easier lot in
every particular, with choice of associates when he desired
them, which was not always, happily he lost most of his gruff-
ness as the old mastiff of the mainmast exposed to all
weathers and with salt-horse for his diet. A stranger accosting
him sunning himself upon some old spar on the strand, and
kindly saluting him there, would receive no surly response,
and if more than mere salutation was exchanged, would probably go away with the impression that he had been talking
with an interesting oddity, a salt philosopher, not lacking in
a sort of grim common-sense.

After being ashore for a period, a singularity in his habits
was remarked. At times, but only when he might think himself
quite alone, he would roll aside the bosom of his darned
Guernsey frock and steadfastly contemplate something on his
body. If by chance discovered in this, he would quickly con-
ceal all and growl his resentment.

This peculiarity awakening the curiosity of certain idle
observers, lodgers under the same roof with him, and none
caring to be so bold as to question him as to the reason of it,
or to ask what it was on his body, a drug was enlisted as a
means of finding out the secret. In prudent quantities it was
slyly slipped into his huge bowl of tea at supper. Next morning a certain old-clothes-man whispered to his gossips the result
of his sorry intrusion overnight.

Drawing them into a corner, and looking around furtively,
"Listen," said he, and told them an eerie story, following it
up with shuddering conjectures, vague enough, but dear to
the superstitious and ignorant mind. What he had really
discovered was this: a crucifix in indigo and vermilion tattooed on the chest and on the side of the heart. Slanting across
the crucifix and paling the pigment there ran a whitish scar,
long and thin, such as might ensue from the slash of a cutlass
imperfectly parried or dodged. The cross of the Passion is often
tattooed upon the sailor, upon the forearm generally, sometimes, though but rarely, on the trunk. As for the scar, the old
mastman had in legitimate naval service known what it was
to repel boarders and not without receiving a sabre mark from
them. It may be. The gossips of the lodging, however, took another view of the discovery, and at last reported to the land-

lady that the old sailor was a sort of *man forbid,* a man branded
by the Evil Spirit, and it would be well to get rid of him, lest
the charm in the horse-shoe nailed over the house-door should
be fatally counteracted and be naught. The good woman, however, was a sensible lady with no belief in the horse-shoe,
though she tolerated it, and as the old mastman was regular in
his weekly dues, and never made noise or gave trouble, she
turned a deaf ear to all solicitations against him.

Since in his presence it was ever prudently concealed, the
old mariner was not then aware of underhand proceedings. At
sea it had never come to his ears that some of his shipmates
thought him a bucanier, for there was a quiet leonine droop
about the angles of his mouth that said—*hands off.* So now
he was ignorant of the circumstances that the same rumour had
followed him ashore. Had his habits been social, he would
have socially felt the effect of this and cast about in vain for
the cause; whether having basis or not, some ill-report is in
certain instances like what sailors call a *dry tempest,* during
which there is neither rain nor lightning, though none the
less the viewless and intangible winds make a shipwreck and
then ask—who did it?

So Orme pursued his solitary way with not much from without to disturb him. But Time's moments still keep descending
upon the quietest hour, and though it were adamant they
would wear it. In his retirement the superannuated giant begins to mellow down into a sort of animal decay. In hard,
rude natures, especially such as have passed their lives among
the elements, farmers or sailors, this animal decay mostly af-
fects the memory by casting a haze over it; not seldom, it softens
the heart as well, besides more or less, perhaps, drowsing the
conscience, innocent or otherwise.

But let us come to the close of a sketch necessarily imperfect. One fine Easter Day, following a spell of rheumatic
weather, Orme was discovered alone and dead on a height
overlooking the seaward sweep of the great haven ·to whose
shore, in his retirement from sea, he had moored. It was an
evened terrace, destined for use in war, but in peace neglected
and offering a sanctuary for anybody. Mounted on it was an
obsolete battery of rusty guns. Against one of these he was
found leaning, his legs stretched out before him; his clay pipe
broken in twain, the vacant bowl and no spillings from it, attesting that his pipe had been smoked out to the last of its contents. He faced the outlet to the ocean. The eyes were open,

still continuing in death the vital glance fixed on the hazy waters and the dim-seen sails coming and going or at anchor near by. What had been his last thoughts? If aught of reality lurked in the rumours concerning him, had remorse, had penitence any place in those thoughts? Or was there just nothing of either? After all, were his moodiness and mutterings, his strange freaks, starts, eccentric shrugs and grimaces, were these but the grotesque additions like the wens and knobs and distortions of the trunk of an old chance apple-tree in an inclement upland, not only beaten by many storms, but also obstructed in its natural development by the chance of its having first sprouted among hard-packed rock? In short, that fatality, no more encrusting him, made him what he came to be? Even admitting that there was something dark that he chose to keep to himself, what then? Such reticence may sometimes be more for the sake of others than one's self. No, let us believe that the animal decay before mentioned still befriended him to the close, and that he fell asleep recalling through the haze of memory many a far-off scene of the wide world's beauty dreamily suggested by the hazy waters before him.

He lies buried among other sailors, for whom also strangers performed one last rite in a lonely plot overgrown with wild eglantine uncared for by man.

BILLY BUDD, SAILOR
(*An inside narrative*)

DEDICATED

TO

JACK CHASE

ENGLISHMAN

Wherever that great heart may now be
Here on Earth or harbored in Paradise

Captain of the Maintop
in the year 1843
in the U.S. Frigate
United States

NOTE: First published in 1924, this last and, next to *Moby-Dick*, greatest of Melville's tales also began as headnote to a poem, the haunting ballad that fills out the last chapter of the completed work. (Completed, but never made into a fair copy for the printer.) The text used here—except in the last lines of the ballad, where alternate readings seem preferable to the editor—is the "definitive" Reading Text prepared by Harrison Hayford and Merton M. Sealts, Jr., and is reprinted by kind permission of the University of Chicago Press (© 1962 University of Chicago).

Interpretive commentaries on *Billy Budd* are legion. Those on record by 1962 are reviewed in Professors Hayford's and Sealts's long introduction or listed in their bibliography. My own thoughts on the story—which now seem to me to *under*-state, if anything, the power and beauty of this "inside narrative" as it lives on in the mind—are written out in *The Example of Melville*, 183-203.

1

IN THE time before steamships, or then more frequently than now, a stroller along the docks of any considerable seaport would occasionally have his attention arrested by a group of bronzed mariners, man-of-war's men or merchant sailors in holiday attire, ashore on liberty. In certain instances they would flank, or like a bodyguard quite surround, some superior figure of their own class, moving along with them like Aldebaran among the lesser lights of his constellation. That signal object was the "Handsome Sailor" of the less prosaic time alike of the military and merchant navies. With no perceptible trace of the vainglorious about him, rather with the offhand unaffectedness of natural regality, he seemed to accept the spontaneous homage of his shipmates.

A somewhat remarkable instance recurs to me. In Liverpool, now half a century ago, I saw under the shadow of the great dingy street-wall of Prince's Dock (an obstruction long since removed) a common sailor so intensely black that he must needs have been a native African of the unadulterate blood of Ham—a symmetric figure much above the average height. The two ends of a gay silk handkerchief thrown loose about the neck danced upon the displayed ebony of his chest, in his ears were big hoops of gold, and a Highland bonnet with a tartan band set off his shapely head. It was a hot noon in July; and his face, lustrous with perspiration, beamed with barbaric good humor. In jovial sallies right and left, his white teeth flashing into view, he rollicked along, the center of a company of his shipmates. These were made up of such an assortment of tribes and complexions as would have well fitted them to be marched up by Anacharsis Cloots before the bar of the first French Assembly as Representatives of the Human Race. At each spontaneous tribute rendered by the wayfarers to this black pagod of a fellow—the tribute of a pause and stare, and less frequently an exclamation—the motley retinue showed that they took that sort of pride in the evoker of it which the Assyrian priests doubtless showed for their grand sculptured Bull when the faithful prostrated themselves.

To return. If in some cases a bit of a nautical Murat in setting forth his person ashore, the Handsome Sailor of the period in question evinced nothing of the dandified Billy-be-Dam, an amusing character all but extinct now, but occasionally to be encountered, and in a form yet more amusing than the original, at the tiller of the boats on the tempestuous Erie Canal or, more likely, vaporing in the groggeries along the towpath. Invariably a proficient in his perilous calling, he was also more or less of a mighty boxer or wrestler. It was strength and beauty. Tales of his prowess were recited. Ashore he was the champion; afloat the spokesman; on every suitable occasion always foremost. Close-reefing topsails in a gale, there he was, astride the weather yardarm-end, foot in the Flemish horse as stirrup, both hands tugging at the earing as at a bridle, in very much the attitude of young Alexander curbing the fiery Bucephalus. A superb figure, tossed up as by the horns of Taurus against the thunderous sky, cheerily hallooing to the strenuous file along the spar.

The moral nature was seldom out of keeping with the physical make. Indeed, except as toned by the former, the comeliness and power, always attractive in masculine conjunction, hardly could have drawn the sort of honest homage the Handsome Sailor in some examples received from his less gifted associates.

Such a cynosure, at least in aspect, and something such too in nature, though with important variations made apparent as the story proceeds, was welkin-eyed Billy Budd—or Baby Budd, as more familiarly, under circumstances hereafter to be given, he at last came to be called—aged twenty-one, a foretopman of the British fleet toward the close of the last decade of the eighteenth century. It was not very long prior to the time of the narration that follows that he had entered the King's service, having been impressed on the Narrow Seas from a homeward-bound English merchantman into a seventy-four outward bound, H.M.A. *Bellipotent;* which ship, as was not unusual in those hurried days, having been obliged to put to sea short of her proper complement of men. Plump upon Billy at first sight in the gangway the boarding officer, Lieutenant Ratcliffe, pounced, even before the merchantman's crew was formally mustered on the quarter-deck for his deliberate inspection. And him only he elected. For whether it was because the other men when ranged before him showed to ill advantage after Billy, or whether he had some scruples in view of the merchantman's being rather short-handed, however it might be, the officer contented himself with his first spontaneous choice. To the surprise of the ship's company, though much to the lieutenant's satisfaction, Billy made no demur. But, indeed, any demur would have been as idle as the protest of a goldfinch popped into a cage.

Noting this uncomplaining acquiescence, all but cheerful, one might say, the shipmaster turned a surprised glance of silent reproach at the sailor. The shipmaster was one of those worthy mortals found in every vocation, even the humbler ones—the sort of person whom everybody agrees in calling "a respectable man." And—nor so strange to report as it may appear to be—though a ploughman of the troubled waters, lifelong contending with the intractable elements, there was nothing this honest soul at heart loved better than simple peace and quiet. For the rest, he was fifty or thereabouts, a little inclined to corpulence, a prepossessing face, unwhiskered, and of an agreeable color—a rather full face, humanely intelligent in expression. On a fair day with a fair wind and all going well, a certain musical chime in his voice seemed to be the veritable unobstructed outcome of the innermost man. He had much prudence, much conscientiousness, and there were occasions when these virtues were the cause of overmuch disquietude in him. On a passage, so long as his craft was in any proximity to land, no sleep for Captain Graveling. He took to heart those serious responsibilities not so heavily borne by some shipmasters.

Now while Billy Budd was down in the forecastle getting his kit together, the *Bellipotent*'s lieutenant, burly and bluff, nowise disconcerted by Captain Graveling's omitting to proffer the customary hospitalities on an occasion so unwelcome to him, an omission simply caused by preoccupation of thought, unceremoniously invited himself into the cabin, and also to a flask from the spirit locker, a receptacle which his experienced eye instantly discovered. In fact he was one of those sea dogs in whom all the hardship and peril of naval life in the great prolonged wars of his time never impaired the natural instinct for sensuous enjoyment. His duty he always faithfully did; but duty is sometimes a dry obligation, and he was for irrigating its aridity, whensoever possible, with a fertilizing decoction of strong waters. For the cabin's proprietor there was nothing left but to play the part of the enforced host with whatever grace and alacrity were practicable. As necessary adjuncts to the flask, he silently placed tumbler and water jug before the irrepressible guest. But excusing himself from partaking just then, he dismally watched the unembarrassed officer deliberately diluting his grog a little, then tossing it off in three swallows, pushing the empty tumbler away, yet not so far as to be beyond easy reach, at the same time settling himself in his seat and smacking his lips with high satisfaction, looking straight at the host.

These proceedings over, the master broke the silence; and there lurked a rueful reproach in the tone of his voice: "Lieutenant, you are going to take my best man from me, the jewel of 'em."

"Yes, I know," rejoined the other, immediately drawing back the tumbler preliminary to a replenishing. "Yes, I know. Sorry."

"Beg pardon, but you don't understand, Lieutenant. See here, now. Before I shipped that young fellow, my forecastle was a rat-pit of quarrels. It was black times, I tell you, aboard the *Rights* here. I was worried to that degree my pipe had no comfort for me. But Billy came; and it was like a Catholic priest striking peace in an Irish shindy. Not that he preached to them or said or did anything in particular; but a virtue went out of him, sugaring the sour ones. They took to him like hornets to treacle; all but the buffer of the gang, the big shaggy chap with the fire-red whiskers. He indeed, out of envy, perhaps, of the newcomer, and thinking such a "sweet and pleasant fellow," as he mockingly designated him to the others, could hardly have the spirit of a gamecock, must needs bestir himself in trying to get up an ugly row with him. Billy forebore with him and reasoned with him in a pleasant way—he is something like myself, Lieutenant, to whom aught like a quarrel is hateful—but nothing served. So, in the second dogwatch one day, the Red Whiskers in presence of the others, under pretense of showing Billy just whence a sirloin steak was cut—for the fellow had once been a butcher—insultingly gave him a dig under the ribs. Quick as lightning Billy let fly his arm. I dare say he never meant to do quite as much as he did, but anyhow he gave the burly fool a terrible drubbing. It took about half a minute, I should think. And, lord bless you, the lubber was astonished at the celerity. And will you believe it, Lieutenant, the Red Whiskers now really loves Billy—loves him, or is the biggest hypocrite that ever I heard of. But they all love him. Some of 'em do his washing, darn his old trousers for him; the carpenter is at odd times making a pretty little chest of drawers for him. Anybody will do anything for Billy Budd; and it's the happy family here. But now, Lieutenant, if that young fellow goes—I know how it will be aboard the *Rights*. Not again very soon shall I, coming up from dinner, lean over the capstan smoking a quiet pipe—no, not very soon again, I think. Ay, Lieutenant, you are going to take away the jewel of 'em; you are going to take away my peacemaker!" And with that the good soul had really some ado in checking a rising sob.

"Well," said the lieutenant, who had listened with amused interest to all this and now was waxing merry with his tipple; "well, blessed are the peacemakers, especially the fighting peacemakers. And such are the seventy-four beauties some of which you see poking their noses out of the portholes of yonder warship lying to for me," pointing through the cabin window at the *Bellipotent*. "But courage! Don't look so downhearted, man. Why, I pledge you in advance the royal approbation. Rest assured that His Majesty will be delighted to know that in a time when his hardtack is not sought for by sailors with such avidity as should be, a time also when some shipmasters privily resent the borrowing from them a tar or two for the service; His Majesty, I say, will be delighted to learn that *one* shipmaster at least cheerfully surrenders to the King the flower of his flock, a sailor who with equal loyalty makes no dissent.—But where's my beauty? Ah," looking through the cabin's open door, "here he comes; and, by Jove, lugging along his chest—Apollo with his portmanteau!—My man," stepping out to him, "you can't take that big box aboard a warship. The boxes there are mostly shot boxes. Put your duds in a bag, lad. Boot and saddle for the cavalryman, bag and hammock for the man-of-war's man."

The transfer from chest to bag was made. And, after seeing his man into the cutter and then following him down, the lieutenant pushed off from the *Rights-of-Man*. That was the merchant ship's name, though by her master and crew abbreviated in sailor fashion into the *Rights*. The hardheaded Dundee owner was a staunch admirer of Thomas Paine, whose book in rejoinder to Burke's arraignment of the French Revolution had then been published for some time and had gone everywhere. In christening his vessel after the title of Paine's volume the man of Dundee was something like his contemporary shipowner, Stephen Girard of Philadelphia, whose sympathies, alike with his native land and its liberal philosophers, he evinced by naming his ships after Voltaire, Diderot, and so forth.

But now, when the boat swept under the merchantman's stern, and officer and oarsmen were noting—some bitterly and others with a grin—the name emblazoned there; just then it was that the new recruit jumped up from the bow where the coxswain had directed him to sit, and waving hat to his silent shipmates sorrowfully looking over at him from the taffrail, bade the lads a genial good-bye. Then, making a salutation as to the ship herself, "And good-bye to you too, old *Rights-of-Man*."

"Down, sir!" roared the lieutenant, instantly assuming all the rigor of his rank, though with difficulty repressing a smile.

To be sure, Billy's action was a terrible breach of naval decorum. But in that decorum he had never been instructed; in consideration of which the lieutenant would hardly have been so energetic in reproof but for the concluding farewell to the ship. This he rather took as meant to convey a covert sally on the new recruit's part, a sly slur at impressment in general, and that of himself in especial. And yet, more likely, if satire it was in effect, it was hardly so by intention, for Billy, though happily endowed with the gaiety of high health, youth, and a free heart, was yet by no means of a satirical turn. The will to it and the sinister dexterity were alike wanting. To deal in double meanings and insinuations of any sort was quite foreign to his nature.

As to his enforced enlistment, that he seemed to take pretty much as he was wont to take any vicissitude of weather. Like the animals, though no philosopher, he was, without knowing it, practically a fatalist. And it may be that he rather liked this adventurous turn in his affairs, which promised an opening into novel scenes and martial excitements.

Aboard the *Bellipotent* our merchant sailor was forthwith rated as an able seaman and assigned to the starboard watch of the foretop. He was soon at home in the service, not at all disliked for his unpretentious good looks and a sort of genial happy-go-lucky air. No merrier man in his mess: in marked contrast to certain other individuals included like himself among the impressed portion of the ship's company; for these when not actively employed were sometimes, and more particularly in the last dogwatch when the drawing near of twilight induced revery, apt to fall into a saddish mood which in some partook of sullenness. But they were not so young as our foretopman, and no few of them must have known a hearth of some sort, others may have had wives and children left, too probably, in uncertain circumstances, and hardly any but must have had acknowledged kith and kin, while for Billy, as will shortly be seen, his entire family was practically invested in himself.

2

THOUGH our new-made foretopman was well received in the top and on the gun decks, hardly here was he that cynosure he had previously been among tnose minor ship's companies of the merchant marine, with which companies only had he hitherto consorted.

He was young; and despite his all but fully developed frame, in aspect looked even younger than he really was, owing to a lingering adolescent expression in the as yet smooth face all but feminine in purity of natural complexion but where, thanks to his seagoing, the lily was quite suppressed and the rose had some ado visibly to flush through the tan.

To one essentially such a novice in the complexities of factitious life, the abrupt transition from his former and simpler sphere to the ampler and more knowing world of a great warship; this might well have abashed him had there been any conceit or vanity in his composition. Among her miscellaneous multitude, the *Bellipotent* mustered several individuals who however inferior in grade were of no common natural stamp, sailors more signally susceptive of that air which continuous martial discipline and repeated presence in battle can in some degree impart even to the average man. As the Handsome Sailor, Billy Budd's position aboard the seventy-four was something analogous to that of a rustic beauty transplanted from the provinces and brought into competition with the highborn dames of the court. But this change of circumstances he scarce noted. As little did he observe that something about him provoked an ambiguous smile in one or two harder faces among the bluejackets. Nor less unaware was he of the peculiar favorable effect his person and demeanor had upon the more intelligent gentlemen of the quarter-deck. Nor could this well have been otherwise. Cast in a mold peculiar to the finest physical examples of those Englishmen in whom the Saxon strain would seem not at all to partake of any Norman or other admixture, he showed in face that humane look of reposeful good nature which the Greek sculptor in some instances gave to his heroic strong man, Hercules. But this again was subtly modified by another and pervasive quality. The ear, small and shapely, the arch of the foot, the curve in mouth and nostril, even the indurated hand dyed to the orange-tawny of the toucan's bill, a hand telling alike of the halyards and tar bucket; but, above all, something in the mobile expression, and every chance attitude and movement, something suggestive of a mother eminently favored by Love and the Graces; all this strangely indicated a lineage in direct contradiction to his lot. The mysteriousness here became less mysterious through a matter of fact elicited when Billy at the capstan was being formally mustered into the service. Asked by the officer, a small, brisk little gentleman as it chanced, among other questions, his place of birth, he replied, "Please, sir, I don't know."

"Don't know where you were born? Who was your father?"

"God knows, sir."

Struck by the straightforward simplicity of these replies, the officer next asked, "Do you know anything about your beginning?"

"No, sir. But I have heard that I was found in a pretty silk-lined basket hanging one morning from the knocker of a good man's door in Bristol."

"*Found,* say you? Well," throwing back his head and looking up and down the new recruit; "well, it turns out to have been a pretty good find. Hope they'll find some more like you, my man; the fleet sadly needs them."

Yes, Billy Budd was a foundling, a presumable by-blow, and, evidently, no ignoble one. Noble descent was as evident in him as in a blood horse.

For the rest, with little or no sharpness of faculty or any trace of the wisdom of the serpent, nor yet quite a dove, he possessed that kind and degree of intelligence going along with the unconventional rectitude of a sound human creature, one to whom not yet has been proffered the questionable apple of knowledge. He was illiterate; he could not read, but he could sing, and like the illiterate nightingale was sometimes the composer of his own song.

Of self-consciousness he seemed to have little or none, or about as much as we may reasonably impute to a dog of Saint Bernard's breed.

Habitually living with the elements and knowing little more of the land than as a beach, or, rather, that portion of the terraqueous globe providentially set apart for dance-houses, doxies, and tapsters, in short what sailors call a "fiddler's green," his simple nature remained unsophisticated by those moral obliquities which are not in every case incompatible with that manufacturable thing known as respectability. But are sailors, frequenters of fiddlers' greens, without vices? No; but less often than with landsmen do their vices, so called, partake of crookedness of heart, seeming less to proceed from viciousness than exuberance of vitality after long constraint: frank manifestations in accordance with natural law. By his original constitution aided by the co-operating influences of his lot, Billy in many respects was little more than a sort of upright barbarian, much such perhaps as Adam presumably might have been ere the urbane Serpent wriggled himself into his company.

And here be it submitted that apparently going to corroborate the doctrine of man's Fall, a doctrine now popularly ignored, it is observable that where certain virtues pristine and unadulterate peculiarly characterize anybody in the external uniform of civilization, they will upon scrutiny seem not to be derived from custom or convention, but rather to be out of keeping with these, as if indeed exceptionally transmitted from a period prior to Cain's city and citified man. The character marked by such qualities has to an unvitiated taste an untampered-with flavor like that of berries, while the man thoroughly civilized, even in a fair specimen of the breed, has to the same moral palate a questionable smack as of a compounded wine. To any stray inheritor of these primitive qualities found, like Caspar Hauser, wandering dazed in any Christian capital of our time, the good-natured poet's famous invocation, near two thousand years ago, of the good rustic out of his latitude in the Rome of the Caesars, still appropriately holds:

> Honest and poor, faithful in word and thought,
> What hath thee, Fabian, to the city brought?

Though our Handsome Sailor had as much of masculine beauty as one can expect anywhere to see; nevertheless, like the beautiful woman in one of Hawthorne's minor tales, there was just one thing amiss in him. No visible blemish indeed, as with the lady; no, but an occasional liability to a vocal defect. Though in the hour of elemental uproar or peril he was everything that a sailor should be, yet under sudden provocation of strong heart-feeling his voice, otherwise singularly musical, as if expressive of the harmony within, was apt to develop an organic hesitancy, in fact more or less of a stutter or even worse. In this particular Billy was a striking instance that the arch interferer, the envious marplot of Eden, still has more or less to do with every human consignment to this planet of Earth. In every case, one way or another he is sure to slip in his little card, as much as to remind us—I too have a hand here.

The avowal of such an imperfection in the Handsome Sailor should be evidence not alone that he is not presented as a conventional hero, but also that the story in which he is the main figure is no romance.

3

AT THE time of Billy Budd's arbitrary enlistment into the *Bellipotent* that ship was on her way to join the Mediterranean fleet. No long time elapsed before the junction was effected. As one of that fleet the seventy-four participated in its movements, though at times on account of her superior sailing qualities, in the absence of frigates, dispatched on separate duty as a scout and at times on less temporary service. But with all this the story has little concernment, restricted as it is to the inner life of one particular ship and the career of an individual sailor.

It was the summer of 1797. In the April of that year had occurred the commotion at Spithead followed in May by a second and yet more serious outbreak in the fleet at the Nore. The latter is known, and without exaggeration in the epithet, as "the Great Mutiny." It was indeed a demonstration more menacing to England than the contemporary manifestoes and conquering and proselyting armies of the French Directory. To the British Empire the Nore Mutiny was what a strike in the fire brigade would be to London threatened by general arson. In a crisis when the kingdom might well have anticipated the famous signal that some years later published along the naval line of battle what it was that, upon occasion England expected of Englishmen; *that* was the time when at the mastheads of the three-deckers and seventy-fours moored in her own roadstead—a fleet the right arm of a Power then all but the sole free conservative one of the Old World—the bluejackets, to be numbered by thousands, ran up with huzzas the

British colors with the union and cross wiped out; by that cancellation transmuting the flag of founded law and freedom defined, into the enemy's red meteor of unbridled and unbounded revolt. Reasonable discontent growing out of practical grievances in the fleet had been ignited into irrational combustion as by live cinders blown across the Channel from France in flames.

The event converted into irony for a time those spirited strains of Dibdin—as a song-writer no mean auxiliary to the English government at that European conjuncture—strains celebrating, among other things, the patriotic devotion of the British tar: "And as for my life, 'tis the King's!"

Such an episode in the Island's grand naval story her naval historians naturally abridge, one of them (William James) candidly acknowledging that fain would he pass it over did not "impartiality forbid fastidiousness." And yet his mention is less a narration than a reference, having to do hardly at all with details. Nor are these readily to be found in the libraries. Like some other events in every age befalling states everywhere, including America, the Great Mutiny was of such character that national pride along with views of policy would fain shade it off into the historical background. Such events cannot be ignored, but there is a considerate way of historically treating them. If a well-constituted individual refrains from blazoning aught amiss or calamitous in his family, a nation in the like circumstance may without reproach be equally discreet.

Though after parleyings between government and the ringleaders, and concessions by the former as to some glaring abuses, the first uprising—that at Spithead—with difficulty was put down, or matters for the time pacified; yet at the Nore the unforeseen renewal of insurrection on a yet larger scale, and emphasized in the conferences that ensued by demands deemed by the authorities not only inadmissible but aggressively insolent, indicated—if the Red Flag did not sufficiently do so—what was the spirit animating the men. Final suppression, however, there was; but only made possible perhaps by the unswerving loyalty of the marine corps and a voluntary resumption of loyalty among influential sections of the crews.

To some extent the Nore Mutiny may be regarded as analogous to the distempering irruption of contagious fever in a frame constitutionally sound, and which anon throws it off.

At all events, of these thousands of mutineers were some of

the tars who not so very long afterwards—whether wholly prompted thereto by patriotism, or pugnacious instinct, or by both—helped to win a coronet for Nelson at the Nile, and the naval crown of crowns for him at Trafalgar. To the mutineers, those battles and especially Trafalgar were a plenary absolution and a grand one. For all that goes to make up scenic naval display and heroic magnificence in arms, those battles, especially Trafalgar, stand unmatched in human annals.

4

IN THIS matter of writing, resolve as one may to keep to the main road, some bypaths have an enticement not readily to be withstood. I am going to err into such a bypath. If the reader will keep me company I shall be glad. At the least, we can promise ourselves that pleasure which is wickedly said to be in sinning, for a literary sin the divergence will be.

Very likely it is no new remark that the inventions of our time have at last brought about a change in sea warfare in degree corresponding to the revolution in all warfare effected by the original introduction from China into Europe of gunpowder. The first European firearm, a clumsy contrivance, was, as is well known, scouted by no few of the knights as a base implement, good enough peradventure for weavers too craven to stand up crossing steel with steel in frank fight. But as ashore knightly valor, though shorn of its blazonry, did not cease with the knights, neither on the seas—though nowadays in encounters there a certain kind of displayed gallantry be fallen out of date as hardly applicable under changed circumstances—did the nobler qualities of such naval magnates as Don John of Austria, Doria, Van Tromp, Jean Bart, the long line of British admirals, and the American Decaturs of 1812 become obsolete with their wooden walls.

Nevertheless, to anybody who can hold the Present at its worth without being inappreciative of the Past, it may be forgiven, if to such an one the solitary old hulk at Portsmouth, Nelson's *Victory*, seems to float there, not alone as the decaying monument of a fame incorruptible, but also as a poetic reproach, softened by its picturesqueness, to the *Monitors* and yet mightier hulls of the European ironclads. And this not altogether because such craft are unsightly, unavoidably lacking the symmetry and grand lines of the old battleships, but equally for other reasons.

There are some, perhaps, who while not altogether inaccessible to that poetic reproach just alluded to, may yet on behalf of the new order be disposed to parry it; and this to the extent of iconoclasm, if need be. For example, prompted by the sight of the star inserted in the *Victory's* quarter-deck designating the spot where the Great Sailor fell, these martial utilitarians may suggest considerations implying that Nelson's ornate publication of his person in battle was not only unnecessary, but not military, nay, savored of foolhardiness and vanity. They may add, too, that at Trafalgar it was in effect nothing less than a challenge to death; and death came; and that but for his bravado the victorious admiral might possibly have survived the battle, and so, instead of having his sagacious dying injunctions overruled by his immediate successor in command, he himself when the contest was decided might have brought his shattered fleet to anchor, a proceeding which might have averted the deplorable loss of life by shipwreck in the elemental tempest that followed the martial one.

Well, should we set aside the more than disputable point whether for various reasons it was possible to anchor the fleet, then plausibly enough the Benthamites of war may urge the above. But the *might-have-been* is but boggy ground to build on. And, certainly, in foresight as to the larger issue of an encounter, and anxious preparations for it—buoying the deadly way and mapping it out, as at Copenhagen—few commanders have been so painstakingly circumspect as this same reckless declarer of his person in fight.

Personal prudence, even when dictated by quite other than selfish considerations, surely is no special virtue in a military man; while an excessive love of glory, impassioning a less burning impulse, the honest sense of duty, is the first. If the name *Wellington* is not so much of a trumpet to the blood as the simpler name *Nelson,* the reason for this may perhaps be inferred from the above. Alfred in his funeral ode on the victor of Waterloo ventures not to call him the greatest soldier of all time, though in the same ode he invokes Nelson as "the greatest sailor since our world began."

At Trafalgar Nelson on the brink of opening the fight sat down and wrote his last brief will and testament. If under the presentiment of the most magnificent of all victories to be crowned by his own glorious death, a sort of priestly motive led him to dress his person in the jewelled vouchers of his own shining deeds; if thus to have adorned himself for the altar and the sacrifice were indeed vainglory, then affectation and fustian is each more heroic line in the great epics and dramas, since in such lines the poet but embodies in verse those exaltations of sentiment that a nature like Nelson, the opportunity being given, vitalizes into acts.

5

YES THE outbreak at the Nore was put down. But not every grievance was redressed. If the contractors, for example were no longer permitted to ply some practices peculiar to their tribe everywhere, such as providing shoddy cloth, rations not sound, or false in the measure; not the less impressment, for one thing, went on. By custom sanctioned for centuries, and judicially maintained by a Lord Chancellor as late as Mansfield, that mode of manning the fleet, a mode now fallen into a sort of abeyance but never formally renounced, it was not practicable to give up in those years. Its abrogation would have crippled the indispensable fleet, one wholly under canvas, no steam power, its innumerable sails and thousands of cannon, everything in short, worked by muscle alone; a fleet the more insatiate in demand for men, because then multiplying its ships of all grades against contingencies present and to come of the convulsed Continent.

Discontent foreran the Two Mutinies, and more or less it lurkingly survived them. Hence it was not unreasonable to apprehend some return of trouble sporadic or general. One instance of such apprehensions: In the same year with this story, Nelson, then Rear Admiral Sir Horatio, being with the fleet off the Spanish coast, was directed by the admiral in command to shift his pennant from the *Captain* to the *Theseus*; and for this reason: that the latter ship having newly arrived on the station from home, where it had taken part in the Great Mutiny, danger was apprehended from the temper of the men; and it was thought that an officer like Nelson was the one, not indeed to terrorize the crew into base subjection, but to win them, by force of his mere presence and heroic personality, back to an allegiance if not as enthusiastic as his own yet as true.

So it was that for a time, on more than one quarter-deck, anxiety did exist. At sea, precautionary vigilance was strained against relapse. At short notice an engagement might come on. When it did, the lieutenants assigned to batteries felt it incumbent on them, in some instances, to stand with drawn swords behind the men working the guns.

6

BUT ON board the seventy-four in which Billy now swung his hammock, very little in the manner of the men and nothing obvious in the demeanor of the officers would have suggested to an ordinary observer that the Great Mutiny was a recent event. In their general bearing and conduct the commissioned officers of a warship naturally take their tone from the commander, that is if he have that ascendancy of character that ought to be his.

Captain the Honorable Edward Fairfax Vere, to give his full title, was a bachelor of forty or thereabouts, a sailor of distinction even in a time prolific of renowned seamen. Though allied to the higher nobility, his advancement had not been altogether owing to influences connected with that circumstance. He had seen much service, been in various engagements, always acquitting himself as an officer mindful of the welfare of his men, but never tolerating an infraction of discipline; thoroughly versed in the science of his profession, and intrepid to the verge of temerity, though never injudiciously so. For his gallantry in the West Indian waters as flag lieutenant under Rodney in that admiral's crowning victory over De Grasse, he was made a post captain.

Ashore, in the garb of a civilian, scarce anyone would have taken him for a sailor, more especially that he never garnished unprofessional talk with nautical terms, and grave in his bearing, evinced little appreciation of mere humor. It was not out of keeping with these traits that on a passage when nothing demanded his paramount action, he was the most undemonstrative of men. Any landsman observing this gentleman not conspicuous by his stature and wearing no pronounced insignia, emerging from his cabin to the open deck, and noting the silent deference of the officers retiring to leeward, might have taken him for the King's guest, a civilian aboard the King's ship, some highly honorable discreet envoy on his way to an important post. But in fact this unobtrusiveness of demeanor may have proceeded from a certain unaffected modesty of manhood sometimes accompanying a resolute nature, a modesty evinced at all times not calling for pronounced action, which shown in any rank of life suggests a virtue aristocratic in kind. As with some others engaged in various departments of the world's more heroic activities, Captain Vere though practical enough upon occasion would at times betray a certain dreaminess of mood. Standing alone on the weather side of the quarter-deck, one hand holding by the rigging, he would absently gaze off at the blank sea. At the presentation to him then of some minor matter interrupting the current of his thoughts, he would show more or less irascibility; but instantly he would control it.

In the navy he was popularly known by the appellation "Starry Vere." How such a designation happened to fall upon one who whatever his sterling qualities was without any brilliant ones, was in this wise: A favorite kinsman, Lord Denton, a freehearted fellow, had been the first to meet and congratulate him upon his return to England from his West Indian cruise; and but the day previous turning over a copy of Andrew Marvell's poems had lighted, not for the first time, however, upon the lines entitled "Appleton House," the name of one of the seats of their common ancestor, a hero in the German wars of the seventeenth century, in which poem occur the lines:

> This 'tis to have been from the first
> In a domestic heaven nursed,
> Under the discipline severe
> Of Fairfax and the starry Vere.

And so, upon embracing his cousin fresh, from Rodney's great victory wherein he had played so gallant a part, brimming over with just family pride in the sailor of their house, he exuberantly exclaimed, "Give ye joy, Ed; give ye joy, my starry Vere!" This got currency, and the novel prefix serving in fa-

miliar parlance readily to distinguish the *Bellipotent*'s captain
from another Vere his senior, a distant relative, an officer of
like rank in the navy, it remained permanently attached to
the surname.

7

IN VIEW of the part that the commander of the *Bellipotent*
plays in scenes shortly to follow, it may be well to fill out that
sketch of him outlined in the previous chapter.

Aside from his qualities as a sea officer Captain Vere was
an exceptional character. Unlike no few of England's renowned sailors, long and arduous service with signal devotion
to it had not resulted in absorbing and *salting* the entire man.
He had a marked leaning toward everything intellectual. He
loved books, never going to sea without a newly replenished
library, compact but of the best. The isolated leisure, in some
cases so wearisome, falling at intervals to commanders even
during a war cruise, never was tedious to Captain Vere. With
nothing of that literary taste which less heeds the thing conveyed than the vehicle, his bias was toward those books to
which every serious mind of superior order occupying any active post of authority in the world naturally inclines: books
treating of actual men and events no matter of what era—history, biography, and unconventional writers like Montaigne,
who, free from cant and convention, honestly and in the
spirit of common sense philosophize upon realities. In this
line of reading he found confirmation of his own more reserved thoughts—confirmation which he had vainly sought in
social converse, so that as touching most fundamental topics,
there had got to be established in him some positive convictions which he forefelt would abide in him essentially unmodi-
fied so long as his intelligent part remained unimpaired. In
view of the troubled period in which his lot was cast, this was
well for him. His settled convictions were as a dike against
those invading waters of novel opinion social, political, and
otherwise, which carried away as in a torrent no few minds
in those days, minds by nature not inferior to his own. While
other members of that aristocracy to which by birth he belonged were incensed at the innovators mainly because their
theories were inimical to the privileged classes, Captain Vere

disinterestedly opposed them not alone because they seemed to him insusceptible of embodiment in lasting institutions, but at war with the peace of the world and the true welfare of mankind.

With minds less stored than his and less earnest, some officers of his rank, with whom at times he would necessarily consort, found him lacking in the companionable quality, a dry and bookish gentleman, as they deemed. Upon any chance withdrawal from their company one would be apt to say to another something like this: "Vere is a noble fellow, Starry Vere. 'Spite the gazettes, Sir Horatio" (meaning him who became Lord Nelson) "is at bottom scarce a better seaman or fighter. But between you and me now, don't you think there is a queer streak of the pedantic running through him? Yes, like the King's yarn in a coil of navy rope?"

Some apparent ground there was for this sort of confidential criticism; since not only did the captain's discourse never fall into the jocosely familiar, but in i'lustrating of any point touching the stirring personages and events of the time he would be as apt to cite some historic character or incident of antiquity as he would be to cite from the moderns. He seemed unmindful of the circumstance that to his bluff company such remote allusions, however pertinent they might really be, were altogether alien to men whose reading was mainly confined to the journals. But considerateness in such matters is not easy to natures constituted like Captain Vere's. Their honesty prescribes to them directness, sometimes far-reaching like that of a migratory fowl that in its flight never heeds when it crosses a frontier.

8

The lieutenants and other commissioned gentlemen forming Captain Vere's staff it is not necessary here to particularize, nor needs it to make any mention of any of the warrant officers. But among the petty officers was one who, having much to do with the story, may as well be forthwith introduced. His portrait I essay, but shall never hit it. This was John Claggart, the master-at-arms. But that sea title may to landsmen seem somewhat equivocal. Originally, doubtless, that petty officer's function was the instruction of the men in the use of arms, sword or cutlass. But very long ago, owing to the advance in gunnery making hand-to-hand encounters less frequent and giving to niter and sulphur the pre-eminence over steel, that function ceased; the master-at-arms of a great warship becoming a sort of chief of police charged among other matters with the duty of preserving order on the populous lower gun decks.

Claggart was a man about five-and-thirty, somewhat spare and tall, yet of no ill figure upon the whole. His hand was too small and shapely to have been accustomed to hard toil. The face was a notable one, the features all except the chin cleanly cut as those on a Greek medallion; yet the chin, beardless as Tecumseh's, had something of strange protuberant broadness in its make that recalled the prints of the Reverend Dr. Titus Oates, the historic deponent with the clerical drawl in the time of Charles II and the fraud of the alleged Popish Plot. It served Claggart in his office that his eye could cast a tutoring glance. His brow was of the sort phrenologically associated with more than average intellect; silken jet curls partly clustering over it, making a foil to the pallor below, a pallor tinged with a faint shade of amber akin to the hue of time-tinted marbles of old. This complexion, singularly contrasting with the red or deeply bronzed visages of the sailors, and in part the result of his official seclusion from the sunlight, though it was not exactly displeasing, nevertheless seemed to hint of something defective or abnormal in the constitution and blood. But his general aspect and manner were so suggestive of an education and career incongruous with his naval function that when not actively engaged in it he looked like a man of high quality, social and moral, who for reasons of his own was keeping incog. Nothing was known of his former life. It might be that he was an Englishman; and yet there lurked a bit of accent in his speech suggesting that possibly he was not such by birth, but through naturalization in early childhood. Among certain grizzled sea gossips of the gun decks and forecastle went a rumor perdue that the master-at-arms was a *chevalier* who had volunteered into the King's navy by way of compounding for some mysterious swindle whereof he had been arraigned at the King's Bench. The fact that nobody could substantiate this report was, of course, nothing against its secret currency. Such a rumor once started on the gun decks in reference to almost anyone below the rank of a commissioned officer would, during the period assigned to this narrative, have seemed not altogether wanting in credibility to the tarry old wiseacres of a man-of-war crew. And indeed a man of Claggart's accomplishments, without prior nautical experience entering the navy at mature life, as he did, and necessarily allotted at the start to the lowest grade in it; a man, too, who never made allusion to his previous life ashore; these were circumstances which in the dearth of exact knowledge as to his true antecedents opened to the invidious a vague field for unfavorable surmise.

But the sailors' dogwatch gossip concerning him derived a vague plausibility from the fact that now for some period the British navy could so little afford to be squeamish in the matter of keeping up the muster rolls, that not only were press gangs notoriously abroad both afloat and ashore, but there was little or no secret about another matter, namely, that the London police were at liberty to capture any able-bodied suspect, any questionable fellow at large, and summarily ship him to the dockyard or fleet. Furthermore, even among voluntary enlistments there were instances where the motive thereto partook neither of patriotic impulse nor yet of a random desire to experience a bit of sea life and martial adventure. Insolvent debtors of minor grade, together with the promiscuous lame ducks of morality, found in the navy a convenient and secure refuge, secure because, once enlisted aboard a King's ship, they were as much in sanctuary as the transgressor of the Middle Ages harboring himself under the shadow of the altar. Such sanctioned irregularities, which for obvious reasons the government would hardly think to parade at the time and which consequently, and as affecting the least influential class of mankind, have all but dropped into oblivion, lend color to something for the truth whereof I do not vouch, and hence have some scruple in stating; something I remember having seen in print though the book I cannot recall; but the same thing was personally communicated to me now more than forty years ago by an old pensioner in a cocked hat with whom I had a most interesting talk on the terrace at Greenwich, a Baltimore Negro, a Trafalgar man. It was to this effect: In the case of a warship short of hands whose speedy sailing was imperative, the deficient quota, in lack of any other way of making it good, would be eked out by drafts culled direct from the jails. For reasons previously suggested it would not perhaps be easy at the present day directly to prove or disprove the allegation. But allowed as a verity, how significant would it be of England's straits at the time confronted by those wars which like a flight of harpies rose shrieking from the din and dust of the fallen Bastille. That era appears measurably clear to us who look back at it, and but read of it. But to the grandfathers of us graybeards, the more thoughtful of them, the genius of it presented an aspect like that of Camoëns' Spirit of the Cape, an eclipsing menace mysterious and prodigious. Not America was exempt from apprehension. At the height of Napoleon's unexampled conquests, there were Americans who had fought at Bunker Hill who looked forward to the possibility that the Atlantic might prove no barrier against the ultimate schemes of this French portentous upstart from the revolutionary chaos who seemed in act of fulfilling judgment prefigured in the Apocalypse.

But the less credence was to be given to the gun-deck talk touching Claggart, seeing that no man holding his office in a man-of-war can ever hope to be popular with the crew. Besides, in derogatory comments upon anyone against whom they have a grudge, or for any reason or no reason mislike, sailors are much like landsmen: they are apt to exaggerate or romance it.

About as much was really known to the *Bellipotent*'s tars of the master-at-arms' career before entering the service as an astronomer knows about a comet's travels prior to its first observable appearance in the sky. The verdict of the sea quidnuncs has been cited only by way of showing what sort of moral impression the man made upon rude uncultivated natures whose conceptions of human wickedness were necessarily of the narrowest, limited to ideas of vulgar rascality—a thief among the swinging hammocks during a night watch, or the man-brokers and land-sharks of the seaports.

It was no gossip, however, but fact that though, as before hinted, Claggart upon his entrance into the navy was, as a novice, assigned to the least honorable section of a man-of-war's crew, embracing the drudgery, he did not long remain there. The superior capacity he immediately evinced, his constitutional sobriety, an ingratiating deference to superiors, together with a peculiar ferreting genius manifested on a singular occasion; all this, capped by a certain austere patriotism, abruptly advanced him to the position of master-at-arms.

Of this maritime chief of police the ship's corporals, so called, were the immediate subordinates, and compliant ones; and this, as is to be noted in some business departments ashore, almost to a degree inconsistent with entire moral volition. His place put various converging wires of underground influence under the chief's control, capable when astutely worked through his understrappers of operating to the mysterious discomfort, if nothing worse, of any of the sea commonalty.

9

LIFE IN the foretop well agreed with Billy Budd. There, when not actually engaged on the yards yet higher aloft, the topmen, who as such had been picked out for youth and activity, constituted an aerial club lounging at ease against the smaller stun'sails rolled up into cushions, spinning yarns like the lazy gods, and frequently amused with what was going on in the busy world of the decks below. No wonder then that a young fellow of Billy's disposition was well content in such society. Giving no cause of offense to anybody, he was always alert at a call. So in the merchant service it had been with him. But now such a punctiliousness in duty was shown that his topmates would sometimes good-naturedly laugh at him for it. This heightened alacrity had its cause, namely, the impression made upon him by the first formal gangway-punishment he had ever witnessed, which befell the day following his impressment. It had been incurred by a little fellow, young, a novice after-guardsman absent from his assigned post when the ship was being put about; a dereliction resulting in a rather serious hitch to that maneuver, one demanding instantaneous promptitude in letting go and making fast. When Billy saw the culprit's naked back under the scourge, gridironed with red welts and worse, when he marked the dire expression in the liberated man's face as with his woolen shirt flung over him by the executioner he rushed forward from the spot to bury himself in the crowd, Billy was horrified. He resolved that never through remissness would he make himself liable to such a visitation or do or omit aught that might merit even verbal reproof. What then was his surprise and concern when ultimately he found himself getting into petty trouble occasionally about such matters as the stowage of his bag or something amiss in his hammock, matters under the police oversight of the ship's corporals of the lower decks, and which brought down on him a vague threat from one of them.

So heedful in all things as he was, how could this be? He could not understand it, and it more than vexed him. When he spoke to his young topmates about it they were either lightly incredulous or found something comical in his unconcealed anxiety. "Is it your bag, Billy?" said one. "Well, sew yourself up in it, bully boy, and then you'll be sure to know if anybody meddles with it."

Now there was a veteran aboard who because his years began to disqualify him for more active work had been recently assigned duty as mainmastman in his watch, looking to the gear belayed at the rail roundabout that great spar near the deck. At off-times the foretopman had picked up some acquaintance with him, and now in his trouble it occurred to him that he might be the sort of person to go to for wise counsel. He was an old Dansker long anglicized in the service, of few words, many wrinkles, and some honorable scars. His wizened face, time-tinted and weather-stained to the complexion of an antique parchment, was here and there peppered blue by the chance explosion of a gun cartridge in action.

He was an *Agamemnon* man, some two years prior to the time of this story having served under Nelson when still captain in that ship immortal in naval memory, which dismantled and in part broken up to her bare ribs is seen a grand skeleton in Haden's etching. As one of a boarding party from the *Agamemnon* he had received a cut slantwise along one temple and cheek leaving a long pale scar like a streak of dawn's light falling athwart the dark visage. It was on account of that scar and the affair in which it was known that he had received it, as well as from his blue-peppered complexion, that the Dansker went among the *Bellipotent*'s crew by the name of "Board-Her-in-the-Smoke."

Now the first time that his small weasel eyes happened to light on Billy Budd, a certain grim internal merriment set all his ancient wrinkles into antic play. Was it that his eccentric unsentimental old sapience, primitive in its kind, saw or thought it saw something which in contrast with the warship's environment looked oddly incongruous in the Handsome Sailor? But after slyly studying him at intervals, the old Merlin's equivocal merriment was modified; for now when the twain would meet, it would start in his face a quizzing sort of look, but it would be but momentary and sometimes replaced by an expression of speculative query as to what might eventually befall a nature like that, dropped into a world not without some mantraps and against whose subtleties simple courage lacking experience and address, and without any touch of defensive ugliness, is of little avail; and where such innocence as man is capable of does yet in a moral emergency not always sharpen the faculties or enlighten the will.

However it was, the Dansker in his ascetic way rather took to Billy. Nor was this only because of a certain philosophic interest in such a character. There was another cause. While the old man's eccentricities, sometimes bordering on the ursine, repelled the juniors, Billy, undeterred thereby, revering him as a salt hero, would make advances, never passing the old *Agamemnon* man without a salutation marked by that respect which is seldom lost on the aged, however crabbed at times or whatever their station in life.

There was a vein of dry humor, or what not, in the mastman; and, whether in freak of patriarchal irony touching Billy's youth and athletic frame, or for some other and more recondite reason, from the first in addressing him he always substituted *Baby* for Billy, the Dansker in fact being the originator of the name by which the foretopman eventually became known aboard ship.

Well then, in his mysterious little difficulty going in quest of the wrinkled one, Billy found him off duty in a dogwatch ruminating by himself, seated on a shot box of the upper gun deck, now and then surveying with a somewhat cynical regard certain of the more swaggering promenaders there. Billy recounted his trouble, again wondering how it all happened. The salt seer attentively listened, accompanying the foretopman's recital with queer twitchings of his wrinkles and problematical little sparkles of his small ferret eyes. Making an end of his story, the foretopman asked, "And now, Dansker, do. tell me what you think of it."

The old man, shoving up the front of his tarpaulin and deliberately rubbing the long slant scar at the point where it entered the thin hair, laconically said, "Baby Budd, *Jemmy Legs*" (meaning the master-at-arms) "is down on you."

"*Jemmy Legs!*" ejaculated Billy, his welkin eyes expanding. "What for? Why, he calls me 'the sweet and pleasant young fellow,' they tell me."

"Does he so?" grinned the grizzled one; then said, "Ay, Baby lad, a sweet voice has Jemmy Legs."

"No, not always. But to me he has. I seldom pass him but there comes a pleasant word."

"And that's because he's down upon you, Baby Budd."

Such reiteration, along with the manner of it, incomprehensible to a novice, disturbed Billy almost as much as the mystery for which he had sought explanation. Something less unpleasingly oracular he tried to extract; but the old sea Chiron, thinking perhaps that for the nonce he had sufficiently instructed his young Achilles, pursed his lips, gathered all his wrinkles together, and would commit himself to nothing further.

Years, and those experiences which befall certain shrewder men subordinated lifelong to the will of superiors, all this had developed in the Dansker the pithy guarded cynicism that was his leading characteristic.

10

THE NEXT day an incident served to confirm Billy Budd in his incredulity as to the Dansker's strange summing up of the case submitted. The ship at noon, going large before the wind, was rolling on her course, and he below at dinner and engaged in some sportful talk with the members of his mess, chanced in a sudden lurch to spill the entire contents of his soup pan upon the new-scrubbed deck. Claggart, the master-at-arms, official rattan in hand, happened to be passing along the battery in a bay of which the mess was lodged, and the greasy liquid streamed just across his path. Stepping over it, he was proceeding on his way without comment, since the matter was nothing to take notice of under the circumstances, when he happened to observe who it was that had done the spilling. His countenance changed. Pausing, he was about to ejaculate something hasty at the sailor, but checked himself, and pointing down to the streaming soup, playfully tapped him from behind with his rattan, saying in a low musical voice peculiar to him at times, "Handsomely done my lad! And handsome is as handsome did it, too!" And with that passed on. Not noted by Billy as not coming within his view was the involuntary smile, or rather grimace, that accompanied Claggart's equivocal words. Aridly it drew down the thin corners of his shapely mouth. But everybody taking his remark as meant for humorous, and at which therefore as coming from a superior they were bound to laugh "with counterfeited glee," acted accordingly; and Billy, tickled, it may be, by the allusion to his being the Handsome Sailor, merrily joined in; then addressing his messmates exclaimed, "There now, who says that Jemmy Legs is down on me!"

"And who said he was, Beauty?" demanded one Donald with some surprise. Whereat the foretopman looked a little foolish, recalling that it was only one person, Board-Her-in-the-Smoke, who had suggested what to him was the smoky idea that this master-at-arms was in any peculiar way hostile to him. Meantime that functionary, resuming his path, must have momentarily worn some expression less guarded than that of the bitter smile, usurping the face from the heart—some distorting expression perhaps, for a drummer-boy heedlessly frolicking along from the opposite direction and chancing to come into light collision with his person was strangely disconcerted by his aspect. Nor was the impression lessened when the official, impetuously giving him a sharp cut with the rattan, vehemently exclaimed, "Look where you go!"

11

WHAT WAS the matter with the master-at-arms? And, be the matter what it might, how could it have direct relation to Billy Budd, with whom prior to the affair of the spilled soup he had never come into any special contact official or otherwise? What indeed could the trouble have to do with one so little inclined to give offense as the merchant-ship's "peacemaker," even him who in Claggart's own phrase was "the sweet and pleasant young fellow"? Yes, why should Jemmy Legs, to borrow the Dansker's expression, be "down" on the Handsome Sailor? But, at heart and not for nothing, as the late chance encounter may indicate to the discerning, down on him, secretly down on him, he assuredly was.

Now to invent something touching the more private career of Claggart, something involving Billy Budd, of which something the latter should be wholly ignorant, some romantic incident implying that Claggart's knowledge of the young bluejacket began at some period anterior to catching sight of him on board the seventy-four—all this, not so difficult to do, might avail in a way more or less interesting to account for whatever of enigma may appear to lurk in the case. But in fact there was nothing of the sort. And yet the cause necessarily to be assumed as the sole one assignable is in its very realism as much charged with that prime element of Radcliffian romance, the mysterious, as any that the ingenuity of the author of *The Mysteries of Udolpho* could devise. For what can more partake of the mysterious than an antipathy spontaneous and profound such as is evoked in certain exceptional mortals by the mere aspect of some other mortal, however harmless he may be, if not called forth by this very harmlessness itself?

Now there can exist no irritating juxtaposition of dissimilar personalities comparable to that which is possible aboard a great warship fully manned and at sea. There, every day among all ranks, almost every man comes into more or less of contact with almost every other man. Wholly there to avoid even the sight of an aggravating object one must needs give it Jonah's toss or jump overboard himself. Imagine how all this might eventually operate on some peculiar human creature the direct reverse of a saint!

But for the adequate comprehending of Claggart by a normal nature these hints are insufficient. To pass from a normal nature to him one must cross "the deadly space between." And this is best done by indirection.

Long ago an honest scholar, my senior, said to me in reference to one who like himself is now no more, a man so unimpeachably respectable that against him nothing was ever openly said though among the few something was whispered, "Yes, X—— is a nut not to be cracked by the tap of a lady's fan. You are aware that I am the adherent of no organized religion, much less of any philosophy built into a system. Well, for all that, I think that to try and get into X——, enter his labyrinth and get out again, without a clue derived from some source other than what is known as 'knowledge of the world'—that were hardly possible, at least for me."

"Why," said I, "X——, however singular a study to some, is yet human, and knowledge of the world assuredly implies the knowledge of human nature, and in most of its varieties."

"Yes, but a superficial knowledge of it, serving ordinary purposes. But for anything deeper, I am not certain whether to know the world and to know human nature be not two distinct branches of knowledge, which while they may coexist in the same heart, yet either may exist with little or nothing of the other. Nay, in an average man of the world, his constant rubbing with it blunts that finer spiritual insight indispensable to the understanding of the essential in certain exceptional characters, whether evil ones or good. In a matter of some importance I have seen a girl wind an old lawyer about her little finger. Nor was it the dotage of senile love. Nothing of the sort. But he knew law better than he knew the girl's heart. Coke and Blackstone hardly shed so much light into obscure spiritual places as the Hebrew prophets. And who were they? Mostly recluses."

At the time, my inexperience was such that I did not quite see the drift of all this. It may be that I see it now. And, indeed, if that lexicon which is based on Holy Writ were any longer popular, one might with less difficulty define and denominate certain phenomenal men. As it is, one must turn to some authority not liable to the charge of being tinctured with the biblical element.

In a list of definitions included in the authentic translation of Plato, a list attributed to him, occurs this: "Natural Depravity: a depravity according to nature," a definition which, though savoring of Calvinism, by no means involves Calvin's dogma as to total mankind. Evidently its intent makes it applicable but to individuals. Not many are the examples of this depravity which the gallows and jail supply. At any rate, for notable instances, since these have no vulgar alloy of the brute in them, but invariably are dominated by intellectuality, one must go elsewhere. Civilization, especially if of the austerer sort, is auspicious to it. It folds itself in the mantle of respectability. It has its certain negative virtues serving as silent auxiliaries. It never allows wine to get within its guard. It is not going too far to say that it is without vices or small sins. There is a phenomenal pride in it that excludes them. It is never mercenary or avaricious. In short, the depravity here meant partakes nothing of the sordid or sensual. It is serious, but free from acerbity. Though no flatterer of mankind it never speaks ill of it.

But the thing which in eminent instances signalizes so exceptional a nature is this: Though the man's even temper and discreet bearing would seem to intimate a mind peculiarly subject to the law of reason, not the less in heart he would seem to riot in complete exemption from that law, having apparently little to do with reason further than to employ it as an ambidexter implement for effecting the irrational. That is to say: Toward the accomplishment of an aim which in wantonness of atrocity would seem to partake of the insane, he will direct a cool judgment sagacious and sound. These men are madmen, and of the most dangerous sort, for their lunacy is not continuous, but occasional, evoked by some special object; it is protectively secretive, which is as much as to say it is self-contained, so that when, moreover, most active it is to the average mind not distinguishable from sanity, and for the reason above suggested: that whatever its aims may be—and the aim is never declared—the method and the outward proceeding are always perfectly rational.

Now something such an one was Claggart, in whom was the mania of an evil nature, not engendered by vicious training or corrupting books or licentious living, but born with him and innate, in short "a depravity according to nature."

Dark sayings are these, some will say. But why? Is it because they somewhat savor of Holy Writ in its phrase "mystery of iniquity"? If they do, such savor was far enough from being intended, for little will it commend these pages to many a reader of today.

The point of the present story turning on the hidden nature of the master-at-arms has necessitated this chapter. With an added hint or two in connection with the incident at the mess, the resumed narrative must be left to vindicate, as it may, its own credibility.

12

THAT CLAGGART'S figure was not amiss, and his face, save the chin, well molded, has already been said. Of these favorable points he seemed not insensible, for he was not only neat but careful in his dress. But the form of Billy Budd was heroic; and if his face was without the intellectual look of the pallid Claggart's, not the less was it lit, like his, from within, though from a different source. The bonfire in his heart made luminous the rose-tan in his cheek.

In view of the marked contrast between the persons of the twain, it is more than probable that when the master-at-arms in the scene last given applied to the sailor the proverb "Handsome is as handsome does," he there let escape an ironic inkling, not caught by the young sailors who heard it, as to what it was that had first moved him against Billy, namely, his significant personal beauty.

Now envy and antipathy, passions irreconcilable in reason, nevertheless in fact may spring conjoined like Chang and Eng in one birth. Is Envy then such a monster? Well, though many an arraigned mortal has in hopes of mitigated penalty pleaded guilty to horrible actions, did ever anybody seriously confess to envy? Something there is in it universally felt to be more shameful than even felonious crime. And not only does everybody disown it, but the better sort are inclined to incredulity when it is in earnest imputed to an intelligent man. But since its lodgment is in the heart not the brain, no degree of intellect supplies a guarantee against it. But Claggart's was no vulgar form of the passion. Nor, as directed toward Billy Budd, did it partake of that streak of apprehensive jealousy that marred Saul's visage perturbedly brooding on the comely young David. Claggart's envy struck deeper. If askance he eyed the good looks, cheery health, and frank enjoyment of young life in Billy Budd, it was because these went along with a nature that, as Claggart magnetically felt, had in its simplicity never willed malice or experienced the reactionary bite of that serpent. To him, the spirit lodged within Billy, and looking out from his welkin eyes as from windows, that ineffability it was which made the dimple in his dyed cheek, suppled his joints, and dancing in his yellow curls made him pre-eminently the Handsome Sailor. One person excepted, the master-at-arms was perhaps the only man in the ship intellectually capable of adequately appreciating the moral phenomenon presented in Billy Budd. And the insight but intensified his passion, which assuming various secret forms within him, at times assumed that of cynic disdain, disdain of innocence—to be nothing more than innocent! Yet in an aesthetic way he saw the charm of it, the courageous free-and-easy temper of it, and fain would have shared it, but he despaired of it.

With no power to annul the elemental evil in him, though readily enough he could hide it; apprehending the good, but powerless to be it; a nature like Claggart's, surcharged with energy as such natures almost invariably are, what recourse is left to it but to recoil upon itself and, like the scorpion for which the Creator alone is responsible, act out to the end the part allotted it.

13

PASSION, and passion in its profoundest, is not a thing demanding a palatial stage whereon to play its part. Down among the groundlings, among the beggars and rakers of the garbage, profound passion is enacted. And the circumstances that provoke it, however trivial or mean, are no measure of its power. In the present instance the stage is a scrubbed gun deck, and one of the external provocations a man-of-war's man's spilled soup.

Now when the master-at-arms noticed whence came that greasy fluid streaming before his feet, he must have taken it—to some extent wilfully, perhaps—not for the mere accident it assuredly was, but for the sly escape of a spontaneous feeling on Billy's part more or less answering to the antipathy on his own. In effect a foolish demonstration, he must have thought, and very harmless, like the futile kick of a heifer, which yet were the heifer a shod stallion would not be so harmless. Even so was it that into the gall of Claggart's envy he infused the vitriol of his contempt. But the incident confirmed to him certain telltale reports purveyed to his ear by "Squeak," one of his more cunning corporals, a grizzled little man, so nicknamed by the sailors on account of his squeaky voice and sharp visage ferreting about the dark corners of the lower decks after interlopers, satirically suggesting to them the idea of a rat in a cellar.

From his chief's employing him as an implicit tool in laying little traps for the worriment of the foretopman—for it was from the master-at-arms that the petty persecutions heretofore adverted to had proceeded—the corporal, having naturally enough concluded that his master could have no love for the sailor, made it his business, faithful understrapper that he was, to foment the ill blood by perverting to his chief certain innocent frolics of the good-natured foretopman, besides inventing for his mouth sundry contumelious epithets he claimed to have overheard him let fall. The master-at-arms never suspected the veracity of these reports, more especially as to the epithets, for he well knew how secretly unpopular may become a master-at-arms, at least a master-at-arms of those days, zealous in his function, and how the bluejackets shoot at him in private their raillery and wit; the nickname by which he goes among them (Jemmy Legs) implying under the form of merriment cherished disrespect and dislike. But in view of the greediness of hate for pabulum it hardly needed a purveyor to feed Claggart's passion.

An uncommon prudence is habitual with the subtler depravity, for it has everything to hide. And in case of an injury but suspected, its secretiveness voluntarily cuts it off from enlightenment or disillusion; and, not unreluctantly, action is taken upon surmise as upon certainty. And the retaliation is apt to be in monstrous disproportion to the supposed offense; for when in anybody was revenge in its exactions aught else but an inordinate usurer? But how with Claggart's conscience? For though consciences are unlike as foreheads, every intelligence, not excluding the scriptural devils who "believe and tremble," has one. But Claggart's conscience being but the lawyer to his will, made ogres of trifles, probably arguing that the motive imputed to Billy in spilling the soup just when he did, together with the epithets alleged, these, if nothing more, made a strong case against him; nay, justified animosity into a sort of retributive righteousness. The Pharisee is the Guy Fawkes prowling in the hid chambers underlying some natures like Claggart's. And they can really form no conception of an unreciprocated malice. Probably the master-at-arms' clandestine persecution of Billy was started to try the temper of the man; but it had not developed any quality in him that enmity could make official use of or even pervert into plausible self-justification; so that the occurrence at the mess, petty if it were, was a welcome one to that peculiar conscience assigned to be the private mentor of Claggart; and, for the rest, not improbably it put him upon new experiments.

14

NOT MANY days after the last incident narrated, something befell Billy Budd that more graveled him than aught that had previously occurred.

It was a warm night for the latitude; and the foretopman, whose watch at the time was properly below, was dozing on the uppermost deck whither he had ascended from his hot hammock, one of hundreds suspended so closely wedged together over a lower gun deck that there was little or no swing to them. He lay as in the shadow of a hillside, stretched under the lee of the booms, a piled ridge of spare spars amidships between foremast and mainmast among which the ship's largest boat, the launch, was stowed. Alongside of three other slumberers from below, he lay near that end of the booms which approaches the foremast; his station aloft on duty as a foretopman being just over the deck-station of the forecastlemen, entitling him according to usage to make himself more or less at home in that neighborhood.

Presently he was stirred into semiconsciousness by somebody, who must have previously sounded the sleep of the others, touching his shoulder, and then, as the foretopman raised his head, breathing into his ear in a quick whisper, "Slip into the lee forechains, Billy; there is something in the wind. Don't speak. Quick, I will meet you there," and disappearing.

Now Billy, like sundry other essentially good-natured ones, had some of the weaknesses inseparable from essential good nature; and among these was a reluctance, almost an incapacity of plumply saying *no* to an abrupt proposition not obviously absurd on the face of it, nor obviously unfriendly, nor iniquitous. And being of warm blood, he had not the phlegm tacitly to negative any proposition by unresponsive inaction. Like his sense of fear, his apprehension as to aught outside of the honest and natural was seldom very quick. Besides, upon the present occasion, the drowse from his sleep still hung upon him.

However it was, he mechanically rose and, sleepily wondering what could be in the wind, betook himself to the designated place, a narrow platform, one of six, outside of the high bulwarks and screened by the great deadeyes and multiple columned lanyards of the shrouds and backstays; and, in a great warship of that time, of dimensions commensurate to the hull's magnitude; a tarry balcony in short, overhanging the sea, and so secluded that one mariner of the *Bellipotent*, a Nonconformist old tar of a serious turn, made it even in daytime his private oratory.

In this retired nook the stranger soon joined Billy Budd. There was no moon as yet; a haze obscured the starlight. He could not distinctly see the stranger's face. Yet from something in the outline and carriage, Billy took him, and correctly, for one of the afterguard.

"Hist! Billy," said the man, in the same quick cautionary whisper as before. "You were impressed, weren't you? Well, so was I"; and he paused, as to mark the effect. But Billy, not knowing exactly what to make of this, said nothing. Then the other: "We are not the only impressed ones, Billy. There's a gang of us.—Couldn't you—help—at a pinch?"

"What do you mean?" demanded Billy, here thoroughly shaking off his drowse.

"Hist, hist!" the hurried whisper now growing husky. "See here," and the man held up two small objects faintly twinkling in the night-light; "see, they are yours, Billy, if you'll only——"

But Billy broke in, and in his resentful eagerness to deliver himself his vocal infirmity somewhat intruded. "D—d—damme, I don't know what you are d—d—driving at, or what you mean, but you had better g—g—go where you belong!" For the moment the fellow, as confounded, did not stir; and Billy, springing to his feet, said, "If you d—don't start, I'll t—t—toss you back over the r—rail!" There was no mistaking this, and the mysterious emissary decamped, disappearing in the direction of the mainmast in the shadow of the booms.

"Hallo, what's the matter?" here came growling from a forecastleman awakened from his deck-doze by Billy's raised voice. And as the foretopman reappeared and was recognized by him: "Ah, Beauty, is it you? Well, something must have been the matter, for you st—st—stuttered."

"Oh," rejoined Billy, now mastering the impediment, "I found an afterguardsman in our part of the ship here, and I bid him be off where he belongs."

"And is that all you did about it, Foretopman?" gruffly demanded another, an irascible old fellow of brick-colored visage and hair who was known to his associate forecastlemen as "Red Pepper." "Such sneaks I should like to marry to the gunner's daughter!"—by that expression meaning that he would like to subject them to disciplinary castigation over a gun.

However, Billy's rendering of the matter satisfactorily accounted to these inquirers for the brief commotion, since of all the sections of a ship's company the forecastlemen, veterans for the most part and bigoted in their sea prejudices, are the most jealous in resenting territorial encroachments, especially on the part of any of the afterguard, of whom they have but a sorry opinion—chiefly landsmen, never going aloft except to

reef or furl the mainsail, and in no wise competent to handle
a marlinspike or turn in a deadeye, say.

15

THIS INCIDENT sorely puzzled Billy Budd. It was an entirely new
experience, the first time in his life that he had ever been personally approached in underhand intriguing fashion. Prior to
this encounter he had known nothing of the afterguardsman,
the two men being stationed wide apart, one forward and aloft
during his watch, the other on deck and aft.

What could it mean? And could they really be guineas,
those two glittering objects the interloper had held up to his
(Billy's) eyes? Where could the fellow get guineas? Why, even
spare buttons are not so plentiful at sea. The more he turned
the matter over, the more he was nonplussed, and made uneasy
and discomfited. In his disgustful recoil from an overture
which, though he but ill comprehended, he instinctively knew
must involve evil of some sort, Billy Budd was like a young
horse fresh from the pasture suddenly inhaling a vile whiff
from some chemical factory, and by repeated snortings trying to
get it out of his nostrils and lungs. This frame of mind barred
all desire of holding further parley with the fellow, even were
it but for the purpose of gaining some enlightenment as to
his design in approaching him. And yet he was not without
natural curiosity to see how such a visitor in the dark would
look in broad day.

He espied him the following afternoon in his first dogwatch
below, one of the smokers on that forward part of the upper
gun deck allotted to the pipe. He recognized him by his general
cut and build more than by his round freckled face and glassy
eyes of pale blue, veiled with lashes all but white. And yet
Billy was a bit uncertain whether indeed it were he—yonder
chap about his own age chatting and laughing in freehearted
way, leaning against a gun; a genial young fellow enough to
look at, and something of a rattlebrain, to all appearance.
Rather chubby too for a sailor, even an afterguardsman. In
short, the last man in the world, one would think, to be over-
burdened with thoughts, especially those perilous thoughts
that must needs belong to a conspirator in any serious project,
or even to the underling of such a conspirator.

Although Billy was not aware of it, the fellow, with a side long watchful glance, had perceived Billy first, and then noting that Billy was looking at him, thereupon nodded a familiar sort of friendly recognition as to an old acquaintance, without interrupting the talk he was engaged in with the group of smokers. A day or two afterwards, chancing in the evening promenade on a gun deck to pass Billy, he offered a flying word of good-fellowship, as it were, which by its unexpectedness, and equivocalness under the circumstances, so embarrassed Billy that he knew not how to respond to it, and let it go unnoticed.

Billy was now left more at a loss than before. The ineffectual speculations into which he was led were so disturbingly alien to him that he did his best to smother them. It never entered his mind that here was a matter which, from its extreme questionableness, it was his duty as a loyal bluejacket to report in the proper quarter. And, probably, had such a step been suggested to him, he would have been deterred from taking it by the thought, one of novice magnanimity, that it would savor overmuch of the dirty work of a telltale. He kept the thing to himself. Yet upon one occasion he could not forbear a little disburdening himself to the old Dansker, tempted thereto perhaps by the influence of a balmy night when the ship lay becalmed; the twain, silent for the most part, sitting together on deck, their heads propped against the bulwarks. But it was only a partial and anonymous account that Billy gave, the unfounded scruples above referred to preventing full disclosure to anybody. Upon hearing Billy's version, the sage Dansker seemed to divine more than he was told; and after a little meditation, during which his wrinkles were pursed as into a point, quite effacing for the time that quizzing expression his face sometimes wore: "Didn't I say so, Baby Budd?"

"Say what?" demanded Billy.

"Why, *Jemmy Legs* is *down* on you."

"And what," rejoined Billy in amazement, "has *Jemmy Legs* to do with that cracked afterguardsman?"

"Ho, it was an afterguardsman, then. A cat's-paw, a cat's-paw!" And with that exclamation, whether it had reference to a light puff of air just then coming over the calm sea, or a subtler relation to the afterguardsman, there is no telling, the old Merlin gave a twisting wrench with his black teeth at his plug of tobacco, vouchsafing no reply to Billy's impetuous question, though now repeated, for it was his wont to relapse into grim silence when interrogated in skeptical sort as to any of his sententious oracles, not always very clear ones, rather partaking of that obscurity which invests most Delphic deliverances from any quarter.

Long experience had very likely brought this old man to that bitter prudence which never interferes in aught and never gives advice.

16

YES, DESPITE the Dansker's pithy insistence as to the master-at-arms being at the bottom of these strange experiences of Billy on board the *Bellipotent*, the young sailor was ready to ascribe them to almost anybody but the man who, to use Billy's own expression, "always had a pleasant word for him." This is to be wondered at. Yet not so much to be wondered at. In certain matters, some sailors even in mature life remain unsophisticated enough. But a young seafarer of the disposition of our athletic foretopman is much of a child-man. And yet a child's utter innocence is but its blank ignorance, and the innocence more or less wanes as intelligence waxes. But in Billy Budd intelligence, such as it was, had advanced while yet his simple-mindedness remained for the most part unaffected. Experience is a teacher indeed; yet did Billy's years make his experience small. Besides, he had none of that intuitive knowledge of the bad which in natures not good or incompletely so foreruns experience, and therefore may pertain, as in some instances it too clearly does pertain, even to youth.

And what could Billy know of man except of man as a mere sailor? And the old-fashioned sailor, the veritable man before the mast, the sailor from boyhood up, he, though indeed of the same species as a landsman, is in some respects singularly distinct from him. The sailor is frankness, the landsman is finesse. Life is not a game with the sailor, demanding the long head—no intricate game of chess where few moves are made in straight-forwardness and ends are attained by indirection, an oblique, tedious, barren game hardly worth that poor candle burnt out in playing it.

Yes, as a class, sailors are in character a juvenile race. Even their deviations are marked by juvenility, this more especially holding true with the sailors of Billy's time. Then too, certain things which apply to all sailors do more pointedly operate here and there upon the junior one. Every sailor, too, is accustomed to obey orders without debating them; his life afloat is externally ruled for him; he is not brought into that promiscuous commerce with mankind where unobstructed free agency on equal terms—equal superficially, at least—soon teaches one that unless upon occasion he exercise a distrust keen in proportion to the fairness of the appearance, some foul turn may be served him. A ruled undemonstrative distrustfulness is so habitual, not with businessmen so much as with men who know their kind in less shallow relations than business, namely, certain men of the world, that they come at last to employ it all but unconsciously; and some of them would very likely feel real surprise at being charged with it as one of their general characteristics.

17

BUT AFTER the little matter at the mess Billy Budd no more found himself in strange trouble at times about his hammock or his clothes bag or what not. As to that smile that occasionally sunned him, and the pleasant passing word, these were, if not more frequent, yet if anything more pronounced than before.

But for all that, there were certain other demonstrations now. When Claggart's unobserved glance happened to light on belted Billy rolling along the upper gun deck in the leisure of the second dogwatch, exchanging passing broadsides of fun with other young promenaders in the crowd, that glance would follow the cheerful sea Hyperion with a settled meditative and melancholy expression, his eyes strangely suffused with incipient feverish tears. Then would Claggart look like the man of sorrows. Yes, and sometimes the melancholy expression would have in it a touch of soft yearning, as if Claggart could even have loved Billy but for fate and ban. But this was an evanescence, and quickly repented of, as it were, by an immitigable look, pinching and shriveling the visage into the momentary semblance of a wrinkled walnut. But sometimes catching sight in advance of the foretopman coming in his direction, he would, upon their nearing, step aside a little to let him pass, dwelling upon Billy for the moment with the glittering dental satire of a Guise. But upon any abrupt unforeseen encounter

a red light would flash forth from his eye like a spark from
an anvil in a dusk smithy. That quick, fierce light was a strange
one, darted from orbs which in repose were of a color nearest
approaching a deeper violet, the softest of shades.

Though some of these caprices of the pit could not but be
observed by their object, yet were they beyond the construing
of such a nature. And the thews of Billy were hardly compatible with that sort of sensitive spiritual organization which in
some cases instinctively conveys to ignorant innocence an
admonition of the proximity of the malign. He thought the
master-at-arms acted in a manner rather queer at times. That
was all. But the occasional frank air and pleasant word went
for what they purported to be, the young sailor never having
heard as yet of the "too fair-spoken man."

Had the foretopman been conscious of having done or said
anything to provoke the ill will of the official, it would have
been different with him, and his sight might have been purged
if not sharpened. As it was, innocence was his blinder.

So was it with him in yet another matter. Two minor
officers, the armorer and captain of the hold, with whom he had
never exchanged a word, his position in the ship not bringing
him into contact with them, these men now for the first began
to cast upon Billy, when they chanced to encounter him, that
peculiar glance which evidences that the man from whom it
comes has been some way tampered with, and to the prejudice
of him upon whom the glance lights. Never did it occur to
Billy as a thing to be noted or a thing suspicious, though he
well knew the fact, that the armorer and captain of the hold,
with the ship's yeoman, apothecary, and others of that grade,
were by naval usage messmates of the master-at-arms, men
with ears convenient to his confidential tongue.

But the general popularity that came from our Handsome
Sailor's manly forwardness upon occasion and irresistible good
nature, indicating no mental superiority tending to excite an
invidious feeling, this good will on the part of most of his shipmates made him the less to concern himself about such mute
aspects toward him as those whereto allusion has just been
made, aspects he could not so fathom as to infer their whole
import.

As to the afterguardsman, though Billy for reasons already
given necessarily saw little of him, yet when the two did happen
to meet, invariably came the fellow's offhand cheerful recognition, sometimes accompanied by a passing pleasant word or

two. Whatever that equivocal young person's original design may really have been, or the design of which he might have been the deputy, certain it was from his manner upon these occasions that he had wholly dropped it.

It was as if his precocity of crookedness (and every vulgar villain is precocious) had for once deceived him, and the man he had sought to entrap as a simpleton had through his very simplicity ignominiously baffled him.

But shrewd ones may opine that it was hardly possible for Billy to refrain from going up to the afterguardsman and bluntly demanding to know his purpose in the initial interview so abruptly closed in the forechains. Shrewd ones may also think it but natural in Billy to set about sounding some of the other impressed men of the ship in order to discover what basis, if any, there was for the emissary's obscure suggestions as to plotting disaffection aboard. Yes, shrewd ones may so think. But something more, or rather something else than mere shrewdness is perhaps needful for the due understanding of such a character as Billy Budd's.

As to Claggart, the monomania in the man—if that indeed it were—as involuntarily disclosed by starts in the manifestations detailed, yet in general covered over by his self-contained and rational demeanor; this, like a subterranean fire, was eating its way deeper and deeper in him. Something decisive must come of it.

18

AFTER THE mysterious interview in the forechains, the one so abruptly ended there by Billy, nothing especially germane to the story occurred until the events now about to be narrated.

Elsewhere it has been said that in the lack of frigates (of course better sailers than line-of-battle ships) in the English squadron up the Straits at that period, the *Bellipotent* 74 was occasionally employed not only as an available substitute for a scout, but at times on detached service of more important kind. This was not alone because of her sailing qualities, not common in a ship of her rate, but quite as much, probably, that the character of her commander, it was thought, specially adapted him for any duty where under unforeseen difficulties a prompt initiative might have to be taken in some matter demanding knowledge and ability in addition to those qualities implied in good seamanship. It was on an expedition of the latter sort, a somewhat distant one, and when the *Bellipotent* was almost at her furthest remove from the fleet, that in the latter part of an afternoon watch she unexpectedly came in sight of a ship of the enemy. It proved to be a frigate. The latter, perceiving through the glass that the weight of men and metal would be heavily against her, invoking her light heels crowded sail to get away. After a chase urged almost against hope and lasting until about the middle of the first dogwatch, she signally succeeded in effecting her escape.

Not long after the pursuit had been given up, and ere the excitement incident thereto had altogether waned away, the master-at-arms, ascending from his cavernous sphere, made his appearance cap in hand by the mainmast respectfully waiting the notice of Captain Vere, then solitary walking the weather side of the quarter-deck, doubtless somewhat chafed at the failure of the pursuit. The spot where Claggart stood was the place allotted to men of lesser grades seeking some more particular interview either with the officer of the deck or the captain himself. But from the latter it was not often that a sailor or petty officer of those days would seek a hearing; only some exceptional cause would, according to established custom, have warranted that.

Presently, just as the commander, absorbed in his reflections, was on the point of turning aft in his promenade, he became sensible of Claggart's presence, and saw the doffed cap held in deferential expectancy. Here be it said that Captain Vere's personal knowledge of this petty officer had only begun at the time of the ship's last sailing from home, Claggart then for the first, in transfer from a ship detained for repairs, supplying on board the *Bellipotent* the place of a previous master-at-arms disabled and ashore.

No sooner did the commander observe who it was that now deferentially stood awaiting his notice than a peculiar expression came over him. It was not unlike that which uncontrollably will flit across the countenance of one at unawares encountering a person who, though known to him indeed, has hardly been long enough known for thorough knowledge, but something in whose aspect nevertheless now for the first provokes a vaguely repellent distaste. But coming to a stand and resuming much of his wonted official manner, save that a sort of im-

patience lurked in the intonation of the opening word, he
said "Well? What is it, Master-at-arms?"

With the air of a subordinate grieved at the necessity of being a messenger of ill tidings, and while conscientiously determined to be frank yet equally resolved upon shunning over-
statement, Claggart at this invitation, or rather summons to
disburden, spoke up. What he said, conveyed in the language of
no uneducated man, was to the effect following, if not altogether in these words, namely, that during the chase and preparations for the possible encounter he had seen enough to
convince him that at least one sailor aboard was a dangerous
character in a ship mustering some who not only had taken
a guilty part in the late serious troubles, but others also who,
like the man in question, had entered His Majesty's service
under another form than enlistment.

At this point Captain Vere with some impatience interrupted
him: "Be direct, man; say *impressed men*."

Claggart made a gesture of subservience, and proceeded.
Quite lately he (Claggart) had begun to suspect that on the
gun decks some sort of movement prompted by the sailor in
question was covertly going on, but he had not thought himself warranted in reporting the suspicion so long as it remained
indistinct. But from what he had that afternoon observed in
the man referred to, the suspicion of something clandestine
going on had advanced to a point less removed from certainty.
He deeply felt, he added, the serious responsibility assumed in
making a report involving such possible consequences to the
individual mainly concerned, besides tending to augment
those natural anxieties which every naval commander must
feel in view of extraordinary outbreaks so recent as those which,
he sorrowfully said it, it needed not to name.

Now at the first broaching of the matter Captain Vere, taken
by surprise, could not wholly dissemble his disquietude. But as
Claggart went on, the former's aspect changed into restiveness
under something in the testifier's manner in giving his testimony. However, he refrained from interrupting him. And
Claggart, continuing, concluded with this: "God forbid, your
honor, that the *Bellipotent's* should be the experience of
the——"

"Never mind that!" here peremptorily broke in the superior,
his face altering with anger, instinctively divining the ship that
the other was about to name, one in which the Nore Mutiny

had assumed a singularly tragical character that for a time jeopardized the life of its commander. Under the circumstances he was indignant at the purposed allusion. When the commissioned officers themselves were on all occasions very heedful how they referred to the recent events in the fleet, for a petty officer unnecessarily to allude to them in the presence of his captain, this struck him as a most immodest presumption. Besides, to his quick sense of self-respect it even looked under the circumstances something like an attempt to alarm him. Nor at first was he without some surprise that one who so far as he had hitherto come under his notice had shown considerable tact in his function should in this particular evince such lack of it.

But these thoughts and kindred dubious ones flitting across his mind were suddenly replaced by an intuitional surmise which, though as yet obscure in form, served practically to affect his reception of the ill tidings. Certain it is that, long versed in everything pertaining to the complicated gun-deck life, which like every other form of life has its secret mines and dubious side, the side popularly disclaimed, Captain Vere did not permit himself to be unduly disturbed by the general tenor of his subordinate's report.

Furthermore, if in view of recent events prompt action should be taken at the first palpable sign of recurring insubordination, for all that, not judicious would it be, he thought, to keep the idea of lingering disaffection alive by undue forwardness in crediting an informer, even if his own subordinate and charged among other things with police surveillance of the crew. This feeling would not perhaps have so prevailed with him were it not that upon a prior occasion the patriotic zeal officially evinced by Claggart had somewhat irritated him as appearing rather supersensible and strained. Furthermore, something even in the official's self-possessed and somewhat ostentatious manner in making his specifications strangely reminded him of a bandsman, a perjurious witness in a capital case before a courtmartial ashore of which when a lieutenant he (Captain Vere) had been a member.

Now the peremptory check given to Claggart in the matter of the arrested allusion was quickly followed up by this: "You say that there is at least one dangerous man aboard. Name him."

"William Budd, a foretopman, your honor."

"William Budd!" repeated Captain Vere with unfeigned

astonishment. "And mean you the man that Lieutenant Ratcliffe took from the merchantman not very long ago, the young fellow who seems to be so popular with the men—Billy, the Handsome Sailor, as they call him?"

"The same, your honor; but for all his youth and good looks, a deep one. Not for nothing does he insinuate himself into the good will of his shipmates, since at the least they will at a pinch say—all hands will—a good word for him, and at all hazards. Did Lieutenant Ratcliffe happen to tell your honor of that adroit fling of Budd's, jumping up in the cutter's bow under the merchantman's stern when he was being taken off? It is even masked by that sort of good-humored air that at heart he resents his impressment. You have but noted his fair cheek. A mantrap may be under the ruddy-tipped daisies."

Now the Handsome Sailor as a signal figure among the crew had naturally enough attracted the captain's attention from the first. Though in general not very demonstrative to his officers, he had congratulated Lieutenant Ratcliffe upon his good fortune in lighting on such a fine specimen of the *genus homo,* who in the nude might have posed for a statue of young Adam before the Fall. As to Billy's adieu to the ship *Rights-of-Man,* which the boarding lieutenant had indeed reported to him, but, in a deferential way, more as a good story than aught else, Captain Vere, though mistakenly understanding it as a satiric sally, had but thought so much the better of the impressed man for it; as a military sailor, admiring the spirit that could take an arbitrary enlistment so merrily and sensibly. The foretopman's conduct, too, so far as it had fallen under the captain's notice, had confirmed the first happy augury, while the new recruit's qualities as a "sailor-man" seemed to be such that he had thought of recommending him to the executive officer for promotion to a place that would more frequently bring him under his own observation, namely, the captaincy of the mizzentop, replacing there in the starboard watch a man not so young whom partly for that reason he deemed less fitted for the post. Be it parenthesized here that since the mizzentopmen have not to handle such breadths of heavy canvas as the lower sails on the mainmast and foremast, a young man if of the right stuff not only seems best adapted to duty there, but in fact is generally selected for the captaincy of that top, and the company under him are light hands and often but striplings. In sum, Captain Vere had from the beginning deemed Billy Budd to be what in the naval parlance of the time was called a "King's bargain": that is to say, for His Britannic Majesty's navy a capital investment at small outlay or none at all.

After a brief pause, during which the reminiscences above mentioned passed vividly through his mind and he weighed the import of Claggart's last suggestion conveyed in the phrase "mantrap under the daisies," and the more he weighed it the less reliance he felt in the informer's good faith, suddenly he turned upon him and in a low voice demanded: "Do you come to me, Master-at-arms, with so foggy a tale? As to Budd, cite me an act or spoken word of his confirmatory of what you in general charge against him. Stay," drawing nearer to him; "heed what you speak. Just now, and in a case like this, there is a yardarm-end for the false witness."

"Ah, your honor!" sighed Claggart, mildly shaking his shapely head as in sad deprecation of such unmerited severity of tone. Then, bridling—erecting himself as in virtuous self-assertion—he circumstantially alleged certain words and acts which collectively, if credited, led to presumptions mortally inculpating Budd. And for some of these averments, he added, substantiating proof was not far.

With gray eyes impatient and distrustful essaying to fathom to the bottom Claggart's calm violet ones, Captain Vere again heard him out; then for the moment stood ruminating. The mood he evinced, Claggart—himself for the time liberated from the other's scrutiny—steadily regarded with a look difficult to render: a look curious of the operation of his tactics, a look such as might have been that of the spokesman of the envious children of Jacob deceptively imposing upon the troubled patriarch the blood-dyed coat of young Joseph.

Though something exceptional in the moral quality of Captain Vere made him, in earnest encounter with a fellow man, a veritable touchstone of that man's essential nature, yet now as to Claggart and what was really going on in him his feeling partook less of intuitional conviction than of strong suspicion clogged by strange dubieties. The perplexity he evinced proceeded less from aught touching the man informed against—as Claggart doubtless opined—than from considerations how best to act in regard to the informer. At first, indeed, he was naturally for summoning that substantiation of his allegations which Claggart said was at hand. But such a proceeding would result in the matter at once getting abroad, which in the present stage of it, he thought, might undesirably affect the ship's company. If Claggart was a false witness—that closed the affair. And therefore, before trying the accusation, he would first practically test the accuser; and he thought this could be done in a quiet, undemonstrative way.

The measure he determined upon involved a shifting of the scene, a transfer to a place less exposed to observation than the broad quarter-deck. For although the few gun-room officers there at the time had, in due observance of naval etiquette, withdrawn to leeward the moment Captain Vere had begun his promenade on the deck's weather side; and though during the colloquy with Claggart they of course ventured not to diminish the distance; and though throughout the interview Captain Vere's voice was far from high, and Claggart's silvery and low; and the wind in the cordage and the wash of the sea helped the more to put them beyond earshot; nevertheless, the interview's continuance already had attracted observation from some topmen aloft and other sailors in the waist or further forward.

Having determined upon his measures, Captain Vere forthwith took action. Abruptly turning to Claggart, he asked, "Master-at-arms, is it now Budd's watch aloft?"

"No, your honor."

Whereupon, "Mr. Wilkes!" summoning the nearest midshipman. "Tell Albert to come to me." Albert was the captain's hammock-boy, a sort of sea valet in whose discretion and fidelity his master had much confidence. The lad appeared.

"You know Budd, the foretopman?"

"I do, sir."

"Go find him. It is his watch off. Manage to tell him out of earshot that he is wanted aft. Contrive it that he speaks to nobody. Keep him in talk yourself. And not till you get well aft here, not till then let him know that the place where he is wanted is my cabin. You understand. Go.—Master-at-arms, show yourself on the decks below, and when you think it time for Albert to be coming with his man, stand by quietly to follow the sailor in."

19

Now WHEN the foretopman found himself in the cabin, closeted there, as it were, with the captain and Claggart, he was surprised enough. But it was a surprise unaccompanied by appre-

hension or distrust. To an immature nature essentially honest
and humane, forewarning intimations of subtler danger from
one's kind come tardily if at all. The only thing that took shape
in the young sailor's mind was this: Yes, the captain, I have
always thought, looks kindly upon me. Wonder if he's going to
make me his coxswain. I should like that. And may be now he
is going to ask the master-at-arms about me.

"Shut the door there, sentry," said the commander; "stand
without, and let nobody come in.—Now, Master-at-arms, tell
this man to his face what you told of him to me," and stood prepared to scrutinize the mutually confronting visages.

With the measured step and calm collected air of an asylum
physician approaching in the public hall some patient beginning to show indications of a coming paroxysm, Claggart deliberately advanced within short range of Billy and, mes-
merically looking him in the eye, briefly recapitulated the
accusation.

Not at first did Billy take it in. When he did, the rose-tan of
his cheek looked struck as by white leprosy. He stood like one
impaled and gagged. Meanwhile the accuser's eyes, removing not as yet from the blue dilated ones, underwent a phenomenal change, their wonted rich violet color blurring into
a muddy purple. Those lights of human intelligence, losing
human expression were gelidly protruding like the alien eyes
of certain uncatalogued creatures of the deep. The first mes-
meristic glance was one of serpent fascination; the last was
as the paralyzing lurch of the torpedo fish.

"Speak, man!" said Captain Vere to the transfixed one,
struck by his aspect even more than by Claggart's. "Speak!
Defend yourself!" Which appeal caused but a strange dumb
gesturing and gurgling in Billy; amazement at such an accusation so suddenly sprung on inexperienced nonage; this, and,
it may be, horror of the accuser's eyes, serving to bring out his
lurking defect and in this instance for the time intensifying
it into a convulsed tongue-tie; while the intent head and entire form straining forward in an agony of ineffectual eagerness to obey the injunction to speak and defend himself, gave
an expression to the face like that of a condemned vestal
priestess in the moment of being buried alive, and in the first
struggle against suffocation.

Though at the time Captain Vere was quite ignorant of
Billy's liability to vocal impediment, he now immediately divined it, since vividly Billy's aspect recalled to him that of a

bright young schoolmate of his whom he had once seen struck by much the same startling impotence in the act of eagerly rising in the class to be foremost in response to a testing question put to it by the master. Going close up to the young sailor, and laying a soothing hand on his shoulder, he said, "There is no hurry, my boy. Take your time, take your time." Contrary to the effect intended, these words so fatherly in tone, doubtless touching Billy's heart to the quick, prompted yet more violent efforts at utterance—efforts soon ending for the time in confirming the paralysis, and bringing to his face an expression which was as a crucifixion to behold. The next instant, quick as the flame from a discharged cannon at night, his right arm shot out, and Claggart dropped to the deck. Whether intentionally or but owing to the young athlete's superior height, the blow had taken effect full upon the forehead, so shapely and intellectual-looking a feature in the master-at-arms; so that the body fell over lenghtwise, like a heavy plank tilted from erectness. A gasp or two, and he lay motionless.

"Fated boy," breathed Captain Vere in tone so low as to be almost a whisper, "what have you done! But here, help me."

The twain raised the felled one from the loins up into a sitting position. The spare form flexibly acquiesced, but inertly. It was like handling a dead snake. They lowered it back. Regaining erectness, Captain Vere with one hand covering his face stood to all appearance as impassive as the object at this feet. Was he absorbed in taking in all the bearings of the event and what was best not only now at once to be done, but also in the sequel? Slowly he uncovered his face; and the effect was as if the moon emerging from eclipse should reappear with quite another aspect than that which had gone into hiding. The father in him, manifested towards Billy thus far in the scene, was replaced by the military disciplinarian. In his official tone he bade the foretopman retire to a stateroom aft (pointing it out), and there remain till thence summoned. This order Billy in silence mechanically obeyed. Then going to the cabin door where it opened on the quarter-deck, Captain Vere said to the sentry without, "Tell somebody to send Albert here." When the lad appeared, his master so contrived it that he should not catch sight of the prone one. "Albert," he said to him, "tell the surgeon I wish to see him. You need not come back till called."

When the surgeon entered—a self-poised character of that grave sense and experience that hardly anything could take him aback—Captain Vere advanced to meet him, thus unconsciously intercepting his view of Claggart, and, interrupting the other's wonted ceremonious salutation, said, "Nay. Tell me how it is with yonder man," directing his attention to the prostrate one.

The surgeon looked, and for all his self-command somewhat started at the abrupt revelation. On Claggart's always pallid complexion, thick black blood was now oozing from nostril and ear. To the gazer's professional eye it was unmistakably no living man that he saw.

"Is it so, then?" said Captain Vere, intently watching him. "I thought it. But verify it." Whereupon the customary tests confirmed the surgeon's first glance, who now, looking up in unfeigned concern, cast a look of intense inquisitiveness upon his superior. But Captain Vere, with one hand to his brow, was standing motionless. Suddenly, catching the surgeon's arm convulsively, he exclaimed, pointing down to the body, "It is the divine judgment on Ananias! Look!"

Disturbed by the excited manner he had never before observed in the *Bellipotent*'s captain, and as yet wholly ignorant of the affair, the prudent surgeon nevertheless held his peace, only again looking an earnest interrogatory as to what it was that had resulted in such a tragedy.

But Captain Vere was now again motionless, standing absorbed in thought. Again starting, he vehemently exclaimed, "Struck dead by an angel of God! Yet the angel must hang!"

At these passionate interjections, mere incoherences to the listener as yet unapprised of the antecedents, the surgeon was profoundly discomposed. But now, as recollecting himself, Captain Vere in less passionate tone briefly related the circumstances leading up to the event. "But come; we must dispatch," he added. "Help me to remove him" (meaning the body) "to yonder compartment," designating one opposite that where the foretopman remained immured. Anew disturbed by a request that, as implying a desire for secrecy, seemed unaccountably strange to him, there was nothing for the subordinate to do but comply.

"Go now," said Captain Vere with something of his wonted manner. "Go now. I presently shall call a drumhead court. Tell the lieutenants what has happened, and tell Mr. Mordant" (meaning the captain of marines), "and charge them to keep the matter to themselves."

20

FULL OF disquietude and misgiving, the surgeon left the cabin. Was Captain Vere suddenly affected in his mind, or was it but a transient excitement, brought about by so strange and extraordinary a tragedy? As to the drumhead court, it struck the surgeon as impolitic, if nothing more. The thing to do, he thought, was to place Billy Budd in confinement, and in a way dictated by usage, and postpone further action in so extraordinary a case to such time as they should rejoin the squadron, and then refer it to the admiral. He recalled the unwonted agitation of Captain Vere and his excited exclamations, so at variance with his normal manner. Was he unhinged?

But assuming that he is, it is not so susceptible of proof. What then can the surgeon do? No more trying situation is conceivable than that of an officer subordinate under a captain whom he suspects to be not mad, indeed, but yet not quite unaffected in his intellects. To argue his order to him would be insolence. To resist him would be mutiny.

In obedience to Captain Vere, he communicated what had happened to the lieutenants and captain of marines, saying nothing as to the captain's state. They fully shared his own surprise and concern. Like him too, they seemed to think that such a matter should be referred to the admiral.

21

WHO IN the rainbow can draw the line where the violet tint ends and the orange tint begins? Distinctly we see the difference of the colors, but where exactly does the one first blendingly enter into the other? So with sanity and insanity. In pronounced cases there is no question about them. But in some supposed cases, in various degrees supposedly less pronounced, to draw the exact line of demarcation few will undertake, though for a fee becoming considerate some professional experts will. There is nothing namable but that some men will, or undertake to, do it for pay.

Whether Captain Vere, as the surgeon professionally and privately surmised, was really the sudden victim of any degree

of aberration, every one must determine for himself by such
light as this narrative may afford.

That the unhappy event which has been narrated could not
have happened at a worse juncture was but too true. For it
was close on the heel of the suppressed insurrections, an after-
time very critical to naval authority, demanding from every
English sea commander two qualities not readily interfusable
—prudence and rigor. Moreover, there was something crucial
in the case.

In the jugglery of circumstances preceding and attending
the event on board the *Bellipotent,* and in the light of that
martial code whereby it was formally to be judged, innocence
and guilt personified in Claggart and Budd in effect changed
places. In a legal view the apparent victim of the tragedy was
he who had sought to victimize a man blameless; and the indisputable deed of the latter, navally regarded, constituted
the most heinous of military crimes. Yet more. The essential
right and wrong involved in the matter, the clearer that might
be, so much the worse for the responsibility of a loyal sea commander, inasmuch as he was not authorized to determine the
matter on that primitive basis.

Small wonder then that the *Bellipotent*'s captain, though in
general a man of rapid decision, felt that circumspectness not
less than promptitude was necessary. Until he could decide
upon his course, and in each detail; and not only so, but until the concluding measure was upon the point of being enacted,
he deemed it advisable, in view of all the circumstances, to
guard as much as possible against publicity. Here he may or
may not have erred. Certain it is, however, that subsequently
in the confidential talk of more than one or two gun rooms
and cabins he was not a little criticized by some officers, a fact
imputed by his friends and vehemently by his cousin Jack
Denton to professional jealousy of Starry Vere. Some imaginative ground for invidious comment there was. The maintenance of secrecy in the matter, the confining all knowledge
of it for a time to the place where the homicide occurred, the
quarterdeck cabin; in these particulars lurked some resemblance to the policy adopted in those tragedies of the palace
which have occurred more than once in the capital founded
by Peter the Barbarian.

The case indeed was such that fain would the *Bellipotent*'s
captain have deferred taking any action whatever respecting
it further than to keep the foretopman a close prisoner till

the ship rejoined the squadron and then submitting the matter to the judgment of his admiral.

But a true military officer is in one particular like a true monk. Not with more of self-abnegation will the latter keep his vows of monastic obedience than the former his vows of allegiance to martial duty.

Feeling that unless quick action was taken on it, the deed of the foretopman, so soon as it should be known on the gun decks, would tend to awaken any slumbering embers of the Nore among the crew, a sense of the urgency of the case overruled in Captain Vere every other consideration. But though a conscientious disciplinarian, he was no lover of authority for mere authority's sake. Very far was he from embracing opportunities for monopolizing to himself the perils of moral responsibility, none at least that could properly be referred to an official superior or shared with him by his official equals or even subordinates. So thinking, he was glad it would not be at variance with usage to turn the matter over to a summary court of his own officers, reserving to himself, as the one on whom the ultimate accountability would rest, the right of maintaining a supervision of it, or formally or informally interposing at need. Accordingly a drumhead court was summarily convened, he electing the individuals composing it: the first lieutenant, the captain of marines, and the sailing master.

In associating an officer of marines with the sea lieutenant and the sailing master in a case having to do with a sailor, the commander perhaps deviated from general custom. He was prompted thereto by the circumstance that he took that soldier to be a judicious person, thoughtful, and not altogether incapable of grappling with a difficult case unprecedented in his prior experience. Yet even as to him he was not without some latent misgiving, for withal he was an extremely good-natured man, an enjoyer of his dinner, a sound sleeper, and inclined to obesity—a man who though he would always maintain his manhood in battle might not prove altogether reliable in a moral dilemma involving aught of the tragic. As to the first lieutenant and the sailing master, Captain Vere could not but be aware that though honest natures, of approved gallantry upon occasion, their intelligence was mostly confined to the matter of active seamanship and the fighting demands of their profession.

The court was held in the same cabin where the unfortunate

affair had taken place. This cabin, the commander's, embraced the entire area under the poop deck. Aft, and on either side, was a small stateroom, the one now temporarily a jail and the other a dead-house, and a yet smaller compartment, leaving a space between expanding forward into a goodly oblong of length coinciding with the ship's beam. A skylight of moderate dimension was overhead, and at each end of the oblong space were two sashed porthole windows easily convertible back into embrasures for short carronades.

All being quickly in readiness, Billy Budd was arraigned, Captain Vere necessarily appearing as the sole witness in the case, and as such temporarily sinking his rank, though singularly maintaining it in a matter apparently trivial, namely, that he testified from the ship's weather side, with that object having caused the court to sit on the lee side. Concisely he narrated all that had led up to the catastrophe, omitting nothing in Claggart's accusation and deposing as to the manner in which the prisoner had received it. At this testimony the three officers glanced with no little surprise at Billy Budd, the last man they would have suspected either of the mutinous design alleged by Claggart or the undeniable deed he himself had done. The first lieutenant, taking judicial primacy and turning toward the prisoner, said, "Captain Vere has spoken. Is it or is it not as Captain Vere says?"

In response came syllables not so much impeded in the utterance as might have been anticipated. They were these: "Captain Vere tells the truth. It is just as Captain Vere says, but it is not as the master-at-arms said. I have eaten the King's bread and I am true to the King."

"I believe you, my man," said the witness, his voice indicating a suppressed emotion not otherwise betrayed.

"God will bless you for that, your honor!" not without stammering said Billy, and all but broke down. But immediately he was recalled to self-control by another question, to which with the same emotional difficulty of utterance he said, "No, there was no malice between us. I never bore malice against the master-at-arms. I am sorry that he is dead. I did not mean to kill him. Could I have used my tongue I would not have struck him. But he foully lied to my face and in presence of my captain, and I had to say something, and I could only say it with a blow, God help me!"

In the impulsive aboveboard manner of the frank one the court saw confirmed all that was implied in words that just previously had perplexed them, coming as they did from the testifier to the tragedy and promptly following Billy's impassioned disclaimer of mutinous intent—Captain Vere's words, "I believe you, my man."

Next it was asked of him whether he knew of or suspected aught savoring of incipient trouble (meaning mutiny, though the explicit term was avoided) going on in any section of the ship's company.

The reply lingered. This was naturally imputed by the court to the same vocal embarrassment which had retarded or obstructed previous answers. But in main it was otherwise here, the question immediately recalling to Billy's mind the interview with the afterguardsman in the forechains. But an innate repugnance to playing a part at all approaching that of an informer against one's own shipmates—the same erring sense of uninstructed honor which had stood in the way of his reporting the matter at the time, though as a loyal man-of-war's man it was incumbent on him, and failure so to do, if charged against him and proven, would have subjected him to the heaviest of penalties; this, with the blind feeling now his that nothing really was being hatched, prevailed with him. When the answer came it was a negative.

"One question more," said the officer of marines, now first speaking and with a troubled earnestness. "You tell us that what the master-at-arms said against you was a lie. Now why should he have so lied, so maliciously lied, since you declare there was no malice between you?"

At that question, unintentionally touching on a spiritual sphere wholly obscure to Billy's thoughts, he was nonplussed, evincing a confusion indeed that some observers, such as can readily be imagined, would have construed into involuntary evidence of hidden guilt. Nevertheless, he strove some way to answer, but all at once relinquished the vain endeavor, at the same time turning an appealing glance towards Captain Vere as deeming him his best helper and friend. Captain Vere, who had been seated for a time, rose to his feet, addressing the interrogator. "The question you put to him comes naturally enough. But how can he rightly answer it?—or anybody else, unless indeed it be he who lies within there," designating the compartment where lay the corpse. "But the prone one there will not rise to our summons. In effect, though, as it seems to me, the point you make is hardly material. Quite aside from any conceivable motive actuating the master-at-arms, and irrespective of the provocation to the blow, a martial court must needs in the present case confine its attention to the blow's consequence, which consequence justly is to be deemed not otherwise than as the striker's deed."

This utterance, the full significance of which it was not at all likely that Billy took in, nevertheless caused him to turn a wistful interrogative look toward the speaker, a look in its dumb expressiveness not unlike that which a dog of generous breed might turn upon his master, seeking in his face some elucidation of a previous gesture ambiguous to the canine intelligence. Nor was the same utterance without marked effect upon the three officers, more especially the soldier. Couched in it seemed to them a meaning unanticipated, involving a prejudgment on the speaker's part. It served to augment a mental disturbance previously evident enough.

The soldier once more spoke, in a tone of suggestive dubiety addressing at once his associates and Captain Vere: "Nobody is present,—none of the ship's company, I mean—who might shed lateral light, if any is to be had, upon what remains mysterious in this matter."

"That is thoughtfully put," said Captain Vere; "I see your drift. Ay, there is a mystery; but, to use a scriptural phrase, it is a 'mystery of iniquity,' a matter for psychologic theologians to discuss. But what has a military court to do with it? Not to add that for us any possible investigation of it is cut off by the lasting tongue-tie of—him—in yonder," again designating the mortuary stateroom. "The prisoner's deed—with that alone we have to do."

To this, and particularly the closing reiteration, the marine soldier, knowing not how aptly to reply, sadly abstained from saying aught. The first lieutenant, who at the outset had not unnaturally assumed primacy in the court, now overrulingly instructed by a glance from Captain Vere, a glance more effective than words, resumed that primacy. Turning to the prisoner, "Budd," he said, and scarce in equable tones, "Budd, if you have aught further to say for yourself, say it now."

Upon this the young sailor turned another quick glance toward Captain Vere; then, as taking a hint from that aspect, a hint confirming his own instinct that silence was now best, replied to the lieutenant, "I have said all, sir."

The marine—the same who had been the sentinel without the cabin door at the time that the foretopman, followed by the master-at-arms, entered it—he, standing by the sailor throughout these judicial proceedings, was now directed to take him back to the after compartment originally assigned to the prisoner and his custodian. As the twain disappeared from view, the three officers, as partially liberated from some inward constraint associated with Billy's mere presence, simultaneously stirred in their seats. They exchanged looks of troubled indecision, yet feeling that decide they must and without long delay. For Captain Vere, he for the time stood—unconsciously with his back toward them, apparently in one of his absent fits—gazing out from a sashed porthole to windward upon the monotonous blank of the twilight sea. But the court's silence continuing, broken only at moments by brief consultations, in low earnest tones, this served to arouse him and energize him. Turning, he to-and-fro paced the cabin athwart; in the returning ascent to windward climbing the slant deck in the ship's lee roll, without knowing it symbolizing thus in his action a mind resolute to surmount difficulties even if against primitive instincts strong as the wind and the sea. Presently he came to a stand before the three. After scanning their faces he stood less as mustering his thoughts for expression than as one inly deliberating how best to put them to well-meaning men not intellectually mature, men with whom it was necessary to demonstrate certain principles that were axioms to himself. Similar impatience as to talking is perhaps one reason that deters some minds from addressing any popular assemblies.

When speak he did, something, both in the substance of what he said and his manner of saying it, showed the influence of unshared studies modifying and tempering the practical training of an active career. This, along with his phraseology, now and then was suggestive of the grounds whereon rested that imputation of a certain pedantry socially alleged against him by certain naval men of wholly practical cast, captains who nevertheless would frankly concede that His Majesty's navy mustered no more efficient officer of their grade than Starry Vere.

What he said was to this effect: "Hitherto I have been but the witness, little more; and I should hardly think now to take another tone, that of your coadjutor for the time, did I not perceive in you—at the crisis too—a troubled hesitancy, proceeding, I doubt not, from the clash of military duty with moral scruple—scruple vitalized by compassion. For the compassion, how can I otherwise than share it? But, mindful of

paramount obligations, I strive against scruples that may tend
to enervate decision. Not, gentlemen, that I hide from myself
that the case is an exceptional one. Speculatively regarded,
it well might be referred to a jury of casuists. But for us here,
acting not as casuists or moralists, it is a case practical, and
under martial law practically to be dealt with.

"But your scruples: do they move as in a dusk? Challenge
them. Make them advance and declare themselves. Come now;
do they import something like this: If, mindless of palliating
circumstances, we are bound to regard the death of the master-at-arms as the prisoner's deed, then does that deed con-
stitute a captial crime whereof the penalty is a mortal one.
But in natural justice is nothing but the prisoner's overt act
to be considered? How can we adjudge to summary and shameful death a fellow creature innocent before God, and whom
we feel to be so?—Does that state it aright? You sign sad assent.
Well, I too feel that, the full force of that. It is Nature. But
do these buttons that we wear attest that our allegiance is to
Nature? No, to the King. Though the ocean, which is inviolate
Nature primeval, though this be the element where we move
and have our being as sailors, yet as the King's officers lies our
duty in a sphere correspondingly natural? So little is that true,
that in receiving our commissions we in the most important
regards ceased to be natural free agents. When war is declared
are we the commissioned fighters previously consulted? We
fight at command. If our judgments approve the war, that is
but coincidence. So in other particulars. So now. For suppose
condemnation to follow these present proceedings. Would
it be so much we ourselves that would condemn as it would
be martial law operating through us? For that law and the
rigor of it, we are not responsible. Our vowed responsibility
is in this: That however pitilessly that law may operate in
any instances, we nevertheless adhere to it and administer it.

"But the exceptional in the matter moves the hearts within
you. Even so too is mine moved. But let not warm hearts betray heads that should be cool. Ashore in a criminal case, will
an upright judge allow himself off the bench to be waylaid
by some tender kinswoman of the accused seeking to touch
him with her tearful plea? Well, the heart here, sometimes the
feminine in man, is as that piteous woman, and hard though
it be, she must here be ruled out."

He paused, earnestly studying them for a moment; then resumed.

"But something in your aspect seems to urge that it is not solely the heart that moves in you, but also the conscience, the private conscience. But tell me whether or not, occupying the position we do, private conscience should not yield to that imperial one formulated in the code under which alone we officially proceed?"

Here the three men moved in their seats, less convinced than agitated by the course of an argument troubling but the more the spontaneous conflict within.

Perceiving which, the speaker paused for a moment; then abruptly changing his tone, went on.

"To steady us a bit, let us recur to the facts.—In wartime at sea a man-of-war's man strikes his superior in grade, and the blow kills. Apart from its effect the blow itself is, according to the Articles of War, a capital crime. Furthermore——"

"Ay, sir," emotionally broke in the officer of marines, "in one sense it was. But surely Budd purposed neither mutiny nor homicide."

"Surely not, my good man. And before a court less arbitrary and more merciful than a martial one, that plea would largely extenuate. At the Last Assizes it shall acquit. But how here? We proceed under the law of the Mutiny Act. In feature no child can resemble his father more than that Act resembles in spirit the thing from which it derives—War. In His Majesty's service—in this ship, indeed—there are Englishmen forced to fight for the King against their will. Against their conscience, for aught we know. Though as their fellow creatures some of us may appreciate their position, yet as navy officers what reck we of it? Still less recks the enemy. Our impressed men he would fain cut down in the same swath with our volunteers. As regards the enemy's naval conscripts, some of whom may even share our own abhorrence of the regicidal French Directory, it is the same on our side. War looks but to the frontage, the appearance. And the Mutiny Act, War's child, takes after the father. Budd's intent or non-intent is nothing to the purpose.

"But while, put to it by those anxieties in you which I cannot but respect, I only repeat myself—while thus strangely we prolong proceedings that should be summary—the enemy may be sighted and an engagement result. We must do; and one of two things must we do—condemn or let go."

"Can we not convict and yet mitigate the penalty?" asked the sailing master, here speaking, and falteringly, for the first.

"Gentlemen, were that clearly lawful for us under the circumstances, consider the consequences of such clemency. The people" (meaning the ship's company) "have native sense; most of them are familiar with our naval usage and tradition; and how would they take it? Even could you explain to them—which our official position forbids—they, long molded by arbitrary discipline, have not that kind of intelligent responsiveness that might qualify them to comprehend and discriminate. No, to the people the foretopman's deed, however it be worded in the announcement, will be plain homicide committed in a flagrant act of mutiny. What penalty for that should follow, they know. But it does not follow. *Why?* they will ruminate. You know what sailors are. Will they not revert to the recent outbreak at the Nore? Ay. They know the well-founded alarm —the panic it struck throughout England. Your clement sentence they would account pusillanimous. They would think that we flinch, that we are afraid of them—afraid of practicing a lawful rigor singularly demanded at this juncture, lest it should provoke new troubles. What shame to us such a conjecture on their part, and how deadly to discipline. You see then, whither, prompted by duty and the law, I steadfastly drive. But I beseech you, my friends, do not take me amiss. I feel as you do for this unfortunate boy. But did he know our hearts, I take him to be of that generous nature that he would feel even for us on whom in this military necessity so heavy a compulsion is laid."

With that, crossing the deck he resumed his place by the sashed porthole, tacitly leaving the three to come to a decision. On the cabin's opposite side the troubled court sat silent. Loyal lieges, plain and practical, though at bottom they dissented from some points Captain Vere had put to them, they were without the faculty, hardly had the inclination, to gainsay one whom they felt to be an earnest man, one too not less their superior in mind than in naval rank. But it is not improbable that even such of his words as were not without influence over them, less came home to them than his closing appeal to their instinct as sea officers: in the forethought he threw out as to the practical consequences to discipline, considering the unconfirmed tone of the fleet at the time, should a man-of-war's man's violent killing at sea of a superior in grade be allowed to pass for aught else than a capital crime demanding prompt infliction of the penalty.

Not unlikely they were brought to something more or less akin to that harassed frame of mind which in the year 1842

actuated the commander of the U.S. brig-of-war *Somers* to resolve, under the so-called Articles of War, Articles modeled
upon the English Mutiny Act, to resolve upon the execution
at sea of a midshipman and two sailors as mutineers design-
ing the seizure of the brig. Which resolution was carried out
though in a time of peace and within not many days' sail of
home. An act vindicated by a naval court of inquiry subsequently convened ashore. History, and here cited without comment. True, the circumstances on board the *Somers* were different from those on board the *Bellipotent*. But the urgency
felt, well-warranted or otherwise, was much the same.

Says a writer whom few know, "Forty years after a battle it
is easy for a noncombatant to reason about how it ought to
have been fought. It is another thing personally and under
fire to have to direct the fighting while involved in the obscur-
ing smoke of it. Much so with respect to other emergencies
involving considerations both practical and moral, and when
it is imperative promptly to act. The greater the fog the more
it imperils the steamer, and speed is put on though at the
hazard of running somebody down. Little ween the snug card
players in the cabin of the responsibilities of the sleepless man
on the bridge."

In brief, Billy Budd was formally convicted and sentenced
to be hung at the yardarm in the early morning watch, it being now night. Otherwise, as is customary in such cases, the
sentence would forthwith have been carried out. In wartime
on the field or in the fleet, a mortal punishment decreed by
a drumhead court—on the field sometimes decreed by but a
nod from the general—follows without delay on the heel of
conviction, without appeal.

22

It was Captain Vere himself who of his own motion communicated the finding of the court to the prisoner, for that purpose
going to the compartment where he was in custody and bidding the marine there to withdraw for the time.

Beyond the communication of the sentence, what took place
at this interview was never known. But in view of the character of the twain briefly closeted in that stateroom, each radically sharing in the rarer qualities of our nature—so rare in-

deed as to be all but incredible to average minds however much cultivated—some conjectures may be ventured.

It would have been in consonance with the spirit of Captain Vere should he on this occasion have concealed nothing from the condemned one—should he indeed have frankly disclosed to him the part he himself had played in bringing about the decision, at the same time revealing his actuating motives. On Billy's side it is not improbable that such a confession would have been received in much the same spirit that prompted it. Not without a sort of joy, indeed, he might have appreciated the brave opinion of him implied in his captain's making such a confidant of him. Nor, as to the sentence itself, could he have been insensible that it was imparted to him as to one not afraid to die. Even more may have been. Captain Vere in end may have developed the passion sometimes latent under an exterior stoical or indifferent. He was old enough to have been Billy's father. The austere devotee of military duty, letting himself melt back into what remains primeval in our formalized humanity, may in end have caught Billy to his heart, even as Abraham may have caught young Isaac on the brink of resolutely offering him up in obedience to the exacting behest. But there is no telling the sacrament, seldom if in any case revealed to the gadding world, wherever under circumstances at all akin to those here attempted to be set forth two of great Nature's nobler order embrace. There is privacy at the time, inviolable to the survivor; and holy oblivion, the sequel to each diviner magnanimity, providentially covers all at last.

The first to encounter Captain Vere in act of leaving the compartment was the senior lieutenant. The face he beheld, for the moment one expressive of the agony of the strong, was to that officer, though a man of fifty, a startling revelation. That the condemned one suffered less than he who mainly had effected the condemnation was apparently indicated by the former's exclamation in the scene soon perforce to be touched upon.

23

OF A SERIES of incidents within a brief term rapidly following each other, the adequate narration may take up a term less brief, especially if explanation or comment here and there seem requisite to the better understanding of such incidents.

Between the entrance into the cabin of him who never left it alive, and him who when he did leave it left it as one condemned to die; between this and the closeted interview just given, less than an hour and a half had elapsed. It was an interval long enough, however, to awaken speculations among no few of the ship's company as to what it was that could be detaining in the cabin the master-at-arms and the sailor; for a rumor that both of them had been seen to enter it and neither of them had been seen to emerge, this rumor had got abroad upon the gun decks and in the tops, the people of a great warship being in one respect like villagers, taking microscopic note of every outward movement or nonmovement going on. When therefore, in weather not at all tempestuous, all hands were called in the second dogwatch, a summons under such circumstances not usual in those hours, the crew were not wholly unprepared for some announcement extraordinary, one having connection too with the continued absence of the two men from their wonted haunts.

There was a moderate sea at the time; and the moon, newly risen and near to being at its full, silvered the white spar deck wherever not blotted by the clear-cut shadows horizontally thrown of fixtures and moving men. On either side the quarterdeck the marine guard under arms was drawn up; and Captain Vere, standing in his place surrounded by all the wardroom officers, addressed his men. In so doing, his manner showed neither more nor less than that properly pertaining to his supreme position aboard his own ship. In clear terms and concise he told them what had taken place in the cabin: that the master-at-arms was dead, that he who had killed him had been already tried by a summary court and condemned to death, and that the execution would take place in the early morning watch. The word *mutiny* was not named in what he said. He refrained too from making the occasion an opportunity for any preachment as to the maintenance of discipline, thinking perhaps that under existing circumstances in the navy the consequence of violating discipline should be made to speak for itself.

Their captain's announcement was listened to by the throng of standing sailors in a dumbness like that of a seated congregation of believers in hell listening to the clergyman's announcement of his Calvinistic text.

At the close, however, a confused murmur went up. It began to wax. All but instantly, then, at a sign, it was pierced and suppressed by shrill whistles of the boatswain and his mates. The word was given to about ship.

To be prepared for burial Claggart's body was delivered to certain petty officers of his mess. And here, not to clog the sequel with lateral matters, it may be added that at a suitable hour, the master-at-arms was committed to the sea with every funeral honor properly belonging to his naval grade.

In this proceeding as in every public one growing out of the tragedy strict adherence to usage was observed. Nor in any point could it have been at all deviated from, either with respect to Claggart or Billy Budd, without begetting undesirable speculations in the ship's company, sailors, and more particularly men-of-war's men, being of all men the greatest sticklers for usage. For similar cause, all communication between Captain Vere and the condemned one ended with the closeted interview already given, the latter being now surrendered to the ordinary routine preliminary to the end. His transfer under guard from the captain's quarters was effected without unusual precautions—at least no visible ones. If possible, not to let the men so much as surmise that their officers anticipate aught amiss from them is the tacit rule in a military ship. And the more that some sort of trouble should really be apprehended, the more do the officers keep that apprehension to themselves, though not the less unostentatious vigilance may be augmented. In the present instance, the sentry placed over the prisoner had strict orders to let no one have communication with him but the chaplain. And certain unobtrusive measures were taken absolutely to insure this point.

24

IN A SEVENTY-FOUR of the old order the deck known as the upper gun deck was the one covered by the spar deck, which last, though not without its armament, was for the most part exposed to the weather. In general it was at all hours free from hammocks; those of the crew swinging on the lower gun deck and berth deck, the latter being not only a dormitory but also the place for the stowing of the sailors' bags, and on both sides lined with the large chests or movable pantries of the many messes of the men.

On the starboard side of the *Bellipotent*'s upper gun deck, behold Billy Budd under sentry lying prone in irons in one of the bays formed by the regular spacing of the guns comprising the batteries on either side. All these pieces were of the heavier caliber of that period. Mounted on lumbering wooden carriages, they were hampered with cumbersome harness of breeching and strong side-tackles for running them out. Guns and carriages, together with the long rammers and shorter linstocks lodged in loops overhead—all these, as customary, were painted black; and the heavy hempen breechings, tarred to the same tint, wore the like livery of the undertakers. In contrast with the funeral hue of these surroundings, the prone sailor's exterior apparel, white jumper and white duck trousers, each more or less soiled, dimly glimmered in the obscure light of the bay like a patch of discolored snow in early April lingering at some upland cave's black mouth. In effect he is already in his shroud, or the garments that shall serve him in lieu of one. Over him but scarce illuminating him, two battle lanterns swing from two massive beams of the deck above. Fed with the oil supplied by the war contractors (whose gains, honest or otherwise, are in every land an anticipated portion of the harvest of death), with flickering splashes of dirty yellow light they pollute the pale moonshine all but ineffectually struggling in obstructed flecks through the open ports from which the tampioned cannon protrude. Other lanterns at intervals serve but to bring out somewhat the obscurer bays which, like small confessionals or side-chapels in a cathedral, branch from the long dim-vistaed broad aisle between the two batteries of that covered tier.

Such was the deck where now lay the Handsome Sailor. Through the rose-tan of his complexion no pallor could have shown. It would have taken days of sequestration from the winds and the sun to have brought about the effacement of that. But the skeleton in the cheekbone at the point of its angle was just beginning delicately to be defined under the warm-tinted skin. In fervid hearts self-contained, some brief experiences devour our human tissue as secret fire in a ship's hold consumes cotton in the bale.

But now lying between the two guns, as nipped in the vice of fate, Billy's agony, mainly proceeding from a generous young heart's virgin experience of the diabolical incarnate and effective in some men—the tension of that agony was over now. It survived not the something healing in the closeted interview with Captain Vere. Without movement, he lay as in a trance, that adolescent expression previously noted as his taking on something akin to the look of a slumbering child in the cradle when the warm hearth-glow of the still chamber at night plays on the dimples that at whiles mysteriously form in the cheek, silently coming and going there. For now and then in the gyved one's trance a serene happy light born of some wandering reminiscence or dream would diffuse itself over his face, and then wane away only anew to return.

The chaplain, coming to see him and finding him thus, and perceiving no sign that he was conscious of his presence, attentively regarded him for a space, then slipping aside, withdrew for the time, peradventure feeling that even he, the minister of Christ though receiving his stipend from Mars, had no consolation to proffer which could result in a peace transcending that which he beheld. But in the small hours he came again. And the prisoner, now awake to his surroundings, noticed his approach, and civilly, all but cheerfully, welcomed him. But it was to little purpose that in the interview following, the good man sought to bring Billy Budd to some godly understanding that he must die, and at dawn. True, Billy himself freely referred to his death as a thing close at hand; but it was something in the way that children will refer to death in general, who yet among their other sports will play a funeral with hearse and mourners.

Not that like children Billy was incapable of conceiving what death really is. No, but he was wholly without irrational fear of it, a fear more prevalent in highly civilized communities than those so-called barbarous ones which in all respects stand nearer to unadulterate Nature. And, as elsewhere said, a barbarian Billy radically was—as much so, for all the costume, as his countrymen the British captives, living trophies, made to march in the Roman triumph of Germanicus. Quite as much so as those later barbarians, young men probably, and picked specimens among the earlier British converts to Christianity, at least nominally such, taken to Rome (as today converts from lesser isles of the sea may be taken to London), of whom the Pope of that time, admiring the strangeness of their personal beauty so unlike the Italian stamp, their clear ruddy complexion and curled flaxen locks, exclaimed, "Angles" (meaning *English,* the modern derivative), "Angles, do you call them? And is it because they look so like angels?" Had it been later in time, one would think that the Pope had in mind Fra Angelico's seraphs, some of whom, plucking apples in gardens on the Hesperides, have the faint rosebud complexion of the more beautiful English girls.

If in vain the good chaplain sought to impress the young barbarian with ideas of death akin to those conveyed in the skull, dial, and crossbones on old tombstones, equally futile to all appearance were his efforts to bring home to him the thought of salvation and a Savior. Billy listened, but less out of awe or reverence, perhaps, than from a certain natural politeness, doubtless at bottom regarding all that in much the same way that most mariners of his class take any discourse abstract or out of the common tone of the workaday world. And this sailor way of taking clerical discourse is not wholly unlike the way in which the primer of Christianity, full of transcendent miracles, was received long ago on tropic isles by any superior *savage*, so called—a Tahitian, say, of Captain Cook's time or shortly after that time. Out of natural courtesy he received, but did not appropriate. It was like a gift placed in the palm of an outreached hand upon which the fingers do not close.

But the *Bellipotent*'s chaplain was a discreet man possessing the good sense of a good heart. So he insisted not in his vocation here. At the instance of Captain Vere, a lieutenant had apprised him of pretty much everything as to Billy; and since he felt that innocence was even a better thing than religion wherewith to go to Judgment, he reluctantly withdrew; but in his emotion not without first performing an act strange enough in an Englishman, and under the circumstances yet more so in any regular priest. Stooping over, he kissed on the fair cheek his fellow man, a felon in martial law, one whom though on the confines of death he felt he could never convert to a dogma; nor for all that did he fear for his future.

Marvel not that having been made acquainted with the young sailor's essential innocence the worthy man lifted not a finger to avert the doom of such a martyr to martial discipline. So to do would not only have been as idle as invoking the desert, but would also have been an audacious transgression of the bounds of his function, one as exactly prescribed to him by military law as that of the boatswain or any other naval officer. Bluntly put, a chaplain is the minister of the Prince of Peace serving in the host of the God of War—Mars. As such, he is as incongruous as a musket would be on the altar at Christmas. Why, then, is he there? Because he indirectly subserves the purpose attested by the cannon; because too he lends the sanction of the religion of the meek to that which practically is the abrogation of everything but brute Force.

25

THE NIGHT so luminous on the spar deck, but otherwise on the cavernous ones below, levels so like the tiered galleries in a coal mine—the luminous night passed away. But like the prophet in the chariot disappearing in heaven and dropping his mantle to Elisha, the withdrawing night transferred its pale robe to the breaking day. A meek, shy light appeared in the East, where stretched a diaphanous fleece of white furrowed vapor. That light slowly waxed. Suddenly *eight bells* was struck aft, responded to by one louder metallic stroke from forward. It was four o'clock in the morning. Instantly the silver whistles were heard summoning all hands to witness punishment. Up through the great hatchways rimmed with racks of heavy shot the watch below came pouring, overspreading with the watch already on deck the space between the mainmast and foremast including that occupied by the capacious launch and the black booms tiered on either side of it, boat and booms making a summit of observation for the powder-boys and younger tars. A different group comprising one watch of topmen leaned over the rail of that sea balcony, no small one in a seventy-four, looking down on the crowd below. Man or boy, none spake but in whisper, and few spake at all. Captain Vere—as before, the central figure among the assembled commissioned officers —stood nigh the break of the poop deck facing forward. Just below him on the quarter-deck the marines in full equipment were drawn up much as at the scene of the promulgated sentence.

At sea in the old time, the execution by halter of a military sailor was generally from the foreyard. In the present instance, for special reasons the mainyard was assigned. Under an arm of that yard the prisoner was presently brought up, the chaplain attending him. It was noted at the time, and remarked upon afterwards, that in this final scene the good man evinced little or nothing of the perfunctory. Brief speech indeed he had with the condemned one, but the genuine Gospel was less on his tongue than in his aspect and manner towards him. The final preparations personal to the latter being speedily brought to an end by two boatswain's mates, the consummation impended. Billy stood facing aft. At the penultimate moment, his words, his only ones, words wholly unobstructed in the utterance, were these: "God bless Captain Vere!" Syllables so unanticipated coming from one with the ignominious hemp about his neck—a conventional felon's benediction directed aft towards the quarters of honor; syllables too delivered in the clear melody of a singing bird on the point of launching from the twig—had a phenomenal effect, not unenhanced by the rare personal beauty of the young sailor, spiritualized now through late experiences so poignantly profound.

Without volition, as it were, as if indeed the ship's populace were but the vehicles of some vocal current electric, with one voice from alow and aloft came a resonant sympathetic echo: "God bless Captain Vere!" And yet at that instant Billy alone must have been in their hearts, even as in their eyes.

At the pronounced words and the spontaneous echo that voluminously rebounded them, Captain Vere, either through stoic self-control or a sort of momentary paralysis induced by emotional shock, stood erectly rigid as a musket in the ship-armorer's rack.

The hull, deliberately recovering from the periodic roll to leeward, was just regaining an even keel when the last signal, a preconcerted dumb one, was given. At the same moment it chanced that the vapory fleece hanging low in the East was shot through with a soft glory as of the fleece of the Lamb of God seen in mystical vision, and simultaneously therewith, watched by the wedged mass of upturned faces, Billy ascended; and, ascending, took the full rose of the dawn.

In the pinioned figure arrived at the yard-end, to the wonder of all no motion was apparent, none save that created by the slow roll of the hull in moderate weather, so majestic in a great ship ponderously cannoned.

26

WHEN SOME days afterwards, in reference to the singularity just mentioned, the purser, a rather ruddy, rotund person more accurate as an accountant than profound as a philosopher, said at mess to the surgeon, "What testimony to the force lodged in will power," the latter, saturnine, spare, and tall, one in whom a discreet causticity went along with a manner less genial than polite, replied, "Your pardon, Mr. Purser. In a hanging scientifically conducted—and under special orders I myself directed how Budd's was to be effected—any movement following the completed suspension and originating in the body suspended, such movement indicates mechanical spasm in the muscular system. Hence the absence of that is no more attributable to will power, as you call it, than to horsepower —begging your pardon."

"But this muscular spasm you speak of, is not that in a degree more or less invariable in these cases?"

"Assuredly so, Mr. Purser."

"How then, my good sir, do you account for its absence in this instance?"

"Mr. Purser, it is clear that your sense of the singularity in this matter equals not mine. You account for it by what you call will power—a term not yet included in the lexicon of science. For me, I do not, with my present knowledge, pretend to account for it at all. Even should we assume the hypothesis that at the first touch of the halyards the action of Budd's heart, intensified by extraordinary emotion at its climax, abruptly stopped—much like a watch when in carelessly winding it up you strain at the finish, thus snapping the chain—even under that hypothesis how account for the phenomenon that followed?"

"You admit, then, that the absence of spasmodic movement was phenomenal."

"It was phenomenal, Mr. Purser, in the sense that it was an appearance the cause of which is not immediately to be assigned."

"But tell me, my dear sir," pertinaciously continued the other, "was the man's death effected by the halter, or was it a species of euthanasia?"

"*Euthanasia,* Mr. Purser, is something like your *will power:*
I doubt its authenticity as a scientific term—begging your pardon again. It is at once imaginative and metaphysical—in
short, Greek.—But," abruptly changing his tone, "there is a
case in the sick bay that I do not care to leave to my assistants.
Beg your pardon, but excuse me." And rising from the mess he
formally withdrew.

27

THE SILENCE at the moment of execution and for a moment or
two continuing thereafter, a silence but emphasized by the
regular wash of the sea against the hull or the flutter of a sail
caused by the helmsman's eyes being tempted astray, this emphasized silence was gradually disturbed by a sound not easily
to be verbally rendered. Whoever has heard the freshet-wave of
a torrent suddenly swelled by pouring showers in tropical
mountains, showers not shared by the plain; whoever has heard
the first muffled murmur of its sloping advance through precipi-
tous woods may form some conception of the sound now heard.
The seeming remoteness of its source was because of its mur-
murous indistinctness, since it came from close by, even from
the men massed on the ship's open deck. Being inarticulate, it
was dubious in significance further than it seemed to indicate
some capricious revulsion of thought or feeling such as mobs
ashore are liable to, in the present instance possibly implying
a sullen revocation on the men's part of their involuntary
echoing of Billy's benediction. But ere the murmur had time
to wax into clamor it was met by a strategic command, the
more telling that it came with abrupt unexpectedness: "Pipe
the boatswain watch, Boatswain, and see that they go."

Shrill as the shriek of the sea hawk, the silver whistles of
the boatswain and his mates pierced that ominous low sound,
dissipating it; and yielding to the mechanism of discipline the
throng was thinned by one-half. For the remainder, most of
them were set to temporary employments connected with trim-
ming the yards and so forth, business readily to be got up to
serve occasion by any officer of the deck.

Now each proceeding that follows a mortal sentence pronounced at sea by a drumhead court is characterized by promptitude not perceptibly merging into a hurry, though bordering

that. The hammock, the one which had been Billy's bed when alive, having already been ballasted with shot and otherwise prepared to serve for his canvas coffin, the last offices of the sea undertakers, the sailmaker's mates, were now speedily completed. When everything was in readiness a second call for all hands, made necessary by the strategic movement before mentioned, was sounded, now to witness burial.

The details of this closing formality it needs not to give. But when the tilted plank let slide its freight into the sea, a second strange human murmur was heard, blended now with another inarticulate sound proceeding from certain larger seafowl who, their attention having been attracted by the peculiar commotion in the water resulting from the heavy sloped dive of the shotted hammock into the sea, flew screaming to the spot. So near the hull did they come, that the stridor or bony creak of their gaunt double-jointed pinions was audible. As the ship under light airs passed on, leaving the burial spot astern, they still kept circling it low down with the moving shadow of their outstretched wings and the croaked requiem of their cries.

Upon sailors as superstitious as those of the age preceding ours, men-of-war's men too who had just beheld the prodigy of repose in the form suspended in air, and now foundering in the deeps; to such mariners the action of the seafowl, though dictated by mere animal greed for prey, was big with no prosaic significance. An uncertain movement began among them, in which some encroachment was made. It was tolerated but for a moment. For suddenly the drum beat to quarters, which familiar sound happening at least twice every day, had upon the present occasion a signal peremptoriness in it. True martial discipline long continued superinduces in average man a sort of impulse whose operation at the official word of command much resembles in its promptitude the effect of an instinct.

The drumbeat dissolved the multitude, distributing most of them along the batteries of the two covered gun decks. There, as wonted, the guns' crews stood by their respective cannon erect and silent. In due course the first officer, sword under arm and standing in his place on the quarter-deck, formally received the successive reports of the sworded lieutenants commanding the sections of batteries below; the last of which reports being made, the summed report he delivered with the customary salute to the commander. All this occupied time, which in the present case was the object in beating to quarters at an hour prior to the customary one. That such variance from usage was authorized by an officer like Captain Vere, a martinet as some deemed him, was evidence of the necessity for unusual action implied in what he deemed to be temporarily the mood of his men. "With mankind," he would say, "forms, measured forms, are everything; and that is the import couched in the story of Orpheus with his lyre spellbinding the wild denizens of the wood." And this he once applied to the disruption of forms going on across the Channel and the consequences thereof.

At this unwonted muster at quarters, all proceeded as at the regular hour. The band on the quarter-deck played a sacred air, after which the chaplain went through the customary morning service. That done, the drum beat the retreat; and toned by music and religious rites subserving the discipline and purposes of war, the men in their wonted orderly manner dispersed to the places allotted them when not at the guns.

And now it was full day. The fleece of low-hanging vapor had vanished, licked up by the sun that late had so glorified it. And the circumambient air in the clearness of its serenity was like smooth white marble in the polished block not yet removed from the marble-dealer's yard.

28

THE SYMMETRY of form attainable in pure fiction cannot so readily be achieved in a narration essentially having less to do with fable than with fact. Truth uncompromisingly told will always have its ragged edges; hence the conclusion of such a narration is apt to be less finished than an architectural finial.

How it fared with the Handsome Sailor during the year of the Great Mutiny has been faithfully given. But though properly the story ends with his life, something in way of sequel will not be amiss. Three brief chapters will suffice.

In the general rechristening under the Directory of the craft originally forming the navy of the French monarchy, the *St. Louis* line-of-battle ship was named the *Athée* (the *Atheist*). Such a name, like some other substituted ones in the Revolutionary fleet, while proclaiming the infidel audacity of the ruling power, was yet, though not so intended to be, the aptest name, if one consider it, ever given to a warship; far more so indeed than the *Devastation*, the *Erebus* (the *Hell*), and similar names bestowed upon fighting ships.

On the return passage to the English fleet from the detached cruise during which occurred the events already recorded, the *Bellipotent* fell in with the *Athée*. An engagement ensued, during which Captain Vere, in the act of putting his ship alongside the enemy with a view of throwing his boarders across her bulwarks, was hit by a musket ball from a porthole of the enemy's main cabin. More than disabled, he dropped to the deck and was carried below to the same cockpit where some of his men already lay. The senior lieutenant took command. Under him the enemy was finally captured, and though much crippled was by rare good fortune successfully taken into Gibraltar, an English port not very distant from the scene of the fight. There, Captain Vere with the rest of the wounded was put ashore. He lingered for some days, but the end came. Unhappily he was cut off too early for the Nile and Trafalgar. The spirit that 'spite its philosophic austerity may yet have indulged in the most secret of all passions, ambition, never attained to the fulness of fame.

Not long before death, while lying under the influence of that magical drug which, soothing the physical frame, mysteriously operates on the subtler element in man, he was heard to murmur words inexplicable to his attendant: "Billy Budd, Billy Budd." That these were not the accents of remorse would seem clear from what the attendant said to the *Bellipotent*'s senior officer of marines, who, as the most reluctant to condemn of the members of the drumhead court, too well knew, though here he kept the knowledge to himself, who Billy Budd was.

29

SOME FEW weeks after the execution, among other matters under the head of "News from the Mediterranean," there appeared in a naval chronicle of the time, an authorized weekly publication, an account of the affair. It was doubtless for the most part written in good faith, though the medium, partly rumor, through which the facts must have reached the writer served to deflect and in part falsify them. The account was as follows:

"On the tenth of the last month a deplorable occurrence took place on board H.M.S. *Bellipotent*. John Claggart, the ship's master-at-arms, discovering that some sort of plot was incipient among an inferior section of the ship's company, and that the ringleader was one William Budd; he, Claggart, in the act of arraigning the man before the captain, was vindictively stabbed to the heart by the suddenly drawn sheath knife of Budd.

"The deed and the implement employed sufficiently suggest that though mustered into the service under an English name the assassin was no Englishman, but one of those aliens adopting English cognomens whom the present extraordinary necessities of the service have caused to be admitted into it in considerable numbers.

"The enormity of the crime and the extreme depravity of the criminal appear the greater in view of the character of the victim, a middle-aged man respectable and discreet, belonging to that minor official grade, the petty officers, upon whom, as none know better than the commissioned gentlemen, the efficiency of His Majesty's navy so largely depends. His function was a responsible one, at once onerous and thankless; and his fidelity in it the greater because of his strong patriotic impulse. In this instance as in so many other instances in these days, the character of this unfortunate man signally refutes, if refutation were needed, that peevish saying attributed to the late Dr. Johnson, that patriotism is the last refuge of a scoundrel.

"The criminal paid the penalty of his crime. The promptitude of the punishment has proved salutary. Nothing amiss is now apprehended aboard H.M.S. *Bellipotent.*"

The above, appearing in a publication now long ago superannuated and forgotten, is all that hitherto has stood in human record to attest what manner of men respectively were John Claggart and Billy Budd.

30

EVERYTHING IS for a term venerated in navies. Any tangible object associated with some striking incident of the service is converted into a monument. The spar from which the foretopman was suspended was for some few years kept trace of by the bluejackets. Their knowledges followed it from ship to dockyard and again from dockyard to ship, still pursuing it even when at last reduced to a mere dockyard boom. To them a chip of it was as a piece of the Cross. Ignorant though they

were of the secret facts of the tragedy, and not thinking but
that the penalty was somehow unavoidably inflicted from the
naval point of view, for all that, they instinctively felt that
Billy was a sort of man as incapable of mutiny as of wilful
murder. They recalled the fresh young image of the Handsome
Sailor, that face never deformed by a sneer or subtler vile freak
of the heart within. This impression of him was doubtless deepened by the fact that he was gone, and in a measure mysteriously
gone. On the gun decks of the *Bellipotent* the general estimate
of his nature and its unconscious simplicity eventually found
rude utterance from another foretopman, one of his own
watch, gifted, as some sailors are, with an artless *poetic* temperament. The tarry hand made some lines which, after circulating
among the shipboard crews for a while, finally got rudely
printed at Portsmouth as a ballad. The title given to it was
the sailor's.

BILLY IN THE DARBIES

Good of the chaplain to enter Lone Bay
And down on his marrowbones here and pray
For the likes just o' me, Billy Budd.—But, look:
Through the port comes the moonshine astray!
It tips the guard's cutlass and silvers this nook;
But 'twill die in the dawning of Billy's last day.
A jewel-block they'll make of me tomorrow,
Pendant pearl from the yardarm-end
Like the eardrop I gave to Bristol Molly—
O, 'tis me, not the sentence they'll suspend.
Ay, ay, all is up; and I must up too,
Early in the morning, aloft from alow.
On an empty stomach now never it would do.
They'll give me a nibble—bit o' biscuit ere I go.
Sure, a messmate will reach me the last parting cup;
But, turning heads away from the hoist and the belay,
Heaven knows who will have the running of me up!
No pipe to those halyards.—But aren't it all sham?
A blur's in my eyes; it is dreaming that I am.
A hatchet to my hawser? All adrift to go?
The drum roll to grog, and Billy never know?
But Donald he has promised to stand by the plank;
So I'll shake a friendly hand ere I sink.
But—no! It is dead then I'll be, come to think.

I remember Taff the Welshman when he sank.
And his cheek it was like the budding pink.
But me they'll lash me in hammock, drop me deep.
Fathoms down, fathoms down, how I'll dream fast asleep.
I feel it stealing now. Sentry, are you there?
Just ease this darbies at the wrist, and roll me over fair,
I am sleepy and the oozy weeds about me twist.

A SELECTED BIBLIOGRAPHY

THE FIRST two volumes in Northwestern University–Newberry Library edition of Melville's writings are in print (as of early 1969) and are admirably designed and edited. This edition when complete will offer students a wholly reliable series of texts and text histories. Meanwhile the Constable "Standard Edition" in sixteen volumes (London, 1922–24; reprinted New York; Russell and Russell, 1963) remains serviceable. In the case of *Billy Budd*, however, the text edited by Harrison Hayford and Merton M. Sealts, Jr. (1962) supersedes all previous printings. Paperback editions of Melville's book-length narratives have multiplied in recent years, especially of *Moby-Dick;* many contain useful introductions and bibliographies. *The Complete Stories of Herman Melville,* ed. Jay Leyda (1949), falls somewhat short of what its title claims, but the texts are sound and the introduction and "notes on sources &c." supply much valuable information.

Leon Howard's biography, *Herman Melville* (1951), and Newton Arvin's *Melville* (1950: American Men of Letters Series) are standard, though Arvin is puzzlingly dismissive of the work of the 1853–56 period. Jay Leyda, *The Melville Log: A Documentary Life of Herman Melville,* 2v. (1951), is a storehouse of essential data; Eleanor Melville Metcalf, *Herman Melville: Cycle and Epicycle* (1953), is a shorter work in the same mode. Brief introductory studies have been published by Jean-Jacques Mayoux (1958), A. R. Humphreys (1962), and D. E. S. Maxwell (1968).

The quantity of biographical, critical, and interpretive writing on Melville that is of genuine value has become immense, and there is no particular sign of a tapering off. In fact a new round of revaluations seems to have begun. The Melville entries in the bibliographical volume of *Literary History of the United States,* ed. Robert E. Spiller and others (3rd edition revised, 1963), and in *Eight American Authors: A Review of Research and Criticism,* ed. Jay B. Hubbell and others (1963), provide comprehensive listings of both general assessments and studies of individual works. The critical bibliography in James E. Miller, *A Reader's Guide to Herman Melville* (1962), contains helpful brief descriptions of standard secondary works. The annual PMLA bibliography may be consulted for the period since 1962. William T. Stafford, ed., *Melville's Billy Budd and the Critics* (1961), and John P. Runden, ed., *Melville's Benito Cereno* (1965), present the critical debates over these controversial tales. Hershel Parker, ed., *The Recognition of Herman Melville* (1967), samples Melville criticism in general from 1846 to 1966. The response to Melville by certain European writers of this century (Lawrence, Forster, Gide, Unamuno, Jean Giono, Camus, Cesare Pavese, Eugenio Montale) has been extraordinary but is not very well represented in current collections of criticism.

A CHRONOLOGY

1819   Born August 1, New York City, third child and second son of Allan Melville, merchant, and Maria Gansevoort Melville.

1819–30   Melville family in New York City, occupying houses on Pearl, Courtlandt and Bleecker Streets and (1828–30) at 675 Broadway; summers in Albany, Boston, the Berkshires.

1830   Allan Melville in financial difficulties; family moves to Albany, Melville attending Albany Academy.

1832   Death of Allan Melville.

1833–35   Melville continues schooling at Albany Classical School and clerks part time in a bank and in his brother's cap and fur store.

1836   "Greater portion of a year" spent at the Pittsfield, Massachusetts, farm of his uncle, Thomas Melville.

1837–38   Teaching school in Pittsfield; family moves to Lansingburgh, north of Albany.

1838–39   Engineering student at Lansingburgh Academy.

1839   Ships on the packet *St. Lawrence,* New York–Liverpool, June to September.

1839–40   Teaching school at Greenbush and Brunswick, near Albany; visits Galena, Illinois. In New Bedford, December 26.

1841   Ships January 3 on whaler *Acushnet* for the South Seas.

1842-44 Jumps ship in the Marquesas; ashore in Tahiti; whaling cruise aboard the *Charles and Henry* of Nantucket; enlists in U. S. Navy at Honolulu aboard frigate *United States;* discharged in Boston, October, 1844.

1846 Publishes *Typee: A Peep at Polynesian Life During a Four Months' Residence in a Valley of the Marquesas.*

1847 Publishes *Omoo: A Narrative of Adventures in the South Seas;* marries Elizabeth Shaw, daughter of the Chief Justice of Massachusetts; establishes residence in New York City; reads "old books."

1849 Publishes *Mardi and a Voyage Thither; Redburn: His First Voyage, Being the Sailor-Boy Confessions and Reminiscences of the Son-of-a-Gentleman, in the Merchant Service;* voyage to England and France, October–December.

1850 Publishes *White-Jacket or The World in a Man-of-War;* moves to "Arrowhead," outside Pittsfield.

1851-52 Publishes *Moby-Dick or The Whale; Pierre or The Ambiguities;* letters to Hawthorne.

1853-54 Attempts without success to get a consular appointment; stories appearing in *Putnam's* and *Harper's.*

1855 Publishes *Israel Potter: His Fifty Years of Exile.*

1856-57 Publishes *The Piazza Tales, The Confidence Man: His Masquerade;* voyage to Europe and Palestine.

1857-60 Lecturing engagements in the East and Middle West.

1860 Voyage to San Francisco via Cape Horn. Unable to find publisher for a volume of poems.

1863 Moves from Pittsfield to New York (East Twenty-Sixth Street) in October.

1866   Appointed district officer in New York Customs House; publishes *Battle-Pieces and Aspects of the War* (poems with prose supplement).

1867   Oldest child, Malcolm, aged 18, kills himself with a pistol shot.

1876   Publishes *Clarel: A Poem and Pilgrimage in the Holy Land*, through the generosity of Peter Gansevoort, his uncle.

1885–86   Retirement from Customs House; death of second son, Stanwix.

1888   Publishes, privately, *John Marr and Other Sailors* (poems).

1891   Publishes, privately, *Timoleon* (poems); finishes work on *Billy Budd*; dies September 28.

1924   Publication of *Billy Budd* and other late writings.